# Summa Angelica

## Leo Vinci

**Visit us online at** www.authorsonline.co.uk

This work is dedicated to the
## 'STAR OF THE MORNING'
of the
## ORDER OF THE MORNING STAR

# A BRIEF OUTLINE

This is a brief outline of the work showing how each chapter adds information to the chapter above, not unlike building a pyramid starting by starting at the top with the one brick, then two, then three until all the chapters are set in place to make a base to support the work.

## Part 1

This is the largest chapter and deals with Angels and Archangels in religion, myth, legend, folklore. It takes in many subjects associated with the angels, Christian, Roman, Greek, Islam, Biblical, Apocryphal, Fallen Angels, Dragons and Serpents, the Guph, the Shekinah, the Bat, Manna the Bread of the Angels, Melchizedek, some Enochian Angels, the Bad Angels, the Orders of the Angels and many words and themes associated with this study. This chapter is divided into sixty–six subtitles.

## Part 2

**The Planet and their Angels**. This chapter adds the information of the angels and the planets they rule, what the planets rule and how to use this.

**Your Personal and Guardian Angels.** This chapter adds information for finding your Guardian Angels, your Auxiliary Angels and the Angel of the Ascendant or Benben Angel, the Six o'clock Angel.

**The Pentagrams of the Angels**. This chapter adds information of how to make a Pentagram of the Angels a general pentagram for you, your home and those living there. The Personal Pentagram of the Angels is a pentagram that is personal to the one who makes it because it is made up from information personal to that individual.

**Your Letters or Invocation.** This chapter adds information of how to make the Letters of Invocation, what to use, how to write them and how these are used using the Angelic Signatures, Seals, etc.

**Pyramid of Personal Power.** This chapter adds information to the above for this is the 'motor' of the work, that which 'drives' it.

**Jacob's Ladder.** This chapter adds information and discusses the 'what,' the 'why' and 'that' which started the writing.

**The Kameas in Angelic Use**. This chapter adds information and discusses the use of the kameas in Angelic Magic, how they are used. The Seals, Spirits and Intelligences; the Olympic Spirits etc. the use of the Hebrew Alphabet.

**The Magical Scripts**. This chapter adds information, discusses the use of Magical Scripts and gives sufficient reliable scripts, enough to undertake the work given in the work.

**The Tables of Planetary and Angelic Hours**. This chapter adds information and discusses how to find the correct hours and days for doing your work and these Tables can be used for many other things. The Tables are easy to use and are supplied at the back of the work.

**Closing the Work.** These are some observations on the work given here, stressing a few of the more important points, some final suggestions to the reader and my leave–taking.

**Diagrams and Tables.** These are mentioned of throughout the work — I did say the outline would be very brief!

# CONTENTS:

**PART ONE: 'The Angels . . .'**

A Brief Outline of the Work.

*PART TWO:* '*... and their Magic.*'

# PART ONE:

# THE ANGELS

'Call. Is there one to answer thee?
To which of the holy ones (i.e. the angels) wilt thou turn?'
*Job* 5:1.

## PART ONE: THE ANGELS ...

## FIRST THINGS FIRST

(NB. Some parts of this chapter, because of its length, have been given sub–headings if it deals with a specific subject, information or angel(s) at any length. This has been done to make it possible for the reader to go to a particular theme or information quickly if they want to but the heading must not be taken to mean that this is a main entry or the only place where such information can be found.)

This work is in two separate parts. The first part is largely concerned with the information that we will use in the second. Therefore, it will aid understanding considerably if Part One is familiar to the reader. Part One of the work could be regarded as 'the theory' of the subject matter in hand, which is 'The Angels  . . . ' of the sub–title. Part Two is 'the practice' that deals with '  . . . and their Magic' of the sub–title. This is why it was said that time spent studying the material of Part One will be useful and valuable to the reader later when they reach Part Two — because we can always deal more successfully with things that we understand or know.

When we start writing about angels we have to decide what are the 'first things' to be considered 'first?' At this early stage, if we begin to ponder the extent and complexity of the journey we are about to undertake, we may never start because we may feel that the task could possibly overwhelm us for the subject is vast and it is not exhausted here. Where do we start in our study of these magnificent creations that have fascinated countless millions of people from so many countries and religions through equally countless centuries — by whatever name they are found called. The subject is a vast one without doubt and somewhat daunting in its scope so, as I have said, perhaps it would be better not to think about it but plunge straight in and become caught up in the tide and follow where it takes us.

Knowing this would be a long chapter I pondered how it would be best to set it all down, not all of the first attempts were thought acceptable so I resorted to an old practise of taking wine before retiring and consider how best to do the task just as I was falling asleep. I awoke during the night and wrote down in a notepad my nocturnal ramblings, which is one way that I sometimes work. In the morning, I read the notes and can only hope I have done them some justice but if I have not, the fault is mine, what follows are the notes as written down. Of course, throughout the work for any *lapsus calami* found I accept full responsibility, it came out as:

'Regard the first part of the work as the well–spring of a stream that will eventually grow into a large river. The river will grow and finally end at the harbour that divides Parts One and Two of the work. The area between the two parts is the dock where all the goods and cargo (= information gathered on the journey down Part One) are stored, sorted and inspected before starting out on the second part of the journey, which is Part Two. These goods are the various sections that have been discussed, the explanations or information additional to the main angelic theme and insert these at strategic points in the river as it flows on.

1

'Do not regard these 'strategic points' in the journey as a dam that blocks the flow of the river. See them more as an 'island' or 'group of islands' where the reader can pause in their travels down to the river's end and its 'harbour.' A rest before they embark out on the open sea, to try to find new lands and unexplored territories that lie unmapped in Part Two. These pauses should not be thought of as breaks in the journey but resting places where the river flows on all sides of the island and the journey can be picked up again once the information the islands give is set out for the reader's use by picking up what 'stores' are needed.

Call these 'islands' — *Shekinah*, *Merkabah Mysteries*, *Melchizedek*, *Bat Qol*, *Lilith*, *Mammon*, *Cabbalistic Angels*, *Heresy*, *Enochia and its Angels*, *Guph* and include the traditions, legends and folklore concerning the subjects of the 'angelic islands.' These 'islands' should be regarded as supply depots for what will be needed for the journey ahead or give additional information that may help. In this way, the long journey will be taken with some breathing space on dry land to pick up extra supplies and these breaks should give additional understanding of the subject.' This is what I have attempted to do according to the notes but whether I have been successful or not, only time will tell.

The words of the sub–title have a purpose and are deliberately composed and divided to show this purpose. The first part is *'The Angels . . . '* and this makes up Part One of the work, the section you are reading now. The second part of the sub–title *' . . . and their Magic'* makes up Part Two of the work, the part we will be studying next. These two sections when put together (as they are on the front page) give us the purpose of the work in one sentence — *The Angels . . . and their Magic.*

To those brought up in the West, despite the rapid movement of populations and the even swifter changing fashions in so many areas of life, which seem to come and go with every passing wind today, this has to be the *Bible.* This is because it is the 'the Book' of the writer, his family, the country where he was born and book from which he was originally taught. However, the angels or 'celestial messengers' are obviously not confined only to the *Bible* or the Christian faith. All religions and religious philosophies have such 'other–world' beings in their pantheon and many have been dealing with them long before Christianity arrived.

This all–important 'middle ground' stands between a nation, a people or an individual at one end and their God or Supreme Being at the other. It is here there could be a chance of contact because this area is intermediate and between the two, common ground where a 'meeting' might be possible because of the desire to 'meet halfway.'

What occupies the middle ground and how can it be used to advantage? This is an important area that we must try to become familiar with so that we do not get lost on our journey. It is like the area of land that lies between a large country — the vast celestial — and a small one — us!

In the religions of Ancient Greece, Rome, Judaism, Christianity, Islam and other the other peoples, the angels act as intermediaries and Divine Messengers, often sent to give instruction, information, to advise, warn, give comfort, rescue, to give commands or chastise the human race or an individual in some way. An angel can act as a protective guardian, a teacher or a divine warrior. Angels can come on behalf of the Power or Source that they serve and they can bring with them the fiat of their Creator to give, bless, advise, protect, punish, rebuke, destroy and to even bring death, natural or otherwise. The Angel of Death is one of the most constant and ever-present of angels in all religions, whatever title is found.

We must not regard angels only as the fluffy artistic creations of the annual Christmas or other religious cards and writings of those who make use of them with similar license. This does not mean that they will not use a form appropriate to what they have to do and if a child sees an angel in this way, it will be so. There would be little point in appearing in such a way as to give to the one they have come to help a heart attack.

Sometimes the dividing line between a good or bad angel, a good or bad daemon is very finely drawn and it can be vague at times to say the least. Perhaps the divine messengers or angels could be summarized as incarnate powers that bridge the 'middle ground' and intercede between the divine and limitless with the mundane and limited, which is where we find ourselves. As will be repeated often throughout this work, there usually seems to be something 'that intercedes between man and God' and this channel of mediation or intervention is recorded as being used by the prophets where one term used was a *specularia*= 'window–pane, a window, a looking glass.' This Latin term is found in botany for Venus's Looking–glass — *specularia, speculum–veneris* — a species of annual herb grown as a garden ornamental for its blue, violet, or white, wide-open, bell-shaped flowers.

The term 'window' is sometimes used in space programmes when launching rockets from the terrestrial into space and the choice to launch is often ruled by having 'an appropriate window' to leave one place for another totally different place. When faced with this unknown region we need all the help we can get and try to find any maps, signposts or footprints left behind by those who have gone before on a similar journey.

Compared to the known age of the planet, the human race has been here a comparatively short time. Most should know by now some of the basic and more obvious rules of life. Putting your hand into a red–hot fire or taking a knife and plunging it into someone's chest would have reasonably predictable results. Even a child can foresee that you would be severely burnt in the first, with an excellent chance of killing someone in the latter and you would usually have to take the consequences of your actions either way as a result.

The reason for these obvious examples is to show that we are to a certain degree usually aware of the likely outcome of a great many of our actions in the world we inhabit. A red light tells us to stop and we all have agreed to this when driving for obvious reasons. However, we do not have to stop, but we do have to take the responsibility for what can happen if we do not get away with it or if it goes dreadfully wrong.

We do not have this advantage when we are dealing with the Angelic World or 'other worlds' that are unfamiliar to us because we are not on familiar terms with the laws of action and reaction that operate in these places, as we should here — 'should' being the operative word. We really do not know their kingdom very well if at all compared to our own. Despite knowing the circumstances and situations of our world, we can still get ourselves into a great deal of trouble and danger at times.

This is why the reader will find repeated many times the need to be respectful, to tread softly, move carefully and to speak quietly. It is easy to transgress laws, regulations and the rules of courtesy, especially when you do not know they exist because you are a stranger in a strange land and this plea is not always accepted in mitigation or litigation. This cannot be claimed as unfair treatment when we are admonished in our place that 'ignorance of the law is no excuse' — a rather stupid axiom. We are not allowed to practise law for the obvious reasons that we know extremely little about it, but we are still expected to know the laws when it is too late and we have transgressed them accidentally — *non sequitur.*

Consider how much more important this would be in the Angelic Kingdom, a far more powerful kingdom than our place in the scheme of things could ever be. Hence, the regular warning to act with prudence, respect and to take nothing for granted. The angels have a patent advantage of knowing their surroundings and ours better than we do. If access to the angelic were easy, very few books of this nature would be written because put simply, they would not be needed, you scarcely need a book to tell you how to go to the next town.

Such works should be regarded as guides that incorporate the accumulated experience of the past, the present and those still attempting to undertake 'the never–ending journey.' Just as early explorers and navigators brought information back to add to existing charts and correct them if found faulty. This helps those who follow, giving greater safety, marking the dangers to avoid and marking any safer and shorter routes to take.

Despite the doctrine of the angels being endorsed by the *Bible* and other religious works, some theologians have suggested that a number of biblical writers created a belief in the angels as a literary expedient. This was done to represent the divine presence as supreme, the only true God and to reduce in importance the gods of polytheistic religions to a subservient position with regard to the divine presence — 'for' and 'against' will be given if it has been found or known about.

Earlier we used a term we regard as important to this work — 'the Middle Ground.' It is this 'Middle Ground' where most of the work (as far as this writer is concerned) is attempted but first you have to know about it and then find it. 'All roads lead to Rome' is still being used but the 'Middle Ground' is not Rome. This will be taken up again later and it is not a difficult concept to understand or follow and even at this early stage it is a phrase I would like the reader to keep in mind while reading what follows.

As said, the angels are not confined to the *Bible*, but this monumental work is the main source of the angelic for those who are mostly of Western origin. As an occidental, I was naturally brought up with the *Bible*, as my family was before me. The *Bible* is ingrained into my being and even if I wanted to, I would not know how to remove it but then why would I want to do that? My personal studies and writings are sometimes pigeonholed by a assortment of names such as 'occult, mystical, magical, pagan, heathenism, insanity and even Black Magic' by occasional zealots who must have their say — these people are always with us it seems, yet I have never dealt in the Negative Arts or Black Magic and never will. My study of the *Bible* has not been lacking in diligence, respect and great interest.

The fact I am attempting to work with the angels does not appear to count to some but perhaps this is because the methods used have not been 'approved' by those who feel that their approval is necessary and to a large extent, I often work alone. This particular approach to such studies may persuade some that I am hostile to the *Bible*, especially when I find fault. I agree that some of my studies look at the work from a different perspective and I arrive, according to them, at a different perception of the work according to the religion that stems from it — it has been interesting to say the least.

I do not with the following statement wish to be deliberately offensive to those of orthodox Christian belief when I say that it is not necessary to consider religion when reading the *Bible*. Whatever view I hold of the work, it has afforded me constant study for many years since a child and my love of it has never diminished. My main dissension in later life is with some of the interpretations and conclusions drawn from *Scripture* by people — not God. Witness the fact that many are now rewriting the Bible to suit their particular views and in their own words, I wonder what would be the outcome if they tried this with some of the other 'holy' works.

> 'Both read the Bible day and night
> But thou read'st black where I read white.'
> ***The Everlasting Gospel*** (c. 1818)
> William Blake 1757–1827. English poet

I have the greatest respect for the work on two very important levels. The first is the remarkable antiquity of the *Bible* and the second is that it is one of the most widely distributed books in history, in addition to being one of the oldest books in continuous publication. A lot of the judgements and conclusions made here will not see eye to eye with the 'agreed interpretation' of those who guide the religion that is taken from but in this respect I am not limited to having to conform to a set of rules I did not make. There could the cry of heretic and some have called me this, which from time to time made me feel I could be on the right track for if you are swimming against the stream, you could be swimming to the source. My feelings in the matter are far better explained than I could ever manage by the English poet and Latin scholar A. E. Housman (1859–1936) to which I can add nothing, which is why such writers are often found in many of things that I write, especially this writer:

'The laws of God, the laws of man,
He may keep that will and can;
Not I: let God and man decree
Laws for themselves and not for me;
And if my ways are not as theirs
Let them mind their own affairs.'
*Last Poems* (1922) No.12

I have long thought that it is best not to confuse what has been or being done in the name of a religion with the religion itself. If that were followed through to its logical conclusion, so many of the things that people admire would be found with dirt on its hands whatever the religion, politics or philosophy. The *Bible* is certainly worthy of anyone's reading or examination.

When I first joined the School my teacher said 'the *Bible* was a wonderful manual of magic if you knew what to look for and where.' This was quite a cultural shock at the time and I know now that is just what was intended to be — would he go or would he stay? Would he be receptive to some of the things that were to follow if he did stay? I stayed and I would like to think I did benefit by staying all those years ago, of course I believe that I did or I would have taken a different course long ago and I have even less time to waste now than then.

The important point I am making is this. Anyone who denies themselves access to the pages of the *Bible* because of their antagonism to the work, the Christian Church in particular or to religion in general is depriving themselves of more than they know because the book is a literary giant, but that is their shortfall not mine.

'He [the translator] will find one English book and one only, where, as in the Iliad itself, perfect plainness of speech is allied with perfect nobleness and that book is the Bible.' On Translating Homer (1861) – Matthew Arnold 1822–88. English poet and essayist

For me, reading the *Bible* as literature places it without question or doubt among the greatest books of the world. I have a special love of the King James Version because it is the one I was brought with and in which is found some of the most glorious prose ever written, we that have it should be justly proud of it and apologize to none. Thomas Babington Macauley put it better when he wrote 'The *English Bible*, a book that, if everything else in our language should perish, would alone suffice to show the whole extent of its beauty and power.' It is a work of sublime literature and its influence is obvious to anyone who listens with a little more care to everyday speech.

People talk of 'forbidden fruit,' of 'sparing the rod' and escaping 'by the skin of their teeth.' They 'wash their hands of something or someone' and say they were saved at the 'eleventh hour' often by their 'guardian angel.' When speaking of the weather, how often do you hear 'Red sky at night, shepherds delight, red sky in the morning, shepherds warning.'

Point out to people this was originally an *agrapha* of Christ in the *Bible* and watch the response. However, Jesus did say 'When it is evening, ye say, It will be fair weather; for the sky is red. And in the morning, It will be foul weather for the day: for the sky is red and lowering.' *Matthew* 16:2–3. Of course, the *New Testament* can only contain *agrapha* or 'unwritten sayings of Christ' as he never actually wrote anything down in the Greek has $\alpha\gamma\rho\alpha\phi o\varsigma$, *agraphos*= 'unwritten' (Thucydides) 'not registered.'

We say someone is a 'Solomon' or a 'Judas' with most knowing that the former is a compliment, the latter is not, calling a woman a 'Jezebel' does not exactly compliment her. We admonish people saying 'do not judge or you be judged in turn' and 'do to others as you would have them do to you' and so forth. We also hear the frequent chestnut among many that Delilah 'cut off Samson's seven locks of hair' when she did nothing of the sort, Delilah never touched the hair of Samson. The list is endless, but I think there is enough to make the point intended that even those who rarely if ever open the *Bible* still use it, often without even knowing it.

'Remember that you are a human being with a soul and the divine gift of articulate speech: that your native language is the language of Shakespeare and Milton and the Bible; and don't sit there crooning like a bilious pigeon.' *Pygmalion* (1916) Act 1. George Bernard Shaw 1856–1950. Irish playwright.

The Christian religion has to be taken into account regarding the main subject matter of this work and this must not taken as an apology, why should it be? Other points of view and information are not precluded because they have great interest to the subject. The *Bible* has moulded much of society in the West and elsewhere, including many of their laws. Sometimes this influence has been for good, while at other times it has a great deal to answer for, as history clearly shows but in this it does not stand alone. To be fair this has always been the same with zealots whatever their cause or country and 'doing God's work' has excused many and much. They always know best and are usually seeking some form of power to take over or take charge of anything and anyone.

History in the main shows where there is great power there is great fault and the greater the power, then the greater the fault can be, though not necessarily. It bears repetition that the hands of any system that seeks power in the world for good or ill are not completely clean — if ever, even today. Once they have got what they want they can afford to be a little more generous, as we all can — *noblesse oblige* indeed — but try to take it away from them! No matter how much people protest to the contrary, which of course they will ' . . . use every man after his desert and who should 'scape the whipping?' *Hamlet* Act.2: Sc.2.

There must be grist for the perpetual treadmills that insist that you show that you are 'up to date,' speaking 'the language of the day' and that you are 'relevant' — if you are alive — you are relevant.

There are so many new 'isms' today and they are breeding faster and greater in the world than any biblical plague. Someone always seems to be thinking up things for the rest of us to obey. This sort of thing suggests that there are people with too much time on their hands and not enough to do with it.

It seems that those who have the Church in their charge today are more concerned with chasing an elusive will–o–the–wisp called 'relevance.' If the religions of today spent as much time seeking

God as they do seeking 'relevance,' they could be a real force for even greater good and something to be reckoned with. This saddens many who are their own priesthood even though they plough a lonely furrow or are but 'labourers in the vineyard.' Let us stop off on an 'island' for a while:

## PAGANISM

Paganism suffered less from such shortcomings because it was generous, perhaps a little too generous and trusting for its own good at times but it was still strong enough to accommodate most people and their tenets within its corpus. Such generosity, though highly desirable, is not always wise and this may have been why paganism was brought low for a while. It is usually the generosity of those who are truly strong, open-handed and share what they have without seeking any recompense because their keyword is the gift of live and let live. The truly strong know that others can take from their light without the light being diminished or dimmed in any way, while the mean of spirit have not yet grasped this tenet.

The truly strong have a generosity with their knowledge and time that often assumes that others know as much as they do. They will as a rule share and give to most that ask from them, despite the fact that their generosity is not always appreciated and frequently taken for granted.

Paganism is far from dead or beaten, as some had hoped it would eventually be. After a great number of years of study and writing, I find it quite beyond my simple ken that Paganism is still being regarded as evil by some and being confused with worship of the Devil, Satanism and evil in general. I would have thought that these infantile objections, for they cannot be considered arguments, would have been dismissed out of hand long ago. They have not so sadly we must make an obvious defence against those who level these trifling accusations. Paganism is none of the above, the philosophy of Paganism (as its name infers) is involved directly concerned in all aspects and regard for the worship of Nature, the stewardship of the Earth and being well–mannered with it. Let us look at the words 'pagan' and 'heathen' a little more the better to understand them — worse things have been worshipped.

Paganism is taken from the words *pagan, paien, payen*, Latin *paganus*= 1. Adj., pertaining to a village. 2. Subst., 1: a villager, a rustic. 2: a civilian as opposed to a military man. 3: a heathen or pagan from *paganus*= a village. The last use of the word dates from the fourth century and it is generally accepted that the first use of the name *pagan* in this particular meaning was in an edict of the Emperor Valentinian in A.D 368. Christianity was first preached in the large towns and because of this and the greater tendency of the people of cities to adopt new opinions and fads; they still do under the pretentiousness of superiority over 'rural folk.' Christianity rooted itself at the great centres of population before greatly affecting the country parts, the cities became Christian while the country people were heathen and the word *paganus* consequently became synonymous with *heathen*.

*Heathen* is found in many languages including the Anglo-Saxon as *hœthen* from *hœth*= 'heath.' In ordinary language, a 'dweller on the heath' sometimes it meant 'an uncivilised man, a barbarian.' Technically (briefly), it is from the Hebrew of the *Old Testament*, 'a gentile, one not a Jew with the further implication being that they worshipped false gods or that, if they worshipped Jehovah, they did so by forbidden methods. *Heathen* is the rendering of the Hebrew word *goim* (goyim)= 'people, nations, foreigners, gentiles, heathens in a special sense.' The Greek equivalent of the Hebrew *goim* is *εθνικος (εθνος), ethnikos (ethnos)*= 'foreign, heathen, gentile' *New Testament*.

In its purest form, paganism could reasonably vie with many of the established religions and I am sure it could even prove a satisfactory alternative to some of them. It is worth repeating that paganism involves a reverence for Nature, the Earth and it upholds the very important belief of individual responsibility and until this particular nettle is firmly grasped by people, I feel little overall progress will be achieved in any form of belief or advancement. Finally, there is a belief and acceptance of the Gods and Goddesses, often found under a Chief Deity. One of the accusations often given against Paganism is that it involves animism, which does not really hold water. Most religions, from the simplest to the most complex include some form of animism, so let us take a brief look at this objection.

*Animism*, from the Latin *anima*= 'breath' or 'soul' is broadly the acceptance of spiritual beings or accepting the spiritual found within matter. If you were to ask most people what they think the angels are, they will consistently suggest they are spiritual beings and not physical. Many biologists and psychologists point out that animism refers to a view that the human mind is a non–material entity that mediates with the body through the brain and the nervous system.

*Animism* as a philosophical theory is the doctrine that most objects in the world have an inner being or spirit, though early races must have accepted some objects as being without spiritual life. They probably considered objects that acted in an unpredictable or mysterious fashion 'as if being alive.' Just as we do when an inanimate object does not seem to obey the rules (even today) saying that some things appear 'to have a life of their own.'

Some writers consider *animism*, as a belief in spiritual beings and a minimum definition of religion. The 18th century German doctor and chemist Stahl (1660–1734) devised the term *animism* to describe his theory that the soul is the vital principle responsible for organic development. However, since the late 19th century the term is now mainly associated with anthropology. One view, remembered early in my studies is still worth taking note of:

*'Qui croit à la Providence et à l'efficacité de la prière doit se rappeler qu'il accepte tous les principes sur lesquels repose la divination antique.' Historie de la Divination dans L'antiquite.* (4 vols.) 1879–82. Auguste Bouché–Leclerq.

('He who believes in Providence and in the efficaciousness of prayer ought to remember that he is accepting all those principles upon which stands archaic divination.')

'The virtues of the heathen, being devoid of grace, can only be looked upon as splendid vices.' *De Carne Christi* – Tertullian. Religion is the common experience shared by a group and it usually requires an arbiter when deciding what is compatible with it. In Catholicism, it is the Pope who performs this office and in other religions, it is often an accepted and recognized priesthood or someone standing at the head of the group or order, which does much the same thing, an archbishop for instance. Occult Groups and Schools often have a leader or teacher to guide them. The best Schools are those where there is a 'contacted' teacher working 'under authority' from higher up the Tree and the 'authority' is working through the teacher.

Mysticism on the other hand is a personal experience rarely shared and usually it requires none to arbitrate on its behalf. I have often thought we should use care when we attempt to cast out the devil within us so that we do not cast out what may prove to be the best in us.

Jupiter, the chief god of the Roman pantheon sends the god Mercury/Hermes to do his expressed bidding of making his pronouncements known to the priesthoods or populace of a forthcoming event or edict. The One God sends the Archangel Gabriel, the Angel of the

Annunciation to do much the same task. The former is paganism while the latter is of 'the true faith.'

Sometimes this makes some people regard the Archangel Gabriel as the Archangel of Communication instead of 'Proclamation' and this can be found. The task of communication has already been allotted and it has long been with the Archangel Raphael. The Archangel Gabriel 'announces' as all angels do and can and this is communication without question at the time, but not communication in all its forms. As said, the Angel of Communication is the Archangel Raphael.

One of the tasks that the planet Mercury undertakes is to act as the 'bearer of news' and it would not be wrong to say that this is one of his main functions, the other being medicine, hygiene and health in general. Mercury/Hermes and his archangel are communication in all forms, including the nervous system of the body that take the required information around the body. This is why, for example in astrology, this function is found under Mercury's sway and not the Moon (= Archangel Gabriel.) The natives of his sign of the Zodiac, Gemini (not Virgo= mainly 'health, medicine and hygiene') are often called the 'news–vendors of the zodiac.' They like to have news first, they like to be first to tell and nothing is too trivial for their interest, even when the 'news' is thought to have become 'mere gossip.'

I should not have to point out that the pagan and classical deities were also under One Supreme God who reigned over all and to whom ultimately all were answerable. However, there was a difference between the angels of the **Old Testament** and the gods of the Greeks, Romans and other nations. The classical pantheon was plurality, not monotheism. I am not the first to suggest that the angels appear to have brought back a form of plurality into monotheism even if it was through the backdoor. This is why, discussed later, some of the early Church Fathers where not happy with the invocation or worship of angels as we are doing with this work but then very little seemed to please the early Church Fathers.

Any notion of angelic equality with the Creator was foiled early in the scheme of things. The Rabbis say the One–God created the angels after the Creation of the World and while the One God was still in solitary splendour. The angels were not created before or during this creative act, because nothing created before Yahweh. God is first and all other matters were secondary, no matter how important they were thought to be.

In the mythology of Eastern and Western nations many events of Nature, good luck, good hunting and fertility, victory in conflict, the overall well–being and prosperity of the people, the fertility of people, animals and crops so many things were under the aegis of a spirit or genius to whom you could appeal.

Today we still have totems in the form of a rabbit's foot, a horseshoe, a 'lucky' shirt' or some item that makes a person feel vulnerable if they are without it or not wearing it. Any good or bad events in the lives of the people or individuals were regarded as being the blessings or curses of individual divinities. Some gods were local to an area and often this is why, particularly with some of the Celtic spirits for example, single inscriptions refer to a god or gods appearing locally and not generally. This is found for example with the god Cernunnos who at times was found only in specific areas.

The god Cernunnos is 'the Horned One' in Celtic religion, he is an archaic and powerful deity and he was extensively worshipped as the 'Lord of Wild Things' and is usually given as a 'fertility and Chthonic' deity. Cernunnos probably had a diversity of names in various areas of the Celtic world, but his characteristics were generally unvarying and were usually found in the region called Gaul, which is now a central region in France. He is prominently figured on the Gundestrup Bowl, which is a beautiful silver bowl showing a mixture of Celtic and Roman influences from Jutland. On this bowl, Cernunnos is accompanied by a boar and purses of money or snakes have been found probably representing regeneration. Cernunnos wears the antlers of a stag, sometimes a stag or the sacred ram–horned serpent accompanies him and these were deities in their own right. He wore or held a torque, which was the sacred neck ornament of Celtic gods and its heroes. On the bowl, horned helmets are figured and some Anglo–Saxon helmets were horned. His kinship and concerns are rather obvious and he is broadly in keeping with the god of Nature, Pan.

These deities acknowledged a superior deity as chief among them, this was unacceptable to Israel because these diverse deities as well as their superior God, enjoyed dignity, worship and divine honours, therefore, these deities were pluralism and false — instead of monotheism and truth.

Jewish mythology claims that every natural manifestation and event resulted from and was under the absolute Will of the One God. This is because the One God was Eternal, Perfect and the Creator of All. Thus, everything was subject to him and to no other. Jewish myth would not tolerate any thoughts or schemes that suggested duality, the plurality of gods or anything else that disturbed or destroyed this absolute Unity.

It should be remembered that the names given to a deity are abstract symbols and ideas necessary to enable the human mind to grasp the thought that the deity exists. The name given does not necessarily describe the composition or essence of a deity. When the early Cabbalists wanted to describe the deity before the universe was created they used the description *Ain Soph* or *Ayin*= 'without end' or *No–Thing*= 'nothing.' It was not an absolute negative void or a negative 'no thing or nothing.' There is something there that is 'unknown to man' and the human mind could not comprehend it, hence the difficulty of finding the right words to explain. It is not there in a material sense —it is — *non est*, a contraction of *non est inventus*= 'he was not found, he (or it) was not found, he (or it) was gone.'

Some say that atheism is terrifying but not as terrifying as the hard–faced tyranny of a single, omnipresent God. This principle is thought to be why many monotheistic religions often fragment and shatter later in their existence and why Paganism with its flexibility refuses to lie down and die as some had hoped. Paganism appeals to some heartfelt need within the human breast that sees a god, goddesses or the gods and spirits in everything and everywhere.

The ministering angels of Jewish myth possess divine power but it is said that they are not independent agents because they do not have independence or Free Will from their Creator. They have no will of their own but the will of their Creator to whom they are obedient and subservient without question or questioning. Needless to say, this opinion brings out the alternative view by expressing a different position. The former view is given as why it was stressed (in early teachings) that the angels were created on the second or fifth day of Creation and that God alone was responsible for Creation in its entirety, not the angels because they were created later and therefore they must be subject to the Creator's will.

'For I the Lord thy God am a jealous God, visiting iniquity of the fathers upon the children unto the third and fourth generation of them that hate me; and shewing mercy unto thousands of them that love me, and keep my commandments.' *Exodus* 20:5. I have long thought 'visiting iniquity' to the 'children unto the third or fourth generation' was a mite spiteful to the innocent for what was after all — 'the iniquity of the fathers' who hated him.

As a primary idea in trying to understand the human condition or existence itself, Nature and the complexity of human society, God has been the object of endless philosophical and theological speculation. There was a long period during which Western culture understood itself and the world mainly through the framework of Greco–Roman philosophy (c.200–1400). We find the notion of God was first formed with the help of Platonic and then by Aristotelian classification.

Greek philosophy had a penchant for the consummate, changeless and eternal realms of being. This religious tradition naturally laid great emphasis on the absolute nature of God. It is no surprise that God was conceived as being pure, completely independent, constant and divine. The active and secular aspects of God exhibited themselves chiefly though the agency of an angelic host, the lives of the saints and good people everywhere. The word 'host' is usually interpreted as bands of angels, not the Sun, Moon or Stars, as said elsewhere, if the 'host' in question is human, it is generally given as such to avoid error.

If you ask a child (even an adult) in later life about angels, they will usually speak of them in biblical terms. This is because it was from the **Bible** more often than not in the West, they were first made aware of the angels. Their ideas regarding angels, their appearance and their powers are normally biblical. Therefore, there should be little or no surprise that we are beginning our journey of discovery mainly with the **Bible** — though of course other angelic sources are not absent from the work. Angels are accessible to all one way or another, sometimes without asking or seeking them. Before we make a start with the **Old Testament** let us deal with three, important terms found in most works of this nature . . . we have come another of our 'islands' spoken of earlier. We will really make speedier growth by stopping on these 'islands' as we progress down the 'river' to gather supplies or stores — this 'island' is called:

## ANALOGY, SYMBOL AND SIGN

In traditional cultures, the power of the symbol and sign were highly esteemed. Magic, Angelic teachings and divination were among the forms used in an attempt to reveal and understand the Will of God or the Gods, including the great forces that control and shape the ends of the world and areas under discussion had their symbols and signs. These ritual forms and teachings carried within them the myths and legends of the culture, including its system of signs and symbols, which gave the seeker access to these myths and legends. It was a place where and individual and the great archetypical images could meet for a while and work together.

In view of the above, it may prove useful to expand and discuss these three small words frequently used in most works of this nature including this one, how they are generally used and are used here.

*Analogy* (in everyday language) is a process of arguing from similarity in known respects — to similarity in other respects. The resemblance of relations between one thing or another and when these resemblances are pointed out together — they are usually connected by the word 'between.'

*Symbol* does not have the same restrictions as the sign. It comes from the Latin, *sybolus/symbolum*, in the Greek, *συμβολον, symbolun*= 'a sign or token by which one infers a thing' from *συμβαλλω, sumballo*= 'to throw together' or 'to compare one's own opinion with facts and so . . . to conclude, infer, conjecture, interpret . . . to make out, understand.' In the Greek sense, 'a casting together, as of a contribution into a common treasury. An object animate or inanimate, standing for, representing or calling up something moral or intellectual; an emblem, a figure a type or representation.' A case in point — 'Salt as incorruptible was the symbol of friendship; which, if it casually fell, was accounted ominous' – Browne: *Vulgar Errours.*

A symbol does not restrict the imagination and as a result, meditation and quiet reflection on a symbol will often bring out the greater depth and potential found inherent within it because sometimes symbols are used to represent ideas or principles, now and then very complex ones that words do not help. So it follows that the greater your 'internal library' — the better and more accurate your chance of doing this will be — because symbols have to work with what they find within individuals. Symbols often go beyond their form for those who can see beyond the symbol and they partake in that to which they point. They can open up degrees of reality that are often closed to the seeker. They unlock dimensions and elements of the soul that correspond to reality, they cannot be created intentionally or invented at will and can either be inner and outer.

*Signs* are strict in their intention and should have no ambiguity by meaning exactly what they say or they would serve no useful purpose. For example, the signs used for poison, radiation, electrocution, keep out and so forth are universal in their message whatever the language. There would be little point in writing a sign warning the motorist that 'the bridge across a deep ravine had collapsed' if the sign was in any way vague regarding the danger because the results would hardly bear thinking about.

This is how these words are used throughout the work and using the broadest of brush strokes they can be taken as: *Analogy*= association, *Symbol*= allegory and *Sign*= representation. We may as well get two other points that are important to the way this method operates, this time regarding the place where our efforts are to be made . . .

## THE MIDDLE GROUND

The reader will find the above title stressed as being indispensable to the writer and the work. The 'Middle Ground' is the area where the majority of your efforts will be concentrated so it would be better to know how to prepare the ground and how it is regarded and used. The focus of the work is nearly always directed to the 'Middle Ground' and again this is why the terminology has been introduced early in the book. So, why is it considered so important?

When two countries adjoin each other, as they must, they have frontiers but these are not technically contiguous. More often than not, there is usually an undeveloped area between them that is not claimed by either country, which is why it is commonly called 'no man's land.' On this unclaimed land only barbed wire, border controls and weeds flourish. This area can sometimes prove very dangerous for anyone found there from either side as they normally have to prove who they are, why they are there, what they are doing there and what it is they want. At frontiers, assessment is made concerning your purpose and the reasons for wanting to be admitted to where you want to go. The guardians of the border usually want to know where you have come from, why you have come, where you are going, what you are taking into the country, how long you are going to stay and all the rest.

In some respects, this may prove a useful analogy for us particularly when the Middle Ground is between the Terrestrial and the Celestial. It is better for the traveller to have some knowledge of the protocol of the place they are trying to go to. A knowledge of signs and symbols is often involved through which you can identify yourself and your intent, who are you attempting to contact and often to get there at all, we sometimes have 'to go very deep within.'

By being there, you often show that contact is being sought to begin with and if you are shown signs and symbols, it would be better if you are able to understand as many of them as possible and to know what they mean. The greater the 'internal library' you possess the more they will have to use to gain a better understanding and it is not trite to say that they can only use what they find. It is obvious that the angels are more successful in our sphere than we are in the theirs, because more angels appear in our 'country' than we are in 'theirs,' which should tell us a lot.

# THE 'LARGE UPPER ROOM . . . THERE MAKE READY.'

There is another important facet of this section that must be taken up before we leave it and that is the large 'Upper Room.' The words used here are from *St. Luke* but they can be found in so many places for those who look as can the 'large room' which, for instance should not be found 'under the Sun.' In biblical use is goes like this, 'For the passover, Christ said to Peter and John, Go and prepare us the Passover that we may eat. And they said unto him, Where wilt thou that we prepare? And he said unto them, Behold, when ye are entered into the city, there shall a man meet you, bearing a pitcher of water; follow him into the house where he entereth in. And ye shall say unto the goodman of the house, The Master saith unto thee, Where is the guest chamber, where I shall eat the passover with my disciples? And she shall shew you a large upper room furnished; there make ready.' *Luke* 22: 8–13. Following the 'man . . . bearing a pitcher' foreshadows the *Age of Aquarius* that will follow the *Age of Pisces* that has 'the fish' as its symbol.

Today for the most there is too much noise and diversion, preventing so many for being still and have some 'empty places' within them where there is nothing and silence — the dread of so many in modern society today. Every minute of the day must be occupied and silence is a black hole into which many are fearful that they will fall and never get out.

If you enter the Middle Ground and leave your invitation to the angels there, then you should make preparations in case they take it up. It is simple good manners and courtesy for if you invited a friend or friends to your home to visit or stay, you would prepare to receive them and 'there make ready.' You must make space and cater for them for the duration of their stay and if having given the offer of hospitality, most would do this.

However, this is on a physical level and can be dealt with easier, however, it appears to be harder on a higher level but it is equally requires good manners and courtesy or you should not extend the invitation. There is a force that makes people feel a need to fill up every moment when awake. While this is not evil of itself, I feel that it has become negative, especially when it starts when young, because noise and being active is equated with enjoying yourself!

Now, what are we getting and I know that some are there already. The 'empty space' where the angels can come is sometimes harder to create than people think but it has to be done. It need not be something that is foreign to the modern mind even though modern life is a noisy, busy, demanding and distracting place and it seems that it is fearful of letting people know the advantages of the alternatives.

'I am not eager, bold
Or strong — all that is past.
I am ready not to do,
At last, at last!'

*Parabola* – St. Peter Canisius 1521–1597,
who founded the Jesuit colony at Colgne.

If everything is filled and there is no 'upper room' to be found within, where can they stay for there is 'no room at the inn.' Now let us move on . . .

*Mal'achim* in the Hebrew is the plural of *mal'akh* or *mal'ach*= 'messenger' found many times throughout. This is a broad term for messengers or ministers and the angels in a unique sense because they are intermediaries or mediators between the spiritual and the material kingdoms. For this reason it is appropriate to try to gain contact and cooperation from these beings as *Legatus*= *a 'Messenger* or *Ambassador.'* Mediation for instance can apply to all of the ten classes of angelic beings found in the Cabbalistic and biblical hierarchies, though most contact usually takes place with the angels and archangels initially. Higher contact (especially in the beginning) is not always immediate but it can be granted in exceptional circumstances and it is certainly not impossible.

However, the two lower orders of angels and archangels should be more than enough for anyone for many lifetimes and please do not use the term 'lower' in a derogatory sense. I dislike the word 'lower' in some usage as it infers something as being 'lesser than.' When you climb a ladder the rung you are standing on is higher than the one just left but lower that the one above it. A rung contains both descriptions within itself depending on the direction you are looking or going. When you climb, you are looking for the higher rung, but when you descend, you are looking for the lower. One direction takes you up, the other takes you down, you are using the same rungs for both directions and this makes them all equally important.

This can be applied especially to the messengers of God in the *Bible*, generally rendered as angels, as well as being designated the *Bene–Elohim* or 'the Sons of the God.' Elohim (singular Eloah, Hebrew= God), the God of Israel in the *Old Testament*. A plural of majesty, the term Elohim has sometimes been used for other deities. It is these mediators that can let you or guide you to the Middle Ground and they can also guide and assist you regarding what you are seeking.

The Middle Ground, where meeting and contact is being attempted has the obviously important word —'middle' — because that means that you go halfway in your attempts and you can do little more in the beginning other than make yourself ready and wait. You 'wait' because you are 'waiting to asked' and you wait until you are asked because it is good manners and arrogance is not a visa. Knowing of the Middle Ground means that you are aware of a point where the borders of the two areas merge and join, a mixture where the two regions are reasonably in balance and neutral.

As a rule in our dealings with others, we usually feel sympathetically inclined to those who are prepared to 'meet us halfway' in any form of dealing such as business deals, personal relationships, friendship, reconciliation and the like. This protocol I am sure will be enlarged upon further as the work progresses.

This is why I feel it would be of advantage if the concept of the Middle Ground was kept in the back of the reader's mind while reading the work. It will guide you and help by placing things in a specific area and context. It is not unlike having a place of safety when we find ourselves on uncertain ground, somewhere we can go back to if we are indecisive of our footing or not sure of the way. Sometimes we have to go back to something that is familiar because it gives us familiarity and time to pause and contemplate our next move. We often do this in life by returning to the known and safe from where we can retrace our path to a new position before going on into the unknown.

We should stop thinking of the Deities and their messengers as absolutely definable beings that can be fitted into neat boxes, labels or notions of our making and not theirs. This is our restricted judgment at work and not their unlimited potential and capabilities, about which we can only dream. There is action and interaction where the Deities are merging and separating at different times and places, which allows their enormously diverse characteristics to become even more prominent or less so if this is what is required.

The Enochian Angel Mapsama tells John Dee (in part): ' . . . But be humble. Enter not of presumption; but of permission. Go not in rashly; but be brought in willingly: for many have ascended, but few have entered.' This statement brings to mind the biblical injunction ' . . . for many are called but few are chosen.' *Matthew* 20:16 and 22:14 and this latter statement is also found repeated and enlarged in the short subdivision devoted to Dr. John Dee and the *Enochia* and its angels near the end of Part 1, (see *Gmicalzoma — An Enochian Dictionary* also published by *Authors OnLine*).

## THE ANALOGY OF THE MAGNETIC FIELD

Many people give the impression they regard heaven and earth as two separate places with the middle ground somewhere between them, which at times is difficult to bridge or even find and here a magnet is a good model. Often when people are asked give a description of a magnet; they often say that it has 'two separate poles' but this is not strictly true. The two poles are not 'separate' and never can be. The magnet has two opposing poles but not separate poles because one pole cannot exist without the other and they cannot be understood independently for the simple reason that if one pole were able to be removed the other cannot exist, more to the point, neither can the magnet.

Something that is a unity is often divided and made dual in speech — even when it is not. People often speak of a country as if it were two separate countries, one country being the north and the other the south, cities and towns are frequently treated in a like manner having an 'East End' and a 'West End.' but these are two areas of the same country, city or town.

There is a magnetic field between the two poles and this is the 'bridge or Middle Ground.' It joins and links the two poles and it is impossible to understand these independently because they are indivisible from the whole. The magnetic field can be thought of as a bridge that joins the two parts. For the 'Middle Ground' to exist it has to be in the middle with something on either side.

A magnet contains the ubiquitous 'trinity' having a North Pole, a South Pole and a magnetic field between the two and it is the magnetic field that we attempt to use. The earth has two opposing magnetic poles, a magnetic field exists between them and we use the magnetic field of the earth to navigate and find our way about the planet among other things.

We use the magnetic field to get where we want to go with the aid of a compass or other instruments, which makes the magnetic field visible for us to use by showing magnetic north from which the other directions can be derived. The poles are at the ends of the magnet whatever its shape and we know as magnetic field is connecting them. The magnetic field can be observed under the right or certain conditions and at school, a sheet of paper was put on top of a magnet, the paper was sprinkled with iron filings and gently tapped to demonstrate the existence of the magnetic field when its pattern was seen through the medium of the iron–filings.

In work of this nature, we have to create the right 'conditions' to get us where we want to go. We use protocol (= 'compass') to navigate the Middle Ground that we hope will take us to where we want be and the required angel to help us to seek our aspirations, give help or solutions to problems that beset us and all that flesh is heir to. On the other hand, it is often in the area between 'the poles' where we can lose our bearings and go astray.

On Jacob's Ladder, the magnetic field went up one side of the ladder and down the other, just as the angels do from the 'pole of heaven' to 'the pole of earth' and back up the other side to complete the circuit. A stronger magnetic field can disturb other magnetic fields and powers unfriendly to your aims can use this interference for their own ends, causing chaos, making us lose our bearings and direction. If you think this may be happen, you could try invoking the additional defence of an appropriate defensive angel to your cause and often this can be of help.

Why this is relevant to us is discussed and explained in greater detail in the chapter *The Link* or *Jacob's Ladder* in Part Two. I sometimes think of the middle ground as a 'magnetic field' and call it the — *Mare Magnes* — this is my poetic term for the place because it is how I believe it operates. ***Mare***= 'a sea, nostrum or Mediterranean Sea' and ***Magnes, Μαγνης, Magnes***= 'with or without lapis, the magnet ('lapis').

My old science master will be turning in his grave how I am using his teachings for something being so unscientific in his eyes, the Middle Ground indeed! Something that cannot be measured, detected by smell or touch, weighed and so on. I will still stick with my difference of opinion with him that Science may be the 'head' of a people but myth legend and folklore are their 'heartbeat' with the angels mediating between these poles and scientists always seem to be the last to know.

Scientists have at last found out how the bee, a creature that science has said for years should not be able to fly, does. This must of great consolation to the bee that has been doing it from pre–biblical times and this has long been an annoyance to me. I thank science for what it has given me and I am both grateful and filled with admiration for science and its many of its works but do not feel the need to put my Soul on its altar for either confirmation or blessing.

## SOME CLASSICAL SPIRITS

Let us look at some of the earlier manifestations of helpful and unhelpful spirits, sprites or whatever name is used for them in classical times. The term ***peri*** from Persian myth is often found and used in the West as a term for a fairy, which many crossword enthusiasts know. They are usually given as a beautiful but harmless presence, whose rank is usually set between angels and evil spirits.

W. S. Gilbert uses the term in the text and the sub–title of the Savoy Opera, ***Iolanthe – 'The Peer and the Peri.'*** In Persian or Iranian mythology, a peri (plural peris) is a fairy–like creature, some say a genie that was thought to have descended from the fallen angels or spirits. It is said that 'they direct with a wand those of pure mind the way to heaven.' However, they are held to be ruled by Iblis (or Eblis), the great evil spirit, though once of good standing, now equated with the Christian Satan.

Next, let us look at some of the public, civic spirits and guardian spirits staying in classical times. This section introduces some of the spirits and gods who are broadly, other than in name or title, shown to be performing similar duties as the angels, acting between the gods and the races of the earth. Many other examples can be found with little difficulty. The important personal Roman household gods were the Lares.

Lar, singular with Lares plural in Roman religion, these were any of the many tutelary deities. Originally, they were the gods of the tilled fields and were worshipped by the entire household at the crossroads where the fields of the family bordered on those of others. Later the Lares were worshipped in the house in association with the Penates, the gods of the storeroom (= 'penus') and as a result the prosperity of the family. The ***Penates publici*** were the 'luck' of the Roman state, originallly brought by Aeneas from Troy and kept at Lavinium. The household Lar (= 'familiaris') was regarded and honoured as the centre of the family and the cult of the family.

In the beginning each household had only one Lar, which was usually represented as a youthful build, dressed in a short tunic, holding a drinking horn in one hand and in the other a cup. However, under the empire two images were regularly found, one set on each side of the central figure of the genius of Vesta, or of some other deity. The whole group came to be called indifferently Lares or Penates. A prayer was said to the Lar/Lares every morning and special offerings were made at family festivals.

These good spirits of the departed, the Lares compitales, were actively thought to work for the well–being of the family and to bring it prosperity. Every family had its 'lord' (= Guardian Angel?) and one of the chief duties of the family 'lord' was to prevent the family from becoming extinct.

The Lares compitales were worshipped as good spirits (= the angels and archangels?) While the malevolent tormentors were the *larvae* (= the fallen angels or demons?)

Lares (= as familiares or domestici) are the tutelar deities of a house, the household gods, whose images stood on the hearth in a little shrine, aedes or in a small chapel, the lararium. *Compitalis*= 'of or pertaining to the cross–ways' also 'a festival annually celebrated at crossroads in honour of the Lares soon after the Saturnalia.' To the household Lares a portion of each meal was offered and the floor was considered the haunt of ghosts. If any food fell onto the floor then it had 'gone to the region of ghosts' and was regarded as having been formally given to them.

The statue of the family Lares was often portrayed as a youth with a drinking horn and cup. The worship of the Lares at Rome was closely connected with that of the Manes (Latin, *di manus*= 'the good gods') or they are connected with Mania, who is thought to be the mother of the Manes or Lares. She was called Lara by some and was invoked at the *Festival of the Lares* and placated by offerings of poppy heads and garlic. We are told the word Lares comes from the Etruscan *Lars*, which is thought to mean 'conductor or leader.' Manes are also the spirits of the dead and they were identified with the ancestors of the family. Later the term became used for the soul of the individual after death. Tombs were often found inscribed *DIS MANIBUS (or DM) SACRUM*, which preceded the name of the deceased showing they were dedicated to the Manes.

The Lares are found divided into two chief classes. The *Lars domestici* mentioned above and the *Lars publici,* the Manes of a house that were raised to the dignity of heroes with the Lars. When people were buried in the house there appears to be little difference between the two.

The Romans originally buried their dead in the house until the *Laws of the Twelve Tables* forbade the practise. These laws were inscribed on twelve bronze tablets — the *Twelve Tables* — that were on open display in the Forum. These were the earliest Roman code of laws and the starting point in the growth of Roman law. They gave provisions concerning legal procedures, debt foreclosure, funerary regulations, inheritance, paternal authority over children, property rights and guidance regarding a variety of major and minor offences. Although many of these provisions were modified or replaced at later times, the *Law of the Twelve Tables* formed the basis of all later private Roman law, which is why the Manes as spirits of the dead were now associated with the place of burial that was set outside the home.

As said earlier, the shrine of the Lares was found beside the household hearth (= under the rule of the goddess Vesta), which was in the atrium in early days. The atrium was the forecourt, hall, entrance–room that part of the house into which you first came after passing through the entrance and it was always covered. The ancient Roman and his children saluted the shrine of the Lares daily with a Morning Prayer and an offering from the table, customarily given after the main meal was finished with a part of the meal being laid on the fire in the hearth. Pious offerings were made to Lares every day and on joyous family occasions when their altars would be decked with garlands, cakes, honey, wine and incense. The *Lars familiaris* (= personal or the family Guardian Angels) were inseparable from the family and when the family moved, their *Lars familairis* went with them.

The public *Lares,* (= state or Guardian Angels of the people), the *Lars publici* are expressly distinguished from the domestic or private Lares. These public Lares were worshipped not only at Rome but also in all towns and places that were governed according to the Roman example.

The Public Lares were patrons of the state who presided over the major crossroads (= 'compita') of the city and in chapels (= 'aediculae'). There were always two *Lares compitales* or *vicorum*, one for each of the intersecting roads. The popular festival that honoured them was the *Compitalia*, which was held either annually or four times each year as both periods are found. The Lares of the whole city were called the *Lares præstistes*. The Lares were invoked as protectors of a journey as guardians of the crossroads (= *Lares viales*), in the country (= *Lares rurales*), in war and on the sea (= *Lares marini*).

The deities in the *Iliad* often threw a mist or shield around their wards in time of danger. Athene (= Athena) protected Achilles and Aphrodite protected Paris from an assault of Menelaus.

In Nabatean inscriptions there is a deity called *Shi'a Alqum* — 'the accompanier of the People,' whose charge was to guard and watch over caravans, as the Greek God Pan did with the Egyptian God Min at Mendes in Egypt. This is not unlike the powerful angel that accompanied the Children of Israel on their journey out of the bondage of Egypt.

At times leading the way as 'a pillar of cloud by day' and 'a pillar of cloud of fire, by night to show the way. When the Egyptians came in pursuit, the pillar of cloud went behind them and came between Israel and the Egyptians and was a 'cloud and darkness to them' and a vanguard to protect them from the Egyptian armies.

Now let us turn to the purpose of giving these particular examples to the reader. I believe that if the Roman deities were removed and replaced with Christian terminology, with the angels replacing the Roman spirits, suggested at certain points, some of these would be taken for delightful Christian rituals or festivals that could be used as a satisfying practice and I judge they would be found without the sin of heathenism. What is more, having removed the 'burning offence of paganism' they would be of great comfort and highly effective to all concerned. I am sure it would be a ceremony approved and practised by many people, even today because there is simply nothing there to give affront — and yet they would. They are gentle rituals and a reverent practise for both family and private worship.

Before we leave the examples, let us take a brief look at some of the guardian spirits, the personal and ancestral of the Teutonic races and bring the examples a little nearer home to our latitudes. In Germanic belief, we find the *Fylgja, Fylgjur* or *Fylgir*, which is Old Norse for 'followers.' These 'followers' were the protective or guardian spirits who attached themselves to an individual. If these guardian spirits wanted to appear to their charge, it was usually in the form of a woman or an animal. The life of the *Fylgjr* was determined by the life of the individual because like their charge, they were not immortal.

The *Fylgja* usually remained invisible and with the death of the human being, they either died or simply disappeared. The foreboding dreams of Old Scandinavia gives evidence of how deeply rooted were the ideas of the *fylgja* because 'the materialization of a man's spirit, in the animal form that had attended him throughout his life, was seen in dreams or it appeared just before death and while their charge was wide awake.'

The *fylgja* is quite distinct from the *hamingja*, which is occasionally called *fygjukona* often described as 'the wise maidens' in the *Eddic Poem* and the word is said to be best translated as 'fetch' or 'wraith.' This was a female tutelary genius that on the death of one member of the family was passed on to another and this is thought to account for the practise of naming a new born child after a recently deceased grandparent or relative. This was done to attach the guardian spirit of the family to the child's fortune. Among the Ashkenazim, Jewish children were named after deceased relatives and not usually after someone living, but other communities do not do this.

These spirits appeared at first as giant women, the offspring of the Norns, who are the *hamingja* of the world. *Hamingja* (= 'the many formed') as the name is from the Old Norse *hamr*= ('form.') As said earlier, the *fylgja* proper is never called *hamingja* with a parallel distinction being made between the personal soul and the ancestral soul, one dies and the other is passed on in the family, this separation is found in the customs of many races.

This particular spirit can be found in Iceland where each family or tribe had attached to it an *aettar–fylgja* and each individual had their *fylgja* that took the shape of a dog. In Iceland, much attention was given to the land spirits (= 'landvoettir'). The pre–Christian law of Iceland demanded that no one must approach the land in a ship that displayed a dragonhead, lest by doing so they frighten the land spirits.

We also have the Slavonic *vjedogonya* who are conceived partly as 'spirits of the house' and partly 'as guardian spirits dwelling in each man.' This possibly comes from the Old Slavic *vetru*= 'wind' showing the 'wind–like nature of the soul.' Again, I find very little here that is not protective and comforting, knowing there were guardian spirits watching over a person's life. Now let us leave these associated examples, put here to show that other countries and races have similar forms.

When the first Christians celebrated the Mysteries of their Faith it was often accompanied by seven lights, the trisagion, some incense and readings from the gospels. These seven lights are symbolic to me of the seven Sephiroth of Cabbala set below the Abyss in some systems (the **Cabbala of the Latter Day Cabbalists – Kircher**) and the Seven Planets of Old and their planetary or Star Angels, the **Seven Angels before the Throne of God** — 'the Angels with the lapis lazuli eyes' is an old tradition. This is why it was thought that wearing a ring of lapis lazuli, a broach, a pendant or even carrying a small piece of lapis lazuli about the person somewhere was not a bad thing for dealing with the angels. This particular stone was a long time favourite long before I took up these studies and lapis lazuli will appear again with regard to the **Ten Words or Commandments** later in the work.

Attention is frequently drawn throughout regarding the predominance of the number 'seven' in the **Bible** and most works of this nature, myth, legend and folklore. In the story of Samson, Delilah finds out the secret of Samson's strength. While Samson slept upon her knees, 'she called for a man, and caused him to shave off the seven locks of his head; and she began to afflict him, and his strength went from him.' The story is found in **Judges** 16:19.

The **Star Angels** are the rulers, lords or masters of the heavenly Spirits of the Stars and the planet is the physical body of the Spirit, which gives the Angel of the Planet. This was the basis for the worship of the Star Angels by a great many of antiquity. This form of worship was taken over by primitive Christianity in a modified form and it still exists in early lists.

An early list of the seven star–angels gives Michael= 'who is like unto God,' Gabriel= 'the strength of God,' Raphael= 'of divine virtue,' Uriel= 'God's light and fire,' Scaltiel= 'the speech of God,' Jehudiel= 'the praise of God' and Barachiel= 'the blessing of God.' They are often referred to as the **Rectors of the Seven Sacred Planets** and it was their divine attributes that may have led to the development of the names by which the archangels are known today. Jewish astrology also links the angels and archangels with the planets. The influence of the time of the birth upon the character and fate of a person, for example in the **Talmud**. Someone born on a Sunday will be either wholly good or bad, because on this day both light and darkness were created. Destiny is thought to come from the planet ruling the hour of the birth of the individual.

Archangel Michael with the Sun, Archangel Gabriel with the Moon, the Angel Aniel (= Angel Anael) with Venus, Angel Samael with Mars, Archangel Raphael with Mercury, the Angel Zadkiel (= Angel Sachiel) with Jupiter and the Angel Kafziel (= Angel Cassiel) with Saturn. In Medieval Europe, the Sun (= Archangel Michael) and the planet Mercury (= Archangel Raphael) were frequently reversed or substituted for each other as given elsewhere.

The Archangel Raphael of the planet Mercury is often coupled with the Sun and the Archangel Michael, which may account why the Sun and the Archangel Michael is found being asked for assistance in medical matters, long in the hands of the Archangel Raphael and the planet Mercury. Though it is accepted that the Sun and Michael rule a healthy heart and the body overall as a healthy organism and without this little can be achieved.

The legendary account of the trisagion and its origins is given by St. John of Damascus (*De Fid Orthodox*). He tells us that Proclus, Bishop of Constantinople in the middle of the fifth century was leading prayers during a tempest when a boy was caught up into the air and taught the trisagion by the angels. The *Four Gospels* regularly have the Winged Man (= Aquarius), the Lion (= Leo), the Bull (= Taurus) and the Eagle (= Scorpio — the Eagle represents the highest aspirations and the Scorpion the lowest of this Sign of the Zodiac) on their cover and pages. These are also the animals of the *Merkabah* (= 'the chariot') of *Ezekiel* and represent the Four Foundations of the Earth, found in the *Old Testament* and extended later.

Many pagan festivals and rituals were given an acceptable veneer to make them agreeable to the *New Dispensation*. This was not a new practice by any means and neither was it exclusive the Christianity, most 'new' religions frequently did this, so this is more a comment than a criticism. Far older religions than Christianity have used the best of the earlier models of worship, after all the earlier models were the shoes into which the new model was trying to step. Such practises were old when Christianity was young or non–existent. This system had one great advantage to commend its use because it presented the weaker, vulnerable new philosophy, which was still liable to rejection with a veneer of familiarity and comfort. New religions lack the authority that acceptance brings and it is, in the beginning at least, usually on its best behaviour. Those that had gone before did likewise in their 'early' stages.

Only the most zealous bigot could find offence in some of the early pagan festivals but more often than not, permission for it to exist had not been authorized by the new and its new leaders. Finding fault and whinging is a way of life for zealots and they are not living to the full unless they are making themselves miserable and everyone else around them to boot — 'misery loves company.' Did we leave out the fallen or evil angels, found in the Christian angelology in the Roman model above? No!

The Lares were the good spirits of the departed and by contrast, the Larvæ were the dead souls who could find no rest in death, sometimes because of guilt or because they had met with some indignity that offended them, such as a violent or untimely death before their allotted span. The Larvæ or Lemures in Roman religion were fearsome and wicked spectres of the dead that appear in grotesque and terrifying forms. They were said to wander abroad as dreadful spectres or skeletons that have returned to the upper world with the sole purpose of injuring or making life misery for the living, to haunt their living relatives and cause them injury. To banish these evil spirits from the house expiatory rites were held on three days of the year.

These three days were the 9th, 11th and 13th of May — the *Festival or Rites of the Lemuria*. On these three nights, the Pater Familias goes to the front door at midnight and outside the house performs a rather splendid but simple ritual (= Service) to keep the Larvæ or Lemures (= 'evil spirits or fallen angels and Satan') at bay. The rites of Lemuria were supposedly instituted by Romulus in expiation for his brother's murder and they required the father of every family to rise at midnight, purify his hands, throw black beans for the spirits to collect and to recite appeals for the spirits' departure. The purpose of the ritual was to protect the family within the house who are under the protection of the Lares (= Guardian Angels) for life. On these three days, all the temples were closed and marriage was avoided.

Now the reader knows why May is traditionally held to be an unlucky month to hold a wedding and it is still avoided by many couples even today. However, it is only the 9th, 11th and 13th of May that was regarded as being unlucky for marriage and not the whole month as usually thought today. The temples were closed on these days, which would have prevented any marriage from taking place in any case. If a couple wanted to really tempt Fate they were usually told to chose Friday the 13th of May for the wedding, if this time was available.

The notion of a guardian spirit that watches over an individual from their birth and directs their actions, they may be friendly or hostile and this was generally entertained by the Greeks. This is perhaps best expressed in the famous fragment of the Athenian Meander who wrote 'By every man at birth a good demon takes his stand, to initiate him into the mysteries of life.' This avowal is not to be regarded as some literary fancy but as an accepted belief, a popular opinion of his day and to many even now. Theognis wisely says ' . . . there are many who have a craven soul, but a good daemon.'

We can appeal to Pindar, a witness of a very different type 'The mighty purpose of Zeus directs the daemon of those whom he loves.' The Catholic 'priest of the stigmata' Padre Pio is reported to have told those who sought his help that if they could not come to him, they should send their Guardian Angel. We are frequently told that he sent out his Guardian Angels to others.

Regarding the Jewish Oracles, Maimonides tells us 'the worshippers of the Teraphim or carved images claimed that the light of the principal stars or planets permeated these through and through, the angelic Virtues, the regents of the stars and planets, talked with them, teaching them many useful things and arts.' Seldenus said 'the teraphim were built and composed after the position of certain planets' and this is almost talismanic in its instructions.

The records of the Hebrews show that the ancient Hebrews consulted oracles, idols, statues, images and so forth, as much as any of the pagan nations and the teraphim was found among their oracular images. The inclination of the Israelites toward idolatry was in part I feel the expression of the collective human longing for a god you can see and be on familiar terms with through the physical senses, much of the 'idolatry' of the Israelites was initially borrowed from their neighbours. They were exposed to a huge amount of polytheistic worship for the period of their reported stay in Egypt and this must have influenced their thinking and actions to some extent at the time.

The Israelites demanded of Aaron that he make them a golden calf fashioned in the Egyptian form of the Apis bull before Moses came down from Mount Sinai forbidding such things. Even in patriarchal times, references are made to teraphim or household gods and at sites of excavation, examples of these statues are found. Terah was said to have 'worshipped other gods than Jehovah, the *kaeiroi* or *kabiri*, in the Hebrew= 'teraphim.' From one viewpoint, the Golden Calf is thought to stand for the secret knowledge that the Jews took from the Egyptians when they left. When Moses came down from Mt Sinai, he destroyed the idol by burning it, grinding what was left of it into a powder, which he scattered on water. The punishment for their idolatry was almost alchemical in its form; Moses made the Children of Israel drink the water. *Exodus* 32:20. Let us look at another important concept from the past . . .

## THE UNKNOWN GOD OR GODS

This is a particularly favourite tenet of mine and I often use it in principle. In polytheistic religious systems, caution is recommended because as there were numerous gods known and worshipped — it may be conceivable that there were some gods who were 'not know by name or purpose to men.' It was considered to be prudent to recognize, pray to or extend offerings to these unknown gods as well as those that were known. In 'the Babylonian Penitential Psalms,' unknown sins are often acknowledged and many unknown gods were addressed lest any, being overlooked, may decide to vent their anger upon the penitent because of this omission — even although the omission was quite unintentional.

It is possible this circumspection accounted for the altar seen by St. Paul in Athens with the inscription, *Agnostos Theos*= the 'unknown god.' *Αγνωστος, Agnostos*= 'unknown, not to be known.' *Θεος, Theos*= 'God.'

Several literary references bear witness to the fact that such altars were both well–known and used. Pausanias refers to them twice in his works. One of these 'altars of gods called unknown and heroes' was seen by him in Athens, he also writes of 'an altar to the unknown gods' at Olympia' where they kept a perpetual fire to Pan. Philostratus and Tertullian both mention altars of the 'unknown' gods at Athens.

Paul, in my judgment showed remarkable ignorance in the *Acts* where we read. 'Then Paul stood in the midst of Mars' hill, and said: Ye men of Athens, I perceive that in all things ye are too superstitious. For as I passed by, and beheld your devotions. I found an altar with this inscription, TO THE UNKNOWN GOD. Whom therefore ye ignorantly worship, him declare I unto you . . .' (17:22–24.) I do not think the Athenians 'ignorantly' worshipped the *Agnostos Theos*. The Athenians and the Greeks knew exactly what they were doing and what they were worshipping. It was Paul who did not know what they or he was doing. The altar was a mark of respect for any possible omission of an unknown deity through ignorance — insurance if you will or must — but that it was being done 'ignorantly,' I think not. I feel the only ignorance being flaunted here belongs to Paul and no other.

There is a clear reference in Lucian, regarding the purpose of the cult of unknown deities. First, specific gods were summoned by name to a gathering as well as the unknown gods, whose altars were propitiated with sweet odours or another formula used in sacrifice when there was uncertainty of name or purpose — 'whether the deity was god or goddess.' The same prudence is established wherever a cult of ghosts was found. As time passes the names of the dead are forgotten, but it was thought they were still able to do harm to the living if they were overlooked or if they felt offended through neglect.

When you attempt work of this nature, you are often trying to contact an entity that is on another level to your own, usually considered to be on a higher level than this one. However, if you do not close the 'door' when you are finished or leave it ajar, an entity not friendly to our level could use this as a means of entrance it or into your life. If you do not 'finish' and 'ground' any work properly, you could find yourself with a veritable *Pandora's Box* on your hands and be left wondering where it came from.

You must remember that Chaos was here first and it wants to come back and claim its own. Order was imposed upon Chaos from without; to Chaos this imposition of Order was the unnatural state of affairs because order is the antithesis of Chaos. At the time of writing, I think there must be many 'doors' that have been left ajar all over the world. Chaos has not only got its foot in the door, but in some circumstances and areas of life here its feet are firmly under the table and I am sure that in some of these it has been invited to join the feast and so I wonder why some are surprised that it accepted the invitation and turned up.

## THE WORD — ANGEL

Let us look at the word 'angel' before going any further as the word is obviously important to us. The word angel is the designation of a class of celestial beings in both the *Old* and *New Testaments* and it is a general term indicating a superhuman, though subordinate being, despite being found in monotheistic religions.

The Hebrew word *mal'akh* and the Greek word *αγγελος, angelos* are words meaning 'a messenger or envoy' or 'generally, one that announces; of birds of augury' or 'a divine messenger, an angel.' Originally, it had little or no distinction between a human or superhuman messenger, other than what was indicated by the text in which it is found, as with *nekr–angelos*= 'a messenger of the dead.' The term *mal'akh* also meant 'a messenger of a king' and it is thought by some that the word may have been taken from the Persian 'angaros' meaning 'a courier.'

In the *New Testament* there is no other word translated as 'angel' other than the Greek given above — *angelos*. Regarding the Hebrew word, it should be noted that in most cases there is usually some distinctive term attached to the word or its use so that there is little doubt whose messenger or what kind of messenger they are. In Ancient Greece in its original use, the Greek word 'angelos' meant a human messenger and not necessarily a superhuman or celestial one. Another word, Latin, *daemon*= 'a spirit, genius' was in current usage and some considered it was better suited for the job, it is also an ancient astrological term that is explained elsewhere. It is a word I use frequently as an alternative to 'angel' especially when used privately — please do not confuse this word with the English word demon with its English connotation, which was derived from it. In the context of this work and others, this word is mainly used by ecclesiastical writers to mean 'an evil spirit or demon.' If a demon is meant, then that word will be used.

*Mal'akh* was considered to be right for an angelic messenger but the Greek word 'angelos' was thought more appropriate for simply a 'messenger' earlier. The other Greek word as said, that could have been used was — *daimon*= 'a god or goddess, fate, destiny, fortune, good or bad, one's genius, one's lot or fortune' and in ancient Greece *daimon* was a supernatural power. The term was almost interchangeable by Homer with *Θεος, Theos*= 'a god.' The distinction seems to be that *Theos* stresses the 'nature of the god' while daimon stressed the 'activity of the god' and personally, it this distinction that I like. The word 'daimon' was usually applied to any sudden or unexpected supernatural intervention that could not be ascribed to any specific deity. In common use, it became the Power that determined a mortal's fate. Therefore, an individual could have a personal daimon that directed their life from birth to death and numerous commentators said that this was exactly what it did.

In Roman mythology, an individual's *genius* was their protecting or Guardian Spirit. It was believed that every human being, family and city had its personal *genius*. The *genius* received special veneration as a household god because it was thought to grant success and intellectual powers to its devotees.

The word *genius* was and still is given to a person with extraordinary intellectual powers, though it is used without much thought and today it is used far too freely and very little thought. The spiritual *genius* of a woman was referred to as her 'Juno' in the past, which is a delightful and most appropriate turn of phrase.

Juno was connected with all aspects of the life of women, most particularly their married life. Among many other titles she was *Juno Lucina* — 'the goddess who brings to light' — and hence the goddess of childbirth, she had a temple on the Esquiline from the 4th century B.C. In her role as female comforter, she assumed various descriptive names but her general festival called the *Matronalia* was celebrated on March 1st. Individualized, she became a female guardian angel especially, as said, during the sanctity of married life that was sacred to her, hence the law that no prostitute must ever touch her altar. As every man had his genius, every woman had her Juno and she represented in a sense, the female principle of life, just as Jupiter was all to the male.

It is possible that birthdays were celebrated to honour the genius or daimon more than the individual. When a personal genius was shown in art, it was often represented by a winged youth. Every place had its genius and at many festivals, sacrifices were offered to them. The *genius* of a place was often represented as a serpent eating fruit.

I personally believe that the word 'daimon' is nearer to our idea of angels than *αγγελος*, *angelos* with respect to its deeper meaning, therefore, many of the opinions expressed throughout will be personal and reflect the way I work and think. Some very famous people in the Greek world of old had their personal *daimon* and it was regarded as their 'good guardian spirit.' Socrates used the name 'daimon' and he said that his daimon told the future to him and while it prevented him from doing wrong, it did not insist that he did what it said because the choice was always his. The daimon of Socrates stood for his higher, spiritual self and the voice of conscience or an instinct that guided the person to fulfil their destiny; later writers took it to personify inspiration. Hesiod designated them 'as spirits of the Golden Age appointed to watch over and guard mankind.' We often find that two *daimons* accompany an individual, one prompting to good and the other to evil. This may be the same genius, whose influence is defined as good and at another time evil.

As said, each individual was declared as having two *daemons* — a good one and a bad one — just as we are said to have two Guardian Angels, though not necessarily one good and one bad. In Greek, the good demon was called an *Agathodaimon*= 'bonus' which, in ancient astrology was 'the last but one of the twelve celestial signs' — appropriately, the Eleventh House of the chart and 'the House of Hopes and Wishes, Serendipity.' The good genius is frequently represented as a youth holding a horn of plenty or cornucopia, a bowl; a poppy, ears of corn and it was to him at Athens that a cup of uncontaminated wine was drunk at dinner. The *Anamalech* was a demon that was the harbinger of bad tidings.

The *Agathodaemon* and the *Kakodaemon* are the Serpent of Wisdom and the Serpent of Evil, because the serpent can be either sage or sorcerer. The dragon is the eternally watchful one and guardian of those treasures that are sacred. It is a ruthless and destructive force to those who endeavour to get by force the riches they have not gained by right and proper title. To secure knowledge, we must know how to tame the serpent that rules the lower worlds and the power that the serpent possesses of sloughing off its old skin, which has a great deal to tell the perceptive, spoken of later.

Greek, *αγαθος, agathos*= 'good.' (Latin *bonus*.) *Αγαθον–δαιμονος, Agathon–daimonos*= as a toast 'to the good genius,' *αγαθα τα, agatha ta*= 'the gods of good fortune and wealth.' *Δαιμων, Daimon*= 'a god or goddess, deity or divine power; one's daimon or genius; one's lot or foturne.'

The Greek, *Κακο–δαιμων, Kakodaimon* = 'possessed by an evil genius, ill–fated, ill–starred, miserable, an evil genius.' The term usually means 'an evil spirit' and these two words have interest to those curious about ancient astrology. *Kakodaimon* was once the name, given by some of the medieval astrologers to the Twelfth House of an astrological chart, which follows and is underneath the House of the *Agathodaemon*, the Eleventh House dealing with matters of 'one's lot, the gods of wealth and fortune, good fortune' for the most, the Eleventh House contains matters and things that are non–material.

The twelfth house designations of old are now rejected by modern astrologers who no longer regard it as the 'the House of Self–Undoing, the House of Sorrows and the House of Secret and Hidden Enemies.' The ruler of 'evil things or the hidden, demonic element' that is inherent in human make up or what the Fates can throw at us at times when they have a mind — but this does not mean I have to reject it. Before Christianity, the use of *angelos* and *daemon* were all but interchangeable with little or no bother. Despite the word 'demon' being derived from the word *daemon* — a *daemon* was not thought of as necessarily being malevolent.

*Δαιμων, Daimon* or *Genius* (Greek) or *Daemon* (Roman) were protecting spirits corresponding to the angel of an individual or their Guardian Angel — the same play with different characters. They were believed to be the agents of Zeus–Jupiter dwelling on earth to fulfil his decrees and administer his justice. The Greek philosophers taught and the Romans believed that these agents were assigned to each mortal at birth. The Romans venerated them as gods most holy, principally on their birthdays, which were naturally also the birthday of the individual, when they offered them libations of incense, garlands and wine.

In the mythology and thought of the Greeks, a daimon was a supernatural power that guided the individual fate of human beings, though sometimes they were called Guardian Spirits. In Homer a *daimon*, which meant the 'allotter of fate' was applied to one of the great gods. In those early days, the word daimon came to mean 'the good or evil daimon of a man that followed him throughout his life.' It was given to the lesser gods and since Plato, the word seems to be conceived as being appropriate to those beings that were 'intermediate between the gods and men.'

As given earlier, daemon or demon came from Greek *daimon* and the Latin *daemon*= 'a spirit.' They were a god, an angel, a celestial power or spirit of varying degrees of other worldliness, ranging from the supreme deity of the hierarchy through the greater gods and down to simple genii and lemures.

Originally, the term applied by and large to a deity but later as said, it was frequently used to describe intermediate beings that stood between the gods and the human. They were agents of the powers and functions of the gods. Philosophers such as Plato divided the daemons into three classes, the first two are invisible while the third class of daimons were clothed with bodies like a mist that was usually invisible, though now and then they made themselves visible for a short period.

In Jewish and Christian use, the word daimon came to mean an evil spirit. In the *Septuagint* the earliest Greek translation of the Hebrew *Bible*, the word daimon was given this interpretation. Daemon was applied to idols and the pagan gods generally in the Latin Vulgate (5th century A.D) also to those spirits who might take possession of individuals. Traditional belief thought these spirits were responsible for sickness and they were expelled by means of exorcism. The Greek, διαβολος, *diabolos*= 'a deceiver, back–biter, slanderer or slandering, the devil and was often found synonymous with demons, devils, the Devil or Satan of the *New Testament*'— in the Latin, *diabolus*.

As said above the *Septuagint* is the earliest extant Greek translation of the *Old Testament* from the original Hebrew, in all probability made for the use of the Jewish community in Egypt when Greek was the vernacular throughout the region.

The name *Septuagint* (designated LXX) from the Latin *septuaginta*= 'seventy' was taken later from the legend, according to a *Letter of Aristaeus*, a contemporary document written by Aristaeus, a Greek official at the Egyptian court of Ptolemy II Philadelphus (285-246 B.C). This tells us there were seventy–two translators (seventy being the nearest round number) doing the work, six from each of the Twelve Tribes of Israel working in separate rooms translating the whole and in the end all their versions were identical or so goes the tale.

As often happens with a lot of the celestial powers and their symbols, many of them have been reduced to insignificance in Judaism and Christianity. For the most part regarded as being evil powers that are hostile to the human race with the One God saying, they should be feared and shunned instead of being revered and respected. The concept of an Adversary, Satan or the Devil is preserved in the title daemones. The ancient Greeks and Romans, however, made a clear distinction between the daemones of the ethereal and spiritual existence and never confused them with any lower, earthbound daemones, who were clearly denizens of the lower astral and physical realms. The ancients refused to have any contact or dealings with this level of existence like anyone else.

Exorcism is the ritual of expelling demons or evil spirits from people, places and those possessed or in danger of possession. The practice was very widespread in ancient cultures and it was usually based on magical ritual. There were special priests in ancient Babylon who destroyed a clay or wax image of a demon in a ritual intended to disable their power or to destroy the demon itself. The *Bible* contains many references to demons and exorcism and in the *New Testament*; evil spirits were expelled by Christ through prayer and at his command. Alterantively, it was someone granted special religious authority, such as a priest or a shaman in Paganism who performs an exorcism today. In the Roman Catholic Church, priests do practise exorcism but it is usually only performed with special priests with special permission and generally as a last resort.

In the broadest of brush strokes, with some repetition, an angel is a messenger of god who can be either good or evil depending on what they are sent to do and from our point of view, they have special powers greater than a human being but less than their Creator. The two major words translated as 'angel' appear almost three hundred times throughout the *Bible* from *Genesis* to *Revelation*.

Sometimes there is only one angel, sometimes two and sometimes it is a host of angels. The Archangel Gabriel, who announced to the shepherds the birth of Christ, was joined by 'a multitude of the heavenly host' all praising God. *Luke* 2:13. It is impossible to separate the *Old* and the *New Testament* when those of the Christian faith use the combined books that are the Christian *Bible*.

The existence of these superhuman beings is as already said, earlier than the *Bible* and spiritual intelligences were conjectured by Plato among others. We have already said that the word angel means 'messenger,' but it has been used in a wider sense of messenger. 2 *Malachi* 2:7 'For the priest's lips should keep knowledge, and they should seek the law at his mouth; for he is the messenger of the Lord of host.' This sentence shows that the designation 'messenger' has been given to priests as it had been to the prophets.

The term 'messenger' has also been applied to the Messiah as sent by God, though *Isaiah* 42:19 has a different views of its interpretation. There is no doubt regarding the opinion of the Sadducees regarding the angels. 'For the Sadducees say that there is no resurrection, neither angel, nor spirit: but the Pharisees confess both. And there arose a great cry and the scribes that were of the Pharisees' part arose and strove saying, We find no evil in this man: but if a spirit or an angel hath spoken to him, let us not fight against God.' *Acts* 23:8–10.

It seems natural that the ancient Hebrews thought of God as being surrounded by a court or retinue of spirits or angels and this may account in part for the use of the plural pronoun in the Creation narratives. There is restraint in referring to them and they are only brought into play when needed during critical times. For the most, the angels are without name and they appeared to have little individuality of their own being known mainly by what they say and/or did.

It seems that some ministering angels have a very ephemeral life. They are created every day from 'a river of fire' called *Nehar di Nehar* and having expressed the praises of the Creator, they return to the river from which they were created. The source of this river of fire is the perspiration of the *Hayyot* who perspire from the task of bearing God's Throne. Companies of angels are created every day and pass, while others remain in existence. Again, we find the close association or suggestion of the two elements of fire and water that is often found associated in connection with the angels, this time it is a 'river' of 'fire.'

Maimonides tells us that even though the angels have form, they have no substance. They are pure spirit and they are not differentiated one from the other by having any variation of body as we have. Any distinction is given only by their spiritual form and their purpose. He informs us that the angels are 'creatures of fire' and when they are in human form with wings this is a feature of prophetic revelation. In the *Zohar*, angels are chaste spirits and in their natural appearance, they cannot materialize in the natural world because the natural world could not hold them. If the angels want to do this, they are obliged to assume the outward appearance of the world.

These angels were created for the daily service of the Eternal, to execute his commands and pass away according to *Hagigah* and the *Book of Enoch*. They are simply agents of God and the means 'whereby communication with man is achieved.' It is held that man could not see God himself and live. In *Exodus* 33:20 it is written 'And he said, Thou canst not see my face: for there shall no man see me and live.' However, according to the *Bible*, some have done this and survived.

The spiritual nature of the angels has been stressed by the early *Old Testament* prophets, especially by Ezekiel and Isaiah in their visionary descriptions. The cherubim and seraphim, two superior orders of angels, are described as winged creatures that guard the Throne of God. The use of wings attached to various beings symbolizes their invisible and spiritual nature. A practice that can be traced back to the ancient Egyptians, who represented their crusading sun-god Horus of Edfu as a winged disk.

Despite the many references in the *Bible* to angels, the *Doctrine of Angels* is not really a significant topic in Christian theology. They are included in descriptions of all that God created such as, 'Praise ye him, all his angels.' *Psalm* 148: 2. We find clues that they witnessed the creation of the world as in the question. 'Whereupon are the foundations thereof fastened? Or who laid the corner stone thereof; When the morning stars sang together, And all the sons of God shouted for joy?' *Job* 38:6. Despite their close association with God, they do share some things with us but being spiritual, the angels are free from many of our limitations, the most obvious being death.

The angels are regarded as sexless and they do not marry. In all their appearances in human form in the *Bible*, they were always taken as being men. In keeping with other writers, I have not found them as women or children in the main source using the *Bible*. The only feminine aspect of note in Jewish hidden and traditional lore may prove the spiritual presence of the *Shekinah* or 'the Glory of God' and the *Bat Qol* — the 'Daughter of the Voice.' Though I am in no doubt angel's can appear as both female and children if that is what was required. I am confident they will appear in whatever form is necessary for the task they have been sent to complete and will use whatever material is to hand. They choose an appearance acceptable to those they are visiting if their visit is benign and they will often assist without upsetting the people they were sent to help, sometimes without even letting them know they have been helped. As said, in this work, they are represented as given in the *Bible*, which is our main source work.

Demons have been and will be mentioned again throughout the work so let us look briefly at some of the salient points regarding them even though this may involve some repetition when gathering such information in one place.

Demons are usually regarded as supernatural beings, forces or spirits that are capable of influencing human lives, generally by evil means and definitely with evil intent. However, the story in the *Book of Tobit* from the *Apocrypha* has a very power demon called Asmodeus who, with the help of the Archangel Raphael, is banished to Egypt, this story appears at various points.

The beautiful Sarah is so beloved by this demon that seven men who had in turn married her, were put to death by the demon the night before the marriage and before its consummation. The *Talmud* tells us that Solomon confined this demon and made him labour in the construction of the First Temple of Jerusalem but other *Haggadic* legends (I believe) portray Asmodeus as a more beneficial figure. The *Haggadah* is a sacred book, its main theme is the delivery of the Children of Israel from the bondage of Egypt and it is, among other things, a celebration of their freedom.

This will taken up later but the point being made here, while looking at demons, is that around the second century B.C when Tobit is thought to have been written, demons were obviously considered capable of sexual love and possessing a devastating and fatal jealousy. This reminds us of the results of the contact of the Sons of God with the daughters of Men in *Genesis* 6:2 and this includes the Jinns among the Arabic nations among others.

Demons play a role in the traditions of most religions and races and they appear in most mythologies and literature. Among the demons of Assyria many were named after the disease they were supposed to afflict people with. In some cases in point, the names of the demons and the illness were or became identical.

There has been a belief from prehistoric times that evil spirits could influence people's lives and this has not departed today by any means. Many races and nations of the past believed that spirits occupied all the elements of nature. Evil spirits or demons were sometimes thought to be the spirits of ancestors who brought affliction to the living. This has resulted in many of our funeral traditions, such as the mourners all dressing alike and in black to confuse a vengeful spirit and to protect specific individuals. Societies who practised ancestor worship sought to sway the actions of both the good and bad spirits.

Many ancient societies, among them Babylon and Egypt, thought evil spirits were responsible for the functions of the body and that demons caused particular illnesses, the medical science of the Egyptians was closely connected with their magic and demonology. The human body was divided into thirty–six parts, a deity presided over each part and it was their job to preserve that part against ill. For example Ra took care of the face, Hathor the eyes and so forth, while Thoth as the God of Medicine had charge overall of the body as the complete organism.

As said elsewhere, disease was considered to be due to demons and certain formulae were used and recited, sometimes it was said over and over again before they were considered successful. Often the patient swallowed the appropriate formulae that had been written on papyrus. Naturally, amulets, talismans and charms were also worn to assist and protect.

Egyptian magic, like many other practices found, could be used for the benefit of people or to their detriment. To the Egyptians a person's fate was fixed at birth and what that was could be found out from the planet under which that individual was born, we mentioned the similar Hebrew practice earlier. The Fate was controlled by the gods who sometimes interfered in it to save a favourite. The individual could, from time to time, overrule the judgment of Fate by the power of specific acts or agencies,

Christian ideas about demons originated from the references to evil beings or 'unclean spirits' in the *Old Testament*. By the Middle Ages, Christian theology had developed an elaborate hierarchy of angels, who were associated with God, while the fallen angels or demons were led by Satan naturally regarded as the original fallen angel. In most English versions of the *Bible*, the term demon is translated as the Devil and in the *New Testament* the term 'demon' is identified clearly with an evil spirit.

Briefly, the angels and demons of Islam are broadly closely related to corresponding doctrines in Judaism and Christianity. The Four Throne Bearers of Allah and four other angels are well known. Jibril (= Archangel Gabriel); the Angel of Revelation, Mikal (= Archangel Michael); the Angel of Nature, 'providing man with food and knowledge.' Israfel is the Angel who places the soul in the body and the angel who will sound the trumpet for the Last Judgment. Izrail is the Angel of Death who takes the breath of life away. As with other religious philosophies we find demons vying for the control of lives and souls. The most prominent and important of these being Iblis, Eblis or Haris (= 'despair'), the Devil, Shaytan or Satan, who entices mortals for his own purposes.

As said, Izra'il is the Angel of Death in Islam (Azrael in Hebrew lore) and he separates souls from their bodies and is one of the four archangels. We are told this archangel stands with one foot in heaven while the other foot stands on the razor-sharp bridge that separates paradise from hell.' Izra'il was the only angel courageous enough to come to earth and face the hosts of the devil Iblis to bring back the materials 'needed to make man.' For this service, he was made the Angel of Death and given a inventory of 'all mankind.'

This angel does not actually know when a person will die until the tree underneath God's throne drops a leaf that bears their name. He must then separate the body and soul after forty days and there are several ways to try avert death but as with most angels with this task, people may 'try' to outwit him but the archangel will prevail in the end. Reciting ritual prayers prevents the angel of death from entering the throat to take the spirit and if they are distributing alms, the angel is unable take them by their hand. However, when the Angel of Death finally comes back with an inscribed apple from paradise or writes the name God in the palm of their hand, the spirit must leave.

Islam developed its own hierarchy of angels and many of these, such as the Archangels Michael, Gabriel and Allah's throne bearers (= a lion, an eagle, a bull, and a man) show their Judaeo–Christian inspiration or origins. Islam has a complex system of demons and their writings outline a band of evil beings called *jinn*, who cause ruin and preside over places where evil activities take place. The first jinni was called Iblis who was cast out by Allah for refusing to worship the first man, Adam mentioned elsewhere.

Two angels in the mythology of Islam unintentionally became the architects of evil. A group of angels were watching sins being committed on earth and they 'ridiculed man's weakness.' God thought they would not fare any better and suggested that some of the angels be sent to earth to see how well they could reject fornication, idolatry, murder and the effects of strong wine. The Angels Harut and Marut were chosen for the trial. Beautiful women seduced them almost as soon as they arrived on earth. Discovering there had been a witness to their sins and not wanting to be found out, they slew the witness. The angels who remained in heaven had to admit that God was right.

The now fallen angels had to face judgement and make penance for the sins and arrogance and this was to be done either on earth or in hell. Harut and Marut decided to be punished on earth and they were condemned to hang by their feet in a well in Babylon until the Day of Judgement. The two angels Harut and Marut are first found mentioned in the Qur'an as angels in Babylon dealing in iniquity. The legend in all probability appeared as an explanation of why these two angels are to be found in these particular circumstances. This story parallels a Jewish legend about the fallen angels Shemhazai, Uzza and Azael as 'the guardian of hidden treasures'

The Anunnaki in Babylonian mythology are a hierarchy of lower angels. These were the Angels of Earth or the Underworld. The star gods who had sunk below the horizon to become the judges of the dead. Under the Anunnaki, it is said there were several classes of genii, some good and some evil.

In the beliefs of Islam, regarding the resurrection of the dead, two Angels (coloured black with blue eyes) called Munkar (Monker) and Nakir, question the deceased regarding the tenets of Islam. These Angels test the faith of the dead in their tomb. After death, the Angels Munkar and Nakir set the deceased upright in their grave. The deceased for instance is asked to identify Muhammad. The righteous will of course know that he is the messenger of God and his prophet, so they will be allowed to rest in peace until the Day of Judgment. Those who are infidels and sinners will not be able to give correct replies and they are beaten by the two angels every day — save Friday — for a period appointed by God and required.

The Archangel Mikal was so overwhelmed at the sight of hell when it was created it is said he never laughed again. Mikal and Jibril were the first angels to obey God's order to worship Adam in Islamic legend. These two Archangels are credited with purifying Muhammad's heart before his night journey from Mecca to Jerusalem and his later ascension to heaven. In biblical literature, Michael is the complement of Mikal.

The Archangel Jibril acts as 'the mediator between God and man' and transmits God's revelations to the prophets — notably Muhammad. In biblical literature, the Archangel Gabriel is the complement of Jibril. In Islam, Israfel — 'the Burning One' — is the Archangel who will blow the trumpet from a holy rock in Jerusalem to announce the Day of Resurrection. The trumpet is constantly poised to his lips, ready to be blown when God so orders. Three times each day and each night Israfel looks down at the vision of hell, he is so overcome with sorrow he weeps so many tears that they would engulf the earth if Allah did not intervene. This is the angel who served as companion to Mohammed for three years, after which time the Archangel Gabriel took over. Israfel is one the four angels that was sent by Allah to bring the seven handfuls of dust for the creation of Adam. In biblical literature, Raphael is given as the complement of Israfel.

***The City of God (De Civitate Dei)*** was written by Saint Augustine's between A.D 413 and 426 and was the saint's answer to Volusanius because it was the pagan philosopher's assertion (in part) that the adoption of Christianity by the Emperor Constantine had led to the Visigoths' sacking Rome in 410. In his lengthy philosophical treatise, Augustine naturally discards the pagan position and as expected translates history through Christian revelation.

The work is in keeping with the judgement that paganism is a creation of the Devil or Satan, a false religion that has been superseded by the only true religion — Christianity. The most famous theme of the work is that of 'two cities,' the Christian city devoted to God while the earthly pagan city (= Babylon) is naturally submissive to the Devil and obeying him. Babylon, exposed as it is to moral quandary and strife, is marked out for certain destruction.

Finally, Christianity decreed that all the pagan and heathen gods were evil, filled with demons and the word daimon/daemon started to take on the unfavourable meaning it now has in the English language. Perhaps with the benefit of hindsight, this also shows the happier choice of 'angel' instead of daemon because the word now has a meaning that the original did not, in fact and it is quite the opposite and this has happened to many words. In English, the name 'demon' has now attained an exactitude of meaning and is now applied to malevolent, evil and supernatural beings. This now makes it a difficult word to use in describing the circumstances reflected in the religion and folklore of other nations especially in earlier and classical times.

When we spoke earlier of famous people having a guiding spirit called a 'demon,' we said that one of the most famous on record was the daimon of Socrates, who forewarned the Greek philosopher of danger. Socrates regularly said that a Divine sign prevented him from taking a particular course of action. This customary sign was made known to him by means of 'a warning voice' and it was emphatic on trifling affairs as well as important matters. Cicero said of Socrates that he 'brought down philosophy from heaven to earth.' This 'warning voice' of Socrates today would probably be called 'the still small voice' and be greatly valued, as was the ***Bat Qol***.

The voice is the concrete expression of abstract thought that is a creative power that has order and energy. The septenary of the Creator is represented and articulated by the seven mysterious vowels of the Greek alphabet that are in agreement with the Seven Heavens. Consonants were considered as being the mystical instruments of sounds or 'voices' that carry the vowels. The consonants gave the vowels a medium of expression in the same way as the spirit can communicate itself through the body.

The Deity often communicates through the use of the voice in the ***Old Testament***. The voice is one of the ways in which a divine presence reveals itself to the mind, as when in the ***Bible***, the Lord revealed himself to Elijah not in the wind, not in the earthquake, not in the fire, but after the fire as — the 'still small voice' — see also ***Bat Qol***.

As said, Socrates said that he was guarded throughout his life by his familiar spirit and this was regarded as being quite normal by most and envied by many. Neglect of the Gods or their messengers does not make them depart and they are always there and ever alert to the needs of people. Neglect may wound them but it does not destroy them because they simply withdraw to watch and wait and we seem to lose them for a time, sometimes I believe for good and this is part of the problem. Today of course, the beneficial 'demon' of Socrates would automatically be thought to be evil and Socrates would stand accused of dealing with or worshipping the Devil or Satan when nothing could be further from the truth.

Demons are widespread and inseparable from the folklore of the world and many of these familiars have characteristic qualities through which they are recognized. The Japanese oni, which is a generic name applied to the powers of evil in Japanese myth are said to bring storm and tempest. In Scotland, kelpies haunted pools and lay in wait to drown any unwary travellers. The *kelpi* is a Scottish god of all the rivers and lakes in the country and often takes the form of a water horse, occasionally grazing on the banks of rivers, at other times it is found in fords and streams. This particular horse is mischievous, invariably malevolent and encourages travellers to jump on his back and then he plunges into the water and drowns them. The 'water horse' in Welsh folklore is cyffyl dwr, in the Shetlands it is called the shooplitee and in the Orkney's the tang or tangie.

The name 'Elohim is almost totally reserved as a title for the 'One True God' in the later evolution of the religion of Israel. *Sebaoth*= 'hosts' in the title *Yahweh Sebaoth*= 'Lord of Hosts' was probably identified with the angels. People once identified the 'hosts' with the celestial stars because the stars were long considered as being intimately linked with the angels. The word 'hosts' was also identified with the armies of Israel, but the context of the sentence would make this distinction clear to the reader.

Now let us look at the term *Mal'akh Yahweh*= 'angel of the Lord' and *Mal'akh Elohim*= 'angel of God.' The *Mal'akh Yahweh* is an appearance or manifestation of Yahweh as a man and the term *Mal'akh Yahweh* is often found compatible with Yahweh. Those who have seen the *Mal'akh Yahweh* say they have seen God as written earlier.

The term *Mal'akh Yahweh* is thought by some commentators to have originally been a courtly and verbal effusion for 'the divine king' but it quickly became a way of evading a crude anthropomorphism. In due time it was used to indicate an angel of illustrious rank. There is another theophany found with the 'man' who wrestles with Jacob at Peniel, because the 'man' is identified with God. This is an example of a theophany and this term is discussed later.

Ancient and medieval peoples at large embraced the influence of the good spirits, angels, evil spirits or fallen angels and during the Middle Ages, theologians developed a hierarchy of angels. These were arranged in the following nine ranks and the list began with the lowest level, which is usually regarded as being the level closest to earth and its people, though 'lowest' is not being used with a derogatory meaning. This order consists of the Angels, Archangels, Principalities, Powers, Virtues, Dominions, Thrones, Cherubim and Seraphim. These nine groups will be dealt with later in the appropriate place.

In many creeds in the Near East before Judaism, angels were frequently documented as gods or lesser divinities. Their presence was taken for granted by the biblical authors. The use of the word 'angel' is sometimes thought to be a way of describing an appearance of God in human form.

As said earlier, *Mal'akh Yahweh* is termed the 'angel of the Lord.' It is difficult in some passages to determine with any degree of certainty whether the 'angel of the Lord' means one of the heavenly servants of the Lord or a power who is higher than the angels, perhaps between the angels and God. Some commentators thought that later writers deliberately substituted 'the angel of the Lord' for 'the Lord' in the **Samaritan Pentateuch**, which differs in a number of ways from the Masoretic text. It is said this was done because it was considered demeaning to Yahweh's prestige to have Yahweh become visible in human guise to run around doing his parochial errands.

The Samaritans are an ancient tribe that descended from Ephraim and Manasseh. They were the last remnant of a Jewish sect that for centuries did not consider Jerusalem to be the central holy place, regarding Mount Gerizim as their holy mountain in Palestine and the one rightful place appointed unto God for his people. This was the main reason of strife with the Jews, because they lived in hostile tension with their Jewish neighbours. The Jews had 'no dealings' with the Samaritans, but Jesus did (**John** 4:6–30.) They are mentioned in the Scripture in the chapters, 2 **Kings**. 17–18.

Although the origins of the Samaritans are clouded in obscurity, they are written about enough for the reader to extend this brief introduction of them should they wish to do so. A frequent point made regarding the Samaritans is their 'disbelief in angels,' however, other writers think this should be taken with some caution as their literary remains show. They often substitute an angel's name for the name of God in their **Targum**

## OLD TESTAMENT

It is very difficult, perhaps impossible, to decide where the borderline between divination and prophecy is drawn. There often seems to be a dislike of the first because it appears to come from the spirit world and as a result, it can be manipulated. The second is regarded as a direct communication from God making it the superior of the two but some regard this as the most difficult, both forms are found in the **Old** and **New Testament** and in both forms, the same general principles are being used.

People are attempting to gain contact with the spiritual or 'other worlds' in order to obtain some special knowledge or benediction. In divination, this knowledge was often established by observing explicit omens or signs though this was not always the case. Sometimes the beings consulted 'possessed or used' the soothsayer in much the same way as mediums are in Spiritualism. The diviner of old and the modern 'medium' tell us that they are simply channels through which spiritual beings speak.

The **Urim** and **Thummin** are often declared to be a form of sortilege or divination giving a simple 'yes' or 'no' answer to questions that were often framed in such a way so as to invite such an answer, still used today using the toss of a coin, though without divine sanction and ruled by chance, nor was this the only form used. The Romans, Greeks, Arabs and the rest of the world used similar systems and we have other signs recognized in the **Old Testament**. There was the 'sign' of Gideons fleece in **Judges** 6:36. In 1 **Samuel** 14:8 ff, Jonathan decided whether or not he is to attack the Philistines by the words that he may chance to hear them speak — 'this shall be a sign unto us' and such practises do not appear to be condemned in the biblical narrative, in some cases signs were given this way.

One of the most important methods of divination that link the Hebrews with most of the other nations of antiquity was through dreams and it differs little (if at all) from the methods of other nations. Usually the dream in a symbolic form appears to be introduced from the outside into the human soul in order to inform or warn in some way and there are many examples of this. See the dream–visions of **Enoch**, the **Book of Daniel** or **Josephus** to name a few.

There is only one reference to an angel, spirits and the demons in the early Hebrew poems. Although some authorities believe this may not be part of the original text and the 'holy ones' found in **Deuteronomy** 33:2 were later presumed to be angels. The word angel is a general term designating a unique entity, but an entity that is considered subordinate in a monotheist religion, for example, Christianity, Islam, Judaism and in some allied religions, such as Zoroastrianism.

Polytheism is the doctrine and belief in a plurality of gods, the spirits of the cosmos or celestial entities under whatever name they may be described. In polytheism, the grades of superhuman beings and helpers are both continuous and often seamless, sometimes making it difficult to see where one ends and the other begins. The creator, most feel, cannot be effectively regarded as being concerned with every infinitesimal function in the universe so frequently general terms such as 'Nature' are found being used. This inferred that other beings or agencies took care of such things at the creator's behest or on behalf of the creator.

In monotheism, there is a sharp distinction of class as well as degree, setting God at one end of the scale with the other superhuman beings at the other, all below being under the will of the One God. These beings are often said to have no will, only the Creator's and the angels are frequently found placed in this grouping. One of the main functions of the angelic was to help the petitioner to make contact with the Deity. To this end, Christianity has Seraphim, Cherubim, Thrones, Dominions, Virtues, Powers, Principalities, Archangels, Angels and the Saints which theology it does not hide. The unity of the Divine is often found wanting through the artifice often used to conceal its shortcomings.

Once we depart from the simple archaic scheme of a Supreme Creator in a universe that is filled with spiritual beings that form chains of command, ranks and a rich diversity of forms, which are elements of the creator. We find ourselves in a labyrinth of abstraction and contradiction, where the patches sometimes show what has been put in place to strengthen the weak material and cover over the faults and holes that have appeared — not unlike software manufacturers really; there really is nothing new under the Sun. The *Talmud* tells us ' . . . every blade of grass has an angel who bends over it and whispers, grow.'

From the deity down to the nature spirits, people looked upon these powers with a degree of trepidation and even now still attempt to be friendly, propitiate them and live with them. It would have been better if these powers were considered as an integral part of the Supreme God because when a light is taken from a candle it does not diminish or lessen the light of the original candle. However, it does carry a part of the unique light to where it is needed most, to those dwelling in darkness or shadows.

Ancient and medieval peoples accepted the wide and overall influence of good spirits or angels and evil spirits or fallen angels and it did not seem to worry them overmuch. They are mentioned by their nature or the task they were performing at the time and not usually by name in the *Bible*. There is a Spirit, who volunteered to become a Spirit of Lying 'And there came forth a spirit, and stood before the Lord . . . I will go forth and be a lying spirit.' 1 *Kings* 22:22. A Spirit of Discord is found in *Judges* 9:23 in the line, 'God sent a spirit of discord between Abimelech and the men of Schechem.' A Spirit of Whoredom is mentioned in *Hosea* 4:12 'which caused them to err' and the Angel of Lust is usually given as Parzulph, who is mentioned again in Part Two. His name in the Hebrew is given as 'two faced' or 'hypercritical.' A Spirit of Jealousy is given in *Numbers* 5:4 where 'the spirit of jealousy came upon him.' I think this is enough to show the point but at least the system appears to be generous in catering for the needs of all.

## SOME ANGELS AND THE CABBALA

For a moment let us depart from Scripture sources to take in some Cabbalistic thoughts, though some would not regard this as a serious departure as the angelic has a prominent role in all this material. For those readers who may be unfamiliar with Cabbala, which does have esoteric

33

connections with Christianity, let us look briefly at a little of the philosophy, the operative word being 'a little.' I would be first to admit that trying to explain this enormous subject and study in a few lines is foolhardy when you see the amount of books and the millions of words that have been devoted to the topic by some very knowledgeable, enthusiastic and intellectual writers. Some would regard the attempt as being tantamount to heresy, if not foolish. However, Cabbala is a very difficult subject to avoid in the Western Tradition coming as it does from the Hebrew upon which so much is built and in both tradition and Cabbala, the angels play a very large and important role.

Cabbala contains within its teachings a diagram called the 'Tree of Life.' This diagram is given in its most familiar form and the one chiefly found and there are other forms such as the **Cabbala of the Latter Day Cabbalists** (see Kircher). Using the familiar form will make it easier to those who know little or nothing of the system and the one they are most likely to find and will I hope make the text here clearer.

This system is a system that can aid people in their attempts to make contact and try to understand the Divine and themselves. The most important work in the beginning starts with us and will assist us to 'connect' to a system that has existed for thousands of years. However, bear in mind one very important precept above all — if you are going to plant this 'Tree,' make it grow and harvest the 'fruit' — you must prepare the soil and make that soil fit for the task you have elected to undertake — the soil required is you and there can be no substitute for the hard work and study needed — but the rewards can be great.

I would be the first to admit that I think the Cabbala has been pulled and twisted over the years to fit some very strange concepts. Here is not the place to discuss this, only to advise that such examples do exist and that they will be found. The Cabbala is very generous to those who seek it and seems to endlessly accommodate itself to peoples needs and it is to the system's credit that it still survives intact in its adaptation for the most. This could prove to be its strength over its very long history.

If you know how and where to look, you will find the Cabbalistic Tree popping up in some very unlikely places, hidden in diagrams and art, it is there in so many places if you seek it. However, to connect yourself to the system you must first know that such a system exists. Then you have to study it and it will teach you how prepare yourself properly to use it. If anyone thinks that this is a five-minute job because they have finished their library book and its a wet afternoon, perhaps it would be better that they did not even attempt it.

You may feel the need or desire for the help and companionship of like minds that are travelling in the direction you want to go, to join them would be a good idea and for the most, you will need neither priest nor priesthood. However, if you link yourself to a good School or Teacher then you should accept the organization and structure of the School and its teachings. If you are not prepared to do this then you should not join because you will be wasting everyone's time including your own. Loose cannons have been known to sink the ship they are on, so their ropes were cut with a sharp axe and they were jettisoned overboard to save the ship. In a crisis or emergency, there can be no sentimentality, only safety, survival for the 'ship' — the Work in hand.

Such paths can be a very lonely ones at times and if this thought bothers you then you should stay in the warmth, safety and comfort of the crowd because such ways do not suit everyone. This is the path for the 'outsider' who ever ploughs a lonely furrow and such a path is not for faint hearts because once you take your light from a large group it can no longer be hidden, no matter how small, it announces to all that you are striking out on your own. There are some that think — better the 'herd' than the 'maverick' — as a rule you know where the 'herd' is going and it can be comfortable I admit but the herd can be stampeded and sometimes take you where you do not want to go — there is usually a price to pay for most things that have value and worth.

The system is closely allied with the angels on practically every level of its working. There is the Jewish enumeration of the ten agencies through which God created the world given in early works as 'wisdom, insight, cognition, strength, power, inexorableness, justice, right, love and mercy' other titles are sometime used. A 'correctly proportioned man, if his body were divided into the decade, each tenth would be the length of his head' so in this I am not included.

Rabbinical angelology is not a pure breed and it owes much to Zoroastrian and Mithric influences. The 'prayers of man, his recovery from sickness, his safety from peril, his circumstances after death' are all placed under angelic domination. There are two main divisions of angels and they were named respectively, *familia shel ma'alah*= 'the heavenly host below' and *familia shel matia*= 'the heavenly host above,' both of which I believe figure in the *Jewish Prayer Book*.

The main spellings of this Work that will be met with are Cabbala, Cabala, Kabbalah or Qabbala and we use the first with a fondness for the rest. This name means 'received tradition.' This was the original term used to denote the prophets and the prophetical teachings were 'received' or 'doctrine received by tradition.' Though another name for Cabbalah I believe is *Hokhmah Mistarah*= 'Secret Science.'

In old Jewish literature the name is applied to the entire body of 'received doctrine or tradition' of mystical and theosophical system developed in the eleventh and twelfth centuries with the exceptions given above. Eventually the meaning of Cabbala underwent a change and it became applied to hidden and mysterious doctrines dealing with the nature of the Deity and his relationship to the world.

Cabbala was a widespread Jewish mysticism in all its appearances, which crystallized in 12th–13th century Spain and Provence around the *Sefer ha–zohar — The Book of Splendour* — now usually the *Zohar* — 'Illumination' or 'Brightness.' This generated the later mystical movements in Judaism. Especially those esoteric religious and philosophical systems that claimed to provide knowledge of God and of the relationship of the universe to God, frequently through the medium of direct mystical intuition, philosophical studies or both. The cult of Elijah is prominent in Cabbalistic literature with some founders of this form of mysticism (c.12th Century) claiming to have received their instruction directly from the prophet.

Cabbala originally determined the legal tradition of Judaism. Later it was used by Jewish mystical tradition, in particular to the system of esoteric mystical hypothesis and practices that developed during the 12th and 13th century. As with other Jewish religious expressions, the system of Cabbala was the basis for revelation of the *Old Testament*. The revealed text was interpreted with the aid of hermeneutic methods that were effective to the Cabbala. *Gematria*, *Notarikon* and *Temurah* are three of the most commonly used methods of letter and numerical symbolism used and they are enlarged a little in Part Two.

The cardinal doctrines of the Cabbala are given as embracing the nature of the Deity, the Divine emanations or Sephiroth, cosmogony, the 'creation of the angels and man,' their destiny and the implication of what is being revealed. There are certain intermediate things, often given as five in all, between God and his people, to which great veneration bordering on adoration are given. Sometimes they are identified with God. Sometimes they are spoken of as personalities and at other times as abstract forces.

These five things are, the Angel Metatron; the *Memra*= 'the Word' of Yahweh; the *Shekinah*; the *Ruach Hakkodesh*= 'the Holy Spirit' sometimes seems to be identical with the *Shekinah* and the *Bat Qol*= 'the heavenly voice through which revelation is given.' The *Bat Qol* is dealt with later.

It is said the world was created by 'ten sayings' and the phrase 'And God said' appears ten times regarding the Creation and as an objection to the cult of anthropomorphism. The *Maamar* or *Memra=* 'Word' to some extent acts as the mediator and becomes the agent or instrument of Creation. This formulates the idea of 'mediators,' whether the Demiurge or Metatron, though this is repudiated by several authorities. Stress was placed on the fact that these could not have been created on the first day, lest any share in the Creation be ascribed to them when creation is by God alone. The Angel Metatron is mentioned by name frequently and some believing that Metatron governs the entire Tree of Life.

I have often wondered if these matters of 'when, how or what' are essential? They did not seem to trouble Johannes Eckhart, better know as Meister Eckhart. I believe the following was taken from *Meister Eckhart* by Pfeffer (1857) John Watkins — I no longer have the book and my notes are a little vague, but not the views expressed and they are another point of view.

'Do not fondly imagine that God, when he created the heavens and the earth and all creatures, made one thing one day and another the next. Moses describes it thus, it is true, nevertheless he knew better: he did so merely on account of those who are incapable of understanding or conceiving otherwise. All God did was: he willed and they were.'

One reason for introducing the subject of Cabbala here is that some occult writer's think of the 'seven churches of Asia' as the 'seven churches of Assiah,' As(s)ia(h) or Asia. 'Assiah' is a Cabbalistic term and it is one of the four levels of the Tree of Life, mentioned above. The Tree of Life contains four worlds and each world below is a lessening of the World above it. Apart from the top world, each of the other three lower worlds diminishes the quality of the emanation above it. Each of the three lower worlds becomes more gross and dense as it descends from the original creation. Finally, the fourth world gathers enough impurity and becomes gross enough to form the world of Physical Matter — the World of Assiah.

The fourth world is the world of Nature and human existence so this does not exactly paint a very flattering picture of our position within the scale of things. Therefore, it is worth remembering this when we get up on our hind legs and consider ourselves as something somewhat special, which we obviously are — to us. We are given our place in the scheme — in as much as it is probably is the only place where we could exist as we are.

Nearly all religions tell us that they or their founder(s) are a road or 'way' from here to a better place and most religions tell their adherents that the religion is a path to something better. I have always thought there is a misconception in the human mind regarding this planet. Many think that we own it, when we are but the stewards. This should sound a warning bell because stewardship can be revoked at any time or a steward can be called to account for their both their good and bad management — give an account upon which the lease will be renewed or cancelled — the legal precedence for this thinking being the Garden of Eden, where there was little room for any argument discussion or appeal it would seem.

**World One** — the highest world — is the **World of Atziluth** of the Divine Archetypes, the *Shekinah* and Union with God. The World of Atziluth is the *World of Emanations* and this title translates roughly into 'the World of Making.'

**World Two** is the **World of Briah** of the highest ranking angels, the cherubim and seraphs, the Thrones and Chariot of God. Ten Mighty angels hold the manifestation of the World of Atziluth, the world above it. The World of Briah is the 'world of creation' and is the realm of the very high Angel of Presence, Metatron. It is through this world that High Magic is powered at its highest level and perhaps this is why relatively few are able to contact it, let alone use it.

**World Three** is the **World of Yetzirah** of the angelic hosts. It does not manifest through a single Being but through the Angelic Choirs or Hosts. The World of Yetzirah is the 'World of Formation.'

With **World Four** we finally we come to our portion in the design of things, this is the **World of Assiah** The World of Assiah is 'the World of Action.' Contact with the world above this is possible, not unlike an 'upper room' an often used phrase in literature of this nature, Christ used it. The World of Assiah of the *Exiled Shekinah* and our world can make contact with the world of the angelic host, the World of Yetzirah and this is the purpose of this work and it is this that we are attempting as others have done before us. In the World of Assiah, the Divine emanations exhibit themselves at their lowest level — if they are able. This may be due in part to what the material they have to work with here and the state of the place, uncomplimentary though this may be to we who inhabit 'the place.'

Contact with the upper Worlds of Briah and Yetzirah is possible, with the chances of contact decreasing as we 'rise upon the planes.' Very few I believe are able to make contact with the World of Atziluth. If you are lucky, you may be 'invited' to do so, but I think this is very, very rare. More important perhaps, if you are able to contact the highest World of Atziluth at Will, then what need have you of this world, unless you have elected to do so?

One of the three deputy Princes (= *Sarim*) of the Ten Holy Sephiroth is Ithuriel — 'discovery of God,' sometimes 'a great golden crown.' Ithuriel is under the suzerainty or ethnarchy of the Angel Sephuriron to whom these three angelic princes are answerable. The other two of the three Princes are Malkiel (= 'God's king) and Nashriel. In the *Sixth and Seventh Books of Moses* there is a powerful angel of the Fifth Seal called *Sephiroth*, which is the name given to the kingdoms of the Cabbala. It is said that this angel is invoked in the 'conjuring rites of Cabbala.'

The Sephirah or Divine Emanations show the stages of the manifestations of God. It is used to explain how a transcendent, inaccessible Godhead — the *En Sof* — can associate to the physical world. A distinction is made between with the first three Sephiroth of the Cabbala, these are 1: The Supreme Crown; 2: Wisdom and 3: Intelligence regarded as the highest and the remaining seven kingdoms are lower or below these three. These remaining seven are 4: Love; 5: Power; 6: Beauty; 7: Endurance; 8: Majesty; 9: Foundation and 10: Kingdom. Linking these kingdoms are the thirty–two paths of wisdom established upon the twenty–two letters of the Hebrew alphabet and the ten primordial numbers that represent the elements of creation.

One consideration regarding Cabbala and the Tree of Life may have occurred to some readers, so it will be dealt with briefly here. If the spirits, angels, archangels and the higher angels are placed in the Four Worlds of the Tree of Life do the 'bad fallen or evil' angels' have a place or 'tree' and do they have a place they can call their own — does light have shadow?

The following is brief as most is here, there are many other important considerations appertaining to this lower tree and indeed as there are even more to the higher trees. Remember, I did say this short excursion into Cabbala is impertinent in its brevity considering the magnitude and importance of the subject and perhaps only a fool would attempt it — guilty as charged and not for the first time! I hope it will help readers to have some knowledge of the subject, no matter how slight if they have none and that is its sole purpose. Those who want to pursue the subject matter fuller and I hope they can find plenty of books to help them on their quest. A fair start for Cabbala would be the works of Dion Fortune, Gareth Knight and a man whose many books I have bought for a long time now — Z'ev ben Shimon Halevi or to use his English name — Warren Kenton.

Please understand, omission does not imply criticism in any way, a list for this particular subject would be lengthy and obviously, I have not read everything.

There is a lower, mirror–image of the World of Assiah (= our world) called the Qliphoth and here can be found the 'evil or averse' Sephiroth= kingdoms and its inhabitants, the *Tree of Evil or Empty, Discarded Shells*. The Qliphoth is not a separate Tree strictly speaking but a coin has two sides and you cannot have one without the other. You cannot pick up one side of a coin without disturbing the other on our level and you cannot leave the side you do not like lying for if you pick up the coin then you pick up its two side. It is the other side of the coin of the Tree of Life at our level and this is why good intentions or deeds can sometimes go wrong, even when only good was wished for or sought.

If someone pointed to your shadow on the ground, you would not say it was someone else's because it could not exist without you and it goes where you go like your 'dark twin.' The only way get rid of your shadow is to keep out of the light — but who wants to live in perpetual darkness and be like one that is blind? The demons or dire angels are considered obscene and among the most defective of forms of existence, the insignificant *Shells or Rinds of Existence* but they are nevertheless, thought of by some as being 'energies and forces most destructive and injurious to man' and denying this does not banish them. This is like putting a nice fence up to hide a rubbish tip, you cannot see it true but it is still there.

This 'Tree of Darkness' also has ten kingdoms resembling the 'Tree of Life' of which it is a shadow or copy. As your shadow is a drab, lifeless copy of you that is lacking in detail, vital energy and all that goes with life, if you greatly animate yourself it will do likewise but if you stop it will because it only imitates having no true life of its own. If you mistake or misunderstand what it is, it can pull you down into its dark kingdom — melodramatic — you choose the path that you will take.

The first three kingdoms of the Tree of Darkness stand in direct opposition to the highest three kingdoms of the Tree of Life. In the Tree of Life, these are at the top of the tree but on the Tree of Darkness — the Qliphoth — they are at the bottom. One of these lower kingdoms is said to be the 'Abode of the Darkness' that in *Genesis*, 'covered the face of the deep.' This kingdom is 'without form and void' and order was imposed on this kingdom from the outside with the *Fiat Lux,* order is not its natural composition and it wants its chaotic rule back.

Therefore, Chaos is forever at war with Order and now and then, as history shows, it breaks through and gains the upper hand and Chaos rules once more. The seven lower degrees, beneath these three, are said to be infernal halls or hells, reversed on the *Qliphoth,* working from the bottom up. Obviously, the lower, infernal tree does not possess any of the Divine Nature of the Tree of Life, which is the Tree of Light and Life. The lower tree is a 'dark shadow' of Darkness and Death, generally thought to be under the rule of the Angel, do not confuse the Angel Samael the Angel of Mars with the Angel Sammael give above.

Dion Fortune said of the Qliphoth, the reverse side of a Sephirah of our Tree, that they were the 'unbalanced and destructive aspect of the Holy Stations themselves.' *Mystical Qabalah*, p.289. In this area, *Qliphoth* is singular while *Qliphah* is plural. When speaking of contact with the *Qliphothic* forces, on page 304 Dion Fortune wisely tells us that 'It is this (= the evil Qliphah) that gives the single–minded zealot his abnormal power.' All zealots are consistently disproportionate in their outlook because they will brook no opposition to their aims or opinions, least of all by reasoning, which appears to all intents and purposes to be an abomination to them and a red rag to a bull. Neither will they listen to any alternative opinions or thoughts that differ from theirs and their driving force, the 'power' or 'drive' that they have called up and accepted as their Master, works through them and 'drives' them to destroy or subjugate anyone or anything that opposes them or it

Every now and then a channel from the World of Atziluth= the highest world, may find a relatively pure channel it can use to send something or someone with direct contact to the World of Assiah= the lower world, ours. There are relatively few people in a generation that have whatever is necessary for this to happen. When then does happen some outstanding creations come to pass in our world. We are sometimes given a genius, a real one such as a Mozart, a Mahler, a Shakespeare, a Milton, a Beethoven, a Michelangelo or a Leonardo da Vinci perhaps. As you can see, this 'channel' is not opened very often, despite the word 'genius' being handed out like sweets to children today, to such an extent that the original word to some has lost almost any real meaning that it had.

Among the best gentile exponents of the Cabbala was the Italian, Pico da Mirandola (1463–1494). The renowned Johann Reuchlin (1455–1522) was also a fervent apostle of the Cabbala and his works were found in the library of Dr. John Dee. Reuchlin completed the *De Rudimentis Hebraicis* in 1506, the first Hebrew grammar written by a Christian, which was of significant benefit to biblical scholarship. With his eloquence, he captivated the greatest minds of his time. At the time, Reuchlin was the foremost German champion of Greek and Hebrew studies. We must mention Henrich Cornelius Agrippa of Nettesheim (1487–1535), Theophrastus Paracelsus (1493–1541) and later, Robert Fludd (1574–1637).

Mirandola believed that 'No science yields greater proof of the divinity of Christ than magic and the Cabbala.' He convinced Pope Sextus of the paramount importance of Cabbala as an auxiliary to Christianity, that his holiness had the Cabbalistic writings translated into Latin for the use of divinity students. Pico's thought is an eclectic attempt to harmonize Judaism, Christianity and Greek philosophy. He classifies all things on three levels. First the Super–celestial, God and the angels, next in order comes the Celestial of the Sun, Moon, planets, stars and terrestrial, the material things beneath the Moon. Last, he called the human race 'the Divine Masterpiece,' because they were capable of mediating in these categories. Individuals possessed the potential, freedom and the power to shape their destiny.

'A magic force put to sleep by sin is latent in man. It can be awakened by the Grace of God or by the art of Cabbala. We find a pure and holy knowledge in us, if we manage to isolate ourselves from all outward influences and allow ourselves to be led by the inward light. At this stage of concentration the spirit distinguishes each object on which it directs its attention, being able to unite itself therein and attain even to God.' Helmont (1577–1544).

We hope the information given here is enough to encourage the reader to take up other paths in their search concerning the angels and the angelic kingdom. The information exists and is there for those who want to find it, more so than even fifty years ago say. It may be asked if I do not intend to enlarge upon information, why introduce it all? I do not see any reason for not adding a few extra 'signposts' for those who would like to extend their journey beyond this work to other themes. This can be done, in part, by showing where people can get a more 'detailed map.' The writer believes that the 'map' given here is more than adequate for the task in hand and I believe those who want to go further will do so and those who do not — will not — it has ever been so.

The work was written to help those who do not know where to start in some areas because they know little about the subject, perhaps not knowing what exists. So, let us continue with those matters relevant to the book that have as their source, the philosophy and tradition of Cabbala and the angelic.

God lives in a solemn seclusion from his subjects and only a favoured few (it seems) may see or have seen his face. Access to him without his grace is punishable by death and his 'officials' execute his Will. He is surrounded by an Angelic Host that is almost military in its hierarchy and assembly that will execute this Will to the letter of the Law.

Those in the immediate presence of God are the Princes of the Countenance, one of whom is the Angel Suriel and the Angel Metatron is another. Metatron has this title because he could behold the countenance of the Supreme Being, whom he served as confidant and he is called the 'Prince of the World.' Each of the seventy nations has a representative in the Court of Heaven of whom the greatest is said to be the Archangel Michael, a Prince of Israel. The representatives or Viceroys of Nature are mentioned elsewhere but let us move next to a mighty angel called the . . .

## ANGEL METATRON

The Angel Metatron is the greatest of angels in Jewish myth and legend and is identified as the Prince or Angel of the Presence, as Michael the archangel, the 'tall angel' or as Enoch after his ascent into heaven. Metatron is a very high–ranking angel indeed and also one of the highest that is taller that all the other angels and one of the Recording Angels. Metatron is likewise described as a celestial scribe 'recording the sins and merits of men, as a guardian of heavenly secrets, as God's mediator with men.' He was found leading Moses in the Third Heaven and encountering the 'tall angel' that is often given to Sandalphon and this could be true for tall he is, but this angel is usually found in the sixth or seventh heaven.

In the lore of the Hebrews, Metatron is one of the greatest angels and as every account regarding the angelic hierarchy shows, there is very little if anything that does not pass through him or that he does not know. All angels stand in the presence of God, but Metatron has been found seated, so some have reflected that perhaps he should be worshipped as having divine power. However, this unique privilege was given to this high angel by Divine permission and it did not include personal worship. It is often given that the angels have 'no back but four faces so as to be able to always see god' — 'and every one had four faces, and every one had four wings.' *Ezekiel* 1:7.

The name Metatron is said to mean 'guide' and 'the measurer of the heavens,' but his name has never been satisfactorily explained. Eleazar of Worms thought it was taken from the Latin, *metator*= 'One who metes out or marks off a place, a divider and fixer of boundaries.' See also *metatorius* and *metatura* both having a similar definition.

The Angel Metatron is held to be the greatest of the entire heavenly host, the first and also the last of the ten Archangels of the Briatic World. Metatron is often termed the 'Prince of Angels, Angel of the Covenant, Chancellor of Heaven and Chief of the Ministering Angels and the Angel of Mankind.' He has been found with the interesting appellation 'boy–angel' though it is said there are well over one hundred alternative names given to him. In a few of the early accounts he is called 'the lesser Yahweh' and this would seem to imply that he is 'second to God' or 'a second God' for his 'number' is the same as El Shaddi, a name of God, which is 314. The latter appellation is established through Hebrew numerology where the consonants that comprise the names Metatron and Shaddai (= 'Almighty') are evaluated according to these numerical values giving both names, the total arrived at is — 314.

He has been called 'the shining light of the *Shekinah*' who 'has a name like that of his Master.' Some sources give Metatron the title of the Angel with the Flaming Sword who protected the Garden of Eden after the expulsion of Adam and Eve but this task has also been given to others. Metatron is the leader of the Invisible Host and his place is immediately beneath the Throne of God. The above are some of his considerable titles for not all have been given only mentioned. 3.*Enoch* has Metatron possessing thirty–six wings and a 'spirit of fire.'

The Angel Suriel — 'God's command' — is found in the immediate presence of God because he is a Prince of the Countenance. He is usually mentioned in the same breath as Ariel, Metatron, Uriel and the like, which is very exalted company to be found in. He is like the Archangel Raphael, a healing angel but he is also an Angel of Death and in this capacity, he was sent to Mount Nebo to bring the soul of Moses to God. Always remember, if an angel can heal and cure then he can also make something worse and take life see the *Zohar* below. His name is frequently found on Gnostic amulets with Peniel, Raphael and Uriel. He is one of the seven angels who rule the earth according to Cabbala.

The Angel Metatron is called a Prince of the World and 'he enters the deeds of men in a book,' which makes him one of the Recording Angels. The *Zohar* tells us that Metatron was the Rod of Moses, which 'from one side came life and from the other, death.'

Traditionally Metatron is the angel who led the Israelites through the wilderness during the Exodus from Egypt, although this assignment is also found given to the Archangel Gabriel. God says, 'Behold I send an Angel before thee, to keep thee in the way, and to bring thee into the place I have prepared.' *Exodus* 23:2, this is often applied to John the Baptist, but more think it refers to Metatron and this is expanded a little later when speaking of the *Tetragrammaton*.

As a Recording Angel, the Angel Metatron is kept particularly busy in one important and great activity — prayer. In the *Zohar,* the Angel Gazardiel is one of the principal supervisor's of the East who 'kisses the prayer's of the faithful and conveys them to the supernal firmament.' According to the *Talmud*, this angel also has the supervision of the rising and setting of the sun and it is his duty to watch that it rises and sets at the correct time each day.

We have already said that each of the seventy nations has a delegate in the court of heaven and among them, 'the greatest is Michael.' It is frequently given that the Angel Metatron is greater than the Archangel Michael, even though the latter has the title archangel. This is because the Angel Metatron is of the world and he sits in the presence of God, while the Archangel Michael is the highest of a nation and the Angel Metatron is given as being greater than the Archangel Gabriel. In the *Yalkut Hadash* Metatron is 'appointed over Michael and Gabriel.'

The *Midrash* is a transliteration of a Hebrew word and is a Medieval Hebrew commentary on the Scripture, given as sermons that use allegory and legendary illustration. They were a means by which the earliest Rabbis investigated Scripture in order to make it surrender its laws and wisdom that is not observable in a casual appraisal. They are books that interpret or comment on the *Scriptures*, because *Midrash* is Hebrew for 'interpretation, to enquire, to investigate, a study or the result of research' with the plural *Midrashim*. The *Talmud* poetically describes the *Midrash* as 'a hammer that wakes the shining light, the sparks that slumber in rock.' *Midrash*. The word Midrash only appears twice and this is in *Chronicles*.

According to a passage in the *Zohar* (*Midrash Ha–Ne'el–am*, the section *Haye–Sarah*), Metatron is appointed to take charge of the soul every day and provide it with the necessary light from the Divine as he is commanded. It is the Angel Metatron who is detailed to take the record of the graveyards from the Angel Dumah, the Angel of Death and show it to the Master. It is Metatron who is destined 'to put the leaven into the bones that lie beneath the earth. To repair the bodies and bring them to a state of perfection, in the absence of the soul, which will be sent by God to its appointed place.'

The Angel Dumah or Duma (Aramaic= 'silence') is an 'Angel of Death, the Angel of Silence and the stillness of death.' The Angel of Silence is given charge of the disembodied spirits. The Angel Dumah is sometimes given as a tutelary Angel of Egypt, the Prince of Hell and the *Zohar* tells us that he has 'tens of thousands of Angels of Destruction' under him. Dumah is a popular figure in Yiddish folklore and he also appears in the Babylonian legends. If there was a plague in the city, one Rabbi suggested that you do not walk down the middle of the road because, if consent has been granted to the Angel of Death to follow his mission, he walks about openly and as a rule 'walks down the middle of the road.' However, if the city has a healthy feeling about it, you should not walk on the pathways because if the Angel of Death has not been granted consent, he creeps about in secret, so stay out in the open.

If a sleeper would say *Psalm* 41 before closing their eyes, they would awake safe in the morning but, upon waking, they should not rub their eyes before they had washed them. This was to give protection from the *Demon of Blindness* that he may not blind them. Demons fed on certain elements during the night so it was thought dangerous to drink water during the night for dread that *Shabriri*, the *Demon of Blindness* should strike them down. The person afflicted may cause the demon to progressively decay by cutting off the syllables from the name of *Shabriri* one by one and pronouncing the shortened name. Thus, *Shabriri, briri, riri, ri*. As the syllables lessened so the danger dwindles away and the danger passes and when the afflicted says the final *ri*, it is said that the demon died. This answers to what is now called sympathetic magic and is mentioned elsewhere, remembering the triangle that is formed by *Abracadabra*, dropping a letter until only 'A is left.

The Hebrew *Mot*, *Duma(h)* and *Sheol* were originally demons or Jinns, corresponding to the Greek *Κερες, Keres*= 'the malignant spirits, the bringers of all kinds of evil' hence 'spiritual blindness, doom, fate.' *Θανατος, Thanatos*= 'Death, who is iron–hearted and hated even by the gods, though sometimes thought a healer for 'only death will ease Hippolytus' pain' and in the Greek, *Αιδης, Aides*= 'unseen, annihilated, invisible, Hades or Pluto, the God of the Nether World.' *Pluto*= 'God of the Underworld' modelled on *Hades* — 'the Invisible One' — *God of Death*. The Roman *Lethum, Mors*= 'Death, a child of Night and the sister of Sleep. Pheonician and Jewish traditions say *Mot* hovered about or over dying people.

The Angel of Death is called Azrael by the Arabians and the ancient Persians call this angel, Mordad. There are very few nations, possibly none, who do not have legends in their literature or lore about an Angel of Death. In Islam, it is said you only see an angel at the moment of death, while in the *Bible* the angels and archangels often appear to proclaim or accompany a death.

The Angel Metatron is often styled *Sar–ha–Panin*= 'The Prince of the Presence,' as well as *Sar–ha–Olam*= 'the Prince of the World.' Metatron, like Enoch in the Apocryphal *Book of Jubilees* is described as 'the heavenly scribe.' Metatron occupies the highest world in *Cabbala* and he alone constitutes the world of pure spirit, as is the garment of *Shaddai*= 'Almighty' that is, the visible manifestation of the Deity. His name, according to the *Zohar* is numerically equivalent to that of the Lord. For the curious, this number is 314 under the Talmudic rule of *Gematria*, mentioned earlier in this section and in Part 2.

The Angel Metatron 'dwells in Him and is the garment of *Shaddai*, which is the visible manifestation of the Deity and his name is numerically corresponds to that of the Lord.' He presides over the visible world, protects the unity, harmony and the turning of the spheres, the planets, the heavenly bodies or the *Yetziratic World* and these are divided into ten ranks that answer to the *Ten Sephiroth*.

The first world (= *the World of Emanations*) is inhabited by spiritual beings of various orders and the first world or the Archetypal Man, in whose image everything is fashioned, is occupied by none. The Angel Metatron governs the visible world and he inhabits the second world or *World of Briah*, which is the first habitable world and he unaided, encompasses the world of pure spirits. He is the Captain of the Angelic Hosts that people the second dwelling place and this angel preserves the harmony of that world and guides the revolutions of the spheres, the planets and all the heavenly bodies.

He is the Captain of the Myriads of angelic beings because he constitutes the entire world of spirits or angels and each of these angels is set over a different part of Creation. One angel has control over a specific sphere with another controlling another heavenly body. One angel has charge of the sun, another the moon, another the earth, another the sea, another fire, another the wind, another the light, while a different angel supervises the seasons. They preside over everything and these angels take their names from the heavenly bodies or part of the Creation over which they are directly concerned. The Archangel Michael the Sun, the Archangel Gabriel the Moon, the Angel Cassiel the planet Saturn and so forth, these are discussed and given later in the work.

They are divided into ten ranks answering to the number of the ten Sephiroth or the Kingdoms on the Tree of Life and these ten Sephiroth are sometimes called the *Intermediaries* between the Unknowable or Invisible Deity and the Knowable, Visible occupiers of the material world — human beings. As said, the *World of Briah* is occupied by the Angel Metatron, 'the world of true spirit and governing the visible world.' In the angelic scheme of the pseudo–Dionysius there are nine ranks of angels given but 'ten ranks' can sometimes be found, discussed at the end.

Metatron plays a paramount role in the operation of the Cosmos and this is because he is a personified emanation of the Deity as 'an ever present guide and an instructor of mankind.' Metatron is credited with being the teacher of the *Torah* to Abraham and was his guide both in Paradise and on earth. The *Talmud* tells us that even in Paradise today the great Angel Metatron teaches those children who died prematurely and who have died without knowledge. Metatron collaborates with God in the teaching of the young. God devotes the last three hours of the day to this undertaking and Metatron has charge of all the remaining hours.

Metatron, in the early myths of the Hebrew's was represented as the Vice Regent of the Creator and it was this mighty angel who transmitted the orders of the One God to Moses as the Angel of the Covenant and the Angel of the Face or Presence and this title is also given to the Archangel Michael. Being the teacher and instructor of Moses Metatron is the Guardian of the Law and Holy Writ. There was obviously a special relationship between the Angel Metatron and Moses.

We must remember that Moses asked Metatron to intercede with God when his death was close because Moses would not give up his soul to the Angel of Death. Metatron had an excellent relationship with Moses according to tradition and it was Metatron that Moses asked to intercede with God to attempt to delay his death. One of the functions of Metatron was 'to facilitate man's access to the Deity' and 'the angels that intercede for man.'

This may be why Moses and Metatron are found at times interchanged. Enoch is often given as Archangel Metatron and Elijah as the Archangel Sandalphon, though some say Elijah was already an angel. We are often given the angelic names of Enoch and Elijah but we are not certain of the angelic name of Moses, which many say he has. He is often called 'angel' by the Rabbis, though this could simply have been a title of respect and love in which they held the prophet. Some texts give the rank of Moses above all the angels — including Metatron.

Tradition often gives Jesus as an angel and there is an esoteric tradition that he was one of the two 'men' (= angels) who appeared with the Lord to accept the hospitality of Abraham, under the terebinth trees at Mamre. *Genesis*.18. There is a Talmudic legend that says the Archangel Michael assumed 'the form of Moses.' Enoch, we are told, was exposed to the process of glory and purification so that later, when he was permitted to return to the earth for thirty days, an angel 'chilled his face' and this was done to darken the radiance of his angelic glory before 'he came down to mingle among men.' (*Slav. Enoch* 36:2).

He is called the Prince of the Universe and is commanded by God the All–Father to create the world. In the myth of Metatron we find the influence of the Demiurge, however, Judaism could never permit this Gnostic doctrine to be taught and those who did so were excommunicated.

It is said in the **Berishith Rabba** 'that the voice of God became Metatron over the waters.' An angel allied with Metatron is the Angel Uzziel — the 'strength of God' — one of the principal angels in rabbinic angelology of the order cherubim, sometimes given as the chief of the Order of Virtues. In the Merkabah mysteries, Uzziel is an Angel of Mercy under the command of Metatron. The angelology of the Rabbi's has the higher ranks of angels under Uzziel who is their chief angel. The **Book of Raziel** tells us he is 'one of the seven angels that stand before the Throne of Glory' and among those 'set over the four winds.'

Metatron, according the **Talmud**, bears the **Tetragrammaton** within himself, this is thought to have been taken from the angel in **Exodus** 23: 21 and gives this unknown angel a name, the italics used in the following are mine of course. 'Behold, I send an Angel before thee, to keep thee in the way, and to bring thee into the place I have prepared. Beware of him, and obey his voice, provoke him not; for he will not pardon your transgressions; *for my name is in him.*' These words make this angel a very powerful angel and Metatron would be an obvious choice for this.

According to some sources, the **Slavonic Book of Enoch** for example, it was the Archangel Michael, originally the Guardian Angel of Israel who was transformed into Metatron — 'the angel whose name is like that of his Divine Master.'

Usually when the angels are mentioned in most works, the word 'angel' is written in lower case but, in **Exodus** 23: 21, it is 'an Angel.' There is little doubt about heeding this angel and obeying him because Metatron has the sum of all the angelic forces within him. We have already said that the letters of El Shaddai and Metatron, by the system of **Gematria** have the same value, therefore, the Almighty and Metatron are considered to be equal by some so if you offend one, you offend the other and take the consequences. Now let us move on to another mighty angel, the half–brother of the Angel Metatron . . .

## ANGEL SANDALPHON

The Angel Sandalphon is a great angel like his twin Metatron, he is a very tall angel and he has been a favourite of mine for many years. Sandalphon means 'co–brother' and he is usually given as the twin brother of Metatron and because Sandalphon is intimately connected with Metatron, he is a high angel who also presents petitions to God. He is often found standing behind the celestial chariot where he weaves crowns from the prayers of suppliants and presents them to his Creator. *Ezekiel* 1.

In the **Greater Key of Solomon** of Mather's, Sandalphon is designated 'the left–hand feminine cherub of the ark.' The Angels Metatron and Sandalphon would be excellent if placed on the lid of the ark, giving a male and female polarity, which would make the Mercy Seat most holy, which it naturally is. Many think of Sandalphon, though given as male is the feminine, left–hand twin or half–brother of Metatron who, in turn, is the male and right–hand of Sandalphon and this would include myself at the time of writing and my present thoughts. Sandalphon is called, with the Angel Cassiel of the planet Saturn, as the 'Angel of Tears'

Sandalphon is a lover of sandals because he wears 'soft footwear' when he stands in the presence of the Lord, though he adopts leather footwear when he stands before the **Shekinah** and some traditions set this angel over the welfare of the birds. As always, I try to seek help from the Hebrew, Greek and Latin language to see if I can gain a better understanding of words because sometimes they can be very revealing, especially if the meaning has changed from the original.

The Greek word, σανδαλον, *sandalon*= 'a small sandal or slipper' or 'a wooden sole, bound on straps round the instep and ankle, a sandal.' The Latin is *sandalium*= 'a slipper, sandal.' *Sandaliarius*= 'of or pertaining to sandals.' The god Apollo as *Apollo Sandaliarius,* had a statue in Sandal–street (= Shoemakers' Street in the fourth region of Rome.) *Sandaliarius* also means 'a sandal–maker.'

Cabbalists consider Sandalphon significant because he causes the separation of the sexes within the unborn embryo and this is why he is found called the *Angel of the Embryo*. Like Metatron, Sandalphon gathers the prayers of the faithful, which he takes to the 'King of Kings.' This he does by transforming 'the prayers of the faithful into a garland' which he raises up 'as an orb.' *Talmud.*

## ARCHANGEL MICHAEL

In the *Bible*, we usually find unnamed angels and messengers until we arrive at the *Book of Daniel* where we find the names of the Archangel Gabriel (8:16) and the Archangel Michael (10:13.) Despite the Gabriel being mentioned first, there is widespread agreement that Michael is the superior of the two angels regarding rank and station for the reason that wherever Michael is found, more often than not, the *Shekinah* is found also, discussed later. Further, of Michael it is said ' . . . but lo, Michael, one of the chief princes, came to help me.' Earlier a voice was heard that said 'Gabriel, make this man understand the vision. So he came near where I stood: and when he came, I was afraid.'

The Archangel Michael or Mikhael in Hebrew — 'who is like God'— is an *Old Testament* name synonymous with Micaiah or Micha. Dr. John Dee called Michael — *Fortitudo Dei* — 'Strength of God.' The Latin, *Quis ut Deus*= 'one like god' is used in association with angelic power and it is called by ancient medieval Hebrew and Christian mystics — Michael — given by some writers saying it is from Hebrew *mi*= 'who' plus *cha*= 'like' plus *el*= 'God or a divinity' therefore 'who is like God.'

Arabic Mikail or Mikhail in the *Bible* and the *Qur'an*. The address used at times for the Archangel Michael in the Roman Church is the *Angel of the Face*. In the seven heavens mentioned throughout at various points, in the sixth heaven the Angel Zebul (= 'habitation or temple') can be found with the Angel Sabath, who rules by day and Zebul by night. The Heavenly Jerusalem, the Temple and the altar upon which the Archangel Gabriel offers his sacrifice.

The Archangel Michael and Gabriel are without doubt the most prominent angels found mentioned and they are often found cooperating in a duty but I feel there would be very little disputing that Michael is probably one of the greatest and major of the angels found. He is chief of the rank of angels called the Virtues and the Archangels, though the reader will find that roles are frequently found overlapping and in this instance, with the Archangels Gabriel and Archangel Raphael.

They assisted, with the Archangel Raphael and the Angel Sammael (= Satan) in the death and burial of Moses. The Archangel Michael as the Guardian Angel of Israel was the angel that instructed Moses. The two Archangels Michael and Gabriel are held to have been 'grooms' at the marriage of Adam and Eve at which God officiated, no less.

As said, in the *Book of Daniel* the name is given to one of the chief 'princes' of the heavenly host, the Guardian Angel and 'Prince of Israel' (10:13), he is also found in *Jude* and *Revelation*. It is probably Michael who is referred to in *Malachi* 3:1 as the 'messenger' and the 'messenger of the covenant.' In the *Talmud*, Michael's association to the other angels is 'the High Priest of Israel on earth.' The Archangel Michael holds the secret of the mighty 'Word' by which God created heaven and earth therefore, it is not unnatural that he is regarded as the direct lawgiver to the prophet Moses on Sinai. 'This is Moses which said unto the children of Israel . . . in the wilderness with the angel that which spake to him in the mount Sina, and with our fathers; who received the lively oracles to give unto us.' *Acts* 7:38.

Naturally, Michael appears in Jewish theosophy as the greatest of all the angels and among the four or seven that surround the Throne of God and the adversary of Sammael 'the enemy of God.' The Archangel Michael is frequently referred to as the 'great captain' or the leader of the heavenly hosts, the warrior who helped the Children of Israel. In the early history of the Christian church therefore, it is not surprising to find that Michael was regarded as the chief of the church armies against the heathen. At Mass, Michael is in charge of the worship and adoration of the Most High and he sends the prayers of the faithful to God as the smoke of the incense.

As said, the Archangel Michael has the secret of 'the mighty word' by which God created heaven and earth (*Enoch* 65: 14) and was 'the angel who spoke with Moses in the Mount.' (*Acts* 7:38.) Numerous commentators tell us it was through Babylonian and Persian influences that names were given to the angels. In the lore of the ancient Persians the Archangel Michael was known as *Beshter* — the *Sustainer of Mankind* — because he was considered as 'providing sustenance to mankind' and this equates him with Metatron according to some observers.

In Hebrew records, we are told that God created four winds or directions and four banners for the armies of Israel. He also made 'four angels to surround his Throne' and these are the Archangels Michael, Gabriel, Raphael and Uriel. Michael stood on the right of the Throne and had accord to the Tribe of Reuben, which was set in the South. Uriel stood on the left of it signifying corresponding to the Tribe of Dan, which was in the North. Gabriel was in front of it, corresponding to the Tribe of Judah as well as Moses and Aaron, who were set in the East, while Raphael was stationed at the rear of the Throne that was in the West and corresponded with the Tribe of Ephraim.

There were symbols on the devices borne by the Hebrew hosts through the desert. Each of the four divisions of the Hebrew host consisted of three tribes making up the twelve tribes in all. The three tribes within a division were known by the name of the principle tribe and it was their sign or device that was used on their banner. The camp of Judah was in the East leading the march. The camp of Reuben was in the South. Ephraim was in the West. The division in the North who brought up the rear was led by Dan.

The traditional symbols shown on the four standards, like totems, are said to have been the lion for Judah (= Leo). For the tribe of Reuben — there was a man and a river (= Aquarius). There was the bull for Ephraim (= Taurus) and an eagle or a serpent for Dan (= Scorpio). It is natural these four standards are considered to have astrological connotations in the belt of the Zodiac as the four Fixed Signs of the Zodiac — the ubiquitous 'four corners of the Earth' mentioned repeatedly throughout the work

The Archangel Michael is considered to be parallel with Vohu mano, which name means 'good thought or mind' and he is 'Ahura's first masterpiece.' Vohu Mano is one of Zoroastrian *Amesha–spentas* or *archangels* — 'beneficent immortals.' There are six immortal holy ones, who represented the personified attributes of Ahura Mazda and therefore they were created by Ahura Mazda, the Wise Lord, to help to govern over creation. These six are Ministers of his power set against the evil spirit, Ahriman, they are usually shown gathered a on golden thrones about Ahura Mazda, attended by angels. They are the everlasting bestowers of good and they are worshipped separately. Each of them has a special month, festival, flower and presides over an element in the world order.

*Ameretat*= represented 'immortality and the spirits of trees and plants' presiding over water and plants and may possibly come to the believer as a reward for partaking of the natures of the other Amesha–spentas.; *Aramaiti*= is 'holy harmony the spirit of devotion and faith, guiding and protecting the believer and as the spirit of the earth' presiding over the Earth; *Asha*= personified the representation of 'righteousness, the spirit of fire'; *Haurvatat*= personifying 'saving health, the spirits of the waters, wholeness and protection.'

*Kshathra Vairya* = has 'rulership over the spirit of metals' is the power of the kingdom of Ahura Mazda and the believer can become conscious of this power in action by being guided by 'excellent order and good mind.' *Vohu Manah*= is representative of 'good thought and spirit of the human race' and he welcomes the souls of the blessed in paradise.

Believers are instructed to 'bring down Vohu Manah in your lives on Earth' through profound love in marriage and toward your fellowman. Consistent with Zoroastrian doctrine because the prophet Zoroaster was (in a vision) guided into the presence of Ahura Mazda by Vohu Manah, any individual who seeks to know 'the Wise Lord' must draw near to him through this immortal. These archangels are also known as the *Amshaspands* and they are splendid archangels that would bring grace and bless any form of religion.

The Archangel Michael is frequently found represented as the 'great captain, the leader of the heavenly hosts, the warrior assisting the Children of Israel. Early in the history of the Christian church, he came to be regarded as the helper of the armies of the Church against the heathen. It was the Archangel Michael — the 'Marshal of Paradise' — who told the Virgin Mother of her impending death. Michael received her soul and bore it to Jesus.

In 590, a great pestilence ravaged the people of Rome, for three days they sang the service through the streets at the order of St. Gregory who conducted a penitential procession to pray for the end of a plague. On the third day Gregory saw the Archangel Michael hovering over the city who finally alighted on the top of the Mausoleum of Hadrian where he sheathed his bloody sword and the plague was stayed. The building was originally called the *Hadrianeum* — the *Tomb of Hadrian* or the *Sepulcrum Antoninorum*, the burial place of the *Antonine* emperors. It was built AD 135-139 and converted into a fortress in the 5th century. It is on the right bank of the Tiber River and guards the Ponte Sant'Angelo, one of the principal ancient Roman bridges. From the incident of the terrible plague and the archangel that surmounts the building, its name was changed to the *Castel San'Angelo* and the building is immortalised in the final act of Puccini's opera *Tosca*.

The Archangel Michael is known as the patron of the grocers, sailors, sick and soldiers he is also the patron saint of Germany. The reader should connect this list with St. George, who is also connected with armies (= soldiers, armies, Richard the Lion–Heart) and he was a 'dragon–slayer' on horseback. There are his marine connections (= sailors, headlands and marine channels bearing his name) and he is initially heard of as 'a purveyor of provisions for the Army of Constantinople,' which is in all probability why he was also adopted by 'grocers' as their saint.

In art, numerous representations of Michael reflect his character as a warrior, he is rarely shown without wings as the conqueror of Satan and he is frequently found in armour. As the Lord of Souls, he bears no arms but carries a balance that has small figures in each pan representing souls being weighed and judged. He often carries a banner and flourishing a sword in combat with or triumphing over a dragon, from the story in the Book (or Apocalypse) of Revelation.

Legend tells us that God forgave Adam his original sin when the First Man was on his deathbed. Michael cleansed Adam's soul of sin and lifted from him God's curse. Adam is said to have composed *Psalm* 104, which is a 'Psalm of Creation.' 'Who walketh upon the wings of the wind . . .who maketh his angels spirits . . .who laid the foundations of the earth that it should not be

47

moved forever . . . appointed the moon for seasons . . .and thou renewest the face of the earth.' As said, the Archangel Michael is mentioned five times in all in biblical and associated texts and his character always seems to in the role of a chief militant. In the **Book of Daniel** Michael is a champion of Tetragrammaton         the Jewish church against Persia. He overcomes the dragon in **Revelations** and contends with Satan, over the body of Moses in **Jude** and it appears this incident was familiar to Clement of Alexandra, Origen and other early writers.

There are many apparitions of the Archangel Michael recorded and many of them have been near the tops of mountains. He appeared at Mont St. Michel in France, where a sanctuary was erected to commemorate the event. The most famous may prove to be the **Michaelion** church near to Constantinople, which was built by the Emperor Constantine in the 5th century.

The Archangel Gabriel calls him 'Michael, your prince,' referring to the Jewish church. In **Enoch** he is styled 'Michael, one of the holy angels who, presiding over human virtue, commands the nations.' Today, the Archangel Michael is now the patron angel or saint of policeman designated so by Pope Pius XII in 1950. Remembering that Michael was adamant on keeping to the absolute 'letter of Holy law and will not permit the movement of a dot or comma of the Law,' it could prove that this is perhaps a fitting appointment.

There was an old English coin called 'an angel' because it had the image of the Archangel Michael in conflict with the Dragon. **Revelation** 7:7. The reverse of the coin had a ship with a huge cross on the mast. It was first struck in France in 1340 and was introduced into England by Edward IV in 1465.

The feast of St. Michael originated in Phrygia and this feast is honoured in the East and the West on September 29th. The feast of the Appearing (or Apparition) of St. Michael the Archangel of the Roman Catholic Church is kept on May 8th. According to legend, the archangel's appearance took place on Mt. Gargano in Apulia, c. 492 and as a result Mt. Gargano became a significant site of pilgrimage in medieval times.

## ARCHANGEL GABRIEL

The Archangel Gabriel — 'God is my strength' — is similar to the Archangel Michael and is an angel of the of the highest rank in the lore of the Hebrews, Christians and Islam (where he is called Jibril). Dr. John Dee addressed the Archangel Gabriel as — **Misericor Dei** — 'Compassionate God.' His various tasks are many that are mentioned both here and throughout the work. The Archangel Gabriel is the only angel with the Archangel Michael to be mentioned by name in the **Old Testament** because we do not include the Book of Tobit in the **Old Testament** because it is an **Apocryphal** work, in which the Archangel Raphael is given. The Archangel Gabriel is important enough to sit on the left–hand side of God and although the title Archangel is used throughout for this angel because he is called angel in the **Bible**.

The prophet Mohammed said that this was the angel that dictated the **Qu'ra, sura** by **sura** to Islam and this angel is the Angel of Truth. However, the records available show a discrepancy or conflict regarding the Archangel Gabriel statements that, if the records are true, seems to have changed his mind with regard to Jesus. He tells Mary ' . . .that holy thing which shall be born of thee shall be called the Son of God' in the **Bible**. A few hundred years later however, we find the same Archangel telling the prophet Mohammed — even though both Mohammed and Islam are always highly respectful and reverential of Jesus — that Jesus is 'only a prophet.'

'And he called to the man clothed in linen, which had the writer's inkhorn by his side; and the Lord said unto him, Go through the midst of the city . . . and set a mark upon the foreheads of men.' **Ezekiel** 9:2–4. This angel is thought to be the 'man clothed in linen' found in **Ezekiel** but it is said that the 'man' was the Archangel Gabriel. According to many sources, the Archangel Gabriel is the angel that destroys Sodom, although he is not actually named.

Gabriel seems to give skill, wisdom and understanding in *Daniel* given earlier in 'Gabriel, make this man understand the vision . . . he said unto me, Understand, O son of man: for at the time of the end shall be the vision.' *Daniel* 8:16. Gabriel told Daniel 'I am now come forth to give thee skill and understanding.' *Daniel* 9:21 and because the Angel Gabriel stood in the Divine Presence, it is customary for both Jewish and Christian writers to speak of him as an Archangel.

In the *Book of Enoch*, the Archangel Gabriel is 'set over all powers' and shares in the work of intercession. In the *New Testament*, Gabriel announces the birth of the Christ though as said, this angel is not called by the title 'archangel' in the *Bible*, though I will continue to use it. Gabriel is set 'over Paradise and over the cherubim's.' The Archangel Gabriel in the *Old Testament* interprets the vision of the ram and the he–goat to the prophet, (*Daniel* 8:15–26). The archangel explains the prediction of the 70 weeks of years (or 490 years) for the duration of the exile from Jerusalem (*Daniel* 9:21– 27). Gabriel announces the birth of a son to Zacharias, who is destined to become known as John the Baptist. *Luke* 1:11–20.

A rather intriguing legend in found in association with the Archangel Gabriel that tells us. 'At the time that Solomon married Pharaoh's daughter, Gabriel descended and stuck a reed in the sea around which gathered a mud bank and upon it, the great city of Rome was built.' (*Sanh.21b*). 'And Solomon made affinity with Pharaoh king of Egypt, and took Pharaoh's daughter and brought her into the city of David.' 1 *Kings* 3:1. The interpretation of the legend is given, because of Solomon's foolishness a new empire was brought into existence that was predestined to bring about the downfall of the kingdom of Israel.

According to the *Targum Pseudo–Jonathan* Gabriel was the man who showed the way to Joseph. In the *Targum* on 2.*Chronicles*, he is named as the angel who destroyed the host of the Assyrian king, Sennacherib. In the canonical chapter of the *King James Version*, we have 'And the Lord sent an angel, which cut off all the mighty men of valour, and the leaders and captains in the camp of the king of Assyria . . .Thus the Lord saved Hezekiah and the inhabitants of Jerusalem from the hand of Sennacherib the king of Assyria.' 2 *Chronicles* 32:21–22, Sennacherib was finally murdered in the temple of his god Nisroch by two of his sons.

There are other candidates for the destruction of Sennacherib that include the Archangels Michael and Uriel, but in the Syrian *Apocalypse of Baruch*, it is the Angel Ramiel who destroys the hosts of Sennacherib. The Angel Ramiel — the chief of thunder' supervises true visions. It was this angel who assisted Baruch with the interpretation of his visions as the 'presider over true vision.'

In the writings of Enoch, the Angel Ramiel is both a holy angel and a fallen angel. He is a chief of thunder, like the Archangel Uriel and has under his charge those souls that will come up for sentence on the last day, according to the *Sibylline Oracles*. He is one of the five angels commissioned for this task, the other four angels being Arakiel, Aziel, Samael and Uriel.

In later writings Gabriel is spoken of as the archangel who regulates the ripening of the fruits of the earth and presides over fire though this is a strange element for an Archangel whose Element is Water and thunder. He is the angel who watches particularly over women when they are with child and all aspects of childbirth and birth. The Archangel Gabriel is an expert linguist and it was Gabriel who taught Joseph the seventy tongues that were spoken at the Tower of Babel. While the confusion of tongues of the Tower of Babel was brought about by the presence of the Angels of Confusion who are seven in all. These angels are described in the *Talmud* as being Angel Abatha — 'the presser of the winepress.' Angel Barbonah — 'annihilation.' Angel Bigtha — another 'presser of the winepress.' Angel Biztha — 'the destroyer of the house.' Angel Carcas — 'the knocker.' Angel Mehuman — 'confusion' and the Angel Zethar — 'the observer of immortality.'

The Archangel Gabriel is the Angel of the Annunciation and it was this Archangel who announced the birth of Jesus to Mary, celebrated on **Lady Day**, March 25th for Christianity. The fire and lamps used in this rite could have their origins with the marriage of Vulcan with Venus, to the Magi watching over the sacred fire in the East and to the Vestal Virgins in the West.

The Archangel Gabriel, sometimes with Duma(h) is the Angel of Dreams or the Angel of Aspirations and Dreams according to the Cabbala, because he is the Angel of the Moon. The **Zohar** calls Gabriel the 'Supervisor of Dreams,' which is a most fitting title.

To most races, dreams have long been significant and in Greece according to Hesiod, 'dreams are the children of the night and the brothers and sisters of Death and Sleep.' Deceptive dreams issue from the Gate of Ivory, whereas true dreams come through the Gate of Horn. Hermes had particular authority over the dream–gods who were subsequently revered through worship.

Every dream was regarded as a combination of truth and falsehood, with the conviction that a dream would be realized according to the explanation placed on it. The Egyptians regarded dreams as 'the shadow of future events' and dreams were interpreted by priests in the temple from their dream books. 'And it will come to pass afterwards, that I will pour out my spirit upon all flesh; and your sons and your daughters shall prophesy, your old men shall dream dreams, your young men shall see visions: and also upon the servants and upon the handmaids in those days will I pour out my spirit.' *Joel* 2:28. The ancient Rabbis said a dream that has not been interpreted 'is as an unread letter.'

The Archangel Gabriel is one of the Archangels of Creation that are found in the sixth heaven according to Enoch. It is Gabriel who is said to have foretold of the birth of Samson and the birth of the Virgin Mary. The Archangel Gabriel stood on the right side of the altar of incense and told Zachariah 'I am Gabriel that stand in the presence of God; and I am sent to speak to thee, and to shew thee these glad tidings.' *Luke* 1:19. The Jews believe him to be 'the chief of the angelic guards' and 'keeper of the celestial treasury.' The Archangel Gabriel undertook a prominent role in the Annunciation, coupled with other traditions extant. It is said that Gabriel guides the soul from paradise and into the womb; once the soul is there, he instructs it for the nine months preceding birth. His feast day is March 24th.

In the **Book of Enoch**, part of the **Pseudepigrapha**. Greek, **pseudographia**= 'false writing, a forgery' from ψευδης, **pseudes**= 'false,' ψευδος, **pseudos**= 'a falsehood,' a prefix signifying 'false, counterfeit' and γραφω, **grapho**= 'to write, to write down.' Couple the foregoing with the comments regarding the **Apocrypha**.

The Archangel Gabriel is one of the seven archangels who stood close to God. The **Qu'ran** often mentions angels who are seen as celestial beings living in a supernal world. Although there are many angels, four are given as archangels and are of particular importance. Gabriel is given great prominence in the **Qu'ran** where he is given the appellation 'Holy Spirit,' and 'Spirit of Truth.'

In Islam, there are four archangels that are important. The Archangel Gabriel is held in the highest esteem in Islam because this Archangel helped to bring the **Qu'ran** to the world. I believe his name is mentioned in the **Qu'ran** only three times, but distinct epithets in that authority is widely recognized as pertaining to him. The Archangel Michael is Israfel (= 'the burning one' in Arabic folklore) who, at the end of time on Judgement Day, will sound the last trumpet because he is also an Angel of Death. This archangel looks into Hell three times during the day and three times at night and he is so moved to grief at what he sees that his tears would deluge the earth, if Allah did not prevent this.

We also find the Archangel Iblis or Eblis meaning 'despair' *Iblis* is derived from the Greek word δοαβολος, *diabolos* or Satan the ***Treasurer of the Heavenly Paradise***, who fell from his high position, because he refused God's command to bow down before Adam. He told God that he was 'made from fire, which element is far superior to the mud of Adam.' His punishment was postponed until the Day of Judgment, then he and his host will have to face the eternal fires of hell but until that time, he is sanctioned to tempt all but true believers to evil. One of the first demonic acts of Iblis, where he is referred to in this context as *shaitan*, Iblis entered the Garden of Eden and tempted Eve to eat of the tree of immortality. Iblis is the cause of Adam and Eve being expelled from the Garden and Paradise.

The exact nature of the *shaitans* is hard to resolve. In the *Qu'ran* and Hebrew mythology, they are evil spirits. Iblis and the *shaitans* whisper evil suggestions into people's ears but (it is said) they have no real power over them. The *shaitans* can only tempt and any success they have depends mainly upon their ingenuity and the weakness of the listener, the devil Iblis is called in Arabic — *ash–Shaytan*.

Ordinary angels are regarded as being superior to human beings generally but inferior to the prophets. An angel though closer to God cannot know God but a faithful human being can, which to me seems to exult people over many of the angels and on this I admit to being divided or cautious.

In the calendars of the Armenian, Coptic and Greek churches, Gabriel is especially commemorated. Later Christian tradition made the Archangel Gabriel the trumpeter of the Last Judgement. A popular figure in art Gabriel is often shown appearing to Mary or with a raised trumpet. Mary is often shown in humility and reverence before this superior being in early art but after the thirteenth century, the whole thing appears to be reversed and Mary is exalted over the archangel — the ***Regina angelorum*** — with Gabriel kneeling before her.

The Archangel Gabriel figures in a legend of Moses the Patriarch. In this legend Thermutis, the daughter of Pharaoh Valid (who had no children) grew fond of the boy whom she found adrift on the Nile and she wanted Moses to succeed the king on the throne of Egypt.

In the following legend, there are slight variations, which we have noted in parenthesis. When Moses was three she took him to the king who playfully put the crown of Egypt upon his head (or the child Moses took the crown and placed it on his head). However, Moses pulled the crown from his head, dashed it upon the ground (and trampled it under his feet). It is claimed that Moses did this because he abominated the figures of the idols engraved upon it. However, this could have been added later as propaganda for the Hebrew dispensation of the One God, to make or strengthen an obvious point.

Those around the king claimed this was a calamitous omen for both the pharaoh and the kingdom saying that the child should be put to death. It had been read in the stars that Moses would be the downfall of the Pharaoh but the king hesitated regarding this. Others believed that the child was too young to know right from wrong and some already thought there was something unusual about this child despite his young years.

A counsellor called Jethro (or the Archangel Gabriel in disguise, sent by God to mingle with the courtiers as a wise sage) made a suggestion regarding the incident. He said a ruby ring and a burning coal (or two basins, one of burning coals and another of precious stones) should be brought and set down before the child. Should Moses choose the ring he knew right from wrong and he should be slain. If Moses chose the burning coal(s), he could not have known and should live.

The signet ring of Pharaoh was brought, which had set in it a large, shining jewel. It was the ring (or a basin of precious stones) that the child would have reached out for it had it not been for the intervention of the Archangel Gabriel. The archangel became invisible and turned the child's hand aside so that he took the live coal and as children do Moses put the live coal to his mouth and was badly burned so that he could not speak distinctly again, but his life was spared.

Aaron did not speak for Moses on matters relating to God but he spoke on behalf of Moses to the people about communal and everyday affairs that involved them. It is said that it also accounts for Aaron being his constant companion because Moses was unable to enunciate the Words of Power properly because they must be accurate in vibration or they could have adverse or calamitous results. This is why it is said that invocations should be carefully spoken and worded. One of the careless traps of invocation is ambiguity, heed the warning never be lax with important words whatever level of your life you are dealing with. Neither should you be careless in everyday speech where most know from experience how slipshod words can often cost people dearly.

We have all been in circumstances were everything is going well and then a careless slip of the tongue brought it all crashing down around our ears at the point of completion and all was lost. This has given us the vernacular but accurate expression 'I've blown it' — this says it all because its 'gone with the wind.' If this can be the result on a mundane level, the cost could be even dearer if you are attempting to deal with any of the higher levels. What can make matters worse is that sometimes the results filter down long after the event has been forgotten and you cannot connect cause with result. Consequently, you are left wondering 'what have I done to deserve this.'

I have in the past had a few accusations levelled at me that I am very pedantic about this particular topic — but this has not deterred me from my opinion in the matter nor will it — as the foregoing shows. Readers have Free Will, they will accept or reject 'according to their Lights' and that is their choice. However, I have long and intuitively agreed with the belief of the Priests of the Egypt that — *the word is the deed* — and I have held this opinion long before I undertook this kind of work and I still cleave to it, definitely so in the important areas of my life, this Work being one of them where I do my best not to default. People who are lax regarding this do not know what troubles they store up for themselves.

This is one of the beliefs of earning or being eventually given your School Name and contrary to common belief this is not something you are given as soon as you join, it is given only when you have earned it by being ready for it and the responsibility that it incures, not before and you may never be given it. If the 'soil' will not support the growth, why waste a good plant that will not grow to its full potential and so be wasted — you waste your time and everyone else's. When in the School, doing School Work or using your School Name you exercise extreme care in what you do, say or write, you never bring disgrace upon it or the School or you will become worthless and cut off.

This legend or tradition is said to explain the lines in Scripture. 'And Moses said unto the Lord, O my Lord I am not eloquent, neither heretofore, nor since thou hast spoken unto thy servant: but I am slow of speech, and of a slow tongue.' *Exodus* 4:10. The Lord continues, 'Now therefore go, I will be thy mouth, and teach thee what thou shalt say . . . Is not Aaron the Levite thy brother? I know that he can speak well . . . And thou shalt speak unto him, and put words in his mouth: and I will be with thy mouth: and will teach you what ye shall do. And he shall be thy spokesman unto the people: and he shall be, even he shall be to thee instead of a mouth, and thou shalt be to him instead of God. And thou shalt take this rod in thine hand, wherewith thou shalt do signs.' *Exodus* 4:14–17.

The prophet Muhammad on his *Night Journey* or *al–Miraj* (= 'the ascent') from Mecca to Jerusalem was guided by the Archangel Gabriel and while there Muhammad met the early prophets, together with Adam, Hermes, Moses, the Archangel Michael and Jesus. He also ascended to paradise where he encountered the majesty of Allah and he was also shown hell. Let us remain with Islam and the Archangel Gabriel.

In Islam, the Black Stone is the sacred stone built into the eastern corner of the Ka'aba, an oblong building in the quadrangle of the Great Mosque at Mecca. There are a number of stories connected with its origin and one tells us it was sent to Earth at the time of the first man Adam. Muhammad declared it had been given to Abraham by the Archangel Gabriel. The Black Stone is essential to Islam and it is revered by all of the Islamic faith, who turn and face Mecca when they pray.

The Archangel Gabriel, who said he 'was speaking with the authority of God,' spoke to the extraordinary remarkable and great English Scholar Dr. John Dee in his contact with the Enochian Angels. Later in the chapter, you will find the communication and more information of what passed between them, where Dee is spoken of a little more fully as I have dealt with John Dee in the work *Gimcalzoma — An Enochian Dictionary (1976, 1992* and *2002)* the last date is the edition published by *Authors OnLine (Authorsonline.co.uk)*.

To close the section regarding the Archangel Gabriel there is a rumour or tradition that the Archangel Gabriel was replaced by God for a period of twenty–one days. It seems that the Archangel Gabriel was told to destroy Jerusalem. The Archangel Gabriel was told to take coals from between the cherubim and cast them on the city to destroy it. In the hope that the Jews would repent, for three years the Archangel Gabriel withheld his mission and for his delay it is said that he was removed his high office for twenty–one days. He was replaced by the Guardian Angel of Persia, the Angel Dubbiel (Dubiel or Dobiel) said to come from *dov*= 'bear' and *el*= 'of God' and in the literature of the Rabbis the bear is a symbol of Persia. 'And behold another beast, a second, like to a bear, and it raised up itself on one side, and it had three ribs in the mouth of it between the teeth of it; and they said thus unto to it, Arise, devour much flesh.' *Daniel* 7:9. The Angel Dubbiel throughout the short interlude of his office made good use of it on behalf of the kingdom of Persia to subjugate other kingdoms under Persia, including the Kingdom of Judah.

He was negotiating further terms of behalf of his charges when God heard a voice pleading with him regard to 'God's children' from outside the curtain, the Archangel being unable to enter the presence of God or pass the holy curtain. God paused giving his seal on Dubbiel's dealings to ask who it was that was speaking outside. He was told that it was the Archangel Gabriel and without more ado God repealed his order of banishment and received the Archangel Gabriel back into his presence, Gabriel's weeks of exile was at an end. Some writers are of the opinion that Dubbiel was an evil angel or a demon.

I believe that I am right in thinking that the Angel of Greece represented by a he–goat, was also said to have gained temporary dominion over the Jews for a short while as did quite a few others throughout their long history, God did not seem to mind giving his people into the 'dominion' of others.

## ARCHANGEL RAPHAEL

Let us turn next to the Archangel Raphael, who is one of the Four Throne Angels. The Archangel Raphael is frequently given the title of the 'Angel of Compassion' and an 'Angel of Creation,' an 'Angel of Joy, Knowledge, Love, Prayer' and he 'presides over the spirits of men.' His name in the Hebrew is given as 'God heals.' Dr. John Dee addressed him as *Medicina Dei —* 'Medicine of God.'

He is also the *Angel of Knowledge and Science*, mindful of guarding those who are young and innocent and this is in keeping with one of his astrological signs — Gemini — ruling among other matters, young children, their needs, their early education and so on. He rules the local neighbourhood and early schooling that usually takes place in their neighbourhood (= 3rd House) while they are young so they are close to their home and their parents (= 4th House). When they grow up there is a good chance that their higher education will be undertaken in the opposite house to the third, the 9th House, when they will leave home and go to university, study law or church among other things, travel aboard to foreign lands and all the other matters under the rule of this astrological house.

It was the Archangel Raphael who brought Solomon his magical ring, a gift of God to help him build the Temple of God, which was engraved with the *pentalpha* (= *pentagram*) that had the power to subdue and coerce the demons to do the work, mentioned elsewhere. Some works give his name as being comprised in the Hebrew from *rapha*= 'to knit together, joining, repairing and mending, curing and healing + *el*= of god, divinity. He is also called 'the Builder of God, the One who Heals.'

The Archangel Raphael is one of the four angels stationed about the throne of God belonging to Seven Spirits before the Throne that are said to part of the four orders of angels, the Seraphim, Cherubim, Dominions and Powers. He is the *Angel of the Evening Winds* and has be mentioned elsewhere as 'the Walker on the Wind' who leaves no footprints. He is on the Cabbalistic Tree of Life as one of its Guardians and an Angel of Prayer. If there is any duality, opposites or conflict, the planet Mercury and his Archangel Raphael often appear as a go–between because he is also the head of the Family of Heralds and although not his only function, it is an important purpose for his existence.

In the *Books of Enoch*, Raphael is 'one of the four presence's set over the all, the diseases and all the wounds of the children of men.' In the *Book of Enoch*, the Archangel Raphael is 'the angel of the spirits of men' and it is his business to 'heal (= rebuild and repair) the earth which the angels (= the 'fallen angels') have defiled.' The Archangel Raphael has many tasks so he is busy and always in motion, it is therefore of little surprise to find that his metal is quicksilver, that adapts and changes to any mould it is found, have little or no shape of its own, a lot like the archangel himself. In some *Apocryphal* books, he is called one of the 'watchers.'

He is the Psycopomp or 'guide of the dead in the underworld' but I have not found anywhere that Hermes/Mercurius cannot travel to or anywhere from which he is barred. Psychopomp has the prefix Greek prefix *psycho.* Ψυχε, *Psyche*= 'breath, the soul, anima especially as a sign of life, spirit' and the Greek πομπος, *pompos*= 'conductor, escort, guide.' A guide or conductor of spirits or souls (= Hermes).

The Archangel Raphael was one of the angels that went with the Archangel Michael and Gabriel to visit Abraham. Because it had been omitted early in life we are told the aged patriarch Abraham suffered great pain through having circumcision in his old age. The Archangel Raphael also rules the sixth house of the astrological chart ruled by the planet Mercury, which is the natural house of Sign of the Zodiac of Virgo, the house of sickness and hygiene among other matters. Therefore, it is no surprise to find the Great Healing Archangel Raphael giving a helping hand to ease the great discomfort and healing of the aged patriarch. Eisenmenger offers us ' . . .among the Jews circumcision was believed to give efficacy to prayer. After circumcision prayer was heard, though previously it might not have been heard.'

'In the Hereafter Abraham will sit at the entrance of *Gehinnom* and will not allow any circumcised Israelite to descend into it.' Ge–hinnom, Greek, *Geenna*, suggested as abbreviated from *Gey Ben Hinnom* — the *Valley of Ben Himmon* — the name for the place of torment for the wicked after death and this is dealt with in its place.

The Archangels are referred to as numbering seven, for example *Revelation* 8:2 and *Tobit* 7:15 and only four are named in the Book of Enoch. These as already given are the Archangels Michael,

Uriel, Suriel (= Raphael) and Gabriel. Raphael is to be found among the saints in both Eastern and Western churches and his feast day is the 24th of October.

There was a pool in Jerusalem called Bethesda, which had five porches. 'In these lay a great multitude of impotent folk, of blind, halt, withered, waiting for the moving of the water. For an angel went down at a certain season into the pool, and troubled the water: whosoever then first after the troubling of the water stepped in was made whole of whatsoever disease he had.' *John* 5:1–4. Some manuscripts give the name as *Beth–zatha*, which is thought to mean 'House of Olives,' though modern thought now thinks it means 'a place with two pools.' The pool was surrounded by five porches or colonnades that gave a covered walkway around it. It was located by the Sheepgate and was the place where the ill and handicapped came in the hope they would be cured, if they could get into the pool at the right time. The angel is not named in the text but my opinion is that there can be little doubt for me that it was the healing Archangel Raphael that 'troubled the water.' It is possible this connection with water and healing may have connected him with the title of the 'Angel of the Baptismal Waters' as it was thought that the water is given its powers of healing from an angel.

In a later *Midrash*, Raphael appears as the angel commissioned to put down the evil spirits that vexed the sons of Noah with plagues and sicknesses after the Flood. Never forget the Archangel Raphael can cure a disease because he has command of the disease and its curing, therefore, should he chose or be commanded to do so, he can mete out disease if he wishes because both are under his command. At the breaking of the fourth seal a rider appeared riding a pale horse and the rider was called Death — who killed 'by plague' among other things.

God commanded an Angel of the Presence to teach Noah all the medicines and the angel did the bidding of his Creator. Noah was taught the use of medicines by the Archangel Raphael, who showed him how to use them with the herbs of the earth and taught Noah the art of preparing medicines from herbs, from roots, and seeds, the healing trees and the reason they were created. It is said that Noah set the words down in a book, the *Book of Noah* possibly one of the earliest treatise on *materia medica*, which book he gave to Shem.

It was from the *Book of Noah*, according to legend, that future generations gained their skills in the healing arts. Some of these learned travellers set out to seek the trees of healing and the wood of the tree of life, which they found 'east of Eden.' However, when they stretched out their hands to take their prize they were touched by the 'flaming sword,' were turned to ashes and the art of medicine left the healers and physicians. As a consequence, medicine and healing was lost for many centuries to the world until a learned man called Hippocrates, a contemporary of Socrates and the most famous of the Greek physicians renewed the knowledge for the benefit of the inhabitants of the earth.

However, even before him perhaps there was one other I admire greatly, the creator of the Step Pyramid at Saqqara — Imhotep — Priest–Physician and regularly compared to Aesculapius (Latin) *Ασκληπιος, Asklepios*, the Greek God of Physicians and healing, who was taught healing by the wisest of the centaurs, Chiron. *Asklepios* was symbolized by a rod with twin snakes entwined around it. The Greeks honoured Imhotep, his medical writings were renowned and his writings were equally respected in Rome by the Emperors Tiberius and Claudius.

The Archangel Raphael helps those who travel as he rules the astrological third house of travel and communication in the astrological chart, the natural house of Gemini. Raphael is the ruler of heralds and some say it was Raphael that bore the 'good tidings of great joy' not Gabriel — Cancer rules home, family, womb and tomb all of which enclose. The birth was under the Archangel Gabriel the Angel of the Moon, all births are but any news and communication about the birth was under the Archangel Raphael — Gemini rules news, communication, writing and making such things known to all by all means available. However, I still stay with the Archangel Gabriel in the matter.

The Archangel Raphael is often shown as a traveller or pilgrim in art, with sandals, water gourd, staff in his hand and a wallet or *panetierre*, hanging on his belt. As Guardian or Protective Angel, he often has a sword with a small casket or vase containing the 'fish charm' against evil spirits but some art has him holding a fish There are some illustrations showing him in his role of Guardian Angel and leading Tobit to safety.

We have mentioned the story of Tobit and Tobias elsewhere, but perhaps a condensed recounting of the tale will not come amiss under the heading of the Archangel involved in the tale. The **Book of Tobit** is found in the **Old Testament Apocrypha**, written around 200–170 B.C in either Hebrew or Aramaic and assembled as a didactic romance, possibly in Egypt. In the Greek translation, the work was popular among Hellenistic Jews and Christians.

The book tells how Tobit, a pious Jew was in exile in Assyria with his son Tobias. Although in exile, he did good for his fellowmen by still observing the ethics and rituals of Israel. Tobit buried the bodies of executed Jews in Nineveh, which was an important *mitzvah* (= 'command/commandment'). In Judaism, the term *mitzvah* is also applied to a good deed and in the above Tobit gave the dead 'the last kindness' because the dead cannot give any reward or thanks to the living for their acts of kindness to them – *Mishnah Pe'ah*. Regarding the *Mitzvah* there are said to be 613 precepts of which 365 are negative (= 'do not ') and 248 positive (= 'do') however, this 'numbering' is a later addition (Medieval?) but the essential variation has long been found in rabbinic literature.

A further classification of the precepts takes place 'between man and God' and 'between man and his neighbour.' Notwithstanding this and his other good works Tobias was made blind when bird droppings fell into his eyes. He regarded this as a test of his faith and his love of God, which he does his best to pass on to both his wife and son.

Sarah, the beautiful daughter of Raguel, a widow whose seven husbands have each been killed by the demon Asmodeus before consummation on their wedding night because of the demon's love for her and so she is childless and she beseeches God to end her suffering. In answer to their prayers, God sends the Archangel Raphael to earth to aid both Sarah and Tobit. The Archangel Raphael in human form and using the name *Azariah*= 'Yahwah helps,' accompanies Tobit and Tobias on their journey. This incident shows that, when the book was written around the second century B.C it is thought, that demons were thought to be capable of sexual and physical love. This reminds us of the love of the Sons of God for the daughters of men in Genesis 6:2 as it was for the Jinn of the Arabs and I am sure as others are, it was by no means exclusive to them.

Tobias and Raphael lodge on the banks of the Tigris, and when Tobias washed in the waters of the river a great fish leapt up, which Raphael told him to catch. From this fish, they took the heart, liver and gall, which they salted well to preserve them. Tobias thought this was pointless but *Azariah* (= Raphael) told him if the heart and liver were set upon a fire, the smoke would drive away evil spirits and the gall was used for healing blindness.

Tobias marries Sarah and that night in the marriage chamber, he remembered what *Azariah* had told him. He put the heart and the liver of the fish on the hot coals, the smoke expelled the demon and he was driven into Egypt. When they reached Nineveh, Raphael told Tobit to take with him the gall of the fish. He uses the gall to anoint the eyes of Tobit, which made them smart and he rubbed them. The white film (= cataracts/blindness?) fell away and he could see again. This again is in keeping with the Archangel Raphael being the Healing Archangel and using the organs of a fish in this manner was a practise of doctors of Egypt where Asmodeus was banished and this why Raphael is often found with fish in art.

In early translations of the **Bible**, we are told that Tobias and Sarah devoted the first three nights of their marriage in prayer, consummating their marriage on the fourth night and this practise became the religious observation of devout Christians during the Middle Ages.

The name of the son Tobias is reality identical with his father Tobit — **Tuviah** in the Hebrew — but to avoid confusion between father and son in English translations the name Tobias was used for the son. A dog follows Tobias on his journey in another version of the tale but while the dog was sacred in Persia, it was commonly scorned by Jews.

It is interesting that a parallel tale of Sarah is found in the **New Testament**, a woman who had seven husbands and no children is also found in **Matthew** 22:23–28. Like Tobit burying his countrymen, a rich man Joseph of Arimathea performed a **mitzvah** for Jesus by asking permission to bury the body after the Crucifixion and 'Pilate commanded the body to be delivered.' **Matthew** 27:57–59, see also **Mark**, **Luke** and **John**. Jews usually consider all good deeds as the fulfilment of a **mitzvah** (plural **mitzvot**) because such actions express God's will. The Torah is God's design for the universe so the obedience to the **mitzvot** brings life and accord to the person, the society and the cosmos. For this reason, the **mitzvot** though mandatory, can be fully and unselfishly carried out in a spirit of devotion and joy.

In the **Book of Tobit**, Raphael is 'one of the seven holy angels (= Archangels) which presents the prayers of the saints and goes before the glory of the Holy One.' (12:15.) The themes in the story, which uses demonology, magic and folklore shows a similarity with ancient Near Eastern narratives from 500 B.C onwards. This tale is thought to show the Persian influence with the appearance of angels and demons.

We will close this section on the Archangel Raphael by introducing another angel that has, among his other titles and duties, the title healing angel the Angel Suriel. There are alternative spellings but this is one mostly found. In **Enoch 1,** he is one of the 'four great Archangels' and in Cabbala and he is found among the seven angels 'that rule the earth.' Suriel is often found on Gnostic amulets with Raphael and other angels. Suriel is a Prince of the Presence, this identifies him with other angels including Metatron and Uriel and because he is an important healing angel, this links him with the Archangel Raphael. However, Suriel is also an Angel of Death and a number of angels have this title. Suriel being among the angels (in some accounts) that were sent to bring back to God the soul of Moses, a story given elsewhere. One important thing to remember regarding the Archangel Raphael is this. If there is any duality or opposites, the planet Mercury and the Archangel Raphael can appear as a go–between because this is one of the foremost functions for his being and, although it is a very important function, by the same token remember it is not the only function, they are legion. In the Cabbala, the 'Angel of Progress' is given to Mercury and the Archangel Raphael and I expect this will be found elsewhere.

## ARCHANGEL URIEL

Next, we come to a favourite angel, one of my important angels as a Guardian Angel and he has long fascinated me — the Archangel Uriel — 'the Fire of God, Flame, Light of Divinity of God is my Light.' Dr. John Dee addressed him as the **Lux Dei** — the 'Light of God.' Specifically, the Angel or Divinity of Light and not only physical light, but light in its spiritual origins, illumination of the intellect and many other associated ideas. Today we usually call him the Archangel Uriel, but he can be found as Archangel, Seraph or Cherub. Uriel is called the Angel of the Abyss, 'the angel set over the world and Tartarus.' Thus, we find Uriel with Raphael as the Angel of Hades, the Archangel Raphael is given charge of the departed souls but the officiating angel of the 'newly dead' was the Archangel Uriel. Uriel is sometimes given rule over the South but he rules the North for much of **Western Traditional Magic**. Uriel is an Angel of the Triplicities of the Zodiac in **Ceremonial Magic**. Michael takes the Fire triplicity, Raphael the triplicity of Air, Gabriel the triplicity of water and although of the triplicity of air perhaps fire, the Archangel Uriel takes up the triplicity of Earth in this position and it is sound.

The Archangel Uriel in the **Apocrypha** is a leading angel, time and again found with the Archangels Michael, Gabriel and Raphael and because of his Hebrew name, he has been identified as an **Angel of Thunder and Earthquake, the Wielder of the Fiery Sword** that expelled Adam and Eve from the Garden of Eden in Jewish traditions. He is the destroyer of the hosts of Sennacherib and as the angel that enlightened Ezra with visions. Generally, he is given as an Angel of Terror, Prophecy or Mystery; yet strange though it may seem (at least to me) despite all the foregoing, Christian tradition by and large pays little attention to this Archangel — which is their loss!

The word 'Abyss,' in the title of Uriel above, comes from the Greek $\alpha\beta\upsilon\sigma\sigma\upsilon\varsigma$, *abyssos*= 1: 'with no bottom, bottomless, unfathomed.' 2: 'the great deep, the abyss, bottomless pit.' It comes from the root $\beta\alpha\theta\upsilon\varsigma$, *bathos*= 'depth' or 'height' as measured 'up or down' and in the **New Testament**, $\tau\upsilon$ $\beta\alpha\theta\upsilon\varsigma$, *to bathos*= 'the deep water.' Latin, *altitudeo*= 'height, loftiness' or 'depth' or 'depth of soul, that conceals thoughts and purposes, unfathomableness, secrecy, reserve.'

This abyss as a concept is consistent in most mythologies. According to the **Edda**, it is the formless void that goes before Creation and the Abode of the Gods for the period of the Long Night of Non–existence, not unlike the Ain–Soph above the Tree of Life, an area that appears to be empty, but do not believe that. With the Akkadians, Babylonians and Sumerians the Great Deep gave birth to Ea, the All–wise, unknowable and vast divine being. In Chaldean cosmogony, it was Tiamat, the embodiment of chaos. Egyptian cosmogony speaks of Nut. Norse cosmogony tells us of Ginungagap — 'the Great Void' or 'the Yawn between' — the chasm of the offspring of Ginn — that was in existence before Existence, the Never–Ending Void or the Abyss of Illusion. It is the gaping void of Norse mythology, deep space as an undreamt of abstraction, without form and emptiness and so forth

According to the ancient Hebrews, The Archangel Uriel is one of the four, seven or ten angels that are stationed about the Throne of Divinity so we must slip back into **Cabbala** because the diverse worlds originate from the **En Soph** and from each other and these worlds maintain the relationship to the Deity.

In part of the **Pseudepigrapha** (explained in the heading **Archangel Gabriel**, see also heading **Apocrypha**) Uriel announces 'I have come down to earth to make my dwelling among men, and I am called Jacob by name.' This statement has long been far from clear but to some commentators it has suggested that Uriel may have become Jacob and if this is true, then Uriel would be the first angel on record to have become a mortal, this is offered without comment.

Uriel has rule 'over clamour and terror' so he is not the easiest of angels to deal with because he is often shown as a stern angel who can punish severely. Enoch tells us that he 'watches over thunder and terror, that he is chief among the seven archangels, he supervises Tartarus or Hell and in this terrible place the punishment is severe for sinners, who are hung over everlasting fires and more so for the blasphemers that also hang over these fires — by their tongues.

 He can be a very unpredictable to deal with at times and therefore a complex or difficult angel, from our point of view of course. Anyone who boasts they have the measure of this Archangel is inviting the proverbial 'bolt from the blue' and what is more, they are very likely to get it.

Anyone who has Uriel for a Guardian Angel will be led along unusual paths with turns of fate that cannot always be predicted. They will never quite know where the lightning will strike next or when and, contrary to the old adage, this lightning quite often strikes more than twice, not only in the same place but sometimes even on the same day. One thing is certain with this angel you quickly learn to expect the unexpected or suffer for any tardiness in learning.

None with this angel taking an interest in their lives will ever be bored — we would love to be now and then — just for a change. Of course, he inclines to make you discontent and bored with mundane life, but you learn to appreciate this at times. I am sure Uriel must be the Occidental equivalent of the Chinese Oriental 'blessing' — 'May you live in interesting times.'

He must not be thought of only in this way. True though it is, because he can also be a most benign angel being the 'Angel of the eleventh hour miracle,' ruling the 11th house of the astrological chart and appearing when all seems lost and you are hanging on by your fingertips, often it is them he appears and gives you his hand. He is the Angel of Magic, Astrology and kindred subjects.

Uriel is mentioned in the Apocryphal book 2 *Esdras* 4:1 and the following chapters. He is the Archangel of Salvation and the figure that enlightens Ezra with visions and interpretations. 'And the angel that was sent unto me, whose name was Uriel, gave me an answer.' Esdras is the Greek and Latin form of Ezra. The second *Book of Esdras* or the *Esdras Apocalypse* is the work in which the writer relates his visions and discourses with the Archangel Uriel. There are two *Books of Esdras* with the second book dated sometime after A.D 70 or for the zealots 70 A.P.C.N (= *anno post Christum natum*, or 'in the year after the birth of Christ'). Uriel, as the quoted line tells us is a disseminator of knowledge, interpretation and an Angel of Prophecy. In *Enoch* 32:1, Uriel is one of the Angel's of Destruction of whom it is said ' . . . when executing the punishments of the world, the Angels of Destruction are given the *Sword of God* to be used by them as an instrument of punishment.' It is also said that the Angels of Destruction helped the magicians of Egypt to counter the miracles performed by Moses and Aaron, in particular when changing the waters into blood. The Angels of Destruction (= 'malache habbalah' – Gustav Davidson) do not necessarily mete out only death because as Angels of Punishment it can take the form of illness, pestilence, plague, misfortune or death and where is the dividing line set for the Angels of Vengence; these angels are many.

The name Uriel in Hebrew means 'Fire or Light of God.' He has been variously identified in Jewish traditions as an 'Angel of Thunder and Earthquake,' the 'Archangel and Wielder of the Fiery Sword' that drove Adam and Eve from Eden, the destroyer of the hosts of Sennacherib and generally an 'Angel of Terror, Prophecy or Mystery.' The Regent of the Sun with the Archangel Raphael and the Angel of the Abyss, I do not think I have missed anything out. Ezra, whom God praised for 'his good character' complained to God concerning His treatment of the Jewish people. Ezra said that they languished in misfortune while the heathens seemed to prosper. It was the Archangel Uriel who came to him to explain 'that all evil must run its course.'

More than two thousand years ago a Messianic Cult hid in the caves in the hills above the Red Sea taking with them scrolls of the *Bible* because they thought Rome may destroy them if they were found. This cult was expecting to be joined by the angels to assist them in their battle against evil because they were preparing for the 'War of the Sons of Light, against the Sons of Darkness.' In these preparations, we find Sariel (= Uriel) as an archangel that is selected as one of the four leaders of the Sons of Light, who are divided into four divisions. When they fight upon their shields will be the name of their particular archangel.

Uriel in legend is sometimes given as the angel that wrestled with Jacob at Peniel but as we have said elsewhere, quite a few angels are thought to have been given this task. Uriel has been identified as one of the angels who helped to bury Adam and Abel in Paradise. He is said to be the angel sent by Metatron to warn Noah of the impending Flood but as always, some of these events have also been given to other angels. Incidentally, while with the subject of the Flood it was the task of the Angel Charbiel, whose name means 'dryness,' to 'draw together and dry up all the waters of the earth.' The Archangel Uriel is to be found in the **Book of Raziel** and Barratt in **The Magus**, tells us that Uriel brought alchemy to the earth because alchemy 'is of divine origin.'

I have never had any doubt about who was sent to bring about the conversion of Saul, later Paul, when he was on the road to Damascus. Paul tells us 'I made my journey, and was come nigh unto Damascus about noon, and suddenly there shone from heaven a great light about me.' A voice told him it was Jesus of Nazareth speaking to him and he was asked why did he persecute him. Saul said he could not see for the 'glory of that light' and he was led by the hand of them that were with him. He was blind for three days and his sight was restored by Ananias. Initially, Paul was extremely zealous in his persecution of 'the disciples of the Lord' and would not be turned from his work by anyone or anything. He was as immovable a zealot and as fanatical as any could possibly be in his task — or so he thought.

Here was Saul going down the road to Damascus, probably on a nice warm sunny day with cloudless skies 'about noon' and these two words are important. When out of a clear blue sky there was a light from heaven that brought him and his secure world down around his knees, a world that he thought was a tower of strength, a fair description and not unlike the Tarot card numbered sixteen in the Major Arcana — the **Lightning Struck Tower**. This card also has a 'clear blue sky' without any clouds, but the strong 'tower of strength' with its narrow windows (= restricted or blinkered outlook?) is brought down and the people dwelling within are brought low with it regardless of station, one is usually illustrated as wearing a crown — in the final analysis destruction and death level all in the final equality.

A favourite astrological theme with the writer is that only an 'irresistible force' (= the planet Uranus and the Archangel Uriel) can move or bring down 'an immovable object' (= the planet Saturn and the Angel Cassiel) and the planet Uranus is the only one who can do this to the planet Saturn. In the words of the justifiably popular song 'when an irresistible force . . . meets an immovable object . . . you can bet as sure as you live, something's got to give.' There is very little that can stand up to the planet Uranus or the Archangel Uriel and in the story of Saul above take a guess in which hour Uranus is usually most active — 'about noon' — as Saul found out to his cost.

However, Uranus also has a weakness for when he becomes bored with the affair or situation he is dealing with, which he usually does or when the novelty wears off, he moves on to something else that is intransigent and needs his instant 'revolutionary' touch. Then guess what, Saturn comes back and finding not one brick standing on another, quietly builds it all up again and so it goes on, perhaps not quite the same, but it is back under Saturn's rule once more because Saturn has and gives — persistence and determination — often underestimated.

Remember some of the things that Saturn rules and its not that surprising to find the truth in this because Saturn is 'patient, practical, thrifty, cautious, timely, responsible, difficult to dislodge, he impedes, he hinders and — he can wait.' Where you find Saturn in any astrological chart — there you will reap what you have sown or are sowing — and he can wait — because he is Time itself. **Retribution** by Longfellow I feel is describing so skilfully the ancient god Saturn more when he wrote; 'The mills of god grind slowly, yet they grind exceedingly small.' The planet Saturn is God's Mill, grinding between millstones, which he also rules.

The Archangel Uriel is credited with bringing Cabbala to earth according to some accounts, which is the key to 'the interpretation of Scripture' and another angel held to have given the gift of Cabbala is Metatron. Because these two mighty angels, Uriel and Metatron are so intimately connected with the Cabbala they may promote the state of **devequt** or **devekut**= 'to cleave to God, attachment or having god always in mind.' In Jewish religious thought, this is an adherence to or communion with God — 'lost to mystical union' because it can denote the ecstatic state produced by such a communion.

In Jewish religious thought, an adherence to or communion with God that stops short of mystical union. The notion of *devequt* seems to be derived from the biblical reference in *Deuteronomy* 11:22, 'loving the Lord your God, walking in all his ways and cleaving unto to him.' The Rabbis understood this as being applied to the *Torah* and its students, saying this is the only possible way of doing this, thinking it impossible to 'cleave to God, Himself.' As others have pointed out, Maimonides develops this idea in the *Guide to the Perplexed* where he thought that the greatest saints could possibly achieve this by their communion with God through their constant thinking and being centred in God through the medium of meditation and prayer throughout the days of their life. When the great saints have their minds solely upon God and serving him at all times very little here seems to be able to lay a hand on them and they seem to be impervious to the ordinary mishaps of human life. It is a crucial concept of the Jewish mystical system called the Cabbala. As a fundamental concept of the Jewish mystical system. *Devekut* was regarded as one of the three highest strengths or values of a mystic — some commentators equate this to ecstasy and the highest stage on the spiritual ladder.

The *Council of Laodocia* (A.D. 348–381) adopted some sixty canons, mainly disciplinary but included in them was the canon that angelic worship was both illegal and idolatrous. It was expressly forbidden to mention the names of angels. Uriel was one of the archangels, during the Church Council in Rome in A.D 745, who was abandoned by the church despite his obvious high rank and the position that he held, which was to me foolish.

At this church council, taken under Pope Zachary, the Archangel Uriel and six other angels were 'reprobated' as 'false or evil spirits and not to be venerated.' The other six angels were Adimus, Inias, Raguel, Saboathe, Simiel and Tubuel. It does seem that they repented their foolishness and reinstated the Archangel Uriel and Raguel, one of seven archangels found in the writings of Enoch, an angel of the earth. He is attributed with taking the patriarch to heaven while he was still living ' . . . and Enoch walked with God.' *Genesis* 5:24, although other angels are given.

This particular Council was unfortunate for the bishops Clement and Adalber who gave instruction regarding the reverence due to these angels and they were both convicted of heresy. The Council forbade the invocation and veneration of any angel other than those given in Scripture that are named as Michael, Gabriel and Raphael. This, however, is not strictly true if we choose to accept Abaddon (= Hebrew) or Apollyon (Greek), who is named in *Revelation* as being 'the angel of the bottomless pit.' (9:11).

Wormwood is considered by many to be an angel despite being referred to as 'a star' but we must remember, the angels were often termed 'stars' and 'celestial' as in ' . . . when the morning stars sung together' and there are other examples.

Although I believe the decision on behalf of the Council regarding the Archangel Uriel was ill–advised, it must be said that there was taking place a genuine attempts to weed out many of the spurious angels that had been introduced through the simple expedience of adding 'el' to the end of a name. This was not the first time this had been attempted without success and some of the earlier attempts went back as far as the fourth century. At its height, roughly between the eleventh to thirteenth centuries, countless angels appeared by making anagrams of Hebrew letters and adding 'el' therefore, some names that can be found in the past may have lacked the support of any lengthy tradition or relevant records.

The word 'reprobate' used above has been the subject of much controversy and the meaning of the word has been assumed to be the antithesis of 'election' though no such word is used in the *Bible* in this sense. In Scripture, 'reprobation' seems to mean something rejected by its lack of worth, not in consequence of any Divine decree, it is something that has failed when put to the proof. In the Greek we have *αδοκιμος, adokimos*= 'not standing the test, spurious (properly of coinage), unproven, base, mean' or of people,' rejected as false, disreputable, reprobate.'

The word 'reprobate' could be used with good effect concerning some of the magical scripts given in some Grimoires extant and a lot of them appear to be little more than the overwrought and overheated imagination of some the medieval magicians of the past. It would seem that if something is around long enough it often assumes an approbation it does not always merit.

A Grimoire is a magical treatise more often than not dealing with black or negative magic. These books often give details of how to invoke the infernal hierarchies. They frequently date from the Middle Ages and the famous of their genre are found with an imposing title such as the **Grand Grimoire**, the **Key of Solomon**. The **Grimoire of Pope Honorius** was published in Rome in 1629 though it is highly unlikely to be the work of a bishop of Rome especially *the* Bishop of Rome, though it has Christian ideas, dealing as it does with the evocation of rebellious angels.

Many pagan deities were transmogrified into angels the better to serve their new Jewish master. I admit I probably would have been little better in this, because I would have coded the name of my favourite Greek gods in particular Pan by adding the simple addition of the suffix 'el' and by now Pan would perhaps have been the official **Patron Saint of Gardeners and of the Wild Untilled Ground**. I doubt if the congregation would have challenged my 'angel.' It only had to get past the higher echelon and I am sure if it appeared in manuscripts often enough, even they would have let it pass just in case it was all right, ever mindful of the 'emperor's new clothes.'

However there already is an angel called Panael on record who is one of the 'angelic guards of the North Wind' and another angel with the same duties, Paniel, whose name is sometimes found on kameas and 'worn as a defence against evil.' These two angels had ideal names for hiding the identity of the God of Nature, Pan, so that he could appear as an 'angel' and be used with the appropriate rituals that would 'look right' if it was questioned. There is more on the subject of 'Kameas' that is mentioned in the above in Part Two.

I find the duty of these two angels 'of the north wind' interesting as one of the ancient signs of the Zodiac the Goat, *Capricornus* or *Aegipan*, which is an appellation of Pan, which is in the North and the 'home of the North Wind' among other things. Did someone get there before me, this is pure speculation of course but appealing to my sense of irony, Pan does mean 'all.'

We often find small churches in England called *Bethel*. This name is derived from the Hebrew letter *beth* meaning 'house, tent' All the Hebrew letters have descriptive names and the Hebrew 'El,' means 'God, the divine or 'God the Mighty One.' This naturally gives the word *Bethel* the meaning the 'House of God' or the 'House of God the Mighty One.'

Adding the suffix 'el' to the name of a pagan god or spirits brought them instantly into the One True Church, acceptable to those who previously used them and these would be those in the congregation who were already comfortable and familiar with these deities. This represents instant conversion or as I prefer to call it 'incorporation' with a minimum of fuss or trouble. When intelligence cannot vanquish something, it usually compromises and incorporates it. As I have said elsewhere, the early Rabbis and the Church Fathers were not the unintelligent of the day and what they could not drive out or send away, they built-in, a sensible Roman attribute such as *elicio*. The symbols of the Archangel Uriel are usually a scroll and a book though he is often portrayed holding a flame in his open hand.

# ANGEL RAZIEL

There is one more angel I would like to touch upon before leaving this section that has taken us in and out of the realms of Cabbala for a time regarding the angels and the angelic. This is the Angel Raziel because he is the 'Angel of the Mysteries' 'the Secret of God' who is mentioned in Cabbala and rabbinical lore, including the writings of Enoch. Sometimes the name is given as Ratziel, but we will use the former as it is more commonly found, he can also be found with other names that include Akrasiel, Gallizure or Saraquel and he is also named as the Chief of the Thrones

The Angel Raziel can be found with the titles 'the Angel of the Secret Regions and Chief of the Supreme Mysteries.' He is said to be the personification, protector and guardian of the second Sephirah, kingdom or emanation of the Cabbalistic Tree of Life — Chokmah= 'Divine Wisdom.'

Raziel is the renowned author of the *Sefer Raziel — The Book of the Angel Raziel —* in which all heavenly and earthly knowledge, directions for the preparation of amulets, talismans among other things have been written. The work contains some one thousand, five hundred 'keys' that profess to unlock the mystery of the world. This work by many is considered to be medieval and thought to be the compilation of a medieval writer, the greatest show of hands being given for Eleazar ben Judah of Worms or Isaac the Blind.

Eleazar (original name Eleazar Ben Judah Ben Kalonymos, 1176–1238) became a rabbi at Worms in 1201 and was a prolific and vigorous writer; he was the author of ritual and Cabbalistic works, though his fame rests chiefly on *Rokeah*. He was a student of angels (now called angelology). Throughout the history of religions, varying kinds and degrees of beliefs have existed in diverse spiritual beings, powers and principles that mediate between the realm of the sacred or holy or the transcendent realm and the profane realm of time, space, cause and effect. Such spiritual beings when regarded as benevolent are usually called angels in Western religions.

These studies not only appeared in his mystic theories of theurgy — the art of persuading or compelling supernatural beings 'to obey one's behest' — and in addition in his writings on the *kavod*= 'divine glory.' This concept was shared by his master Judah ben Samuel the Hasid, who wrote a mystical work, existing only in records on the subject. Eleazar believed that the *kavod* (= 'a ruling angel) was an emanation of God and an aspect of God, while God himself was transcendent and unknowable.

In the tradition of Cabbala, an oral version of the book 'existed' so it must have been written down at some point. The keys of the *Book of Raziel* were not able to be understood by any other angel, but in the *Targum Ecclesiastes,* we are told that 'each day the Angel Raziel, standing on Mount Horeb, proclaims the secrets of men to all mankind.' (10:20.)

Legend and tradition tells a different story saying that Raziel gave the book to Adam, whom he taught but the other angels were envious at not being included, stole the work and threw it into the sea. Raziel is the Angel of the 'Secret Region and Master of the Supreme Mysteries'. This work is held to be a Secret and Consummate Book that was the origin of all, along with the Hebrew letters. It was brought down from heaven by Raziel, he entrusted it to Adam, and this gift established Adam in a superior position to many of the celestial beings, though this excludes the messenger that brought it down to Adam and after whom it was named. Adam was cautioned to conceal it and he seems to have studied the work in silence and committed it to memory.

Tradition again tells us that Adam was clasping this work when he was exiled from Eden and eventually Adam lost the work. This book, probably more than most, has many mysteries attached to it. The *Book of Adam and Eve* is a pseudepigraphic work extant in Greek, Latin and Slavonic versions, though it was probably written in Aramaic or Hebrew originally. It deals with the lives of

Adam and Eve after their expulsion from the Garden of Eden and it also deals with their remorse, death and promised resurrection. It records that God appointed three angels to administer to Adam, these were the Angel's Aebel, Anush and Shetel, who roasted meat and mixed and cooled his wine for him.

As said above, the angels were jealous that Adam had been given this work instead of them, so they stole it and cast it into the sea. God ordered Rahab a primordial angel of the sea (sometimes he is found being called a demon) to bring it back. The name Rahab means 'violence' and his name is often used as a symbolic name for Egypt. Legend has God destroying Rahab later because he refused to separate the waters at the time of the Creation but another legend has Rahab destroyed (a second time?) for trying to hinder the Hebrews from escaping across the Red Sea. Rahab is occasionally found as an Angel of Death.

It must be admitted Rahab did appear to have a special talent for upsetting God and perhaps this is why he is found being called the Angel of Insolence. He is said to be connected with the Semitic myth of Tiamat, a destroyer of God's order in the universe. 'Art thou not it that hath cut Rahab, and wounded the dragon.' *Isaiah* 51:9. Tiamat of Mesopotamian (Babylonian) myth is the Spirit of Chaos and the Deep over which he had sway that was without any form of law and order. Orpheus said that Chaos existed first, eternal, vast and uncreated. Chaos was not dark nor light, moist nor dry, hot nor cold but all things intermingled. Tiamat was the personification of salt water (= 'bitterness') and combines with Apusu the god of fresh water (= 'sweetness.') This creation myth is echoed by another ' . . . darkness was upon the face of the deep; and Spirit of God moved upon the face of the waters.' *Genesis* 1:2.

The Babylonian deity Marduk (Hebrew= *Merodach)* was the chief deity of Babylon, a solar 'god of the spring sun.' In the creation epic in a battle, Tiamat is killed and split into two parts from which Marduk makes heaven and earth. However, if Rahab was destroyed at the Creation, who was it that gave back the *Book of Raziel* to Adam after it was fished out of the sea. As these were later events to the Creation, was Rahab only punished earlier or restored to life later?

The *Book of Raziel* passed from Adam to Enoch who it is said by some put the work out under his name as the *Book of Enoch*. Because the *Book of Raziel* was first owned by Adam, the Angel Raziel is often found being referred to as 'Adam's Angel.' We should point out that Adam is sometimes named as an angel being called the 'bright angel.' in the *Talmud* he was conceived androgynous, being created in the image of God — who was likewise androgynous.

The *Book of Raziel* is found next with Noah who is quite a fascinating figure over an above his task of building the ark and surviving the Flood. He was born of unusual circumstances and custom has it that he was exceptionally white skinned with white hair falling over his shoulders. Noah was also unusual because in a time of large families, he was an only child upon whom his mother doted. He was tenth of the antediluvian patriarchs in direct descent from Adam. His father was Lamech and his grandfather was Methuselah. Being a contemporary of Adam it is said that he lived in sight of the Garden of Eden and Noah took a vine on the Ark that was given to him by Adam. His father placed him under the teaching of his father Methuselah because he knew that his son was destined for greatness, but he did not know for what or why.

He knew his son was God's and not his because he arrived into the world marked by already being circumcised. His father Lamech did not really know what to do with his son or how to serve him best for his life knowing he was so special. He went to his father, Methuselah who was the longest living of the antediluvian patriarchs, for advice.

'And he (= Lamech) said to him (=Methuselah): "I have begotten a strange son: he is not like man but resembles the children of the angels of heaven; and his nature is different and he is not like us, and his eyes are like the rays of the sun and his countenance is glorious.' *Book of Enoch*.

Chapter CV. 'And all the days of Enoch were three hundred, sixty and five years.' *Genesis* 5:23–24. The 365 'days of Enoch' denote the length of the solar year or Zodiac, a symbol of the Great Cycle of Life through which the Soul's development is accomplished.

This in turn sent Methuselah to visit Enoch for advice and as mentioned above, the Book that would eventually be given to his great grandson at an appropriate time, which he had already seen. When he returned from Enoch, Methuselah took the boy under his wing for extensive teaching for the work that he had to do. From Enoch and Methuselah, he was taught much. Each period of old had it's 'Master of the Animals' and today we would probably use the term 'Shaman.' With all the diverse forms of life that were aboard the Ark, animals, birds, insects and so forth Noah would need to be well versed in this particular craft to survive the journey with his precious cargo and keep it intact.

When God decided to destroy the world, many reasons were given for this. A strong incentive was considered to be that the angels had mated with people of the earth and some of them were therefore privy to information about the Divine Mysteries to which the uninitiated had no right to possess being as yet not evolved and ignorant, so they may use the knowledge without wisdom. Noah as such did not meddle over much in the Divine Mysteries — he only learnt them and obeyed them. It was his burden to carry them over to the new people when the ordeal of the Flood would finally end.

When Noah was instructed to build the Ark, Latin *arca*= 'a box or chest,' he was given a book 'encrusted with sapphires' by an angel and he learned how to build the Ark with its help. It is interesting to note the word in the 'ark of bulrushes' used for the basket in which Moses was set afloat on the Nile. *Exodus* 2:3. The Book contained all that would be necessary for what he had to do when the ordeal of destruction was over and when the Ark finally landed on Mount Ararat, Noah stepped forth to give thanks and make sacrifice. Muslim tradition holds that it was on Mount Ararat where Adam met Eve after their punitive parting during which time he was a nomad on the face of the earth and he was conducted to the summit by the Archangel Gabriel

It is said that Noah did not make the sacrifice because his body was imperfect by a fall that affected his hip. Tradition has it that the king of the beasts was not well and Noah, being late with his dinner, he hit Noah with his paw and knocked him down for his tardiness. This injury caused Noah to limp afterwards. We are told that Noah planted Adam's vine on landing, with some help from Satan, who saw this as a possible way to establish himself within the new order. It seems hard for a number of people to accept that Satan was just there and they feel that he must always 'be accounted for' and this is discussed in greater detail elsewhere. The Rabbi's say that the fiend Satan buried a lion, a lamb and a hog at the foot of the first vine planted by Noah and that Man received from the wine ferocity (= the lion), mildness (= the lamb) or wallowing in the mud (= the hog).

Finally, the ***Book of Raziel*** found its way to Solomon who derived and acquired his own remarkable knowledge of magic and his great power over demons with its help. The demons were able to assume human form or any form at will. They lodged in trees, caper bushes, gardens, vineyards, in ruined desolate houses and places that were 'dirty.' People were advised not to enter any of these places alone 'on the eve of Wednesday and Saturday' because to do so 'was considered to be dangerous' and so it should be avoided 'Have respect unto the covenant. For the dark places of the earth are full of the habitations of cruelty.' *Psalms* 74:20.

The whole world is filled with evil spirits and harmful demons that not only assail people but animals, dogs are especially predisposed to possession and another account adds 'woman in confinement' to the list. The evil spirits shun the light and prefer darkness therefore night is a particularly dangerous, subsequently it was advised not to walk abroad during darkness when alone. To avoid the sunlight the evil spirits search for shaded places and there are 'five shadows that are hazardous because of evil spirits.' The shadow of single palms, the shadow of the lotus tree, the caper, the sorb bush and the fig tree. The common rule is that the more branches the tree has, the more dangerous will be its shade. If it has thorns, the danger is greater but the one exception to this is the Service tree despite it having thorns.

The names of God, the archangels, the angels and the name of Solomon make a significant contribution to early Jewish magic, which was particularly rich in charms, amulets, talismans and the like. Jewish magic has never been anything but the invocation of the benefic powers through the use of the holy names of God and his angels and the *Talmud* is among the first to make a distinction between black and white forms of magic. The *Bible* prohibited the use of black magic under the penalty of death at times. If white magic was used in the service of religion or to further religious needs, its use was often overlooked. We often find the angel's names combined with the names of the heathen god's. Important among the angels were the names of the Archangels Gabriel, Raphael, Uriel and Michael — the 'Conqueror of the Dragon.'

The four Archangels Michael, Gabriel, Raphael and Uriel are above all others in rank and dignity, excluding such angels as Metatron, Sandalphon and other obvious exceptions. These four archangels are permitted near the Divine Throne of Light. Michael is on the right, Gabriel on the left; Uriel in front of the throne and Raphael behind it. Of the seven Archangels, these four Angel Princes have the advantage of being able to enter within the *pargod* or 'the Veil,' while all others heard the commands of God while remaining outside the Veil.

Later Jewish tradition gives the Archangel Michael as the Angel of Mercy; the Archangel Gabriel as the Angel of Justice; the Archangel Raphael as the Angel of Healing and the Archangel Uriel as the Angel of Illumination. Elderly Jewish friends, a long time ago, told me of an old prayer that was used especially before going to sleep and a trace of it may still remains in the Hebrew *Prayer Book* but I do not know for sure. Say the following. 'In the name of the Lord, the God of Israel, may Michael be at my right hand; Gabriel at my left, before me Uriel, behind me Raphael and the *Shekinah* of God (or 'the divine presence of God') be above my head.' This is a very powerful prayer of great simplicity and beauty, equal to the Lord's Prayer in my view.

In the Western traditional practise of magic, the Archangel Michael was frequently called upon for his healing powers as were other archangels and angels mentioned above. The four directions in positive Western Magic have their Guardian Angels and the stations of the above prayer are a little different from that given above. The Archangel Raphael was positioned to the front of the operator (= the East and the Element of Air) the direction that they should be facing. The Archangel Gabriel behind them (= the West and the Element of Water). The Archangel Michael on their right (= the South and the Element of Fire) and the Archangel Uriel on their left (= the North and the Element of Earth). This is the practice of this work and for many Western traditions and this arrangement is further reinforced in Part Two.

Around 3000 B.C when they marked certain important set points in the heavens, the two equinoxes and the two solstices, the 'Four Royal Stars of Persia' could be found and of course, these four mighty stars, although very slow moving, for example Aldebaran has been in Gemini from around 1285 A.D are naturally still with us. In brackets, I have put the approximate whole degree longitudes given for the years in 2002+.

*Aldebaran* (9° Gemini) was the Watcher of the East, marking the Vernal Equinox. Warlike Aldebaran is one of the *Four Guardians of Heaven*, sentinels that watch over the other stars. This is one of the four ancient key stars in the heavens also called the Archangel Stars. The Archangel Michael (= *Aldebaran*) the Watcher of the East — the Military Commander of the Heavenly Host.

Some commentators have considered them as 'horses' and associated them with the legendary *Four Horsemen of Apocalypse* of *Revelation* and the four horses and chariots found in *Zechariah*.

'I saw by night, and behold a man riding upon a red horse, and he stood among the myrtle trees that were in the bottom; and behind him there red horses, speckled, and white. Then said I, O my lord, what are these? And the angel that talked with me said unto me, I will shew thee what these be . . . these are they whom the Lord hath sent to walk to a fro through the earth, and behold all the earth sitteth still, and is at rest.' 1:8–11.

The oldest known zodiac was measured from Aldebaran's rising in April because it marked the beginning of the Babylonian year. It was known as the 'Forecaster,' the 'Star of the Tablet' and 'the Follower' who forever follows the Pleiades. The 'restorers to health' of the Hopi Indian Tribe appealed to the 'Broad Star' — *Aldebaran* — for help.

In all astrological works, this star is regarded as a fortunate star. It was sacred to the god Nabu, who recorded on a tablet the decisions taken at the Spring Congress of the Gods. Nabu (*Old Testament*= Nebo), a son of Marduk, occupied a very high rank in the Babylonian pantheon as the god of writing, education, literature and wisdom, his attribute being a writing stylus. Nebu is without doubt Mercury, whether Nabu or Nebo being the scribe of the *Tablets of Destiny*.

*Antares* (9° Sagittarius) was the Watcher of the West, marking the Autumnal Equinox. To the Chinese, Antares was the 'Heart of the Green Dragon.' While in Egyptian astronomy Antares corresponded to the goddess Selket (the Scorpion goddess — not Sekhmet) who was the Guardian of the Dead and Guardian of the Canopic Jars. She uses her magic spells against the enemies of the Sun God, cognate with Isis to some, proclaiming the sunrise throughout her temples at the autumnal equinox around 3700–3500 B.C and this star was the symbol of Isis in the pyramid ceremonies. One of the four Guardians of Heaven and sentinels that watch over the other stars.

*Fomalhaut* (3° Pisces) was the object of sunrise worship about 500 B.C in the temple of Demeter at Eleusis and foretold of eminence, fortune and power. Found in the mouth of the Southern Fish, the Arabic *Finn al Hut* — 'the Fish's Mouth' — has long been a name of this star and to the Arabic nations it was known as 'the First Frog.' Fomalhaut represented the Archangel Gabriel and was the Watcher of the South, marking the Winter Solstice. As a Royal Star of Persia, it was *Hastorang* in 3000 B.C.

*Regulus* (29° Leo) was the Watcher of the North who marked the Summer Solstice. Regulus was long considered to be supreme and the leader among these Four Guardians, the leader of the Four Royal Stars and seen as one of the Four Guardians of Heaven. Copernicus gave us the name Regulus, but in antiquity, it was known as *Cor Leonis* — 'the Lion's Heart' — 'the Royal One in the Lion's Breast' — who regulated all things in the heavens. For example, if it is found in the 10th House of a birth chart, it can make 'an astrologer to kings, people in high station and noble men.'

The foregoing does not follow Western practice given earlier and above. Four leaders of the stars were produced by Ahura Mazda and they were made the Guardian Stars of the stars in the area over which they presided. *Tasoheter* — the Archangel Michael (= *Aldebaran*) the Watcher of the East and the Vernal Equinox; *Satavaesa* — the Archangel Uriel (= *Antares*) the Watcher of the West who conquers evil for Ahura Mazda; *Hastorang* — the Archangel Gabriel (= *Fomalhaut*) the Watcher of the South and the Winter Solstice. Last but not least is *Vanant* — the Archangel Raphael (= *Regulus*) the Healing Archangel, the Watcher of the North and the Summer Solstice.

As said earlier, we shall be dealing with the four Archangels Michael, Gabriel, Raphael and Uriel in greater detail in Part 2 and the manner in which we will use them is given there. In Egyptian and Jewish temples, these significant points were represented by the four colours of the curtain hung before the *Adytum.*

Let us take a look at the word *adytum* the better to understand it, because it is an alternative for the word 'temenos' used later and explained. *Adytum* (plural *adyta*) is Latin from Greek, αδυτος, *adutos*= 'not to be entered and αδυτον, *aduton*= 'the innermost sanctuary. A shrine, the innermost and most sacred part of a temple, the holy of holies.' The Greek τεμενος, *temenos*= 1: 'At first, a portion of land cut off and assigned as the domain to kings and chiefs.' *Homer.* 2: 'A piece of land dedicated to a god, the sacred precincts' in it stood the temple. Τεμενιος, *Temenios*= 'on' or 'in the sacred **precincts'** — at Syracuse, Apollo of the Temenos; Τεμεντις, *Temenitis*= 'the height' on which was the Temenos of Apollo. *Sophocles.* Τεμ Νειλοιο, *Tem Neiloio*= 'The Sacred Valley of the Nile.' I think this is enough to put these words and their origins into perspective and give their use.

As said, the adytum was 'not to be entered and the innermost shrine of a temple.' The holy of holies or 'sanctum sanctorum' was comparatively universal and found in the architectural plans of practically all the temples of the ancient nations. It often contained a sarcophagus or an image of the god to whom the temple was dedicated frequently as a symbol of regeneration, resurrection and initiation. The Jews, when they became monotheistic in their religious beliefs and practices, made the *adytum* the symbol of their national monotheism, exoterically and esoterically, a symbol of generation rather than regeneration. Yet the true meaning can be read in the story of David dancing before the ark, for the dance was essentially a Bacchic rite, whose meaning was unfolded only in the Mysteries. The above terms are taken up in more detail in Part 2.

As said earlier, common in the architectural plans of temples and sacred places of all ancient nations was the *Holy of Holies* or the *Sanctum Sanctorum.* In keeping with the religious mores of the race concerned, it often contained a coffin or sarcophagus and/or a figure of the god to whom the temple was dedicated. This was usually a symbol of regeneration, resurrection and initiation. In the Pyramid of Cheops, the King's Chamber is thought by some as being a form in principle of an Egyptian *adytum.* The aspirant for initiation and the representative of the solar god lay in the sarcophagus. The aspirant was thought to be a symbol of the revitalizing spark flowing into the bountiful womb of nature and from where, after a 'mystic death,' he emerged renewed once more.

Two apocryphal works written in the name of Enoch are extant. The *Book of Enoch*, compiled from documents was written about 200–50 B.C. While the other work, the *Book of the Secrets of Enoch* is from approximately A.D 1–50 and it is thought that a large part of the *Book of the Secrets of Enoch* was first written in Greek. This may be inferred from statements as 'And I gave him a name (= 'Adam') from the four substances: the East, the West, the North and the South.' (30: 13). It is said that Adam's name is derived from the initial letters of these four quarters of the earth and the initials making up Adam's name are stressed below. Of course, this derivation would be impossible in the Semitic but it is an interesting concept.

| GREEK: | ENGLISH | MEANING: |
|---|---|---|
| Ανατολη | Anatole | 'a rising, rise of the sun, or the stars — the quarter of sunrise, East.' |
| Δυσις | Dusis | 'a sinking or setting of the sun or stars — the quarter in which the sun sets; the West.' West.' |
| Αρκτος | Arktos | 'a bear, the great bear, Ursa Major the North Pole, the region of the bear or generally — the North.' |
| Μεσημβρια | Mesembria | 'midday, noon, when the sun is at the meridian, the parts towards noon— the South.' |

While with the name of Adam, we again repeat that not all the angels were amicable to the creation of Adam and the reaction of the Angel Azazel, mentioned elsewhere was to refuse to bow down before Adam at God's command. This is referred to in the appropriate places throughout the work and neither was this angel the only one to demur.

When Moses went up Mount Sinai to be given the Torah, God protected him from the resentment of the angels by spreading a cloud over him to hide him. When Moses arrives at the Gates of Heaven, the Guardian of the Gates, the Angel Kemuel, admonishes Moses for trying to enter heaven but when Moses tells him he has come to receive the Torah, the gates fly open of their own accord. The Angel Kemuel had to permit Moses to enter seeing that it is God's will. The Angel Kemuel — 'helper' or 'Assembly of God' —was the angel 'who stands at the windows of Heaven as mediator between the prayers of Israel and the princes of the seventh Heaven.' *Gustav Davidson*.

The angels however, were not pleased to see the *Torah* pass into human hands. Seeing Moses they cried to God for help but God tells them, that Moses has come for the *Torah*. A great cry rose from the angels because the *Torah* was made before the world was created and they said 'how can such a precious treasure pass into the hands of a mere man?' God tells them that this was the reason for it being created. God pulls Moses into heaven where God, like Sandalphon, is found 'weaving' crowns on the letters of the *Torah* and after other sights and teaching, Moses is delivered back to the top of Mt. Sinai to return to the people.

The *Talmud* tells us 'the universe was created as the habitation of man and all that it contains was provided for his benefit.' The ministering angels spoke to God asking. 'What is man that thou art mindful of him, and the son of man that Thou visitest him? For thou hast made him a little lower than the angels (*Psalm* 8:4). For what purpose is this source of trouble to be created?' God replies (in part) that he had stocked the earth well with the fowl of the air, the fish of the sea, sheep, oxen and beasts, what pleasure would He have if there were none to see and share them with Him.

In this world, 'the uniqueness of man' is equated by the *Talmud* to 'the uniqueness of God' in the universe and it lies in 'man's freedom of choice.' Nature follows its laws and angels their missions, but 'man is his own master.' In St. Paul's doctrine, the original sin of Adam made sin an basic part of human nature and the rabbis considered man a wondrous and harmonious being. The duality of his nature was explained by the existence of a good and bad impulse personified by two angels, the ***Yetzer ha-tov*** and the ***Yetzer ha-ra'*** that enters each life after its birth.

'It is the duty of man to overcome his evil inclination.' The Rabbis thought the struggle against 'evil inclination' was a never–ending one in this life. The ***Yetzer ha-tov*** is 'the good inclination' and the ***Yetzer ha-ra'*** is 'the evil inclination.' The Rabbis have always had (I feel) a realistic and down–to–earth view of life on earth and its people. They were well aware of the constant struggle against temptation and the tendency to evil but felt it could be kept under control if it was really desired and one strong control to attain this was the ***Torah***.

It is not (I believe) even suggested that 'evil inclination' could or should be destroyed by anyone, but it was 'breaking the evil inclination' that was both desirable and possible. This is quite a large and important subject. It should be associated with the comments of the earlier chapter ***The Word — Angel*** and any of the many references to ***Guardian Angels***.

The universe is perceived as being populated by two classes of beings in the ***Talmud***. Those above are the ***Elyonim*** — the angels, with the human race below — the ***Tachtonim.*** To this I am (without authority and some impudence) adding the term 'the middle ground' to the area that is between and separating these two classes, because it is not. Nor is it empty or to be regarded as separating them and I am sure it does not. Bear in mind, the enquiry of the angels by the Rabbis was not undertaken to 'invent intermediaries between God and the world.'

The true purpose of the angels it has been said was only for the glorification of God. If the people see the sovereign of the land being given the highest honour and reverence, which they considered correct, then what honour and respect should they accord to 'the King of the Universe' who bestowed his glory upon his creatures and created all.

The angels, as said elsewhere, were considered 'more perfect creatures than man' but, as they themselves were created, they could never hope to achieve the perfection of God, even though they were worthy to stand in close proximity to the Throne of Glory. While a great deal is to be found about the angels in the Rabbinic teachings, the depiction of a Celestial Court where God is the King and nearby him a multitude of ministers serve him is in the ***Bible*** as ' . . . I saw the Lord on his throne, all the host of heaven standing by him on his right hand and on his left.' Other examples are easy to find in the ***Bible*** where the angels are found as helpers and messengers to the Most High.

Attempts to summon the angels has resulted in many and various forms of magic over its long and at times chequered history, in particular the practice of skrying, which is now commonly called crystal gazing. When it is called crystal gazing, it gives the false impression that it can only be done with the aid of a crystal ball but this is not true and this is why I prefer the old name of skrying. Skrying was often used to try to foresee the future or to gain advice and guidance regarding present problems, the future and its outcome from those entities the seeker considered wiser and having greater wisdom than themselves regarding such matters.

This was attempted by skrying into a pool in natural surroundings or even a bowl of water to begin with, which you can still used because you do not need a crystal ball, which often seems to distort what is seen by virtue of its shape. All you need to do is to fill a suitable container with clean water to which has been added the smallest pinch of salt. You can use a crystal container because crystal is ruled by the Moon, as is water in general, the act of skrying and the various forms of clairvoyance, sometimes working with the planet Neptune and the Angel Asariel.

Exorcise the salt and water individually before mixing them together to clear them of any inherent impurities because you do not want to mix impurities in when they are combined. Next, you bless the water and the salt individually to consecrate them to your purpose. When this is done, they are combined which is a simple enough exercise, the combination when mixed is now said to make for greater authority and power, greater together than when they were separate. Some bless the saline mixture before they use it and this can only be helpful.

If you intend to keep your skrying water holder for skrying only, then it would be well to obey a few simple temple rules. Keep the container for this work only and do not use it for anything else, there is little point in using it as a spittoon between your periods of skrying and thinking that it will be acceptable when you take it up again for this work — would you do so.

However, you obtained the container, whether it is a suitable one you had to hand or one that you have bought from a shop, before you use it wash it and then wash it and soak it well in water to which a generous amount of salt has been added this time. Dry it with a clean cloth, I find clean kitchen towels are best because they can be used once and thrown away after use. You wrap your receptacle in a clean cloth to store it away. Doing this is to prevent whatever you are using from becoming contaminated by secular vibrations, which do not usually help in these matters or what you are attempting to do.

Apart from the blessing of the Church, you have Holy Water with which to fill your container. You could use a container of suitable colour depending on whom you are trying to contact with your skrying, which is a good practise but perhaps this would be gilding the lily a little too much and heedlessly complicating a simple task. A nice crystal container for the water for this work is best.

Another good medium to use for this work is something like a large sheet art or cartridge paper that is matt black, readily obtainable from most art shops, which is better than a gloss surface for the simple reason it does not have distracting reflections. A sheet of strong matt black cartridge paper fixed to a flat board will do nicely. Stand it up like a screen or a black window, which it is and through which you are trying to look or just 'through and beyond' the surface colour, try not to regard the window as being solid — more like looking through a window and out into the darkness. When looking at your black square, look into it, beyond or through it — *but not at it*. 'For now we see through a glass, darkly.' 1 *Corinthians* 13:11 remember that we 'see through a glass darkly.'

Use the still surface to concentrate your thoughts but do not strain or try to force the process as that will be counter–productive to your intent. Likewise, you need not be in total darkness for the obvious reason you would not be able to see the skrying medium that you are using, though bright lights are not recommend. Sometimes skrying is helped by placing a small light behind you or out of sight, so that it does not directly reflect on the surface of the water, the black square or into your eyes. A small natural soft light, such as a night–light, oil lamp or candle, helps both your eyes and you in your efforts — above all relax.

Whenever you can, leave the water you are going to use in a window or somewhere where the light of the moon can fall on the water to 'charge' it, especially during a waxing moon and as close to New Moon as possible. If this cannot be done do not worry about it, the Moon is there and the time is right. Leave the Full Moon alone and do not use the three days before the New Moon — because this is 'the Dark of the Moon' that 'is not favourable to man and his affairs because they could be reversed.' Do not be discouraged if you cannot do this as it is a talent not given to everyone, but we all have it to some extent and it can be developed with practise and patience. Some have it more so than others, nevertheless, do not give up after five minutes either, because if this is the impatient way you are going to approach the matter it would be better you do not start. Sit quiet, at the same time if you can, You should keep trying to develop whatever talent you have, but give it a fair crack of the whip, I feel we have become too much of an 'instant everything' society and for whatever we need — just add water — otherwise its not fun.

It always takes a lot of practise to do anything worthwhile. First the desire, then the practise then hopefully the results and remember few are successful with everything we want to do.

The Chinese used polished mirrors for skrying, while the Greeks and Romans used bronze mirrors, a **speculum** (= 'a mirror, a window or metallic reflector.') When children did skrying, a theurgist mirror was sometimes used and this was occasionally simply a bottle of clear water in which pictures would appear for the child to see and replies given by them to the questions asked.

I am sure that peaceful pools and silent lakes would have been used for this work in early history because these were natural elements in their natural place. The undines, the spirits of the Element of Water were probably invoked to come to the aid of the skryer. I am sure the nymphs of the woodland glades, where the natural pools had formed would also be invoked before the skrying began and may even come and watch. Such an invocation would be done to consecrate the setting and to ask for permission, guidance and help in what was being attempted. If you find a clear natural pool or holy well call upon Pan first then ask the permission of the undines to take some water home in a bottle for any future attempts. There is no need to use salt to purify this water or bless it when it is taken from a natural place and not out of a tap. I used for quite a time water taken from **Dicken's Well** (= **Richard III**) from Bosworth Field.

It is thought the use of a crystal or stone may have begun sometime during the fifteenth century and this led to the term 'crystal gazing.' Dr. John Dee and Edward Kelly used a 'stone' for this, which is on display in the British Museum. It was know sometimes as the 'Angelical Stone' and Dee said it was given to him by the Archangels Raphael and Gabriel. We know that Dr. Dee sometimes used a crystal because he recorded in his diary on 25th of May 1581 — 'I had a sight offered me in **crystallo** and I saw.' Dee and Kelly dealt with the angels and Enochia is a system of angelic magic that included appearances from Michael, Uriel, Gabriel and other angels, this information is extended later.

A sixteenth century manuscript tells us that good and bad angels can appear but you will know them by their appearance. 'The good angels are dignified powers of light and in countenance very fair. Beautiful, affable, youthful, smiling, amiable and usually flaxenish or gold coloured hair, without any of the least deformity either of hairyness in the face or body or any crooked nose or ill-shaped members. Their garments or vestures without spot of blemish and always embrace the word mercy.'

'The angel would be appropriately welcomed and then he must be questioned with the given formula to verify he is who he says his is and he must give satisfactory reply before he can depart. We are told that 'if the angel gives you an unsatisfactory answer or remains silent, make a humble request to the visitant for answers.'

Should there be a failure in the operation then, we are instructed 'there are the nine great Celestial Keys and angelic Invocations that could be used for calling forth to visible appearance, the governing angels.' These 'are Metatron, Raziel, Cassiel, Sachiel, Samael, Michael, Anael, Raphael and Gabriel.' These include the seven planets of old astrology, omitting Raziel and Metatron. Again, the seven angels and others with their magic will be found again in Part 2, subtitled ' . . . and their 'Magic.'

Solomon achieved an important place in Jewish magic and he often appears as 'the Lord and Master of the Spirits.' According to the **Talmud**, magic and sorcery were thought practices that belonged to the heathen nations and they obviously did not wish to pollute the Jewish community with it or as little as possible, considering Egypt as the home and font of magic and sorcery. 'Ten measures of sorcery descended to the world; Egypt took nine measures and the rest of the world took one.' (**Kid.** 49b).

It was alleged that Solomon sealed the spirits in a great bottle, which at one time was displayed in Jerusalem along with his magical ring. Many claimed that Solomon had discovered the working source of magic, which he infused into his magical rings. He expounded the virtues of plants, stones and much use was made of his name. His seal and portrait sometimes shows him as a dragon–slayer on horseback, not dissimilar to Horus of the Egyptians and subsequently as some writers believe — St. George.

According to tradition, the Temple of Solomon was built on seven pillars and guarded by the mighty Angel Metatron. The one thing Solomon feared was the spirits and demons would stop building the temple upon his death. They were only kept at the task by the potent power of his magical ring. 'So that there was neither hammer nor axe nor any tool of iron heard in the house, while it was in building.' 1 *Kings* 6:7.

Solomon spent much time within the incomplete temple in deep prayer and meditation and when he was at prayer, neither spirit nor human would approach him for sometimes this would last a month or more. If a spirit did approach him, it was destroyed by a heavenly fire from on high that guarded him during these times. I would say this is the Archangel Uriel at work because 'magic' and a 'heavenly fire from on high' are two of the matters that are under his to command. As said elsewhere, the Archangel Uriel can be seen in the major trump of the Tarot No. 10, The 'Lightning Struck Tower' or the 'Bolt from the Blue.' As long as Solomon kept the commandments of God, he held absolute control over the demons and their leaders. When he fell into sin then the demons were his master and not he theirs.

Every day in the garden of Solomon a new tree grew and Solomon would ask the tree the reason for its having been created. Once, when Solomon saw a new tree he asked his usual questions and the tree told him to cut a staff and to lean upon it for the destruction of the temple was nigh. Solomon knew that the temple could not be destroyed while he lived so he tacitly understood that the tree was warning him of his impending death. He made the staff as told and used it to lean on and support his body during his prayers and meditations.

He prayed to God that his death be hidden from the spirits so they would work to complete the temple and God granted Solomon's wish. An angel took his soul while his body remained in its customary attitude of ardent prayer and none dared to approach him for it is said for a year and the temple was finally completed. God then sent an insect to gnaw the staff from within a little each day and the staff eventually crumbled under the weight of Solomon's body and he fell. The spirits knew that Solomon was dead and they fled or flew away — but the temple was finished. These demons it is said, like the Jinn's of the Arabs and the Assyrians, carried out their work at night but the moment the cock crew their were gone and did not work. This has made some authorities to think about the incident of Peter and his denial of the Christ before' the cock crew thrice' and to speculate regarding a connection.

## THE RECORDING ANGEL

In Cabbala there is an omnipresent and very important angel who is found in many religious philosophies called — the 'Recording Angel.' We do not hear much about this angel but we have already mentioned Metatron, the Archangel Michael earlier in this respect and the Angel Azrael is another of these angels. At the creation of Adam, in Arabic tradition, Michael, Gabriel and Israfel failed to contribute 'the seven handfuls of earth required to create the body of Adam.' It was the Angel Azrael who succeeded in completing the task by bringing the earth required, so he was given the duty of disconnecting the body from the soul upon death.

The same tradition tells us Azrael is 'forever writing in a large book and forever erasing what he writes.' What he is 'writing' in the large book is the birth of a human being and he 'erases' their name upon their death. Other examples of this particular order of angel will be found in the religions of other civilizations.

Recording Angels are charged with keeping records of all events both celestial and earthly and very few nations are found without this angel. One thing that may have perplexed early people was how did God, who was pure spirit and infinite deal with substance called matter, which by comparison was corruptible, impure and limited. It is thought from this came the conception of a being that was semi–human and semi–divine, who stood on a low rung of the Divine Ladder. Someone who was able to connect with the creatures of the earth without detriment and who had the authority to deal with these problems of the material plane, coming as they do between the Deity and the corporeal

In other words an archangel or angel who could bridge the vast abyss between the world and its people (= the World of Assiah and below?) and God (= the World of Atziluth and above?) Again, we come upon the Middle Ground that needs a way to span the abyss that exists between the celestial and the corporeal. The angels are some of the guides that can bridge the 'Middle Ground,' especially when it proves too much for individuals to deal with without some kind of help.

The work of the Recording Angel in Judaism is to keep an account of the deeds of nations and individuals and to present these records (sometime in the future) to the Heavenly Father. The presentation of this record can take place during the lifetime of the nation or an individual but it was usually presented after death in the case of the individual. Upon this record depended the rapture or suffering that is to be apportioned in the after–life.

One early text tells us. 'When a man sleeps the body tells the soul what has been done during the day. The soul then reports to the spirit, the spirit to the angel, the angel to the cherub, the cherub to the seraph, who finally brings the record to Yahweh.' An old Hebrew prayer, pronounced upon waking from sleep in the morning starts with words 'O Lord, who revivest the dead . . .' — Sleep was held to be a sixtieth part of death and the Rabbis considered prayer to be something superior and more than simply entreating for material wants.

Three passages in the *Old Testament* show that the duties of a Recording Angel appear to be well established and any italics found in the following are mine. First we have *Malachi* 3:16. 'Then they that feared the Lord spake often one to another: and the Lord hearkened, and heard it, and *a book of remembrance was written* before him for them that feared the Lord.'

Second, in *Ezekiel* 9:3–4. 'And he called to the man clothed with linen, which had a writer's inkhorn by his side; and the Lord said unto him. Go through the midst of the city, through the midst of Jerusalem, and *set a mark upon the foreheads* of the men that sign, and that cry for all the abominations that be done in the midst thereof.' The man 'with the inkhorn' is one of six angels sent to exact punishment of those who were defiant in Jerusalem. The mark was discriminating for he told them to smite those without pity who do not have the mark, whether they be young or old, maiden or little children. Was this the same 'mark' use to distinguish Cain so that he should be protected?

The third passage is in *Daniel* 12:1. 'And at the end of time shall Michael stand up, the great prince which standeth for the children of thy people: and there shall be a time of great trouble, such as never was since there was a nation even to the same time: and at that time the people shall be delivered, every one that shall be *found written in a book*.'

When you read these three passages together with an awareness of a common theme, an underlying scheme appears and I am sure that more can be found elsewhere. At some time in the future, divine judgement will be apportioned and all will reap what they have sown, according to the record kept. The Recording Angel is often given as the Archangel Michael, but as said elsewhere, there are quite a few angels who assume this title.

Rabbi Akiba ben Joseph (A.D. c.50–c.132), although he does not mention the Recording Angel, outlined this accounting very well between a human being and their Maker: 'Everything is given on pledge and a net is spread for all living. The shop is open and the dealer gives credit, and the ledger lies open; the hand writes; and whosoever wishes to borrow may come and borrow; but the collectors regularly make their daily round and exact payment from man whether he be content or not; and they have that whereon they can rely in their demand; and the judgement is a judgement of truth, and everything is prepared for the feast.' *Mishna*, *Aboth*, iii, 16.

In Islam, every believer was attended by two angels called the Kiramu'l katibin, 'Guardians and Noble Scribes' the right angel contemplates and dictates and the one on the left records, upon the death of the individual this record is given to Azrael, the Angel of Death for perusal and the reckoning. This example shows this principle can be found in quite a few religious philosophies and serves much the same purpose.

## THE CABBALISTIC LORD'S PRAYER

When that most beautiful of prayer's, the Lord's Prayer or *Pater Noster* of the *New Testament* is spoken in the version I prefer. It is obviously Cabbalistic but especially the closing lines because the speaker and teacher giving the prayer and teaching us how to pray was thought to be a rabbi. These closing lines of the prayer cover the four lowest kingdoms or Sephirah of the *Tree of Life*. 'For thine is the kingdom (= 10th kingdom: Malkuth), the Power (= 7th kingdom: Netzach) and the Glory (= 8th kingdom: Hod).' The placement of these three kingdoms makes them surround the 9th kingdom= Foundation (= 'for ever') then 'earth' the prayer with the right hand pointing down to the earth by passing the point where you started by passing them through the 10th kingdom: Malkuth, see the diagram at the rear and the explanation next.

Using the *Finger's of Horus*, raise the two fingers of the right hand upright, the first and middle fingers. Draw the other two fingers into the palm, put the thumb on top of them in benediction and saying 'for thine is the Kingdom,' touch the solar plexus with the two fingers. Next, 'and the power' touch the right shoulder, 'and the glory' touch the left shoulder and with 'for ever' touch the heart. 'For ever' implies a foundation upon which to build something that is strong, secure and will last. Finally go through the Kingdom of Malkuth and say 'Amen' — 'so be it' — this ends and earths the prayer, which is closed by making it 'earth' to complete and close the circuit.

This is best done by passing the hand through the area of the solar plexus to go through the position of 'Malkuth, the Kingdom' again (see the diagram), which is where you started. You began the 'circuit' from Malkuth and you complete the 'circuit' by going through it and putting your hand to your side with the fingers pointing down to the earth and the Chthonic Gods; drop to the left knee and touch the earth/floor. The power has now like the escaped fox — 'gone to earth.' This touching the earth or floor is something that was done in most of the rituals of the Chthonic Gods and it is both practical and respectful.

If the final part, the essential 'earthing' is not practical because it may draw unnecessary attention to yourself and what you are doing. After completing the 'circuit' when going through the 10th Kingdom of Malkuth again, remain standing and simply put the hand down to your right side with the extended fingers or your open palm pointing downwards and say the 'Amen.'

In classical times when praying to the celestial gods the palms where turned upwards, but for the chthonic gods the palms would be turned downwards to face the earth. Sometimes the prayers to the Earth Gods would be undertaken standing in a small pit or hole — 'having your feet planted in the earth like most living things.' I have used the ending of this potent prayer to 'close' many things of life. Sometimes, if I am somewhere with people I do feel happy with, or I feel uncertain about things I use this ending to 'close things.' It can be done privately without giving offence or drawing attention to yourself.

## A CAUTION

Throughout the sections earlier and elsewhere in the work, we have mentioned various Archangels and Angels that are or have been given the addition assignment of being an Angel of Death. This is a task given to many angels with some quite surprising and unexpected, to me at least. It should be obvious that each and every race has these servants of the Creator, whatever they choose to call them. They have not been given a section to themselves but brought in at appropriate points in the text when and where it was necessary because, no matter how they perform their duty, the conclusion is the same or the designation given them would have little meaning and be pointless.

In the writings of the Hebrews, there are some ten or twelve angels at least who have this particular duty or it is asked of other angels as and when it is needed for reasons only the Creator knows. We have already pointed out earlier that one of tasks of Satan is as an Angel of Death, which gives him certain rights and privileges including 'testing the righteous' with regard to their steadfastness and this seems to annoy people when he exercises his rights. Perhaps knowing that Satan has the power of his station as an Angel of Death perhaps this explains the following:

'For I verily, as absent in the body, but present in spirit, have judged already, as though I were present, concerning him that hath so done this deed, in the name of our Lord Jesus Christ. When ye are gathered together, and my spirit, with the power of our Lord Jesus Christ, to deliver such a one unto Satan for the destruction of the flesh, that the spirit may be saved in the day of the Lord Jesus.' 1 *Corinthians* 5:4.

In other words, he is not tormenting or chastising with great pain, but releasing by death so that the spirit can be released by the disintegration of the flesh that keeps the spirit bound to its early station against its will — 'that the spirit may be saved into day of the Lord Jesus.' Satan has long been a legitimate angel with allotted tasks and work for him to do — the 'Tester' — for the one who sends him.

Only on very rare occasions, folklore, myth and legend would have us believe that this particular angel ever been outwitted in his principal task. However, do not count on it that he can be outwitted, remember he has been playing this game longer than we have and there is little that has not been tried or that he does not know about, remember he was called upon to deal with the death of Moses, though Moses was a very special case. Now when we come to 'the devil' we can find the following pact.

The working of a charm is often subject to certain conditions and a cleric was freed from a demon that took possession of him as long as he did not eat flesh nor perform any priestly functions. If he broke either of these conditions, which he did, the demon again took possession of him and this was called 'making terms with the Devil.' Those who made such compacts rejoiced in trying to outwit the foolish Devil by fixing an impossible condition or date for his return and payment, saying come 'when Christ is born again of Mary' or 'when Christ shall write a new Gospel' or call on the Greek calends. The Greeks do not have calends in their months but the Romans have and would pay their bills, rents, taxes etc., on the calends — the first of the month. If the Romans said, they would defer payment to the Greek calends— *ad Græcus Kalendas* —that meant never!

Despite the given purpose of this work, these individual angels are not included in the practical section in Part 2 and it is only in Part 1 where reference to them is found. Death assumes many guises and comes in various forms and few are they who know them all. Often he is a friend that is known to the person dying so that they will go with him. So then, what is the 'caution' that is being offered in the subtitle above. Simply this, leave these angels well alone and do not attempt to invoke or deal with them in any way, shape or form. They will come on their own at their appointed time, sometimes welcome and sometimes not and few know of the time of their coming and I would think very few would want to.

They are not angels you experiment with or attempt to call up 'in fun,' which is the reason for doing far too many things at the time of writing as far as I am concerned — these are very serious angels. As many good Schools wisely advise their students 'gates' can often be opened by chance and sometimes without even knowing that this has been done, other than coping with the results of doing it.

Closing them is much harder and sometimes very difficult, the more so if you do not know that you have managed to open the 'gates' in the first place no matter how slight and there are 'gates' best not tampered with and best left closed. Closing and securing both Temple and ritual is the most important part of the Work even though not the most glamorous and it is the part that is likely to be neglected in the rush to get away when the rituals are over — but only the foolish would neglect something so essential. Would you walk out of your house at night leaving every door and window unlocked for several hours or all night? If you did, what or whom may be waiting for you when you returned and should you be surprised.

Let us make one thing crystal clear between the reader and the writer so that there is no doubt in anyone's mind regarding the matter. Is this put here to be dramatic or theatrical on paper? A literary ploy used to titillate the gullible and sell books by being vague and boding a dramatic and theatrical evil because of the nature of the subject in hand? No, that would be far too easy, I have seen it done in the past but not by the writer, it never will and to a certain extent with a lot of situations, quite unnecessary. Always keep one thought regarding these particular angels in the front of your mind if you are tempted to try to deal with them.

Whether the exercise is successful, by accident or foolish bravado and if they do decide to come and see who has been imprudent or courageous enough to call upon them — some tell us that they rarely if ever return empty–handed — I do not know about this for I have never been tempted to try nor never will. Some knowledge I can take for granted. This warning of itself could be an over–dramatic caveat from the past by an inflamed medieval imagination. I for one am not prepared to test the water in this way because that would be the equivalent of testing the depth of the water with both feet, which is not usually recommended.

The *Talmud* considers that Death is the strongest thing that God has created in the Universe and as such, it cannot be overcome even though 'the ten strong things that have been created strong can . . . because death is stronger than them all.' Numerous outward appearances are assumed by Death and it is written that 'nine–hundred and three varieties of death have been produced in the world' but I am in little doubt that we may have now added a significant quota to this through methods of our devising.

There are accounts on the process of dying and in one, the angel has a drawn sword in his hand on which a drop of gall is hanging over the pillow of the dying, when the one dying sees the angel they open their mouth in surprise and the angel lets the drop fall. Another is roughly along the outline that when death comes to someone the Angel of Death comes to take away their soul (= *Neshamah*). The *Neshamah,* more often than not is found linked with blood that is the vitality and life of both humans or animals.

It is explained as being like a vein that is overflowing with blood, it has other lesser veins that spread out and dispersed all over the body. The angel takes the top of the this vein and he removes it out from the body. If the person dying is righteous then the Angel of Death extracts it very gently — not unlike 'taking a hair from milk.' However, if the person was wicked it is taken like 'whirling waters at the entrance of a canal.' When this vein has been removed, the person dies and the spirit comes forth and settles on their nose until the body decays. The Angel Dumah then takes it 'to the Court of Death among the spirits' where, step by step, the righteous progresses to the presence of the *Shekinah* and the unrighteous.

Now, as far as I am concerned, I feel that any responsibility I have in the matter, rightly or wrongly has been fulfilled and the subject is closed. Now let us land on another 'island' in our journey.

## SALT AND HOLY WATER

Having introduced Holy Water in the above, let us take another little diversion by looking at the very important Element of Earth — Salt and when salt in joined with the Element of Water it is both useful and sacred combination, so better to understand it. Salt has been used since earliest times as a condiment for food. In the *Bible* it is asked, 'can that which is unsavoury be eaten without salt?' *Job* 6:6. It was mixed with the fodder for cattle, as a preservative in incense, though take care with this. Salt is given as an antidote against the effects of the heat and service personnel are given salt tablets when serving in a country with a very hot climate where salt loss of the body is greater than usual. None of this has changed in modern times; only the amount used is questioned by being excessive most of the time.

Salt found great acceptance among the Hebrew worshippers. All meat offerings were required to be seasoned with salt and because it was important, it was sold in large quantities in the Temple market. A large quantity of salt was kept in a special chamber assigned for its storage in the Temple. The Hebrews had an inexhaustible supply of salt on the southern shores of the Salt Sea. 'All these were joined together in the Vale of Siddim, which is the salt sea,' *Genesis* 14:3. The 'salt sea' is now called the *Dead Sea* for obvious reasons.

The salt lake features prominently in Jewish history. It is associated with Abraham, David, Lot, Solomon and the defenders of Masada. The first Dead Sea Scrolls were found at Qumran on the North–Eastern Shore. The Dead Sea is called — *Buhayrat Lut* — the 'Sea of Lot' to the Arab people and *Yam ha–Melah* — the 'Salt Sea' to the Hebrews. The salt lake is on the border between Israel and Jordan. Its shoreline is the lowest point on the Earth's surface, being on average 1300 feet below sea level. The lake is some 405 square miles in area, 46 miles long and about ten miles wide. Its depth ranges from a maximum of some 1,310 feet at the North to less than nine feet in the South. The density of the Dead Sea keeps swimmers afloat because it is about seven times as salty (nearly 30% by volume) as the ocean. Only simple organisms can live in its saline waters while the area is hot and dry with annual rainfall of about two inches.

Christ told his disciples. 'Ye are the salt of the earth; but if the salt has lost its savour, wherewith shall it be salted? It is thenceforth good for nothing, but to be cast out, and to be trodden under foot of men.' *Matthew* 5:13. He further tells us ' . . . for every one shall be salted with salt fire and every sacrifice shall be salted with salt. Salt is good: but if the salt have lost his saltness, wherewith will ye season it? Have salt in yourselves, have peace one with another.' *Matthew* 9:49.

Salt is a symbol of truth and the truth should be sought because without truth there cannot be any progress. Truth is 'an ingredient in the spiritual man' and 'When the desires are sacrificed for love of the higher qualities, truth (= salt) permeates the lower nature (= earth).'

There is so much folklore and myth on the subject of salt and because it has always been held in high esteem, it seems to indicate a more significant use of salt in the past that has been neglected, while the outer rituals and practices have remained. The Latin word *salus* gives us 'a being safe and sound; sound or whole condition, health welfare, prosperity, preservation, safety, deliverance and so forth.' So many of these attributes were attached to the Goddess Salus, a Roman divinity whose temple stood on one of the summits of the **Quirinalis**.

This Goddess was the personification of health, prosperity and the overall public welfare among the Romans. In some of these, she answers very closely to the Greek Goddess Hygieia, the attendant of Asclepius and so it is that Salus in art is often represented by the same elements and frequently appeared on coins feeding the sacred snake from her patera. The patera (in Classical Antiquity) was a round plate, dish, saucer (sometimes shown with a handle) or goblet used by the Greeks and Romans in their sacrifices and libations. However, Salus also represented prosperity in general — *Salus Publivs Populi Romana* — the reason for her important temple.

In public, she was worshipped on the 30th of April in conjunction with Pax, Concordia and Janus. Her counterpart among the Sabines is the Goddess Strenia and *strenæ* were gifts given by the Romans at the New Year with the customary good wishes, these were made up of branches of bay and palm, sweetmeats made of honey and figs or dates — with the wish that the year may bring only joy, health and prosperity.

Each year, when the Consuls entered office, signs were taken by the high–priests for the fortunes or otherwise of the republic during the following year, these were called the *augurium Salutis*. There is a great deal of custom regarding salt to be found that shows the importance in which it was held. To 'share bread and salt' in some countries is a unique bond of friendship even today. To honour Salus midwives put a pinch of salt into the mouth of a newborn child. The Romans and Greeks took particular concern to ensure that their sacrificial cakes and salt were thrown on the altar fires together.

Great care was taken not to arouse the wrath of the Goddess Salus by allowing salt to fall to the ground though carelessness, but of course, nothing sacred should be allowed to touch the ground. Like the Goddess Fortuna, Salus is represented with a rudder and a globe at her feet. Sometimes seated pouring a libation from a *patera* (= 'a broad, flat dish used in offerings, a libation saucer or bowl') upon an altar around which a serpent is winding itself.

In Rome, Salus rings dedicated to the Goddess Salus were worn by many as a protection against disease, infection and to ensure prosperity and welfare. They were engraved with a pentagram that was surround by mystical letters and the symbol of healing — a coiled serpent. An old practise of writers of the Middle Ages was to put a pentacle or five–pointed star on the first page of their manuscripts to ensure good fortune for their work and it can still be done — even on computers for those with imagination.

The foregoing has just briefly touched upon the interesting subject and the value in which salt, a commodity we hold so commonplace today, was held in the past. I hope it has served its purpose in this respect.

As practiced in the Roman Catholic Church, the **Rite of Holy Water** is practically the same as that of the ancient Egyptians in that the water, which has been blessed or consecrated is used to sprinkle the worshippers and objects used during the ritual or service. It seems reasonable that it was adopted from the **Ancient Mysteries** and that it became a symbolic rite of external purification.

In Egypt and Rome, it 'accompanied the rite of bread and wine.' Holy water was sprinkled by the Egyptian priest on his gods, the sacred images and the faithful either by being poured or sprinkled. A brush has been found, believed to have been used for the same purpose as it is today — as an asperger. *The Cake of Isis* was placed upon the altar and we are told that they were identical in shape with the consecrated cake of the Roman and Eastern Churches.

We are further told that 'the Egyptians marked this holy bread with St. Andrew's cross.' The **Presence** bread was broken before being distributed by the priests to the people and it was hypothetically thought to become the flesh and blood of the Deity — this does sound a little familiar. The miracle was wrought by the hand of the officiating priest, who blessed the food' and that the bread offerings bore upon them the imprint of the fingers, which is the mark of consecration.'

Holy water may not be something that was taken over by the Christian Church from pagan practises, even though I have written many times over the years that this was a frequent practise in the past. It possibly continued the Judaic practise of consecration — making holy or setting apart for divine purposes. *Exodus* 19:14 records how, prior to the giving of the *Ten Words or Commandments*, Moses consecrated God's people, which involved washing their clothes. 'And Moses went down from the mount unto the people, and sanctified the people; and they washed their clothes.' Elsewhere in Scripture, anointing with oil and sprinkling with the blood of the sacrifices were used to make both people and objects holy.

There is a consistency of symbolism in these rituals and some think, anticipating the supreme sacrifice of the Christ from whose wounds flowed the 'water and blood' when the soldier 'pierced his side.' *John* 34:19, by this repentant sinners are cleansed and set aside apart for God. Many Christians may regard the method of creating Holy Water that includes the prayers of blessing as being symbolic of the power of God to cleanse and wash away evil than any form of magical powers, despite the 'miracles' that Christ performed.

Salt is used in alchemy for a fundamental principle of nature, a member of the triad mercury, sulphur and salt, corresponding to spirit, soul and body or to fire (or air), water and earth. Paracelsus regarded these as the mystical elements of all compound bodies. All forms of matter were reducible to one or other of them — everything was a sulphur, a mercury, a salt or a compound.

The **Philosopher's Stone** was regarded as being a compound of all three. Ancient thought regarded such elements as fundamental principles, which are found manifesting on different planes, nor did it make hard and fast distinctions between physical and non–physical. Modern thought however has given a fictitious reality to physical objects and regards the ancient use of the terms as being purely metaphorical. The veneration shown to salt was not a simple deification of its physical virtues, but a recognition of the principle of salt in nature of which ordinary salt is regarded as being a physical representation.

The well–known use of salt to give 'savour' (*Matthew* 5:13) and the preservative qualities of salt prove it to be a physical manifestation of an important principle. It gives such phrases as 'bread and salt' and 'the salt of the earth' and used as a medium of friendship and trust in 'to take salt with someone, show that such phrases and the principles behind them are not used simply as figures of speech but a use of salt in its more fundamental sense. For the same reason it played an important part, along with other materials, in sealing contracts, sacrificial and ritual ceremonies. See below.

The Roman Catholic Ritual of the Exorcism of salt, promulgated in 1851/2 under the sanction of Cardinal Engelbert, Archbishop of Marlines and of the Archbishop of Paris, runs — 'The Priest blesses the salt and says: 'Creature of Salt, I exorcise thee in the name of the living God . . .

become the health of the soul and of the body. Everywhere where thou art thrown may the unclean spirit be put to flight' this reflects or otherwise the Cabbalistic or Occult versions.

Holy water should have some grains of 'blessed salt' mixed with it to be truly effective. Since Norman times a stoup (= a stope or basin) has been built in the entrances of churches. The Holy Water is placed in these receptacles for the use of the congregation as a ritual cleansing before entering the church with the water and salt mixture being blessed by the priest. As a symbol of purification, the people entering the church dipped their fingers in the holy water and sprinkled themselves with it. In Anglo–Saxon stoup is *steap*= 'a cup' and in the Dutch, *stoop*= 'a gallon' because it was also a measure, as with 'a pint stoup.' There are of various forms of stoup, some being set into the wall, standing on a socle and they were often flamboyantly decorated. A socle is 'a plain block or plinth, forming a low pedestal to a statue or column.'

It may seem strange to some that we should discuss the Element of Water, what is there to discuss? Water is one of the primary cosmic elements having countless manifestations. Its most fundamental meaning is that of the great mother of all, the feminine receptive principle over which and in which broods the fire of spirit. In accordance with Thales (640–546 B.C), one of the **Seven Sages of Greece** who held that 'everything is contained in water' therefore 'the Universe is explicable in terms of a single principle;' as with other ancient philosophers, salt is the first principle of things. Of course, this is not water on the material plane, but in a figurative sense for the potential fluid contained in boundless space. This was symbolized in ancient Egypt by **Kneph**, the 'unrevealed' god, who was represented as the serpent — the emblem of eternity — encircling a water urn with his head hovering over the waters, which he nurtures with his breath. This god has brought to the minds of many the opening lines of the opening lines of the Bible in **Genesis**: 'And the Spirit of God moved upon the face of the waters.' In the Norse, there is the honeydew, the food of the gods and of the creative bees on the **Yggdrasil** that falls during the night upon the tree of life from the 'divine waters, the birthplace of the gods.'

Water corresponds with soul, representing the middle world between spirit and fire on the one hand, and matter and earth on the other. It corresponds to the astral plane as compared with the physical and here we see its quality of instability, mobility, having no fixed shape but adapting itself to other shapes, dissolving solid bodies and re–precipitating them. It corresponds to the intellectual nature as contrasted with the spiritual and the physical. It should not have to be pointed out that water and fire are two of the essential elements of life, as are their correspondences the Sun (= Fire) and Moon (= Water).

In holy water — **Aqua Benedicta** — the salt represents wisdom and the water, human nature. When salt and water are combined, they represent the nature of Christ. In Christian and Jewish practice, ritual ablutions were prominent. When water and salt are exorcised, they were withdrawn from the 'power of Satan' that since the 'Fall' has 'corrupted and abused even inanimate things.' The use of holy water among the Christians is know to be very ancient and was probably taken from earlier practises. The eight books of the **Apostolic Canstitutions** of St. Clement of Rome (flourished c. 96), contains a formula for blessing water that it may have power 'to give health, drive away diseases, put demons to flight and so on.'

The Greeks blessed fresh water on the first of the month and sprinkled the people with it. The Romans sprinkled themselves with the **Aqua Lustralis** or they were sprinkled with it by the priest, showing that the symbolism and rite is a very old one. **Aqua**= 'water' and **Lustralis**= 'relating to purification from guilt or the appeasing of the gods, lustral, a sacrifice, a purification, a propitiatory offering.'

Water has long been used as a medium of purification and you only have to witness its extensive use in baptismal rites or its use in whatever ceremony is being used. Salt is a creature of the Element of Earth. Water is the Spiritual and salt is of the physical plane. These two elements are powerful in their own right when they are used effectively. When they are combined, their effectiveness is far greater than when they are separate, combining the two with due ceremony combines two planes or spheres. As said, first, the salt is exorcised then the water, then the salt is blessed then the water and then the two are amalgamated and blessed in their new combination for greater power. It is as simple as that but it must be done with due ceremony and respect.

## ST. GEORGE AND THE ARCHANGEL MICHAEL

Although Saint George is not *Old Testament* or *New Testament* material, he is important to the country of my birth, England, to many others and to me. I did contemplate setting him immediately after the Archangel Michael earlier with whom he is at times intimately linked, some thinking he originated from the Archangel Michael. However, I did not want the grouping of the Archangels and Throne Angels to be broken when I gave them earlier. Further, setting St George there may have suggested to some that he was to be included in this special group of Archangels or Throne Angels. The thing to remember is that St. George is not being dealt with as an angel. However, the angels seem to have taken a particular interest in him because of this close association with the Archangel Michael.

When the Pro–consul Dacian tortured George of Capadocia in the persecution of the Christians under Diocletian, he had him bound to a wheel filled with sharp knives but two angels came from heaven and broke the wheel into pieces. After many more cruel attempts to kill him that seemed to have no effect, the Pro–consul finally had him beheaded in A.D 303, a death we are told that he readily embraced. His body was taken to Lydia by three of his men, it was buried there and later the Emperor Constantine built a church over the tomb. His worship is very ancient in the East and the Greeks give St. George the title of 'the Great Martyr.'

George is said to have been born to a noble Capadocian family and his martyrdom at Lydia in Palestine seems to be regarded as fact. It has the testimony of two early Syrian church inscriptions and in a canon of Pope Gelasius I dated A.D 494, where St George is referred to as 'one held in reverence.'

Although there is for the most part a lack of any historical connection between St George the Martyr and England, the Council of Oxford in 1222, ordered that his feast day April 23rd should be celebrated as a national festival. I believe this feast has recently been raised to a *Solemnatas* called in English 'a solemnity,' which is a feast of the greatest importance, which it should be! When he retired from military service, there is a legend that he paid a visit to Britain but sadly nothing can be found to sustain this, so it could be more an fervent yearning than a fact. In the 14th century, he became the Patron Saint of England on the instigation of the Order of the Garter, which is England's highest honour granted by Edward III in 1330. In his *History of the Order of the Garter*, Ashmole says that in the sixth century, King Arthur placed a picture of St. George on his banners and Selden tells us that St George was the adopted patron saint of England in Anglo–Saxon times.

Little attention seems to have been given to him in Europe until the Crusades when, because of the aid he gave to Godfrey of Boulogne, his fame as the saint of the military was established. When Richard I known as the 'Lionheart' or Richard Cœur de Lion so called from the prodigies of personal valour performed by him in the Holy Land (1157, 1189–1199) during his Holy War. He placed his army under the protection of St. George and naturally, the saint became more popular in England after the Crusades. He is the patron saint of soldiers and sailors, the protector of rocky and 'dangerous coasts that are liable to flood.' He is invoked for the 'mentally infirm' though this connection evades many, including me. St George is the patron saint of Genoa, he is found prominently around St Marks Square and Venice generally and naturally, he is found in England. The god Kalvis of the Baltic region is often found associated with St. George.

The god Kalvis is found in other places in Baltic religion, the heavenly smith is usually associated with a huge iron hammer. A smith in the tradition of the Greek Hephaistos and other smiths. Kalvis also seems to have been a dragon killer, a function in which he was superseded by the Christian St. George. Each morning Kalvis hammers a new sun for Ausrine (Latvian= Auseklis). Kalvis creates the dawn and a silver belt and golden stirrups for Dievo suneliai (Latvian= Dieva deli) 'who were known as the 'Heavenly Twins' and the morning and evening stars. The big iron hammer of Kalvis was used to aid the sun that was freed from imprisonment and this god was honoured by the Lithuanians up to the turn of the 15th century. Kalvis it seems was also a dragon killer, a task in which he was superseded by the Christian St. George, who became the patron saint of England and is one of the most popular saints among the Baltic races.

It should be unnecessary to labour the obvious connection between Saint George and Saint Michael (= the Archangel Michael) and this is St. George's connection with 'the angelic.' Michael not only holds the keys to the Kingdom of Heaven but his is possibly the earliest recorded slaughter of the dragon. This could naturally make him the model of our St George and the other Christian paradigms that have followed.

George is from the Latin **Georgius** and from the Greek **Γεοργος, Georgos**= 'a cultivator of the earth'; **geo**= 'earth' and **εργον, ergon**= 'a cultivator of the earth.' There has long been a custom in England to give all farmers the familiar name of 'Farmer George' because 'farmers, through their physical labour, were thought to urge or work the earth to yield her produce.' The poetry known as 'georgic' is poetry relating to husbandry, agriculture, treating of rural affairs and, of course, the most famous of the category are as you would expect the four books written of Virgil — the **Georgics**. Perhaps the most familiar word we use in English is 'geography,' which is from the Latin **geographia**, from the Greek **γεωγραφια, geographia** from **γεω, geo** for 'earth,' **γειος, geios**= 'belonging to the earth' and **γραφια, graphia**= 'to write, a description' making 'geography' or 'a description of the earth.'

At one time, there was the Festival of the Sacred Plough in Britain and the first sod was turned in Cornwall to the ritual words 'In the name of God let us begin.' The Emperor in China turned the first sod of earth and this was a customary ritual of the ruler in many countries and by many races.

Some of the marine connections of St. George have mentioned above and many Channels still bear his name in many countries. St George's Channel is a strait separating south–east Ireland from Wales and joining the Atlantic Ocean to the Irish Sea in the North. The ensign of the Navy is a red cross on a white background, which is the national flag of England and St George. This ensign was originally known as a **Christofer** or **Jack**. There has long been a connection of St. George with water to encourage growth of fields and meadows and the woodland fungi — *calocybe gambosa* — known as St. George's Mushroom

This connection is frequently shown with the annual act of clothing a male as the Green Man or Green George in leaves, corn, vines and so on. Sometimes an image was used instead of the man and either water was poured over him or he was thrown into water at the end of the ceremonies. Throwing the **Green George** into water to give him a good soaking was done to gain the favour of the water–sprites to do likewise to the land to make the meadows green in summer. Many of the spring celebrations in Europe on St. George's Day were obviously charms for rain and water generally.

The most popular legend of St George tells of his combat with the dragon. A pagan town in Libya was terrorized by a dragon, (said to represent the Devil or Satan by the Church). The inhabitants tried to appease it with offerings of sheep at first and then sacrificing members of the community. Finally, the virgin daughter of the king (said to represent authority and the Church) was chosen by lot and she was taken to wait her fate by the monster. George arrived, killed the dragon and converted the entire community to Christianity.

It is interesting to these Isles that some traditions actually have George being born in Coventry and 'he is reported to have been marked at his birth (forsooth!) with a red bloody cross on his right hand.' H. O. F., *St. George for England*, p.15. This may have connection with a ballad found in the *Reliques* of Percy, *St George and the Dragon*. If true, George was the son of Lord Albert of Coventry, his mother died at his birth, the baby was stolen away by 'the weird lady of the woods' and she brought him up to deeds of arms and valour.

We are told that his body held three marks, the first was a dragon on his chest, the second was a garter around one of his legs and the last was a 'blood red cross on the arm.' The maiden that he saved, Sabra the daughter of the king of Morocco and Egypt who did not want her to marry a Christian so he sent George to Persia with instructions that he should not come back. However, he made good his escape from that trap and carried Sabra back to England with him where (it is said) she became his wife and they lived together in great happiness in Coventry until their deaths. There are other, similar tales of which the above is only one. George is mentioned by St Jerome (331–420), St. Gregory (540–604) and the Venerable Bede (672–735) in his martyrology as well as among other writers.

He is the patron Saint of England by adoption as many saints are and he has been so for too long to dismiss him, as some do simply by saying he 'is not of these shores.' The fact that he is by some being attacked shows that he is important, why attack someone who is effete of unimportant? If it comes to the point that Saint George was 'not born of these shores,' well, neither is Saint Andrew (= a Galilean) or Saint Patrick (= Romano–British). Only Saint David was really born in the country of which he is the patron Saint — Wales. St George can be found in many unexpected places and he is venerated in all of them.

The Gallacian bishop and pilgrim traveller Arculf was the earliest Christian explorer and an observer of any importance to witness the rise of Islam (c. AD. 680). Arculf is the first to mention the column of Jerusalem, which was claimed to mark 'the centre of the Inhabited Earth,' which later became one of the favourite wonders of Palestine. He gave many valuable accounts of the principle sites of Judea, Galilee and of other places. He drew many useful drawings and plans; he refers to the Caliph Moawiya I (A.D 661–680) rescuing 'the *sudarium* of Christ from the Jews.' *Sudarium*= 'a cloth for wiping perspiration, a handkerchief.'

Laodicea ad Lycum in Asia Minor was one of the oldest homes of Christianity and the seat of one of the Seven Churches in Asia of the *Apocalypse*. Pliny asserts that the town in older times was called Diospolis and Rhoas. St. George of Diospolis (= the 'City of Light') was hailed by early Christians as 'the Mighty Man,' the Sun of Truth' and the 'Star of the Morning.'

The title *Epistle to the Ephesians* is found in Iraneus, Tertullian, Clement of Alexander and in all the earliest Mss. However, Marcion (c.A.D 150) used and recommended copies with the title *To the Laodiceans* or the *Pauline Epistles to the Laodocians and the Alexandrians*. Some think the words 'in Ephesus' was probably lacking from the original address and it was inserted from the suggestion of the title.

A kermess was originally a Mass on the anniversary of the foundation of a church and often peformed in honour of its patron — the word being equivalent to 'Kirkmass.' They were commonly held in the Low Countries and Northern France and they were accompanied by much dancing, great feasting and many sports. They still survive though now they are little more than country fairs because the old allegorical representation is forgotten.

The kermess we are interested in is (or was if no longer kept) the *Mons Kermesse*, which was held on Trinity Sunday was called the *Procession of Lumecon*. The hero of this festival is Gilles de

Chin. Gilles slays the fearful monster/dragon because it is the captor of a princess in the Grand Place and this, as with so many others are is really the story *Saint George and the Dragon*. Before leaving St. George we must touch upon St. George and angelic armies, though we shall look mainly at what may prove the most famous of the all . . .

## ANGELIC and PHANTOM ARMIES — ARTHUR MACHIN and THE ANGEL of MONS.

Phantom armies are not new on the battlefields of the world and there are many incidents recorded of them. They made a brief but highly dramatic appearance to the British ranks during their calamitous retreat from Mons on August of 1914. Their appearance is thought by some to be the result of a story by Arthur Machen — *The Bowmen*. However, this story was published in the *Evening News* in London on September 29th 1914, a little while after the event.

This story had immense power with the public and from the story (it is claimed), we get the famous story of the *Angels of Mons*. In the story, a solder recalls that he once read on a plate in a restaurant the motto *Adsit Anglis Sanctus Georgius* — 'May St. George be a present help to the English.' He invoked the motto and it was immediately answered by the Agincourt bowmen of 1415, who showered arrows into the enemy, but the officers of the enemy found no wounds on their dead. Several German prisoners captured later asked the same question 'who was the officer seated on a large white horse.' St. George he was for England, St. Denys was for France was the war cries of the troops of the two nations in 1415. For the English it was — *'St George!'* — while for the French it was — *'Montjoys St. Denis*!'

In his written field notes dated September 5th, three weeks *before* the story went to the paper and public, Brigadier–General John Chartris referred to stories among his troops of angelic sightings at Mons. In press reports, the survival of the Old Contemptibles was attributed to the direct intervention of St. George and his angels. These are not all the facts of the events and there are is a lot more that can be found readily enough for the curious, but it is enough and people must make of them what they will, according to their lights. Machen explains the Angels of Mons as being his own work and fiction. Harold Begbie published *On the Side of the Angels: The Story of the Angel of Mons — An Answer to 'The Bowmen.'* A collection of all the accounts he could gather of those who were there, it was an attempt to show true or false that they did not appear to be simply the creations of Machen's fertile mind. As said, there are still plenty of accounts available for those who are inquisitive about the matter and want to make up their minds.

I have been using the motto *Adsit Anglis Sanctus Georgius* for more years than I care to remember and the years really do not matter and long before I knew of the *Angel of Mons* story. It has been used in invocations, letters, letter headings, writing and books including this one for a long time now. The motto was given to me by an old friend with its interpretation, which he said was 'in dog Latin' and I have used it from that day onwards. The last well–attested account of a phantom host in the clouds in the British Isles was in June 1745 at Souter Fell and now we must leave the phantom or angelic armies. The other element in the story of George is the dragon, which could almost fill a small book but let us take a brief look at its symbolism because of its connections not only with St George but also with the Archangel Michael.

## DRAGONS and SERPENTS

Dragon is from the Greek δρακων, *drakon*= 'a dragon or serpent of huge size, a python. Homer, etc.' Latin *draco*= 'a sort of serpent, a dragon,' *draconigena*= 'dragon–born (poetic) as with *Alexander the Great* whom Olympias was said to have conceived by a serpent.' Known to scholarship as a mythical monster, a huge lizard, winged, scaly, fire breathing, doubtless originating with the memory of an actual prehistoric animal, dragon is often found one and the same with serpent.

The dragon and the serpent appear in various events in cosmic world history or suggesting various terrestrial or human qualities and either creature does at times signify spiritual immortality, wisdom, re–embodiment or regeneration. In the triad of the sun, moon and the serpent or cross, the dragon often represents the manifested Logos and hence is frequently seven–headed. As such, it is in conflict with the sun and sometimes with the moon but this conflict is merely the duality of the contrary forces essential to cosmic stability.

The dragon itself is often dual and may be paired with the serpent, as with *Agathodaimon* and *Kakodaimon* given earlier, the good and evil serpents seen on the caduceus of Hermes/Mercury. Again the dragon is regarded as being two–poled with having a head and a tail, Rahu and Ketu in India, commonly described as being the moon's north and south nodes in European literature, the moon thus is a triple symbol in which a unity conflicts with duality.

One of the most persistent and universal myths has the Sun God or God of Light struggling with the dragon and ultimately defeating it. Many say this myth symbolizes the descent of spirit into matter and the eventual subjection of matter by spirit in the course of an ideal evolution.

Some of the dragon myths belong to Bel (later Merodach) and the dragon *Tiamat* in Babylonia and the Hebrews; *Fafnir* in Scandinavia and among the Greeks, the *Python* that was conquered by Apollo. The two serpents killed by Hercules at his birth; the fight between Ahti and the evil serpent in the Kalevala and there are many other such stories. In the Christian Apocalypse, the dragon plays a great part but it has been often misinterpreted as evil with Satan or the Devil. Let us add a little flesh to some of the above.

*Bel* (= Greek, Latin) *Baal* (= Chaldean) from the Semitic ba'al 'chief or lord.' He is one of the supreme gods of the Chaldeo– or Assyro–Babylonian pantheon. The second of the triad composed of Anu, Bel and Ea who are associated with the three divisions of the universe, heaven, earth and water. The various names of Bel/Baal in the *Old* and *New Testaments* show the different aspects to which he was related.

*Merodach* (= Hebrew) or *Marduk* (= Babylonian) is the guardian deity of ancient Babylon, the local *Bel* (= 'lord') of later times. Originally, he was a solar deity but he was elevated to the supreme rank in the Babylonian pantheon under Khammurabi (c. 2250 B.C.) The priests transferred a lot of the features and many of the heroic acts of Bel to Marduk and so he became known as the slayer of the serpent Tiamat. Marduk was also regarded as 'the creator of the world and mankind' previously these had been attributed to Bel.

*Fafnir* is a mythical dragon that is found in the Norse *Edda*. Fáfnir killed his father for his treasure of gold, which had been cursed by the dwarf Andvari. Fáfnir then took the appearance of a dragon and he guarded the gold on Gnipaheden. His brother Regin wanting the gold persuaded his charge, the hero Sigurd, to kill the dragon and cook its heart for him but Sigurd when doing this burnt his finger. Instinctively putting it in his mouth, he found as soon as the dragon's heart-blood touched his tongue, he was able to comprehend the language and messages of the birds. This is in keeping with the tale of so many other stories especially Irish and Celtic and may be an allegory featuring the development of intelligence. Many myths feature slaying a dragon or the serpent of wisdom to obtain a treasure of gold (= wisdom), which in many cases carries with it a curse, showing the need for great discrimination in its use.

The Python/Dragon was a monstrous serpent produced by Gaea, Gaia or Ge that haunted the caves of Parnassus. It was slain by Apollo with his first arrows so among the Greeks the python is associated with Apollo who stands for order, justice, law and purification that was obtained by the penance he undertook for this crime. His characteristic as a nemesis of evil is shown by his bow, which Apollo used as an infant to slay the Python and he was consequently called Apollo Pythius. He is the deity who wards off evil, the healer, father of Asclepius who is frequently identified with him. As a god of divination, he particularly associated with the Oracle at Delphi and the other principal seat of his worship was at Delos, which is his birthplace.

Apollo is the patron of music and song, of new civic foundations and protector of crops and flocks. His lyre is the sacred heptachord or having seven strings as the Sun making the seven planets of old. The *Septerion* is a festival celebrated every nine years at Delphi, in memory of the slaying of the serpent Python by Apollo and his purification, which took place in the laurel grove of Tempe to which he returned after nine years of penance.

Ahti is the Finnish god of water who is usually portrayed as an old man who aids fishermen and Ahti is also a name for *Lemminkainen*, called the *Dragon of Knowledge* in the *Kalevala*.

Others that could have been included are Asclepius Serapis, Pluto, Knoum and Kneph are all deities with whom the attributes of the serpent have been associated. The foregoing are all the accredited healers, the givers of health both spiritual and physical often coupled with enlightenment.

In the Apocalypse of Christianity, the dragon is found playing a large part, but more often than not it has been misinterpreted as being only evil in the same way that Satan or the Devil has been seen as the antagonist of the Divine and of all individuals. The dragon symbol then is both cosmic and human in its function and it may stand for the Powers of Nature, which 'first overcome man' and 'over which he must in the end prevail.'

The dragon in its higher or superior sense means, among other things, Divine Wisdom especially where the serpent is used for terrestrial wisdom and adepts or initiates were frequently called 'dragons.' A *Dragon of Wisdom* is normally an adept, one of the wise and is a skilled magician traditionally — of whatever path. In Chinese Buddhism, the term is used for the genii of the four quarters called in China, the *Black Warrior*, the *White Tiger*, the *Vermilion Bird* and the *Azure Dragon* — these are the *Four Hidden Dragons of Wisdom*.

The dragon is the eternally vigilant one being the guardian of the sacred treasures. The dragon is the ruthless destroyer of anyone who attempts to gain by force the riches to which they have not won the title. To gain knowledge, we must know how to discipline the serpent that rules the nether worlds. In initiations the individual seeking enlightenment has to meet face-to-face their lowest, strongest passions and these are often found in their material form at the time. The seeker must conquer them or become a victim to them once roused — one or the other — having undertaken to embark on this particular goal. There are few if any halfway houses open for those who fail because they do not have a foot in either camp — a form of limbo, from people whose knowledge is limited and ever repetitive — having left one place and not yet reached the another.

The student should have a clear idea long before reaching this particular point just how much they are prepared to sacrifice for their aims or leave it well alone. If the individual is triumphant, they take on the spiritual serpent in its other aspect of the *Dragon of Wisdom*. This is to be seen in the sense of regeneration in that snakes shed their skin and emerge from the struggle renewed and symbolically purified after sloughing off the old, leaving it behind, growing and progressing in a new form.

The tyro, through their training, hard work and sacrifice endeavours to shed the old individual and emerge from the Work as one who is new — until the next growth that will surely come and keep on coming. The tests may start all over again because only a fool would say that this task is an easy one or can be evaded if the challenge is accepted. This form of advice has long stood the test of time and is as old as the ancient Schools that originated the principles in the first place.

In the early stages — although being alert in all stages would not come amiss to the wise — it is important for the student to learn to differentiate between impulse and intuition because they often appear to be the same but they are not and great care is needed to differentiate between them or the student could be deceived or mislead.

Intuition is important because it is 'tuition from within,' 'in–tuition' or from the 'inner voice or guide' that can give knowledge of great significance. This is because intuition often comes from higher levels and it is then when inner or inside tuition becomes true intuition and takes over the direction of their lives — impulse is not.

If you are not certain take time to pause if the situation or circumstances will allow you to do so, but try to make time no matter how short it is. If this is done and dispassionate criticism applied, I repeat no matter how short this may be, impulse will generally lose its force because as a rule, impulse is connected with the self, its needs and it is more transient than people think.

Intuition on the other hand increases in strength and develops with greater clarity in the interval taken between thought and action, again no matter how slight interval — impulse declines and wavers — intuition develops and is reinforced through the waiting.

The serpent is typically a dual symbol. In the beginning of Creation, it is these two poles that initiate spirit and matter with interaction between the downward forces of the one and the upward forces of the other. Intelligence may represent a sage or a thief, which he does because Hermes/Mercury rules both. In the play a *Winter's Tale* (Act 4). Autolycus tells us 'My father name me Autolycus' and that he was 'litter'd under Mercury . . . to have an open ear, a quick eye and a nimble hand, is necessary for a cut–purse (= thief).' The serpentine wisdom may be found working on every plane of materiality. The perverse will of people may turn natural forces to evil purposes and we have already spoken of the good serpent and the bad, the *Agathodaemon* and *Kakodaemon* because the serpent can equally be either — sage or sorcerer.

The reverence for the serpent was nourished to some extent by a dread of it and this may have survived initially from rituals that began their existence as a form of fetish worship. The form of the serpent handed down from age to age was probably thought of as the complement of magical powers. There are few places on the earth that are not occupied by serpents or where it has not at some time or other been given some form of worship, respect or fear by the populace. The strange beauty of the serpent gives it a fascination or an abhorrence that is hard to explain, but usually it is one or the other.

Most other forms of life walk, run, leap, hop, jump and the means can usually be understood, but the serpent glides and the means of doing so cannot be seen. The serpent is quiet, sometimes possessing a deadly venom that can bring instant or painful death and with other qualities and faculties that account for its being regarded by many as bordering on the supernatural above all other life forms and of course, there is the Garden of Eden in the back of the mind of so many, even if they will not admit it.

Its custom of attaching itself to human habitations may be traced to the belief of its guardianship. It was believed by some to be a reincarnation of a dead man's soul, a messenger from the gods so while it has been worshipped by the Chinese and Egyptians, it was demonised by the followers of Zarathustra, the Jews, Islam and Christianity.

The Hebrew's on the other hand were open worshippers of snakes, until the reign of King Hezekiah and the original brazen serpent of Moses had remained in existence until his time. In consequence of the idolatrous worship offered to it by the people . . . 'He removed the high places, and brake the images, and cut down the grove, and brake into pieces the brazen serpent that Moses had made; for unto those days the children of Israel did burn incense to it: and called it

Nehushtan (= 'brass') 2 *Kings* 18:4–5. See also the Serpent of Brass in *Numbers* 21:4 and mentioned elsewhere. Many mythologies have women with serpent's hair or tails that all have magical powers, from Medusa, Lilith the Hebrew sorceress onwards, again another subject for fuller treatment but not here.

When the ancient Egyptians personified the powers of nature, they gave the evil powers the shapes of noxious animals and reptiles such as snakes and scorpions. The principle enemy of the natural body was the worm and from earliest times it seems that a huge worm or serpent was chosen by the Egyptians as the type of power that was particularly hostile to the dead and the foe that fought the Sun God. Many world mythologies have some form of Serpent but I think the foregoing is enough to show the point being made regarding this fascinating creature that has found connections with the angels and being a creation that has kept us in its thrall for so long.

Next, we are going to look at some important aspects of the *Old Testament*, Jewish traditions, the *Talmud* and so forth regarding matters connected with the angels. The traditional first wife of *Adam* was *Lilith*, the mating of the angels with 'the daughters of the earth.' The *Bread of the Angels* that sustained the Children of Israel, in their wanderings in the desert — *Manna*. The *Tetragrammaton* or the *Sacred Name of God*, a beautiful concept called the *Shekinah* or *Glory of God* with the *Bat Qol* or 'daughter of the voice.' Finally, we shall touch upon the *Merkabah Mysteries* or the *Riders of the Chariot* and a few more things besides — such as Satan or the Devil, because wherever we are, he is never far away — when God builds a church, Satan builds a chapel.

## LILITH

In the mythology of the Hebrews, Islam and Christianity, the winged female demon Lilith is a Demon of the Night. She takes wing at night seeking newborn children to kidnap or strangle and she is not averse to sleeping males to seduce them for one purpose — the production of demon sons and if this is not enough for you then there is more.

Lilith, Hebrew from *layil*= 'night,' but modern scholars appear to associate her with the Sumerian *lulu*= 'wantoness' explaining that she encourages lust. In Cabbalistic allegory, Lilith or Lilitu is given as Adam's first wife and created as he was, unlike Eve. In context she seems to be an Assyrian spirit of the wind with wings and long hair. She is appropriately branded as the 'night–hag' or as the *Meyalleleth*= 'the howling one,' but this does not mean that she was ugly. In the *Talmud* she is described as being an attractive woman 'with long wavy hair.'

> Not a drop of her blood was human.
> But she was made like a soft sweet woman.'
> *Eden Bower*: D.G. Rossetti

In the parables of Cabbala and the Talmud, she is called the female reflection of Sammael; Sammael–Lilith or man–animal united creating a being called —*Hayoh Bisha* — the Beast or Evil Beast. (*Zohar* ii, 255, 259), Lilith, the wife of Adam. Lilith appears to be against life or life that is not under her control and domination. The hatred of the Jewish arch–demon and fierce female spirit against children when born is both malicious and spiteful just as she is against all pregnant women or those in confinement, because she is the 'child–snatcher.' The *Zohar* tell us she is most powerful when the Moon is waning. Lilith is considered to be the female reflection or consort of the Angel Sammael — the Angel of Death or the angel who is called the 'Poison of Death.' The Angel Sammael is regarded as Satan in *Scripture* with many commentators claiming Lilith was his wife.

As written elsewhere please take note the double 'mm' in the name Sammael and do not confuse him with the Angel Samael, the Angel of Mars who will be mentioned later, this will probably be repeated because it is important. Sammael was clothed in the phantom or shadow image of an Ox from whence we get the cloven hoof, while Lilith is clothed as a Mule, which is sterile. Sammael and Lilith can unite as one when they are called 'the Beast' or 'the Evil or Wicked Beast.' Later, in the Cabbala she becomes the Demon Queen.

Lilith or 'the Liliths' in commonplace Talmudic thought are nocturnal apparitions of female life forms that normally appear at night to haunt human beings. The Rabbis portray these creatures as assuming female form, being elegantly dressed and lying in wait for children by night. These Jewish fables, which have direct reference to female Elementals and other denizens of the astral and lower astral levels agree with to the Roman and Greek *empusa* and *lamiae*. The Arabian *ghulah* (= masculine *ghul*) are entities of monstrous character dwelling in the sandy deserts, awaiting men and will destroy them if possible the other creatures of the night, the succubus and succubae.

*Empusa* — The *empusa* is a monstrous spectre that was believed to devour human beings. They were able to assume many different forms and were sent out by Hecate to frighten travellers. However, according to Philostratus, if the traveller insulted the *empusa*, it usually fled into the night uttering a shrill sound like the *lamiae* but if they were successful in their intent, they would eventually devour their human lover.

*Lamiae* — The *lamiae* and *mormolycia* assume the form of a beautiful women for the purpose of attracting young men, sucking out their blood and eating their flesh and they are usually numbered among the *empusae*

As a protection against the evil wiles of Lilith during childbirth, magic circles were drawn on the walls of the birth room and on the floor. This is also found in the revised and enlarged *Practical Book of Candle Magic*. The names of the three dread angels whom Lilith 'must obey' were written within these circles. Their names are sometimes found on talismans, amulets, charms, cameos or drawn in charcoal, particularly willow charcoal because the willow is a tree of the Moon ruling birth, conception, the affairs of women and is very potent in such matters as a result.

All these are the concerns of the Moon and are under the rulership of the Archangel Gabriel who extends his wings over all pregnant mothers because this archangel is especially concerned with birth and early childhood. This is why the Archangel Gabriel is always found associated with the Virgin Mother of Christianity.

The names of the three dread angels are *Sanvi*, *Sansavi* and *Semengalef* (sometimes *Sinoi*, *Sinsinoi* and *Semengalaf*, other names do exist, but I use the ones given here). These were the three angels that God sent after Lilith to bring her back when she refused to be with Adam. She had gone off to consort with demons by the seashore of the Red Sea and she was told if she did not obey these angels, then one hundred of her offspring would be slain each day.

The angels it is said were going to drown her in the Red Sea but she pleaded for her life and they relented and let her live because Lilith gave them her solemn oath that she would not give vent to her hatred against *any* child where the names of these angels were displayed or their talismans used. The formula written is 'Let not Lilith enter here' with the names of the three angels and 'Adam and Eve' to which is added — 'barring Lilith.'

Alternatively, it is written 'protect this new–born child from harm' and this can still be found written on the walls of the birth chamber in some parts of the world even today. Amulets of the three angels placed in the four corners of the room, the bed and so forth. It is said, after the birth, if a child laughed while it was sleeping, this was taken as a warning that Lilith was near at hand. To make her (or any demon) depart simply tap the child softly on its nose, see below.

The hatred of Lilith is venomous against children and she will endeavour to vent her spleen against a girl until she is eight days old, but a boy is threatened until he is twenty days old. *Talmud* legend tells us she was wife to Adam before Eve and tradition says that she refused to be 'under Adam' and this has made her attractive to some forms of thinking common today. The *Talmud* says regarding her: 'It is forbidden for a man to sleep alone in a house; and whoever sleeps alone in a house will be seized by Lilith.' (*Shab.* 151b).

The bed of those who have just been married is made secure by tossing four coins on the bed with the words — 'Adam and Eve' or 'Avaunt thee Lilith.' In other legends, she is held to be the mother of Cain, but regarding one theme all the legends agree — Lilith appears as the *Spirit of Isolation*, negative, rejected and filled with a consuming hatred and vengeance against most forms of human life, particularly marriage, families and children.

As said, the protection of the birth chamber, the mother and child is still be undertaken in some old parts of Poland and Russia where old safeguards do not die easily. The *Book of Raziel*, which contains the description of the holy circle and pictures of these angels, was used as an additional safeguard being placed under the pillow of the expectant mother.

Two female demons that live in constant strife and enmity with Lilith are the she–demons Makhlath (= 'the dancer') and her daughter Agrath. The strength of demon Agrath is at its most powerful on Wednesdays and Saturdays. According to legend when the prophet Elijah met Lilith, he made her disclose the names she used while she was among mortals and active in her evil and hatred, many are know but I do think all have been given.

In the *Talmud*, there is a unique angel called Lailah whose name means 'night.' In *Job* 3: 3 he tells us 'let the day perish wherein I was born' but continues 'and the night in which it was said, there is a man–child conceived. Let that day be darkness, let not God regard it from above . . . neither let the light shine upon it . . . let darkness and the shadow of death stain it . . . and on.' A cult associated with Lilith survived among some Jews as late as A.D 7th century

The Angel Lailah is sometimes found connected with Lilith and he is considered to be her equal in wickedness but it has to be pointed out that other records are not all bad. The *Zohar* tells us the Angel Lailah is 'the angel appointed to guard the spirits at their birth.' This angel presides over human conception in its earliest stages and the embryo is brought before the Divine Throne through his mediation, where its future is determined. Its station in life is settled, who will be the marriage partner and so on. At the command of God, a spirit enters the sperm, which is restored to the womb of the mother and there the child rests with its head between its knees.

One interpretation tells us that Lailah takes a small seminal drop and places it before the Holy One. He asks 'the Sovereign of the Universe' what is to become of this drop.' Should it become strong or weak, wise or foolish, rich or poor? Though notice not if it is to be 'wicked or righteous.' This brings to mind the very wise Talmudic maxim 'All is in the hands of Heaven — except the fear of Heaven.' God decides its fate but not the moral character. 'Behold, I set before you this day a blessing and a curse . . . a blessing if ye obey the commandments . . . a curse if ye will not obey the commandments . . . etc.' *Deuteronomy* 11:26 and 'See I have set before thee this day life and good, and death and evil . . . etc. 30:15.

This (commentators say) perhaps made the Israelites think that God had set two ways of life, the way of life and the way of death and they could walk in whichever of the paths that they decide on. 'Chose life that both thee and thy seed may live.' 30:19.

Next, after the fate of the child is decided, two angels (= the Guardian Angels) are set to watch over the baby who has a light burning over its head and by this light the child can see from one end of the world to the other. In the morning, an angel takes the child to Paradise and shows it the righteous or those who have lived a virtuous life in this world. In the evening, the angel takes it to hell and shows the child the torments of the wicked that await those who sin.

At the appropriate time, the angel commands the child to come forth by striking it lightly near the nose or just under the nose and this extinguishes the light above the child's head and makes it forget whatever it saw while it was in the womb of its mother. Have you ever wondered what that hollow is on your upper lip, under your nose? Legend tells us that this is the mark that is left where the baby was lightly tapped by the angel. Whatever the child learns afterwards is a mere recollection of the knowledge garnered during life as an embryo. According to the legend, most children come into the world crying for the reason that they do not want to come here because at the time of their birth they know what to expect. We do not know how we got here and it is even harder to find the way back.

This is reminiscent of the wisdom of Shakespeare, who knew a thing or two, given in **King Lear** where he gives to Lear the words. 'Thou must be patient: we came crying hither: Thou knows't, the first time we smell the air, we wawl and cry . . . When we are born, we cry that we are come to this great stage of fools.' Act.4: Sc.6.

The Guardian Angels are not the only angels that are involved in the birth of a child. When the child is ready to enter the world, other angels take an interest in the event of the birth even though they may play only a very small part in its future. Who your Guardian and Personal Angels are will be given in Part 2. Temporarily at the time among those present at the birth are the angels of the mother, the father and the angels of those who are in attendance who are helping at the event but this information is less important than the personal angels that belong to the new–born child from birth to death. Some people attend us only once at birth and for the most, they are unknown to us even though this scene could possibly vie with Prospero's island for spirits in attendance.

It is the Personal Angels that we are concerned with and again this subject is dealt with in Part 2. The balance book for the new life has been audited, the account opened and the stamp of 'Free Will' is affixed and this 'stamp' marks the bearer to accept or reject the account, the debits, the credits, the profit and loss at the end of all when the account is closed, which is fine while we are living it. However, the account of the life is audited at death to see how well the account was managed while it was open — lastly comes the result of the audit and the reckoning.

## THE MATING OF THE SONS OF GOD

The mating of the 'Sons of God' with the women of the earth and the 'daughters of men' is one of the interesting sections in the **Bible** so let us look at some of the more interesting aspects of it. Many explanations are offered in support of how and why the angels or 'Sons of God' came to earth and what is thought to be the reason for their coming here.

In one version, the 'Sons of God' descended from Seth who was Adam's third and favourite son, while the 'Daughters of the Earth' are said to have come from the line of Cain and of course, this made them wicked. Considering the trouble Cain and his descendants are said to have wreaked on God's grand design, I have always wondered why God let Cain live after his slaughter of Abel and protected him with a special mark so that none should slay him for what he had done.

The reality of demons is not disputed and their existence is commonly acknowledged by countless races and nations and this is possibly through the influence of Babylonian and Jewish belief of the period, which attempts to account for them in a world created by the One–God. In fact, the certainty in the spirits of evil was such a firmly held belief existing among both the educated and uneducated classes that the **Talmud** appears to legislate for them. 'Three things cause a person to transgress against his conscience and the will of his Maker and these are Gentiles, an evil spirit and the pressing needs caused by poverty.' *Eru. 41b*.

The origin of these demons or harmful spirits gives a difference of opinion. One tells us that they are part of God's creation and were among the ten things that were created on the eve of the first Sabbath and included in these 'ten things' are the *mazzikin* or 'harmful spirits.' However, as the Sabbath followed before their creation was complete they are without bodies because God had already hallowed the Sabbath and no work could be done, even His, so they are thought of as disembodied spirits. They are not fallen angels, neither are they of the ancient heathen gods, but are intermediate 'between the angels and man' but as a rule they are usually considered to be evil by inclination.

There are variations of this explanation that perhaps should be considered and one example is given as. They are the souls of evil men transformed by God into a malevolent appearance as a punishment. The men who built the Tower of Babel consisted of three categories. The first class said let us go up to heaven and live there, the second said let us go up and practise idolatry, while the third said let us go up and declare war on God. God disseminated the first class, the second class God confounded their tongue and the third class he turned into apes, spirits demons and devils of the night. *Sanh.*109a.

To obtain the assistance and help of these powers, certain means had to be devised. Gifts or sacrifices were made to win them over and to try and gain control over them. Maimonides, when he interpreted the line in the *Bible*. 'They sacrificed unto devils (=*shedhim*), *Deuteronomy* 32:17 says the gift most agreeable to them was blood. Their willing help was accomplished by giving them the blood of the sacrifice. The practitioner must also partake of the blood, thus 'sharing the food of the evil spirits and becoming their accomplice.' Naturally, such sacrifices were not limited only to blood and the magician among other things used candles and a knife with a black handle. *Shedhim* seems to be understood by the translators of the *Septuagint* as 'demons,' but it was also made parallel with 'foreign gods.' Some saying that the root *shed* became a general term for 'demon' in later Judaism.

In one version of the 'mating' about two hundred angels and their leaders came down on Mount Hermon in rebellious mood against God. We are told they seduced the girls and taught them charms and enchantments, especially 'the charms of trees, which were to play a part in witchcraft.' The willow for example was sacred to Hecate the Mother of Witches, Hera and Persephone, all death aspects of the Triple Moon Goddess were worshipped and honoured by witches.

The willow was the meeting place of witches and when a witch began her career, it was to the willow that she went. She would sit on one of its roots and take a solemn oath to foreswear God, his angels and all those things that are sacred and holy. She would write her name in a book that the Devil would present to her using her blood. By this act and the vow she made she was irredeemably lost and had consigned her soul to the torments of hell where she would be condemned to eternal damnation.

After the rebellious angels had finished with the human women, they next taught the men a few sins that they could call their own. One angel taught the art of astrology, another how to make swords, another abortion and yet another — writing (?) The angel who taught them the art of coats of mail and swords is said to have been the angel who had seduced Eve. The children of this union grew to enormous size and strong but the experiment turned out badly with some adding that it all ended in cannibalism.

Another version has the angels or the Angels Harut and Marut, came to earth with God's expressed permission before the Flood when wickedness was most rife and showing no sign of flagging. The angels said they would like to try and do something to help the situation. God was not happy with this suggestion and told them if they came to earth to live, they would most certainly be corrupted by its inhabitants and their conduct, so it seems God did not have too much faith in his 'other creations' either.

The angels said they would do all within their power to establish the name of God and his goodness again and reluctantly God let them go to see if they could survive temptation. Because they were two of the angels who showed their displeasure at the creation of Adam, perhaps they would be better able to survive the test of Adam's seed.

The angels failed the test miserably and they were corrupted by the women they befriended and 'fell in love with the women.' They were duly punished by God as he promised he would if they failed. Some records say that the Angel Harut hangs head downwards from heaven while the Angel Marut is chained behind' the dark mountains' or in the desert, where he will remain until the Day of Judgement. These Angels were met with earlier in the paragraphs referring to Islam.

The Kenites given by some as the descendants of Cain, were pupils of these angels and according to the **Book of Jubilees,** they corrupted the descendants of Seth and caused the Flood. It is thought the Kenites may have been a wandering guild of smiths who, similar to the once itinerant tinkers of today, wandered abroad giving their services wherever they were needed and some commentators connect the word 'kenite' with ('copper')–smith in both the Arabic and Aramaic.

Among the names of the arch–demons the names of Satan and Azael are found, but they play a comparatively small part in the matter. Azael is given greater prominence than Satan and a great number of the names are not found in canonical literature. The character of demons and spirits is sometimes rather vague though not in the **Book of Enoch**. In this work, the angels who had fallen in love with women of the human race appeared to use their powers principally as a means of deception and sorcery.

The early 'befriending' moved quickly on to physical contact and this is the point where the various accounts generally and broadly merge to produce the 'giants' of **Genesis**. These giants included the **Anakim,** an ancestor race of old Canaan whose size terrified the spies sent out by Moses and Goliath of Gath is thought to have descended from these people.

In the biblical text Goliath is not spoken of as being a 'giant' but he is thought to have stood over nine feet and the name given to a prehistoric race that occupied Moab was the **Emim** (= 'terrible men.') They were also called the Rephaim and the Nephilim. 'There were giants in the earth in those days; and also after that, when the sons of God came in unto the daughters of men, and they bare children to them, the same became mighty men, which were of old, men of renown.' **Genesis** 6:4. Another passage tells us that Goliath of Gath was slain by Elhanan of Bethlehem in one of David's conflicts with the Philistines 2 **Sammuel** 21: 18-22. This may be a transcription slip as the parallel 1 **Chronicles**. 20:5 avoids the inconsistency by giving 'Elhanan . . . slew Lahmi the brother of Goliath.'

**Nephilim** appears to be a transliteration of a word from Hebrew of unknown etymology, although it is usually found rendered as 'giants' or 'a race of extraordinary size' or associated with 'hairy men or satyrs.' They are only mentioned twice in the **Old Testament**. It is said that the Greek transliteration of the Hebrew gave the word '**nephilim**' and modern translation usually identifies with the Anakim and Rephaim. Some writers have taken the Hebrew **naphal**= 'to fall' when referring to the **nephilim**= 'the fallen ones.'

They became the fallen angels who mated with the daughters of the earth and their theomachy has been carried on to this day. **Θεος, Theos**= 'God.' The first element in many words derived from the Greek referring to the Divine Being or divinity' and **μαχη, mache**= 'battle, fight or combat' giving 'a fighting against the gods or God, as with the battle of the giants with the gods in ancient mythology and here in the **Bible**.' The translation of the word **nephilim** is uncertain and none of the terms translates into 'giant,' so we cannot be sure the *Nephilim* were people of gigantic stature. However, Christ taught later that the angels do not have carnal relationships or marriage *Luke* 20:34–35 but this is not clear-cut and was this only for the 'fallen angels.'

In Medieval European folklore, the incubus is a male demon who seeks sexual intercourse with sleeping women. Its female counterpart is the succubus who sleeps with men and tormented them. Latin *incubus* = 'nightmare,' *in–cubo* = 'to lie in' or 'upon a thing.' More than one legend tells us the incubus and succubus was a fallen angel. Union with an incubus was thought to lead to the birth of demons, deformed children and witches. In the literature of witchcraft of the Middle Ages, the word incubus was often used for those who were thought to have the devil as a paramour. The legendary wizard Merlin is said to have been the offspring of such a union being without father.

We can assume because they are fallen angels they were obviously able to have carnal knowledge, relationships and marry even though Christ says, the angels do not indulge in these things.

Some early Christian mythology tells us when the angels fell man was created to fill the gaps in the angelic host. A vast amount of Jewish literature hints at the belief of a reserve or storehouse of souls for future creation — the *guph* —this is dealt with later. These souls were obliged to enter the womb and the body of the child therein. The souls objected and protested because of the uncertainty and risk of being born into human life — but to no avail.

Another version tells us God has created an abundance of souls that will one day occupy a human body. There was a storehouse or 'Treasure House in Heaven' where these souls were drawn together. Souls remain there until the impetus arrives for them to go down to earth where they will be coupled with a human body. Some myths tell us that they are hidden 'under the throne of the All–Father.' Only when each and every one of this store of souls — 'created at the Beginning of Time' — have been 'set upon the earth and left its body will the Redeemer be free from his incarnations on earth.'

Some of the souls sent to earth are commanded to occupy a human body as a punishment or the termination of a right or privilege. This was a trial for some souls and a chance to show their strength in adversity. In the struggle of the soul against the passions and instincts inherent in corporeal matter, the soul is given the opportunity to reveal its true worth. It can exercise the divine gift of Free Will to remain faithful to its divine origins or alternatively — betray them —again and again!

As said throughout, there are usually two Guardian Angels who watch over their charge. Islam tells us that all have two Guardian Angels as does traditional Christianity and the tasks of these angels are with slight variations, reasonably uniform. In some cases, one Guardian Angel is thought to be the accuser and the recorder of evil deeds and some literature regards this Guardian Angel responsible for the person's evil inclinations. The other Guardian Angel records the charitable acts, keeping faith with God along with their other virtues and on their death these two accounts are set against each other and a reckoning is taken.

In passing, some practices are done in accordance with the phases of the Angel of the Moon, the Archangel Gabriel. Work on some levels of 'magic' operate through the lunar 'tides' of the Moon that wax and wane like the tides found in nature and they are used by practitioners for their work. Therefore, care should be taken to use the correct 'lunar tide' for what is being attempted. For example, you should not launch a boat on a tide that is ebbing or has ebbed. The water should at least be under the boat and deep enough for the boat to float if you want to get somewhere, which seems reasonable.

The most potent protection and safeguard is the protection of the Divine against spirits and harmful demons. A sure way to achieve this protection is said to be obedience of God's Commandments. If you perform one precept then 'one angel is assigned to him.' If you obey two precepts then 'two angels are assigned to him' and if you perform all the precepts then 'many angels are assigned to him.' 'He shall cover thee with his feathers, and under his wings shalt thou trust' . . . 'For he shall give his angels charge over thee, to keep thee in all thy ways.' *Psalm* 91:4 & 11. It is said that these angels are and individuals guardians from evil. In the *Talmud*, when a man goes to the synagogue on the eve of the Sabbath, two ministering angels go with him, 'one good and the other evil.'

The Talmud tells us that 'the angels go with a man wherever he goes, with one exception' — when he has to go to attend to his natural functions. However, before he enters the closet he should request pardon of the angels for the reason that he has to take his leave of them for a time.

When the child is ready to be born the Guardian Angel is said to 'turn out the light in the baby's head,' which makes all argument against being born forgotten and pointless. The Guardian Angel then gives the child a light tap on the nose or usually just under it and this was given earlier when we dealt with the Angel Lailah.

As said earlier, the life ordained for it is shown to the child. The child is forewarned of what lies in store for it before it is born and because it may choose not to undertake certain events, lessons or trials in their life what was shown is erased and not remembered them. At times, we do 'remember' of course, people, places, circumstances and so forth and to account for them we call such times — *de ja vue*. I have been lucky in my life to have some people I cannot really remember meeting because it seems they have always been there and it was more as a 'meeting again.' There are signs to help and 'maps' that can guide the life, but they must be looked for, found and the knowledge gained how to use them for the best.

One of the fallen or evil angels became the evil spirit Asmodeus that had a habit of strangling newborn children if he was allowed to get close enough to them. Asmodeus became an demon of anger, despair, jealousy, lechery, revenge and, if that was not enough, his burning ambition was to wreck new marriages, encouraging husbands to perform acts of adultery and preventing close 'acquaintance' between husband and wife. He often portrayed as having three heads, a bull, a ram and an ogre, the feet of a cock all considered sexually insistent symbols, with ugly wings riding a dragon a Christian symbol of an equally lecherous goat–like Satan. He is, therefore, naturally one of the leaders in Satan's guile and traps. Those who sought him out or called upon him were clearly advised to be respectfully bareheaded before he arrives.

It is thought that Asmodeus originally had his ancestry in Persia and he was incorporated into Jewish lore where he not only became an evil spirit but placed high and powerful in their legends. The Hebrew name is *Ashemedai* (= 'the destroyer') and this is thought to have come from the Persian *Aesham–dev* (= 'the demon of lust.') It was Asmodeus in the *Book of Tobit*, who slays the seven bridegrooms of Sarah, before the Archangel Raphael sent him on his way to Egypt. Asmodeus is the child of Lilith and that accounts for a lot. Asmodeus in other stories was the result of an incestuous relationship between Tubal–Cain and his sister Naamah. Tubal–Cain was the first artificer in bronze and iron and this is thought to be the link of the fallen angels with Cain.

The connection with Cain is considered to be why the workers in the (then) new and magical arts of working with and manipulating metal were greatly feared in the past. Their home and place of work was frequently set outside the village confines in some communities and this accounted why tinkers at one time were a wandering race, travelling from place to place, plying their craft and having no permanent or particular place of residence.

They were always being 'moved on' wherever they tried to settle. They were once thought to be powerful in the arts of magic and this is why, when we assert we do not care a damn about the results of something, we often say 'I don't care a tinker's cuss (= 'curse') or dam.' The 'cuss' seems to be the earlier version but if you used 'dam' — this was the clay or dough used by the tinker to keep the solder in place over the repair and when the solder was set, the 'dam' was thrown away as being worthless. At one time the tinker was called 'a man who 'tinks' or beats a kettle to announce his occupation and that he is open for business.' This relationship with Cain is said to have implanted within the human race the inherent trait to murder and Cain's original sin was visited upon those who are thought to have descended from him — or having his blood.

Upon being banished, Cain complained to the Lord that any that found him would kill him for his crime so the Lord marked him to prevent this from happening. 'Therefore whosoever slayeth Cain, vengeance shall be taken upon him sevenfold and the Lord set a mark upon Cain, lest any finding him should kill him.' *Genesis*.15. To me this is not unlike some of the conditions originally attached to Satan and his office — see *Job* and *Satan* later.

However, the request and its granting has always been somewhat of a puzzlement to me and gives some difficulties with the story and I am sure I am not the only one to think this. God curses the murderer but protects him by placing a mark on him that will protect him from death at the hands of others. Because of this possibility, the mark of God is set on his head for all to see and protect him. Perhaps Gods commandment 'Thou shalt not kill' was the result of Cain's action. The **Ten Commandments** are stated twice in the **Old Testament**. The first time is when God gave them to Moses in **Exodus** 20:17 and in **Deuteronomy** 5:6–21, where Moses reminds his people of their covenant in a renewal ceremony in which he reminds them of their substance, meaning and binding legality.

Of course, in the original language, they are called the 'Ten Words' and this gave us the title and name 'Decalogue.' We are told that they were written on 'two tablets' and in keeping with others, I do not believe each tablet had five of the Commandments written on them. I believe both tablets had the full ten 'words' written on them. The first tablet belonged to God and was his side of the covenant bargain, which is why it was placed in the **Ark of the Covenant** under the direct protection of the writer of the tablet because it was a 'covenant.'

A covenant is a binding pledge of great importance in the relationships between individuals, groups and nations having social, legal and religious consequences. In this case, the covenant is primarily concerned with a special religious sense in Judaism and Christianity.

The second tablet was given to Israel that was the recipient of the covenant. Most receipts given in commerce have a minimum of two identical sheets, one being a copy of the original top copy and some receipts have three or more sheets according to the system being used.

The Ark of the Covenant (Hebrew= **Aron Ha-Berit**) in Judaism and Christianity was an ornate wooden chest of acacia wood, which was gold-plated inside and out. The lid was of solid gold on which were fixed two cherubim with outstretched wings the tips of which met in the middle. It had four golden rings through which two staves of acacia wood could be placed to carry it. In biblical times housed the two tablets of the Law given to Moses by God.

The Ark rested in the Holy of Holies inside the Tabernacle of the ancient Temple of Jerusalem and was only the high priest of the Israelites on Yom Kippur, the Day of Atonement. The Levites (priestly functionaries) carried the Ark with them during the wanderings of the Hebrews in the wilderness. Though later scholars, from the descriptions given think it would have been too heavy to actually carry. Following the conquest of Canaan, the Promised Land, the Ark resided at Shiloh and from time to time, it was carried into battle by the Israelites. It was taken to Jerusalem by King

David and eventually placed in the Temple by King Solomon but the final fate of the Ark is unknown.

The word 'covenant' — Latin *convenio*= 'to come together, meet together, assemble' — is an interesting word. However it is used, it usually is an agreement whereby a party or parties makes stipulations that binds another or others to perform, give to or do something for them. In Scripture, theology, etc., it is an engagement entered into between Jehovah and some other being or person. There are a vast number of passages in the *Old Testament* and a few in the *New Testament* that speak of covenants, too many to go into here but easy to find in Scripture, with many forms in the legal profession, the word has a long history.

Cain is sometimes identified by some with the serpent in the Garden of Eden. The *Bible* says he belongs to the evil one 'Not as Cain, who was of that wicked one and slew his brother.' 1.*John* 3:12. Tubal–Cain is a son of Lamech and Zillah and is described as 'an instructor of every artificer in brass and iron.' *Genesis* 4: 22. The name is of uncertain etymology and nothing more is recorded of him. Tubal's brother was Jubal–Cain the inventor of the lyre, flute, stringed and wind instruments. Josephus says of Jubal–Cain that 'he cultivated music.'

## MANNA OR THE 'BREAD OF ANGELS':

Manna is a remarkable substance that is found in *Numbers* 11:7–9 where we are told ' . . . there is nothing at all, beside this manna, before our eyes . . . and the manna was as coriander seed, and colour thereof as the colour of bdellium (silent 'b'). And the people went about, and gathered it, and ground it in mills, or beat it in a mortar, and baked it in pans, and made cakes of it: and the taste of it was as the taste of fresh oil. And when the dew fell upon the camp in the night, the manna fell upon it.'

Manna possessed a wonderful fragrance, but the manna that was given for consumption to the people on the Sabbath was a thousand times greater than this. Bdellium is the name of several trees and shrubs, chiefly the *balsamodendren* that yields a gum–resin similar to impure myrrh. Bdellium is the name of a gum that is regularly used as an ingredient of incense. An earlier work on incense is now being extended and revised and will be republished later.

In Hebrew folklore, manna was thought to come from heaven and was the food of Celestial Beings and with this, we are back into the realm of pre–Israelite paganism. In *Psalm* 78:23–25 we find 'Though he commanded the clouds from above, and opened the doors of heaven, And had rained down manna upon them to eat, And had given them of the corn of heaven. Man did eat angels food.'

We find the 'bread of angels' mentioned in *Apocryphal* works, for example the *Wisdom of Solomon* and later rabbinical lore that tells us manna took on the taste of the food enjoyed by the person that was eating it. Whatever was the preferred food of someone, manna took on that taste and saying further that it was 'agreeable to every taste.' In *Psalm* 105: 40, we are told 'The people asked, and he brought quails, And he satisfied them with the bread of heaven.'

This is reminiscent of the *Grail Feast* and the *Cauldron of Dagda*, known as *Undry*, one of the treasures of the *Tuatha de Danann*, a cauldron that 'leaves no one unsatisfied.' The important cauldrons in Celtic tradition were without doubt used at large feasts to supply food and drink and some of these cauldrons were said to have a capacity of between fourteen to seventeen gallons, which is remarkably large. In mythological tradition, they were often connected with other–world feasting and especially with rebirth and resurrection.

The above has parallels in classical works in the ambrosia and nectar that was the food of the gods. According to Hesiod and Aristotle 'honeydew' came directly from heaven, Columella was adamant that it sprang 'from the morning dew' and in the Finnish *Kavala* (Rune 15), a bee is instructed to bring it from heaven. Ambrosia was considered as the 'food of immortality' and in liquid form, it was nectar. In Celtic lore, some of the food or fairy food has been spoken of in much the same way, especially by those who undertook journeys to the Underworld.

Manna was the miraculous food that sustained the people of Israel during their forty years of wandering in the wilderness and those who followed Israel out of Egypt and mixed in the crowd were not the 'chosen people' and called 'the Intruders.' From the time of the Exodus from Egypt to their entering the land of Canaan, we are told 'They did eat manna, until they came unto the borders of the land of Canaan.' *Exodus* 16:35.

The main details concerning manna can be summarised from *Exodus* Chapter 16. Manna rained from heaven for forty years. When the dew fell during the night upon the camp, the manna fell upon it. When the dew had disappeared, it lay upon the surface of the ground as small as hoar–frost. (*Verse* 14). It resembled white coriander seed in appearance. It tasted as wafers made with honey and each took according to their eating habits. (*Verse* 31). It melted with the heat of the sun and had to be gathered in the early morning. (*Verse* 21). It was a substitute for bread (*Verse* 12). It was like coriander seed and the colour of bdellium, capable of being baked in pans, made into cakes and boiled. It was ground in mills or beaten with a mortar and tasted like oil. (*Numbers* 11:7). Any manna that had not been used by the morning stank and was corrupted with worms. (*Exodus* 16:20). On the day before the Sabbath, a double quantity was gathered because on the Sabbath, none fell at all. However, this manna kept until the Sabbath, it did not stink neither did it have worms. (*Verse* 23–29.) See also chapters in *Numbers*, *Deuteronomy* and *Joshua* among others.

Some say the word manna comes from the Hebrew *'man'* — an expression of surprise. It is said when the Israelites saw manna for the first time they cried out — 'what is it?' *Exodus* 16:15. Some scholars object to this saying this is not a Hebrew word but Aramaic. Modern commentators hold the word is from the Hebrew word *manan*= 'to allot,' which makes manna an 'allotment' or 'a gift,' or 'God's gift to his people' and there was undeniably an element of 'allotting or measurement' in its distribution, see below and the later tale of Moses.

A gold pot of manna was preserved in the sanctuary for it is written 'Take a pot, and put an omer full of manna therein, and lay it up before the Lord, to be kept for your generations.' *Exodus* 16:33. An 'omer' is a measure of capacity and used for apportioning the manna to each person. An omer represented one day's ration of manna said to be approximately five pints of dry weight by today's Imperial weight reckoning — whatever it is under the occupation of Brussels!

'And after the second veil, the tabernacle which was the Holiest of all; which had the golden censer, and the ark of the covenant overlaid round about with gold, wherein was the golden pot of manna, and Aaron's rod that budded, and the tables of the covenant; and over it the cherubims of glory shadowing the Mercy Seat; of which we cannot now speak of particularly.' *Hebrews*. 9:4.

The measure given to each individual for the day appears to be borne out by a legend of the time. Tradition tells us that a man complained to Moses that his neighbour had stolen his slave. The accused man insisted he had legally bought the slave and as a result, the slave was rightfully his property. Moses told them that he would resolve the matter in the morning. In the morning, the allotted manna found before each tent was measured and the measure for the slave was before the tent of the first man and the slave's original owner. This was proof the slave had not been sold, the thief was made to return the slave to the lawful owner and he was punished accordingly. *Midrash Agadah*.

Countless efforts have been made to explain the substance manna satisfactorily. The explanation that has gained the most credence was that the manna is the exudation of the Tamarisk tree, the *el–tarfah* of the Arabs — *tamarix mannifera*. This tree does produce a sweet–tasting fluid, due to the action of small insects and the fluid dropped to the ground where it formed small grains that disappear when the sun became hot. However, this tempting explanation does not fully satisfy the demands of the description of the 'Bread of Angels' in *Scripture*, which space limits, so briefly.

The production of the sweet–tasting liquid from the Tamarisk tree is uncertain and sometimes it does not produce any liquid at all. The manna of Moses was produced for a large number of people every day for forty years. The main harvest of the tamarisk is around the period of June or July, Moses started to support the people with manna in May and it was gathered all the year around, daily and without a break. The amount required to feed such a large number of people obviously far outstrips the production of the trees found there — then or now.

The 'manna' of the tree hangs on the tarfah twigs until it drops to the ground, while the Hebrew manna rained down from the heavens. Both melted in the heat of the sun but the tree 'manna' can be kept for months, while the manna of Moses bred worms and stank if kept more than a day. The product of the tamarisk tastes like honey, but the manna of Moses was like cake and honey. The 'manna' of the tree cannot be boiled, ground in mills, pounded in a mortar or made into cakes, while that of Moses could. The 'manna' of the tamarisk has none of the nutritious properties of a meal and although it was used with bread, it could not be used as a substitute for bread and the manna of Moses is said to have been used as a substitute for bread for forty years.

Rabbinical sources mention the 'bread of angels' and said with the restoration of the 'pot of manna' will come the arrival of the Messiah. Manna is mentioned in the *New Testament* in *John*, *Hebrews* and *Revelation*.

Manna is said to have served the purpose of teaching Israel of its total dependence on the Lord of the Covenant. 'And he humbled thee, and suffered thee to hunger, and fed thee with manna, which thou knewest not, neither did thy fathers know; that he might make thee know that man doth not live by bread only, but by every word that prodeedeth out of the mouth of the Lord, doth man live.' *Deuteronomy* 8:3 and 16.

In the *Bible* there are seven names used for heaven so natural it is often specified that there are seven heavens and these are *Vilon*, *Rakia*, *Shechakin*, *Zebul*, *Maon*, *Machon* and *Arboth*. The third heaven, *Shechakin* is the heaven where the millstones are located to grind manna for the righteous, it is said. 'he commanded the skies above and opened the doors of heaven (= *Shechakin*, the third heaven); and he rained down manna for them to eat. And had given them of the corn of heaven. Man did eat angels' food.' *Psalm* 78:23–25.

The first heaven *Vilon* comes from the Latin *Velum*= 'a curtain, a veil or cloth.' We are told the only purpose of this heaven was to cover the light of the sun during the night so that the stars and Moon that shine from the second heaven Rakia may be seen. Naturally, this veil or curtain was withdrawn again in the morning. In Arboth are found the Law, Justice and Charity, the Treasures of Life, Blessings and Peace, the Souls of the Righteous and the *Guph* — the souls that are as yet unborn and the dew that will revive the dead.

The above was thought to be echoed by Christ when he would not yield to the Devil's temptations, applying the word in its absolute sense. 'It is written, Man shall not live by bread alone, but by every word that proceedeth out of the mouth of God.' *Matthew* and *Luke* 4:4.

The Church of Pergamos is promised for 'him that overcometh.' He will be given 'to eat of the hidden manna, and will give him a white stone, and in the stone a new name written, which no man knoweth saving he that receiveth it.' *Revelation* 2:17. Hidden manna is sometimes thought of as the spiritual gifts of a triumphal church in its communion with Christ. Jesus spoke of himself as the 'true bread from heaven in *John* 6:32, and consequently manna is a Christian symbol for the

Eucharist. I think there is enough here to help the reader regarding the 'Bread of Angels' and to add to it if they wish

## TERAPHIM

At the beginning of this long chapter, we wrote about the classical spirits and it will help if you try to keep them in mind regarding the *Old Testament* icons called *teraphim*. This term is often translated in the *Old Testament* as 'household gods' though sometimes the term found used is 'familiar spirits' and for something to be 'familiar,' it has to be known in the first place.

Many nations brought images of the gods into the house and set them in the family shrine because they were believed to have the power of warding off evil spirits and some believe that the teraphim were in the house to pray to, encourage good luck, good health and good wealth, the main three wishes of people. Conceivably the teraphim was originally an idol that in later biblical times was regarded as or acted more like a charm or talisman with magical significance as suggested in *Zechariah* 10:2, quoted below.

To many the teraphim and their worship is proof of the original polytheism of the Israelites. The word is always plural and there was enough magical power being used at Pharaohs court from the staff of Aaron, whose 'greater' magic defeated the Egyptian magicians in what was, whatever you chose to call it, a duel of magic and magicians. We have already mentioned that gazing at the golden serpent, erected by Moses was done to be cured of the bites of the 'fiery serpents'

What is called 'sympathetic magic has always existed and strangely, in spite of our presumed sophistication over these naive earlier races, it is still going strong. The success or otherwise of this form of magic depends for the most part upon the association of ideas. The fundamental hypothesis is that to produce a result you usually had to imitate it. Therefore, to burn or otherwise injure anything belonging to a person is to affect its owner in a similar way. This is why many Schools in the past advised their students to dispose of personal and bodily material carefully for to burn hair, nail clippings or the like of a person was to burn them.

The likeness of someone could be mutilated, pierced with pins or nails to cause them pain and suffering. To destroy a portrait or a photograph was to bring devastation to that person. It is possible there has never been a period, up to the time of writing, in magic or divination that has not involved the conviction that spirits, more powerful and knowledgeable than we are, not only exist but they could be contacted by using appropriate means to assist us in our wishes, for good or ill.

Sympathetic magic is clearly shown in *Samuel* 6. When the Philistines took the Ark of God, they set it up in the temple of Dagon. In the morning they found Dagon had fallen on his face before the Ark. Briefly they were made to suffer, the land was covered with mice and the people afflicted with tumours or *emerodes*= an old form of the word 'haemorrhoids.' They resolved to sent the Ark back to the Israelites but, following the instructions of their priests, they fill the Ark with five golden images of the tumours and five of the mice.

By means of these, they clearly expected to be liberated of both their torment and their tormentors. The golden images of the evil were thought in some way to have the influence of getting rid of the thing that the images stood for. This practise has not died out even today, witness the models of various parts of the body that have been healed and crutches from the lame hanging in many places of worship in gratitude from the one who was restored to health, in particular at holy wells or trees.

We find the word 'teraphim' more in the Hebrew than in the Greek/English translation. As said 'teraphim' is plural in form and never seems to appear in the singular, although in 1.*Samuel* below, a single figure is used and described. The human form of the teraphim is inferred by Michah, see below and although teraphim were principally though to be small idols, some were obviously life size or Michah could not have placed a teraphim in David's bed to make it appear that David was still sleeping in it. Therefore, it has been suggested that some may have been more akin to life like mummies than crude wooden images.

The teraphim were also 'made' by Micah in *Judges* 17:5 where they are differentiated from 'a graven image and a molten image.' They were also asked or inquired of by King Nebuchadnezzar as in *Ezekiel* 2:21— 'He consulted with images.' In *Zechariah* 10:2, it is said 'For the idols have spoken vanity, and the diviners have seen to lie, and have told false dreams.' They are first mentioned by Laban in *Genesis* 3:30, calling them his gods he asks ' . . . yet wherefore hast thou stolen my gods?'

'Molten' is a term applied to images and other objects, which were fashioned by pouring fused or molten metal into a mould and this method was evidently used to make the Golden Calf, see *Exodus* 32:4. A graven image is also found under the word 'idol.' An idol is properly the visible representation of an object of worship, but the word is frequently used of the object of worship itself, whether visible or invisible. The are many kinds of idol and included in these are words descriptive of idols as with carved images, graven images, molten images and so forth, today idols are called after what they do, film, sport, singers and so on and we make enough of these to worship, 'heroes' and 'legends,' in enormous numbers every year.

Many early Christians thought idols were inhabited by devils and evil spirits, a view that may possibly have its source in *Corinthians* 10:20. 'That the idol is anything, or that which is offered in sacrifice to idols is anything? But I say, that the things which the Gentiles sacrifice, they sacrifice to devils, and not to God; and I would not that ye should have fellowship with devils . . . '

It seems evident from the texts of *Ezekiel* and *Zechariah*, that the teraphim were used for divination and they were used by Micah in his attempt to establish a new priesthood, see below and *Judges* 17:5. Whether the word 'teraphim' is translated as 'idol, idolatry or image' or sometimes not even translated, the passages containing the word show that it generally means a figure in human form or frequently an idol. One other thing to note is whenever the teraphim are mentioned they are as a rule associated with some form of religious use and neither the teraphim or how they were being used was spoken of with approval.

Regarding the Jewish Oracles, Maimonides tells us that the worshippers of the teraphim carved images, claiming that the light of the principal stars or planets permeated the teraphim through the angelic virtues and the regents of the stars and planets, so that they talked with them and were taught by them many useful things and arts. Seldenus said that 'the teraphim were built and composed after the position of certain planets.' Maimonides or Moses Ben Maimon (1135–1204) the Jewish philosopher is generally acknowledged to be the greatest of the Jewish sages, Talmudist and codifier of the Middle Ages. He wrote in both Hebrew and Arabic and his greatest work is the *Guide to the Perplexed* (1190).

The main versions of the *Talmud* are the Palestinian and the Babylonian versions that came from their Academies. There are differences in language between the two representing the two dialects of Aramaic, which are different. They do however overlap to a significant degree. The *Babylonian Talmud* includes more material than the *Palestinian Talmud* and to some commentators this makes the *Babylonian Talmud* the 'more significant.'

The teraphim may have been talismans that were kept in the family shrine — 'and Rachel had stolen the images that were her father's and hid them . . . Rachel had taken the images, and put them in the camel's furniture, and sat upon them.' *Genesis* 31:19. The theory of some commentators is that the teraphim may have some tribal or family significance. The family teraphim may have conferred on those who owned them the rights of inheritance among other things and this may be why they were jealously guarded.

Earlier writers think Rachel stole the teraphim simply to secure their good luck and protection. One fact is certain, when Rachel took the teraphim from her father Laban pursued her in great anger, so it was evident that he placed great value upon them and it may also show one thing more. The incidence of the teraphim shows that Rachael and her family had not completely cut themselves off from what would be termed today as heathendom or paganism, even though the teraphim had no countenance in *Genesis*.

We have mentioned that the teraphim are mentioned regarding Micah's attempt to establish a private priesthood, 'And the man Micah had a house of gods' (*Judges* 17:5) and when the Danites moved to Laish, they stole Micah's teraphim and ephod for oracular use. 'Do you know that there is in these houses an ephod, and teraphim . . . And these men went to Micah's house, and fetched the carved image, the ephod, and the teraphim, and the molten image.' *Judges* 8:14–20, 31.

We are told the ephod symbolizes the true religion and its priesthood. The ephod is the garment worn during religious services connected with the tabernacle or temple, which is connected to the Urim and Thummim, the sacred lots, which some believe were used to discover the will of God. 'And thou shalt make the robe of the ephod all of blue.' *Exodus* 28:32. We read 'like sortilege or divination by lot, which was a very common method of divining among the Arabs and Romans, some were of the opinion that the Urim and Thummim were simply two stones put into the pocket attached to the high priest's ephod. On them 'were written some such words as "yes" and "no" and whichever was taken out, the alternative word upon it was looked upon as the divine decision.' *Witton Jones* (1897).

Flavius Josephus, the Jewish historian, writes that divination by Urim and Thummim ended some time during 2 B.C. Others regard the teraphim as a symbol of idolatry into which they should not fall, because it could cause the ruin of their place of worship. This explanation seems odd because if something is 'idolatry' and against the tenets of your religion, why keep it, let alone use it?

*Hosea* 3: 4 seems to speak of the teraphim as inseparable from the office of religion. 'For the children of Israel shall abide many days without a prince (he *Prince of Israel* is the Archangel Michael), and without a sacrifice, and without an image, and without an ephod, and without teraphim.' In these lines, they appear to be given importance for something that was considered idolatrous, even at the time. Like the ephod the teraphim were consulted for divination and their domestic or private cultivation, not in public use may have accounted for their relative immunity.

Teraphim are usually thought of as small idols the kind placed on altars or special places in the house and the Greeks (initially) and the Romans had similar figures, possibly portable, made of wood draped with robes with their heads made of marble, clay or wax. The Sibylline books ordered them in 399 B.C in a Roman festival called the *Lectisternium*. Sacrifices being of the nature of feasts, the Greeks and Romans particularly in times of great distress, which is the reason for the solemnly inviting the gods to the feast. They placed images of the gods reclining on couches with tables and food before them as if they were partaking of the things that were being offered in sacrifice — a freewill offering.

The figures or *capita deorum* (= 'bundles of herbs) were laid on a *lectus* = 'a couch for reclining on at meals, an eating couch.' A table was set before them on which people placed a meal. Sometimes these banquets were given to the gods generally as 'festivals of prayer and thanksgiving,' which were called supplications, both friends and strangers were invited to come in to the open table, which was supplied the householder 'each according to their ability.'

Josiah attempted to rid the country of teraphim, mediums, divination and wizards but his reforms did not last very long, see 2 **Kings** 23:24. Fascinating though the subject is it is time now to leave it and return to our subject, even though we have far from exhausted this one.

## TETRAGRAMMATON

We have introduced the term Tetragrammaton and technically speaking any word of four letters is a 'tetragrammaton' but not the Tetragrammaton used in Cabbala or by Cabbalists because they apply this term only to the ineffable name of God — YHVH — translated by the English biblical translators as Jehovah. The four–letter name of God being revealed to Moses formed from the Hebrew, consonants *yod, hey, vau* and *hey* or y h w h, consequently YHVH in the common English rendering. Tetragrammaton is the Hebrew name of God reduced to four letters and it will help to discuss this a little to add to our knowledge. It comes from the four consonants that make one of the most important and highest names for God and the word we use for this four letter name, the Tetragrammaton comes from the Greek, *tetra*= 'four' *gramma*= 'a letter of the alphabet' so this words gives us 'four letters of the alphabet.'

Following the Exile, 6th Century B.C and especially from the 3rd century B.C onwards, Jews ceased to use the name Yahweh. Judaism became a universal religion through its proselytising in the Greco–Roman world, the more common noun *elohim*, meaning 'god' tended to replace Yahweh to make obvious the worldwide sovereignty of Israel's God over all others. Simultaneously, the divine name was increasingly thought of as being too sacred to be articulated. It was replaced vocally in the synagogue ritual by the Hebrew word *Adonai* (= 'My Lord') and this was translated as *Kyrios* (= 'Lord') in the *Septuagint*, the Greek version of the *Old Testament*.

It is used as a personal name of the God of Israel. God in Hebrew is *Elohim* and God Almighty is *El Shaddai*. In Rabbinical literature the Tetragrammaton is known as *Ha–Shem*= 'the Name' or *Shem Hamephorash* meaning both 'the special Name' or 'the explicit Name' spoken only by the High Priest of the Temple. The letters forming this special name are as said the Hebrew equivalent of the English letters Y, H, V and H, or YHVH, which is the usual English rendering that is usually translated as 'the Lord' following the Greek, *κυριος, kyrios*= 'having power or authority over, lord or master of  (**Latin**= 'dominus') the Gods, the head of the family.' *Κυριακος, Kyriakos*= 'of or for a lord or master: especially belonging to the Lord (Christ). The word *κυριος, kyrios* has been assumed to be where the Teutonic word *kirk, kirche*= *church* came from, but authorities question why this Greek word was adopted by Northern nations rather than the Latin *ecclesia* so it is as a rule thought unverified.

The Hebrew and older form that exists is J, H, V and H is based upon *yod* — 'y' being written as *jod* — 'j.' The YHVH is mainly given here because it will be the one the reader will usually will find — 'the one who is, that is, the absolute and unchangeable.' The name appears in the *Ten Words or Commandments* and JHVH is the name that the Jews were 'not to take in vain.' They regarded the name so holy they would not pronounce it, instead they would read/see the word and say Adonai= 'Lord.' In Hebrew text, there are three names of God prominent in use 1: *El*; 2: *Elohim* and 3: *JHVH* and it is thought that these to the early Christians may have suggested a Trinity.

It is common to articulate the name as Yahweh (pronounced= *Yarr*–wuh). Most translators give Yahweh as 'the LORD' and they often use capitals to distinguish the deity from the same word 'lord' when it is used for the earthly ranking. Jehovah was imperfectly translated from the Masoretic Hebrew text. The word consists of the consonants *JHVH* or *YHVH* combined with the vowels of a separate word that were spoken as *Adonai* (= 'Lord'). Hebrew originally was a written consonant script with the vowels being supplied by the reader. Much of the information given here comes as a direct result of the Jewish observance of never pronouncing the name as it is written but as *Adonai* — 'the Lord.' There is, however a tradition that the unique pronunciation was handed on by the Sages and Teachers to their disciples every so often — once or twice every seven years (*Kid.* 71*a*).

It is a matter of speculation what the original vowels may have been and the pronunciation has been lost. When in time the name YHVH became too sacred to be pronounced, the original vowels were forgotten. It is thought the name was originally spoken Jaweh or Yahwe that is usually spelled Yahweh in modern practice. This name is thought by some to be the verb *hawah* or *hajah*, meaning 'to be' and interpreters from the past, defining the word in an abstract meaning, suggesting 'He who is' or the 'I am,' which could associate it with *Exodus* 3:14. 'And God said unto Moses, I AM THAT I AM: and he said, Thus shalt thou say unto the children of Israel, I AM hath sent me unto you.'

The interpretation of texts such as *Exodus* 20:7, 'Thou shalt not take the name of the Lord thy God in vain,' and ' . . . the Iraelitish woman's son blasphemed the name of the Lord, and cursed.' *Leviticus* 24:11, the Divine name became judged too sacred for careless utterance and according to the *Mishna*, those who do so will have no portion in the 'World to Come.' Some of the names of God are descriptive of the actions of God according to Maimonides and this includes the title Adonai, which expresses the 'lordship of God' much as given earlier for 'Lord.'

The Mishna (Hebrew= 'repeated study/teaching') is given as the oldest authoritative post–biblical collection and codification of Jewish oral laws, systematically compiled by numerous scholars (called *tannaim*) over a period of about two centuries. The Mishna supplements the written or scriptural, laws found in the *Pentateuch*. It presents various interpretations of selective legal traditions preserved orally since at least the time of Ezra (c. 450 B.C.)

The meaning of the Tetragrammaton is not spoken or written for the reason that this Divine name gives a clear indication of the essence of God, 'this name has no derivation because no created thing is associated with Him.' The Tetragrammaton in Cabbala contains all the Sephiroth and their innumerable combinations of Divine manifestations and it is said these have magical power and anyone who know how to draw upon this power can work miracles.

It is said the scribes, when they read aloud substituted 'Lord' and wrote the vowel markings for 'Lord' into the consonant framework — JHVH — to remind future readers. Another suggestion is that the translators of the Hebrew, not realizing what the scribes had done or why, read the word as it was written. The Jewish historian and antiquarian Josephus belonged to a family of priests and in his *Antiquities* he is reluctant to talk about the *Tetragrammaton* in explicit terms. He writes 'Whereupon God declared to him (= Moses) His name, which had never been discovered to men before, concerning which it is not lawful for me to speak.' *Antiquities* II. Xii 4.

Non–Jews, particularly those of the Christian persuasion combined it with vowels, which were set under the consonant letters of Hebrew, including the *Tetragrammaton* and in error they were combined and constructed a new word form — *Jehovah* — which is an accepted word now and universally used, even though the name does not exist anywhere in the Hebrew tradition or language. Most biblical scholars today prefer to render it simply as YHWH or JHWH, which is nearer the original being without the vowels.

The evidence of the Greek Church fathers appears to give the forms *Jabe* and *Jao* as being traditional. There were also shortened Hebrew forms of the words with Jahu used in proper name. JAH is found in the *Psalms*, 'Extol him that rideth upon the heavens by his name JAH, and rejoice before him.' (68:4). There has been a great deal of speculation regarding the meaning of the name Yahweh. We can take some consolation that this speculation has been going on for a long time and has not been explained satisfactorily even now. Even in the *Bible* itself, as pointed out above in

105

*Exodus* 3.14, thought to have been written about the period 800 B.C. It is also shown that God had been known by other names by the ancestors of the Jews. God tells Moses he is Yahweh, but he came to Abraham, Isaac and Jacob as God Almighty (= *El Shaddai*) 'but by my name Yahweh I was not know to them.'

People sometimes concealed their names for a variety of reasons. Names become more potent when they are pronounced, for to the written name is added the power of vibration. Most names of things differ in different languages, yet even these names can gain power by acquaintance. There are natural names of vibration for things, to know the real name of a power gives you mastery over it and enables you to stir up that power or 'call it up.' For this reason great secrecy in the past among initiates was preserved regarding the real names of angels, archangels, powers, deities and the like.

Nations of the past always kept the names of their chief gods secret, especially the supreme god of the pantheon. They gave them a 'public' name because the name represents the essential character of a being whether divine or mundane, but not the secret name. The Romans used a practise known as *elicio* 1: 'to draw out, entice, to lure forth.' 2: 'To call forth, call down a god by religious rites, to raise, to conjure up a departed spirit by magic.' In conquest they would sent people ahead to find out the secret names of the gods of their enemies before any attack was made and they promised to build these gods a temple in Rome to give them honour and service if they would come over to them — no fools these ancient Romans.

Witness the scrawl or scribble on many of the letters you get today from the 'gods' of organizations, large or small. There is something written that they call a signature and it may well be their signature, but it could be anyone because it means nothing. With this type of letter I do not believe they want you to know who signed it, for that would give you the power to know them, find them, speak and write to them with all the resultant personal responsibility this would bring to the writer — the practise is not new so is there really anything new under the sun?

Jewish Law draws a reasonable distinction between wrongs that are done wilfully and those done involuntarily. However, no such allowances are made for profaning the heavenly Name because this was regarded as the most heinous of crimes and a sin against the relationship that existed between God, and Israel, for which there was no forgiveness. 'Whoever profanes the Name of Heaven in secret will suffer the penalty of it in public; and this, whether the heavenly Name be profaned unintentionally or in wilfulness.' *Aboth* iv.5.

A name is not just a convenient label in the manner that most use or think it is. It was regarded as indicative of the nature of the person or object to which it belonged. This is why such particular veneration and respect was attached to 'the special Name' even when used 'in secret.' It was common for parents to think carefully about the 'given name' of a child and these were seldom chosen at random. The 'family name' showed your family, tribe or clan, but careful thought went into the given name by especially choosing a name with regard to the qualities traditionally inherent in it that the parents hoped would be adopted by the child in the future.

A practise of the past was giving a 'middle' name that was not always used or even given out by being omitted or just the initial used. This is a remnant of a magical name representing the 'essence' of the individual and kept occult or secret so that sorcerers and their kind could not work their evil against the individual to attack them.

This is why I am repeating here some lines given earlier and taken from the section on the most powerful Angel Metatron: 'Behold, I send an Angel before thee, to keep thee in the way, and to bring thee into the place I have prepared. Beware of him, and obey his voice, provoke him not; for he will not pardon your transgressions; *for my name is in him*.' These words make this angel a very powerful angel and Metatron would be an obvious choice for this.'

Names are often mystical, mostly when given in works of this nature and many names are found given, in particular the names given to the Creator. Sometimes (just a thought among the other thoughts), I feel there could be hiding among all the names known, the one that may well be that special name, the chief name close in description to the Divine Essence and Power that the name really represents. Many deities are found with so many names and these often represent an attribute of that deity but — is it 'the most important name?'

If one could understand the Divine Essence sufficiently enough to grasp what this right name with its important vibration may be such knowledge could wield a potent spiritual awareness and control in the one who sought after and found it. Most nations, races have long believed and Occult Schools teach this, it has a long history. If the exact and proper name of spiritual entities and things could be found and used then it could wield a tremendous power — but this a concept that has to be properly taught, understood and most important of all — used — no wonder they hid it.

The *Shem Hamephorash* is 'the distinctive Name' and Cabbalistic expression for the Great Name, which is said (by some commentators) to have been enunciated by the High Priest in the Holy of Holies. It is also said that Jesus was accused by some Jews of having stolen this name from the Temple by using magical arts and of using it in the production of his miracles or magic.

As explained above, the four–letter name of Jehovah was secret and should not be used, spoken, communicated and as it cannot be spoken, then each has to work to discover what it is or hope it will be revealed to them for it is the greatest of all the Names. The greatest expansion of the permutations is considerable to expound it to its fullness and the greatest is expanded to 72 letters — the *Shem Hamephorash* — for each of these 72 angels or genii have qualities and offices that originate from the Creator.

The titles of these 72 angels are the Creators attributes, virtues and grace and as far as we are concerned, they act as the Vice Regents of the Creator and they are found distributed through time and seasons. Whether they are in their world or ours, they are forever looking inwards towards the source of their being.

Substitute words are not new. Masonic ritual tells us that the Master's Word was lost with the death of Hiram Abif. King Solomon and King Hiram saw eye–to–eye that a replacement should be used until the true one is revealed, the Pythagoreans possessed 'an ineffable Word' and many more examples could be added. We have already discussed above that for the Jews, Adonai is spoken as a substitute for the *Tetragrammaton*, incorrectly transliterated in the *Bible* as Jehovah, which should I believe always be pronounced as Adonai. The early Cabbalists were anxious to conceal the real Mystery name of the Eternal from the profane and the profaning. Ancient names were more often than not given as symbols or representations of the original if known.

The *Christian Apocalypse*: tells us: 'To him that overcometh will I give to eat of the hidden manna, and will give him a white stone, and in the stone a new name written, which no man knoweth saving he that receiveth it.' *Revelations* 2:17.

The 'white stone' is Latin — *Alba Petra* — the significance of this in a genuine initiation and confirms the purification of the adept–initiate. The granting a new name proclaims the adept–initiate is reborn through the Rites of Initiation and is therefore, new born to the old self. They would be given a new name, besides that of an adept–initiate. Obviously, no one knows the new name except the one who receives it. The foregoing by no means exhausts this fascinating and very deep subject but — it is too much to be undertaken here, but if it has made the subject known a little more then I feel it may have served some purpose.

# SHEKINAH

An important topic we must take into account in anything dealing with the angelic is the beautiful concept of the *Shekinah* and she has been designated 'an angel' from time to time and if she has not, she ought to be. Afterwards we will take up the subject of the *Bat Qol* because she is often found linked with the *Shekinah*.

The *Shekinah* is said by some commentators to be a transliteration of a Hebrew word, *shakhan* 'to dwell, that which dwells, the one who resides' or 'the bride of the Lord' or 'God dwelling in a particular place, a divine name wherever it is.' When you read the words 'to dwell' or 'dwelling' with regard to the *Shekinah* and although it is difficult to explain, try not to think only of a material space for the *Shekinah*. Maimonides tells us that the term 'dwelling' need not have a suggestion of physical space, but can be used in the sense of a durable relationship. Seek to visualize the *Shekinah* as attaching itself to a particular place or space, the 'attachment' can be either transitory or enduring because the *Shekinah* comes to exemplify Gods presence in the world. This is best expressed in 'And let them make me a sanctuary, that I may dwell (= *ve–shakhanti*) among them' as given in *Exodus* 25:8.

Further, the *Shekinah* could not only attach itself to places, but to people, their souls because she is often called this, their bodies, their homes and so on to which it gave a Divinity and its removal was a great loss and mourned. The *Shekinah* is a visible manifestation of God's glory or presence, a special light or 'created glory.' A favourite metaphor is to refer to the 'light' or shining' of the *Shekinah* as with 'May the Lord cause the light of His countenance to shine upon thee' in *Numbers* 6:25. As the Sun can light every corner of the earth with its light, so the *Shekinah* of God can make its presence felt everywhere.' *Sanh*. 39a.

The *Shekinah* is an emanation or a dwelling; referring both to the primordial celestial emanation and to the Sephiroth, collectively regarded as the cosmic Tree of Life. In Jewish religious and mystical thought, the *Cloud of Glory* or a veil that surrounds a spiritual or divine manifestation. In the Cabbala, *Shekinah* is used in a cosmic sense of the Creator or God's Glory — termed the Superior *Shekinah* — or the *First Splendour*, the Divine or Spiritual Essence that emanates from *Ayn Soph*, which it envelopes as a veil and from which originates the hierarchy of the Sephiroth. The inferior *Shekinah* is connected with the tenth or lowest Sephirah, Malkuth (= Kingdom or Dwelling), which is equivalent to the material or physical universe, as the vehicle or carrier of all the chains of command of the Sephiroth.

If we carry the idea a little further, we could say the *Shekinah* shrouds the human being and becomes their vital aura, the intermediary of all the higher principles. The *Shekinah* could be thought of as equivalent to the Holy Ghost in the Christian Trinity as it was with the early Christians whose Holy Spirit was feminine, just as Sophia was with the Gnostics.

When Moses came down from Sinai after forty days and nights, after the renewal of the covenant with the 'tablets of stone like unto the first.' We will pick the story up with ' ... when he came down from the mount, that Moses wist not that the skin of his face shone; and they were afraid to come nigh.' Further ' ... and the children of Israel saw the face of Moses that the skin of Moses' face shone: and Moses put a vail upon his face again, until he went in to speak with him.' *Exodus* 34:27–35. The *Shekinah* may have inspired the benedictions of the priest, the Lord told Moses to tell Aaron and his sons to bless the people and as given above, 'The Lord make His face to shine upon thee, and be gracious unto thee.' *Numbers* 6:25.

The word entered Christian theology from its use in the *Targums* and rabbinical literature. It describes the immanent presence in the physical world of the transcendent Deity. There is uncertainty regarding the precise time when the different *Targums* — 'translations' — as the

Babylonian versions of the *Old Testament* are generally called were composed in the sixth century after the Babylonian captivity. Hebrew was being replaced by Aramaic as the generally spoken language among the Jews, so it became necessary to explain the meaning of the readings from the Scriptures.

The *Targums* were translations of the *Scripture* from the Hebrew into other languages, especially Aramaic and were reasonably literal translations or paraphrase of portions of *Scripture* used in the synagogues of Palestine and Babylon. Only a small portion of the many *Targums* that were produced for oral use has survived, for obvious reasons. It is generally accepted that spoken interpretations were presented to the people before the written accounts came into being, much in the manner of myths that became legends when they were written down, spoken of elsewhere.

*Shekinah* is in almost continual use in the *Targums* as is the repeated phrase 'And I will dwell among the children of Israel.' *Exodus* 29:45. In the now respected *Targum Onkelos* the foregoing phrase is rendered as 'I will cause my *Shekinah* to dwell in the midst of the children of Israel and I will be their God.' We find in *Habakkuk* 2:20 'But the Lord is in his holy temple.' This is rendered in the *Targum* as 'Jehovah was pleased to cause His *Shekinah* to dwell' and I prefer the Targum version thinking it the better one, but this is personal and is given to show the point we are making. The well–known *Babylonian Targums* are *Onkelos* for the *Pentateuch* and *Pseudo–Jonathan* for the *Prophets*.

When the reader finds the words the '*Shekinah* rests' in or on, it can be taken to mean that 'God dwells.' Some believe the presence of the *Shekinah* is implied in the passage of *Matthew* 18:20. 'For where two or three are gathered in my name, there am I in the midst of them' or 'the *Shekinah* is in the midst of them.' In keeping with others, I repeat that I believe the expression to remember for the most part is that the *Shekinah* is taken as 'dwelling' and the 'dwelling' is granted, it is never commanded because it cannot be.

Although the word is not used in either *Testament*, I feel it is reasonable to say it clearly originates more from the *Old Testament* than the *New Testament*, especially in those passages that describes God as 'dwelling among' the people or 'resting' in a particular place. Adam's sin and the later sins of mankind were the cause of the *Shekinah* (= 'the Divine Presence') or the immanent aspect of God, being exiled to the lowest kingdom on the Tree of Life. The *Shekinah* was divorced from God in the final Sephirah, which is the tenth kingdom of Malkuth. The term '*Sephirah*' for the kingdoms or emanations is a common name for them, Sephirah is singular and Sephiroth is plural.

The word *Shekinah* is feminine, therefore, the Cabbala considers the *Shekinah* to be the female aspect of Divinity. It symbolically expresses the idea of the restoration of harmony as the reunion of the male and female aspects of the Divine. In *The Secret Doctrine of Israel*, A. E. Waite tells us 'she is the guide of man on earth and the womanhood which is part of him.' She has been given the title of 'the liberating angel' who delivers the soul in all ages. The *Shekinah* is 'ever near to man and never separated from the just.'

The *Shekinah* is held to be the 'outer garment' of the Torah — the 'Holy Law.' Many of the Jewish Rabbis think that the sins of the world were born when the *Shekinah* was exiled from her source and rightful place with God because she is considered his feminine aspect. A man must be like a bridegroom and court her gently and with great skill or she will fly away. She speaks to him unseen at first, as one hidden behind a curtain and to whatever understanding he has and encourages his insight and learning.

'If he is lucky, he will catch a glimpse of her so that he will know her face' — lucky man if this is so. Her earthly form is the mother with whom the father should lie on the Sabbath and from this coupling would come enough strength to sustain and bless the lives of the family until the Sabbath comes again. The *Shekinah* is a very beautiful concept therefore it is hard to explain and for those who do understand her, no explanation is necessary.

There are many examples regarding the *Shekinah* that could be chosen, 'And let them make me a sanctuary; that I may dwell among them.' *Exodus* 10:8 and this again gives an example of 'dwelling' among the people. God dwells in heaven primarily but he can also dwell on earth, in a place that has been specially prepared for him. This important principle is stressed in Part 2. The preparation of the *temenos* and inviting the angels to accept your work as a 'bridge' across that important but sometimes elusive middle ground will be addressed later.

In a more restricted use, the term is also applied to the *Shekinah Glory*. The first appearance of the *Shekinah* is when God led Israel from the bondage of Egypt. He protected them by a pillar of cloud and fire. (*Exodus* 13.) God appeared in the cloud over the atonement cover of the Ark. (*Exodus* 13 and 14.) This is the visible pillar of fire and smoke that dwelt in the midst of Israel at Sinai. 'And mount Sinai was altogether on a smoke, because the Lord descended upon it in fire: and the smoke thereof ascended as the smoke of a furnace, and the whole mount quaked greatly.' *Exodus* 19:18.

There is a reference to the *Shekinah* when Israel is guided through the wilderness in *Exodus* 40:35. The *Shekinah* appears to be lost for a while with the defeat of Israel, at the hands of the Philistines. The wife of Phineas named her son I'chabod (= 'inglorious' or 'the glory has departed'), which is why its use as an exclamation. He was born immediately after she heard the news that her father–in–law and husband had been slain and the Ark of God had been captured. 'And she said, the glory is departed from Israel: for the ark of God is taken.' 1 *Samuel* 4:22. The Glory returned when it filled the temple of Solomon once more. (1 *Kings* 8:10.) Ezekiel visualized its leaving the result of sin before the destruction of the temple. 'Then the glory of the Lord departed from off the threshold of the house, and stood over the cherubim.' (10:18.) Judaism confessed its absence from the second temple — see the *Bat Qol* below.

The *New Testament* naturally says that it reappeared in the Christ who ascended in a cloud of glory. 'And when he had spoken these things, while they beheld, he was taken up; and cloud received him out of their sight,' see *Acts* 1:9.

Perhaps the theophany most descriptive of this is when Moses finished the work of the Tabernacle. 'Then a cloud covered the tent of the congregation, and the glory of the Lord filled the tabernacle. And Moses was not able to enter into the tent of the congregation, because the cloud abode thereon, and the glory of the Lord filled the tabernacle . . . For the cloud of the Lord was upon the tabernacle by day, and fire was on it by night, in the sight of all the house of Israel, throughout all their journeys.' *Exodus* 40:34–38. The cloud, the Holy Spirit, covering the Tabernacle has been identified as either the *Shekinah* or the Angel Metatron.

Whenever or if the *Shekinah* or the Heavenly Presence appears it must be received bare–foot. Joshua was told to remove his sandals. 'And the captain of the Lord's host said unto Joshua, Loose thy shoe from off thy foot; for the place whereon thou standest is holy. And Joshua did so.' *Joshua* 5:15 and so it was that the priests ministered in the Temple barefoot.

Many times you can read that the 'Heavenly Presence rested over Israel' and often its connection with the west for 'by decree of heaven, the *Shekinah* dwelt in the west' often with regard to the western walls, ramparts and Temples of a city. The Heavenly Presence has never departed from the Western Wall of the Temple, 'there he stands behind our wall.' *Song of Songs* 2:9. The Western Wall is the only remaining wall of the Temple area and therefore has been revered by the Jews for many centuries as a most holy place. Statements are often made about such matters such as the Western Wall as *Aggadah*, which is that aspect of Judaism, especially the literature of the *Talmud*, that deals with non–legal topics or in later parlance legends and not *Halakhah*, the legal side of Judaism, Jewish rules, regulations and the Law.

Rabbinical sources use the term *Shekinah* more as a specific reference than these *Old Testament* examples. In the *Targums* the words 'Shekinah, the Word of God' and the 'Glory of God' are used as corresponding to each other. The word *Shekinah* became a comprehensive term for the presence of God in any form and it is used here as a designation for God or a part of him, as with his hand or face. Only in later rabbinical sources does the *Shekinah* become a separate entity created by God as an intermediary between Him and his Creation.

I feel there is little doubt that the divine presence of the *Shekinah* smoothes any potential progress or possibility of any intimate contact of God or the Lord with the world of human beings or individuals — if it is granted. It is a sign that God has stretched forth his hand downwards to the earth and anyone who thinks that such an extraordinary contact is theirs to command at their personal bidding will swiftly find 'the handwriting' on their wall — MENE, MENE, TEKEL UPHARSIN — and deservedly so.

Prayer and the study of the sacred is one of the foremost channels of an individual or individuals to becoming more receptive to the *Shekinah*. Transgressions have the inverse result of driving her away to a point of non–existence for the reason that in such an atmosphere for she can neither survive nor stay. The Rabbis instruct that 'whoever sins in secret, presses against the feet of the *Shekinah*.' *Kid.* 321a

The *New Testament* frequently alludes to the *Shekinah* in principle, although the term *Shekinah* as such is not used, God's presence in the *New Testament* is frequently associated with the 'light and glory.' There are many examples that start with 'and the glory of the Lord shone round them.' *Luke* 2:9. The *Gospel of John* tells us of the word made flesh, dwelling among men who beheld his glory. 'And the Word was made flesh, and dwelt among us, (and we beheld his glory, the glory as of the only begotten of the Father), full of grace and truth. (1:14), all of these models testify to the presence of God or an Angel of his Presence. .

There is an obvious allusion to the *Shekinah* used in the description of the theophanic cloud of the transfiguration narrative. 'While he yet spake, behold, a bright cloud overshadowed them: and behold a voice out of the cloud, which said, This is my beloved Son, in whom I am well pleased; hear ye him.' *Matthew* 17:5, an example of the *Bat Qol* making its presence known to those who where capable of hearing it.

Let us give two final examples. Paul identifies Christ as the *Shekinah*, 'For in him dwelleth all the fullness of the Godhead bodily.' *Colossians* 2:9. 'For God, who commanded that the light shine out of darkness, hath shined in our hearts, to give the light of knowledge of the glory of God in the face of Jesus Christ.' 2 *Corinthians* 4:6.

We draw the reader's attention to an explanation already mentioned of 'an appearance or manifestation of God,' a theophany, frequently referred to as the '*Shekinah* Glory.' Another example, like that of Moses and the tabernacle already given, is when 'the glory of God' filled the finished Temple of Solomon.

Later rabbinical literature (as said earlier) made the *Shekinah* a separate entity and 'an intermediary between God and man.' How would the *Shekinah* be recognized if it did appear? This question is easier to pose than answer but if the *Shekinah* did elect to appear and it is a rare occurrence, it is unmistakable, unforgettable and without any doubt — it is a light like no other. You would want it to come repeatedly, if it will. In attempting to describe such an occurrence, we do come upon the limitation of words wonderful though they are, regarding a few matters.

I would remind the reader of one of the descriptions of the *Shekinah* given at the beginning of this section — 'that which dwells.' These are excellent words to remember here. Try to imagine your room being 'coated' with light and lit by it, as if every surface, nook and cranny was luminescent from within itself and generating its own light. The room is filled with a light that does not appear to have any point of source and there are no deep shadows as when using a single or several light sources.

It is similar to what can be achieved with the finest indirect lighting reflected from the ceiling where the source cannot be directly seen though it can be easily discovered with the **Shekinah**, you cannot do this. The room becomes dull and very commonplace when the **Shekinah** leaves and the 'light visibly leaves or is withdrawn because it does not go out as when switched off.' The light becomes very ordinary and mundane once more and in occult literature, this may be the 'Celestial Light' of which some speak when they say it is a 'light that shimmers around certain mystical visions.'

This has a parallel story in classical literature of the birth of Dionysus, the son of the supreme god Zeus and his latest romantic conquest, Semele. The wife of Zeus, Hera tricked Semele to demand to see Zeus in his full divine glory and splendour. Hera knew that her husband had promised Semele he would grant all her wishes and against his better judgement, he granted her this wish, just as Hera had planned. Semele died as a result of her wish to see the glory and power of a light and radiance that was not earthly. Dionysus was saved by Hermes because Zeus opened his thigh placed the child inside and stitched the wound up until the child was born to start his adventures in the world.

Remember I did point out 'the limitation of words' but as said, words are all we have and we must do the best we can when such limitations arise as they must. If you do witness this materialization, you will know it without doubt because it cannot be mistaken for anything else and you will know. If you are this fortunate in this matter and try explaining what you have seen and experienced to another, especially when it lacks any form of physical counterpart.

## THE BAT QOL

Here we take up briefly another immanence of the Divine, the **Bat Qol** (**Bath Qol** and **Bath Kol** can all be found) — 'the Daughter of the Voice'— 'an echo.' This is the name given in the literature of the **Talmud** and Jewish mysticism to a communication from heaven.

The **Bat Qol** is another of the feminine aspects of the Divine frequently mentioned in conjunction with the **Shekinah** and she is sometimes designated as a Guardian Angel and she is another of the supernatural ways used of 'communicating the will of God directly to man.' This was especially so when the end of the Hebrew prophets had come. The Holy Spirit had come to a close for Israel and the **Bat Qol** is used in the Cabbala to signify the female side of the logos, the daughter of the primordial light, the **Shekinah** and she is equivalent to the Chinese Kuan–Yin and all the other gentle voices in other religions or philosophies. It also represents the wisdom that was received by initiates — often heard as a quiet, still voice that was hard to hear above clamour — this unique wisdom being the **Daughter of Universal Wisdom**. Do not forget the daemon of Socrates that guided him — 'A rose by any other name . . .' and this is extended a little below.

The **Bat Qol** in Rabbinic literature is used to represent the 'direct divine voice' and it differs from the **Holy Spirit** in that it can reveal itself to any individual or group, rather than exclusively to a small number of individuals or groups after extensive religious or occult instruction that can result in spiritual development.

There are many examples to choose from such as when Solomon had to arbitrate which woman was the true mother of the disputed child, the mother who would rather her child went to the wrong woman that it should be divided by the sword. Tradition holds that the **Bat Qol** announced to

112

Solomon that the woman who wanted to child to live was the mother of the child and 'they saw that the wisdom of God was in him.' 1 *Kings* 3:23–28

We find, in the difficult sphere of personification, as with the various terms used for God, **Shekinah** (= 'dwelling') when used as an abstract noun, that they are often used with vast latitude. Sometimes it is expressed as a radiant indication of the presence of God found in the concrete 'dwelling' such as the Tabernacle (= *mishkan*) — but the term is not restricted to this use and these things come when they will — whether we hear them is another matter.

We have already given the following example, 'And there came a voice from heaven saying, Thou are my beloved Son, in whom I am well pleased.' *Mark* 1:12. This could be described by the Rabbis as the **Bat Qol** speaking as the voice was regarded as divine and it announced the will of God.

Let us repeat some lines from earlier regarding the 'daemon' as they are appropriate here. Some very famous people in the Greek world had their personal *daemon* and it was regarded as their 'good guardian spirit.' Socrates used the name 'daemon' and he said that his daemon told the future to him and while it prevented him from doing wrong, it did not insist that he did what it said because the choice was always his. The daemon of Socrates stood for his higher and spiritual self and the voice of conscience or an instinct that guided the person to fulfil their destiny, later writers took it to personify inspiration. Had Socrates been a Hebrew, he would probably called it his **Bat Qol**.

The **Bat Qol** may have been a form of divination among the ancient Jews because, it is said, after appealing to the **Bat Qol** the first words uttered by her were regarded as prophetic. 'Everyday the **Bat Qol** goes forth from Mt. Sinai and makes a proclamation saying — 'Woe to creatures for contempt of the *Torah*, for whoever does not labour in the *Torah* is said to be under the divine censure.' The **Bat Qol** is the 'still small voice' of Christianity and she can, especially today, be drowned out by the noise she has to contend with and because of this we must listen very carefully or set some time aside for her.

A suggestion regarding the **Bat Qol** that I have used in the past to students may prove valid here. I simply pointed out that some of the greatest composers in the world only managed to write one Violin Concerto, some wrote a few, some many and a number of composers none because it is a very difficult medium of composition. When you see the vast number of string desks that make up a full symphony orchestra, perhaps the bulk of the orchestra. It must have been a complex format to write in such a way that the solo violin could be heard above the sounds of the other strings and not be drowned out because the instruments, particularly the violin section, which are so closely related in quality of sound to the soloist that they often accompanied.

I feel this case in point is similar to the **Bat Qol**, which is a small voice trying to be heard over so many other instruments of the same quality of voices in our lives which today seem to be getting even more raucous by the hour. At some parties, I have sometimes gone to the side or to the edge of the groups of people there because at times it does sound like a *Tower of Babel*. It would take great skill to hear 'a still small voice' under such circumstances. Greater skill to know that it was present and an even greater skill to hear what it was trying to say. This is not a criticism of parties, merely an example, though I must admit I have often pondered why noise and loud volume is so often associated with 'enjoying yourself.' I have a companion, often we sit and read, sometimes we say very little unless she or myself want to say something but it is so pleasant.

Prophecy ended with the prophets of the Second Temple. In its place there was the **Bat Qol** — a 'second voice.' A kind of Divine echo heard within the precincts of the temple or given in answer to questions or queries put to heaven by the Rabbis. As said earlier, I suppose the Christian equivalent, in the broad sense is the 'still small voice,' which was not heard in the wind, earthquake and fire by Elijah in 1 *Kings* 19. The 'inner voice' we are always being told to listen for when we are silent and personally, I feel there may be little between all of these apart from the words being used.

## THE GUPH

This is another word we have used in association with the angels and the angelic — so far. Each of the pieces we deal with is like the pieces of a jigsaw puzzle and when they are fitted together they will give us a more of the picture and the more we know, we hope the better will be our understanding — well that is the theory being attempted.

The *Guph* — sometimes *Guff* or *Guf* — is an interesting word and it belongs to a very fascinating concept. What follows is a short introduction to the material. Books dealing with the *Talmud* teach the pre–existence of souls as we have already mentioned the names of the seven heavens earlier in the chapter *Manna or the Bread of Angels*. The seventh heaven is *Aroboth* and in this heaven are stored 'the spirits and souls which have still to be united to bodies.'

There is a universal belief with respect to the *Guph* that the time of the Messiah cannot dawn until these unborn souls have had their appointed time on earth. The *Guph* is the storehouse where these unborn souls are stored in the celestial realms while waiting their time to don their 'coats of skin' or to inhabit a human body. It is said and we have mentioned it that these souls are very reluctant to do this and struggle hard to avoid it. In simple terms, the time of the Messiah or Son of David will not come to an end until all the souls that are stored in the *Guph* have been used up and the storehouse is empty. (*Jeb.*62a).

The soul is the spiritual driving force within the individual and it has the potential and power to raise the individual higher than the level of the animal kingdom or basic human existence. The soul can lift an individual up through ideals and insight, encouraging them to decide on good and to reject evil, preferring compassion to cruelty and indifference, hatred to love and all the obvious selections and pairing that can be made regarding such matters. Raising the person above the physical and the mundane, to heighten and free the power of the soul and all that this entails for its period in the physical body. Only a genuine consciousness of this precious gift enables the life to be influenced indirectly at first and finally directly by the Divine Will.

Some of these ideas are thought to explain the presence of the soul given to an individual upon conception before being sent to the corporeal because 'how can unsalted meat not go bad' for it cannot be preserved. It is possible that this is the fundamental meaning in *Job* 10:12 of 'Thou hast granted me life and favour, and thy visitation (= conception) hath preserved my spirit. And these things you hid in thine heart.'

Salt is regarded as special as we have said and there is a great deal in *Scripture* that mentions salt, symbolically and practical in both the *Old Testament* and the *New Testament*. Christ in *Mark* 9:49–50 tells us. 'For every one shall be salted with fire, and every sacrifice shall be salted with salt. Salt is good: but if the salt have lost his saltiness, wherewith will you season it: have salt in yourselves, and have peace one with another.'

The following was briefly introduced earlier but it also belongs here to enlarge this section so it has been abridged. A vast amount of Jewish literature hints at a belief of a reserve or storehouse of souls to be used for future creation. From the storehouse, these souls are obliged to enter the womb and the body of the child therein. The souls object and protest because the knowledge of their fate is known to them and mercifully wiped before physical birth so they know the uncertainty and risk of being born into human life — but to no avail.

God has created an abundance of souls that will occupy a human body one day. There is a storehouse — the **Guph** or **Treasure House in Heaven** — where these souls are drawn together, they remain in the **Guph** until the momentum arrives for them to go down to earth where they will be coupled with a body. Some myths tell us that the souls are hidden 'under the throne of the All–Father' and as said earlier, only when all of these souls — 'created at the Beginning of Time' — have been 'set upon the earth and left its body will the Redeemer be free from his incarnations on earth.'

Some of the souls sent to earth are commanded to occupy a human body as a punishment or as the termination of a right or privileges already gained and wasted. This was a trial for some souls and a chance to show their strength in adversity. In the struggle of the soul against the passions and instincts inherent in matter, the soul is given the opportunity to reveal its true worth. It exercises the divine gift of Free Will to remain faithful to its divine origins or alternatively — betray them and suffer the consequences. God tells us that 'He is pure, as is his abode as is the soul that I give to you.' He tells us that if you return the soul to Him in the same state of purity as when it was given, all well and good however, if it is not then 'I will destroy it before you.'

## THE MERKABAH MYSTERIES

The 'Merkabah mysteries' belongs to the mystical literature of the Jewish religion. It may require some account no matter how brief because it is generally acknowledged as being the earliest recognized form of Cabbalistic Literature. This material incorporates a great deal regarding angels and concerns. These works are concerned with the **Merkabah** or **Throne Chariot of God**. Merkabah was the name given by the prophet Ezekiel for the chariot that bore up 'enthroned man' in his meditation and ecstasy.

The tracts for this particular work are taken from what are called the **Hekhaloth Books**. These books include description of the heavenly palaces or halls (= **hekhaloth**) through which the seeker will have to pass on his way to the Merkabah. The most significant of these works are the **Greater** and **Lesser Hekhaloth**.

Merkabah mystics experienced ecstatic visions of the celestial hierarchies and the throne of God. In Merkabah mystical literature of the **Greater Hekahaloth**, the ascent of the visionary's soul is portrayed as a hazardous journey through seven spheres or 'heavenly dwellings' that are all protected by hostile angels. The visionary's goal was to behold the divine throne situated on its chariot.

These works contain lengthy descriptions of the secret names and seals that the seeker or initiate will have either with them or securely fixed in their mind and these can secured his safe passing through the heavenly halls. Every stage of his ascent requires a different seal and/or sacred name with which he confronts the demons of the new portal reached and attempting to enter.

Merkabah initiates were restricted to a select few with precise moral qualities and they were required to prepare themselves by fasting and other strict training. The study of the 'Throne Chariot of God' has a long history of fascination for some seekers. A successful visionary journey depended, in part, on the use of specific magical formulas called seals that were used to appease the angelic gatekeeper of each heavenly dwelling, usually in the form of a discussion. This all suggests the use of an experienced teacher or a specialist School of proven worth.

It is in this body of literature where the last stages of the mystic's upward journey (sometimes downward) are also summarized. There we find descriptions of what he may expect to come upon as he passes through the sixth and seventh gates of the halls. The majority of these descriptions are presented as discussions held between the gatekeeper of the hall and the mystical traveller. The literature of the Merkabah mystics is extensive but it was always a little difficult to find, very little was published or translated but this may have improved by now.

The term Merkabah means God's Throne Chariot and refers us to the chariot of Ezekiel's vision. The Merkabah mystic or the Merkabah Rider had only one aspiration, which is entry into the throne world of Merkabah, which is no simple task, having the need to pass through the seven *hekaloth* and heavens to reach the seventh and final hall. This is accounted as being one of the hardest and difficult tasks to undertake for 'throughout the entire experience the traveller was threatened with death' or to paraphrase the words in *Steppin' Wolf* — 'the price of a ticket is your mind.' The reward sought in all this was the ecstasy of seeing the vision of the Merkabah. This stems it is said from 'Man's need to witness or experience the Divine.'

Let us extend this and this could include some repetition in another form. From the Hebrew, *merkabah*= 'chariot.' The *Zohar* says the *Eyn Soph* makes use of the One, the manifested Heavenly Man, as its chariot but the *Eyn Soph* is the Boundless and as earlier writers have commented, it cannot come into individual relationship with anything. They thought it was a ray of the bythos (= 'depth') of *Eyn Soph* that used the manifested Heavenly Man as a chariot.

With the aid of ecstatic mysticism and making the Merkabah or Chariot the focal point of total meditation, it was held that these visionary mystics could rise through these series of heavenly halls. This study of truth may have some bearing on the title and philosophy of the seventh card of major arcana of the tarot — 'The Chariot' — because they had to find seven palaces and these were beyond the seven heavens, palaces or temples, which all had to be traversed. These were arranged as concentric circles with the Merkabah at their centre as the focal point, because the Merkabah is not only the chariot of God but his Throne. Set in front of the Throne of God is a curtain that protects the angels from the Divine Radiance of God. On this curtain is written the history of the world from Adam to the epoch of the Messiah.

The 'chariot' of Ezekiel was a medium by which the pious, the 'riders of the chariot' or the 'Merkabah riders' could rise to the Throne of God, from which rivers of fire flow and where a revelation was said to be vouchsafed them. The aim of the chariot rider was entry through the gates to these 'halls.' With seals, mysteries, prayers, the help of angels, magic and sometimes asceticism such as fasting, it was claimed that this objective could be accomplished. The human soul could be uplifted and realize unity with the Divine World Soul.

However, although the angelic gatekeepers that guard these heavens were not entirely antagonistic to those who sought this, neither were they cooperative to those who approach them because they were set there 'as barriers between God and man.' The term chariot is also used to refer to the visible planets as vehicles of the planetary deities, as with the chariot of Apollo or Phoebus. In the nine chariots of the stars around the pole star, even the human body is called the 'chariot' of the 'inner charioteer' who is the genuine being or true ego, the ego that is not turned inwards, but outwards.

*Ezekiel* in the *Bible* is a book filled with symbolism and divine allegories. St. Jerome calls the *Book of Ezekiel* 'a labyrinth of mysteries' and at one period, the Jews would not permit anyone to read the work who had not reached thirty years of age — the first astrological Saturn return in the birth chart — this is when a planet completes its cycle by returning to the position in the birth chart that it held when the individual was born so it is different for individuals according to their birthday.

In the *Apocalypse*, the angels are found riding in chariots 'and man can find a place with them' but only if he is chaste and for this he must conquer his temptations, which will arise as malignant spirits trying to stop him in his purpose. It is said that he can only master these malignant spirits with magical formulas, prayers and the help of the angels. The 'traveller' has to pass through seven palaces that lie beyond the seven heavens to reach or achieve a visionary experience of the Merkabah or the Throne of God. The mighty Angel Metatron himself is said to have his throne at the Gate of the Seventh Heaven.

The Angel Rikbiel YHWH is one of the prince's of the Merkabah angels for he is an angel appointed over the *Merkabah* (= the 'divine chariot or wheels.') The Angel Rikbiel is said to be set higher than Metatron as one of the 'great Crown Princes of heavenly judgement.' If we were able to get this far, we may possibly also meet the Angel Galgaliel an angel who governs 'the wheel of the sun.'

The Angel Galgaliel is the head of the order of Galgalim or 'spheres,' which is an order of angels held equal to the cherubim and equated with the Ophanim, which are called 'the wheels of the Merkabah.' There are the *Ophanim, the order of the Seraphim* and the holy *Chayyoth* (Hebrew= 'living creatures'), the ministering angels, the Throne of God, exalted and high that 'abide above in the clouds.' The foregoing may explain why so few genuinely reach such exalted heights and if they have, they remain silent about it for the most for there are probably few they can talk to. This may also be why they are so hard to find — finding the 'dreamers' about these regions is easy, they will usually find you or anyone else who will listen to them, which should ring warning bells.

Ophanim (later called galgallim) is from the Hebrew and it is thought to come from *ophan*= 'a wheel, to turn or revolve, the many eyed ones' and Enoch speaks of them as the 'ofanim of the fiery coals.' These are the 'wheels' seen by Ezekiel and by John in *Revelation*. They are employed in the *Sepher Yetsirah*= the *Book of Creation*. The *Ophanim/Ofanim* are shown turning the celestial bodies, particularly the planets and the angelic hosts that give the heavenly bodies their unique character and power, they have command over their movements in space and time. In the *Zohar* (ii 43a), the *Ophanim* comprise the *World of Yetzirah*.

*Hayyoth* (sometimes *Chayyoth*) means 'holy or heavenly beasts' and they are a class of Merkabah Angels and ranked with Cherubim, found in the seventh heaven as Angels of Fire. They support the Throne of Glory. Enoch tells us they are found by the River Chebar and there are only four *Hayyoth* in all but according to the *Zohar*, there are thirty–six and they hold up the universe. They are found in Ezekiel's mystic vision and play a major part in celestial regions as given by the Rabbis.

In Rabbinical circles, only specifically selected and highly trained disciples were permitted to engage in these exacting mystical disciplines also known as *Ma'aseh Merkabah* — 'Work of the Chariot' — and there are works that speak of these mysteries. They embody long descriptions that deal with the secret names, the seals and how to search out the necessary guardianship to protect the rider from the demons that would beset him and seek his destruction in his attempt to ascent — does this discourage you? I think it is meant to do just that.

As can be seen from this very brief description, you just do not to take a stroll to the *Merkabah* on a sudden impulse or because you u are bored and looking for something to do. This work is hard, long and involves long preparation working with special angels, the use of talismans and unique conjuration's, which were sometimes spontaneous in trance rather than using a fixed formula, ritual robes and even then results are still not guaranteed.

The 'perils of the soul,' which the adept could come upon during their ascent through the various hallowed spheres are described clearly enough in the ancient texts. If the initiate successfully ascended through the worlds, kingdoms and palaces, with its protective guardians they would arrive at the absolute world and if they were found to be deserving and having enough merit. They could finally stand in wonderment and trembling before the consummate and blinding vision of the Divine Splendour — which may explain why such true people are so thin on the ground or even in a century.

It is thought that many of the rituals of later Cabbalism may have had their origins in this early mysticism, so it follows as always that there are those who disagree with it all. Later Cabbalism concerned itself more with extended prayer and meditation rather than attempting a mystical ascent to God. The **Book of Enoch** could prove an excellent place for further information, as would **Ezekiel** 1:4–28. The esoteric teachings and practises of the **Merkabah** mystics have somewhat fallen into disuse, but as said some of the **Merkabah** traditions and documents have been absorbed into the Cabbala and can be found if you look for them and more **Merkabah** works are available than in the past.

The Merkabah chariot, regarded as a vehicle should be considered and make use of in two ways. Briefly, the first is naturally as the chariot it is. The Cabbalists make use of the ten Sephiroth as 'a chariot' for ascending and descending through the diverse worlds detailed in the Cabbala, these worlds are in point of fact the ten Sephiroth. 'Adam Qadmon' or the 'Heavenly Man' is identical with the ten Sephiroth therefore, he is deemed an entity infused the spirit of the Divine Hierarchy or the Supreme.

Secondly, **Merkabah** is the secret wisdom or knowledge about which we are told 'without the final initiation into the **Merkabah** the study of the Cabbala will always be incomplete.' **Merkabah** can only be taught in 'darkness, in a deserted place, and after many and significant trials.' Past commentators tell us that **Merkabah** is given out only as a mystery and was communicated to the candidate orally — 'face to face and mouth to ear' — an old way of doing things when things were done through Teachers and Arcane Schools. The Secret Wisdom or Knowledge is regarded as being a 'chariot because what people call the Esoteric Wisdom is the medium that is used for the communication to human consciousness of the mysteries of the universe and subsequently to the individual.' These comments are not intended to discourage anyone regarding this particular matter. If this short foray into the subject has reinforced earlier comments that this is not a subject to be taken up by someone because they are bored or have some time to spare, a favourite phrase — then that may be all to the good!

## SATAN/THE DEVIL/ANGEL SAMMAEL

In the **Bible**, the life of Satan is given roughly from his original creation, to his disobedience and his eventual destruction, which is clearly foretold. If we took all this as read, we would have only touched upon the matter here, there would be little to write about regarding this fascinating angel for angel he is, simply because his story has already been written, its path is set and the end is foretold.

Broadly speaking the story is set out as follows. Satan is an angelic creation who, before the creation of the human race, rebelled against the Creator and became the antagonist 'against God and man.' Satan, as previously pointed out is a Hebrew term meaning 'adversary or accuser' and he was for the most part unknown to Hebrew thought before the **Babylonian Exile**. The concept of Satan made its way into post–exile literature as a product of **Zoroastrianism**, becoming an opponent of God. Satan came into eminence more with **New Testament** writing.

We are told that Satan was 'full of wisdom and perfect in beauty. Thou hast been in Eden the garden of God . . . thou art the cherub that covereth and I have set thee so; thou wast upon the holy mountain of God; thou hast walked up and down in the midst of the stones of fire. Thou wast perfect in thy ways from the day that thou was created, till iniquity was found in thee . . . they have filled the midst of thee with violence, and thou hast sinned: therefore I will cast thee as profane out of the mountain of God: and I will destroy thee, O covering cherub, from the midst of the stones of fire . . . thine heart was lifted up because of thy beauty, thou hast corrupted they wisdom by reason of thy brightness: I will cast thee to the ground . . . etc.' *Ezekiel* 28:12–15. 'How are thou fallen from heaven, O Lucifer, son of the morning! How art thou cut down to the ground, which didst weaken the nations! For thou hast said in thine heart, I will ascend into heaven, I will exalt my throne above the stars of God . . . etc. *Isaiah* 14:12. This gives a some idea of the splendour and elevation of Satan before he fell from his high station.

We are shown him drawing to his cause a great multitude, perhaps about 'a third' of lesser celestial creations as in *Revelation* 12:4, to become the 'Tempter' or the 'Evil One.' The fallen angels or demons fit into two general classes — those who are 'free' and those that 'are bound.' The former roam with their prince and leader as in *Matthew* 12:24. 'The Pharisees heard it, they said, this fellow doth not cast out devils, but by Beelzebub the prince of the devils.'

The angels or demons that are bound are obviously guilty of even greater wickedness because they are confined in Tartarus as in 2 *Peter* 2:4. 'God spared not the angels that sinned, but cast them down into hell (= *Tartarus*), and delivered them into chains of darkness, to be reserved unto judgement.'

In *Genesis* 3, the Fall of Satan condemned the people of the world to his wiles and his judgement was forewarned in Eden when he was cursed for it (v. 15) and this judgement was accomplished at the Cross and Satan continues to reign as usurper, ' . . . if our gospel be hid, it is hid to them that are lost.' 2 *Corinthians* 4:4. Satan continues to tempt people and accuse them but he is to be expelled from heaven ' . . . and the great dragon was cast out, that old serpent, called the Devil, and Satan, which deceiveth the whole world: he was cast out into the earth, and his angels were cast out with him. *Revelation* 12:10. Satan is to be confined to the abyss for one thousand year and, he will make one last attempt to lead his armies against God. 'And when the thousand years are expired, Satan shall be loosed out of prison, and shall go out to deceive the nations, which are in the four quarters of the earth, Gog and Magog, to gather them together to battle: the number of whom is as the sand of the sea. *Revelation* 20:8.

The result of which will be his final doom because ' . . . the devil that deceived them was cast into the lake of fire and brimstone, where the beast and the false prophets are, and shall be tormented day and night for ever and ever.' *Revelation* 20:10. Of course, more than one thousand years has passed for Satan to be 'loosed' out of prison, perhaps he already has seeing what is going on in the world for as said, we are in the second millennium now.

Satan's present work is widespread and destructive and it is said that God permits this evil activity for the time being and all demons must do the bidding of Satan. The unsaved are largely under Satan's authority and he rules them through the evil system of the world over which he is the head and of the unregenerate are a part and Satan is in continual conflict with them, seeking to tempt them to corrupt and destroy their lives.

Gog and Magog are mentioned only twice in the *Bible*, several times in *Ezekiel* in Chapters 38 and 39 but once only in *Revelation*. The first mention is in the opening *Ezekiel* 38. This makes Gog an individual and a prince of Meshec and Tubal, who ruled over the land of Magog that was situated distant from Palestine. However, it was said that the inhabitants of this land would attack Jerusalem in a final effort to cause the downfall of God's people and Ezekiel is told to tell Gog of the overwhelming defeat God has planned to inflict on him and his people. The last reference is to 'Gog and Magog' in *Revelation* that was given earlier. Attempts to identify Gog and Magog to an historical ruler have not met with much success and what is found has usually been regarded as unconvincing.

In *Revelation* they are coupled with Satan and previously with 'the godless nations.' Satan here is going to immobilize Gog and Magog (= the nations of the world) against God, his angels and saints for 'the final conflict.' 'For I will gather all nations against Jerusalem to battle . . . then shall the Lord go forth, and fight against those nations . . . etc.' (cf. *Zechariah* 14). In one instance it is a physical attack on Jerusalem by the forces of hostility while symbolically, it is occasionally thought of as the 'final conflict between good and evil.' In *Revelation* they are thought two powers under Satan and in later literature they were personified as two conventional figures that are opposed to the people of God and the latter is mainly as people know them, two giants of medieval legend and this is how we will close this short discussion.

Gog and Magog are the remnants of an unnatural alliance that produced a race of giants. They were captured and brought to London in chains. They were brought to a palace that stood on a site that would be where the Guildhall will stand and in this palace where they had the duties of porters. I believe that this is in part the narrative of Caxton, some dispute it but it is thought that the Guildhall had their effigies of Gog and Magog in the time of Henry VIII.

Bishop Hall in his *Satires* 1597–8, speaks of the old figures as then in their places in the Guildhall. Stow mentions the older figures as representation of a Briton and a Saxon. In earlier times it was often said 'they represent the ancient British giants' Gog and Magog. The original effigies were destroyed in the 1939–45 War and they were replaced in 1940 but we are told that these fourteen foot plus figures are no match for the originals whose lances alone 'weighed around one half of a ton.'

Brewer says it was the Great Fire that destroyed the original effigies that were carved again in 1708 by Richard Sanders. Children were told the story that when these giants hear the clock on St Paul's strike twelve, they would come down from their pedestals and go into the hall for their dinner. One thing that is certain is that their mystery is not completely solved even today or here. Now we must get back to the true subject of this chapter as the foregoing is only here by association.

It is hard, in fact well nigh impossible to separate the *Old Testament* and the *New Testament* at times especially when dealing with the *Bible* and this is the case now that we have come to that very absorbing entity known as Satan in the *Old Testament* and the Devil of the *New Testament*.

The 'fallen angel' identified as Satan could take a fair size book of his own and then some more and in all probability, he would merit it. However, we can only take some of the most important points here regarding this, for the most part, interesting angel for angel he was or still is and he plays a significant role in any work of this nature where the angels are concerned.

I wrote of him in an earlier work on *Pan, Great God of Nature* already mentioned. I cannot, however, assume that the reader has read the other work. Therefore, we will take some of the salient points regarding this intriguing angel with some additions. He is an angel as many indirect references show.

The first thing we must again draw attention to is that angel known as Sammael, a name that is often given to Satan, is not to be confused with the Angel Samael, the angel of Mars as we have said throughout, because they are two separate angels and not one and the same. Though pronounced the same the former name contains a double 'm' while the latter has only one in the name and the Angel Samael is given in greater detail in Part Two. Satan, as said elsewhere, is identified with the devil (= *diabolos*) and the term 'devil' occurs more frequently in the *New Testament* than the name Satan does. In the *Koran*, I believe the proper name *shaitan* (= 'Satan') is used

We spoke earlier at length of the Greek *Agathodaemon*, the good genius to whom at Athens a cup of pure wine was drunk at dinner. In one of his many forms he is given as the cosmic Christos, the serpent of eternity and this in the human mind becomes the serpent of *Genesis*. After the fall of Mediterranean civilizations, he was converted into the Christian Satan and Satan has as many sources as sins — they are endless.

The Angel Sammael, in Hebrew and Chaldean is the Prince of Darkness, the Angel of Death or called 'Poison.' Sammael is alleged to be the prince of the lowest world of *Qliphoth* (= shells), which is divided into ten degrees producing the lowest hierarchy of the Cabbalistic system corresponding to the ten Sephiroth.

The Talmud states, on the other hand, that 'the evil Spirit, Satan, and Sammael the Angel of Death, are the same' (*Rabba Batra, 16a*). In addition, the Angel Sammael corresponds to the biblical serpent of the *Tree of Knowledge of Good and Evil*. He is also termed the chief of the *Dragons of Evil* and he is generally thought to be responsible for the hot scorching wind of the desert known as the *simoom* or *simoon*. In Arabic, its name is the *samum*= 'a sultry, pestilential wind which destroys travellers,' coming from *samma*= 'he poisoned' or *samus*= 'poisoning' as it darkens the air with the sand it raises. In Algiers and Italy it is called the *Sirocco*, in Egypt the *Kamsin* and in Turkey the *Samiel*.

As with many (or all) the cosmic forces or energies, the Angel Sammael is dual possessing in his highest aspects divine attributes, in his lower aspects possessing material or infernal elements. The same duality is present in human nature. In conjunction with Lilith, Sammael is represented as 'the Evil Beast' as her entry shows.

In many of the old myths, Satan under a variety of names often appears as the benefactor of mankind. Prometheus, Venus-Lucifer and the Serpent of Genesis all took something, usually without permission and passed it on to those below as many myths and legends attest. Christian theology either through misinterpretation or misunderstanding of the keys to its own holy writings has perverted many symbols into something that they were not intended to be. The Serpent of Eden was not the Devil, neither was sex the sin of the human race, nevertheless abuse of spiritual, intellectual and psychic power was.

Judas Iscariot, the disciple of Christ betrayed him and later committed suicide. He was a form of Adversary or Satan being the polar opposite of what is most sacrosanct. His treachery therefore is the discharge of his function and his reason for being in the tale, even though the character has become a narrative of betrayal and crime. There is an old mystical axiom that 'every Saviour has his Judas' every Messiah his Adversary. In fairytales, these are often twins, one is evil, the other is good and a plot of mistaken identity, while good and evil fight the good fight is a frequent theme.

The rebellious angels are said to have been swayed by pride with some thinking they were as great and powerful as the Creator. In their rebellion and later Fall they took down with them several of their companions. At their head was the one who is known as the Angel Sammael or Satan. He was first among the seraphim and one of the peerless of the created beings. A terrible war ensued that became the 'War in Heaven.' The host of Sammael was opposed by the angels led by the Archangel Michael who finally defeated Sammael, Satan or the old dragon/serpent.

The jealousy of Sammael knew no bounds and he was particularly irritated by the favours heaped upon the first created man. He refused to give Adam either homage or worship and plotted with other angels to bring about Adam's downfall. Sammael was held to be responsible for encouraging the original sin that brought about the expulsion of Adam and Eve from the Garden of Eden. We have already spoken of his connection with Lilith who is held to be Adam's first wife, but that was less than successful.

For his sin of disobedience, Sammael was driven out of Heaven but he did not leave without a struggle. This resulted in the **War in Heaven** where Sammael attempted to take the Archangel Michael down with him when he fell by holding on to Michael's wings. God saved Michael and from this event Michael was given the name **Plethi** = 'the rescued.' The **War in Heaven** resulted in one third of the stars or the heavenly host falling. A third part of the trees, sea life, rivers, sun, moon, stars and the like was destroyed or died when the trumpets of the Seven Angels sounded in **Revelation**.

When Satan fell, we are told it was to assume autonomy from God. 'And there was a war in heaven: Michael and his angels fought against the dragon; and the dragon fought and his angels, and prevailed not; neither was their place found any more in heaven . . . he (= Satan) was cast out into the earth and his angels were cast out with him.' **Revelation** 12:7–10. It does make me wonder why God sent Satan here to earth. Why did he not simply destroy him for disobedience as others have been destroyed for less? Satan has been developed from the authorized tempter of Job who works with God to Paul's 'false apostles, deceitful workers transforming themselves into apostles of Christ,' with Satan changing himself 'into an angel of Light.' Satan in **Job** and **Chronicles** is simply 'the Accuser' and an agency of God's will, but under Persian sway he begins to assume an importance that almost rivals God.

With the fall of this band of angel's we find death, envy, malice, pride and a multitude of other sins, coming into the world. God makes use of Sammael or Satan to test good men, chastise the bad and in this way, the Free Will divinely given to man is tried and tested. The human race knew the difference between good and evil, the result of eating the fruit and now they could choose. When Sammael is successful, he appears before the heavenly tribunal as prosecutor. For most of the inhabitants of the earth it is lucky God restrained him and set a limit to his power.

The name of Sammael is said to be derived from **sam**= 'poison' and **el**= 'of god or Divine' — the 'venom of God.' Another suggestion is that the name comes from the word **simme**= 'to blind or deceive' or **semol**= 'left,' because 'he stands on the left side of men' and it is the left ear into which he whispers. Sammael is thought to be identical with the Angel of Death. Rabbinical legend has the beautiful Sammael as the father of Cain but not Adam. Sammael seduced Eve and the child she bore, Cain, was unlike any other child of the earth. Cain is another fascinating and misunderstood mystery that needs unravelling one day.

Most Christians are warned to on their guard against Satan who is 'the prince of the power of air that now worketh in the children of disobedience.' **Ephesians** 2:2. Further, if Satan is of the 'power of air' then he should have little trouble with speech or communication and he will be very 'subtil.' However, the Hebrew word, **ha–satan**= 'adversary' represents **any adversary**, but when it is used as a title or proper name it has the article prefixed — 'the adversary.'

When the name Satan is written in the Hebrew without the article it could be disputed if it is the 'enemy of souls' that is meant. We meet the word Satan some thirty times in the **New Testament**, where the word is interchangeable with **diabolos**= 'devil,' a word that primarily has the meaning of 'a slanderer or accuser' and there is little doubt that Scripture recognizes the Devil or Satan as a distinct personality.

The Hebrew word **shed** is thought to be a 'loan word' from the Babylonian for 'demon and it has been designated the 'deities of foreign people degraded into the position of demons.' Therefore, we find 'they sacrificed unto devils, not to God; to gods whom they know not.' **Deuteronomy** 32:17 and 'Yea, they sacrificed their sons and their daughters unto devils.' **Psalm** 106:37.

We have mentioned elsewhere the Black Moon Lilith, the blood sucking night–hag of **Isaiah**. In folklore, she is **Lilatu** or **Ardat–lili** and she is a nocturnal demon of Babylon whose existence continued as Lilith. She is sometimes found in astrological charts being used by some astrologers and she is a seductress and shows the House in the chart where temptation can show itself because she is the temptress who is out to upset the *status quo*. She is equivalent to the vampire and in rabbinical literature Lilith was the first wife of Adam but leaves him to become a demon and to spawn others like herself. She is also the Sumerian 'goddess of desolation.'

The *Book of the Secrets of Enoch* identifies Satan with the Serpent. It describes his revolt against God and his expulsion from heaven. This work is an apocryphal book that was translated around the 10th or 11th century from the Greek into the Slavonic. It tells of Enoch's rise and his passage through the seven heavens and his homecoming. It incorporates his address to his son and tells us of his next ascent.

In the *Jewish Targums*, Sammael (= in later Judaism, Satan) 'the highest angel that stands before God's throne, caused the serpent to seduce the woman' and the birth of Cain is attributed to a coupling of Satan (= Sammael) and Eve. The *Book of Enoch* represents Satan as the ruler of a rival kingdom of evil and his servants have three main duties — to tempt, to accuse and to punish. Irenaeus ascribes Satan's fall to 'pride and arrogance and envy of God's creation.' However, it should be remembered that history is usually written by the 'winners,' we rarely hear what the 'losers' have to say in the matter either in the past or now if it comes to that.

Some have questioned there was the Fall of the Angels, what follows may involve some repetition, we are left in little doubt about the matter in 'And the angels which kept not their first estate, but left their own habitation, he hath reserved in everlasting chains under darkness unto the judgement of the great day.' *Jude*.6. The existence of the powers of evil is not doubted in 'For we wrestle not against flesh and blood, but against principalities, against the powers, against the rulers of darkness of this world, against spiritual wickedness in high places.' *Ephesians* 6:12.

It is not the first time we have said there is still a great deal about the angels we do not know. Neither must we forget there are ranks above them about which we know even less. Many believe there is a real kingdom of evil that is a grotesque parody of the angelic kingdom. Naturally, according to the *Bible*, this kingdom and its master will be defeated (*Colossians* 2:15) and finally condemned. (*Matthew* 25:41.)

The old Hebrews had no such devil as the Christian Devil though the word Satan is nearly always used in the ordinary sense of 'adversary or tester.' In *Job*, Satan is an emissary of God, one of his sons, charged with a mission to test the people of the earth. The original Hebrew God is supreme, author of both good and evil. Nevertheless, with the later Hebrews, the idea underwent modification and the notion of an evil deity arose, possibly from an adoption of Persian dualism acquired during the captivity. At the time when the Gospels were written, it is evident that the idea of a prince of darkness was very real and ever–present, though the story of the temptation of Jesus is evidently a picture of the triumph of an initiate over the forces of terrestrial nature.

After the Jews became acquainted with the presence of this great and malignant entity Satan, they began to identify all physical and moral evils with him and he was in some cases identified with the god Pan, who was in form at least ready made and perfect for the task he was to be given or represent in form. This entity is thought to have been Ahriman or Angra Mainyu or 'evil spirit,' the corruptor, the disturber of order in the cosmos, the corruptor of the mind. The personification of the evil spirit in the world, the chthonic god of darkness or the Evil Principle. He is the antagonist of Ahura Mazda the god of light who was an object of worship, the antagonism between these two entities was central to the teachings and Zoroaster, who said that the world was a theatre of war, stressed the necessity of choosing between the two and the moral obligation of cooperating with the forces of good to vanquish evil.

Between the New Year and the *Day of Atonement*, Satan was particularly active, enticing the Israelites during the 'days of penitence' when they are asking God to grant them forgiveness for their sins. However, on the **Day of Atonement** Satan is powerless to do anything against them and sound of the shofar (= the ram's horn) 'confounds Satan.' The letters of **Ha–Satan** (= 'the Satan') has a numerical value of three hundred and sixty–four. This number explains that for three hundred and sixty–four days of the year Satan has the power to be in opposition to them, but on the **Day of Atonement**, he is powerless because it is the three hundredth and sixty–fifth day.

In the account of the Fall in the Garden, we meet a mysterious agent of evil called 'the serpent' that creates more questions than answers and this makes it even more fascinating. It is a ridiculous conclusion to suppose this was a conventional serpent and the sort of reptile that we know because for one thing it had the power of speech that equalled Adam himself. It was endowed with reason and wisdom that was perceptibly superior to Adam. It is strange that Adam's ruin was effected by one the 'beasts of the field' that he had just named. The narrator of the tale also assumes that Adam and Eve possessed the faculty of speech because Adam used it to name all the beasts and birds, so obviously there was also reasoning.

In the **Apocryphal Book of Adam and Eve**, the Angel Joel instructs Adam to name all the creatures of the earth, though in **Genesis** 2:19–20 it is God himself that gives the task to Adam and it was Joel that 'allotted our first parents a seventh part of the earthly paradise.' The **Book of Adam and Eve**, although in Greek, Latin and Slavonic versions is thought most likely to have come from Hebrew or Aramaic originally. It tells the lives of Adam and Eve after their expulsion from the Garden of Eden and deals with their repentance, death and the promise of resurrection. The later Jews, however, supposed before the Fall, that the animals could speak and they had all one language. (**Jubilees** 3:28; **Antiquities**, Josephus).

The serpent appears to possess a obvious malice towards God and the cause of this is unknown because it is not recorded that I know, though there are hints to be found. It is strange why the 'serpent' was permitted to work its wiles in the Garden of Eden and was allowed to engage in its 'evil' because I feel, to an all–knowing God, surely the outcome of the incident was without any doubt predictable. May we infer that the temptation was meant to happen perhaps an early test for God's new creations? If it was, then there should be no condemnation of the event or the outcome, for the outcome was the chance being taken with the testing if Free Will was involved.

Another curious aspect of the story is that God condemns and curses the serpent saying 'upon thy belly thou go, and dust thou shall eat all the days of thy life.' **Genesis** 3:14–15. If the serpent was a normal serpent surely, it was already crawling on its belly, so it was not much of a curse or a punishment for what it had done, yet this curse is said to be why serpents crawl on their belly. I would be the first to agree that this 'serpent' was far removed from being able to be called 'normal' so this poses the question what form did it take before the curse was pronounced.

The wording of the curse seems to suggest that whatever was 'cursed' was standing on its feet or at least upright at the time and not crawling around on its belly so perhaps it was not even a serpent but regarded as such because of its actions. As said, if it was a serpent, the curse would not have been a punishment or cause 'the serpent' actual inconvenience, which is what curses are supposed to do. As already said it obviously had the power of speech, not usually given to 'normal' serpents — 'and he said unto the woman' and 'now the serpent was more 'subtil' than any beast of the field which the Lord God had made' and this makes it superior even to them and the Lord God made it — but for what purpose?

'And the woman said unto the serpent,' so the serpent could hear and understand what was being said so they were obviously speaking the same language. The serpent could reason or knew more than Adam and Eve because it told the woman that if you eat the fruit you will not die but 'ye shall be as gods, knowing good and evil . . . and a tree to be desired to make one wise.' **Genesis**

3:1–6 and it was something they did not know. Remember, the serpent said they would 'be as gods' and not that they would become gods, only like them.

You sometimes wonder what or who did Eve see and talk with in the Garden, which was called 'the serpent of wisdom?' Did she look into the eyes of one of God's most beautiful creations, a special angel of whom Eve said 'the serpent beguiled me' — what the Serpent Wisdom gives could beguile many — because surely there is wisdom of knowing the difference between good and evil? Did Adam take the fruit because of who sanctioned the act of eating it? Was it an angel who was later punished for his pride in trying to interfere with Gods creation, impatient of the sometimes slow process of evolution and wanting to make things move faster?

Graham Greene made the same important point in *The Power and the Glory*: ' . . . but I'm a bad priest, you see I know — from experience — how much beauty Satan carried down with him when he fell. Nobody ever said the fallen angels were the ugly ones . . .' I am not sure it was Satan that Eve saw in the Tree. Satan was the name of the 'scapegoat' of the time and tradition has him called Satan after the Fall, for everyone usually seems to be so much wiser after the event.

Depending on your point of view, the serpent appeared to have little or no enmity towards Adam and Eve. As said, it is possible that the serpent wished to hasten their evolution by encouraging them eating the 'forbidden fruit,' by telling them it would open their eyes and make them equal to the gods or 'as gods' — not God — but 'ye shall be as gods.' The serpent being older and wiser probably knew that evolution could be a slow process and it may have been the serpent's impatience in the matter we are dealing with in this. Some think the words — 'knowing good and evil' was added to this by a later writer but to become a god I think requires a little more than simply 'knowing good and evil.'

In most myths, it is frequently necessary, if they are to keep their new standing, heightened spirit and being, to renew this by eating more of the 'fruit' that gave it to them in the first place at set intervals. Only then could they, mortals 'as gods' keep what they had gained, including their temporary immortality. I agree that this was not mentioned or hinted at in the original tale, so perhaps I am making unnecessary difficulties where they do not apply.

In many myths and legends the means of becoming a god is jealously guarded. There are usually dire penalties for those who unsuccessfully try to reach this particular goal.

The Chinese God of Longevity is shown carrying some peaches about him and a child or some children are trying to reach these exceptionally unique fruits. The peaches of longevity only grow and ripen every three thousand years in the Celestial Orchard. Someone who eats the fruit will attain this enormous life span before it is necessary for them to eat the peaches again — three thousand years later to be exact — when the fruit would grow again and not to renew them meant death.

Look at the penalty poor Prometheus had to pay for the Divine 'gift of fire' that he gave to us. A further example, taken from the annals of the Norse and Teutonic myths, concerns Innun. Through the wiles of Loki, Innun was abducted and could not dispense the heavenly apples to the gods, so they grew old daily and were in danger of dying. Loki who was the cause of the trouble was forced to arrange her return and was punished for the trouble he had caused — a troublemaker who is punished and apples once more. Now let us leave these associated examples, put here to show that other countries and races have similar forms of myth and return to Satan and the Devil.

'The serpent' or 'dragon' is old usage in Christianity for Satan, yet Christ admonishes us 'Behold I send you forth as sheep in the midst of wolves: be you therefore as wise as serpents and harmless as doves.' *Matthew* 10:16. Serpents have long been objects of veneration in many religions and philosophies but in the Judeo–Christian religion serpents are more often than not used to represent evil and the Devil/Satan in particular.

As mentioned, a new religion often reversed the beneficial deities of the old religion it was trying to replace by denigrating its pantheon as pagan, false and evil. Making the former good into evil was the customary practise and an ancient one whatever the religion by often making the chief deity, the devil of the new. However, when something is being constantly blamed and maligned without let or hindrance it makes me suspicious of the reasons for doing so and what they intend to put in its place — as they will. What is being maligned and why is it important that this is done? I have often thought this particular technique was a 'distraction' or a smoke screen and wondered what was being hidden or displaced. A long time ago, this made me wonder that perhaps the serpent may not be as bad as he is being shown.

The association with the serpent started in the **Garden of Eden**, it continued throughout to the last book **Revelation** and much of it generally speaking appears to be bad. In ancient mythology, the serpent was frequently used as an emblem of the intelligence of God and sometimes the subtlety of the Evil One. It was almost as if the serpent and God were two sides of the same coin. 'As Moses lifted up the serpent in the wilderness, even so must the Son of man be lifted up.' **John** 3:14. The serpent has long been an emblem of wisdom **par excellence**. The symbol of sin and sinning curled up into a circle, holding its tail in its mouth that is 'time without end.' We read: 'As there is a serpent below, which is still at work in the world, so there is a sacred serpent above which watches over mankind in all the roads and pathways and restrains the Power of the impure serpent.' (**Zohar**), **Secret Doctrine in Israel**. A.E. Waite.

We come to this learning by analogies and so find that the word — 'serpent' — is a veritable gold mine of symbolism and interleaved with subtle hints and clues. There is a meaning within it that words cannot always define, which can be destroyed by taking them too figuratively and dissecting it until it cannot be put back to together again thus laying them open to ridicule by the uninitiated. The symbolism of the serpent is again a box that has a smaller box, within a smaller box, within a box . . . 'Now the serpent was more 'subtil' than any other wild creature that the Lord God had made.' **Genesis** 3 ' . . . 'that the Lord God made.' However, we must leave this for the time being

I do not intend to give a list of all the 'evils' that are placed on Satan's back for they are widely known and it would take too much space. He has had so much heaped on his back over the centuries it is a wonder he can get up to any mischief at all or even get up with the burden he carries. The reality of Satan's temptation cannot be questioned for one moment by those who accept the **New Testament**. What is troublesome regarding Satan is to define the precise limits and the permitted range of this 'roaring lion?' Many think the only thing that should be ascribed to this fallen angel is a moral influence because he is the 'tempter and adversary,' we can always say 'no' to his tempting or any form of temptation for that matter and perhaps that is the rub — the ball is in our court. If we give in and accept Satan's temptation, perhaps the enquiry should be — is the 'giving in' Satan's fault or ours? Almost daily, I hear people criticise the quality of television seen the previous night. The arbiter that all sets have is the programme switch to look at something better and the final arbiter is the off switch, both of which are controlled by us and not the television companies.

If we look at many of the entries for Satan, we find ascribed to him abortions, curdled butter and milk, cakes that do not rise, earthquakes, failed crops, fires that fail to light, violent storms, frightening the children, you name it and if it inconveniences or annoys you — Satan was responsible. If you did wrong and are found out, say Satan made you do it and forgiveness followed quickly. He takes on most of the medieval fancies, which lead to the numerous wild superstitions of magic and much of the finger pointing and settling of ancient scores through accusations of witchcraft that resulted in the pointless deaths and needless persecution of so many women, the old wise ones of the village or town in particular throughout past history. Perhaps the only 'sin she committed' was talking to her cat or cow while she milked it. I have never milked a cow, but I have talked frequently at great length to all my cats and can hardly pass one.

When presenting the case against Satan it is quite remarkable what is left out or conveniently omitted. My research brought me to an early conclusion early in life that by the careful omission of facts and the deliberate stressing of others, any case or cause could be proven if the writer or teacher so wishes it and is clever enough with words. 'Bright is the ring of words, when the right man rings them.' *Songs of Travel* – Stevenson. I want to assume the role of **Promotor Fidei=** 'promoter of the faith' for a short time, though in reverse as the subject under scrutiny is perhaps not seeking sainthood.

This is customarily known by the more popular title of playing 'the Devil's Advocate' as a result, considering the accused, I must point out that by playing 'the Devil's Advocate' — because of the subject matter, no pun is intended. The reason for the effort is to try to get a little more balanced view by removing some of the emotion of the past and no, I am absolutely not suggesting any form of worship of Satan or the Devil with all that it entails in popular fancy.

Some of the highest angels such as the seraphim are usually given six wings as their description demands, whereas Satan is normally found with twelve wings. We will take the 'sins' of Satan as read because there can be few that do not know of them or can imagine what they would be, if not by deed then implication. Instead, let us look at a few of the facts that are left out of the case.

It is strange that we find so few direct and positive statements regarding Satan in the *Old Testament*. It is a fact that Satan is seldom mentioned in the *Old Testament*. Satan is mentioned fifty times in the *Bible* (Robert Young's *Concordance*), fifteen in the *Old Testament* and thirty five in the *New Testament* with the Devil more and mainly in the *New Testament*. The serpent is mentioned as the one who tempts Eve in *Genesis* . In *Job*, there is an angel who acts as a heavenly prosecutor and here he is called Satan but there is nothing in the context of the book to show that he is evil or even an outcast in any way. The *Old Testament* appears to have no clearly developed doctrine regarding Satan but this all changes with the *New Testament* where Satan appears to be frequently identified with narratives in the *Old Testament* Satan as 'the tempter of man, the tester or adversary' and as we know that Satan is frequently called 'the devil' (not devil or a devil) in the *New Testament*.

Devils as such have long existed in many lands, they are not new to the world and its affairs and Satan seems to be an officially sanctioned 'tester or adversary.' It looks as if he is doing his appointed task quite well, which may be why he is reviled so much because he is successful at his task.

The precedence for this statement is given very early in *Genesis*, when God asked Adam if he had eaten of the forbidden tree and Adam gave his reply 'The woman whom though gavest to be with me, she gave me of the tree, and I did eat.' Therefore, God asked the woman about it and she replied. 'The serpent beguiled me, and I did eat.' Who was left to take the blame, after all it was a somewhat limited cast?

Take the example of the Archangel Michael when disputing with the Devil (= Satan) over the body of Moses. 'Yet Michael the archangel, when contending with the devil when he disputed about the body of Moses, durst not bring against him a railing accusation, but said the Lord rebuke thee.' Why was this? What prevented the Archangel Michael an angel of highest exaltation from using his mighty powers against the Satan? Michael is one of the highest of the archangels and we have already been told that he had crushed Satan in the *War in Heaven* and that he was triumphant over Satan. If that is true then Michael must be more powerful than Satan. However, it would seem there was a special relationship attendant upon Satan and the Lord that was clearly understood and Michael could not overstep the mark. The Archangel Michael is the strict upholder of the letter of the Law that he will not break or transgress it by as much as a single dot or comma but was there a limitation imposed of which we do not know.

There is one limitation mentioned in *Leviticus* 24:15 'Whosoever curseth his God shall bear his sin.' Others, under the influence of the *Secret Learning* agree with a law that forbids man from reviling the gods of the heathens. The *Zohar* tells us, whosoever curses strange gods which 'God has imparted to all nations shall bear his sin.' In *Ecclesiasticus* 21:27 we also find — 'When the ungodly curseth Satan, he curseth his own soul' and these are not light words.

In the legend dealing with the death of Moses we are told that Moses was loathe to die despite the one hundred and twenty years he had lived and he argued most eloquently against his death. Most of the angels whom God instructed to draw out his soul balked at the task and gave good reasons why they could not do the assignment given. Finally, God sent the mighty Angel Sammael (= the Chief of all the Satan's according to the *Talmud*), who was filled with delight at the prospect of being the instrument of death to Moses.

Sammael put on his great sword to finish the task and strode off with great strength of mind, nevertheless even he came back to God saying he was unable to utter the words of death for Moses, because the soul of Moses was so pure. In the end, God went to Moses who finally agreed to death but his soul refused to leave the body and God finally withdrew the soul of Moses with a 'Divine kiss,' while the angels, heavens, the sun, the moon, the stars, the constellations and the earth wept with the children of Israel.

The site of the grave of Moses is unknown but it is said to be opposite the place where Moses had buried the Angel Peor or Haron, after the destruction of the idolatrous Golden Calf that so angered God. If the Hebrew nation sins against God, the Angel Peor rises from the earth to destroy them but on seeing the grave of Moses, he returns with all speed into the earth and does not trouble them.

There is an extra–canonical apocalyptic work of the *Old Testament* called the *Assumption* or *Ascension of Moses*, a book of prophecy regarding the future of Israel. The book is written as if spoken by Moses and addressed to Joshua before the law–maker dies and it is said to be founded upon *Deuteronomy*. I have not seen the work but research says that a fragment of the work (1861) recounts the conflict between Michael and Satan concerning the body of Moses. Satan carries out three functions — 'he seduces men, he accused them before God and he inflicts the punishment of death' and Satan is excellent in all of these, but especially in the arts of seduction and few, even the Creator himself at times, has been subjected to his mesmerism and beguiling because he is 'subtil.' We are told it was Satan who convinced the children of Israel that Moses was dead on Sinai and he was to blame for the creation of the *Golden Calf.* (*Shab.*)

There is an important comment that tells us that Satan, the *Yetzer Ha–ra* (= 'evil impulse/inclination'*)* and the *Angel of Death* are one and the same and this account may explain an important and the mystifying agreement regarding God and Satan. It clarifies to some extent why God allows Satan to be vital and not to destroy or hinder him in his given tasks. Death we are told is the strongest force that God has created in the Universe and as such, it is very rare if ever to find that this power has been overcome or got the better of, only love has occasionally managed it.

The Rabbis recommended 'Let not a man open his mouth against Satan.' (*Ber.* 45a.) This is generally explained as meaning that you should not say anything regrettable that may recoil upon you. This is not unlike God's special protection of Cain so that none will kill him despite his crime of murder, which the later Commandments of God to Moses would forbid outright.

The *Talmud* felt the need to make comment regarding this problem so there is a frequently told tale in old Hebrew of a man called Pelimo that is mentioned in the *Talmud*. Pelimo would cry each day that he defied Satan saying 'An arrow in the eyes of Satan' that is, more or less 'I defy thee Satan.' Finally, Satan had enough of this and decided he would visit him on the eve *Day of Atonement* as an old man and a needy beggar. In this guise, Satan asked him ' . . .on such a day as this all people are inside their houses, must I stand outside?'

The 'old man' was let in and given a loaf of bread, he caused so much trouble and was so objectionable in the home of Pelimo, finally Satan dropped to the floor as if dead. The cry went up that Pelimo had killed the old man and the poor Pelimo fled his house in great distress with Satan hard on his heels and was found hiding in a closet. Satan was so upset by the state of the man that he made himself known to him and asked him why did he always speak of him in this way. Pelimo asked Satan how should he speak of him. Satan told him that he should say 'May the Compassionate One rebuke Satan.' When Jesus rebuked Peter, he told him 'Get thee behind me Satan: for thou savourest not the things that be of God, but the things that be of men.' *Mark 8:33.*

The opening of the *Book of Job* tells us that the 'sons of God came to present themselves before the Lord, and Satan came (also) among them.' I have put the word 'also' in parenthesis deliberately because it would be my addition within this sentence if I chose to edit it for reasons that suited me. I have always been suspicious in view of what follows that this small word was an addition by some scribe to make it seem that Satan was the uninvited guest to the feast that he should not have been there, he was unwanted, he should not be there and therefore an intruder. It seems to suggest that Satan had trespassed where he had no right to be. Perhaps it was done because it did not agree with the thoughts of later times, so I think it may have been inserted at a later date, but the operative word in all of this reasoning is — 'I think.'

One small word inserted or comma in the wrong or the right place in a Last Will and Testament can often make the difference between getting everything, little or nothing. Because commas and full stops can change the meaning, they were often omitted in important legal testimonies or documents.

Sometimes a little judicial editing is simply propaganda and it is astonishing what can be justified in the name of 'Truth.' My favourite explanation of it is a frequent quote and according to Pooh Bah, 'It is merely corroborative detail, intended to give artistic verisimilitude to an otherwise bald and unconvincing narrative.' *The Mikado*, libretto by W. S. Gilbert.

Propaganda has been used from the beginning of time and even as I write, propaganda is alive, healthy and doing very nicely thank you. Its organized and methodical use began with tribal and world rulers, Governments, the Church or any vested interest, so it has an excellent pedigree and history. Remember what the writer Mark Twain advised. 'Get your facts first, and then you can distort them as much as you please.'

Now we must come back to our story of Job and our discussion of Satan. I believe that Satan was invited with all the other 'sons of God,' the '*bene–ha–'elohi*,' or 'beings of the Divine Order,' which is the old name applied to them in *Genesis*. The 'sons of God' of *Job* 38.7 are often identified with the 'morning stars who sang together.' They are shown as being free to walk through the earth whenever they will. God even asks Satan where he has been and Satan tells God he has been 'going to and fro in the earth, and from walking up and down in it.' It is an old suggestion that the 'sons of God' congregated to pay court to Yahweh at periodic intervals.

The term was used as the title of a member of the Divine Court whose duty as God's nomadic inquisitor was to gather information about people as he travelled around the earth. Satan is obviously a member of the group that was permitted to go about their duties freely because he was appointed. The Lord was praising Job and he asked Satan 'hast thou considered him?' To me these words have always seemed tantamount to a direct challenge, the Lord is asking Satan has he tested Job and if not — why not?

This seems remarkably like a counter–challenge and very plain speaking for a dismissed and disgraced angel and Satan says, 'Doth Job fear God for naught? Hast thou not made an hedge about him, and about his house, and all that he hath on every side? Thou hast blessed the work of his hands, and his substance is increased in the land. But put forth thine hand now, and touch all that he hath, and he will curse thee to thy face.' Satan obviously feels the 'rules of the game' are biased in favour of Job because of the protection of God, the challenge was not worth his time and effort, the venture was not a fair one and it was biased so much that it excluded any chance of success. God is shown here to be responsible for the challenge because Satan rejects the challenge as meaningless.

With these words Satan is not tempting Job — but God is! However, God takes up the challenge and he even sets the rules. 'And the Lord said unto Satan, Behold, all that he hath is in thy power; only upon himself put not forth thy hand.' At this point Satan leaves the presence of the Lord. This to me seems to point to a very special relationship or at least a clear understanding existing between God and Satan, which God has possibly accepted, devised or created.

In the visions of *Zechariah*, the angels play a great part and they are sometimes spoken of as 'men.' Sometimes as *mal'akh* and the *Mal'akh Yahweh* seems to have a certain primacy among them. *Zechariah* 1:11f. The **Old Testament** refers to Satan as the prosecutor of God's celestial court. At the trial of the High Priest as well as 'the angel of the Lord' came 'Satan standing on his right hand to resist (=speak against or prosecute) him.' *Zechariah* 3:1.

A number of commentators say that Satan can only be in one place at a time and this seems to assume that he must have countless agents to do his behest and this appears to have been used to some advantage. The righteous are attended by good angels so naturally, the wicked have the evil angels as their companions and this gave rise to the following advice in the **Talmud**. If you know that a good man is going to take a journey that you are going to take, either start out three days earlier or three later so that you will be in his company and those of his beneficial angels. Naturally, if he is a wicked man and you are taking a similar route, again start out three days before or three later. This time with the object of not being in the company of the wicked man because Satan's evil angels will be in this mans company.

There is another angel called Mastema, an 'Angel of Hostility and Adversity' and he is an 'Accusing Angel.' This angel is found as the devil in the **Book of Jubilees** and we have already spoken of this **Apocryphal** work, often called **The Little Genesis**. The **Book of Jubilees** was written or compiled around the time of the Second Temple period and it deals with the revelations of the Angel of the Presence to Moses when he ascended Mount Sinai for the second time. Some judge that the work may have been of early Essene origin.

The Angel Mastema is in the service of God and according to this work, his duties are very much the same as Satan with whom he is often compared. Mastema tests people's faith for he is 'an Accusing Angel, the Prince of Injustice and Evil, an Angel of Adversity.' It was Mastema, as leader of the evil spirits who slew the first–born of the Egyptians and it was this angel who tested Abraham. However, some works say that it was Mastema who was on the side of the Egyptian sorcerer's in their battle with Moses and Aaron when they appeared before Pharaoh to perform their magic.

Mastema has legions of evil spirits that he uses to plague the inhabitants of earth and he is said to be responsible for many of the woes to which we are exposed. He is said to be subject to God but he is the 'Father of All Evil.' Legend tells us Mastema at the time of his punishment appealed to God and succeeded in his request that some of his demons are spared God's wrath and about a tithe was saved. These were permitted to serve Mastema to exercise his power 'on the sons of man.' Mastema is another example of a 'rebel angel' who remains part of the cosmic scheme in which he is used to test the loyalty of people, especially the righteous.

There is no attempt here to refute Satan's sins because there are too many for me to do that, though I feel that some of them may have been added for spite. As said earlier, if you do something and you are found out, blame Satan — the 'scapegoat. Just say Satan made you do it and you will be clear of all blame, not be held responsible for your actions — somewhat weak perhaps, but repentant and forgiven. At one time only young princes had 'whipping boys' that took the whip for the prince's misdemeanours, but Satan appears to be more egalitarian and it is all a little too easy I feel. In *Job* and the ***Chronicles***.

Under Persian influence, it was thought that Satan begins to assume far greater import almost to the point of contending with God by acting as 'the Tempter' and the personification of every urge to do harm and evil. Like an equal opposing force, he defies God and seems to brings back plurality to a monotheist religion to which the One God appears to turn a blind eye.

Many pages would be required to describe the strange and sometimes fanciful opinions that have been advanced regarding our subject by Jews, Christians (both heretical and orthodox), Islamic and others. I feel it should be pointed out that some communities denominated Christian still perpetuate and favour the sometimes utterly unscriptural notions about the matter in hand. It seems that if evil exists someone has to take the blame and the blame cannot be given to God even though he 'created everything.' If he did not then he could not be regarded as supreme and the 'One God' because there is something or someone outside him, who can challenge or disturb his Creation and live to tell the tale.

Satan and the Devil are found in many shapes and sizes in folklore and the Devil was developed mainly by Christian theology. In early religions, especially the Persian system of dualism the powers were good with Ahura Mazda while Ahriman came afterwards and created all the evil and he was represented by a serpent. The Jews it seems possessed no idea of a devil as the instigator of evil before their confinement in Babylon and their acquaintance with Chaldean and Persian ideas. Asmodeus is Persian more than Jewish although this devil is associated and included in Jewish lore, probably more as an Evil Spirit. He is invoked with the head uncovered or he will trick you and if he does decide to call make sure you are barefoot. The ***Magic of the Abra–Melin*** tells us 'some Rabbis say that Asmodeus was the child of the incest of Tubal–Cain and his sister Haamah, while other say he is a demon of impurity.'

Next, the Devil/Satan was degraded over the centuries and in medieval times he came in many guises, some of them distinctly grotesque. It seems that the form of Pan was perfectly made for this purpose because it has lasted the longest with his horns, half man, half goat and the cloven hoofs. Other names to mention that are under suspicion are Wayland Smith a cunning worker of metals, like tinkers the children of Cain and feared in earlier times; Hephaistos who, like Satan and Lucifer is sometimes shown as lame in the left foot, the result of their fall from heaven.

This list could be extended to quite some length but enough is here to show the point and the Christian story tellers have transformed the dull demons of yesteryears into Satan and given him

131

countless attendants and various fiends a new lease of life and some, like the Devil, are none to bright it seems.

The Devil/Satan is generally personified in folklore as a poor witless creature that is effortlessly cheated or outwitted in the end by anyone who takes him on and with the simplest of artifice. It looks as if the Devil/Satan is oblivious to many of the things on this planet that a young child would know. Though it should be pointed out that it is usually the Medieval Devil/Satan who gets such bad publicity and stories abound concerning him, but in the films and stories of today, he is getting a much better press and he even manages to win now and then.

In one tale, he helps an architect to build a very difficult bridge and sorts out his problems, his payment is the soul of the first living creature to go across it. The bargain is struck but they cheat the poor Devil by driving, cats, dogs, fowl, hares, goats and pigs across the bridge first. Even in the phrase the 'Devil take the hindmost' is because he usually gets the shadow of the last man in the race, who more often than not escapes though existing without a shadow for the rest of his days. It makes you wonder how evil was able to achieve the hold it has with such an ineffective leader or how he ever got the job in the first place, perhaps more to the point, having got the job how did he ever manage to keep it?

It is difficult to associate this seemingly weak and ineffectual creature with the Angel Sammael — the **Venom of God** and believe that they are the same angel. It bears repetition to say that although we are advised to be on our guard against the 'assaults of Satan, we have not been authorized to treat him 'with contempt.' **Zohar**: Part 2.

God is usually represented as good and Satan as bad and they are made diametrically opposed to each other. Their relationship has been polarized by Christianity and given only two ways of looking at all problems, big or small, black or white with no shades of gray in between. Such opposition has automatically drawn the One God into the world of duality, however unintentional and I am sure it was not intended. It has made the One God one side of the coin with Satan or the Devil the other side. Pick up the 'coin' and you automatically pick up the opposite side because you cannot pick up one without picking up or disturbing the other side — it is a problem — perhaps you just have to accept both sides and deal with them and when you start doing that the tension lessens. The one thing the One God cannot be is plural or he would not be the One God, this is part of the problem with the angels.

Any suggestion of duality or plurality does not help the suggestion of Christ to 'Be ye therefore perfect, even as your Father which is in heaven is perfect.' **Matthew** 5:48. As I said earlier before the Exile, it was thought that Yahweh did everything and was responsible for everything both good and evil quoted elsewhere, several times. The conclusion of this is that 'the evil itself may have been channelled through spirits but Yahweh 'was responsible for it' and 'its creator,' furthermore presumably, those who acted on his direct orders could not be held responsible.

There are many Angels of Death chief among these angels is Azazel (= 'God strengthens') for Azazel is claimed to be one of the chief angels of the Fallen Angels. It was Azazel who 'taught men to fashion swords and shields.' Azazel, according to Jewish legend is the angel who rebelled against the order to bow down to Adam. Azazel asked God 'Why should a son created of smokeless fire bow down to a son of clay, a creature of dust?' Therefore, God cast him out of heaven, made him into a devil and changed his name to Eblis, who is the equivalent of the Christian Satan according to other religions.

Another important Angel of Death was mentioned earlier in the section on 'Metatron' — the Angel Dumah — and we will repeat some of his important points here. Dumah is Aramaic for 'silence' so naturally he the 'Angel of Silence' and 'the stillness of death.' The Angel of Silence is given charge of the disembodied spirits and he is, according to the **Zohar** given as 'chief demon' of

Ghinnom (= Hell). He has countless attendants under his charge and he punishes the souls of those who are sinners. The Angel Dumah is the tutelary Angel of Egypt, Prince of Hell and Vindication.

We have not exhausted even now all the angels by any means that are called 'fallen angels' nor have we spoken of them all. I admit my fear of Satan at Sunday school was real, when I was very young. It would also be truthful to say that although I feared him I was fascinated by him because he was so interesting. I do not know if it was the intention of the artist, it was his eyes that I remember and they were not evil and at Sunday school when all we children were asked who was their favourite disciple, perhaps foreshadowing my future research — I said Judas, which did not go down very well in one so young. I now know this was because Satan is an 'outsider' or someone who could not be accommodated satisfactorily into the scheme of things, he was someone who did not fit in and what is more important, he made those who did fit somewhat uncomfortable at times.

Before we leave Satan, the Devil and their 'fallen angels,' let us take a short trip to North Yorkshire where fossil bones were found called 'fallen angels' and thought to belong to the fallen angels that were cast out of heaven for their rebellion. These were the fossil bones of the *Saurians*= 'a reptile or lizard–like form, one of the order of *Sauria*. A lizard or lizard–like creatures.'

Here I have taken some of the facts here that are not always mentioned in Sunday Schools about Satan or the Devil and I doubt they are mentioned now, as then. The formative years of life can be marked so easily because naturally when we are young we trust those into whose keeping we are placed. This is not always a bad thing, depending on who is doing the 'keeping' and most usually do their best according to their lights and I would be the first to admit this subject would be a difficult problem to solve. What is given early can at times be very hard to undo in later years if you want to, which wastes much time that could be put to better use.

There is no hidden intent or agenda in what is being written here, just the personal feeling that Satan is not as bad as he is painted. Further, I feel he does not automatically polarize the twin aspects of good and evil. If the reader does not agree with what has been written they can of course accept or reject as they see fit and I find no difficulty with this. The one thing that identifies a great many devils, imps, Satan and the Devil are horns, we can find these creatures without them but invariably they seem to have them. These have long fascinated me and they lead me on to another associated hobbyhorse of mine linked with the subject and theme of the next section of this section.

I have had a long fascination and love affair with Pan, metaphorically speaking. I find it very easy to protect him if he needed defence, which he does not. However the one thing he cannot completely deal with I feel is neglect. I have long respected him and Pan is very easy to get on with within well–defined and reasonable confines. He is a very old god, perhaps one of the oldest and I for one would never presume to think I can teach him anything. Even to contemplate trying to teach the Oldest God anything would a presumption I could never justify and I seek him out to learn, I have little to give him. So let us set down a few more details of this heaven sent model for Satan or the Devil.

Min is an Egyptian god who is strongly identified with Pan by the Greeks especially at Panopolis. Min was the guardian of the desert roads and protected travellers in the desert and some suggest these functions were later transferred to the god Pan. Travellers would never leave on any commercial venture without first invoking the aid of Min or Pan to grant them a safe return and a successful venture. This is a frequent theme in folklore and the old religion in which many examples of guardian spirits are to be found. At Mendes in Egypt, the gods Pan and Min were worshipped in the form of a goat — the *Goat of Mendes* that is beloved of horror films and writers of black magic tales.

The appearance of Pan has long given the assumed fallen Angel of Satan or the Devil its present form — mentioned throughout. Yet another source for this humiliation is the figure of Baphomet, he too has the appearance of a goat. Baphomet was a mystic term of medieval times that was like the god Pan, often found identified also with the Goat of Mendes.

The Templars of Malta were accused of worshipping Baphomet as an idol that was a representation of the Devil/Satan. Baphomet was commonly taken as a sign of the beginning of initiation and/or wisdom. Over the years, however the figure of Baphomet has become contaminated, misunderstood and I feel the key to its genuine significance may have been long been lost. Card 15 of the Major Tarot is sometimes thought to have taken up the appearance of Baphomet and labelled — 'the Devil.' Many writers have suggested the veiled significance of the figure of Baphomet and while some are promising, others are fanciful in the extreme to which I am not going to add my portion.

Pan, the Greek God of Nature is usually shown with the horns and hoofs of a goat. However, Pan's mentioned relationship with the **Goat of Mendes** is only thus far, that the latter is a talisman of immense occult power representing the 'creative force of Nature' and one thing that has always puzzled me is why did they not take the Pipes of Pan.

They took his appearance, half man and half goat, the cloven hoof, the 'rank smell' of the goat, the gross procreation, the unbridled passion that led this creature to be always chasing the nymphs and so on, but they left the plaintive music, but the church of the time was never enamoured of any music other than their own. Of course when dealing with Pan we must always bear in mind that animals, flocks and pasturage were extremely important matters of his pastoral age, they were vital to a point of life and death. Another point is sometimes omitted and very important regarding him was that he was also called the **God of the Hyle** and this is not only 'woody or wooded.'

Horns, real and symbolic, are found a great deal in myth, legend, folklore and the **Scriptures**. They are often used as a symbol of courage; might and aggressiveness especially when they are attached to a number of animals, the ones that will not let anyone or anything stand in their way. The altar in the tabernacle had horns set on the four corners, now frequently replaced on modern altars by decorative tassels. If these horns were seized by a fugitive, they were granted sanctuary that could not be violated.

In the apocalyptic and prophetic books of Christianity and other religions can be found dragons and other monsters with horns, the number of horns possibly has some symbolic allusion in **Revelation** the red dragon had 'seven heads and ten horns.' See 12:3. It is accepted that they are a symbol of a natural generative power, which is a characteristic of several symbolic animals, as the ram, the bull, the cow, the goat and so on, who are either defensive or productive.

Before glasses and goblets, drinking was from a horn and the symbolism of this skilfully combines both the male and the female in one symbol. To drink with someone it was offered to the wine–bearer, point down so that it was receptive, receiving the wine to be drunk and containing it — the feminine. However, if there was animosity with the drinking partner, the drinking horn would be turned over and stood on the table point up, it could neither receive or contain any wine. The horn stood on the table erect, challenging and unreceptive of the amenable wine and leaving little to the imagination of what it was telling the other person or people what they could do — the masculine.

Horns as said, were found in Greece with Pan, the god of natural generation, procreation and fertility. They were also plentiful among his satyrs, fauns and the rest. In Judaism, the goat was the scapegoat standing as the sacrifice to bear away the burden of the people's sins. Satan or the Devil is shown with horns, in a similar sense though he can represent the lower aspect of nature that can sometimes disgrace us, but in popular belief horns, hoofs and a tail are looked upon as bestial elements that cause fear and Pan did produce 'panic' and in the process giving us the word.

The moon is the oldest and most explicit symbol of productive generation and has long been described as having horns especially in her most productive and growing phase — New Moon to First Quarter. Primarily, because after this period the horn diminishes to create the full Moon and after the fullness of the Moon, comes the decrease in size and girth, which is self–explanatory really even though done in less than nine months.

Astrologically, when a planet is elevated in a Sign of the Zodiac, it said to represent the highest point of expression of that planet. The Moon is elevated in Taurus for here she is well placed. When she is in Taurus, she is next to the sign of Aries and both signs are symbolized by animals with horns. Aries has the horns of the male ram and these are the active principle of Nature particularly at spring ruled by the planet Mars. Taurus represents the passive and receiving principle in Nature. Therefore it should be ruled by the gentle Eastern cow, an animal having those beautiful long horns, being female and under the rule of Venus — not I feel by the bull —further, the Ram (Aries) and the Bull (Taurus) when together as they are in the zodiac it would not I feel make for peaceful neighbours.

Crescent comes from the Latin *crescere* meaning 'to increase,' the moon in its first quarter or the circular arc or lune. This is a symbol of the moon that is, in its highest significance, the Queen of Heaven, Diana, the Great Mother of the Earth — as the sun is the Great Father of All. It is associated in Egypt with Isis, in Greece and Rome with Aphrodite and Venus, in Asia Minor with Astarte or Astaroth and numerous lunar goddesses are repeatedly shown with the horns similar to the cow, even in Tarot cards. In the Roman Catholic Church, Mary is at times shown standing on the crescent moon. When Venus–Lucifer became transformed into Satan, its crescent became the horns of the Christian Devil. The lunar crescent symbol finds parallels with the ark or *argha* and appears in the Egyptian symbol of the Solar Boat. Showing that the Moon is the Chariot of the Sun when she carries the Sun's light during the hours of darkness, to show her children that the light of the Day Star has not left them in darkness. This is short and it may seem to have taken us from the subject of this section but its purpose was to expand a few points regarding the subject in hand.

## LUCIFER

### 'Angels are bright still, though the brightest fell.'

Before we close this section, permit me to make a personal statement regarding Satan that is not intended to convince the reader or anyone else for that matter of anything. It is set here because it tells the reader where I stand — not where I want the reader to stand.

Let us start with the relevant lines from *Isaiah*. 'How art thou fallen from heaven, O. Lucifer, son of the morning, How art thou cut down to the ground, which didst weaken the nations' *Isaiah* 14:12. To me this has always felt more like a question than a statement of fact, so I felt the exclamation mark is wrong and the reason why I have removed it.

This is a misreading as far as I am concerned that has almost permanently identified Satan with Lucifer, who was the original 'Son of the Morning.' It is claimed that Satan before he was driven from heaven for his pride was called Lucifer. In ancient times Lucifer was the name given to Venus as the 'Day Star, Son of the Morning' or the 'Son of Dawn' of Babylon. I believe I am right in saying that the writers in the *Old Testament* did not distinguish between the fallen angels and the angels that remained dutiful, as said many times, Satan in the beginning simply meant 'adversary or tester' as shown in *Job*. The Church Fathers, in the belief that the verse in *Isaiah* contained an allusion to the fall of Satan from heaven, attached the name Lucifer to Satan see below. St Jerome and other Fathers used the name Lucifer (= 'light') and identified it as a synonym for the Satan/Devil (= 'darkness') and this theme was reinforced later by John Milton in *Paradise Lost*.

In the book *Revelation* of John the Divine, we are told ' . . . and he that overcometh, and keepeth my works to the end, to him will I give power over the nations . . . even as I received of my Father. And I will give him the morning star.' 2:26–29. 'I Jesus have sent mine angels to testify unto your these things in the churches. I am the root and the offspring of David, and the bright and morning star.' 22:16. Originally in the teaching I was given Lucifer meant a star, the 'Morning Star' — *Helel ben Shahar* —the 'Light–bearer.'

A.E. Waite tells us in his work *Holy Cabbalah*, p.276 speaking of the *Zohar*. 'As a conclusion to this part, it seems desirable to say that the Zhoharic prince of demons is never compared to the morning star or any other luminary in heaven. I do not remember that the word *Ilyh* (= Day–Star), Lucifer occurs anywhere in the text as a synonym of Satan.'

A part of any written work consists of the opinions of the writer regarding the subject matter of the book or they would not be writing it. These opinions and views, the reader's view of these opinions can make the writer a fine one to some and a complete idiot to others. However, I have now reached that comfortable age in life where I am reasonably inured to the twin onslaughts of flattery or abuse — *Sine Ira Et Studio*. I remember what an old school master said to me in the last year of his school life when he retired. He said: 'If you hear that someone is speaking ill of you, instead of trying to defend yourself you should say "He obviously does not know me very well, since there are so many other faults he could have mentioned." ' He told me this was a quotation of Epictetus, a Stoic philosopher of the 2nd century A.D and found in *Enchiridion*. I was pleased that he wrote it down for me before he left and I regret not listening more, as usual.

Many works and writers give Satan the title of the 'Prince of Darkness' while Lucifer is the 'light–bearing angel' therefore quite the opposite and there is no darkness there — only Light. We are however told that Satan can appear 'as an angel of Light' in 'For such are false apostles, deceitful workers, transforming themselves into apostles of Christ. And no marvel; for Satan himself is transformed into an angel of light. Therefore it is no great thing if his ministers also be transformed as the ministers of righteousness; who end shall be according to their works' 2 *Corinthians* 11:15.

It should be remembered that in this passage we are being told Satan can *appear* as an angel of light, while Lucifer *is* an Angel of Light. Lucifer is a special case and he is not for me connected in any way with Satan. *Lucifer*= 'light–bringing or bearer.' *Lucifer*= 'Light–bringing, light giver.' The morning star, the planet Venus, φωσφορος, *phosphoros*' (Greek). *Lucetius*= ' Light–bringer, a surname of Jupiter and Juno.' *Lucifico*= 'To make bright, to brighten.' *Lucificus*= 'Light–making, light–giving.' *Lucifluus*= 'Light–streaming, light–beaming, brilliant.' there is nothing here to do with darkness or the lack of light and evil. The name of Lucifer was applied to Satan by St. Jerome and other Church Fathers as other commentators point out, Gustav Davidson among them. It would almost be another book to enter into this discussion fully.

> 'It is Lucifer,
> The son of mystery;
> And since God suffers him to be,
> He, too, is God's minister,
> And labours for some good
> By us not understood.'
> Epilogue – *The Golden Legend* – Longfellow.

A *Hymn of Heavenly Love* by Edmund Spencer has Lucifer as 'the brightest angel, even the Child of Light.' As said earlier, originally Lucifer meant a star, the 'Morning Star' — *Helel ben Shahar* — or the 'Light–bearer.' This is a name for Venus in the morning when the planet appears above the horizon before sunrise, that she is called 'Son of the Morning.' Stars that appear in the morning before the Sun has risen are called 'matutine' (Latin *matutinus*= 'belonging to the morning') and included in the 'matutine' stars are the Moon, Mercury and Venus.

In the evening, Venus often appears as the brightest object in the sky. When this planet is in the Western sky after the Sun has set, she is usually called Hesperus. When any planet sets in the evening, just after the Sun, this is called 'vespertine' (Latin *vespertinus* from *vesper*= evening.') Some have said it is the crescent moon and others Jupiter who are this, though his epithet the 'Morning Star' is quite apt with the appositional 'Son of the Dawn' and now we now we must start to draw this section to a close, so finally.

There are those who feel that the application of the name Lucifer to Satan is flawed, even though it is universally taught that they are one and the same, but quite often if something is mentioned in the *Bible*, then it has to be accounted for in some way. Lucifer i.e. the Morning Star' which is used as a title of Christ as is the name 'Bright Morning Star' as Jesus has called himself. 'I Jesus have sent mine angel to testify unto you these things in the churches. I am the root and the offspring of David, and the bright and morning star.' *Revelation* 22:16

'We have also a more sure word of prophecy; whereunto you do well that ye take heed, as unto a light that shineth in a dark place, until the day dawn, and the day star arise in your hearts: knowing this first, that no prophecy of the scripture is of any private interpretation. For the prophecy came not in the old time by the will of man: but holy men of god spake as they were moved by the Holy Ghost.' 2 *Peter* 1:19.

The name Lucifer is remarkably only mentioned once in the Bible and found in *Isaiah*. Lucifer is the Latin word translated from l l y j = 'the shining one' according the Robert Young, which is the concordance I use for biblical study firmly believing it to be the best. *Helel* is not given as a name because it is obvious that it is a description but it was made into a name in the Latin and that name is Lucifer. The practise of applying the name Lucifer to Satan has existed I believe from around the third century A.D.

We are told that the connection of the two could in part have its source in the *New Testament*, 'And he said unto them, I beheld Satan as lightning fall from heaven,' *Luke* 10:18, which was thought to acceptably explain the *Old Testament*, 'How art thou fallen from heaven, O Lucifer, son of the morning!' *Isaiah* 14:12 and so Lucifer became linked with Satan. It has also been commonly taught that before Satan lost his War in Heaven that his name was Lucifer so the two are one and the same. As a result, Lucifer became synonymous to the name of Satan and the Devil, but I for one do not think that this explanation or others have cleared the matter up and as with some others, I feel the explanations are inaccurate.

If the one spoken of in *Isaiah* 14:12 is not Satan, then perhaps we should start to consider other solutions to the question or at least review the questions that arise because of this. I feel the interpretations given are still not satisfactorily explained and merely accepted. Later writers of the Bible added or subtracted to put any discrepancies right. Much of the difficulty with the *Bible* is that they did not take particular note of the final lines that close this monumental work.

'For I testify unto every man that heareth the words of the prophecy of this book. If any man shall add unto these things, God shall add unto him the plagues that are written in this book: and if any man shall take away from the words of the book of this prophecy, God shall take away his part out of the book of life, and out of the holy city, and from the things which are written in this book.' *Revelation* 22:18–19 — rightly so!

# MAMMON

One quite famous god or angel of medieval folklore is the (Angel) Mammon (Aramaic= 'riches') who in the writings of Agrippa is placed among the devils. The name of this angel has passed into the English language as the personification of greed and riches. This word appears to have been borrowed from the Aramaic in the times of Jesus and the early Church, though used by the Jewish settlers in communities near the Red Sea when referring to wealth or property. He was given as a god of avariciousness and worldliness originally — the 'idol of gold' — but this is not strictly true. This is what we have now but not what we had.

The attributes of Mammon have been somewhat misrepresented and blurred over the centuries to suit the purpose of the times perhaps and there is not really a great deal written about him. There are some representations found of him, the word 'representations' has been chosen with care because it is the belief of the writer that the results found are a 'representation' of how the writer or artist sees him according to what they have read about him. Witness the image of Mammon in *The Magus* by Barrat, which has always left me dissatisfied in many ways because it looks like a made up thing of how a supposed demon should look because of what he is supposed to be or did.

In Greek he is *Μαμμωνας*, *Mammonas*= 'Mammon, a Syrian god of riches; hence 'riches, wealth, N.T.' However, despite the above the word is not Greek nor is it found in the Hebrew *Bible*. It is a Hellenised form of the Aramaic and the name Mammon means 'wealth, riches, money.' In the Hebrew, some authorities have taken it as meaning 'that on which man trusts' while another prefers 'that which brings man into safety,' yet another 'that which is distributed' and so forth and so far any suggestion of 'greed and avariciousness' has not entered into it.

We are told 'in the time of Alexander, the trade of the world' was in the hands of the Phoenicians and Aramaeans' with evidence to show 'that in both languages mammon was the word for money.' In the Aramaic Targums the word is often found and taking one example given from *Judges* 5:19: 'They took no gain of money.' (*Authorized Version*). 'They accepted no *mamon* of silver.' (*Aramaic*).

We are told that the phrase 'mammon of the unrighteous' was 'quite common in Jewish literature' and in the pre–Christian *Book of Enoch* the wicked say: 'our soul is satiated with the unrighteous mammon, but this did not prevent our descending into the flame of Sheol.' 63:2. In the Targums this was given as 'money earned through deceit or fraud' so we find: 'He that is greedy of gain troubleth his own house.' *Proverbs* 15:27.

The phrase 'Make yourself friends by means of the mammon of the unrighteousness' in *Luke* 16:9 (the parable of *The Unjust Steward*) makes some wonder to whom Christ was speaking. Some think that Jesus was talking to the Pharisees and publicans more so than his twelve because later in *Luke* 16:14, there is ' . . . the Pharisees also, who were covetous, heard all these things: and they derided him.'

The advice Christ appears to have given to the Pharisees appears to be that they should make compensation to God by acts of generosity. This is felt to be more suitable to the Pharisees rather than his twelve, who without doubt did not have much 'mammon' of any sort but he could advising them on the correct use of 'mammon' should they get it? However, if it was, the phrase would still of had the same meaning as in Jewish literature. Naturally, there are those who take an a different view and the difficulty in the above is to whom was Christ speaking?

Mammon is thought to be personified in the Greek as *Πλουτος*, *Ploutos*= *Plutus*= 'wealth, riches, treasure, the giver of wealth and the god of riches' and this often included an 'abundance of crops and the treasures of the earth' or the treasures of his kingdom. Plutus is associated with Demeter at Eleusis and his connection with Demeter does not only concern crops, because Plutus is the son of Demeter 'who enriched men with the fruits of the earth' and her beloved Iasion that Zeus killed out of jealousy. Plutus was born at Crete and Demeter and Kore (= Persephone) sent Plutus to those whom they favoured. It must be given again not to confuse Plutus with Pluto as some have. Plutus is clearly distinguished from Pluto as being the god of riches.

Shakespeare uses Plutus correctly with no confusion for in *Julius Ceasar* he has Cassius say ' . . . within a heart dearer than Plutus' mine, richer than gold.' Act 4:Sc.3. Speaking of the overwhelming bounty of Timon, a lord points out ' . . . he pours it out; Plutus, the god of gold, is but his steward.' *Timon of Athens*. Act 1:Sc.1.

Hades in Greek mythology, received dominion of the lower world the prince of the underworld Hades — 'the Unseen or Invisible.' He is regarded as the enemy of all life, heartless, inexorable 'and hated by both gods and men.' Sacrifice and prayer are usually of no avail with this god and so he is only worshipped in very exceptional circumstances and he is generally not shown in Greek art, though more out of fear than not knowing how to depict an 'invisible ruler.'

Hades never took part in the councils or gatherings of the gods, in their wars or the affairs of either heaven or earth and this only seems to have made him all the more terrifying. As *Pylartes* — 'the closer of the gates' — he watched over the entrance to his kingdom to ensure that any who entered could turn and leave. Because he is ruler of the interior of the earth and the treasures hidden within his kingdom, he is occasionally called Pluto and coupled with Plutus (= 'riches') and his Roman counterpart of the underworld — Orcus a chthonic god of the Romans, fashioned upon the Greek god Hades.

However, he does have a lighter side and a milder nature and in this, he is often shown as being 'the giver of wealth' and called Pluto. This is because it is from the depths of the earth that corn and its attendant blessings are produced and as old as Hesiod is the advice to those who plough the earth to call upon the 'Zeus of the Lower World' as well as upon Demeter.

Hades is one of the sons of Kronos, lord of the underworld — the *House of Hades* — because the name is always of a person, never of a place and Hades seems to have almost no cult to call his own. His name arises here and there and the most well–known is Pluto — 'the Rich One' — it is this name that obviously associates him with Plutus.

Plutus comes with Mirth and Peace to the house, which the bearers of the *eiresione* visit. The *eiresione* was among the first–fruits offerings given at the *Pyanepsia*, a festival at the end of October to honour the departing god of summer, Apollo. The *eiresione* is a branch of olive or bay, bound with purple and white wool and hung about with the autumn fruits, pastries and small containers of honey, wine and oil. Statues have been found of the goddess Eirene (= 'peace personified') holding the infant Plutus.

Zeus is said to have made Plutus blind so that he would not bestow his favours only on righteous men exclusively, but he would distribute his gifts blindly without any regard to merit, which does bring to mind 'I have seen the wicked in great power, and spreading himself like the green bay tree'. *Psalms* 37:35. Another tale tells us Zeus blinded Plutus 'because he distributes his gifts without choice or only to the righteous.' The god of riches Plutus, in the literature of the lyric poet Timocreon of Rhodes is consigned to Tartarus because 'his blindness makes so much trouble.'

In the Latin *Plutus* is 'the giver of riches.' Plutus is often represented as a boy with a cornucopia or Amalthea's Horn — 'the horn of plenty.' Mammon, according to the *93 Visions of St. Francesca* 'holds the throne of this world' and this seems to have changed very little in the intervening centuries. The writers of the gospel wrote the Aramaic word *mamona*= 'riches' in Greek letters and in the Scriptures, originally, which have given Mammon his bad name thereafter.

He was personified in the *New Testament* as 'the evil of wealth,' yet wealth of itself is not evil though the way it is used can be. The biblical interpretation of Mammon was taken up literally by medieval writers and he has become a Fallen Angel, an arch–demon and a Prince of Temptation. In the ***Dictionnaire Infernal*** of De Plancy, Mammon is specified as being 'Hell's ambassador to England' — thank you! It was a short step to bring him in line with the Christian Beelzebub, Lucifer and Satan though the medieval view tells us that Mammon was a Syrian god.

Medieval scholars of demonology often attributed the Seven Deadly Sins to a hierarchy of seven arch–demons and in this list, Mammon can usually be found lurking. To Lucifer is given Pride, Mammon is Avarice with Asmodeus as Lechery. Satan is Anger, Beelzebub is Gluttony, Leviathan is Envy and Belphegor Sloth. As well as tempting men to sin, the fallen angels or devils caused many kinds of disasters, whether natural and accidental. Like the demons and evil spirits of Nature in primitive beliefs, the fallen angels were regarded as the agencies of accidental deaths, disease, earthquakes, famine, war, pestilence, plague and all variety of emotional and mental disorders. Anyone afflicted with a mental disease was regarded as being 'possessed by demons.'

The angels obviously make up a liberal division of the *familia* of God among whom strife from time to time broke out, as it can in all good families worthy of the name, but this particular strife also disturbed the peace upon earth. They belong to the celestial family and God does very little without consulting them about it, he does listen but the final decision in all matters rests with him and it is shown that he has overruled their objections in the past. Because of this, we are told of a Rabbi who added this rather delightful, but practical petition to his prayers each day. 'May it be thy will O Lord our God, to grant peace in the household above and the household below.' (***Ber***. 16b). The term *Familia* is 'a house and all belonging to it.'

Many people quote the line from the following in ***Luke*** 16:13: 'No servant can serve two masters; for either he will hate the one, and love the other; or else he will hold to the one, and despise the other. Ye cannot serve God and mammon' and the line many people quote is the last one.

Mammon in the first quotation is presented as a strong rival to God and a test of the loyalty of the disciple. The riches of the world now or the promise of them in the next world has always presented a perplexing dilemma because it questions which of the two masters will receive the obedience and which the disobedience. Mammon has lost none or little of his strength over the intervening years.

However, this is not the only quotation regarding Mammon in ***Luke***. A parallel phrasing makes this evident. 'Make to yourselves friends of the Mammon of unrighteousness . . . If then you have not been faithful in the unrighteous mammon, who will commit to your trust the true riches.' ***Luke*** 16:9–11. The god Mammon in the ***Bible*** does not seem to bear a negative evaluation because despite Mammon being thought 'unrighteous,' you are still exhorted to make friends with him perhaps so that you can be unfaithful to him or learn to master both him and his gifts. When someone gains money, they should not be taken possession of by worldly and material things, but 'possess them as if they possessed them not.'

The message may be that if you cannot handle money properly, become its master and not its servant, you may not be able to handle the 'true riches' of the spirit? If 'true riches' were granted, would the individual squander them in the same way earthy riches can be if they cannot control them? If you were given riches, would you know how to handle them? It is a palpable fact that people who cannot handle their finances very well do not seem to be able to handle life very well because vast riches can overwhelm people.

How then will you handle 'true riches' if you were given it. My mother's view of money drummed into me when young was simple — 'First you make it, then you make it last' — this I have always tried to do. The question, human nature being what it is, that comes to mind is having made friends with Mammon and gained his gifts perhaps we would not be ready to give them up for something less material and more spiritual?

Mammon is sometimes found as a 'demon of avarice, he is often found as a fallen angel ruling in Hell as an arch–tempter. *Luke* 16:13 seems to present him as a power that is hostile to God saying 'ye cannot serve God and mammon,' with the emphasis on 'serve' him — yet the pursuit of wealth is not condemned. Milton also has him as one of the fallen angels in Hell and 'the least erected Spirit that fell from Heaven' who, even when he was in heaven his thoughts were always downward bent:

> ' . . . Admiring more
> The riches of Heav'ns pavement trodd'n gold,
> Than aught, divine or holy, else enjoyed
> In vision beatific.'
> ***Paradise Lost.***

One of the most persistent misquotes of biblical text tells us that 'money is the root of all evil.' This more often than not is used as a form of rebuke by those who do not have a money 'root' and is often directed with contempt against those who do. The relevant line is 'For the *love* of money is the root of all evil.' 1 *Timothy* 6:10. My italics obviously, but in the correctly quoted line the stress has been shifted from the money, to the person involved with it because they may love money above all other things, possibly to a point of evil, something that has not been unknown. Money does not appear to be as bad as frequently thought and it is more the attitude to money that causes the trouble.

We are frequently told that money and trouble go together and this seems to have been recognized early but is it 'the love of it?' It is a fair statement that if you want to find the value of money — try borrowing some! The biblical and pulpit condemnation of money over the centuries does not seem to have had much effect because Mammon is as alive and kicking as he has always been, with plenty of disciples wishing to worship at his shrine asking and seeking his blessings. Mammon can even be found as an angel now and invoked by some — while remaining a fallen angel to others and he is always an interesting angel or god either way. This discussion has been raging for years, I think it will long continue and I cannot see what has been written here will be the final word on the matter by any means.

## SHEOL

Sheol is a word of uncertain etymology and in ordinary use means 'a chasm, a ravine, the underworld' or 'the world of the dead' In the *Old Testament* it is the place under the earth where the dead gathered, a place of shadows, where there is complete silence and a place where existence as we know it is no more. The synonyms used for Sheol are 'death, the pit or destruction (= *Abaddon*).' In many philosophies, it is called the *Land of Forgetfulness*, a place where they no longer praise god. The book of *Job* tells us 'Sheol (= Hell) is naked before him (= God), and destruction (= *Abaddon*) has no covering.' (26:6).

Sheol, in *Old Testament* thought, differs from the later doctrine of Hell or Gehenna (dealt with below) because Sheol was the place where the dead gather without discrimination because all are there, saints and sinners, good and bad, royalty and commoners because to die simply meant 'to join those who had gone before.' The region of the shadow of the dead in the *Old Testament* is on the whole translated as hell or the pit. It was considered as the common abode both of the righteous and the unrighteous, where life was continued as a shadowy, wavering or a dim reflection of earth life. Those in Sheol have no part in life of the earth, neither is there any knowledge or productive work there (*Ecc.*9).

Death is not looked upon as being a natural event because it goes against Gods gift of life. Sheol in the *Old Testament* was the place everyone went to at death because it was the final destination of all — not unlike a place of gathering and punishment, the place of departed souls. Sheol can be thought of in several ways, it is a place from which people can save themselves and a place where the wicked are taken at death and the righteous can be saved from Sheol. The original idea was an evolving idea of an emerging belief in a future life that was later superseded by a new and more unique viewpoint.

It was a common belief among ancient peoples including the Israelites that the soul or spirit after its departure from the body continued to live. Sheol was considered to be at the opposite extreme to heaven and those who went there were frequently said 'to descend' or 'to go down,' which was the opposite of going 'up to heaven.' It was said to have doors or gates and once a person has entered through the Gates of Death, there is no return. Once inside all were equal with no social distinctions because the Angel of Death is a great leveller — in the final analysis all get the equality that many crave.

In the Greek, Charon, the son of Erebus and Nyx has the duty of ferrying the souls of the deceased who have had the rites of burial, over the Rivers Styx. His payment for this task was the coin that was placed in the mouth of the corpse though in other philosophies coins are placed on the eyes — 'to pay the ferry man.' In time, Charon became regarded as a figure of death and the Underworld. As such, he survives as Charos or Charontas — the Angel of Death — in Modern Greek folklore.

The Witch of Endor 'brought Samuel up out of the earth' so that king Saul could consult him in time of crisis, even though necromancy was strictly prohibited by the Laws of Moses and even by the laws of Saul regarding the matter, but in his case, it seems even he relaxed the penalty. This has the implication that those in the underworld, though disconnected from the living, appear to be familiar with and take an interest in, the affairs of the living above them. It must not be concluded because of this that Samael was 'in hell' because he was merely 'brought up' from a place below the earth. Samuel had simply been 'gathered unto his people.' The same words are used in *Deuteronomy* ' . . . as Aaron thy brother was gathered unto his people.' 32:51. King Hezekiah of Judah was 'sick unto death' and laments in his sickness. 'In the noontide of my days I must depart; I am consigned to the gates of the grave (= *Sheol*); I am deprived of the residue of my years.' *Isaiah* 38:10. Such lines strengthen the idea of the 'gates of death, going to his people and going down.'

Gehenna was introduced above and this is a transliteration in English of the Greek form of the Aramaic. Gehenna must be carefully set apart from the other terms used on the subject of the after life. The main difference between Sheol and Gehenna is that the former may in certain conditions lead to the latter as an extreme. Whereas Sheol is a region of inactivity and stillness, Gehenna is both the region and a state of dissolution.

Similar to the *Old Testament*, Sheol is a temporary place that lies between death and resurrection, though Maimonides thought it a place of 'punishment and total annihilation.' Tartarus is given once only with 'hell' used in the *King James Version* and it identifies the place where the angels who fell in the revolt of Satan. 'For if God spared not the angels that sinned, but cast them down to hell (= Tartarus), and delivered them into chains of darkness, to be reserved unto judgement.' 2 *Peter* 2:4.

Tartarus, Son of Aether and Gaia, who by his mother became father of the giants Typhoeus and Echidna. In the Greek, *Ταρταρος, Tartarus*= 'a dark abyss, as deep below Hades as earth below heaven, the prison of the Titans, later, the Nether World.' Other names for **Tartarus** as a deity are Pluto, Hades and Dis — all referring to the underworld. The early conception of the underworld Hades was to a great extent modified by the continuous communication between Greece and Egypt.

In turn, the Romans were fascinated with the thoughts of the Greeks and Virgil has given detailed particulars of the Nether World called **Orcus**, which is divided into five regions of which the last is the place of the blessed **Elysium**. As a place in the **Iliad**, it was one of the four regions, Orcis is far below the earth as heaven or Olympus was above the earth. Into Orcus were thrust the Titans who rebelled against Olympus and in later times Orcus became synonymous with Hades. Much as the Fallen Angels were thrust into Hell.

It would not be unfair I feel to say that the Hell of the early Christian fathers and the Christian religion in general can to some extent, be traced back to **Amenti** of the Egyptians, **Sheol** and **Gehenna** of the Jews and **Orcus** of Virgil. The 'hells' of other religions and many offshoots are part of this connected web. In Scandinavian Valhalla with its purgatory, **Niflheim** and the everlasting **Tartaris** and **Nastrond** are merely variations of the same ideas, save in one important point. In the Northern models there is often a cutting, icy wind with ice and snow possibly representing the Norseman's idea of misery, takes the place of the unquenchable and eternal fires of punishment. Tradition has it that Judas is allowed to leave the pit of fire once every year and go to the snows to cool himself as 'a reward for his sole act of kindness' — though what this was is not given.

In all these regions there is one inflexible stipulation, if for any reason you are sent or travel there while living — you should completely refrain from eating and drinking while there. In the Greek **Hades**, Persephone broke the rules and took a few seeds of a pomegranate or Hades knowing the rules, slipped the six seeds under her tongue and she was condemned to stay there during the autumn and winter months six months in all, one month for each seed. In the **Kalevala** of the Finnish peoples, Wainamoinen astutely abstains from taking any drink or food while he was among the dead.

This condition must not be thought of as being limited only to places of the dead, an old and well–established magical lore admonishes you never to eat or drink anything in any house of which you are not certain or feel uncomfortable. This is according to the widespread idea that if you eat anyone's bread or take salt with them you establish communion and enter into kinship with them. If you make this offer in your house, you have invited the receiver into your home and you have given them the right to be there. A legend from Gascony tells of St Peter sending a prince on a mission for him in the nether regions, with great caution he gives him enough bread for his needs with strict instructions not to eat anything while there.

Many of the early races watched the Sun travel westward over land and seas to sink each evening into an abyss of fire 'to its death' and this is why so many of the dead were buried in the West, as with Western banks of the Nile wotj the living on the Eastern banks in the East. Sometimes the paradise of a race was set in the heavens and it was reached through the 'Path of the Dead' — know to us as the Milky Way.

Gehenna, also called Gehinnom, the abode of the damned in the afterlife in Jewish and Christian eschatology and the doctrine of final things. Named in the **New Testament** in Greek form from the Hebrew **Ge Hinnom**, meaning 'valley of Hinnom.' The Valley of Ben Gehinnom is a deep valley that divided the tribes of Benjamin and Judah and is a yawning ravine to the south west of Jerusalem, sometimes called 'the valley.' It was notorious for the idolatrous practises carried out there by the Israelites during the reigns of King Solomon in the 10th century B.C and King

Manasseh in the 7th century B.C and this continued until the Babylonian Exile in the 6th century B.C. Later it was made a refuse dump and a permanent place of burning to discourage the reinstatement of such sacrifices. The imagery of the burning of humans supplied the conception of 'hellfire' both to Jewish and Christian thoughts of death and the afterlife and it became a symbol of an accursed spot *par excellence* and of eternal punishment — a place where God can destroy the body and the soul. It is mentioned several times in the *New Testament* as a place where fire will destroy the wicked

One practise was infant sacrifice associated with the rites of Moloch or Molach, an Ammonite god who was worshipped with human sacrifice. ' . . . which is in the valley of the children of Hinnom, that no man might make his son or his daughter to pass through the fire of Moloch.' 2 *Kings* 23:10. The ravine earned for itself the reputation of great iniquity. This made it a name for any place of ultimate retribution for the wicked and regarded as a symbol for a place of punishment in the future world. It was Josiah that brought these practises to an end.

Some think Gehenna is symbolically represented in part on the Tarot card called the *Magician*, who raises the Wand of Will above in his right hand upwards to heaven, while the left hand downwards to the earth a symbolic gesture that often indicated the Chthonic Gods.

This is often interpreted as giving the seeker the simple choice — 'To Gehenna or the Throne, he travels fastest who travels alone.' This sentiment was sometimes used by Schools suggesting that the study of the spiritual, mystical or magical study is at times a lonely affair but having less luggage to hold you back your progress can be quicker because of it, there is less to distract the seeker or hold them back.

Not many can travel with you because few sometimes none, are at the same stage of the journey as you are whatever that is and few understand you. Quite often in the beginning, you have plenty travelling with you because in the early stages there is usually ample company. Soon there are those who break away and go ahead as the runners in the race start to get thin with a lot behind you and a fewer ahead. They are also looking for someone to travel with and help them, this is natural, we have all done it. Looking ahead on the road for someone to travel with for a while to broaden your knowledge about what is ahead, discussion, seeking new knowledge and to keep you company for a while. This too is perfectly natural and in the order of things.

## ABADDON OR APOLLYON

Although the *New Testament* seems to take little interest in the idea of an angelic hierarchy, there is little doubt that traces of the doctrine can still be found. Clear distinctions of good and bad angels are met with and among the 'evil' angels, we find Abaddon or Apollyon. 'And they had a king over them, which is the angel of the bottomless pit, whose name in the Hebrew tongue is Abaddon, but in the Greek tongue hath the name Apollyon.' Some modern writers are of the opinion that Apollyon is not Satan though a number of them feel he may be an evil or fallen angel, a destroying angel, the Angel of Death, perhaps even Asmodeus of the Jews.

The word *Abaddon* in Hebrew, Chaldee and Syrian is said to come from the verbal root *abad*= 'to perish, be cut off' denoting 'destruction, place of destruction, abyss; the region of the dead.' This Hebrew word occurs six times in the *Old Testament* and when it does it is usually referring to a 'the place of the dead.' It often serves as a synonym for Sheol and it is variously translated as 'death, destruction, the grave or hell.' Abaddon is not a person but the process of decay, destruction and loss. By synecdoche, the word is made the name of Sheol and it may be that from this came the later identification with the Angel of Destruction or Death.

It is possible that the Greek word *Απολλυων, Apollyon* has been derived from the same verb as *απολλυμι, apollymi*= 'to destroy utterly, kill, to slay' of things, 'to destroy, demolish or waste' sometimes 'to be lost, slip away, vanish.' The term in Greek admits that in all growth there is an corresponding energy for destruction or dissipation. Apollyon is given as 'destruction, laying waste' (*Revelation* 9:11) because the ideas given appear to have been 'made flesh' or personified as 'the angel of the bottomless pit' and so translated as 'the destroyer.' Thus, Abaddon, Apollyon, Hades and Orcus all signify the Underworld, many old writers speak of 'the sheol of Abaddon.' The Hebrew word Abaddon only occurs once in the *New Testament*.

Originally, it is thought that *Apollyon* may have been a mystical term of significance but in Christian times, the term became an pseudonym for Satan. Such changes often meant the original meaning was not to someone's liking because it did not having a nuance that was suitable for them or the circumstances at the time, so the meaning was changed to make it so. If changes are made to be disparaging then it quite often meant the original meaning possibly did not.

When the abyss was opened, smoke issued from it and from the smoke locusts of an extraordinary character came forth and these locusts were thought to be under the rule of their king, *Abaddon*. Some believe that these locusts were symbols of a destructive Power because locusts are destructive by nature and their king was the presiding and controlling spirit over them. Others think the locusts are symbols for men and that would make their king a man because they are described as 'their faces were as the faces of men.'

The fact that *Abaddon* is called an 'angel' may mean nothing because the word angel has been applied to men or those having 'the appearance of men' or simply 'a messenger' in the past. In this case, their king 'which is the angel of the bottomless pit' tells us what he was and where he rules. Various interpreters believe Satan or the Devil is not intended here, so naturally there are those who think that he is. Usually, however, whenever Satan is mentioned in *Revelations* it is very distinct and there can be little doubt about who is really meant. Nowhere in *Revelations* is Satan designated by the terms used here. As the reader will see that speculation involved in this has still not been satisfactorily resolved regarding this angel to this day and this that makes him intriguing. According to Mathers, *Abaddon* is a name for God, Moses invoked this angel to bring down the destructive rain over Egypt and he was called up after the fifth trumpet was sounded in the vision of St. John.

## NEW TESTAMENT

Separating the *Old Testament* and the *New Testament* is easier said than done and without doubt, it is probably not possible to draw a hard and fast line between magic and religion. It is easy in the *Bible* in as much as there is a clear break between the two, but the overlap between them is sometimes enormous. In most religions whether they are early or late, there is a residue, perhaps even a continued existence of magic and in the more advanced development of magic, admitted or not, there may be found the initial stages of religion. Polytheism was a natural outgrowth of animism and the gods of polytheism were the highest and most noble of the spirits within the philosophy, which was certainly a religion and before we go in into the next part let us take a look at the word 'religion.' It is not the boring subject some think.

Religion is written practically the same in most European languages. It comes from the Latin *religio*= 'reverence for God (the Gods), fear of God, connected with a careful pondering of divine things.' *Piety*, *religion*: namely, both pure and inward piety and that which is manifested in religious rites and ceremonies. Hence the rites and ceremonies as well as the entire system of religion and worship, the *res divinae* or *sacrae* were frequently called *religio* or *religiones*, consequently *religio* or *religiones* may very properly be used for religion, according to the preconceptions of it.' *Latin–English Lexicon*; Andrews (1855).

*Relego=* 'to gather together, to collect again' *re=* 'again' and *lego=* 'to lay, to arrange, to gather.' *Objectively:* 'The outer form and embodiment which the inward spirit of a true or false devotion is assumed' or 'a system of doctrine and worship regarded by its adherents as of Divine authority.' *Subjectively:* 'The feeling of veneration with which the worshipper regards the Being he adores, specially the intense veneration which the Christian has for the Trinity, with the moral results to which that veneration leads.'

*Darwin*, (*The Descent of Man*): ' . . . considers that the feeling of religious devotion is a highly complex one, consisting of love, complete submission to an exalted and mysterious superior, a strong sense of dependence, fear, reverence, gratitude, hope for the future and perhaps other elements. No being, he thinks, could experience so complex an emotion until advanced in his intellectual and moral faculties to at least a moderately high level.' Other entries are present but these are the main ones from *Lloyd's Encyclopaedic Dictionary* (1895).

Briefly, magic may perhaps be defined as the attempt of an individual(s) to have communication with spiritual beings and to try to influence them for their advantage and/or assistance. This rests upon a widespread belief even today that the powers in the world on which the well–being of an individual or a people depends is controlled by spiritual agents and these mediators can be conciliated or made friends with, through words, deeds, supplication, ritual, lights, incense, gifts, prescribed behaviour, approved attitudes and so forth.

Further, in this, there is something akin to religious worship and prayer; perhaps it may depend on the direction you have chosen to view the same thing, the view that you take, remembering the tale of the blind men describing an elephant. Indeed magic and religion appear to have numerous similarities that to many made all magic an incipient religion, there is an appeal to spirits who are thought to be more powerful and wiser than the people appealing to them, the superiority of Spirit compared to material matter must have been almost intuitive to a number of early people. The methods employed to secure what is desired are nothing other than supplications of goodwill to the beings that are being consulted. Incantation or invocation is only prayers and in this, the key stress is laid upon the method of utterance, rather than on the moral condition of the agent being used.

Plants, wood, herbs, drugs and so forth, when burnt to appease or please the good spirits and seek protection against the evil ones can be compared with sacrifices, especially those that use incense, found in many branches of both the Jewish practice, the Christian Church and countless others. Whatever it is, in every case something is being done with a view of propitiating and encouraging spiritually elevated beings to be active on our behalf with guidance, protection and support.

Magic is often regarded by some authorities as being unethical and this corresponds with their view that the beings being 'trafficked with' are likewise unethical. For those who deal with the One God, who is believed to be just, holy and the only true God that is above all others, it is required or without question demanded, that they must not deal with anyone other than the One God. This is precise in the early conformity with the One God and it is demanded (in all five times) that 'Thou shalt have no other gods before me.' *Exodus* 20:3, see also *Exodus* 34:14; *Deuteronomy* 4:24; 5:9 and 6:15.

In the above quotations, the important part is that it admits (at the time) there were other gods before the One God and therefore they could be a challenge or why insist that the other gods should not be dealt with. Further, no likeness of these gods must be used as images. Neither must their altars or groves be used, these should be destroyed and they must not be served in any form whatsoever.

The punishment for doing so or breaking the covenant is both terrible though honest, ' . . . for I the Lord thy God am a jealous God, visiting the iniquity of the fathers upon the children unto the third and fourth generation of them that hate me; and shewing mercy unto thousands of them that love me and keep my commandments.' *Exodus* 20:5–6. Though, God's punishment on innocent children for so long after their parents original sin seems rather harsh as we have said elsewhere, however the contract is clearly stated regarding the matter and it was up to the individual to accept or reject the terms. From the foregoing, it seems that the One God was seeking adherents to his cause and offering a contract if his offer was taken up.

Next, let us take some of the questions that may occur to people having been expressed by other writers. These can be grouped into three broad areas with variations within the groups. Did magic precede religion and is it a stepping–stone to religion? Is magic a retrograde step retreating from religion, a rejection of religion in favour of magic? Is magic a total removal and a denial of religion in the strictest sense? The latter is an old view of course, most theologians would cleave to this stance without any deviation and some episodes in history have recorded how inflexible this rigorous view has been in history.

Martin Luther said of witches, who naturally exercised their power to the detriment of all in his day. They spoiled a farmer's eggs, his butter, prevented fires from igniting and everything else that went wrong in people's lives. It caused Luther to proclaim 'I would have no pity on those witches, I would burn them all.' Nevertheless, even today the question remains, is it possible to remove all traces of magic from religion.

The Jewish religion has its phylacteries and mezuzah's that are sometimes used as countercharms and as methods of protection against demons for the possessor, their families, their property and most nations have help similar to these and none is being singled out in any way. There are those who would say that such use denies their higher purpose of reminding those who wore the tefillin or passed through a door of their duty, love and service to Jehovah — and this is not denied. However, the mezuzah serves to shield the house and to protect those within. However, I do not think Maimonides would have approved of the practise of fitting them to the doors of cars in an attempt to prevent accidents or hanging them around the neck as a talisman, amulet or charm, yet I have read of this being done at the time of writing.

There is the oracle of *Urim* and *Thummim* and as said, these are objects of uncertain description that were kept under the breastplate and vestments of the high priest of the Israelites. They seem to have been used to obtain and simple answer of 'yes or no' from God, not unlike casting lots, while the magic of Moses is very prominent in *Genesis* to name but a few examples. Christians were not averse to magical charms, the incantations and charms addressed to the Trinity and relying for results on the use of the Triune names but I have often wondered what the mind-set would have been if it had been a magician who had turned water into wine? In Islam 'the Satan's taught men magic.' Other examples are given throughout and are easily found.

I repeat, despite the examples given that no particular religion or race is being singled out for censure or criticism, which is not my intention. In many cases, I simply observe matters and touch upon them. As already stated, all magic is a form of religion and without doubt, the true magician does not seek to use force in the exercise of their art, something which many would regarded as being counter–productive, including me.

Christianity developed a hierarchy of angels that was firmly based on the Judaic tradition and enlarged. In addition to the Angels, Archangels, Seraphim and Cherubim five other spiritual angelic groups were sanctioned in the church by the fourth century. These five groups are named in the *Letters of Paul* in the *New Testament* and they are the Virtues, Powers, Principalities, Dominions and Thrones. Together these make up a Hierarchy or the Choir of Angels and they form the basis of this work. This does not mean any angels that do not belong to this hierarchy are not discussed or valid. This group forms a familiar and stable centre from which we work and if it is fitting, all will be discussed in the appropriate place.

In the *New Testament* over one third of the references made to the angels are to be found in the *Book of Revelation*. The angels in *Revelation* are either glorious, mystical or grotesque but they definitely cannot be confused with the human race in any way. The language used to describe the angels in these visions is often difficult to interpret or explain and this in part is because the *Book of Revelation* is metaphorical and without any doubt — mystical!

The Latin *Paracletus* and the Greek word *Ραρακλητος, Paracletos, Paraclete*= 1: 'A calling to one, a summons to assist.' 2: 'An exortation, calling upon, imploring.' 3: 'To comfort, to console.'

Paraclete is a fine word, which is given various useful translations from the *Greek Testament* into English as the foregoing shows. The simplest transliteration is 'one who is called to someone's aid' or 'one who advocates for another' and who acts on another's behalf as a mediator, an intercessor or a comforter. Christ is often called a Paraclete because, as a high priest of Melchizedek, he speaks for the people to the God his father.

Christ is often substituted for the angels as the mediator between God and man by some and he has been thought to be an angel himself. In the *Epistle to the Hebrews*, special emphasis is laid on the fact that the angels are created subordinate to Christ. ' . . . being made so much better than the angels, and he by inheritance obtained a more excellent name than they . . . who maketh his angels spirit . . . and let all the angels worship him.'

I like using the word Paraclete for the angels because I feel the meaning of the word is right for them as in — 'calling to one, a summon to assist' — this to me is a perfect description of the angels. Another example: 'The spirit, the Paraclete, shall teach you everything.' *John* 24:26 (*Old Syriac Version*.) The word in the A.V of the Bible is found mostly in *John's* gospel where Christ declares that the Holy Spirit will come from the Father when he departs. The Paraclete is also called the 'Spirit of Truth' that will lead people into the truth and assist them to respond to the message of Jesus. Its a pity the word is seen less and less today but it seems to have gone the way of so many good words.

Some sects believed Christ was God who during his time on earth was like an angel with a phantom body through which he took the appearance of a man. One such sect was the 12th century Albigenses or Cathars. They were of course 'a heretical sect' of Christians who flourished in Southern France near Albi and Toulouse during the 11th–13th centuries and the term 'heretical' meant that they did not toe the official line. The Albigenses displayed a consistent anti–Catholic approach and criticism in their beliefs. They had different sacraments that included the *consolamentum* (= 'baptism of the spirit.') As said, they believed Christ was God, but they believed that while he was on earth he was an angel using a spectral body that took on the aspect of a man. They believed the established Christian church with its corrupt clergy and enormous material wealth was the agent of Satan and should be shunned — a palpable and dangerous heresy without a doubt — so it is obvious they had to go and perhaps the sooner the better.

The Christian church did attempt to win over the Albigenses by peaceful methods in the beginning. However, when it was thought that every attempt made to 'convert them to the true path' had failed, Pope Innocent III launched the *Albigensian Crusade* (c.1209–1229), under the elder Simon de Montfort. Thousands of people were slaughtered, including many that were not Albigenses — just in case. When those in charge of the military asked the religious authority how would the soldiers know who were the Catholics in the towns. They were told ' . . . kill them all, God will know his own.' The movement was finally crushed in 1244 at Montségur, the infamous climax to the *Albigensian Crusade*. The fortress was besieged for ten months and finally two–

hundred and fifty–five heretics were burned to death. This 'crusade' is probably one of the most bloody and infamous episodes in religious history.

The Jewish Qumran sect or Essenes was another sect who saw the world as a battleground. To them, the world was an arena of a powerful struggle between the Spirit of Truth and the Spirit of Wickedness. This latter Spirit was an angelic power that was opposed to God and called Belial (= 'the unholy one'). Belial, in the Qumran texts, is called the *Spirit and Prince of Darkness*. In the *Bible* wicked men are described as a 'man of Belial.' (2 *Samuel* 16:7.) Belial's men are the 'floods of ungodly men' (= *nachalei belial*) in *Psalm* 189:5.

Cerinthus (c. AD 100) was a Christian heretic who allied Jesus with the angelic, but not as St Paul would have it. He preached the world was created by a subordinate deity called a *demiurge* or the angels and one of the angels gave Moses the Ten Commandments. He said Jesus was the natural son of Mary and Joseph and that the Spirit of God — called the 'Christ' — came down upon Jesus at his baptism empowering him to accomplish miracles and proclaim the unknown Father. The spirit of Christ departed from Jesus before the Passion and the resurrection. This is Gnostic thought and again to the church it was heretical. The Gnostic religion was a major contender during the Roman Empire and a strong rival of the sect that became Christianity. So let us take a brief look at . . .

## A LITTLE GNOSTICISM

The Demiurge was the supernatural maker of the world who is subordinate to the Supreme Being or God. From the Greek $\Delta\eta\mu\iota\upsilon\upsilon\gamma\varsigma$, *Demiourgos*= 'one who works for the people, a skilled craftsman and the Maker of the World.' $\Delta\eta\mu\iota\upsilon\varsigma$, *Demios*= 'belonging to the people, elected by the people' and $\varepsilon\rho\gamma\upsilon\nu$, *ergon*= 'a work,' an 'artisan, craftsman, manual labourer' or 'one who makes works for the people.

In Plato's *Timaeus,* the Demiurge was the creator of the world and the builder of the material universe. In Gnosticism, the Demiurge was the architect of the world and a being that is quite distinct from the supreme God and inferior to him. The demiurge is a name given by the Platonian philosophers to an exalted and mysterious agent by whom God was supposed to have created the universe. He was the chief of the aeons or lower order of spirits and was looked upon as the author of evil. He corresponds to the *Logos* or *Word* of St. John and the Platonic Christians of the Early Church. The Demiurge figures conspicuously in Gnostic systems of philosophy.

The Gnostics thought the true God was too far above this level of existence to pay it that much notice. This of course left the world of matter at the mercy of the demiurge and this, according to the Gnostics, left them trapped in a world without the True God. The demiurge is often thought of as a wayward but impotent angel who keeps people in his thrall through ignorance and illusion. In Orphite Gnosticism *Iadalbaoth* appears as Yahweh in the *Old Testament*, Cabbala and Gnostic law and *Iadalbaoth's* angels are called *archons. Iadalbaoth* is usually called the *First Archon of Darkness* and as the demiurge, he occupies a rank directly beneath the 'unknown Father.' Many equate *Iadalbaoth* with Sammael as the Fallen Angel Satan or the Devil.

The Gnostic sects professed Christianity but their beliefs diverged sharply from the faithful of the Early Church. They rejected the literal or traditional interpretations of the Gospels. The Christ, the divine spirit or angel entered the body of the man Jesus and the Christ could not die on the cross — only Jesus because he was of the physical, while Christ was of the Spirit and could not be slain. This naturally gives an alternative meaning (for some) when Jesus asks *Eli, Eli, lama sabachthani* (= 'My God, my God why hast thou forsaken me') on the cross? Jesus (= the *physical*) is asking Christ (= the *spiritual*) why he had forsaken him in his great time of need — why had he been sacrificed. 'And the sun was darkened, and the veil of the temple was rent in the midst. And when Jesus had cried with a loud voice, he said, Father, into thy hands I commend my spirit: and having said thus, he gave up the ghost.' *Luke* 23:45–46; Jesus gave the 'spirit to his Father,' while 'he gave up the ghost.'

'But men must know, that in this theatre of man's life it is reserved only for God and angels to be lookers on'. *The Advancement of Learning* (1605). Francis Bacon 1561–1626. English lawyer, philosopher and essayist.

*Γνωσις, Gnosis (silent 'g')* = 'an enquiry, a judgement, knowledge especially of a deeper kind' or 'revealed knowledge' promised a secret knowledge of the divine realm. Gnosticism ' . . . which professes to restore to mankind the lost knowledge of God.'

The movement appears to have greatly declined by the third century and was regarded as extinct by the sixth, but I believe it is far from dead. It has been disputed whether there are allusions to either nascent or fully developed Gnosticism in the New Testament and some writers profess to find them. I believe many churches today have been resurrected based upon and using Gnostic principles and there are some good works regarding them available now.

Most of the sources about Gnosticism in the past came from Christian anti–Gnostic texts because these diatribes provided extensive quotations in accusation, citing the works destroyed from which they were taken. However, new discoveries at *Nag Hammadi* and other sources have added considerably to the Gnostic library and they are worth anyone's time and effort — in my opinion of course! *The Gospel of Thomas* and *The Gospel of Mary* make a good introduction to the subject and there are some excellent writers to be found. We have been brief regarding the subject remember, the heading does say 'a little' and the selected aspects of the philosophy, because the reader now has easy access to many works dealing with the subject today than in the past, should they wish to go beyond what is given here.

## THE THEOPHANY

This is another important word used for an appearance of God in human form, which is expressed in the ecclesiastical term 'theophany.' This word is from the Greek *Θεος, Theos*= 'God' and *φαινω, phaino*= 'to appear' or 'God appearing or delivering his message, a visible manifestation of God or a god to man.' 'Theophany' (pl. *theophanies*), the term is frequently found in religious works.

The word has the meanings of 'the manifestation of God to man by actual appearance' or 'an appearance of God in visible form, temporary and not necessarily material, though sometimes appearing so.' It is the second explanation that the writer favours most. There are also auditory manifestations of God because he does not necessarily have to be seen. *Theo* is the first element in many words derived from the Greek referring to the Divine Being or divinity as with the word 'theology.' From the Latin and Greek *θεολογια, theologia,* = 'a speaking about God,' *Θεος, Theos*= 'God' and *λογος, logos*= 'a word;' *lego*= 'to speak' therefore, *theologos* = 'speaking about God,'

Visible manifestations include the voice of God that was heard in the Garden of Eden though God was not seen. (*Genesis* 2.) Moses heard God through the flames of the burning bush and again God was not seen, nor did the flames consume the bush (*Exodus* 3.) There were the various fires, smoke and thunder on Mount Sinai. (*Exodus* 9.) There was an angel who appeared in human form. (*Judges* 13.) There was the still small voice (= *Bat Qol*) that spoke to Elijah that was not in wind, earthquake or fire. (1 *Kings* 19.) At the baptism of Jesus by John, there was a voice from heaven — 'this is my beloved son in whom I am well pleased.' (*Matthew* 3) and many others

It has been pointed out it is the message that is important and although the physical display is often magnificent its main purpose could be to impress the recipient and to stress clearly where and from whom it came. The main thing to remember about a *theophany* is that it is God who takes the initiative more often than not on a temporary basis and while using them and he often does not reveal himself, in part or fully. It is suggested the reason why *theophanies* do not appear to be quite so important in the *New Testament* is that Christ was regarded as a *theophany* made flesh and not temporary, not a fleeting visitation but permanent for the time granted for the purpose for which he came.

## THOMAS AQUINAS

'An angel can illuminate the thought and mind of man by strengthening the power of vision, and by bringing within his reach some truth which the angel himself contemplates. *St. Thomas Aquinas.*

Now let us spend a little time with Thomas Aquinas (1224/25-1274) — the 'Angelic Doctor.' Thomas Aquinas (Italian: *San Tommaso d'Aquino*) was born of a noble family in Roccasecca, near Aquino. He was educated at the Benedictine monastery at Monte Cassino and at the University of Naples. Thomas, in the year of his father's death in 1243, while he was still an undergraduate and despite starting his schooling in a Benedictine Order, joined the Dominican Order. His mother was fiercely against this association and in a vain attempt to make him abandon his chosen course. She restrained him within the family castle for more than a year, finally giving in when his resolution would not waver. She liberated him in 1245 and he journeyed to Paris to continue his education where he came under the influence of St. Albertus Magnus, individually discussed later.

He said 'All I have written seems to me like so much straw, compared to what has been revealed to me.' Thomas shared his master's great esteem for the ancient philosophers, in particular Aristotle and the later Arabic and Jewish thinkers. He cherished and welcomed truth wherever he found it and he used it to illuminate and enrich Christian thought. For Thomas reason and faith cannot gainsay each other because they both come from an identical divine source.

Aquinas is regarded as the one who set out the Roman Catholic doctrine concerning the angels and while others have given calculations for the numbers of the angelic host, Thomas maintains the sum is so great that it is beyond human ability to even count them. He thought the angels had the power to imitate God and we, the human race, could only achieve this to a very inadequate degree.

He believed the angels were 'pure intellect, neither male nor female, but able to assume whatever form they like.' If God was 'pure,' which to Thomas was an equivalent term for 'spirit' then the angels were equally free from matter. Some believe, because some of the 'angels' were reputed to have 'begat' giants from their association with the 'daughters of men,' the term 'pure' should only be applied with any exactness to God.

Thomas Aquinas favoured a wordless exchange of angelic thought and the term he used for this was 'illumination' between the angels, rather than any spoken language as some have declared. The only language to converse with the angels, according to the ancient Rabbis was naturally Hebrew, if you were for Islam then the Archangel Gabriel spoke Arabic, for the Catholics it was Latin and so on.

Let us present a few of the salient points given by Thomas Aquinas in his ***Tractus de Angelis***. This may prove at variance with some things already given but if we can differ in our interpretations, opinions and inferences, the Saints have the same privileges. The angels are incorporeal and therefore they are not composed of form or matter. The Angels exceed human beings in numbers, just as they exceed them in perfection and because they are not physical, they are incorruptible. They are naturally a distinct species because they differ in rank. Angels can assume an airy body that does not exercise the functions of life; thus, they do not eat as Christ did after his resurrection.

Saint Thomas set the angels as mediators 'between the mind and Will of God and the minds of men.' He appears to look upon the angels as a bridge and thought that without this 'bridge,' the separation between God and his creation was too great to span and a link could not be made. This seems to be borne out by Thomas to some extent because he said that man is situated by his existence at the juncture of two universes — 'like a horizon of the corporeal and of the spiritual.' The writer has already mentioned the importance he attaches to the 'middle ground' and of using the angels as a pontifex or bridge. In organized religion, this 'link' is the elected leader of that religion or the one who has made the 'contact' with the source of the religion or teachings. This should be so for any School of Occult teaching, if possible, if not then the leader must be a caretaker and guide, a useful service performed until someone with a proven ability to make true contact for the School is found.

In the Roman Catholic Church, this link or bridge is naturally the office of the Pope who is the pontiff. The word ***pontiff*** is from the Latin ***pontifex***= 'the bridge–builder.' From ***pons***= 'a bridge, a path' and ***facio***= 'to make.' This was a title given to the more illustrious members of the Roman Colleges of Priests and is believed to be taken from the Roman pontifices who had charge of the ***Pons Sublicius*** in Rome. The ***Pons Sublicius*** was an early defensive wooden drawbridge and it is the first known bridge to be built in Rome and defended by Horatius. The name ***Pons Sublicius*** was taken from the wooden piles (= ***sublicae***) on which it was built.

On the Ides of May, stuffed figures called ***argei*** (= twenty seven images of men made of rushes, perhaps replacements for earlier human sacrifices) were thrown into the Tiber from this bridge. At the time of Tiberius the office and title, ***Pontifex Maximus*** (= 'controller of the State religion') was bestowed as a matter of course upon the Emperor on his accession but this is now the title of the Pope. Now let us return once more to the views of Thomas Aquinas.

As already said, the angels are incorporeal and not created of matter and form. The angels can assume an aerial body but have no need any of the functions of the physical life. Thomas said the angels could not be in several places at the same time. The angels with their natural powers have a knowledge of God that is 'far greater than men can possess, though even though their knowledge of God is still imperfect.'

Aquinas tells us the angels have restricted knowledge of future events. They possess will and their will is free, but it differs from the intellect. Although they have knowledge of good and evil, their will is under the guidance only of good and so is void of all passion. They can gain merit and through it attain to perfect bliss, even before reaching this state. They are incapable of sin. Their beatitude is perfect so they are incapable of improvement. The knowledge or awareness of the angels is through classifications and the higher angels are effected by even simpler and fewer divisions than the lower angels. Thomas dealt with and discussed so many of the knotty problems and points regarding the angels that he was called ***Doctor Angelicus*** (= 'the Angelic Doctor.') It was often said of him 'Doctor says that it depends upon circumstances' so he was often called the 'Angel of the Schools.'

Thomas Aquinas expressed his views of the evil spirits saying in summary that their sin was pride and envy for the Devil wanted to be equal to God. The demons were not naturally evil but fell through using their free will. The fall of the Devil was not concurrent with his creation because this would make God the cause of evil. He tells us this despite God saying in *Isaiah* 'I am the Lord, and there is none else. I form the light, and create the darkness: I make peace, and create evil: I the Lord do all these things.' (45:7.) Of which I am sure that he was well aware. He tells us the Devil/Satan was the greatest of all the angels and his sin prompted the fallen angels by incitement — not compulsion. The number of the fallen angels is small compared to the angels who persevered. The demons have a dual habitation — 'hell where they torment the damned and air, where they provoke men to evil.'

Saint Thomas Aquinas (1224–74) synthesized religious and philosophical thought during the Middle Ages and he was canonized in 1323. He had little learning of Greek or Hebrew and was untutored in history but his prolific writings, some eighty works in all, show an intellectual power of the highest order. He exerted an immense intellectual sway throughout the church. Thomas Aquinas died on his way to the Council of Lyons and the feast day of St Thomas is March 7th.

## ST. ALBERT THE GREAT — ALBERTUS MAGNUS

Albertus Magnus was mentioned when we spoke of Thomas Aquinas because he was the teacher Thomas Aquinas. We are told that the angels are infinitely numerous ' . . . thousand thousands ministered unto him, and ten thousand times ten thousand stood before him.' *Daniel* 7:10. St. Albert the Great (1206–1280) was more precise saying there are exactly 399,920,004 angels. There was once a belief that to get into heaven you had to force your way past the angels that hindered your getting there. Albertus Magnus was a German medieval scholar, philosopher, churchman and scientist who is usually best known as being the teacher of Thomas Aquinas, but this is a little condescending for he should also be remembered in his own right of which he is worthy because he was outstanding and a very erudite man — remember he taught Thomas Aquinas and although Aquinas was an exceptional student on all counts, it was not the other way round.

Albertus Magnus was a Dominican bishop and philosopher and he was well known enough in his own right. A proponent of Aristotelianism at the University of Paris, he established the study of nature as a legitimate science within the Christian tradition. In 1941,by papal decree, he was declared the patron saint of all who cultivate the natural sciences. He was the most prolific writer of his century and was the only scholar of his age to be called 'the Great' and remember, this title was given and used of him before his death.

The teachings of Albertus Magnus exercised a great influence and in his time had even greater renown than Aquinas his illustrious pupil. According to the English philosopher Roger Bacon, Albertus Magnus was equal in his time to Aristotle. Magnus as a theologian was outstanding among the medieval philosophers but some commentators, with the benefit of hindsight (that makes many things easy), now say he was not as innovative as his star pupil Thomas.

In his *Summa Theologiae* (c.1270), Albertus sought to reconcile Aristotle and the Christian teachings saying human intelligence could not challenge revelation, but he upheld the philosopher's right to investigate the divine mysteries. Albertus was accepted as an authority equal to Aristotle in philosophy and he was known as *Doctor Universalis* — the 'Universal Doctor' — because of the enormous breadth of his knowledge and his extraordinary studies.

He studied at Bologna and Padua and entered the Dominican order in 1223. He taught at Cologne and lectured from 1245 at the Paris University where Thomas Aquinas was his pupil and

Aquinas followed him to Cologne 1248. Thomas became Provincial of the German Dominicans in 1254 and he was made bishop of Ratisbon in 1260 and two years later, he resigned and he eventually retired to his convent at Cologne.

Thomas Aquinas was sometimes called (by his fellow students) the 'dumb ox of Cologne' because of his somewhat thickset appearance, coupled with the fact that he was rather reserved and serious for one so young. Magnus prophetically told them that 'this ox will one day fill the world with his bellowing' — and he did! Albertus died in Cologne on the 15th of November 1280. He was beatified in 1622. In 1931 and he was declared a Doctor of the Church, a title given regularly since the Middle Ages to Christian theologians of outstanding merit and acknowledged saintliness. The Saint's Gregory, Ambrose, Augustine and Jerome were the original 'four doctors' *par excellence*. However, the list has now been increased to over thirty. The feast day of Albertus Magnus is November 15th for his work in natural science and his life and works are worth study for those inclined because he is impossible to dismiss.

## The ANGELS — VIEWS from other SOURCES — FOR and AGAINST

To show there was division and disagreement among the early writers let us take a number of views for and against, regarding the angels.

The Greek theologian St. John of Damascus (c.675–c.749) is an Eastern monk and theological doctor of the Greek and Latin churches whose treatises on the veneration of sacred images placed him in the forefront of the 8th century Iconoclastic Controversy and whose theological synthesis made him a paramount intermediary between Greek and medieval Latin culture.

His writings frequently show signs of the teachings of the Areopagite, following Dionysius in his organization of the heavenly hierarchy (***De Fide Orthodoxa***. ii. 3). In his writings, John gives a description of angels and he defines a number of points regarding them. 'An angel then is an intellectual substance, always mobile, endowed with free–will, serving God, having received according to grace, immortality in its nature, the form and character of whose substance God alone, who created it, knows.'

The German Dominican mystic Tauler (c.1300–61) was a famous preacher and director, especially of nuns. The Dominicans were popularly known in England as the 'Black Friars' from the black mantle worn over their white habit. His extant sermons put emphasis on the indwelling of God within the human soul and he describes in detail the Mystic Way, which he regards as consisting mainly in the practice of the virtues principally abandonment and humility to the will of God. Tauler stresses that union with God is essential not though so much for its own sake but more for the benefits that it produces in the soul. He followed the Dionysian classification of spirits but expressed himself with much reserve regarding the character and nature of angels. A passage from his sermon given on a Michaelmas Day tells us:

'With what words we may and ought to speak of these pure spirits, I do not know, for they have neither hands nor feet, neither shape nor form nor matter. What shall we say of a being which has none of these things, and which cannot be apprehended by our senses? What they are is unknown to us, nor should this surprise us, for we do not know ourselves, our spirit . . . how then could we know this exceeding great spirit, whose dignity far surpasses all the dignity which the world can possess? Therefore we speak of the works which they perform towards us, but not of their nature.'

The second century apologist Athenagoras, in parts of his ***Apology*** tells us the duty of the angels is implementing the supervision of God over the things ordered and created by him. God has overall providence of the whole, with parts assigned to the angels. (***Apol***.24). He also writes of the

154

fallen angels and speaks of one angel in particular, Satan, who is hostile to God, and ponders the difficulty he has with this belief. He tells us that Satan was created like the other angels but he is counter to the good of God.

Apologists' is the name give (especially to Christian writers) who about c.120–220 A.D first addressed themselves to the undertaking of making a rational defence and recommendations their faith to outsiders, presenting the case for Christianity to Non–Christians and those who dissent from it. They had to contend with pagan philosophy and the general outlook that it influenced and in particular Jewish opposition.

The opinion of Ambrose and Jerome is that the angels were created before the material world and both say the cardinal sin of Satan was pride. Ambrose recommends invocation to the angels. Though others did not forbid prayer to the angels some like Theodoret, the Bishop of Cyrrus, Syria (A.D. 42) agreed with those who abstained from prayer to the angels.

Theodoret, answering pagan criticism that Christians worship spiritual beings as well as their God, said that Christians do believe in invisible powers, but they do not give them worship. He said these beings are incorporeal and unlike the pagan deities, they are sexless. Further, they were employed in worshipping God and 'furthering the salvation of man.' Didymus supports Theodoret regarding the cult of angels and the churches dedicated to them. Didymus said that churches are found in many towns and villages dedicated to and under the patronage of the angels and men were prepared to undertake long pilgrimages to win angelic intercessions.

Origen (c.185–254) expresses the view the world has need of the angels, who are set over animals, elements and plants. A Guardian Angel protects the individual from the Devil but if the individual falls, they lose the protection of their Guardian Angel and come under the power of an evil angel. Angels present the prayers of the faithful to the Deity, but Origen says the angels should neither be invoked nor worshipped.

Origen maintained that all spirits were created equal but through the exercise of their free will, they developed in hierarchical order and some fell into sin and so became demons or soul, imprisoned in bodies. Death does finally decide the fate of the soul, which may turn into a demon or an angel. This ascent and descent goes on until the final Apocatastasis, when all creatures, even the devil, will be saved. *Αποκαταστασις, Apokatastasis*= 'complete restoration; Theologically: Final restitution.' The doctrine that in the end all free ethical creatures — 'angels, men and devils' — will be saved.

Anselem disputes the idea that man was created with the intention of supplementing the number of angels decreased by the fall of Satan and his companions. He rejects this saying 'mankind is made for itself and not simply to replenish individuals of another nature.' He argues it is permissible to hold any views as long as it was not contradicted by Scripture.

Augustine of Hippo (A.D 354–430) tells us the angels are '*invisibilis, sensibilis, rationalis, intelectualis immortalis*' and ' . . . they are spirits of an incorporeal substance.' He considers that the designation 'angel' referred to their office and not the nature of these spirits. Those angels who did not fall received 'an assurance of perseverance.' Despite his saying the angels received their creation from the Holy Spirit and 'the gift of grace,' he does not seem to favour a cult of the angels. He tells us they do not desire our worship — '*honoramus eos caritate non servitute*' — but that we with them should worship their God and ours. Augustine refuses to identify 'the sons of God' with the angels as others have done. He considers the sin of the fallen angels was pride and Satan fell at the very beginning of his being.

Augustine tells us in his works that the angels form the heavenly division of the *City of God* and this part of the Holy City gives assistance to the division below. Some writers say that Christ brought the reign of the angels to an end. Augustine tells us the angels 'administer to Christ, the

Divine Head of the mystical Body who is in heaven, and to the members of the Body who are on earth.'

'This is what happens in the Church: the angels of God ascend and descend upon the Son of Man, because the Son of Man to whom they ascend in heart is above, namely the Head, and below is the Son of Man, namely the Body. His members are here; the Head is above. They ascend to the Head, they descend to the members.'

The form given above is reminiscent of the movement in Jacob's vision at Bethel in the *Old Testament*. In this vision, the angels are ascending and descending between God and the people of earth and as mentioned in the chapter *The Link* or *Jacob's Ladder*, it may be the first recorded moment in time that the flow of contact had been in both directions, ascending and descending between the celestial and the earth.

The main office of the fallen and evil angels is 'to deceive men and bring them to perdition' and 'they occupy themselves with the practise of divination and magic.' It seems, however, their power is limited and that God uses them 'for the chastisement of the wicked, the punishment of the good for their faults and for the purpose of testing them.' On the other hand, the good angels tell us of the will of God. They offer up to God our prayers, watch over us, love us and help us and they even have care over the 'unbelieving nations.'

Peter Lombard (c. 1100–60) was bishop of Paris whose *Four Books of Sentences* (Sententiarum libri IV) was the standard theological text of the Middle Ages. He was the 'Master of Sentences' and his is said to be the first systematic theologian of the West. He devotes ten sections in his great achievement, the *Four Books of Sentences* probably written in 1155–8 to the subject of good and evil spirits and they are divided into four books on 1: the Trinity; 2: the Creation and Sin; 3: the Incarnation and the Virtues and 4: the Sacraments and the Four Last Things.

He follows the Areopagite, dealing with a wide range of subjects, among them the Creation, nature, free–will and the Fall. He deals with the liability to sin of angels and deals with demons in the magical arts.

He questions whether Michael, Gabriel and Raphael are individual spirits or orders. Whether man has a good or bad angel assigned to him and so forth. The work gained almost immediate acceptance and it was immensely popular, though naturally not to all. The *Four Books of Sentences* served as the basis of theological studies not only in Paris, where Lombard was named Bishop of Paris just before he died, but also in most of the European universities of medieval times. His concept of the sacraments was to become fundamental to both theology and dogma. His work was finally superseded by the *Summa Theologica* of Thomas Aquinas, a systematic theology of Christian doctrine in philosophical terms that was an attempt to reduce religious truth to an organized system.

The word *Summa* = 'the main thing, chief point, principle matter, the summit, a compendium' — originally was the title of many reference books, which could be on a choice of subjects and not wholly theology. It was a term used by medieval writers and it was a form of investigation developed in the 12th century that began with a compilation of opinions held by churchmen and philosophers. It came to denote a compendium of theology, philosophy and the like and these *compendia* were used as handbooks in Schools. The *Sentences* were short reasoned expositions about the main truths of Christian doctrine. In the early stages, the *Summae* were books of *Sentences*.

In the Middle Ages, they took on the new meaning of being a critical explanation of a text of a literary work, but especially Scripture. It was an exposition, an interpretation or explanation of the *Bible* — an *exegesis* — Greek εξηγησις, *exegesis* = 'a statement, narrative, explanation, interpretation.' As said above, Peter Lombard's work *The Four Books of Sentences* is probably the most famous of the *Sententiae*. Just as the *Summa* of Thomas Aquinas — *Summa Theologica* — is conceivably the most famous of the *Summae*. If any reader was not familiar with the term, they know now how (in spirit at least) this work got its title — *Summa Angelica*.

Gregory the Great follows the hierarchy of Dionysius closely, giving nine orders of angels as *Angeli, Archangeli, Virtutes, Potestates, Pincipatus, Dominationes, Throni, Cherubim* and *Seraphim*.

St John Chrysostom tells us the nature of the angels is superior to ours and it cannot be understood by us. St John Chrysostom possessed great eloquence and gravity. The proficient nature of his preaching gained for him the reputation of being one of the greatest orators of the Early Church and the name *Chrysostom* is taken from the Greek *Χρυσοστομ, (Latin= aurum)*, *χρυσος, chrysos= gold + mouthed?*) 'Golden–mouthed' was first used of him in the 6th century and is why he is esteemed as the *Patron Saint of Orators*.

Basil 'the Great' (c.330–379) tells us that the sanctity of the angels is due to the activity of the Holy Spirit. The angels are less inclined to sin than we are though they are not incapable of committing sin and he considered this case proven by the fall of Lucifer whose transgression was envy and pride. Guardian angels were consigned to individuals, churches and nations, but Basil said Guardian Angels are driven away by sin 'as smoke drives away bees, bad odours and doves.'

Justine Martyr (c.100–165) assumes a cult of angels and Cyril of Jerusalem is of the opinion 'that certain of the fallen angels had obtained their pardon.'

The theologian Tertullian (c.160–c.225) tells us, like Origen, that baptismal water is through the ministry of angels and 'it receives its healing properties from an angel.' The purification is because a spirit, described as *angelus baptismi arabiter* prepares the path for the Holy Spirit. Marriage, which has received the blessing of the Church, is 'announced by the angels and ratified by the Father.' Tertullian alludes to the fall of the angels corrupted by their own free will; from these sprang the race called demons and Satan is their chief. These demons are the origin of all diseases and disasters. They beguile men into idolatry to obtain for themselves their 'proper food of fumes and blood.' Angels and demons are widespread, both have wings and both are invisible to the senses.

Lactinius (c.240–c.320) the Christian apologist, who was later tutor to Crispus son of Constantine, has an interesting doctrine. He tells us before the creation of the world God produced a spirit like himself (= *the Logos*). Then he made another being in who 'the disposition of the Divine origin did not remain.' This being of his will was corrupted with evil and gained for him another name. 'He was called by the Greeks *διαβολος, diabolos*= 'slanderous, backbiting' and 'the Slanderer, the Devil (*New Testament*). Some call him criminator' because he reports to God the faults to which he tempts us and the Jewish appellation of Satan is 'the Accuser.'

In early times, as the above shows, the cult of the angels did not gain automatic assent and they met with considerable hostility from some prominent ecclesiastical writers. With the angels being creations of God, I am left wondering why and what they are objecting to regarding them. It is almost as if some were saying that God made a mistake in creating the angels and that they were not wholly acceptable for varying reasons. God certainly created the angels before those who are objecting about them and you would think the fact that God had created them would be enough for these critics for the most. These people, by objecting to the angels are saying that they know better than the Creator about his creations or the necessity of their creation and think them of little value in some instances. 'What is man, that thou art mindful of him . . . Thou madest him a little lower than the angels.' *Psalm* 8:5 and *Hebrews* 2:7.

The Council of Nicæa (A.D 787) and how it dealt with the question of angels has been mentioned several times. They seem to have the same opinion about the demons. John said that Christians both depicted and venerated the angels and his views seem to have won the general agreement of the council. The decision was taken that the cult of angels, which for many had been a private devotion having met with significant opposition in some quarters, now received the official sanction of the church. Angelic worship could now be regarded as part of the *doctrina publica*.

At the Reformation, Protestant theologians kept the doctrine of good and evil spirits and they even accepted that good spirits mediate on behalf of human beings, yet prohibited any formality or ceremony of invocation regarding the angels, which I find somewhat odd. At the beginning of the nineteenth century, there was a noticeable revival in the credence of angels that encouraged attempts to try to communicate with them once more.

The foregoing gives some idea of the how angels were regarded in the past. Today the whole situation has changed and angels appear in a diversity of forms that varies from a maiden aunt to someone who lets you have their parking space just when you need it and I feel there is a danger if this approach if it is taken too far or if it already has been. I have read of the angels being made the cause or reason behind so many things and some of them are fairly ridiculous and trivial if the matter is given a second thought.

In the sacred texts and in the religious heritage of most nations, the angels are often loving at times and at other times stern and reprimanding, now and then fearful, often dazzling and these Messengers of God were sometimes quite threatening. Quite often, they have brought people to their knees and that could be telling them something. This is the paradigm of the angels to which we have to return because it is now demanded that the angels become the comforters of our every problem or distress, no matter how slight or trivial. It would sometimes seem the more trivial the problem the better — 'need a tap washer mended do not bother to call a plumber — call an angel!'

The angels must be as *our* equals and intervene for us against every petty annoyance in our lives so that we are not troubled or bothered by any dilemma or stress because it is their job to either prevent this or solve it. Is your neighbour playing their radio too loud? Invoke an angel and they will annoy you no more after all — it is *your* right, *their* job and the *reason* they were created! This to me reverses the purpose of this work. It is not we who must go across the Middle Ground to see if we can make contact with the Angelic Hosts — it they who must come down and stop at our border and on their knees, beg to be let in. I do not want to be here when patience is at an end — for it is patient but not limitless.

Angels are not pet poodles who are invoked to intervene in your life at every whim or fancy and to run after us hand and foot because we do not want to be troubled by anything. Perhaps this is why for much of the time they do not bother paying any attention to us. We ourselves quickly tire of a constantly importuning child or someone who is always demanding, wanting things and seeking attention and if people do this too often, we feel we are being used and the same for out patience.

The *I Ching* — the *Book of Change* — comments on this, as mentioned in the chapter *Letter to the Angels* where we have written on similar lines. 'The reader should remember the interpretation attached to Hexagram 4 — *Youthful Folly*. The oracle cautions that at the first time of asking guidance will be given and the seeker will be told, but if the oracle is asked repeatedly then the seeker is importuning. They have become irreverent, annoying, they will not be told anything and any further questioning will be ignored.

The angels obviously must be sent by a Will and Power far greater than we possess or will ever know. We can only request, supplicate and plead but we cannot command because the angels are not ours to command, we do not own the angels not even our Guardian Angel(s) and there have been times I have apologised to mine. Put simply — we do not have either the power or authority to command them to do anything — we can only request and hope they will give us of their time and consideration. The angels belong to the Celestial sphere of the heavenly and the One that created them, primarily to do Heaven's work. They cannot be considered in earthly terms in any way, shape or form, they belong to their Creator.

Naturally, we speak of them in earthly terms at times because these are the terms of reference we use here and understand, but doing this does not make them 'earthly.' We repeat the angels are 'God's Angels' and 'belong to the Celestial.' Acceptance of this simple fact alone would, the writer believes, begin to put the matter on a more appropriate setting and better perspective than it appears to be at the time of writing.

Of course, in writing this, I do not include in this the countless people who do regard the angels in this appropriate light by giving due respect to a greater and far older wisdom. Its a matter of having the perspective right, being respectful — 'even when you are wrong you can decent.'

People are often surprised when they find out how few 'angelic letters' are actually written by me during a year, sometimes none. The 'angelic letters' written in the past were mainly to ask for assistance to help me to cope with a matter, not to ask the angels to do it for me and this guidance was only sought after my efforts had failed and I could see no other way out.

Of course, I have asked them to take something away from me because I felt I could not struggle with it any more and I may well do so in the future. I asked because I thought the problem threatened to overwhelm me and I would go under. There is, however, a recorded precedence for such an appeal — one, it was set in a garden called *Gethsemane* and requested by a far greater strength or evolution than I will ever possess. We all need help at times when things appear too much. The angels must have something to say and do or there would be little point in their coming and the term 'messenger' would no longer apply.

When I was younger and was given the original School Courses on the Angels I was guilty (for a time) of sending so many angelic letters it would have clogged up any Postal Service — Celestial or otherwise. I wanted so many 'toys' to play with and there seemed to so many that I could choose from at the time — all I thought without any effort from me and there just for the asking and taking for I was young and did not have a lot of money at the time. I soon realized that I could have a lot of things with a little more hard work and ingenuity but of course, the crux of the matter was that I really wanted them for nothing! This is why with the benefit of hindsight that I am recommending restraint without 'casting the first stone' for I am not in a position to cast it.

In these material days, when the world seems to be becoming more incoherent by the hour — by the minute as you get older — the angels are 'fallen' angels indeed, but not in the biblical sense or how it sounds. They have fallen to a shadow of their former greatness and glory. It seems that everything, the angels included, must be brought down to the physical level and this suggests an extreme form of vanity and pride, the kind that so often goes before a fall in some important areas of a life and if that comes — what a fall it will be. This is why I do not think we can snap our fingers with every vagary or caprice in our lives and expect an angel to come running at our behest. I do not think we can do this whatever the religion or religious philosophy. We should heed *Montaigne* — 'Man is certainly stark mad; he cannot make a flea, and yet he will be making gods by the dozen.'

Science, not with the approval of everyone, is so busy trying to remove God or the Gods from everything in sight and this is usually done so that it can replace what was originally there. Little wonder we cannot find our God or his angels in anything any more and we wonder where has all the magic has gone — it withdraws but does not die. I repeat, I give science its due and thanks for all the things that it has given me, this computer and word processor and the graphics without a shadow of doubt. To the ancient races, their gods were ever present in everything they saw, touched and felt, in water, air, clouds, fire, earth and all they had around them..

At least this particular accusation cannot be levelled at most of the Pagan beliefs and its adherents jealously guard their Gods and protect what these Gods in turn have served and protected, rivers, trees, woodlands, its flora and fauna and life. Their lives were directed to filling these 'empty places' with divinity and awe, most of these things today are now just empty places, who is there left to protect them? Pan has been dismissed but not gone — 'not lost only mislaid' as written in a letter from the author William S Burroughs to me about the Pan book, a short while before he died, which was very generous of him, appreciated and valued.

Most people today want to be a little too comfortable with their Gods, and I do not think this is something the ancients would have approved of, let alone understood. I do not believe the ancients would have accepted the idea of being too comfortable or too friendly with the Gods. Neither do I think they would consider this was the purpose of their religion or their Gods.

In the **Wind in the Willows**, I have long considered that Kenneth Grahame got this balance and response perfect in favourite lines for me. When Pan comes among the animals Ratty is asked by Mole if he is 'afraid of Pan?' Ratty says he is not. 'Afraid?' murmured the Rat his eyes shining with unutterable love. 'Afraid! Of Him? O never, never! And yet — and yet — O, Mole, I am afraid!' It is the repetition and pause over the words 'and yet — and yet,' with the slight hesitancy of uncertainty, discomfort and fearful of over familiarity that often leads to disrespect that you hear in the written word. A disrespect that is perhaps a little too prevalent today.

These feelings are natural of the great respect and love when in the presence of the Divine, which gives it its authenticity to large extent. The selfless desire to give service to Pan without any thought of recompense is what makes this beautifully balanced response of Grahame's little 'Ratty' ring true for me. The ancients would have understood this relationship even now, despite the intervening years. Further, who wants over–familiar gods? Everyday, the media gives me so many gods. Including more superheroes, heroes and legends than I can shake a stick at or can ever hope to cope with — all demanding homage, obeisance and money — lots of money — my reply is unprintable.

St Francis de Sales advises us to ' . . . make friends with the angels, who though invisible are always with you. Often invoke them, constantly praise them and make good use of their help and assistance in all your temporal and spiritual affairs.' — **Introduction to the Devout Life**. Records show that the angels are sometimes far from the comfortable messengers many would try to make them appear today. William Blake, within his walled garden in Lambeth used to act out (naked) with his wife, the story of the Creation. He professed to have spoken to angels and believed them to be 'the personification of great power' but not necessarily 'the personification of goodness.'

We have said throughout that if the angels were God's agents for blessings, then they can also be the instruments of his curse, chastisement, ruination and death. If we include the **Apocryphal** books, we find a prayer being offered that an angel might destroy the Greeks (**Maccabees**) as an angel destroyed the Assyrians (2 **Mac**.11). In 'the place of punishment,' Enoch saw angels administering torture (**Slav. Enoch**.10.) The angels, not demons and devils — **Demon Est Deus Inversus**. There is a belief that on the Day of Judgement an angel will be appointed 'avenger.' (**Assump. Mos.** 10) and these Apocalyptic Angels to some are the Enochian Angels.

An angel of God has been given the order to cut a sinner in two (***Book of Susanna***.) The Word of God is said to have been an active Angel of Vengeance on the night of ***Exodus*** (***Wis***.18.) Two angels came down from heaven to bind a hostile king (3 ***Mac***.6.) When Jerusalem was destroyed, four angels stood at the four corners with lamps and accomplished its ruin (***Apoc. Bar***.7.) There is an angel whose chief function was death (21) and from the few examples given here, there seems little doubt that whatever needs to be done for good or evil, there is an angel for the task in hand that will do the work of their Creator.

Angels are often found as supreme warriors and thousands of the Archangel Michael's enemies have perished beneath his flaming sword because 'of his righteous wrath.' This description agrees with this archangel being put forward as the leader of the Angelic Host. In the services of the Roman Catholic Church, St Michael is invoked as a 'most glorious and warlike prince,' the 'vanquisher of evil spirits' and the 'receiver of souls.'

Many of the attributes of the Roman god of war, Mars, have been assumed in part by the Archangel Michael, the Leader of the Heavenly Hosts. During the early period of the church, the characteristics of the gods of many countries and people were transferred to angels and saints during the Middle Ages. However, far too much stress has been placed upon Mars as a God of War and Destruction. Initially he was a great God of Nature and it was this aspect that people called upon first, yearly at the time of Spring — the war part came later from Ares who is associated with him.

In the section of ***St. George and the Archangel Michael***, we mentioned the god Kalvis of the Baltic region of Eastern Europe, who is the heavenly smith in the tradition of the Greek Hephaistos with whom he is usually associated bear this god in mind regarding Michael and George.

The name Michael has been thought to be an appellation for the Son of God and it is natural that Christ is always meant by any angel named as his minister. Michael is frequently called the Angel of the Covenant because he represents the authority of the Angelic Kingdom, not just a messenger that is transmitting commands, but speaking as the Word in all its fullness and power. The Archangel Michael is the ***Angel and Instrument of God's Law***.

The great female aeon of Gnostic lore is the ***Pistis Sophia***= 'faith and knowledge' and in the ***New Dispensation*** the Holy Ghost or Spirit= 'the Comforter,' the third person of the Trinity is often regarded as female in its activities. In the ***Gospel according to the Hebrews*** in the ***Apocrypha***, we have the Lord speak of 'my mother the Holy Ghost' who took him to Mount Tabor. Mount Tabor is an important hill east of Nazareth. This mountain is traditionally the Mountain of the Transfiguration but this is uncertain as the ***New Testament*** does not mention it by name and this mountain was thought to have been already been built upon, even at the time of this event. Churches and shrines are built there now to commemorate the ***Transfiguration***.

The angels are stronger and wiser than human beings and their power and their knowledge is limited only by God. 'Bless ye the Lord, ye his angels That excel in strength, that do his commandments, Hearkening unto the voice of the Lord.' ***Psalm*** 103:20.

We refer to the statement given earlier that those who look upon the face of God will not live. On at least two occasions, those who saw an angel said they saw God. Jacob asks the angel, with whom he had wrestled, 'Tell me I pray thee, thy name?' 'And Jacob called the name of the place Peniel: for I have seen God face to face, and my life has been preserved.' ***Genesis*** 32:30.

From this it would not unreasonable to assume that Jacob expected to lose his life because he had seen the face of God and was still living, see ***Exodus*** 33:20. In many writings Peniel — 'the face of God' is the Angel of Jehovah, the antagonist of Jacob, though the ***Zohar*** identifies this angel as the Angel Sammael yet others say it was the Archangel Uriel. In Cabbala Peniel (or Penuel) is an angel of the third Heaven and his day is Friday.

In *Judges* 13:22 we are told 'And Manoah said unto his wife, we shall surely die, because we have seen God.' Many commentators believe that the angel represented God so abundantly that in dealing with the angel, people thought without doubt that they were dealing with God himself. Some of the old theologians thought that the Angel of Jehovah was the second person of the Trinity in differentiation from the created angels, but this idea has no real credence in the *Old Testament*.

An important question that is often raised is when were the angels created. The Scriptures give us very little to work with on regarding this subject, so we have to take from where we can get it. The Jesuit historian and theologian Dionysius Petavius (1583–1652) tells us, 'The most ancient Fathers especially the Greeks and Romans' held that the angels were created before the heavens and all material things.' Naturally, as with most things in life, there is a contrary opinion. Thomas Aquinas writes that the heavens were created first and the angels set in the heavens and since his time, this has been commonly held among the Romans. The creation of the angels was held by early Rabbis when the parting of the waters occurred on the second day — 'in the waters' of the *Psalms* was thought to be their habitation, while others think the fifth day to be more appropriate for their creation.

The Lateran Councils were a series of Councils held at the Lateran Palace in Rome from which naturally they got their name. These were convened it seems from the 7th to the 18th centuries. It was the Lateran Treaty of 1929, between the Italian government and the Holy See, which determined the site of Rome as the capital city of Italy and it also established the Vatican City as a sovereign state. It is the Council of 1215 that interests us most because this council declared that God created the angels and material beings *'simbul ab initio temporis'* (= 'at the same time from the beginning') though many theologians still think that the Council left the question open.

At the Second Council of Nicæa (A.D 787), the nature of angels was again discussed. At this Council, a book written by John, Bishop of Thessalonica was read and the conviction was advanced that angels were not altogether incorporeal and invisible but endowed with a thin ethereal or fiery body. These and similar views met with general approval overall and sanction was given to the custom of depicting and venerating the angels.

John had the same opinion about the demons but said that Christians did depict and venerate the angels and his views seem to have won the general agreement of the council. The decision was taken that the cult of angels, which had been for many a private devotion and encountered considerable opposition from some quarters, had now received the official sanction of the church. The veneration and worship of the angels could now be regarded as part of the *doctrina publica*.

In dealing with the nature of the angels, many of the early Fathers considered them as tangible beings. To account for this opinion is not difficult if we take the history of the marriages between the 'sons of God' and the 'daughters of men' as given in *Genesis* 6:2. However, we must use some caution regarding the subject because there are some who think that the 'sons of God' may have meant 'pious men.' The trouble with this is do we have a statement of genuine history and conviction or an expedient fudging to explain a textual anomaly after it had happened.

The theme of intercourse between deities and mortals is not new and it has a long history to support it. This was once regarded as being prevalent and was not limited to any one country, nation or time. It was thought that special characteristics were passed on through sexual intercourse and that these qualities could pass from one partner to the other and to their offspring. Therefore, intercourse between a god and mortal women or the goddesses and a mortal man was assiduously discouraged and strictly forbidden. It was prohibited for fear that the Divine would become human and the human Divine.

This possibility appeared to bother Yahweh because one of the things it could give the human partner was the benefit of eternal life. Old commentaries tell us that Yahweh said 'his spirit will not be duplicated among men.' He dealt with this eventuality promptly by limiting the span of human life to a maximum of 'one hundred and twenty years,' the reputed lifespan of Moses.

It was commonly believed by the Greeks that if a mortal consorted with a goddess he had to be put to death. We are told of the Cretian legend of Molus, who was a son of Minos and brother to Deucalian. It is said that he attempted to rape a nymph and later he was found without a head. In Crete, there is a Cretan festival in which they show an image of a man without a head, who was called Molus (*Plutarch*: *De Def. Ora* 13).

In another case the father of Aeneas — Anchises — was waylaid by Aphrodite on Mount Ida but he was hesitant to associate with her because 'no man ever remains sound who consorts with a goddess.' Anchises does marry Aphrodite and from the union Aeneas is born. He is strictly prohibited from making known the name of the mother but he naturally boasts of his wife by name to his friends and for this offence, he is either blinded or made lame by means of lightning.

Now back to *Scripture* and the question in hand. In *Matthew* 22:30, Jesus speaking of the angels tells us 'for in resurrection they neither marry, nor are given in marriage, but are as the angels of God in heaven.' These lines, because of the authority from where they come, tell us that the angels do not marry. This statement can obviously exclude the interpretation that says that the 'sons of God' is a synonym for the angels. There was marriage between the 'sons of God' and 'the daughters of men' because the sons of God saw that 'they were fair,' though this is found in the *Old Testament* in *Genesis* 6:2 and not in the *New Testament*.

At the *Seventh General Council Nicæa* of 787, the Patriarch Tarasius argued that the angels could be portrayed in paintings because 'they were circumscribed and they had appeared to many, in the form of men.' The General Council gave no censure to his arguments, restricting itself to the undemanding conclusion that it was lawful to portray angels in pictures and declared its adherence to the doctrine on the veneration of images. Many of the Fathers deny that the angels have bodies, as do most of the modern theologians. The Fourth Lateran Council separates the angelic natures from the corporeal natures by saying that any opinion to the contrary (according to Petavius) is 'proximate to heresy.'

Most believe the angels are quite capable of assuming the appearance of human bodies to which at times they seem to become intimately attached. In their body, they move and portray their own invisible nature or demeanour to God, as passages of the Scripture show. Angels often appear as 'men' including the Angel of Yahweh and they are spoken of as discharging the various functions of human life. The angels do appear to eat and drink for the Lord appeared to Abraham on the plains of Mamre. 'Lo, three men stood by him . . . and he took butter, and milk, and the calf which he had dressed, and set it before them under the tree, and they did eat.' *Genesis* 18:8.

Angels walk because the angels who came to visit Lot at Sodom did. 'And while he lingered, the men laid hold upon his hand, and upon the hand of this wife, and upon the hand of his two daughters . . . and they brought him forth, and set him without the city.' *Genesis* 19:16. I think if they had taken Lot and his family out of the city by supernatural means it would have been written as such. It hardly needs proving that they can speak but a clear example is 'so I answered and spake to the angel that talked with me, what are these, my lord? Then the angel that talked with me answered and said unto me . . . and so forth.' *Zechariah* 4:4.

If, for the moment, we set aside the cherubim and seraphim the angels are not usually spoken of as having wings. Wings abound in the opening chapter of *Ezekiel* 1 and we know that they are high beings described as having 'the likeness of four living creatures.' In this chapter, not only are there wings but also the 'wings are stretched upwards' (1:11) and two 'covered their bodies.' They all had two wings 'which covered on this side, and every one had two which covered that side of their bodies.' (1:22) ' . . . And when they went, I heard the noise of their wings, like the noise of great waters' and ' . . . when they stood, they let down their wings.' (1:24).

Nonetheless, despite wings not always being mentioned, the angels do appear and vanish very quickly. 'And the angel of the Lord appeared to him' . . . and a little later . . . 'Then the angel of the lord departed out of his sight' see *Judges* 6:12 and 21. They are said to 'fly' though this could simply mean 'quickly' after all we used the term 'I must fly' though we do not in reality fly as if having wings, we just move quickly. The use of wings and placing them on various beings was probably done to symbolize their invisible and spiritual nature. This is not only Christian but a practice that can be traced back to the ancient Egyptians, who represented the battling sun–god Horus of the city of Edfu (on the Nile near Aswan) as a winged disk and the city was called during its history — 'the Exultation of Horus.'

The angels are shown to exercise some fairly miraculous powers so I cannot see that flying would present them with any particular difficulty and I cannot see any reason for their being left out by having no wings. The trouble is that human beings tend to associate everything with the earth plane and its physical laws. Each world has its laws and I am sure you have been amazed at some of the things you have managed in dreams, have accepted what happened there or the people and creatures you have met. Yet, because it is the 'world of dreams' you do not take these particular activities amiss or question them, because they seemed perfectly normal for where you were at the time — they only seem odd from the viewpoint of waking.

Many examples of this are shown in *Revelation*, which the readers can find for themselves starting with *Revelation* 7:1 onwards. There are too many examples to quote regarding this particular point, but angelic powers almost pass by default if you accept the existence of the angels. The angels do fly, because John heard an angel making his proclamation in a loud voice while 'flying through the midst of heaven, saying . . .' *Revelation* 8:13.

In *Revelation* 10:1–3, an angel is described as follows. 'Another mighty angel come down from heaven, clothed in a cloud: and a rainbow was upon his head, and his face was as it were the sun, and at his feet as pillars of fire: and he had in his hand a little book open: and he set his right foot upon the sea, and his left foot on the earth, and cried with a loud voice, as when a lion roareth.'

This symbolism is often used for Card 14 of the major arcana of the Tarot, it is similar in detail allowing for personal alterations at the whim of the designer or creator of the pack and there are so many today. I do not think there is no doubt that this is where it possibly came from. This card is titled *Temperance* and sometimes the title the 'Angel of Temperance' is used in some packs. The Waite–Rider pack has this winged figure with his right foot in water and his left foot on dry land. There is a rainbow around its head and the symbol of the sun is set on his brow.

At the feet of the angel on the card sits the Lion and the Eagle, the old symbols for two of the Fixed Signs of the Earth, Leo (= the Element of Fire) and Scorpio (= the Element of Water) the two elements found repeatedly associated with the angels and the Celestial. The angel is pouring what appears to be 'water' from the gold urn in his right hand, while he holds a flaming torch in the left hand and the angel is being connected with the Elements of Fire and Water. In the folds of his robe, just below the band under his neck are found the Hebrew letters of the Tetragrammaton — IHVH. One meaning of this card is given as 'The Holy Guardian Angel institutes the test's and trial's that guide us onward along the Path of Attainment.'

There is a special association found in both the *Bible* and elsewhere, between the angels and the heavenly bodies as when the Lord answers Job. 'When the morning stars sang together, and the sons of God shouted for joy?' *Job* 38:7. Mentioned above there is the strong connection between the angels and the Elements of Fire and Water. 'And another angel came out from the altar, which had the power over fire . . . And I heard the angel of the waters say . . .' *Revelation* 14:18 and 16:5, there are other examples. The Hebrew word for 'heaven' is **Shamayin** and this is explained as being a combination of **sham** and **mayin** ('the place where there is water') or **esh** and **mayim** ('fire and water') and from these elements the celestial region was created. The Chinese practise of **Fung Shiu** popular today, comprises of the Chinese characters for the elements of 'fire and water'

The Element of Fire is considered the most sacred of the elements in many religious philosophies and is often used to show purification as with the burning away of dross, the desires and passions in the life of an individual or living thing, for death is cold and the enemy of life.

This is too intricate a subject to be dealt with here and it would lead us a long way from our brief — even for me to justify and I willingly admit when writing I am over and over again something of a nomad. I do go down the main thoroughfare leading to my destination but there are so many interesting side streets that are hard to resist and I fear I am now too set in my ways to change my tack, but fortunately, this seems to upset reviewers and critics more than it does the readers, who seem to be the more adventurous — wanting what is written and not how its written.

The Element of Water is another weighty subject regarding symbolism and it is another of the sacred elements. Water is often given as the great symbol of Truth and the medium in which creativeness takes place. 'I am the great God who created himself, that is to say, I am Water, that is to say, Nu the father of the gods, as others say, Ra the creator of the name of his members which turned into the gods.' *Papyrus of Hunefer, XVII.* One example of this from Scripture presents itself very early in the work. 'And the Spirit of God moved upon the face of the waters.' *Genesis* 1:2.

## APOCRYPHA

We have often mentioned the *Apocrypha* when speaking of the angels because these books are a rich source of information regarding the angels. Perhaps it may be well to know a little more about it for those who do not know of these valuable books that well. I have always liked the *Apocryphal* books because they seem to have a greater freedom which is not always present in the canonical books, which you feel have been subjected to closer scrutiny for their content as if to make sure it is 'right.' You feel there has probably been some judicious editing here and there to support the vested interest in the works of *Scripture*. The better to present the best argument for the religion it championed. This is not an accusation against its use in religion, propaganda is not only used for religious ends, most religions have used it and still do, they are not the only ones.

*Αποκρυφος, Apokryphos*= 'hidden, concealed, concealed from, in secret, unknown to, obscure, hard to understand,' *αποκρυφω, apocrypho*= 'as the foregoing.' *Αποκρυπτω, Apokrypto*= 'to hide from, to keep hidden from, to hide from sight, conceal.' Some writers say it was coined by St Jerome, the 5th century biblical scholar. He gave it to those biblical books received by the church of his time as part of the Greek version of the *Old Testament*, but not included in the Hebrew *Scriptures*, a clear elucidation. The books of the *Apocrypha* in Christian usage have long been ambiguous. They are thought to date from the period around 300 B.C to A.D. 70 though mostly from 200 B.C. to A.D. 70, before the definite separation of the Christian Church from Judaism.

During the 19th century, the *Apocrypha* assumed a much greater importance in biblical studies. With the development of biblical studies of historical sources the *Apocrypha* has shed important light on the period between the end of the *Old Testament* narrative and the opening of the *New Testament*. When I was at school, I was told that the *Apocrypha* was a 'bridge' between to two *Scriptures* and it covered the 'break' between the two parts. The term is an interesting topic of enquiry, is worthy of separate study and would repay any worthwhile effort but we can only touch upon its importance.

Apocryphal books of the *Old Testament* were sometimes included in the Roman Catholic and Orthodox *Bibles* as *deuterocanonical* (= 'added to the earlier canon'). The books of the *Apocrypha* are often missing from *Bibles* today, which is a pity but the *Apocrypha* and its books can be bought separately. Why the term 'apocryphal' was applied to these books is not secure, perhaps it was because of their relatively late source. They were thought less authoritative than the other books of the *Bible* and these books were not referred to by Christ or his apostles, which is a good enough reason for some. The Rabbis of Judaism wisely called them *'outside books'* but I have long thought of them as being 'books for outsiders.'

It is thought by some that the expression *apocrypha* was at first given to those writings that were considered esoteric writings, chiefly those that were only for private instruction that had a greater, more profound significance than exoteric writings. However, with the increase of false esoteric Schools that increasingly brought the works into disrepute it began to gather its later meaning of spurious or doubtful. People were not averse to altering any book to make their point or plead their cause and I can understand the concern of the early Church Fathers in taking a cautious position regarding what they accepted as being authentic.

The early Fathers often applied the word *apocryphal* to indicate the forged books of heretics or any that savoured of doubtful veracity. Perhaps they appropriated the name from the heretics who flaunted their 'apocryphal' or 'hidden' wisdom of these writings. It was about the end of the second century that the dubious and unfavourable meaning became connected to the word but I think this was used more in derision and a spirit of indignation than a wish to speak or write accurately.

Commentators tell us that the apocalyptic works are parts of the *Bible* and that they are Jewish and Christian books that embody an apocalypse or revelation, given through a symbolic vision of the future. Apocalyptic literature often applies to the final period of world history and describes the final conflict between God, the powers of evil and obviously the old adversaries of Satan, the Devil, Lucifer and all the rest. The battle often culminates in a world cataclysm and sometimes there is a messianic figure that is responsible for the conquest and subjugation of evil.

Often the authors narrate history up to their time in symbolic form as with the 'Visions of Daniel,' then they present a vision of future salvation to be established by God at the end of the present world. Archetypal examples are the books of *Daniel* and *Revelation*. Passages, such as *Isaiah* Chapters 24–27, *Zechariah* chapters 9–14 and *Mark* in Chapter 13 has Christ referring to *Daniel*, they all belong to this distinct class of literature.

Other examples are *Enoch*, *Jubilees* and the *Apocalypse of Baruch* or *Barukh* in the Jewish pseudographa and the *Apocalypse of Peter* in the Apocryphal *New Testament*. The *Apocalypse of Baruch* is a work attributed to Baruch the scribe of Jeremiah. In the Syrian account are found the visions of Baruch on the eve of the destruction of Jerusalem and what followed. In the Greek are found Baruch's journey through the heavens number of heavens visited by Baruch some commentators giving the number as five, while others say it is possible that he originally saw seven heavens.

Writers and visionaries like Baruch visit the heavens to see its secrets, the dwellings of souls and angels and like others examples, the *Apocalypse of Baruch* is one such example. The Ethiopic version contains stories of Baruch and Jeremiah during the devastation of Jerusalem. The literature of the *Apocrypha* is frequently concerned with the source of information about the heavenly world, the places of the damned and redeemed souls, such visions record secrets hidden from others and these sources can sometimes prove highly significant

Apocalyptic literature is usually pseudonymous and often composed under the name of someone eminent and respected and books such as *Daniel* and *Enoch* are examples. *St. John*, however, is the author of *Revelation* in the *New Testament* and plainly wrote under his name and he gave exactly what he saw. Some apocalyptic writings, especially the *Apocalypse of Adam* and others in the literature of Gnosticism, contain elements drawn from Greek mythology as well as Jewish tradition and the *Bible*.

*Tobit*, mentioned before, is an interesting apocryphal book in that it gives us the name of the Archangel Raphael, telling us he is one 'of seven holy angels' that attend the throne of God. In *Enoch* Raphael is one of 'the Watchers' and one of the 'Presence's set over all the diseases and wounds of men.' In the *Zohar* Raphael is charged to heal the earth . . . through him the earth provides a home for man, whom he also heals of his maladies.'

The Archangel Raphael has long been a healing angel and he is the angel invoked in illness and medical matters, which is why the caduceus of Mercury, which is also the planet of the archangel, appears on most medical badges, medical services, ambulances and hospitals and in most countries. The caduceus of Mercury appears on most organizations that deal with communications in most of its forms, though this no longer applies in the United Kingdom. What we now have representing the main organization of communication at the time of writing I do not have a clue, but those who modernize for the sake of it — seldom seem to know either!

The longest book is *Ecclesiaticus* and it is probably the most valued, written about 180 B.C. The writer of *Ecclesiaticus* appears well versed in the 'Wisdom' material of the *Old Testament* here follows a brief example of the kind of material found. 'Great travail is created for every man and an heavy yoke is upon the sons of Adam, from the day they go out of the mother's womb, till the day that they return to the mother of all things.' *Ecclesiaticus* 40:1. This apocalyptic book is also known as the *Wisdom of Ben Sira* being written by Ben Sira an ancient author of 2 B.C and translated into the Greek by his grandson contains moral teachings and despite having a hesitant approach towards the work, the other works of the *Apocrypha* and the *Talmud* quote it.

The book *Susanna* is 'a homily in the honour of virtue, against corruption in high places' and was used as the basis for one of Handel's most beautiful eponymous oratorios. Many chapters in the *Apocrypha* have wonderful titles such as *Bel and the Dragon*, *The Song of the Three Holy Children* among others. The Apocryphal work *Bel and the Dragon* contains two stories of Daniel's contact with pagan cults. In *Bel* Daniel reveals the footprints of the priests by sprinkling flour on the floor, left after removing the sacrifices set before Bel by entering through a secret door. While in the 'Dragon' he brings about the death of the dragon worshipped by the Babylonians and he does this by feeding it a combination of fat, hair and pitch.

The *Agrapha of Jesus* is a book of sayings that are attributed to Jesus that were not included in the Gospels. These are preserved, for example, in the *Acts of the Apostles* ' . . . and to remember the words of the Lord Jesus in the *New Testament*, how he said, 'it is more blessed to give than receive.' (20:35). The *Gospel of Thomas*, the *Apocryphal New Testament*, the *Apostolic Canons*, Gnostic literature, the *Talmud*, and Islamic sources. In early tradition, there was a book of the sayings of Jesus that was attributed to St Matthew.

There are a few individual demons, spirits and angels in canonical literature, but in the literature of the *Apocrypha*, they abound thank goodness, censorship came later. In the apocryphal writings of the Jews, composed approximately A.D.100 or earlier, we find that a belief in spirits, angels and demons preserved and enhanced, though there is a great difference between them at times. Many writers in the apocryphal books still keep the old sympathy (almost pagan) of crediting everything manifest to a spirit and the whole course of Nature was carried out by a spiritual or angelic agency and this is similar to Greek and Roman thought, which I have always found attractive. As D. H. Lawrence said, 'The Romans and Greeks found everything human. Everything had a face, and a human voice. Man spoke and their fountains piped an answer.' — *Fantasia of the Unconscious*.

Some apocryphal literature does not refer to angels, while in others the belief in the angelic and the demonical agencies is carried to great lengths. There is obviously a moderate use of these beliefs in some works and some of the more important characteristics of apocalyptic literature can be roughly listed as follows:

1: The literature is frequently written under an assumed name.

2: An apocalyptic work is often attributed to an earlier respected or established figure, such as a prophet or a saint and this is usually thought to be done to give the work a semblance of authority and credence.

3: There is a belief that God will keep his promises regarding the covenants given to the people in the *Bible*.

4: There are opposing orders of angels, spirits and demons.

5: There is a faith in a heavenly paradise, which is reserved for the virtuous and the just in a future age.

6: There is a belief in the Messiah.

Of the apocryphal works the best known are *Enoch* and 2 *Esdras* but some books of the *Bible* or parts of them have been considered to be apocalyptic books by some scholars and among the canonical books are mentioned *Daniel* and *Revelation*.

The 'Messiah' in Christian and Jewish theology is the *Anointed One*. In Christian theology, this has the additional condition that it is 'the Christ' or Jesus. The *Anointed One* is the Hebrew name for 'the promised deliverer of mankind who will all worship the true God' and in the doctrine of *Cabbala* the Messiah will come when the holy sparks (= the spiritual illumination inherent in all things) have been liberated from the realm of the demonic powers.

The term Messiah was assumed by Jesus and given to him by the later Christian faith. The English word is derived from the Hebrew *mashiah* meaning 'anointed.' In the *Septuagint*, the Greek version of the Hebrew *Bible*, 'Messiah' is translated as *Christos*, from which 'Christ' is derived. Therefore, the name Jesus Christ identifies Jesus as the Messiah, although Judaism of course stresses that the Messiah is yet to come. The idea of the Messiah blends the Hebrew ideal of a King David with the priestly tradition of Moses, which gives the desired Priest–King, though today 'Holy Blood' has now given way to 'Holy Oil.'

Myriads of angels attend the sun (*Slav. Enoch*.14) and they regulate the course of the stars (Ch. 19). A myriad of angels attends the sun on his course through the heavens (*Slav. Enoch*.11) and at sunset, four hundred angels take the Crown of the Sun to God, returning it to the sun in the morning. Angels guard the habitation of the snow and they keep the treasuries of oil, (Ch. 6). So we find there are spirits of dew, of fog, of hail, the hoar–frost, of rain, the sea (Ch. 5) and their respective 'treasuries.' Spirits or angels control the lightning and even cause the pause before the thunder is heard. (*Eth. Enoch* 60.) In the Slav. *Enoch*, the angels kept the Garden of Eden and it was the angels who built the ark. (*Eth. Enoch*. 67.) Many of the elements mentioned above can be found in *Psalm* 148:7–10.

'Praise the Lord from the earth,
Ye dragons, and all the deeps:
Fire, and hail; snow and vapours:
Stormy wind fulfilling his word:
Mountains, and all hills:
Fruitful trees, and all cedars:
Beasts, and all cattle;
Creeping things, and flying fowl.'

We mentioned in the section on '*Manna — the Bread of the Angels*' — the seven designations for heaven in the *Bible* because it is said that there are seven heavens. Found in the heaven *Machon* (6) are the 'treasuries of snow and the treasuries of hail, the loft full of harmful dews, the lofts of the round drops (= 'which harm plants'), the chamber of the whirlwind and storm, the cavern of noxious smoke, the doors, which are made of fire' and so on for the rest and all the foregoing makes me comfortable.

A favourite title for God is given as 'Lord of the Spirits' in the *Book of Jubilees* written about 100 B.C. An apocryphal Jewish work sometimes called *The Little Genesis*, *The Apocalypse of Moses* or the *Testament of Moses* reinterprets the contents of these canonical books. The second book is said to have been given to Moses by an angel when he had ascended Mount Sinai. Much of the historical account chiefly of a legendary character is added to the biblical account of *Genesis* and *Exodus* to proclaim the superiority of the *Torah*.

The writer of the *Book of Jubilees* also speaks of the spirits of cold and heat, darkness, fire, wind, hail, snow, frost, thunder, summer and winter (*Jubilees* 2:1). He calls them angels and the 'fathers of spirits.' (10:5) He names them 'watchers', which is an old name for the angels. The Angel Rahtiel is the Angel of the Constellations and the Angel of the Stars is Kakabel (or Kokabiel) whose duties include 'instructing his fellows in astrology.'

As said earlier, the writer of the *Book of Jubilees* uses an old term for the angels, particularly the Archangel Raphael by calling them 'Watchers' and the 'Fathers of Spirits' and who could quarrel with making angels and spirits representative of the wonders of Nature? For those interested in these particular angels the above will give those readers a starting point from which to start any future studies.

The angels or archangels that are called the 'Watchers' are a very high order of angels. We are told in Hebrew they were called *Irin* and *Grigori*= 'watchers' and tradition has it that these Sephirah never sleep because they were created to see that nothing goes amiss with God's Creation and they are constantly checking this. According to the *Book of Jubilees*, 'the Watchers' were sent to earth to teach the children of men, but once on earth they cohabited with the mortal women — 'the son's of God' of *Genesis*. The Angel Baraqijal is one of the Grigori who mated with the women of the earth, for his trouble he was demoted to the nether regions as a demon and 'a teacher of astrology.' Biblical scholars seem to be in overall agreement that the *Book of Jubilees* was written by a single unknown author who may have been a Pharisee or a Levite priest.

The books of the *Apocrypha* should be read according to the *Thirty–Nine Articles* as 'an example of life and instruction of manners' but they 'should not be used to establish doctrine.' nevertheless The apocryphal books are, important sources for Jewish history and religious developments. Their historical sources are being increasingly recognized and used in modern times. Now we must stop because this is not an investigation of the *Apocrypha* and its books, but for those who have not examined these works and having interest in the angelic, the effort I feel would be worth it as much of great interest to our present subject can be found there.

# SOME COMMENTS ON THE DECALOGUE, THE TORAH AND THE ARK — BRIEFLY

In Judaism, the Torah consists of the first five books of the Hebrew ***Testament***, which is the beginning of the Christian ***Old Testament***. In the Greek and Christian ***Bible***, these five books are called the ***Pentateuch*** and ascribed to Moses. ***Pentateuch*** is from the Latin *pentateuchus* and from the Greek πεντα, *penta*= 'five' and τευχος, *teuchos*= 'a tool, a book' hence= ρεντατευχς, *pentateuch*, collectively called in the Hebrew, the ***Torah***= 'the Law' or the ***Pentateuch***. The ***Pentateuch*** contains the traditional history of the world from the Creation to the death of Moses. They embrace the Covenant of the Hebrew people with the One God and the rules for religious observances, guidelines for social behaviour and naturally include the ***Ten Commandments*** given by God to Moses.

In the Latin, ***Decalogus, Decalogue*** and the ***Greek Δεκαλογος, Dekalogos*** from δεκα, *deka*= 'ten' and λογ'ος, *logos*= 'a word, a discourse'= '***Ten Words***' to the Ten Commandments. The Ten Commandments given by God to Moses on Mount Sinai. They were first introduced into the Liturgy of the Church of England in the Prayer Book of Edward VI in 1552. Many commentators prefer 'words' to 'commandments' as they said to be the 'ten words of creation.' These fit in with the ten Sephirah of the Cabbala and many other examples can be found. There is a ***Midrash*** comment that 'the first five' are 'between man and god' while the remaining five are 'between man and his neighbour' to suggest that religion and ethics are equally essential in broad strokes.

The ***Torah*** is among the holiest and beloved of the sacred writings of the Jews. Those Jews, who know each book making up the ***Torah*** by the first significant word of the Hebrew text, call it ***Shemot*** (= 'Names.')

The synagogue was originally the place where the Torah was read and elucidated and in synagogues today, the term 'Ark' is given to the repository for the Scrolls of the Law used in the sacred service. The Scrolls of the Torah are written by hand in the original Hebrew and placed in the Ark of the Covenant in all synagogues. The Scrolls are sacrosanct by the pious. Not one word, letter or space must be misplaced, lost or transformed and this is the reason why they are written by hand by scribes expressly trained for this most sacred and exacting task, though some commentators say this does not protect it from errors that may have already crept in and are being repeated.

Every synagogue maintains several scrolls, which are normally protected by a covering of rich fabric with silver decorations. Obviously, the Scrolls of the Torah are taken care of and given the greatest respect, reverence and sanctity. There is a special holiday in honour of the Torah, known in Hebrew as ***Simhat Torah***= 'rejoicing in the Law.'

On the eve of ***Simhat Torah*** and throughout the day all the scrolls are taken from the Ark and carried around the synagogue in procession, accompanied by singing, dancing and general high spirits. The children take part and they are called up to read a portion of the Torah. They are then blessed by the assembly and given apples, sweets and other treats.

In the ***Old Testament***, the ***Ark of the Covenant*** was the chest that contained the ***Tablets of the Law*** as given to Moses. The original Ark was built under the direction of Moses during the time the Israelites were wandering in the desert and it is frequently mentioned in the ***Bible***. The ***Ark*** is described in ***Exodus 25*** as being a chest of acacia wood covered with gold. It was also known as the ***Ark of the Law***, the ***Ark of the Testimony*** or ***the Ark of God***. The Chest was in length 2˙5 cubits= 3 ft. 9 in. (?) and its breadth and height was 1˙5 cubits (= 2 ft 3 in.?) It was carried by poles that were set in rings set in the long sides when it was needed to be moved or transported, though same commentators question this as the weight would have been enormous, see also elsewhere.

The Ark lay in the ***Holy of Holies***, the hallowed enclosure of the tabernacle and the Temple in Jerusalem. Various sources tell us that the Chest contained Aaron's rod, a pot or omer of manna and the stone tablets of the Ten Words. The Ark symbolized the pact of faith made between God and the Children of Israel on Mount Sinai. An 'omer' may mean a 'heap or mound' and was a measure for dry things. An omer was a tenth part of an *ephah* (= as a dry corn measure), which is 'about five and one tenth pints' in old works and in imperial measures. The omer was used for measuring the daily allowance of manna for each person.

The *Ark of the Covenant* is undeniably one the most sacred relics of the Hebrew nation but they were not the only nation to possess or use something in this manner. Nomadic Arab tribes transported their ancestral gods in a chest of wood, which was to be found in a special tent on the backs of their camels and this was a well–established practise as others have pointed out. It is likely that the other tribes may have had their own sacred chest for their sacred objects, as *Judges* 20:27 could show ' . . . for the ark of the covenant of God was there in those days.'

## THE ANGELS, THE ELEMENTS OF NATURE AND THE ZODIAC

The *Book of Enoch* and the *Book of Jubilees*, speak of spirits of cold, darkness, fire, hail, heat, summer and thunder. For example, the forces of Nature are represented by viceroys and these two works accord in making spirits of the entire incidents of Nature, while in a different vein from these, the *Testaments of the Twelve Patriarchs*, 'make spirits of man's immortal tendencies.'

The *Testaments of the Twelve Patriarchs* is a pseudographical writing that maintains to acquaint us with the message that each of the twelve sons of Jacob gave to his descendants on his death–bed. It is a matter of dispute if the work is Christian in origin or Jewish. The dates by and large given for the work are around 2 B.C. (= if Jewish) or from around A.D. 200 (= if Christian.)

The Angel of Snow is Shalgiel, Rahab is the Prince of the Sea, the Angel of Lightning is Bardiel and the Angel of the Wind is Ruhiel. The Angel Yurkemi is the Prince of Hail and legend has it that it was this angel who offered to put out the fire for the three men in the fiery furnace. The Archangel Gabriel objected to this saying that Yurkemi's help was not enough to do this.

The Angel of Hurricanes is Zamiel, while Lailah is the Angel of Night and Conception and this angel is spoken of elsewhere. Shemshiel is the Angel of the Day and Ofaniel is the Angel of the 'Wheel of the Moon,' sometimes regarded as identical with Sandalphon. Sui'el is the Angel of Earthquakes while Zakkiel is the Angel who holds 'Sway over Storms.' The mighty Archangel Sandalphon presents the petitions to God as the angels intercede on behalf of people but once it was said they only know Hebrew, so prayers should not be said in Aramaic.

There are seven *Apocryphal Spirits of Deceit* and I wonder if these could be connected with Cabbalistic lower World of the Qliphoth, which has been mentioned in the appropriate place. These seven Spirits of Deceit are 'the Spirit of Fornication, of Insatiableness (= 'who resided in the belly'), of Fighting (= 'resident in the liver and gall'), of Obsequiousness and Chicanery, of Pride, of Lying, Fraud and Injustice. We sometimes find added to these 'deceits,' Theft and Acts of Rapacity. *Reuben* 2:1. The purpose of these spirits was 'to lead men into manifold sins and afterwards to take revenge upon them'. *Levi* 3:2. The evil spirit that a man served was said to wait for his soul as it left the body at death and to plague it. *Asher* 6:5.

For those readers who are interested in the angels that have sway over Nature we give another list. It can be found, in one form or another in various books such as Peter de Abano – *The Heptemaron* and of course, Davidson's *Dictionary of Angels*, which should be in the library of anyone who professes any love or interest in the angels. This book was given to me as a present and it was Gustav Davidson's book that started my passion for the angels in the first place. We have taken the following lists from Book 2 of Barrett's *The Magus*.

The year is divided into four quarters and these divisions are obviously, Spring, Summer, Autumn and Winter. Each of the seasons has a Head or Controlling Angel and their serving angels.

The Angels of Spring are Amatiel, Caracasa, Commissoros and Core
The Controlling Angel of the sign of Spring is called Spugliguel
The name of the earth in Spring is Amadai.
The names of the Sun and Moon in Spring are,
The Sun is Abraym and the Moon is Agusita.

The Angels of Summer are Gargatel, Gaviel and Tariel
The Controlling Angel of the sign of Summer is Tubiel.
The name of the earth in Summer is Festativi.
The names of the Sun and Moon in Summer are,
The Sun is Athemay and the Moon is Armatus.

The Angels of the Autumn are Guabarel and Tarquam.
The Controlling Angel of the sign of Autumn is Torquaret.
The name of the earth in Autumn is Rabinnara.
The names of the Sun and Moon in Autumn are,
The Sun is Abragini and the Moon is Matasignais.

The Angels of the Winter are Amabael and Cetarari.
The Controlling Angel of the sign of Winter is Attarib.
The name of the earth in Winter is Geremiah.
The names of the Sun and Moon in Winter are,
The Sun is Commutoss and the Moon is Assaterim.

The angels of the months and the twelve Signs of the Zodiac are given next. It must be remembered these are astrological months that usually start halfway through the civil months and the month includes the beginning of the following month. They take their name from the month that begins the astrological sign and the sign starts when the Sun enters the first degree of a Sign of the Zodiac. Mars rules the sign of Aries that begins around the 19th of March when the Sun enters that astrological sign and ends around the 19th of April in the next Sign of the Zodiac.

Despite the overlap of the astrological month over two civil months, the angel is regarded as the ruler of the first month named. See the list given below. The month that rules the astrological year begins on the first day of Spring and the list below follows the astrological year and not the civil year, which starts on the 1st of January. The astrological year starts with the Spring Equinox starting in Aries on March the 21st (usually) and extending into first part of April and so on.

The other thing that should be noted about the list used below is that the Seven Ancient Planets are used and it does not use the planets Neptune, Uranus and Pluto because even though there, they had not been discovered. This gives the completely male Sun one Sign of the Zodiac, Leo and the completely female Moon one Sign of the Zodiac, Cancer. The remaining five planets have two Signs of the Zodiac each — one male/positive and the other female/negative to manifest through.

The terms positive and negative are never used in a disparaging manner because they are equal forces and simply manifest in different and seemingly opposite ways. In the practice of today Neptune takes Pisces from Jupiter, Uranus takes Aquarius from Saturn and Pluto, the last to be discovered in 1930, takes Scorpio from Mars. Therefore, it is it is simple to adjust the list to modern use if you wish to do so; this is done in Part Two.

Mars 21–Apr 20. The Angel of March — Aries the Ram — is the Angel Samael.
Apr 21–May 21. The Angel of April — Taurus the Bull — is the Angel Anael.
May 22– Jun 22. The Angel of May — Gemini the Twins — is the Archangel Raphael.
June 23–July 23.The Angel of June — Cancer the Crab — is the Archangel Gabriel.
July 24–Aug 23. The Angel of July — Leo the Lion — is the Archangel Michael.
Aug 24–Sept 23. The Angel of August — Virgo the Virgin — is the Archangel Raphael.
Sept 24–Oct 23. The Angel of September — Libra the Balance — is the Angel Anael.
Oct 24–Nov 22. The Angel of October — Scorpio the Scorpion — is the Angel Samael.
Nov 23–Dec 21. The Angel of November — Sagittarius the Archer — is the Angel Sachiel.
Dec 22–Jan 20. The Angel of December — Capricorn the Sea–Goat — is the Angel Cassiel.
Jan 21–Feb 19. The Angel of January — Aquarius the Water Carrier — is the Angel Cassiel.
Feb 20– Mars 20. The Angel of February — Pisces the Fishes — is the Angel Sachiel.

The Hebrew word **mazzaroth**, found in *Job* 38:32 is often translated as 'the twelve Signs of the Zodiac.' Some authorities have taken the word originally to denote 'lodgings' and this accords with 'house' as used in modern times of the twelve areas through which the sun appears to pass or 'lodge' for a time. The Rabbinical zodiac appears chiefly, but not wholly, to accord with the Zodiac of Bardesanes (? A.D 170), which may have been that of the Chaldeans. The year was divided into twelve months from an ancient date. The early signs were: the Lamb, the Bull, the Two Images, the Crab, the Lion, the Ear of Corn, the Balance, the Scorpion, the Great Image, the Kid, the Bucket and the Fishes and the zodiac of the Meneans resembles this zodiac almost exactly. Bardaisan or Bardesanes was born at Edessa (155–223?) and is often given as a Syrian Gnostic even though this is thought to be doubtful. He was an extremely learned man, a great writer of hymns and most of his works appear to have perished apart from a few, though his school survived his death for a time

Birthstones are used in Part Two with the practical work and are often set in jewellery but sometimes I do not feel the right stones are used. The Sign of the Zodiac Cancer and its angel can be found with a red stone recommended, which are stones of 'fire' by colour alone and this seems inappropriate for a 'water' sign. Red stones are more in keeping with Mars, the 'red planet,' not the white or silver Moon. A red Moon or 'blood on the Moon' has always been held an ominous sign in most cultures. The stone jet and burning a black candle was given for Libra in one work read, instead of Capricorn, which colour and stone is in keeping with Saturn but not gentle and light Venus. I do not believe that Venus would own a black stone, mineral or colour.

The Signs of the Zodiac and their angels can have several stones under their rulership, giving the angel two or more variations if they have two Signs of the Zodiac and if you are using these. I would use a single stone as follows, with alternative suggestion set in brackets. The reader may find this list at variance with other lists found, which is the reason why it is here. I naturally use the list of my School with which I agreed or I would not have accepted it or given it here and I have found it sound over the years or I would have discarded it.

Aries — Angel Samael= Ruby (garnets, jasper, bloodstone, cornelian red stones generally). Taurus — Angel Anael= Emerald (light green stones in general, not dark). Gemini/Archangel Raphael= Agate yellow (all yellow stones in general). Cancer — Archangel Gabriel= Pearl (moonstone, opal, crystal, though sometimes the emerald can be used, white–milky stones in general, sometimes glass, especially crystal). Leo — Archangel Michael= Diamond — the 'highest stone' for the 'highest planet–angel. (Amber, cat's–eye, orange or golden varieties of any stone in general the Sun being a fire planet, which is why the ruby is sometimes found here). Virgo — Archangel Raphael= Agate green (dark yellow stones in general).

Libra — Angel Anael= Sapphire, (lapis–lazuli turquoise, rose quartz, blue diamonds, jade, nephrite, light blue generally). Scorpio — Angel Azrael= Tourmaline (or dark red stones in general). Sagittarius — Angel Sachiel= Amethyst (all purple, lilac or violet stones generally). Capricorn — Angel Cassiel= Jet (garnets, smoky quartz, coral, obsidian, ivory). Aquarius — Archangel Uriel= Chrysoberyl (or any stones that are multi–coloured, flecked with colours or a mixture). Pisces — Angel Asariel= Aquamarine, (beryl, all green stones, especially artificial stones that are green or blue. For example, a paste emerald could be used for the Angel Asariel because the stone is not what it seems it is representative of something else. However, this does not prevent you from using good quality artificial stones for the angels to represent the genuine because not everyone can afford real diamonds, sapphires, rubies, emeralds and so the like. It is your intent that you make sure is genuine, try to 'fake' that and you can forget it and may as well go and do something more useful, more of this in Part 2.

## THE FOUR FIXED SIGNS OF THE ZODIAC

Let us return briefly to the Four Fixed Signs of the Zodiac, which are often called 'the Foundations or Corners of the Earth' and most likely the 'Four Watchtowers' of Enoch and the Enochia of Dr. John Dee and Edward Kelly. The Four Fixed Signs of Taurus (= Element of Earth), Leo (= Element of Fire), Scorpio (= Element of Water) and Aquarius (= Element of Air) and astrologers regard them as the 'four pillars of the astrological chart' because these fixed signs hold up any astrological chart because they are its foundation — they 'fix it' and give it stability but stability can turn into inertia if understanding and knowledge is not employed with a good measure of common sense. Naturally, these stars are found in the writings of other races.

The important star Aldebaran is a star of the first scale and the principal star in Sign of the Zodiac for Taurus the Bull. Aldebaran is one of the four Royal Stars of the ancient Persia and it roughly pointed out the equinoxes and solstices around 4000 B.C. Aldebaran corresponded to the Spring Equinox with the others being Antares for Scorpio= the Summer Solstice, Regulus for Leo= the Autumn Equinox and Fomalhaut in the Southern Fish= the Winter Solstice. They have come down to us though the Hebrew and Semitic writings as the Archangels Gabriel, Michael, Raphael and Uriel, as well as being used in the Christian symbols of the four evangelists given next.

These four signs are found in the creed of the Christian churches to represent the four evangelists. In the *Treatise on Angel Magic* (*Harley* Ms. 6482) in the British Library. In the chapter 'Of Numbers, their power and virtue, the Four Sacred Animals are *Leo* (= 'a lion'), *Aquila* (= 'the eagle'), *Homo* (= 'a human being') and *Vitulus* (= 'a bull–calf).

These are the symbols of the Four Evangelists Mark, John, Matthew and Luke. Matthew, the Man or Aquarius; Mark, the Lion or Leo (= the symbol of Venice with St. George); Luke, the Bull or Taurus and finally John, the Eagle or Scorpio. The sign of Scorpio as said was often represented by an eagle in old times in its highest form its lowest form is the Scorpion skulking and hiding under rocks to strike.

An old Jewish proverb tells us. 'There are four which are the highest in the world, the lion among the wild beasts (= *Leo*), the ox among the tame cattle (= *Taurus*), the eagle among the birds (= *Scorpio*), man among all creatures (= *Aquarius*) but God is supreme over all.' Again, the parenthesis shows where I have placed the astrological interpretation in the proverb. The

Babylonian astrologers are mentioned by a passage in *Isaiah* when he tells them. 'Let now the astrologers, the stargazers, the monthly prognosticators stand up and save thee from these things that shall come upon thee.' *Isaiah* 47:13.

These four fixed signs have the four Elements within them, representing as they do Earth, Fire, Water and Air. The four Elements are represented in the opening lines of the *Bible* in *Genesis*. 'In the beginning God created the heaven and the earth (= Earth) and the Spirit (= Air) moved upon the face of the waters (= Water). And God said, Let their be light (= Fire). And God saw the light, that it was good.'

The ancient Hebrews held that when death came to a man the four sides (= the Elements) quarrelled among themselves. This is because the body that contains the soul taken from the *guph* is born from the 'four sides' and when the Four Elements of Earth, Air, Fire and Water begin to separate at the time of death and the soul is finally separated when death occurs.

In the section that dealt with the Archangel Michael was found the symbols and devices that were borne by the Hebrew hosts in their long journey through the desert. Each of the four divisions of the Hebrew host consisted of four groups of three tribes making up the twelve tribes. The three tribes of each division were known by the name of the principle tribe whose device the group used. The camp of Judah was in the East leading the march; the camp of Reuben was in the South. Ephraim was in the West; the division in the North who brought up the rear was led by Dan.

The traditional symbols shown on the four standards like totems were the lion for Judah, for the tribe of Reuben — there was a man and a river. There was the bull for Ephraim with an eagle or a serpent for Dan. It is natural to think that these four standards are concerned with astrology, the belt of the Zodiac and the Four Fixed Signs of the Earth. The ubiquitous 'Four Corners of the Earth' and by now they should have become old friends in their familiarity.

The four signs were sometimes thought the 'four cornerstones' of early Christianity, when it did not mind showing some of its pagan borrowings and truths. For a religion that has such a hatred of paganism it seems to have borrowed a great deal from and sometimes without as much as a by your leave. Aquarius as most know is the 'Sign of the Water–carrier.' An early Gnostic Christian sect was called *Encratites* or the 'Continent' because they abstained from animal food. The sect was founded by Tatian, an Assyrian who became a Christian under the influence of Justin Martyr. It was in existence in the last part of the second century, though not every sect using the name was under Tatian.

This sect was also called *Aquarians* or the *Aquarii* because they regarded wine as evil and they would only use water to celebrate the Eucharist. Regarding this particular sign of the zodiac there is another interpretation that can be taken from its symbolism. Christ is often said to herald the beginning the Aquarian Age, which comes after the Age of Pisces or 'the Fishes' by equinox precession. The Piscean Age was the Age of his birth and the sign of the religion formed in his name because Christianity as we know it today and already said is not a religion *of* Christ, but *about* Christ mainly due to Paul.

Solomon was credited with an extensive knowledge of astrology as well as magic. This is confirmed in the *Apocrypha* in the *Wisdom of Solomon*. 'For he hath given me certain knowledge of things that are, namely, to know how the world was made, and the operation of the elements. The beginning, ending, and midst of the times: the alterations of the turning of the seasons: The circuits of years, and the positions of stars.' 7:17 and this work, along with others, belong to what is know as the 'wisdom literature' of the *Bible* and the *Apocrypha* and these books were usually based upon respect, a fear of God with a knowledge of and obedience to the Commandments. Jewish astrologers were held to read 'the heavens as a book' because they had long regarded the heavens as a book.

# SOME GENERAL OBSERVATIONS

The *Psalms* are a fruitful orchard in which to gather information about angels. Such as what they do, how they act and so on. The information below is taken from this one source.

8:5 the text reads, 'What is man, that though art mindful of him? For thou hast made him a little lower than the angels.'

34:7 tells us that Yahweh gives his protection to those that fear him. 'The angel of the Lord encampeth round about them that fear him, And delivereth them.'

35:5 tells us that God lets his angel pursue and persecute the wicked, 'Let their way be dark and slippery: And let the angel of the Lord persecute them.'

78:49 tells us that God cast upon the Egyptians his anger and indignation and his angels are the personification of this. 'He cast upon them the fierceness of his anger, Wrath, and indignation, and trouble, by sending evil angels among them.' This appears to bear out the statement at the beginning that God has at his command both good and evil angels and that he uses both to do his bidding.

89:7 infers that God is surrounded in heaven by a council or hosts of angels, 'God is greatly to be feared in the assembly of the saints, And to be had in reverence of all them that are about him.'

91:11 tells us that the angels are guardians and protectors, 'For he shall give his angels charge over thee, To keep thee in all thy ways.' This strengthens the Guardian Angel(s) tenet that the angels have 'charge' over a person and to be 'kept' that person in 'all thy ways.' This does not seem to suggest a short time but for life.

103:20 tells us that the angels are expected to do the Lords commands and listen to his word. 'Bless the Lord, ye his angels, That excel in strength, that do his commandments, Hearkening unto the voice of his word.'

103:21 here they are spoken of as 'ministers' and 'his hosts.' Given as 'Bless ye the Lord, all ye his hosts; Ye ministers of his, that do his pleasure.' 148: 2 gives the instruction to 'Praise ye him, all his angels.'

104:4 tells us it is God 'Who maketh the clouds his chariot: Who walketh upon the wings of the wind: Who maketh his angels spirits; His ministers a flaming fire.' Here again we find the angels connected with the Element of Fire.

With the *Book of Daniel*, the angels come to the fore again and here they are considered as being be exalted 'far above mankind.' 'Gabriel, make this man to understand the vision. So he came near to where I stood: and when he came I was afraid, and fell upon my face.' *Daniel* 8:17. 'And when he (= the Archangel Michael) had spoken such words unto me, I set my face toward the ground and I became dumb.' *Daniel* 10:16. The division of the angels into ranks appears with greater effect in Daniel.

The angels are thought to be pure spiritual intelligence and for this alone they are deemed as being superior to mankind who, being composed of a body and soul, will know death. They are immortal because death involves the separation of the body from the soul. The angels can only be destroyed by or with the authority of their Creator.

Their knowledge depends upon images given to them by God, unlike that of human beings whose knowledge is slowly gained and for the most by means of the five senses, which are far from perfect. The angels do not reason as we do because the keenness of their intellect enables them to see by intuition the principles involved in all things. We see 'through the glass but darkly' most of the time or not at all. Some commentators say that the angels do not know the future so this means that some will say they do. The angels know of the future on a cosmic, universal, national and individual level for clearly their Creator can choose to reveal it to them and my view is they do know the future compared to us.

They are messengers and a messenger usually has something to pass on or there would be little point in their making the journey or using the title. They obviously know a great deal more than we do, the human race are not privy to because it is hidden from us. They can move from one place to another with a dispatch impossible to the inhabitants of this place.

During 'the time of their probation' Lucifer (not Satan) and many 'angels fell.' It is hard to resolve the exact nature of their sin, but Petavius tells us it was 'a desire of absolute dominion over created things, and a hatred of subjugation' and from such thoughts we find Lucifer given to say ' . . . better to reign in Hell, than serve in Heaven.' — *Milton*. It is said that the rebel angels were at once deprived of all their supernatural gifts and thrust into hell without pardon, while the angels who had persevered were at once rewarded with everlasting bliss. St. Gregory the Great said the perfection of the angelic nature made their sin unpardonable.

I am doubtful that even the angels that 'fell' were deprived of 'all of their supernatural gifts' when they became the 'fallen angels.' There would be little point of Scripture warning us against the wiles and entrapment of the rebel angels, Satan or the Devil, if they were 'deprived of their supernatural gifts.' What would there be to warn us about because what could they do? You only fear something or someone who is more powerful than you are and more so if they also possessed supernatural powers upon which they can call.

Similarly, how can they in truth be answerable for our sins? They can suggest, lure, flatter, cajole, make false promises of rewards and powers, lie, cheat and tempt us if you will to the course of action they want us to take and they are clever I am sure. The media of advertising does this sort of thing everyday of our life, but we do not have to accept it or act on the suggestion or buy what is being offered. Some advertising put out today is little more than legalized mugging but at least it is a 'mugging' over which we are in charge and we need not let it happen — because we can say no! If the rebel angels did not have any powers to force us to follow them, then it is we who chose to follow their 'tempting.' So, who is really to blame, the human race — or an impotent angel without any power to call his own? I am sure we will be returning to this theme again.

*Scripture* gives relatively few particulars about the way God dealt with the human race prior to Abraham. The first mention and evidence of the angelic family in the *Bible* are the cherubim who guarded the entrance to Eden, remember cherubim not cherubs — an angel of the air — in the *Zohar*, 'Cherub is the chief of the order of cherubim.' (G. Davidson.) After God had expelled Adam and Eve from the Garden of Eden, he set the cherubim 'at the East of the Garden of Eden' with 'a flaming sword, which turns every way, to keep the way of the tree of life.' *Genesis* 3:24. According to some writers, these beings were personified winds. The elements of wind and fire are often mentioned in context with the cherubim. The angel who expelled Adam and Eve is sometimes named as Iofiel, Jofiel or Jophiel, a companion of the mighty Angel Metatron. The Angel Iofiel is also given as the mentor of the sons of Ham, Japhet and Shem, the sons of Noah.

Before the Exile of the Hebrews, Jewish thought gave Yahweh three classes of aide in attendance, the cherubim, spirits and the seraphim. The cherubim and seraphim were the Guardians of Paradise and the servants of Yahweh. These Spirits were the courtiers of Yahweh and they were sent on duties by him, but they actually play a very small part in matters. Yahweh on special occasions appeared personally to accomplish his purpose and at such appearances we find the 'angel of Yahweh' or the 'angel of God.' The seraphim find a parallel in the Assyrian sculptures, which are frequently shown in the act of fertilizing the sacred palm tree and the inhabitants of Paradise have a strong resemblance to the guardians of the Tree of Life.

Apart from the cherubim, no other spirits appear in the early part of *Genesis* and Yahweh deals directly with individuals as in the story of Abraham. It is only when we arrive at *Genesis* 16:7 that we come upon the words 'the angel of the Lord.' In all passages containing the 'angel of Yahweh,' the LORD, Yahweh himself, has come on some special mission. There seems to be little clear distinction between Yahweh and his angel.

It must be remembered in early thought the spirits were considered as being rather vague, they were considered to have no moral character and were thought neither angel nor demon. They seemed to take their character from the duty they were given to perform so it is possible that the good and evil angels were one the same angels. The one who received the angel did not know what duty the angel had been sent to perform on behalf of Yahweh — a blessing or a curse. At first Yahweh alone was responsible for whatever was performed in his name. However, as time progressed this was modified to give the responsibility to someone else such as ' . . . sending evil angels among them.' *Psalm* 78:49.

Sometimes my thoughts are that the 'evil angels' should have probably been called 'angels of evil' more because of their assignment, 'angels who inflict chastisements as ministers of God.' Just as we change our opinion of people according to what are going to do, especially when done to us personally. The cherubim were represented symbolically on the *Ark of the Covenant*. One of the twin cherubim set on each side of the Mercy Seat of the Ark is called Jael (or Joel) and the other cherub is named as Zarall. Occult tradition tells us that Jael is an angel that governs Libra in the Zodiac.

'And thou shalt make a mercy seat of pure gold: two cubits and a half shall be the length thereof, and a cubit and a half the breadth thereof. And thou shalt make two cherubims of gold, of beaten work shalt thou make them, in the two ends of the mercy seat; one cherub on the end of this side, and another cherub on the other end on that side: out of the mercy seat made he the cherubims on the two ends thereof. And the cherubims spread their wings on high, and covered with their wings over the mercy seat, with their faces one to another; even to the mercy seatward were the faces of the cherubim. *Exodus* 37:7–9.

Sometimes I feel modern writers tend to be rather sarcastic regarding the pictorial representations of angels, especially those with downy wings, plump and dimpled and the like and they even suggest that those who consider the angels in such a way are rather simple–minded. A winged form of angels is given very early in *Scripture* and winged angels are symbolically represented on the Ark of the Covenant. These angels have wings according to the biblical descriptions and they must have a model somewhere?

One reasonably recent article wrote 'contrary to angel lore they (the angels) are not plump and dimpled with the wingspan of an albatross' and with this I fundamentally agree. However, I think angels can appear in whatever form is required of them. If an angel appeared to a child, it would probably assume a form the child thinks the angels take because in that 'form' they would be recognized and accepted. Angels in my view will appear in a form that is acceptable to the beholder and suitable to the time. What would be the point of appearing in such a way you give the person you have come help a heart attack. My teacher said that 'Death always came as a friend, someone you know, trusted or knew perhaps even as a dead friend or parent, otherwise you would not go with them and fight, especially if it was obviously the Angel of Death in all his glory — all the way.'

We made the angels into 'dimpled' cherubs and transformed them from the fearful cherubim of Eden to what can sometimes only be described as docile pets? We created this compliant set of 'angels' by clipping their wings and making them fall to earth, some perhaps for a second time, others for the first. These are the 'angels' with which I take exception because whose importance is being enhanced by such imagining? This form of angel has been removed so far from their Creator I doubt if even he would recognize them as being his own, but people for the most are comfortable with them.

Gustav Davidson in his *Dictionary of Angels*, gives us examples of Angels of Anger, Annihilation, Chaos, Chastisement, Confusion, Corruption, Fire, Hell, Iniquity, Lust, Persecution, Perversion, Prostitution, Vengeance and many, many more. These angels have been deliberately chosen from the lists available because they are not exactly the stuff of Christmas cards and neither are they angels that would make us feel comfortable and in charge of things. If additional argument is needed regarding the existence of such angels — remember that Death and Satan are also angels.

We have said repeatedly that the first mention of angels in the *Bible* comes early. 'So he drove out the man; and he placed at the East of the Garden of Eden Cherubims and a flaming sword which turned every way, to keep the way of the tree of life.' *Genesis* 3:24. This was not exactly a welcoming committee for Adam should he attempt to return to try to assume his former state or estate and if he had the flaming sword would have been used without doubt. The angels were telling Adam and Eve in no uncertain terms — stay out or take the consequences.

How many people, faced with a half–human, half–animal figure with horns on its head, human features, naked torso and the lower half of a goat would shriek 'Satan' or 'the 'Devil' and head for the hills. Had they taken to time to look, enquire and confirm — always try to confirm — they may realized they had a golden opportunity to meet the Greek God of Nature, Pan. Of course, I do not counsel that you take everything on face value, St. Paul is not wholly wrong in saying many an evil spirit will assume an acceptable form to gain acceptance. None should be foolish and believe anyone who tells them that the Path of Knowledge is easy. Gaining discrimination is never easy here or there, it is not like instant coffee where you only add water and of course, whatever you do today, it must always be 'fun.'

I feel the signs that the angels can and do give us are sometimes dismissed, ignored but more likely they are basically overlooked because the angels frequently use what is to hand, so the message or answer can appear somewhat ordinary at times, so it could not possibly have come from an angel. You must not think that the heavens must always open complete with heavenly choir and trumpets when contact is made with an angel that being the only way they can display themselves to people.

This has been so in the past and could be again, but I feel that this kind of display is rare — but this would preclude the 'strangers' we entertain unawares. Perhaps it is an understandable form of wishful thinking that they ought to show themselves in a spectacular manner; after all, what now passes for 'normal' you can see every day. In some passages in *Scripture*, angels have been reported simply as men clothed in white or shining garments, ' . . . two men stood by them in shining garments.' *Luke* 24:4.

They will come in a form that is best suited for the time, circumstances and the person. The Archangel Gabriel 'flew swiftly' and 'came quickly' but the *Bible* does not say that Gabriel had wings and in fact, the *Bible* does not even say that the Angel Gabriel is an Archangel. Some angels in *Scripture* are given wings as in ' . . . each one had six wings.' *Isaiah* 6:2. 'And every one had four wings.' *Ezekiel* 1:6 and *Isaiah* includes mainly seraphim. While in *Ezekiel*, much of *Daniel* and *Zechariah* we have cherubim and something or someone possessing wings was a very ancient emblem of the Spiritual, remember that both tradition and the *Bible* give Satan *twelve wings*.

Great speculation has been made at various times about the wing measurements and muscular strength of an angel. How large would the wings of an angel need to be according to the weight of

179

a man for an angel to fly and it seems that creating the wings is fine apart from their weight. The problem is said to lie with the pectoral muscles needed to 'drive them' because they are not sufficient to do so in the human frame. If they could be increased at least threefold or more for a ten stone body then the human frame could possibly fly but for one thing. What does all this speculation matter for wings are on an angel — not a man, they are not human beings and it is a vanity to think they can be likened to us in any way. These speculative exercises usually end with the preposterous statement that the wings would not work and so an angel cannot possibly fly!

As given above, the most important detail missing from this rather meaningless conjecture is that the 'wings' in enquiry are on an angel, not on a man and the disparaging comparison looks like an attempt to drag them down to our level, which is another vacuous and vain speculation. Although angels are found in our world they are not born of our world and in truth they do not belong here, they only visit us. They do not use physical laws nor have to, as we must because our laws are the only ones we have to live by. I feel they have little if any difficulty in coping with here. However, the reverse is a different matter, when we try to deal with and function within their place and laws, we live in possibly the 'heaviest' place in the scheme of things, see the section on Cabbala and the descent down the Tree of Life. This kind of cavalier attitude is, as far as this writer is concerned, why some find it difficult to access the angelic world.

For many years, the humble bumble–bee was regarded as not being capable of flight according to the laws of science and scientists. Yet it does fly and what is more, it flies in our world using the same scientific principles that says 'it should not be able to fly.' My daily paper has recently told me that scientists now believe they have discovered the secret of the bee's flight and they have had long enough to find it out. It appears to have something to do with the special mechanism of the wings, it has just recently been seen and it was there all the time. This must be very comforting for the bee because it now has official scientific sanction for something it been doing since biblical times and it never even knew that it needed this sanction since it was living as Nature intended — as I frequently say, science is usually the last to know.

I am extremely appreciative to Science for what it has given me to make my life easier and healthier than those who have gone before me — but my soul is my own and not theirs. In spite of the fact that my soul has not been 'approved' or sanctioned by science either, so obviously it cannot exist! The German physicist and philosopher Lichtenberg in his *Aphorisms* tells us, 'If an angel were ever to tell us anything of his philosophy I believe many propositions would sound like two times two equals thirteen.'

This form of speculation is a modern day *quodlibet*. Latin, *quodlibet*, 'Wither it pleases or (poetically) to any place whatever.' English, *quodlibet*= 'Not restrained to a particular subject; discussed at pleasure for curiosity or entertainment.' Historically it was a topic for philosophical or theological discussion or an exercise in this.

The most famous example of this form of discussion comes from the scholars of the Middle Ages was — 'How many angels can dance on the point or head of a pin?' They can all dance on the head of pin because, being angels with no measurable mass as we know it, the problem does not exist, we make a lot of problems exist I feel. Consequently, we can assume this was a *quodlibet* done 'for pleasure.' My teacher used to say ' . . . done for pleasure, go to hell, it is a complete waste of everyone's time more like it because in the end what does it matter and what has it demonstrated?'

The term 'angel' is not used in *Ezekiel*, though there are many supernatural 'men' executing the duties of an angel, marking the idolaters for destruction. 'And he called to the man clothed in linen, which had the writer's inkhorn by his side; and the Lord said unto him, Go through the midst of the city . . . and set a mark upon the foreheads of men.' *Ezekiel* 9:2. The 'man clothed in linen' is thought to be an angel and that this angel was the Archangel Gabriel. The Archangel Vretil, found in *Enoch* 2 is the archangelic keeper of 'the treasury of the Sacred Books', he is reputed to be 'more wise than the other archangels' and we are told that Vretil 'dictates while Enoch writes.' The Archangel Vretil is another candidate for being the unnamed 'man clothed in linen' and he is equated with many high angels including Uriel and Enoch.

Perhaps the first definite allusion to an angel by title is in the account of Hagar's flight from Sarah, her mistress. 'And the angel of the Lord found her by a fountain of water in the wilderness.' *Genesis* 16:7 and 9–11. In *Genesis,* there is an account of three men visiting Abraham and it is distinctly said the Lord then appeared to him in Chapter 17. In Chapter 19:1, two of the men who had thus been with Abraham are identified with the two angels who came to Sodom, where they are mistaken for men. Their appearance in human form is shown by the remainder of the narrative. In Verse 15, the Hebrew has the definite article and they are called 'the angels.' It is thought the ambiguity between 'angel' and 'man' in this incident may have led a *New Testament* author to later add the caveat, just in case the 'men' are angels. 'Do not neglect to show hospitality to strangers, for thereby some have entertained angels unawares.' *Hebrews* 13:2, though I do agree with it principle. The angel of the Lord interferes to prevent the slaying of Isaac as a sacrifice by his father. *Genesis* 22:11. There is the famous vision of Jacob who sees angels ascending and descending a ladder that reached from the earth to heaven, with the Lord God of Abraham standing above it. This vision is given a chapter later because it is felt to be important. *Genesis* 28:12. In the other books of the *Pentateuch*, angelic agencies and appearances are not so much mentioned as inferred and again, this may be because such things were an accepted part of life of the time.

The angel of the Lord appeared to Moses from within the burning bush. The Angel Zagzagel is named 'a Prince of the Presence' and he is said to have taught Moses, as he is a teacher of the angels. This angel is frequently given as the 'Angel of the Burning Bush' as is the Archangel Michael. In the *Midrash Petirat Mosheh*, the Angel Zagzagel (other spellings are used) was joined by the Archangels Michael and Gabriel when the Holy One came down from heaven to take the soul of Moses and to assist in burying the patriarch. Zagzagel — 'the righteousness of God' — in the writings of the rabbis is an angel of benevolence, mercy, memory and chief of the *Order of Dominations*. This angel bears the standard of the Archangel Michael and assists him when he goes into battle. Although other names are given, Zagzagel is usually given as the angel that held back the arm of Abraham when he was about to sacrifice his son Isaac.

In the matter of Moses and the burning bush, there is little doubt as to the identity of the angel because he is called both 'Jehovah' and 'God.' *Exodus* 3:2. In *Judges* 2:1–4, although this chapter begins by saying it is 'the angel of the Lord' who is speaking. The angel quickly starts speaking of himself as being the one who brought the people into the land. 'Which I sware unto your fathers; and I said, I will never break my covenant with you.' This appears to be 'the Lord' himself speaking, not the angel, unless it was this particular angel who had made the covenant and brought them into the land but it is more likely that the 'angel' and the Lord are one.

The 'angel of the Lord' who accompanied the Israelites on their journey out of Egypt was obviously an angel whose duties were defence and protection. When the Egyptians were pressing hard upon the Israelites, the angel changed his position from vanguard (= 'defence') to rearguard (= 'protection'), because he placed a cloud between the hunters and the hunted. Divine protection is not new of course. The Hittites believed their armies were escorted by a deity named Yarris and this god could hide the warriors from their enemies in times of danger.

*Proverbs* 24:17–18 reads 'Rejoice not when thine enemy falleth, and let not thine heart be glad when he stumbleth: Lest the Lord see it, and it displease him.' In the *Talmud,* the Rabbis tell us God does not rejoice when the wicked come upon destruction and the noble expression is shown in a legend of the Rabbis that tells us that the angels wanted to sing at the overthrow of the Egyptians who were drowning in the Red Sea. However, God is said to have rebuked them saying: 'The work of My hands is drowned in the sea, and you would offer Me a song!'

*Psalm* 103:20 gives us some idea of what the duties of an angel are and it refers to their strength and power. 'Bless the Lord, ye his angels, That excel in strength, that do his commandments, Hearkening unto the voice of his word.' In *Psalm,* 104:4 we are told of the creation of angels, because it is set out as one of the acts of the power of the Lord. 'Who maketh his angels spirit.' In the *Epistle to the Hebrews,* we are told that the angels 'are they not all ministering spirits, sent forth to minister to them who shall be heirs of salvation?' 1:14.

Some passages refer to the moral perfection of the angels. 'I know that thou art good to my sight, as an angel of God.' 1 *Samuel* 29:9 and because of the moral perfection of angels, Paul warns Christians against false teachers disguised as angels in *Galatians* 1:8. Neither was he surprised at the success of false prophets 'for Satan himself is transformed into an angel of light.' 2 *Corinthians* 11:14, their appearance is enough in the biblical encounters to distinguish them from ordinary people and there is usually little doubt who they are or from where they have come.

The saints Peter and Paul took great pains to emphasize that Christ's victory was the defeat of the angels, Paul did not seem happy with the angels and he did not appear to trust them completely. Despite the reservations above *Luke* 22:44 tells us that Jesus did wish that the cup would be taken from him but only if God willed it, 'And there appeared an angel unto him from heaven, strengthening him.' It may be worth pointing out that at this critical time in Christ's life it was an angel that came to strengthen Jesus because the critics of the angels (Peter and Paul) were fast asleep when needed. Three times Jesus came to them and each time the disciples were sleeping, causing Jesus to say to Peter 'Simon, sleepest thou? Couldest thou not watch for one hour?' Peter or the angels who would you choose?

Jesus said he could call upon his father for the help of the angels in the Garden at Gethsemane. 'Thinkest thou that I could not pray to my Father, and he shall presently give me more than twelve legions of angels? Nevertheless, how then shall the scriptures be fulfilled, that thus it must be?' *Matthew* 26:53. In this, Jesus does not say he will command the angels to attend, but that he 'will pray' to his Father who will 'give' them to him. I think the trust of the Christ in the angels far outweighs any mistrust Peter or Paul regarding them because they are the lesser voice to the writer. It seems that the human mind or ego starts imposing its will upon matters early in things or from the beginning but it need not be.

A term which is sometimes used for the angels in the Hebrew is 'bird,' while heaven or the 'bosom of God' is called the 'Bird's Nest.' These particular terms may explain the lines in *Ecclesiastes* 10:20, 'Curse not the king, no not in thy thoughts; and curse not the rich in thy bedchamber: for a bird of the air shall carry the voice, and that which hath wings will tell the matter.' We may conclude from this it is an angel 'which hath wings' and it is they who 'will tell the matter' without having to ask to whom the matter will be taken.

The Catholic Church is more prudent than most of the other Christian denominations regarding the angels. The Catholic Church not only acknowledges the existence of angels but actively encourages their adherents to try to communicate with and respect these angelic beings. They are wise in knowing the first steps of any venture are often the hardest to take and anything that assists the venture should be encouraged.

Further, if the 'angelic step' proves too high for their adherents to mount upwards or if this may prove a deterrent, then the Church provides an important and more accessible 'step up' to assist the seeker. This intermediate step is the office of the saints, which could rightly be thought of as the step below the angels and a smaller step leading to the desired objective. The saints are even closer to us and being human may understand our weakness and foibles the better for it. Other Christian denominations do admit the existence of angels but it is in an almost apologetic voice that is half–hearted in its commitment, encouragement or trust, which I feel is to their detriment.

The angels not only serve God in heaven, they also defend nations, countries, churches, people and many other matters of import to life on this level. The angels offer up the prayers of the faithful, particularly those prayers that ascend to heaven during Mass. Every human being on earth has at least one angel who watches over them and most individuals, as written throughout, have two angels as their Guardian Angels, who watch over them, which is the belief of this work. These angels defend their charge from evil but because of free will can only counsel against undertaking evil, help them in prayer, suggest good thoughts and try to guide their charge along beneficial paths but only in rare cases, insist that anything is done.

At the close of life, if they are to be saved they present the soul of the one who was in their protection and guidance to God. 'Likewise, I say unto you, there is joy in the presence of the angels of God over one sinner that repenteth.' *Luke* 15:10. The Churches should give the angels the veneration, honour and respect, which is their due and many do I am glad to say. It is accepted by most that the angels are acquainted with things that pass on earth, so the Church and congregation beg in their prayers for their compassionate office and intercession on their behalf, many feel they are easier to talk to.

In *Colossians*, Paul condemns the 'religion of angels' saying. 'Whether they be thrones, or dominions, or principalities, or powers all things were created by him, and for him: and he is before all things, and by him all things consist.' (1:16.) Many scholars believe that in doing this Paul may possibly have been warning against the 'Gnostic error' prominent in his time, less so than in ours, that considered the angels to be the creators of the world of which he obviously disapproved or he was making an over–zealous defence of the Creator. He does not explain how far the Guardian Angels have been divested of their purpose, in view of the all–embracing sufficiency of Christ and his Spirit, for believers.

## CRY HERESY!

In religion, sometimes regarding the angels, the word heresy has been raised at various times. The disciples had Divine sanction from their Master and the Source that gave it to him, but this did not always make their life easy. Neither were they sheltered in this 'vale of tears,' though they were given understanding of why things were being done, the purpose of their suffering and knowing that does help. It is when you do not know why and all seems pointless that total despair starts to set in. Victor Frankl said in principle — he who has a 'why' to live for can bear with almost any 'how' and Victor Frankl is a very wise man and therefore worth reading.

The angels (as we have said) did not always have a smooth passage, especially with the early Church Fathers and many angels in the past have felt their wrath. Sometimes it would appear that the angels got it from both ends, the celestial and the earthly, the 'celestial' had the authority — but what authority did the earthly have?

The principal meaning of the word 'heresy' was originally 'religious error, departure from what is held to be true doctrine' and the rules of heresy have always existed in the church and not only in the Christian Church. A heresy is anything that is counter to the dogma of a particular church or religion with a wilful adherence to an error of faith by a 'baptised person' who (by baptism) has accepted the teachings of the church against which formal denial or doubts are now being expressed. This also includes the rejection of the agreed rules and principles of an organization, brotherhood, political and the like. Naturally, any form of disobedience, contradiction or questioning was deemed to be unacceptable and as a result a heresy, in politics in particular there are many 'heresies' and they come under different names, though disobedience/treachery is usually high on the list.

Before Christianity was established in the Roman Empire, the heresy of Christianity was regarded as a crime against the State, the Roman gods and therefore punishable by civil and religious law to the full extent and power of the State, history is not short of examples. In modern times, as we have already said, the term heresy is now used for anything that is regarded as a 'disruptive or unorthodox opinion' or someone who differs from 'what is thought to be best for the majority and upsetting the *status quo'* and it is now applied to politics, business or any group of people that has an agreed agenda or purpose with a specific aim or direction. Unacceptable heresy is still alive and kicking with exclusion or removal in some way the punishment for having private and unacceptable opinions.

The Roman Emperor Decius (c. A.D 200–251) ruthlessly persecuted the Christians and incense became the symbol of shame of those the Christians who renounced their faith. Retraction of the heresy of Christianity and other sins in Rome meant that the heretic had to prove their renunciation by burning some grains of incense on the altar of the gods of the State, before a religious image or to the Emperor or his image. Those Christians who renounced their faith in this manner were known as *Thurificati*. This was a symbolic act of apostasy because it tested the individual's loyalty to the State and loyalty to the State meant loyalty to the State religion and the emperor. This act of renunciation may prove one of the main reasons why incense was rejected by the early Christians, which would be reasonable because of the association and the treachery of such an act.

However, the expression did not start out with this particular burden attached to its name. The term 'heretic' originally meant a belief 'arrived at by oneself.' Latin, *hæresis* with the Greek αιρεσις, *hairesis*, (1) 'a taking, a choosing, choice,' (2) 'the thing chosen: later, a philosophical principle or set of principles.' Sense (1) αιρεω, *haireo*= 'to take,' (2) is *from αιρεομαι, haireomai*= 'to take for oneself.' The word started out in life meaning simply making 'an act or choice.' Secondly, it was used for 'a thing chosen' and it came to stand for 'a set of philosophical principles.'

Finally, the ecclesiastical writers and authorities tightened the religious restrictions upon the word and 'heresy' became for the most part religious. The meaning of the word became more rigid and fervent as time progressed. The meaning of the word has gone from 'making a free and private choice' to a serious crime and punishment — not unlike many words of today really, where the few are still dictating to the many as to what will be spoken, written, read or thought with a reckoning for any non–compliance or deviation to their wishes and we are still accepting this.

The English word heresy does not appear in the *Old Testament* and it is found only four times in the *New Testament* with 'heretic' only once in the religious meaning of today. In Christian doctrine, it is unequivocally an error of doctrine and it seems it is upon the following passage alone that the modern ecclesiastical use of the word is founded. In *Acts*, it means 'a difference in methods of worship.'

In the following, it is clearly an error of doctrine and its consequences are equally clear. 'There shall be false prophets and false teachers also among you, who privily shall bring in damnable heresies, even denying the Lord who brought them, and shall bring upon themselves swift destruction.' 2 *Peter* 2:1. Here as said above, heresy courts retribution unless it is recanted and forgiveness for error is sought, so here we those who sin and those who claim the authority to forgive. It is a subject and worthy of more study but now let us leave heresy and deal with . . .

# MORE INFORMATION GATHERED ABOUT THE ANGELS

The birth of John, the forerunner of Christ was foretold by an angel. 'And there appeared unto him an angel of the Lord standing on the right side of the altar of incense . . . and thy wife Elizabeth shall bear thee a son, and thou shalt call his name John.' *Luke* 1:11. Another angel was sent to Mary to be a sign of the birth of her son and to give his name. 'And in the sixth month the Angel Gabriel was sent by God unto the city of Galilee . . . shall be called the Son of God.' *Luke*.1:26. An angel of the Lord instructs Joseph in a dream and giving him the name by which the child shall be called ' . . . and thou shalt call his name Jesus.' *Matthew* 1:21.

An angel announces the birth of Christ to the shepherds. 'And there were in the country shepherds abiding in the field, keeping watch over their flock by night. And, lo, the angel of the Lord came upon them, and the glory of the Lord shone around them.' Other angels join the song of praise at the birth *Luke* 2:9. The warning that delivers Jesus from the sword of Herod is given by an angel who appears to Joseph in a dream, to take the baby and flee to the land of Egypt. When King Herod dies, an angel comes to Joseph, again in a dream as this seems to be the method of angelic communication for Joseph, to take the child back to Israel. *Matthew* 2:13 and 19.

After the temptation of Christ, angels administer to him, ' . . . and, behold, angels came and ministered unto him.' *Matthew* 4:11. Even the Devil alludes to angelic protection if Christ would cast himself down from the pinnacle. 'He shall give his angels charge concerning thee: And in their hands, they shall bear thee up, lest at any time thou dash thy foot against a stone.' *Matthew* 4:6.

With regard to the above, I would like to take a modified example from a recent work called *Pan — Great God of Nature*. The quotation from the *New Testament* regarding the temptation of Jesus by Satan given above is easy to find and tells us that the spirit led Jesus into the wilderness to be tempted by the Devil. In this section the Goat–like Devil takes him to a high mountain, shows him all the kingdoms of the world and their glory, and tells him all this he can have if he will fall down and worship him. This produces the line 'Get thee behind me Satan . . . man shall not live by bread alone . . . and so on.'

In the work of Pan mentioned, a minor Greek myth given by Ennius in his translation of the *Sacred History* of Evemerus and preserved by the Christian father Lactantius was quoted. We are told of the young Jupiter being led to a high mountain by the god Pan. The mountain is called the *Pillar of Heaven*, the young Jupiter ascends the mountain with the old god Pan showing him the way and when they reach the peak, they contemplate distant lands as Pan points them out to the young Jupiter. On the mountain, Jupiter sets up an altar to Coelus or Uranus (= 'heaven) and on this altar, he makes his first sacrifice. It was here that he looked up to the heavens as we now call it . . . and so on.' *Divine Institutions* – Lactantius.

Any representation of this scene would show a young god standing with a demon or devil, horns, half-goat and half–man, little tail, cloven hoof next to both is an altar and sacrifice on a high mountaintop. To a Christian eyes this could only mean that the Devil was tempting the young god and asking to be worshipped in return for the kingdoms of the earth to which the 'Devil' was pointing.

To the Pagan, however, Pan as 'Lord or President of the Mountains' was in his natural habitat and as the old god what would be more natural than his being there with the young Jupiter and showing him the kingdoms in his realm — not Pan's or the Devil's realm — the kingdoms belonging to the young god, Jupiter! Does it sound just a little familiar, of course it does. Last quote from *Pan*: ' . . . the early Christian Fathers spent much time manipulating the Pagan gods into demons and devils for their own purposes. They seemed to have little other thought but to ridicule the old mythologies, but failed to recognize the quality of their own.' Is my bias for Pan showing once more — good!

As said earlier, in the agony of Christ, in the Garden at Gethsemane another angel appears, 'And there appeared an angel unto him from heaven, strengthening him.' *Luke* 22:43. He told one of those with him, on his arrest, to put up his sword. 'Thinkest thou I cannot now pray to my Father, and he shall presently give me more than twelve legions of angels? But how then shall the scriptures be fulfilled, that thus it must be?' *Matthew* 26:53.

The resurrection of Christ was announced by angels. 'And, behold, there was a great earthquake: for the angel of the Lord descended from heaven . . . His countenance was like lightning, and his raiment white as snow: and for fear of him the keepers did shake, and became as dead men.' *Matthew* 28:2

We have said that Christ is a mediator and St. Paul speaks of Christ as being the 'one mediator between God and men, the man Christ Jesus.' 1.*Timothy* 2:5. Christ as man is far from God — *distat a Deo* — and in nature far from men in the dignity of grace and glory. Christ, therefore, as man is most truly called mediator.' St. Athanasius wrote 'a mediator became necessary that things generated might come to be.' In *Galatians* Paul writes ' . . . and it was ordained by angels in the hand of a mediator.' 3:19.

Let us go back to the *Old Testament* for a moment. Moses is often called a mediator and this was a familiar title of Moses with the Jewish writers. His office as mediator soon appears in print, 'I stood between the Lord and you at that time, to shew you the word of the Lord: for ye were afraid by reason of the fire, and went not up into the mount.' *Deuteronomy* 5:5. The doctrine of the angels and their mediation is asserted in the beautiful passage of Elihu's speech in *Job* 33:23, which has been placed at the beginning of Part Two. This is an earlier rendering, which I prefer. The *King James Version* of our quotation is given as:

> 'If there be a messenger with him,
> An interpreter, one among a thousand,
> To shew unto man his uprightness
> Then he is gracious unto him, and saith
> Deliver him from going down to the pit:
> I have found a ransom.'

There can be little doubt in the alternative version heading Part Two regarding the *Old Testament* words 'to mediate.' An angel interceding with God on behalf of men, μεσιτης, *mesites*= 'a mediator, umpire, arbitrator,' μεσιεια, *mesieia*= 'mediation, negotiation' and μεσιτευω, *mesiteuo*= ' to act as mediator.' Another word noted in this grouping is μεσηρης, *meseres*= 'in the middle, midmost.' These words all have a bearing on the scheme of the very important *Middle Ground* of the work that was written about early in the chapter, because every word is 'in the middle or between' and this is what mediators, umpires, intercessors or arbiters are, they 'negotiate between' by being in the middle of two things.

Regarding the quotation taken from, *Job* 5:1, which heads this section, again an earlier translation. Today this gives the word 'saint' for 'angel' and this why I have chosen the earlier version and not the new, for comparison:

'Call now, if there be any that will answer thee;
And to which of the saints wilt thou turn?'

An eminent Protestant scholar comments on the above passage. 'They (= the angels) appear as intercessors for men with God, bringing men's needs before Him and mediating on their behalf. This work is easily connected with their general office of labouring for the good of men, especially of the pious; still it is here for the first time ascribed to them' Dillman, commenting on *Job*, p. 44.

As said earlier, Paul in his letters rebukes the worship of angels and writes disparaging remarks regarding the ranks of angels. Paul lays greaer emphasis in this epistle upon the leadership of Christ. This, as pointed out earlier, may have been to counteract the Gnostic philosophy of worshipping angels, thought by some 'to be pretentious.' This leads others to suppose that Christian doctrine was suffering a serious decline through some general 'Gnostic' theory. The angels play an important part in Gnostic systems regarding intermediary powers (*aeons*, *principalities* and the rest) at the hands of Gnostic theologians. See Paul's *Epistle to the Colossians* 1:15 ff.

Old writers tell us the Egyptians believed that 'every man had three angels attending him.' The followers of Pythagoras believed that we have two and the Romans gave us a good and evil genius or daemon. From Sheridan, in his notes to *Persius* (1739), we are told. 'Every man was supposed by the ancients at his birth to have two *Genii*, as messengers between the gods and him. They were supposed to be private monitors, who by their insinuations disposed us either to good or evil actions. They were also supposed to be not only reporters of our crimes in this life, but registers of them against our trial in the next, when they had the name of Manes given to them.'

In Roman mythology, a *genius* was 'the begatter' and was a guardian spirit who protected the individual from the beginning to the end of their life. We spoke of this in greater detail earlier in the *Old Testament* section. Every living person was bequeathed a particular genius to which yearly offerings were made, generally on that person's birthday for that was when they acquired their guardian and this is why I said earlier that it is likely the celebration was the individual's 'begatter,' more than the individual.

As well as the individual's genius, there were genii that protected tribes, towns, places and the Roman State. A particularly important genius was the *Genius populi Romani*, the *Guardian of Rome*. The achievements of an individual were often attributed to the guidance of their personal genius, which is the inborn power of their life. Sometimes the genius of a dead person is mentioned or the occasional dedication is found to 'the daemon of the departed.' This is the divine guardian who, being from another world, still watches over and guides a human.

This is thought to be what Christ is referring to regarding children in *Matthew* 18:10. 'Take heed that ye despise not one of these little ones; for I say unto you, That in heaven their angels do always behold the face of my Father which is in heaven.' Though generally accepted by the Fathers, it was first clearly defined by the popular theologian, Honorius of Autun (d.1151), a prolific writer who is thought to have lived in England for a time. He held that each soul is entrusted to an angel at the moment the soul is introduced into the body. We will be taking up the question of the personal Guardian Angels in greater detail as said in Part 2.

When Peter was imprisoned in Jerusalem he was rescued by 'the angel of the Lord' who led him from captivity and then left him. When Peter arrived at the house of Mary, the mother of John, many people were praying there. The damsel Rhoda said Peter was at the gate because, although she did not open the gate, she knew his voice. She was not believed at first and they said 'it is his angel.' *Acts* 12:15. Realizing that it really was Peter in the flesh, they opened the door and let him in.

This example features the belief that when a Guardian Angel appeared on earth it takes the form of the person they guard. Many people hold the view that this is how the Angel of Death appears to us at the last, as suggested earlier. He comes as someone we know and trust or we would not go with him and fight him all the way, as some obviously do.

A particular form of Jewish foreshadowing regarding death was the 'study of the shadow' on the moonlight night of *Hosha'anah Rabba*. If a man loses his shadow on this particular night, he will be dead within the course of the year. It is possible this belief is the origin of the old statement 'for their shadow has departed from them' in *Numbers* 14:9.

Shadows have a somewhat ill-omened folklore in the *Talmud*, which tells us of the five to avoid. Spirits avoid bright sunlight and speedily find the shadow so is follows that evil lurks in them so to complete the statement they are: the shadow of a solitary palm; of lotus trees; the caper tree; the sorb bush and the fig tree and it naturally follows that the more branches the trees have, the more hazardous its shade.

Angelic guardianship was current among the Jews and was based upon a true doctrine therefore angelic concern was not regarded as speculative but usual. The *Feast of the Guardian Angels* — the *Angelorum Custodum* — is undertaken on the 1st of March and was first observed in Spain. The *Feast of the Guardian Angels* was instituted and admitted to the Roman calendar under Paul V in 1608 at the request of Ferdinand of Austria, afterwards emperor. Later the date was changed, though not in Germany and some areas of Switzerland by Clement X in 1670. The interest taken by the angels or heaven in the welfare of the human race is plainly expressed in *Luke*.15, in the parable of the 'lost sheep.'

Angels were frequently found in groups of four or seven 'And after these things I saw four angels standing on the four corners of the earth, holding the four winds of the earth.' *Revelation* 7:1. In *Genesis*, they are styled 'men' — *mal'akh* because 'angel' does not occur in *Ezekiel*. In the *New Testament*, St Mark tells us of the *agrapha* of Christ. 'And then shall they see the Son of Man coming in the clouds with great power and glory. And then he shall send his angels, and shall gather together his elect from the four winds, from the uttermost part of the earth to the uttermost part of heaven.' (13:26.)

In the above, the four angels were ' . . . holding the four winds of the earth.' A great deal of importance was placed upon the four winds and their direction by the *Talmud* because there creation was essential and so both are mentioned throughout. The most important direction was the North because 'darkness' comes to the world from the North. The Hebrew word *ruach* can be translated as either 'wind' or 'spirit' and it is early in *Genesis*. 'And the spirit (= 'wind') of God moved on the face of the waters' but before the 'spirit' came on the scene it is written that 'darkness was upon the face of the deep.' The four winds blow every day and the North Wind blows with them all and if this were not so, the commentators tell us, the world could only exist for a short time.

In the Hebrew commentaries, the North Wind is regarded as being neither manifestly hot or cold and for that reason it moderates all the other winds and makes them tolerable. In October on the last day of the *Feast of the Tabernacles*, all present would take note the direction the smoke from the altar took because there was detailed predictions according to which direction it took and it ended with the words that if the smoke went to the East — 'all were happy' but if the smoke went to the West — 'all grieved!'

Frazer in *The Golden Bough* writes of a fire festival of Europe (in some Germanic countries) that took place on the first Sunday in Lent. He tells us the young people go around all the houses gathering straw or brushwood, which they would take to a high prominence. There they would stack the kindling around the bole of a slender beech tree to which they had fastened a piece wood at right–angles in the form of a cross and this construction was known as the 'castle' or 'hut.' They would set the 'hut' on fire and then they would march around it with heads bare carrying torches and praying aloud. Sometimes a straw man was placed in the hut and burnt with it. The people at the festival took particular note in which direction the smoke of the fire went, for example, if it drifted across the fields, this was taken as a sign that the future harvest would be plentiful.

The 'angels of the Seven Churches of Asia Minor' in *Revelation* 1–3 have been variously explained in the work and we will add our 'widow's mite.' Some believe these are angels in the ordinary sense as with the remainder of the chapter. Some think these angels are the representatives (or bishops) of the churches, while others believe it is more likely they are the personification of the spiritual character or the 'invisible bishops of each church.' Some others think they are Guardian Angels standing in the same relationship to the churches, as the 'princes' in *Daniel* stand to the nations, being the personification of the churches. This idea is found in Old Persian thought. Seven angels plus three of the Trinity to make ten and the magic of the ten angels will be taken up in the final chapters of this introduction.

Often outlined in Jewish mythology are the seven heavens first mentioned in the section *Manna — the Bread of the Angels* and these can also be found in quite a few older works, but you must be prepared to find different spellings to what is given here. These are described in various ways and the number seven with its symbolism, traditions, folklore and so on could almost fill a small book on its own. As we said earlier, the Hebrew term for heaven, *Shamayim* is a combination of *sham* and *mayim* and the explanations are given in the section — *Angels —Views from other Sources — For and Against*.

The First Heaven, *Vilon* is said to be like a house that has it curtains drawn. Those who are inside the house can see everything that happens outside, but those who are outside cannot see into the house or see the occupants that are watching them. Through the windows in this heaven, the ministering angels watch the 'children of men,' the mortal race and everything they do. They can see who is walking in the path of Righteousness and who are not. The ruler of the First Heaven is given as Gabriel.

The next heaven of interest is the second. In the Second Heaven, *Rakia* we find the planets, the fixed stars and the constellations. It has twelve windows that accord to the twelve hours of the day and night. Three hundred and sixty–five angels are appointed to take care of and serve the Sun in this heaven. These angels conduct the Sun from window to window during the day as it turns around the world and they guide the Moon before the windows during the night. The rulers of the Second Heaven are Raphael and Zacahriel.

Finally of interest to us here is the Sixth Heaven called *Makon* in which is found 'the hosts of angels who sing hymns of praise during the night.' The chief ruler of the Sixth Heaven is Zachiel, with Zebul during the daylight hours and Sabath during the night hours.

The rulers of the Third Heaven, *Shechakim* have the chief angel Anahel, with the princes Jabriel, Rabacyel and Dalquiel. The ruler of the Fourth Heaven, *Zebul* is Michael. The ruler of the Fifth Heaven, *Maon* is Sandolphon or Sammael, of the Seventh Heaven, *Araboth* is Cassiel, making the seven heavens in all that are named as *Vilon, Rakia, Shecakim, Zebul, Maon, Machon* and *Araboth*.

Apollo and Minerva presided over Athens, as did Athena from whom it got its name. Bacchus and Hercules ruled over the Boeotian Thebes. Juno was set over Carthage. Venus presided over Cyprus and Paphos with Apollo over Rhodes. Mars was the tutelary god of Rome, Neptune of

Taenarus with Diana over Crete and so forth. This short list is enough to show that the idea of gods, goddesses or angels ruling a person, a people, a country or a nation is far from a new.

Moresin tells us 'that Rome, in imitation of Gentilism (= paganism), has fabricated such kinds of genii for guardians and defenders of cities and people. Thus, the Roman Church has assigned St. Andrew to Scotland, St. George to England, St. Denis to France St Egidius to Edinburgh. St. Nicholas to Aberdeen. Popery has in many respects closely copied the heathen mythology. She has the Supreme Being for Jupiter, she has substituted angels for genii, and the souls of the saints for heroes, retaining all kinds of daemons. Against these pests, she has carefully provided her antidotes. She exorcises them out of waters, she rids the air of them by ringing her hallowed bells and so on. The Romanists have similarly assigned tutelary gods to each member of the body: as, for instance, the arms are under the guardianship of Juno, the breast of Neptune, the waist of Mars, the reins of Venus; and so on.' Therefore, it would seem not every one approved or agreed with this aspect of Christendom.

Now, let us return to the *Old Testament* for a while to *Daniel*. I did say from the beginning that you cannot keep the two books separate for long and the associated subjects are scattered throughout them both and not conveniently found in one place. Each nation has a 'prince' or archangel appointed to attend to its welfare. There is 'a prince of the kingdom of Persia,' *Daniel* 10:13 ' . . . lo, the prince of Grecia (= Greece) shall come . . . and there is none that holdeth with me in these things, but Michael your prince.' 10:20–21. This makes the Archangel Michael a 'prince of Israel' and 'one of the chief princes.' (10:13) A similar idea (it is suggested) may be found in *Isaiah* 33:2–24, which dates from around 335–333 B.C. Instead of Michael it is 'the Lord who is our judge, the Lord is our lawgiver and the Lord is our king; he will save us.'

When we come to *Daniel*, we come upon a new feature, which is found in none of the other canonical books of the period, the angels begin to have names and the name usually has meaning. First, we have Michael already mentioned. His name appears only five times in all, three times in the *Book of Daniel* where he appears in human form to Daniel. The remaining times are in *Jude* and the *Apocalypse*.

In *Jude*, he is designated as 'Michael the archangel' and is the only one in the *Bible* to whom this title has been given because as said previously Gabriel is never called archangel in the *Bible*, only angel. The main difference between Gabriel and Michael seems to be that Michael is the Guardian Angel of Israel the High Priest in Heaven and Michael is more preoccupied with the affairs of Heaven. Gabriel is a powerful and active messenger of God who comes from Heaven to execute Gods will. There is more information regarding Gabriel in the non–Canonical writings of the Jews.

Some say Michael is the only archangel, despite the *Book of Tobit* saying there are seven of archangels and with this the Rabbis agree. Luther and many other reformers maintained that Michael was none other that 'the Angel of the Covenant and the Word' or 'the logos of St John.'

It is thought giving formal names to the angels was a feature prevalent in some of the *Apocryphal* works and marked a further step forward in the development and understanding of the angels. Others have argued against the Divine authority of these portions of *Scripture* because of the fact special names are assigned to the heavenly host.

According to these writers, the names of the angels are said to have been derived from heathen sources and can be traced back to the time of the Israelites in Babylon so naturally, other writer's say this opinion rests upon no solid foundation. It cannot be denied the doctrine concerning angels was from very early times, prevalent in a remarkably pure form among the Israelites. Jewish thinking concerning the angels was greatly changed and without question greatly enriched after the Babylonian Exile (597–538 B.C.)

The Babylonian Captivity (or Babylonian Exile) was the deportation of the Jews from Palestine to Babylon by King Nebuchadnezzar II and their release in 538 B.C by the Persian King Cyrus and a great number of Jews remained in Babylon and did not bother to return to Palestine at the end of the Exile and so became part of the Diaspora or body of Jews dispersed among nations outside Palestine. In the history of the Roman Catholic Church, the term 'Babylonian Captivity' is often used regarding the residence of the (Anti–) Popes in Avignon from 1309 to 1377. The Diaspora was the dispersion of the Jews among the Gentiles mainly in the 8th–6th century B.C or any Jews who were dispersed in this way, though it now applies to any group of people similarly dispersed, sent into exile or away from their home. The etymology is from the Greek *διασπειρω, diaspeiro=* 'to scatter' or 'to scatter abroad.'

In ancient Israel, there was the problem of the 'One God' for which there had to be a satisfactory resolution. It has been suggested by some that some Israelites were able to accept the idea of 'the many gods' and they solved the problem simply by turning 'the many gods' into angels — apart from one — naturally. The many serve the one God and the One God is a jealous God and will have none before him. The other course taken is that the lesser gods and angels could be called the 'Sons of God,' which reasonably assumes that the angels would naturally take a masculine form because they are described 'as men' in most of the records of the past, the female is found but most of the angels of both the *Old and New Testament* were male.

If we recall the different archangels who are princes and guardians of nations in *Daniel*. Some believe this assigned to them the role they were already performing as the 'natural' gods of that particular 'heathen nation' at the time. The division of the angels into ranks and the belief in archangels may have originated from the subjugation of the heathen gods to Yahweh. Many or most religions have a extensive history of absorbing what they could not destroy or replace either by incorporation and renaming and a similar practise regarding the sacred trees of the heathens and pagans was to carve a cross on them to rededicate the trees to Christianity — rededicate them?

When special names were applied to these heavenly messengers, it was thought this was done by Divine revelation to give emphasis and magnificence to the both the messenger, the messages they brought and who they brought it from. We find the angel who appeared to Daniel announced himself as being Gabriel — 'the mighty one of God.' There are other examples to be found with a *Concordance of the Bible* and a little effort. I believe I have already said that for serious study, Robert Young's *Analytical Concordance* is the version recommended and my personal choice.

As said, before the Exile, it was thought that Yahweh did everything for himself and was responsible for everything, both good and evil ' . . . Shall there be evil in a city, and the Lord hath not done it?' *Amos* 3:6. 'I am the Lord, and there is none else. I form the light, and create the darkness: I make peace, and create evil: I the Lord do all these things.' *Isaiah* 45:7.

The evil may have been channelled for its execution through spirits but it was Yahweh who was ultimately responsible for it, as with the persuasion of Ahab. 'Who shall persuade Ahab, that he may go up and fall at Ramoth–gilead?' The Lord asked who would do this and he was given different advice. A spirit came forth to the Lord and said 'I will' and 'I will be a lying spirit in the mouth of all his prophets' . . . and the Lord said . . . 'go forth and do it.' 1 *Kings* 22:19–23.

After the time of the Exile to attribute evil to God, would have been dishonourable and ignoble, so any incident of evil was ascribed to the agency of demons, evil or fallen angels. However, when the 'One God' triumphed over the many gods, belief in these did not conveniently disappear overnight. They had to be dealt with, neither were they easily dismissed because they are still here with us and very active we are told. The gods of those worshippers who were hostile to Israel and in opposition to the prophets were denounced in the sacred books and reduced to the rank of demons.

One of the main differences between Jewish myth and those of other nations, whether East or West was the multiplicity of gods, spirits and angels of the latter. In early mythologies, most of the occurrences of Nature were looked upon as manifestations of separate, independent divinities whose duties were to attend and guide such matters. Pan, Faunus, Silvanus, the Nymphs, the Dryads, the Hammerdryads, Sylphs, Cernunnos and so on dealt with the realms of Nature in Greece and Rome and you knew where to go or who to contact for what you wanted.

Now Nature has no gods to protect her as the old gods did because it was they who kept the vandals in check because these Gods protected their kingdoms with a vengeance. Now there are no guardian spirits to perform these tasks because if anyone attempted to invoke them they would be automatically branded heretics.

These old deities recognized a superior God that they acknowledged as their Leader and he was over all with his balancing consort, but they also enjoyed individual honour, dignity, worship and a great deal of individual freedom within a more flexible model regarding their allotted tasks. This puts them out of step with the early Jewish model where everything comes from a Supreme, Perfect Being and Creator who is Eternal and from whom everything comes.

This suggests that the ministering angels who populated Jewish myth were not independent powers and neither did they have Free Will, save only to be disobedient or fall from grace it seems. They are the compliant agents of and subject to the Will of the One Supreme God. Teachers in Jewish myth of the Talmud, for the most, were eager to avoid any idea that could lead to any taint of duality or plurality insisting that the angels were created either on the second or fifth day of Creation. The angels were not created before God or at the same time as the first day of Creation.

The belief in higher beings, which were of greater perfection than the human race, is common to antiquity. The 'angelology' of the Jews may prove the result of the conflict constantly waged between monotheism and polytheism but as frequently said, the cult of polytheism did not conveniently go away, it never does which is most inconsiderate of it and it lingers in the minds and thoughts of people. This is why converting the 'heresies' of a dissenting people can be an uphill struggle; even with those who are thought to have been converted. There always seems to be a deep residue of old memories left that will not go away and conveniently die. It is always there like a 'voice crying in the wilderness.'

To this writer, the study of angels is a compromise between the One and 'the many' and as such it is a problem that is still going strong. I repeat what I said a few pages back because it bears repetition. When intelligence cannot vanquish something, it usually compromises and incorporates it and thereby hopes it will resolve the conflict. The early Rabbis and the Church Fathers were not the unintelligent of the day. There has long been an acceptable custom of making the chief or popular god(s) of a vanquished religion the devil(s) of the new religion. The populace had to be shown the error of their ways and the old gods must be discredited by showing the people how they have been deceived by these abominations.

Take one important example, the God of Nature Pan. I admit freely that he has long been a favourite but gentle 'cause' of mine, Pan was happily roaming the hills of his beloved Arcadia in Greece and a god beloved by most of the population. He was a god that brought a great outpouring of love from the people because he was accessible. There was no running away for Pan because he stayed with his kingdom, his people and his responsibilities and running from him was a waste of time, where could you go and he can run faster than you. The pagan gods did not disappear to some unknown, inaccessible place that was only approached through a priesthood. Men and women were fundamentally their own priests and priestesses and as repeated said Pan had the appearance that made him perfect for his new role in the *New Dispensation*.

We have spoken of this before and I did warn the reader I was biased regarding this matter. What is this 'appearance' revered by so many? Pan is man down to the waist and nestling on his head are the horns of a goat. From the waist down he has the legs of a goat, a small tail and cloven hoofs — and what a blessing they have been. He plays plaintive music on the syrinx or the Pan Pipes, which he invented. This description minus the pipes and the music are familiar and, if you will forgive the unintentional pun also spoken of before, he must have been heaven sent for the role he was to be given. I repeat I have long been puzzled why they did not make use of Pan's syrinx in some way, but perhaps they could not as Pan's music would not suit these joyless people because Pan had too much life, fertility, primitive life and the soul of Nature in it because it was unspoiled and true to its cause.

From time immemorial, the belief has existed that dark and deserted places were inhabited by unfriendly spirits. Pan naturally loved this kind of place with a dislike of the cities and the masses, who I do not think he liked very much. Often when you see Pan represented in art especially in groups, he is often on the edge of things, on a ledge, slightly higher sometimes, apart, watching, waiting and perhaps the first to go because he could slip away virtually unseen.

He was plainly a truly pagan in the true sense of the word, someone from the *paganus*= 'the country.' Because Pan was born in the country, loved the countryside was the god of Nature and haunted the wild lonely places — of course he was a pagan, what else should he be? However, until Christianity was formed and established, Christ was to all intents and purposes a pagan because during his lifetime, Christianity did not exist and he did not really initiate the faith that was to take his name. Christianity is a religion *about* Christ not *of* Christ, because it was not created by him as teacher and prophet, though he was made both.

Pagan was a beautiful term until the city dwellers (of the time) made the word to mean something less worthy and derogatory. This was usually done to enhance the theoretical superiority and sophistication of city life and city dwellers and considering the rural areas and its people as being 'behind the times' and slow and sometimes I do not think this attitude has been completely eradicated in some respects. Whenever Christ was troubled, he quickly left the cities, its people and went out into the desolate *paganus*, for forty days and forty nights on one occasion. 'Desolate' here meaning without people, their noise and the paper–thin glamour that holds their lives together.

Even today, when city life gets too much for some people they nearly always say the same thing, 'I must get away for a few days and recharge my batteries' and this accounts for so many of the holidays homes of the English — in the country. Getting away from what that had depleted their 'batteries' in the first place with its demands for constant attention.

With the conversion to Christianity the city–dwellers designated non–Christians as 'pagans' and made the word a stigma, backward and derogatory, which had to be eradicated on behalf of the new God, with what I call the 'come on in the water's lovely' syndrome. It was the same for the 'heathens' that lived on the heaths that received similar treatment. I am not against cities, some of them are places of great beauty and they refresh the soul but they are being taken over and becoming harder to find.

The cities then as now were always the first to take up the latest fads and fashions in the belief that they know best. The fact that cities were just as quick to drop things and take up something new at the drop of a hat also speaks volumes — then as now. Sometimes, to sell their produce in the city the 'farmers and rustics' had to be 'converted' to Christianity before they could do so, which they did for the day and then, after selling their goods, they went back to the old religion and their familiar gods and places.

The countryside was slower to adopt change because they thought it was unnecessary and in many cases, it was change for the sake of it and quite often transient. What need did these people have for 'this city life' — then or now? The land and Nature changed very little, they knew her timing, her ways, her moods and especially when Mother Nature was found allied to the male priest. An ancient saying has it that: 'A goddess cannot dwell in her shrine unless there is a priest to offer an acceptable sacrifice' and Nature must always have her Green Man or Green George.

The belief was kept alive of how in olden times, these pagan spirits had been appointed 'to bring men to ruin' and it was conveniently forgot that some of the angels were sent by their God to perform the selfsame tasks. So was born part of the doctrine that would contribute to an arch–enemy of righteousness, which was Satan (*Old Testament*) or the Devil (*New Testament.*) Considerable amounts of the world's thoughts and sleepless nights have been taken up with this particular creation since it all began so long ago and he has already been discussed. He held their interest then — he is still holding it now. Next, let us stay a short while with one of the most fascinating names and individuals connected with the angelic in the view of the writer ...

## MELCHIZEDEK

One of the first questions regarding Melchizedek is the hardest to answer. Is Melchizedek a god, God, an angel, an archangel, one of the higher or highest angels above all the angels and archangels, a king, a priest or a man? It would seem that our 'first question' has become eight questions in all. Melchizedek — 'the god Zedek is my king' — whom the psuedo–Dionysus called 'the hierarchy most beloved of 'God' and Epiphanius calls Melchizedek 'an angel of the order of Virtues.' According to the pseudo–Tertullian, Melchizedek is a 'celestial virtue of great grace who does for heavenly angels what Christ does for man.' In the mythology of Phoenicia, Melchizedek is called Sydik and he is 'the father of the seven Elohim or angels of the Divine Presence' all of the above is a very impressive list and it warn us that we are dealing with a very special entity.

Melchizedek (Melchisedec or Melch–Zadok) is referred to twice in the *Old Testament*, though he is a prominent name in the *Epistle to the Hebrews* in the *New Testament* and that covers a very extended period of biblical time, literally from the beginning to the end, from *Genesis* to *Revelation*. In *Genesis* 14, Melchizedek is the priest who blesses Abraham on his return with the people and goods recovered from the eastern kings as 'Melchizedek king of Salem brought forth bread and wine, and he was a priest of the most high God' and Abraham gave him tithes. In *Psalm* 110, Melchizedek is the head of a messianic order of priests. In *Hebrews* 5–7 in the *New Testament*, he typifies the priesthood of the Messiah and he is often found identified with Jesus Christ. Melchizedek's priestly pre–eminence is applied to Christ who is thus the heavenly high priest 'of the order of Melchizedek for ever' and remember this implies that Christ is 'of the order,' part of it and not in charge of it — the Order belonged to Melchizedek.

*Hebrews* 7:4 tells us, 'Now consider how great this man was, unto whom even the patriarch Abraham gave the tenth of the spoils. And verily they that are of the sons of Levi, who receive the office of the priesthood, have a commandment to take tithes of the people according to the law, that is, of their bretheren, though they come out of the loins of Abraham: but he whose descent it not counted from them received tithes of Abraham.'

Melchizedek is the King of Righteousness, a king of Salem and sometimes he is thought to be a symbol of 'the Higher Self' in the human condition. The name is explained by some commentators as *malchi–tsedeq* in the Hebrew from *melech*= 'king' and *tsedeq*= 'righteousness,' giving 'My king of righteousness.' This may be referring to the ancient king/priest–initiates, often the founders of races and nations as well as eponyms cycles and the representatives of spiritual power. The name afterwards became generic (*Psalms* 110:4 and *Hebrews* 7) where a Messianic theory is hinted at and Jesus is described as 'a high priest after the Order of Melchizedek' and this shows one who has reached a high degree of initiation within it, probably the senior or highest position. Melchizedek is frequently identified with the sun, moon and the narrative of Jesus Christ.

The Mesopotamian kings raided the settlements of the five kings near the Dead Sea. As well as the massacre and the taking of possessions, they captured the nephew of Abraham, Lot and his family. Abraham led the attacking force against the Mesopotamians and he brought back the stolen possessions and the family of Lot.

On his victorious return, Abraham was greeted by the grateful kings and Melchizedek who gave him bread and wine. Some Christian scholars say by doing this Melchizedek prefigured the Eucharist with the bread and wine symbolizing spiritual goodness and truth. 'And wine that maketh glad the heart of man, and oil to make his face to shine, and bread that strengtheneth a man's heart.' *Psalm* 104:15. Bread is often given as a symbol of spiritual food of the soul, namely truth and the substance of goodness, the staff of the higher life. 'For the bread of God is that which cometh down out of heaven, and giveth life unto the world.' *John* 6:33. Bread is often given as being spiritual, celestial and the food of angels, which as manna came down from heaven.

Melchizedek also gave his blessing as 'priest of the most high God.' *Genesis* 14:18. The offering of bread and wine symbolized the world above and the world below — the symbols of sustenance and blessings of these worlds. Abraham gives Melchizedek a tithe because he 'gave him a tenth of everything' and when Abraham gave Melchizedek this tithe, he acknowledged the higher spiritual rank and/or secular rank of Melchizedek as a patriarchal priest.

One of the things suggested in *Hebrews* 7:3 is that his priesthood was distant and not received from any priestly pedigree. It is interesting to speculate if Melchizedek was uprooted from paganism with its many gods or was his knowledge of the monotheistic Hebrew God by direct revelation. Melchizedek must have been someone of great importance yet we are almost in total ignorance regarding his parentage, the length of his life, if he had any descendants and so forth. He is so mysterious regarding his person, his office and what this was that a great deal of speculation, some of it very outlandish, some founded and unfounded, has been made regarding him and still is.

He has been identified by later Jewish tradition with Shem, Ham or Japhet. Some draw a parallel between Melchizedek and Christ saying that Christ belonged to 'a tribe of which no man gave attendance at the altar.' Others have suggested 'he was an incarnate angel or other superhuman creature who lived for a time among men and that he foreshadowed the Christ as an early manifestation of the Son of God.' However, if he 'lived for a time among men,' it must be pointed out that it seems to have been a very long time spanning as it does the *Old Testament* to the *New Testament* as it has, where was he from the first entry in *Genesis* to the last in *Revelation*? Of course, he may only put in appearances when it was essential to the events happening on the cosmic stage and wherever he was at other times, would appear to be of greater import than here.

He has been connected with the Holy Spirit and it was prophesied of the Messiah that he would belong as a priest of the order of Melchizedek. The writer of the *Epistle to the Hebrews* repeatedly tells us the prophecy was fulfilled in Christ. In *Psalm* 110, he is referred to as a prototype of the Messiah and this in all probability demonstrates that Melchizedek foreshadowed Christ. *Psalm* 110 is often called by commentators one of the 'enthronement psalms' and these psalms were thought to be used at the coronation of the kings of Judah and the Christ when he was invested with both royalty and priesthood as a priest–king, as told in ' . . . and he shall be a priest upon his throne.' *Zechariah* 6:13. These were the times when we had Priest–Kings as rulers, before the Church made Holy Oil greater than the Holy Blood or *Sangreal* — the 'blood royal' making the church the more powerful and gaining control over both king and their subjects.

He appears greater than Abraham or his descendants and Christ is also a 'king of righteousness.' We are unable to make any definite statements, thoughts or opinions but I feel that few limits can be set regarding this particular personage, as with the Messiah. I repeat, we know very little of him save that he was someone of great importance and was obviously considered remarkable, respected and a lot of other things that simply make him all the more fascinating, mysterious and the reticence of Scripture regarding him is however, in itself significant and revealing.

The foregoing is canonical Christianity and we have not entertained any mythology or paganism regarding Melchizedek. There is a Christian mythology and the following is taken from *The Book of the Cave of Treasures* (Leipzig 1888), which is a compilation of Syrian narratives or tales.

A sect called the Melchizedekites asserted that Melchizedek was an incarnation of a Divine Power or Virtue. Their founder suggested that Melchizedek was a heavenly mediator for the angels. This was to meet the line, 'For verily he took not on him the nature of the angels; but he took on him the seed of Abraham' and he permitted the name Melchizedekites to be attached to his followers.' *Hebrews* 2:16, so it is not unreasonable to regard him as a teacher with followers or disciples.

This sect suggested that Melchizedek was the Holy Ghost and they thought of him as the Word and Spirit of God, the Second Person of the Trinity who came to make Christ the Third Person. This at least would explain why Christ is often referred to as a priest of the Order and not the other way around. This sect penetrated as far as Rome at the end of the second century. One legend has Melchizedek at his birth as an antediluvian baby who was 'glorious of countenance' and 'having the seal of priesthood on his breast.' It is said that his birth is a mystery but he was born to an aged mother, the wife of Nir, who was Noah's brother and this 'supernatural offspring' was preserved by Michael. Another version makes him the grandson or great–grandson of Shem and this may account for the legend that has him feeding the animals on the ark. Another suggestion is that all this was an attempt to give him a pedigree because he was said to have none.

Melchizedek is said to have buried Adam with the aid of Shem. An old legend has Noah and his sons carrying the body of Adam from the *Cave of Treasures*, the first grave of Adam onto the Ark (*The Book of Conflicts of Adam*) where it was sealed against access. 'After Adam, and Eve leave the Garden of Eden and at God's command, gold, frankincense and myrrh are brought by angels, dipped in water by the Tree of Life and given to Adam as tokens from the Garden and these are the sacred treasures of the cave.' *The Book of the Conflicts of Adam*.

These three tokens were regard as 'spiritual wisdom' (= gold), 'grace' (= frankincense) and 'peace' (= myrrh). They were imbued and vitalized by 'truth' and 'life' from being dipped in the water by the Tree of Life. Shem, Ham and Japhet 'brought gold, incense and myrrh.' These 'three gifts' will appear again in the *New Testament* at the birth of the Christ.

The angel of the Lord is said to have met them and escorted them to the centre of the earth where 'the four corners parted to form a cross.' In the centre, they placed the body of Adam. The four parts drew quickly together 'and the door of the created world shut fast.' This place has four names, the first is *Karkaphtha* — 'the skull,' the second is *Gaghulta* — because it was round.' The third is *Resiphta* — 'downtrodden' as Satan's head was crushed there and *Gefifta* — 'because all the nations were to be gathered to it.'

The next morning Melchizedek constructed an altar of twelve stones and presented the sacrifice of the bread and wine that Shem had taken from the Garden of Eden. The wine was obviously the Wine of Life, which according to Jewish mystical traditions has been kept in Paradise for the devout since the Creation of the world, 'wine preserved in the grape from the six days of Creation.'

It is said that Melchizedek stayed there as the priest of the shrine but he could build no house, animal sacrifices were forbidden and the only oblation was the bread and wine. His dress was lion's skin and he cut neither his hair or nails. There are other traditions that Adam was buried at Golgotha.

I hope the reader will now be more alert to the presence of Melchizedek and his angelic connections in *Scripture*. They will no longer regard this mysterious figure as someone that puts in a fleeting appearance in the *Old Testament* and is mentioned again in the *New Testament*. There is a tremendous span between these two events, which makes Melchizedek a mystery waiting to be solved and one that should not be neglected, he is far too important for such treatment.

Melchizedek used bread and wine for the sacrifice in the *Old Testament*. At the last supper Christ broke bread saying it was his body and, although he would touch no food or fruit of the vine. He said that the cup was 'the *New Testament* in my blood, which is shed for you' and that they should 'do this in remembrance of me.' *Luke* 22:17–21 and this is usually taken to mean that Christ and Melchizedek were of the same priestly order.

The 'Angelic Man' is a symbol of the Spiritual Earth and this is represented by the tenth Sephirah of the Cabbalistic Tree of Life, Malkuth the Kingdom and Government in Harmony. Therefore, we find bread and wine, products of the earth, for the Israelites and Christians. The gifts of Shem, Ham and Japhet were gold, frankincense and myrrh, as they were at the birth of Christ later, while the wine and bread of Melchizedek were used at the imminent death of the Christ.

Is Melchizedek an angel? No, not according to anything found in Scripture, though he is obviously a priest of the highest rank with a long span of life, none in the *Bible* if human have lived such a length of time. Legend has him this and more, possibly an angel, probably the harbinger of the *New Dispensation* and higher than many mentioned in those pages and this is brief I agree but so we must leave him. *Hebrews* 7:1 has him ' . . . King of righteousness, and that also King of Salem, which is, King of Peace; without father, without mother, without descent, having neither beginning of days, nor end of life; but made like unto the Son of God; abideth a priest continually.' As said at the beginning, Melchizedek is according the *Enoch* 2. A supernatural son of Noah and on the Ark was 'the feeder of the beasts.' In the mythology of the Phoenicians, he is the father of the *Seven Angels of the Presence* and with respect, this I find an extremely auspicious family by all accounts.

## SOME OF THE 'BAD' ANGELS

Now let us look at one of the 'bad' angels and perhaps the most famous is the one called Beelzebub or Beelzebul in the Greek *Βεελζεβουβ, Beelzeboub* usually written Beelzebub 'the fly–god, a god worshipped in the Philistine town of Ekron. 2 *Kings* 1:3; an evil spirit (Beelzebul); Figuratively: any person of fiendish cruelty, who is so nicknamed by his adversaries or in contempt of moral sentiment, appropriates the appelation to himself and cherishes it as if it were an honourable title.'

Beelzebul from *Baal*= 'lord of' and *zebul* in the *Old Testament* 'a habitation,' in the *Talmud*= 'dung' probably signifying 'lord of dung' making Beelzebul (not Beelzebub) the correct reading in the *Old Testament* passages. Given as 'one of the chief gods of the Cannites, 'a god of fire and fertility.'' This gives the popular name of Beelzebub — 'the Lord of the Flies, the Lord of Chaos' and 'the Lord of Dung.' Others think that Beelzebul means 'Lord of the House' and it refers to the region of air over which Satan presides. Beelzebub was used against Jesus by his enemies. The *Gospel of Nicodemus* has Christ thanking Beelzebul (= archaic form *Be–Elzebub*) despite the objections of Satan with whom a few say he is definitely not to be confused, for letting him take Adam and the other saints 'in prison' with him to heaven. In gratitude, Christ gives Beelzebub 'dominion over the underworld' because — 'a gift demands a gift!' He hath Beelzebub and by the prince of devils casteth he out devils . . . How can Satan cast out Satan.' *Mark* 3:25. Jesus calls himself Beelzebub, lord of the house.' Naturally, the 'house' means the temple or the house of God and Beelzebub was the means of casting out devils.

Some commentators connect the name Beelzebub, the popular form with the Syrian word *beeldebobo* meaning 'an adversary' so he was thought originally to be a Syrian god. The appellation 'adversary' is frequently used regarding Satan. The Jews (= the Pharisees) call Jesus 'Beelzebub,' lord of the dung heap, to explain his ability to cast out demons. 'He casteth out devils through Beelzebub, the chief of the devils.' *Luke* 11:15.

Beelzebub appears, like Asmodeus, to have become a mighty demon at the hands of Cabbalists and Christians. To the Hebrews he was the Prince of Demons, while to the Christians he is second only to Satan, a fallen angel who is Prince of Devils and Demons. He is a demon who inspired great fear and power and those sorcerers who invoke him place themselves at great risk, Asmodeus often appears as an enormous fly.

At the time of the Inquisition he was the master of the witches with whom he copulated in demonic possession with whom they danced and he did not stop with witches, even the nuns were not safe and nor was Urban Grandier, who it is claimed paid the price. The leaving of Beelzebub was often accompanied with a vile stench that lingered — and lingered — and . . !

Another class of demon is the *sefrim*= 'the hairy ones.' Azazel is a creature of uncertain identity sometimes given as 'a demon, a devil, satyrs' or 'he–goats' who like Azazel were thought to inhabit the wastelands and ruins. Some suggest it could be a deity that resembled a goat. 'The wild beasts or the desert shall meet with the wild beasts of the island, and the satyr shall cry to his fellow.' *Isaiah* 34:12. Passages portraying the desolation of Babylon say 'But wild beasts of the desert shall lie there; and their houses shall be full of doleful creatures; and satyrs shall dance there.' *Isaiah* 13:21.

Next, we have Azazel ('entire removal') or 'Scapegoat' is a name used for one of the goats selected for the service of the *Day of Atonement* ceremonies and it is a little bit of a mystery around which more mystery has been added. Azazel has been discussed much as to the meaning of the word being rendered 'scapegoat,' which is found nowhere else in *Scripture* and one or two things present themselves for consideration. We must dismiss the thoughts of some that it is some evil being who had in some way to be propitiated because the later the goat was not slain so there was no sacrifice to 'Azazel.'

Aaron sent away the live goat and the messenger that accompanied the live goat had to wash his clothes and bathe himself before he could enter the camp again. It is not, however, the name of the goat, because that was qualified as being 'unto Azazel' and was not slain in sacrifice. The second goat was 'unto Jehovah' and this goat was slain by Aaron in sacrifice. It is almost as if the goat for Jehovah was to bear the wrath of death as the spotless victim, while the goat for 'Azazel' was to witness in life and living that the blood of atonement had been accepted. The carcass of the goat for the sin offering with the bullock also, were burned 'their skins, their flesh and their dung.'

However, we can read in the *Book of Enoch* Azazel is conceived as being chained in the wilderness into which the scapegoat was led. The high priest by confession transferred his sins and those of the people onto the goat, which was then taken into the wilderness. Then, as now, this expressed the belief that a sin belongs to the power or principle that sent it and for eradication to be complete, it must include sending the sin back its source.

We have discussed elsewhere that Yahweh said he was responsible for both good and evil until a separate source was created to take this duty off his hands. At the beginning the scapegoat was set free to go into the wilderness and this has caused some to think, myself included, whether it would have been better had it been called it the 'escape goat' or 'scapegoat. Later it is thought that the goat was killed by throwing the animal over a cliff. The Arabs degraded the gods of the heathen to jinn (see below) and attributed to them the hairy characteristics of animals, so these satyrs may be heathen deities and transformed in like manner. In the *Epistle of the Hebrews* it is written and claimed that Christ as the Messiah in the *New Testament* of the Christian faith was the 'sacrifice of blood' and 'the scapegoat' so that ' . . . their sins and iniquities I remember no more.'

Gustav Davidson gives Azazel as 'one of the chiefs of the fallen angels and *Revelation* speaks of one third of the heavenly host being involved in the fall.' This angel taught the males 'how to fashion swords and shields' and educated the females about 'finery and the art of beautifying the eyelids' and the story goes that the women were in competition for the supplies of rogue and other ornaments provided by Azazel, the most ingenious of the angels. The women delighted in drawing him and the others into even more dangerous forms of 'physical contact' from which we are told, we got the giants including the Emin, the Gibborim, the Anakim and the Nephilim — enough mischief for several millenniums I think.

In Rabbinic literature, Azazel is the scapegoat even though he is not actually named and he is found in the *Targums* and *Leviticus* also. Iraneus designates Azazel as 'that fallen and yet might angel.' Azazel is another of the angel's in Jewish legend that refused to bow down before Adam and for his refusal, he was dubbed 'the accursed Satan.' It has further been suggested that Azazel was an ancient Semitic pastoral god of the flocks, degraded and demoted to the level of a demon — a familiar story.

*Leviticus* 17:7 under the section 'sacrifices' prohibits any future sacrifice to the satyrs and this statement must be taken to say that sacrifices had been offered to them in the past. 'And they shall no more offer their sacrifices unto devils (= satyrs).' 2 *Chronicles* 11:15 is concerned with Jeroboham's arrangements of priests for the high places ' . . . and he ordained him priests for the high places, and for the devils (= satyrs) and for the calves that he had made

In Middle Eastern Arabic folklore and mythology, the jinn are supernatural spirits or demons who are below the angels. The angels were made of pure bright gems; the jinn were made of fire and a 'man was made of clay.' The jinn are composed of fire or air and can assume both animal and human form for good or evil. If they are good, they are beautiful, sometimes tame, friendly and found in or near the homes of human beings but if they are wicked, they have an hideous appearance. The *ghul* is a treacherous spirit and a shape–changer, the *ifrit* are diabolic or evil spirits and the *si'la* are treacherous spirits of consistent form.

It is said that their correct and correct form is that of a serpent but they can assume human or animal form at will. Often they are invisible and it is not their form that is seen, more what they do. The prefer to live in barren sandy places like deserts that are unapproachable by people or living in holy trees, mountains, damp and dark places or under the earth in fact anywhere, though we are told that citron in the house keeps any demons at bay.

The jinn were originally believed to have been nature spirits and the source of madness as we have said elsewhere. They are not pure spirit but corporeal beings more like beasts than men. They are represented as hairy with an animal form having the mystifying power of disappearing and reappearing at will and they live in air, flame, below the earth in inanimate matter, such as rocks, ruins and trees, underneath the earth, in the air and in fire. Often on the roofs of houses where they throw rocks at those who pass by. They will steal clothes, food or anything else that they want so when anything went missing they were usually blamed — at least they blessed thieves and their labours. They eat and drink as we do and being male and female, they marry and produce children and sometimes this involves human beings who have parallel bodily needs.

Although they live longer than humans, they do in due course die. The jinn are mischievous spirits who take pleasure in punishing people for wrongs done to them, even when it was unintentional. Accidents, sickness, insanity, diseases and especially 'the inspiration' of poets, singers and prophets are ascribed to the Jinn and is said to be the result of their efforts. Those that know the proper magical procedure are said to be able to control the jinn for their ends with the appropriate knowledge, they are found in works such as the Arabian Nights, and as a result, they are frequently known as a **genie** in the West. Now let us go back to some additional . . .

## CHARACTERISTICS OF THE ANGELS

We are shown that one angel can be given duties or commands from another by sending them on diverse tasks. 'And behold the angel that talked with me went forth, and another angel went out to meet him, and he said unto him, Run, speak to this young man saying . . . ' *Zechariah* 2:4. The Angel of Yahweh appears here as a Guardian of Israel since he protects the priest, who is the representative of the Hebrew nation.

There are few nations who do not have seven mighty Angels, Archangel, Spirits or Powers. The Egyptians had their 'Seven Mystery Gods' while the Hindu have their 'Seven Sons of Aditi.' We have already mentioned the Seven Amshaspends of the religion of Zoroaster. Among the Hebrews, there were Seven Archangels or Sephiroth and it was the same with Christianity and Islam with their Seven Archangels.

The seven angels of Ezekiel have been and may be identified with to the 'seven eyes' of Yahweh, 'For behold the stone that I have laid before Joshua; upon one stone shall be seven eyes.' *Zechariah* 3:9. In *Tobit*, a leading part in the drama is played by the Archangel Raphael and he confirms seven angels. 'I am Raphael, one of the seven holy angels, which present the prayers of the saints, and which go in and out before the glory of the Holy One.' *Tobit* 12:15. There are two things that should be noted in this example. The first is that Raphael tells us there are seven angels who 'go in and out' before God. We can assume from this they are archangels because they have the authority and rank to do this. The second thing to note that strengthens this supposition is that these angels appear 'before the glory (=*Shekinah*) of the Holy One.' Remember the *Shekinah* may often be being suggested by the use of the word 'glory.' 'The glory of the Holy One' (see above) and 'shall come in the glory of his Father' (see below), this was discussed elsewhere.

Christ was humbled in the physical body on earth and the angels we are told, were subject to him after the resurrection. 'Who is gone into heaven, and is on the right hand of God; angels and authorities and powers being made subject unto him.' 1 *Peter* 3:22. In the coming glory of Christ, the holy angels will accompany him. 'For the Son of man shall come in the glory (= *Shekinah*) of his Father with his angels; and then he shall reward every man according to his works.' *Matthew* 16:27.

Christ had a very special association with the angels and the line ' . . . with his angels' makes you wonder if he was allotted a company of angels for his personal use or whether he had taken charge of the existing angelic Host? The angels were with him at every stage of his life from the announcement of his birth, warning his parents of danger during the journey to Egypt, supporting him when he was in critical need at *Gethsemane*, proclaiming his resurrection from his tomb and taking him up to heaven. Each of these reported important stages of his life found angels present and although the word 'Guardian Angels' seems a little inadequate when applied to him, it may be that 'guardian angels ' were probably performing that function by reporting continuously to the Father regarding his Son. We can only touch upon some of the many quotations taken from the

*Revelations of St. John the Divine*. In the next section referring to angelic operations and visions, only chapter and verse numbers are given.

In the opening verse, an angel is sent to *St. John the Divine* as a messenger, 'who bare record of the word of God.' (1:1.) John sees a 'strong angel' proclaiming in a 'loud voice, Who is worthy to open the book, and loosen the seals thereof?' The angel is referring to the *Book with Seven Seals* (= *the Book of Raziel*?) John finds ' . . . four angels standing on the four corners of the earth, holding the four winds of the earth,' (7:1) followed by sealing the foreheads of the servants of God.

Winds are frequently used in much the same content as spirit and breath and are expressed by equivalent or matching words in various languages. In the *New Testament*, Jesus uses the allegory of wind for spirit in the lines: ' . . .the wind bloweth where it listeth, and thou hearest the sound thereof, but canst not tell whence it cometh and whither it goeth: so is every one that is born of the Spirit.' *John* 3: 8, with ordinary winds we know where they come from and where it is going. With the Greeks, 'the cave of the winds was the earth and the winds were the winds of the spirit, the circulation of the universe represented as winds.'

The admonition of God out of the whirlwind speaks of the cornerstones of the earth. God asks Job 'Who is this that darkeneth counsel by words without knowledge? Where was thou when I laid the foundations of the earth . . . Whereupon are the foundations thereof fastened? Or who laid the corner stone thereof. When the morning stars sang together, And all the sons of God shouted for joy?' *Job* 38:1 and this quotation has been a frequent example throughout the work.

In the *Bible*, four horses are found and in *Zechariah,* they are red, black, white, grisled and bay horses, the term 'horse' is found infrequently used for angels. When the angel is asked what they mean? The angel tells Zechariah that, 'These are the four spirits of the heavens, which go back and forth from standing before the Lord of all the earth. The black horses, which are therein, go forth into the North Country; and the white go forth after them; and the grisled go forth toward the south country, And the bay went forth, and sought to go that they might walk to and fro through the earth. *Zechariah*. 6.

Another explanation for using the horse as a symbol of speed and spirit may be because in early times the horse was regarded as the swiftest animal on earth and in some mythologies they had wings, just as trees were among the tallest growing structures known at the time. The Hebrews had several words for a horse and chariots, horses were dedicated in olden times to the sun — 'And he took away the horses the kings of Judah had given to the sun.' 2 *Kings* 23:11 and we can find horses represented as winged and a sacred emblem in Assyrian sculptures including Pegasus of the Greeks. The Horse–Gate, one of the gates of Jerusalem was perhaps contiguous to the royal stables or where there was a horse market and there were 'six hundred chosen chariots of Egypt' pursuing Israel when they left Egypt. *Exodus* 14:7.

In the 'Temple of the Holy City' of *Ezekiel*. 41:18 we find the Babylonian and Assyrian motifs of the palm tree coupled with the cherubim. 'And it was made with the cherubim's and palm trees, so that a palm tree was between a cherub; and every cherub has two faces; so that the face of a man was toward the palm tree on the one side, and face of a young lion toward the palm tree on the other side: it was made through all the house round about.'

These 'two faces' found on either side of the palms appear to be or to have some astrological symbolism in them. The face of the 'man' standing for the sign of Aquarius and the face of the 'young lion' for the sign of Leo. These two astrological signs are 180 degrees apart and being opposite in the circle of the heavens, they naturally face each other in the belt of the zodiac.

The old astrological interpretation of the word 'aspect' is given as 'to behold' because things that stand opposite to each other 'behold' each other. One symbol used for the other two fixed signs of the zodiac being a bull. This is a title given to **Merodach** (= **Marduk**) the sun–god who when he passed through the twelve signs was known as **Guddi–bir** — 'the Bull of Light.'

The fourth fixed sign is Scorpio is represented either by the eagle, which is an early sign for Scorpio as well as the scorpion. As we have said elsewhere the eagle represents the heights and the highest to which the Sign of Scorpio can attain, soaring high into the clean, clear air, watching all below with an eagle eye and this is the positive Scorpio. The negative Scorpio is the scorpion, lurking around under rocks, watching and striking from ambush, always with a sting in their tail of venom. Scorpio rules the natural eighth house of the astrological chart — the House of Death. Do not expect a true native of Scorpio to accept the biblical injunction — 'Vengeance is mine sayeth the Lord.' Scorpio will usually concede that this is so, but will often add the rider, silent or otherwise ' . . . this is proper Lord — but after me!'

Aries the Ram is now said to open our year but not at the time of which we are writing due to the procession of the equinox. Taurus was the opening sign of the primitive Arcadian year and the sign was called 'the bull that guides the year.' This symbol may have been represented by the golden calf created and worshipped by the Israelites when they thought Moses was not going to return to them from Mount Sinai and why they used the symbolism. Gold is the metal of the Sun, which is an incorruptible metal and planet in its highest aspect, the Archangel of Light, Michael and this is why the fallen angels could not corrupt the Archangel Michael to be dishonourable to his Creator or abuse the Divine Law. Everything was done to the letter of the Law or nothing, further the Sign of the Zodiac Leo is a Fixed Sign and the 'fixed signs' rarely if ever bend or break and if they do they bear the scars for a long time to come, like the earth after an earthquake.

When Moses eventually came down from Sinai with the Tablets of the Law he found the people worshipping the Golden Calf. The anger of Moses waxed greatly though his was nothing compared to the anger of God. The Lord without delay sent down five Angels of Destruction and Punishment to destroy Israel. Moses invoked the Patriarchs to come to his aid and with their help Moses was able, to some extent to appease the wrath of God, enough so for God to withdraw three of the Angels, *Af*= 'Anger, *Hemah*= 'Wrath' and *Kezef*= 'Death.'

Moses was able to hold back the Angel Mashit(h) (= 'Destruction') and this only left him to deal with the Angel Haron or Peor (= 'Anger'.) Moses subdued Haron and buried him under the earth. The patriarch kept him under control by pronouncing the name of God over him, because Haron tried to rise and destroy the Hebrews every time they sinned against God, mentioned earlier.

## SOME MORE OF THE ANGELS

Jewish prayers to the planets are thought to date from the third or second century B.C and in these special angels and demons are assigned to different astrological bodies. The association of angels with the planets was a connecting link with magic then as now, a point of contact where people could go. This is not unlike tuning in to a specific radio programme that is broadcasting the information that you want to know about and hear. The would be little point in tuning in to 'history' if the subject being sought was 'weather.'

The worship of the heavenly bodies was very widespread in ancient religions and this is sternly condemned in the **Bible**, which also shows that the Israelites were not averse to what was called idolatrous worship. The creation narrative begins with the establishment of two great lights — 'the greater to dominate the day and the lesser to dominate the night.' In **Deuteronomy** we find ' . . . and when you look up to the sky and behold the sun and the moon and the stars, the whole heavenly host, you must not be lured into bowing down to them or serving them.' 4:19.

Maimonides has the Sun, Moon and stars singing to the Creator as they orbit around the earth. The stars and spheres are said to be intelligent beings that are gifted with life and stability. They recognize the One God and like the angels, they glorify him, they sing his praises and acknowledge that the angels are superior to them. The ancient notion of the 'music of the spheres' as usual is better described by Shakespeare. 'There's not the smallest orb which thou behold'st, but in his motion like an angel sings, still quiring to the young–eyed cherubims.' *Merchant of Venice*. The word *quire* is an older spelling now not used for *choir*= 'in concert or chorus; to sing harmoniously' — making a *chorister*= *quirister*.

The Angel Masleh was said to be the medium by means of which the power and influence of the *Word of God* came down into the Zodiac because the Angel Masleh is the *Angel of the Zodiac*. Masleh is credited as being the angel who initiated Chaos so that it produced the Four Elements. The Sabeans held that each planet was occupied by a spirit as a star–soul (= angel?) and calculating the conjunction and opposition of the planets made prediction of the future possible. The Angel Masleh is alleged to accept the power and authority of the Logos when it descends into the sphere of the Zodiac.

Yet 'I run before my horse to market,' if we deal with the magic of the angels here and too early. These matters are dealt with in greater detail in Part 2. Let us take an incident from the *New Testament* that has always had an astrological overlay and an association with the Zodiac among other things, this is also dealt with in the section referring to the 'upper room.' It may be an example of the Word of God 'coming down' and working through the Zodiac as mentioned above or was it a matter–of–fact *Bat Qol*?

When the feast of the Passover was drawing near, Christ sent Peter and John ahead to prepare for the day of the unleavened bread. When they asked him, where they should prepare the feast Christ told them. 'Behold, when ye are entered into the city, there shall a man meet you, bearing a pitcher of water; follow him into the house where he entereth in. And ye shall say to the goodman of the house. The Master saith unto thee, Where is the guest chamber, where I shall eat the Passover with my disciples? And he shall shew you a large upper room furnished: there make ready. And they went, and found as he had said unto them: and they made ready for the passover.' *Luke* 22:7–13.

This incident as said is regarded by some occultists and astrologers as future events casting their shadow before them. In this example the eventual arrival of the Aquarian Age (= Aquarius the Water Carrier or a Man carrying an Urn or Pitcher) moving from the Piscean Age, whose sign is 'the fishes,' which is the early symbol and sometimes a secret sign of Christ and Christianity. The man who met the disciples 'showed them the way' as the Sign of Aquarius and his planet is thought to do, usually it is a new way that replaces the old and outmoded with something better, because such things are under the guidance of the Archangel Uriel. It is not change for the sake of it as this is a negative Uranus working at his worst. Uranus existed in biblical times and probably exerted some guidance, we had to wait to be aware of and use, the things that Uranus gives and have the means and materials to use them — electronics, computers, space travel and the like. Look at the ideas Leonard da Vinci 'invented' in his books that cast their shadow before, but it was not until the materials required to do so appeared that made these basic ideas practical and put into practise.

The angels were once identified with the stars though there is no attempt in the canonical books, as there was in the past, to define the nature of angels or to tell the substance of which they are composed, see the example given in *Job* 38:7. The terms 'host of the height' is given to them in *Isaiah* 24:21. In the *King James* it is given as 'the host of the ones that are on high.' This is thought by some scholars to be a modification of the pre–Exile phrase, the 'host of heaven' that was frequently applied to the stars, the sun, the moon and the planets.

These particular stars had been worshipped during the last years of the Judean monarchy. 'And they shall spread them before the sun, and the moon, and all the host of heaven, whom they have loved, and whom they have walked, and whom they have sought, and whom they have worshipped.' *Jeremiah* 8:2. The sun, moon and stars were considered as gods before the prophets opposed their worship.

As the close of the Exile drew near, Yahweh was confirmed as being supreme over them. 'I have made the earth, and created man upon it: I, even my hands, have stretched out the heavens, and all the host have I commanded.' *Isaiah* 45:12. 'Thou has made heaven, the heaven of heavens, with all their host, the earth, and all things that are therein, the seas, and all that is therein, and thou preservest them all; and the host of heaven worshippeth thee.' *Nehemiah* 9:6. These quotations are said to show it is the stars that worship Yahweh and that people should do likewise.

In both the East and the West about one fifth of all churches built are dedicated to the holy angels. The Archangel Michael is one of the two angels mentioned by name in the *Bible*, the other being the Archangel Gabriel. The Archangel Raphael is given in the *Tobit* in the *Apocrypha*. The *Feast of Michael*, *Michaelmas* or *Michael's Mass* is one of the most ancient feasts and it was noted in the sixth century *Leonine Sacramentary*, this is the earliest surviving book of prayers for the Mass and exists in a MS of the 7th century and preserved in Verona. It is on September 30th and this is the day of dedication of a church of Michael in the *Via Saleria* some six miles from Rome.

A later festival of Michael is May 8th and this date is connected with a famous apparition of St. Michael on Mount Garganus in Apulia, this vision has been placed in the year 493 by the ecclesiastic historian Baronius (1538–1607). The Greek Church keeps a festival of Michael on November 8th and this is connected with a church at Arcadius built by Constantine. Legends of the apparition of the Archangel Michael are connected with all three sites.

Because of St. Michael's traditional office as leader of the heavenly armies, veneration of all angels was eventually incorporated into his cult and with the revision of the *Prayer Book* in 1662, the name St. Michael was added the supplement 'and all angels,' which the Roman Church keeps on September 29th known as *'Dedicatio San Michaelis Archangeli'* — Michaelmas Day, which is also the birthday of the great Englishman, Admiral Lord Nelson. This is mentioned in the so-called martyrology of St. Jerome — as the Dedication of St. Michael and the Feast of all the Angels. In the East, the feast of St. Michael is on September 6th with the feast of the angels generally in November. In the Anglican Church, its proper name is the Feast of St. Michael and All Angels.

Michaelmas was a great religious feast During the Middle Ages and various popular traditions were attached to the day, which coincided with the harvest in a great deal of western Europe. It was customary to have the Michaelmas goose for the feast on Michaelmas and in some areas cutting the last sheaf of corn was known as 'cutting the gander's neck.' In Yorkshire, after the harvest had been gathered safely in, the farmer would give to all that helped him 'an entertainment' called 'the Innin Goose.' In the past there was an old saying 'If you eat goose on Michaelmas–day you will never want for money all the year round.' In Ireland, to find the ring hidden in a Michaelmas pie meant that person would soon be married

It is recorded, in the time of Edward IV that in 1470 in Herefordshire, 'one good goose fit for a lord's dinner on the feast of St. Michael' was due as part service or rent for land. Therefore, 'John de la Hay was bound to render to William Barneby, Lord of Lastres, in the county of Hereford for a parcel of demesne lands, one goose fit for the Lord's dinner on the fast of St Michael the Archangel.' In France, they eat their goose upon St. Martin's Day.

From the breast–bone of a goose eaten on the eve of Michaelmas it was said you could tell what kind of winter it would be. The breast–bone ' . . .when picked, it must be held up to the light, and the white marks then discernible betoken snow, the darker ones, frost and cold weather.' It should also be remarked that the front part of the bone foretells the weather before Christmas, the hind part the weather after Christmas.' *Cleveland Glossary*–Atkinson, (1868). A poem published in 1575 mentions a similar custom, showing that folklore, religious ideas and old customs are often found in tandem and lie deep within people and thus are difficult to eradicate:

'And when the tenants come to pay their quarter's rent
They bring some fowle at Midsummer, a dish of fish in Lent
At Christmas a capon, at Michaelmass a goose;
And somewhat else at New–yeares tide, for feare their lease flie loos.'
*Gascoigne.*

Let us stay for a while with some of the folklore inspired by the Archangel Michael and his Feast of All–angels in the British Isles to show how the angels and the angelic infiltrated everyday life. In Ireland, the Pooka was essentially a November spirit and elsewhere November was pre–eminently the time of All–Hallows or All–Angels. The time of Hallows or Michaelmas was sometimes known as Hoketide a festival in England that was sometimes held upon St. Blaze's Day 'near to Candlemas' on the 3rd of February. 'Call upon God and remember St. Blaze' was the Archangel Michael's charm when fires were lit on his night. In England, Michaelmas is one of the quarter days and it was traditionally marked by the election of magistrates, the beginning of the legal and university terms, the collection of quarterly rents and one of the important matters under the guardianship of the Archangel Michael — the Law and its administration — 'to the letter.'

During this period people would light bonfires or make 'blaze's' for 'lighting souls out of Purgatory.' In Wales, a huge fire was lit by each household. Into the ashes of the bonfire, every member of the family would throw a white elphin or 'Alban' stone, while kneeling in prayer around the dying fire.

One of the features of Michaelmas, in Scotland of old was making and baking an 'enormously large bun made with many ingredients' and this cake belonged to the Archangel Michael and took its name from him. Everyone from each family, domestics or strangers all had their portion of this form of shrew bread to gain a tithe of protection from the Archangel Michael throughout the year.

There was a widely held belief it was unlucky to gather blackberries after October 11th or Old Michaelmas Day. This is because Satan was thrown out of heaven by the Archangel Michael on the first Michaelmas Day and he fell into a blackberry bush much to his chagrin. He curses the berries on each anniversary of this day, he spoils the berries by throwing his cloak over them, spitting on them or with less finesse 'wiping his tail on them' and whoever foolishly gathers or eats the berries after this date will have bad luck.

A kitten born just after Michaelmas is called a 'blackberry cat' and tradition holds that the cat was created by Noah on the ark. It would seem that Noah did not take two of these with him, even though they were prized by the Egyptians and others greatly, especially for protecting the corn after harvesting. Those who lived on the ark came to Noah to complain of the rats and mice that were eating the food and plaguing the travellers. Noah passed his hand down the back of the lion, the king of beasts sneezed and the cat came forth from his mouth and killed the rats and mice. The travellers on the ark had peace from the rats thanks to the creation of the cat. Early pilgrim badges were often made in the image of the Archangel Michael.

Now let us leave our short sojourn with the folklore that has included the Archangel Michael given to show how the angels have influenced so many aspects of our everyday life in the past and research will show how they have an effect on many other areas of our lives in the present and research will produce similar results. Now we will take brief note of the system of Angelic Magic that is known as . . .

## ENOCHIA, ENOCHIAN ANGELS AND ENOCHIAN MAGIC

In the chapter dedicated to *The Magical Scripts* in Part 2, the reader will be referred to a magical script called the *Enochian Alphabet* (all scripts and diagrams are at the end of the book) and it may be as well to set this into context by giving a very short summary of Enochian Angelic Magic here.

From the personal diaries of Dr. John Dee (1527–1608), I spent a wonderful time compiling a dictionary in 1976 of the some nine hundred odd words that were recorded in a language known as 'Enochia.' The volumes of Dr Dee are held in *Manuscript Library* of the *British Museum Library* and the volume was hand–written by John Dee.

For the first hour, I simply held the volume, looking at the pages without really reading them and did no work because not only had John Dee written these pages he had held them as they were his, not a facsimile, the real thing. I asked a very sympathetic and understanding staff did they think I could run fast enough to take it home with me. They said they did sympathize with me, but it really did have to stay on the shelves and be looked after. I think they had met people like me before and so were prepared and generous.

This Enochian system included some powerful spiritual entities — the Enochian Angels and Spirits. The resulting *Enochian Dictionary* was entitled *Gmicalzoma. — 'It means what is says – when you know what it means.'* This work was my *Ficus ad Mercurium*, you never forget your first book and of course, it has been mentioned before and the third imprint is published by the present publisher *Authors OnLine*. The Enochian magic, spirits, the Enochian Angels and the magical system was produce from the nature of the magic and the Work of Dr John Dee and Edward Kelly with the claim being made that it is the magic used by the patriarch Enoch from where it gets its name.

A statement given by the Enochian Angel Ave to John Dee told him: 'Now hath it pleased God to deliver this Doctrine again out the darknesse: and to fulfill his promise to thee, for the Books of Enoch' so it was the books of Enoch that Dee was obviously seeking and he had obviously asked for the knowledge that they contained.

In 1992, I was able to enlarge the original into a new edition of the work with a much larger biography and suggestions for pronunciation among other things, though none can claim to know how Enochia is pronounced as tape recorders were far into the future. The suggestions for the Enochian pronunciation were based upon the work of a well–known school of the past, this is explained the new edition.

The additions in the new work were made to my original information regarding Dee and Kelly, the commentary and contribution to the work naturally, because I do not have the authority nor has it been given, to interfere with the original Enochian work of Dee and Kelly. Their work is not mine to interfere with and nor would I want to though again I believe others have done this but I have not seen of them so I cannot comment. Despite the long intervening years between the original and today, I have always respected the 'moral copyright' of John Dee.

Dee worked on Enochia with the help of a very unusual but some think, dubious man called Edward Kelly (1555–1597) who became his seer or skryer because Dee had little talent for mediumship and whatever people think of Kelly, he did genuinely seem to 'have the second sight.' We cannot go into the unsettled relationship between these two men here and it was stormy at times. Few men could have been so different and in so many ways, but there are many instances of such partnerships in life. However, it is considered by many that John Dee was the 'saint' while Kelly was 'the sinner.' One thing is certain that Fate brought them together for their task, that was strengthened I am sure by Dee's wages to Kelly of £50 per annum — a princely sum at the time.

One thing is certain, these two men did not construct their communications with the spirits and Angels, as it is so complicated and extensive, not the kind of thing you commit to memory. I think both believed absolutely in the truth of what they were doing. John Dee believed them to be the dutiful servants of God, who were under the authority of the Christ, precisely as Dee considered himself to be at all times, though he was slandered as a dealer in magic and with devils.

At times Kelly was remarkably honest, even voicing his mistrust and suspicion of them at times. He thought that they were quite capable of deliberate deception and let it be noted that this mistrust was mutual. It often appeared that the spirits and Angels seemed to treat Kelly with a somewhat amused disdain and functioning through him to work with John Dee. Kelly I feel did not help matters by asking one spirit for some money for a while, getting the reply that she had 'swept it all outdoors' so could not help him, that he was rather self–seeking regarding such matters I feel is not unfair comment.

Furthermore, Kelly was searching for 'the red powder.' This fabled 'red powder' had the power to 'turn base metals into gold.' He purchased a small portion from an innkeeper knowing what it was and spent the rest of his life trying to get some more or finding out how to make it. Many commentators feel this is why he endured the insults of the Enochian spirits for so long in the hope that they would tell him.

The angels who presented themselves included the Archangels Michael, Gabriel, Raphael as well as Ave, Mapsama, Nalvage and the others. There was a 'spiritaull creature, like a pretty girle of 7 or 9 yeares of age who asked Dee 'give me leave to play in your house.' She said 'I am a poor little Maiden, Madini.' The book that introduced Enochia upon an unsuspecting world in facsimile form was *A True and Faithful relation of What Passed for Many Year between Dr. John Dee . . . and Some Spirits'* by Meric Casaubon. (*Antonine Publishing Co*. 1974) The original work was first published in London in 1659. The work of Casaubon covers the dates 1582–87 of the Enochia and spiritual communications and the work is still available either in a reprinting or facsimile copy. If the reader finds quotations regarding John Dee's work with just page numbers given, it is from the above edition.

Because I am highly defensive of Dee and thinking him a genius in the true sense of the word and not the debased coin of today. It has to pointed out that Casaubon was not a friend of Dee and that he thought Dee's work 'a Work of Darkness.' He writes further. 'So much for Dee himself. But of his Spirits a greater question perchance may be moved: If evil, wicked, lying Spirits (as we have reason to believe, and no man I think will question) how came they to be such perswaders to Piety and godliness, yea, such preachers of Christ, his Incarnation, his Passion and other mysteries of the Christian Faith, not only acknowledged, but in some places very Scholastically set out and declared . . .The Divels we know even in the Gospel did acknowledg, nay in some manner proclaim Christ to be the Son of God . . .The Divel is very cunning; a notable Politician. S. Paul knew him so.' The phrase 'and no man I think will question' smacks of over–confidence because I believe he was wrong. We have so many people today in all forms of the media, sometimes you do not even know who they are, but they claim to speaking for me and others, saying 'I am sure I am speaking for others or everyone' on matters about.which we have not been consulted.

Casaubon's work was published as a warning to those who thought they did not need to heed the authority of Kings, Bishops and the like and who went the way of their thoughts and thinking. I doubt if Casaubon had a greater humility and piety in the Christian faith than John Dee. Though it must be given that Casaubon did write that Dee 'commanded' the sprits and he did not make a 'contract' with them, which is very generous of him indeed.

Many people and some famous, then and now, think Casaubon's work had the sole purpose of slandering Dee. Yet, who would know of Meric Casaubon today, if it were not for his work against John Dee, bright though Casaubon proved to be in his time, he would be a footnote in history. His father Isaac had even greater honours in the world because Isaac's honours occupy many pages in some reference books, which the son did not or could not match, even though as said, he was not a fool in learning and knowledge, credit where credit is due. However, he appears to be somewhat self–seeking, poor Dee seemed to attract such people in death as he did in life and there where many who abused this most trusting man.

Who today disparages the efforts of the great scientist Sir Isaac Newton (1643–1727) just because he studied astrology as well as science? When Halley, the discoverer of the comet, expressed his doubts about astrology, Newton is said to have given him the now famous remark — 'Sir, I have studied it, you have not!'

Dee was a respected authority on optics, navigation, astronomy, mathematics, geography, science, horology, the fine arts including music, literature. He was the editor of the first English translation of Euclid's *Elements*, art, architecture and many other learned matters.

Dee possessed an awesome intelligence and he was Under Reader in Greek at the newly founded Trinity College and friend of Abraham Otelius and Gerardus Mercator the great cartographer. He was no mean cartographer himself and knew that England's future lay in the accuracy of its navigation. He corrected the star maps in great detail, knowing their importance. It is known that Tycho Brahe sent a copy of his 'latest book' to the 'most noble and illustrious Dee,' requesting his opinion of his work and Tycho Brahe was no fool. In 1550, Dee was giving lectures on Euclid at the University of Paris, which caused a sensation and all of this at the ripe old age of 23 years old. He petitioned the Crown to preserve old and unpublished records of England's past, anticipating the British Museum Library (where many of his manuscripts rest) by many years.

His private library, open to all serious seekers and students at his ever–open house at Mortlake, was the envy of many of the universities of the day because it was an impressive library, which always kept him poor. He had one of the most accurate clocks in the kingdom remarkable for its time with what we now take so much for granted. He invented navigational equipment, a 'paradoxical compass,' which he claimed would correct chart errors. Erecting astrological charts was acceptable practice as astrology and astronomy had not yet parted company and alchemy and chemistry were still bedfellows. The library was open to all earnest seekers of knowledge so I have never understood how such a generous soul and an illustrious son of England could be ignored and overlooked so casually by history. Now, is my blatant, though quite unnecessary, bias and defence of John Dee showing itself to the reader, like it always is for Pan? Splendid!

Dee started to take an interest in 'natural magic' and he used this term to mean that 'it stemmed from God and therefore good, opposing black magic that was evil.' Taken from the diaries the Angel Ave told Dr. Dee given earlier. 'Now hath it pleased God to deliver this Doctrine again out of the darknesse: and to fulfil his promise with thee, for the books of Enoch.' Of course, again as said, this line tells us how the system got its name of *Enochia*.

Dee never doubted the contact with the angels and I have always been fascinated by the words 'hath it pleased God to deliver this Doctrine again out of the darknesse.' An important part of the work deals with the *Four Watchtowers of the Earth* and their angels, which stand sentinel of the extremes of our universe and they locked out the *Forces of Chaos* and their mighty angel, the Angel Corozon, whose hordes are described as 'the stooping dragons.' Yes, we are back with dragons and serpents that never seem to be far from any work of this nature. The watchtowers are described to John Dee by the Angel Ave:

'The 4 houses, are the 4 Angels of the Earth, which are the 4 Overseers, and Watch–towers, that the eternal God in his providence hath placed, against the usurping blasphemy, misuse, and stealth of the wicked and great enemy, the Devil. To the intent that being put out to the Earth, his envious will might be bridled, the determinations of God fulfilled, and creatures kept and preserved, within the compass and measure of order.' (Page 170.)

The above are wise words and at times, I have wondered if some practising Enochia have tried to lift the latch and peep through a crack in the door — did they succeed? To raise the opposite force is amazingly easy, just say 'do not' and without delay you have 'do,' say 'do not do this' and in an instant you have 'do this.' What is more, I cannot believe that I am the only one to ask these questions, I am sure I am not. If some wanted to see what is on the other side to only open a 'crack' would be enough, but while they were looking out, trying to satisfying their curiosity, what may have come in? Chaos needs only a hairline fracture for its purpose — to upset the 'measure of order.' If the locks, bars, bolts and defending Forces of the Watchtowers — 'the Chief Watchman, is a mighty Prince, a mighty Angel of the Lord' — are on our side, putting them there was planned to keep out what is on the other side and protect what is inside from it. This is clearly stated to John Dee in the above ' . . . and creatures kept, within the and preserved compass and measure of order' and not within the measure of disorder?

The angels told John Dee these hostile forces, are under command of the Angel Coronzon and that the name Coronzon is the authentic heavenly name of Satan. The Angel Ave tells John Dee of the *Four Watchtowers of the Earth* in the entry for *Wednesday*, Junii 26, *a Meridie*. 1584 and what follows is part of the entry starting at the heading and repeating the above . . .

I expound the Vision

'The 4 houses, are Angels of the Earth, which are the 4 Overseers, and the Watchtowers, that the eternal God in his providence hath placed, against usurping blasphemy, misuse, and stealth of the wicked and great enemy, the Devil. To the intent that being put out to the Earth, his envious will might be bridled, the determinations of god fulfilled, and his creatures kept and preserved, within the compass of measure and order.
*What Satan doth, they suffer; And what they wink at, he wrasteth: But when he thinketh himself most assured, then feeleth he the bit.*
*In each of these Houses, the Chief Watchman, is a mighty Prince, a mighty Angel of the Lord: which hath under him 5 Princes (these names I must use for your instruction. The seal and authorities of these Houses are confirmed in the beginning of the World.)* (Page 170.)

The Four Watchtowers are of the Four Elements of Air, Fire, Water and Earth and are represented on our level by alphabetical squares. Each of these towers has within its King and his Elemental hierarchy. They are given, through the angels, Angelic Calls or Keys for communication with the thirty Aethyrs or Airs. The towers bring to mind the ever-present 'foundations of the earth' given in *Job* 38, which has already been pointed out many times elsewhere because they are so difficult to avoid.

A reliable source that I trust told me (privately) that the respected founder of a long established and reputable Occult Society in England said that 'you should never attempt to look the Angels of the Watchtowers directly in the face.' Aleister Crowley is said to have invoked the Kings and Elements of the Four Watchtowers at Boleskine with dire result, dire because it was believed that he could not close them down properly, though this was said in an unconfirmed exchange but considering the source, most likely. The painted representations of the Four Towers used, to the best of my knowledge have never been found.

One interesting entry in the diaries of Dee I include because it has bearing on the form of our work. It takes place between Dee, Kelly and the Angel Ave and is well worth observing. This entry will be introduced again, I am sure in any appropriate place in Part 2 of this work.

Dee -       As for the form of our Petition or Invocation of the good Angels, what sort
            should it be of?
Ave -       A short and brief speech.
Dee -       We beseech you to give us an example: we would have a confidence, it should be
            of more effect.
Ave -       I may not do so.
Kelly -     And why?
Ave -       Invocation proceedeth of the good will of man, and of the heat and fervency
            of the spirit: And therefore is prayer of such effect with God.
Dee -       We beseech you, shall we use one form to all?
Ave -       Every one, after a divers form.
Dee -       If the minde do dictate or prompt a divers form, you mean.
Ave -       I know not: for I dwell not in the soul of man.
            (Page 188.)

I feel John Dee acted with great restraint with what he had been given by the Enochian Angels and I personally feel that he would never act on his own with the material or try to use it without having been given consent to do so and this was probably why he was chosen to do the work. He made a meticulous 'magical diary' or record of his work, which is a perfect model and an example of what a magical diary should be, all students of the Occult should take note. Keeping a 'magical diary' is stressed enough throughout the work and no doubt will be again. Dee was mentioned in the subheading of the **Archangel Gabriel**, where he had contact with the great Archangel Gabriel, who told him that he 'is speaking with authority of God' and he tells the good doctor, concerning God's words and intention and God's words are:

'I have chosen you, to enter into my barns: And have commanded you to open the Corn, that the scattered may appear, and that which remainineth in the sheaf may stand. And have entered into the first, and so into the seventh. And have delivered unto you the Testimony of my spirit to come.

For, my Barn hath been long without Threshers. And I have kept my flayles for a long time hid in unknown places. Which flayle is the Doctrine that I deliver unto; you: Which is the Instrument of thrashing, wherewith you shall beat the sheafs, that the Corn which is scattered, and the rest may be all one.

(But a word in the mean season.)

If I be Master of the Barn, owner of the Corn, and deliverer of my flayle: If all be mine (And unto you, there is nothing: for you are hirelings, whose reward is in heaven.)

Then see, that you neither thresh, nor unbinde, untill I bid you, let it be sufficient unto; you: that you know my house, that you know the labour I will put you to: That I favour you so much as to entertain the labourers within my Barn: For within it thresheth none without my consent. (Page 161.)

As I have written, I do not believe that John Dee would attempt to use the material given without having full permission through the Enochian Angels and from their Creator to do so. In notes written some time ago now, I wrote that I did not think (as the above quotation shows) that permission did not appear to have been given to Dee. I believe it to be so plainly written, I could not see how anyone could miss it, because ' . . . unto you, there is nothing for you are hirelings, whose reward is in heaven' but great affection is shown to Dee 'That I favour you so much as to entertain the labourers within my Barn.' John Dee was a scrupulously genuine and honourable man, whose word once given would not be broken. Having accepted a duty it would be fulfilled to the last jot and tittle and this is in all probability why the angelic work was given to him in the first place — he could be trusted with it and even if he broke the mould by which he lived and did try to use it, he would certainly not abuse it, but I do not think he did this nor would have attempted it.

The instructions are clearly given in the above and elsewhere in the work — 'within it thresheth none without my consent.' The Angel Mapsama insisted the he should not use the 'keys' without permission even though they had been delivered to him and he should go not in rashly but to enter 'by permission' and be 'brought in willingly.'

Has someone attempted what was forbidden to Dr. John Dee and further, do I believe that it has done without the requisite permission being given? I feel this could be so and again I do not believe that I am the only one to consider this possibility by any means. However, let me make one thing clear regarding the above statement and they are the important words, they are the words 'I feel and 'I believe.'

I think one man could have attempted 'to thresh' and 'unbinde the corn' and this could be Aleister Crowley and his *Aeon of Horus*. The Greek name for one of the oldest and most powerful gods of and old and powerful nation — who had the original form of the falcon or hawk —I love this god's protective form and brought him in a reproduction back from Egypt.

I think few were equipped to deal with the Enochian material, but I think Aleister Crowley would be high among them. His work *Liber XXX AERUM vel Sacculi sub figura* CCC–CXVIII being on the *Thirty Aethyrs, the Vision and the Voice* in the *Equinox* Vol. 1, No 5 (1911) or reprinted in the book, the *Vision and the Voice*; Sangreal Foundation (1972) is available for the curious.

I further feel there are other people experimenting and attempting in their own way similar exercises that may involve trying to undo the locks rashly and not invited to enter by permission. It only needs the slightest crack opened in the Gates of the Watchtowers, even unintentionally or by chance that stand sentinel against Chaos, to let in what they were put there and locked to keep out.

I repeat, the Enochian Angel Mapsama tells John Dee (in part) ' . . . But be humble. Enter not of presumption; but of permission. Go not in rashly; but be brought in willingly: for many have ascended, but few have entered.' (145–46) The latter part of this commentary brings to mind the biblical injunction ' . . . for many are called but few are chosen.' *Matthew* 20:16 and 22:14.

Dee's work now usually takes its place among the 'apocalyptic' literature and Crowley was of the opinion, in the *Confessions of Aleister Crowley* – Symonds/Grant, that 'much of their work (Dee and Kelly) still defies explanation.' I believe that even now, a good deal of it still defies explanation.

The revelations and keys of invocation are full of apocalyptic pronouncements that are easy enough to find, the destruction of the world by an angry God, the Antichrist and so forth. If you use the word 'apocalyptic' to many people, they usually say as I did once that it is a time of destruction, death, plague, famine and being at the receiving end of an angry and very wrathful God. To a certain extent, this is true but these things are not all that the word can mean as said elsewhere. Always remember that the word 'apocalyptic' originally included such things as 'to forecast and predict, uncovering or disclosing . . . a revelation' making the book of *Revelation*, a revelation of the future that includes 'famine, pestilence and plague' — because that is what is being predicted.

**Apocalypse:** This is found in most languages and is from the Latin *apocalypsis*, Greek *αποκαλυψις apokalupsis*= 'an uncovering, a revelation,' in the *New Testament* 'the Apocalyse.' *Απο–καλυπτο, apo–kalupto*= 'to uncover, to disclose, reveal, to reveal one's whole mind, made known.' From *απο, apo*= 'away from' of the mind, 'alien from' my heart and *κρυπτο, krupto*= 'to hide, cover, conceal, keep secret.'

**Generally:** 'an uncovering, disclosing or revealing that which was hid. **Specially:** The visions recorded in the last book of the *Bible, Revelations*, which receives both its Latin and Greek name from the fact that its contents mainly consist of a revelation or the *apocalypse* (= 'revelation') of future events previously hidden from mental cognisance.

**Apocalyptic:** Pertaining to a revelation or containing one. Especially belonging to the last book of the *Bible — Revelation*. The opposite to *apocalypse* is *apocrypha*, which is constructed in somewhat the same manner.

In broad brush strokes, *Apocalyptic Literature* (fourteen books in all) means revelation or unveiling. Apocalyptic books claim to reveal things that are normally hidden from sight and mind or to reveal the future.

The *Apocrypha* are the biblical books received by the early Church as part of the Greek version of the *Old Testament* but not included in the Hebrew Bible, the Church received these writing from Hellenistic Judaism, especially it is said that of Alexandria. The Christian usage of these works has always been a little ambiguous though it seems to be a little more relaxed today.

For the curious, who may not know the full fourteen works involved the full list follows. Those who do know can ignore this paragraph. Most of these books were composed during the two centuries immediately preceding the birth of Christ, though some were penned or at least interpolated at a later period up to 70 A.D before the definite separation of the Church from Judaism: 1: *Esdras*; 2: *2 Esdras*; 3: *Tobit*; 4: *Judith*; 5: Additions or the rest of *Esther*; 6: *The Wisdom of Solomon*; 7: *Ecclesiasticus*, called the *Wisdom of Jesus the Son of Sirach*; 8: *Baruch* with the epistle of Jeremy; 9: *The Song of the Three Holy Children*; 10: *The History of Sussana*; 11: *Bel and the Dragon*; 12: *The Prayers of Manasseh (Manasses), King of Judah*; 13: *1 Maccabees* and 14: *2 Maccabees*.

Dr. John Dee and Sir Edward Kelley will be picked up again in Part 2. The foregoing is audacious in its brevity of a highly complex system and subject, just as it was with the Gnostic and Cabbala material earlier. Nevertheless, we are dealing with an Angelic System of Magic so it has a place here, no matter how brief the mention. Being brief can be done to some extent because there are now many books available on the subject so that the reader will be able to expand the material with little difficulty, according to the lights of the interpreter of the system if they wish to do so, though the choice of who they read will have to be theirs. More important, those who may have been unaware of this particular angelic system will now have some idea of the information to seek and I must stop because many more facts of Dee and Kelly are coming into mind seeking to be heard. Now let us return the Angels and take up the . . .

# THE ORDERS OF THE ANGELS

In this section, we will discuss the nine orders of the angels. Dealing with them is not a simple matter because of the differences found in the various authorities and sources. What makes matters worse is that information is sometimes quite meagre with reference to some of the angelic orders, but this may prove in part to be because they have very little or less to do with the lower ranks lower down being near to God and as a result they have less to do with the earth and its inhabitants. Later Jewish and Christian speculation followed on from the lines of angelology of the earlier apocalypses, the angels that play an important part in Gnostic systems and in Jewish literature and Cabbala.

Religious thought among theologians concerning the angels, especially during the Middle Ages, developed a hierarchy of angels and I feel this is valid because even in the most uncomplicated organizations today there is an order or chain of command. Mystical texts often view the angels as emanations of the Divine Light. Maimonides, the foremost medieval Jewish philosopher, equated the angels with the incorporeal Intelligences of Aristotle. He wrote in both Hebrew and Arabic and his greatest work is the *Guide to the Perplexed* (1190) in which he tries to harmonize the thought of Aristotle and Judaism.

Much current thought then and now concerning the angels was influenced principally by the theory of the angelic hierarchy set forth in *De Hierachia Celisti* of the pseudo–Dionysius, a work that influenced St Thomas Aquinas. Immediately below God were the seraphim, cherubim and thrones, in the cosmos itself are found the dominions, powers and virtues and below these in or close to our world were found the principalities, archangels and angels. These are three triple ranks of angels that prompted the Italian poet Tasso (1544–1595) – *Jerusalem Delivered* to write 'In heaven above. The effulgent bands in triple circles move.'

The *De Hierachia Celisti* and such creeds and confessions do not formulate any authoritative doctrine of angels and modern rationalism has been inclined to dispute the reality of such beings nevertheless the pseudo–Dionysius was the first writer to formulate an angelic hierarchy. However, not everyone regards the angels as a subject about which we have sufficient reliable knowledge to do so, from the Early Church Fathers to now.

There is a rather unclear statement by St. Paul in his *Epistle to the Ephesians* that does not help the matter in hand, perhaps intentionally. 'In Christ, when he raised him from the death, and set him at his own right hand in the heavenly places, far above all principality, and power, and might, and dominion, and every name that is named, not only in this world, but also in that which is to come: and hath put all things under his feet, and gave him to be the head over all things to the church, which is his body, the fullness of him that filleth all in all.' 1:21–23. Commentators dispute that either Paul did not know all of the ranks and mentioned only those he knew so naturally others argue that Paul deliberately concealed the true numbers of the ranks.

The scheme of pseudo–Dionysius who, following Platonic and Neoplatonic tradition that had an attachment for the number three, is as follows. The celestial hierarch is divided into three orders, with three ranks within each order. This is regarded as the 'hierarchy of illumination' with (obviously) 'the highest rank being nearer to God and the lowest rank closest to man and all angels are the interpreters of those above them.'

John A. Mehung (c.1240–1305) tells us. 'Observe the three parts into which God has divided the first substance. Of the first and pure part, He created the Cherubim, Seraphim, Archangels and the other angels. Out of the second, which is not so pure, He created the heavens and all that belongs to them; of the third, impure part, the elements and their properties.'

It is thought the three orders of each triad are equal to each other but distributed into a first, second and last power. This is said to interpret Isaiah's vision, when writing of the seraphim's, 'And one cried to another, and said, Holy, holy, holy, is the Lord of hosts.' (6:3.) This ordering is thought to show that 'the first impart their knowledge of divine things to the second, the second to the third and so on.' Not unlike the rungs of a ladder, each rung you climb takes you up and each rung you descend takes you down.

The principle of continuity however, seems to demand the existence of Beings that are intermediaries between God and his creation below and the angels are thought of by many as a being a way of approaching a difficult, sometimes unfriendly and distant God. As the world becomes more incoherent and hostile, the angels have come in once more to fill what seems to many to be an ever–widening gap that people feel they cannot always bridge successfully without needing whatever help they can get.

We have come back to using words that suggest the need to 'bridge the middle ground' though seeking the middle ground first would be a more profitable venture. We need help to span the hiatus that lies between these two areas, which we have to either traverse, connect with or find. This area is far from familiar ground and like any area that is strange or unfamiliar, it is easy to become disoriented or lost. Every region has its mores and you have to learn them if you intend to try and succeed there. Part of the fascination of going to another country is the different customs, language, food, money and the like. Well, it used to be a fascination until those nameless 'people,' who now appear to run our lives, like the One God from unattainable and inaccessible heights, decided that every place you leave will be exactly the same as the place to which you are going — just to make things less interesting and easier for them to run and they will know where everyone is and what they are saying, doing or not doing.

Having mention, Dionysius the Areopagite (A.D 1) who is often confused with the Pseudo Dionysius, let us look at what we can find regarding this biblical figure and a contemporary of St. Paul. The Areopagite acquired a notable posthumous reputation principally through confusion with later Christians similarly named. The biblical one is first quoted in the sixth century and very little is known of him apart that he was converted to Christianity through St Paul's preaching. We read in *Acts*.17:34 that after Paul addressed the men of Athens on the Hill of Mars. 'Paul departed from among them, Howbeit certain men clave unto him, and believed: among the which was Dionysius the Areopagite.' In the 2nd century A.D, he was held to have been the first bishop of Athens and by the 9th century he has been identified with St. Denis of France.

Dionysius the Areopagite was a prominent citizen of Athens and he must have been a man of some importance to be a member of the *Areopagus*, which was the Supreme Court of Athens. The *Areopagus* was a hill northwest of the Acropolis in Athens that overlooked the marketplace; it was also known as the Hill of Mars. The *Areopagus* was also an ancient court of nine, thirty–nine or fifty–one judges, the exact number is not known and it varied, that met there. They were invested with great dignity and charged with the care of the morals of the city and the state treasury. Five centuries before Paul's address Socrates faced his accusers here charged with denigrating the Greek gods. They usually met at night in the open air on the Hill of Mars.

One suggestion is that they got their name because Mars was the god of bloodshed, war and murder, which were crimes generally punished by this court. They met in the open air because they took heed of a law of Athens that said it was not permissible for the murderer and the accuser 'to be under the same roof.' They met at night to hear the case and pass judgement because it was believed they would not favour the plaintiff or the defendant if they could not see them.

Corruption among other things was one of the reasons given why the court and the high positions were finally abolished. Dionysius was thought to be the first bishop of Athens and was put to death there as a martyr in the reign of Domitian, emperor of Rome. For several centuries there have been 'writings' given out under the name of Dionysius the Areopagite. These works were of a mystical–religious character, which had considerable influence in the Middle Ages whose fame added extensively to Dionysius the Aeropagite and not the original and unknown writer, now usually given as the pseudo–Dionysius.

Some Greek writings of the Middle Ages in about 500, probably in Syria were looked upon as the works of a 6th century Neoplatonist who became the pseudo–Dionysius and these are the works originally assigned to Dionysius. These writings are now universally considered a forgery, which is why they are now designated the pseudo–Dionysius. They became important in the theology and spirituality of Eastern Orthodoxy and Western Catholicism. They established a distinct Neoplatonic trend in a large part of medieval Christian doctrine and spirituality, especially in the Western Latin Church, which has decided aspects of its religious and devotional nature up to the present time. The Neoplatonists sought to provide a sound intellectual basis for a religious and moral life, one that lies beyond all experience, the dualism of Thought and Reality.

Included in this corpus of writing are *The Celestial Hierarchy, The Ecclesiastical Hierarchy* and *The Mystical Theology*. The first book deals with the orders of angelic beings and the latter to their earthly complements. *The Divine Names* is a treatise on the biblical names of the Deity and what they teach concerning the nature and attributes of God and expounds a form of intuitive mysticism.

The treatises of Dionysius in which he speculates that everything that exists — the model of Christian society, the degrees of prayer and the angelic world itself — are structured as triads and are images of the eternal Trinity. In this, he introduced a new meaning for the term — 'hierarchy.' The sway of these works is clearly seen in *The Divine Comedy* of Dante, the works of John Milton and others.

'He gives the symbolism of many things and explains the significance of the human body when given to celestial beings.' For example, the feet are ascribed to angels 'to denote their unceasing movement on the divine business, and their feet are winged to denote their celerity.'

The Areopagite's significance in the history of mysticism is not due to anything that he wrote but to writings 'wrongly' attributed to him from the sixth century to the 16th century. Erasmus was among the first to cast doubt upon the assumption that Dionysius was the author of these writings. To date historical research has not been able to identify the unknown author who assumed the name of the *New Testament* convert of St. Paul. There is an enormous literature of the pseudo–Dionysius that was first heard in A.D. 533, at the second Council of Constantinople.

Angelic ranks are implied in the *Bible* where we have the Archangels in, 'Yet Michael the archangel when contending with the devil he disputed about the body of Moses.' *Jude* 9. The principalities and powers are mentioned in 'I am persuaded, that neither death, nor life, nor angels, nor principalities, nor powers? *Romans* 8:38. Finally we can find the thrones and dominions in ' . . . all things created, that are in heaven, and that are in earth, visible and invisible, whether they be thrones, or dominions, or principalities, or powers.' *Colossians* 1:16. Therefore, it was reasonable to assume that the angelic ranks had been in existence for some time.

The angelic hosts, who commanded and directed others were divided into ranks and distinguished from the common mass. Just as the human hosts had commanders and a hierarchy so the archangels were the commanders of the hosts. In the *Testament of Levi*, the Angel of the

Presence is distinguished as an archangel to whom the angels made their summary of what was happening below.

In some Slavic literature when the Lord sits upon his throne, the heavenly host stood on ten steps according to their rank. Four of the angels were designated 'Angels of the Throne' or 'Throne Angels' and these are usually given as Michael, Gabriel, Raphael and Uriel. Sometimes the Angel Phanuel (or Penuel) is substituted for the Archangel Uriel. Phanuel is the Archangel of Penance and one of the four Angels of the Presence.

The works of the pseudo–Dionysius had great influence in the Roman Church, especially on the mystics. St. Jerome gives the ten *Divine or Mystical Names* — *Decem Nomina Mystica* — in almost the same order as given in Cabbalistic writings 'by which the Hebrew's designate God.' In the *Conflict of Adam*, which is thought to be older than the *New Testament*, there is an angelic hierarchy that is almost identical with Dionysius. The sixth rank sometimes has the title 'Sovereignties' instead of 'Powers.'

Earlier we mentioned Picus da Mirandola, who is regarded by some as the first true Christian student of Cabbala. He gives nine hierarchies that are different to Dionysius to which we have added a few brief notes to try to help matters:

*Cherubim* are originally Assyrian or Akkadian and the word is thought to mean 'one who prays or intercedes.' They are often seen as Guardian Spirits at the entrances of temples or palaces. They have a human face with bodies of a sphinx or a bull with huge wings and were not given angelic power by some commentators. They are found on the Ark covering the Mercy Seat with their wings, in Solomon's Temple and in *Revelations*. Dionysus says they are the Guardians of the Fixed Stars. Islam has them formed from the 'tears of Michael' that he shed over the sins of the faithful.

*Seraphim*. Enoch tells us these have four faces and six wings, they are four in number analogous to the 'four winds of the world.' (3.*Enoch*.) The Seraphim are not in the *New Testament* by name, but they are there. 'And the four beasts had each of them six wings about him; and they were full of eyes within; and they rest not day and night, saying, Holy, holy, holy, Lord God Almighty.' (*Revelation* 4:8). One of their duties was to encompass the Throne of God and chant the trisagion — 'Holy, holy, holy.' The prince who ruled them includes Metatron and Michael among others, but their original prince is held to be Satan before his fall.

*Chasmalim* or *Hashmalim*= the 'hayyot or living creatures' are equated with the dominions. Their chief Angel is Hashmal who surrounds the Throne of God. He is a 'fire–speaking angel' who lives in the Cabbalistic *World of Formation*, under the command of Metatron.

*Arliam* or *Erelim*= 'the valiant ones,' which is taken from 'behold the valiant ones will cry without' in *Isaiah* 33:7. They are appointed over the fruit, grain, grass and trees, they are said to correspond to the Thrones.

*Tarsisim* or *Tashishim*= 'the brilliant ones' are said to apply to the seventh kingdom of the Cabbalistic Tree of Life.

*Ophanim (Ofannim)* a term in Hebrew= 'wheels,' for the order of Cherubim.

*Ishim*= angels composed of snow and fire and this order is not mentioned by Dionysius. They are equal to the *Bene elim*= 'the sons of God,' the angels or archangels who constantly sing the praises of God, see *Genesis* 6:2, who are often equated with the Thrones. Their function is to praise the Lord. They are a high order of angels and Moses met them in the fifth heaven according to Maimonides.

*Malachim*= 'kings' corresponding with the Virtues and finally we come to the:

*Elohim* is where Dionysius positions the angels. *Elohim* in Hebrew stands for Jehovah — YHWH= comprising of the feminine '*eloh*' and the male '*im*' forming 'elohim.'

The reader will see variations in the list order, according to who is giving the list. This why at times we have to use terms such as 'as given' or 'he gives,' for example those of St. Ambrose or Jerome, Gregory the Great, Moses Maimonides, the *Zohar*, Mirandola above and others.

The hierarchy of the angels of pseudo–Dionysius is divided into three triads and most of the divisions of pseudo–Dionysius seem to appear in St. Paul, who mentions thrones, dominions, principalities and powers. *Colossians* 1:16. ' . . . when he raised him from the dead, and set him at his own right hand in the heavenly places, far above all principality, and power, and might, and dominion.' *Ephesians* 1:21. 'To the intent that now unto the principalities and powers in heavenly places.' 3:10. In *Peter* 3:22, 'by the resurrection of Jesus Christ: who is gone into heaven, and is on the right hand of God; angels and authorities and powers being made subject to him.'

In the Western Roman Catholic Church, there is the Angelus, which is short for the Angelus bell. In the Latin, *Angelus domini nuntiavit Maria*. This is a devotional exercise celebrating God and the Incarnation, in which the angelic salutation three 'Hail Mary's' are uttered, three times a day and three times each time (= usually at 6 a.m., noon and 6 p.m) making nine times daily in all. There are three divisions of three, one for each division of the three angelic orders of angels, according to some commentators.

We will be taking the angelic order that is the most popular so in keeping with others and my School Teachings because we follow the *Celestial Hierarchy* and St. Thomas Aquinas in *Suma Theologica* because after so many years it is like an old jacket that has grown to fit and become very comfortable. They were classified in the following nine ranks, beginning with the highest; we have the *Seraphim*, *Cherubim*, *Thrones*, *Dominions*, *Principalities*, *Powers*, *Virtues*, *Archangels* and *Angels*. Sometimes a tenth station is added, below the ninth for the 'Blessed Souls' but this is the choice of the user.

The addition of the tenth station as given above also applies to the ten kingdoms, emanations or Sephiroth, as given in the Cabbalistic section given earlier. Barrett in his *Magus* extends the list from nine to twelve with the addition of (10) the *Innocents*, (11) the *Martyrs* and (12) the *Confessors*.

'But we see Jesus, who was made a little lower than the angels for the suffering of death, crowned with glory and honour; that he by the grace of God should taste death for every man.' *Hebrews* 2:9. Suffice to say what follows is a hierarchy of illumination, which places the highest rank immediately below God and the lowest rank above us.

Seven orders only are listed in some works, St Jerome only gave seven ranks by omitting the Principalities and Virtues and this number seven always has something to recommend it. In particular, in magical or occult connotations we usually find the number seven prolific with symbolism, for example in *Revelation*. Remember in this section the most popular lists are taken, variations are extant, the reader will meet with them and if you sometimes find things a little confusing at the higher levels the reader can take comfort that St. Augustine said that he did not know the difference be the higher ranks of the thrones, dominion, principalities and powers and the Psuedo–Dionysus said that only God knows the true number of the angels, their duties and their ranks, however, we start with the . . .

# SERAPHIM

In the first order of the triple levels with the first to the third, we start with the seraphim that are closest to God. In Christian angelology, the seraphim are the highest–ranking celestial beings within the hierarchy of angels. Early Hebrew thought seems to give Yahweh only three ranks of servant before the Exile. These three were the Seraphim, the Cherubim and the Spirits. The Cherubim and Seraphim were the 'Guardians of Paradise' and the attendants of Yahweh. *Isaiah* shows they were not angels in the sense of 'messengers' but attendants and composite figures. The spirits were in the role of a steward that could be sent on missions by Yahweh, though they appeared to play a very small role in the overall scheme of things. Enoch tells us that there are only four Seraphim, one for each of the four cardinal directions.

Seraph, plural Seraphim, Hebrew= 'burning one.' A celestial being with six wings referred to in a vision by the Hebrew prophet Isaiah. They are one of the highest in the nine–fold orders of angels and they are especially gifted with love and associated with light and purity. In Jewish, Christian and Islamic literature, the seraphim are variously described as having two or three pairs of wings and serve as a Throne Guardian of God. Seraphim in the *Old Testament* appear in the Temple vision of the prophet Isaiah as six-winged creatures praising God in what is known in the Greek Orthodox Church as the Trisagion= 'Thrice Holy' — 'Holy, holy, holy is the Lord of hosts; the whole earth is full of his glory.' *Isaiah* 6:3, this is expanded further in the chapter.

We find the Seraphim or Seraph mentioned only twice in the *Bible* and in one chapter only, so we have very little to work with and from the account given in *Isaiah*, we cannot tell how many seraphim Isaiah saw. It is obvious from the account that there were at least two as the following shows. Isaiah says that 'each one had' so there was at least two seraphim, perhaps many more but as said the suggested number has long been four.

'Above it (= the Lords throne) stood the seraphim's: each one had six wings: with twain he covered his face, and with twain he covered his feet, and with twain did he fly. *Isaiah* 6:2–4, according to Enoch II the had 'four faces.' We are being told that with two wings the seraphim covered his face, with another two his feet and with the remaining two he flew. This is a rare occasion, perhaps the only one, when we are told that an angel has wings that were used for flying.

The prophet spoke with the seraphim with familiarity but it is strange that they are not mentioned anywhere else. One of the Seraphim is described as having a live coal in his hand that he had taken from the altar. With this coal he touched the prophet's lips saying 'Lo, this hath touched thy lips; and thine iniquity is taken away, and thy sin purged.' *Isaiah* 6:7. It is traditionally thought that this order of angels has dominion over the Element of Fire, which element is both cleansing and sacred

Many suggestions regarding the meaning of the word 'seraph' are found but I have not included these simply because none of them have been satisfactorily resolved and therefore they could confuse more than clarify. Most of them are rejected by someone for one reason or another, so there seems to be little point. We only mention that some make of the name 'bright' or 'burning,' which again is in keeping with their traditional dominion over the Element of Fire, while others think it means 'lofty or 'noble,' which they are. Their figure has been connected with the serpent–like beings of Oriental mythology, for example the *sarrapu* of the Assyrians and the Egyptian *serref*= 'guardian griffins.'

The name has also been derived from the 'serpentine' movement of lightning= 'flying serpents' and ' . . . for out of the serpent's root shall come forth a cockatrice, and his fruits shall be a fiery flying serpent.' *Isaiah* 14:9. Finally, ' . . . the viper and the fiery flying serpent.' *Isaiah* 30: 6. In Isaiah's inaugural vision, the seraph is symbolic of human figures, expressing their ardency to God.

The cockatrice is the translation of *tzepha* or *tziphon* in *Proverbs* 23 and *Isaiah* 11:8 and it is usually used when a highly venomous reptile is represented.

The cockatrice was regarded as a fabulous species of serpent supposed to be hatched from the egg of a cock and the name belongs to no identified serpent and now appears only in the works of ancient compilers and heraldry. Among the latter, it is usually figured with a crest and some snakes have this appearance so it is thought possible that some of these by description could be meant by the words *tzepha* or *tziphon*, with modern commentators giving the **King James Version** as 'serpent, adder or viper.'

The only thing that does seem positive regarding the seraph is that they were an order that was usually the highest of the celestial beings and similar in nature to the Cherubim. Their principal area of service was around the divine Throne of Power intoning the trisagion.

The Trisagion is sometimes called the Seraphic Hymn (see Cherubim below). Trisagion, Greek neuter of *τρισαγιος, trisagios* from *τρις, tris* of *τρεις, treis*= 'thrice, three times or three and *ἅγιος, hagios*= '*holy*' giving '*thrice holy*' in the refrain 'Holy God, Holy and Mighty, Holy and immortal have mercy upon us.' One of the doxologies of the Eastern Church, repeated in the form of versicle and responses by the choir in certain parts of the liturgy and so called as shown from the triple recurrences of the *ἅγιος, hagios*= 'holy.'

The seraphim are said to be Angels of Fire, the burning ones, of life, they are for the most part ardent in their love of all things Divine and their desire is to aid those beneath.

There is no mention of them by name in the **New Testament** though they are fully described by inference in **Revelations**. 'And the four beasts had each of them six wings about him; and they were full of eyes within: and they rest not day and night, saying, Holy, holy, holy, Lord God Almighty, which was, and is, and is to come.' (4:8). The ruling prince of the Seraphim has included Michael, Metatron but originally it was said to have been given to Satan before the Fall, where some of the angels defected with him.

Supposing popular opinion to be right we know practically nothing of the Seraphim, other than what is told us in the single passage in **Isaiah**. If, however, they are identified with the Cherubim, then their appearance and station is similar to the Seraphim. They are a distinctive order of existence for which accepted belief and the ingenuity of Jewish and Christian writers have invented a minute account. The Christian theologian and Minister General of the Franciscans, St Bonaventure (c. 1217–1274) was noted for his spiritual writings and he was called the 'Seraphic Doctor.' In art, the four-winged Cherubim were painted blue to symbolize the sky or the celestial and the six-winged Seraphim were painted red to symbolize fire. Now let us move on to the . . .

## CHERUBIM

It is recommended the reader keeps the above order of Seraphim, in mind when reading this order because they have much in common and the dividing line between them is sometimes hard to determine or know where one begins and the other ends. Cherub is the singular of Cherubim and they are give as Angels of Air in the Cabbala. Thomas Aquinas tells us in his **Summa** that 'the first angel who sinned was not a seraph, but a cherub.' Cherubiel or Kerubim is the eponymous chief of the order of Cherubim, though the Archangel Gabriel is also regarded as being the chief of the order, perhaps a guardian or overseer.

In Jewish, Christian and Islamic literature, a celestial winged being with human, animal or birdlike characteristics that functions as a throne bearer of the deity. In Christianity, the Cherubim rank among the higher orders of angels, celestial attendants of God that continually praise him

The Cherub and Cherubim are winged creatures mentioned in the **Bible** and the **Bible** is the only positive evidence we have on the subject. It should be remembered that Hebrew thought regarding the Cherubim has varied at different periods of history. They belong to an order along with the Seraphim and the angels. Some scholars argue that the term 'cherub' had its origins in Akkadian mythological texts in the word *karibu*= 'intercessor, to bless or pray – one who prays or intercedes.'

However, a description of the Cherubim in the ***Old Testament*** puts more emphasis on their remarkable mobility and their role as throne bearers of God. This could suggest that their functions are limited, however, ancient Middle Eastern mythology says that these celestial beings serve both important liturgical and intercessory functions in the angelic hierarchy. ***Kirubu*** is the synonym of the 'Steer–god,' whose winged image filled the place of guardian at the entrances of Assyrian palaces.

Most however, say we have no inception of the Cherubim before Eden, the word for a Cherub remains obscure and like other words involved in this subject, it is still not settled despite the time and discussion that has passed regarding them.

There is thought to be no Hebrew root from which the word Cherub can be directly derived. Experts tell us that there are similar roots in Syrian and other languages, though they throw little light upon the subject. I make no claims to being an expert on languages at this level so like my readers I have to depend in some areas of my studies upon the deliberations of those who are held to know more on such matters.

Philo the Jew regarded them as emblematic of the creative and kingly attributes of God. By some they are viewed as the chariot steeds of Jehovah and by others 'the accompaniments of his chariot throne.' Some think Cherub is a 'combination of the highest properties of creature life' that is united or connected with Divine Life. The Cherub is not regarded as a totality but symbolic of the component parts.

The Cherub has four symbolic parts. The ox represents the productive and generating power of the Godhead. The lion is distinctive of the prerogatives of ruling and judgement. The eagle portrays the omnipresence and omniscience. While the man depicts the potential of heavenly wisdom, hence the Cherubim 'are typical of redeemed and glorified manhood.' It should to be noted that God dwells between them as found in 'Thou that dwellest between the cherubim.' ***Psalm*** 80:1. God rides on them as found in ' . . . he rode upon a cherub, and did fly: Yea, he did fly upon the wings of the wind.' ***Psalm*** 18:9. At this late stage it should be unnecessary to be point out that the 'four symbolic' parts of the cherub are our old friends the Four Fixed Signs of the Zodiac and the four Pillars of the Earth. All mentioned many times previously because it is really rather difficult to get away from them.

The above passage is thought to hint at their origins. They are the personification of the storm cloud and the wind. Enoch said the Seraphim were four and they corresponded 'to the four winds of the world.' God sat upon them, just as the pagan gods stood on the backs of animals. It is no surprise to hear this order of angels referred to as the 'cherubim of glory shadowing the mercy seat.' ***Hebrews*** 9:5

They are commonly represented in the art of Mesopotamia as a griffin that is a creature half lion and half eagle. We have already mention that the lion or Leo is the opposite sign of the Zodiac to the eagle, the old symbol for Scorpio. Again, these two signs are two of the 'Four Corners of the earth.' Although the evidence is not supported in the ***Bible***, some think the sphinx may go back to this idea or that we got it from the Egyptians.

Many Assyrian sculptures and Egyptian monuments have a strong similarity to the Cherubs. The Cherubs also bear a resemblance to the Hittite griffins in body and have similar duties as guardians of sacred articles, artefacts and buildings. The Egyptians portrayed human winged figures kneeling between outspread wings, and facing each other is found in the zodiac sanctuary at Dendera.

This almost agrees with the version of the Cherubim of the Hebrew sanctuary and it is because of these that the Cherubim are associated with the griffins. The Cherubim were not thought of as angels in the early lore of Canaan. In the early tradition of Islamic lore, it was thought the Cherubim were created from the tears of the Archangel Michael who shed them 'because of the sins of the faithful.'

Who was first with this fabulous creature is (for many) still unresolved. Nevertheless like the *ideé fixé* created and used by the composer Berlioz from the same fixed representative themes in his music, this could also be also be applied to the fixed ideas found repeated among the ancient peoples and their philosophies even when they were separated by time, countries and oceans. The Cherubim are mentioned for the first time in the story of Adam and Eve where they appear as executors of the Divine Will regarding 'our first parents.' They are the Guardians of the Gates of Paradise to prevent the return of Adam and Eve after their expulsion to prevent their return and before this incident there is no description of the Cherubim before Eden, on which we can draw. There is a partial one taken from those of Moses that were made upon the Mercy Seat.

Moses was told to make two Cherubic figures and that they be placed on the lid (= *kapporeth*) of the Ark of the Covenant. They were made of gold and it is usually accepted they were in human form and they looked towards each other with their wings stretched inwards with wing tips touching over the ark to form the Mercy Seat. The Cherubim on the *kapporeth* formed the throne of God of which the ark was the footstool. From between these two Cherubim, God answered Moses and the leaders of the people when they consulted him on important matters. 'And there I will meet with thee, and I will commune with thee from above the mercy seat, from between the two cherubim which are upon the ark of the testimony, of all things which I will give thee in commandment unto the children of Israel.' *Exodus* 25:22.

The Cherubim found in Solomon's Temple were worked in olive wood in 1 *Kings* 6:23 'And within the oracle he made two cherubim's of olive tree, each ten cubits high.' We know their height, the length of their wings that they stood upon their feet and faced each other and there were two in number. It is impossible to deny the resemblance of detail which exist between the monuments of Egypt and Assyria and the Cherubim's of Moses and Ezekiel, the comparison is hard to dispute and suggests that one took it from the other though an alternative thought occurs. The symbols appear to belong to most ancient ages and they could have been carried and dispersed in many directions from the plain of Shinar and afterwards adapted because they appear to be found even at the Gates of Paradise. Philo the Jew regarded them as emblematic of the creative and kingly attributes of God.

It is natural, since the sanctuary represented Yahweh's dwelling place on earth, that the inner covering stretching over the tabernacle, as well as the curtain before the Holy of Holies, which was also embroidered with Cherubim. There were two large Cherubim in the Holy of Holies in Solomon's temple and they were figures most likely in human form, made of olivewood overlaid with gold and keeping watch over the Ark. There were figures of Cherubim on the inner walls of the sanctuary. Lions, oxen and cherubim were engraved on the bases of the ten brazen lavers that stood in the courtyard of the Temple.

One of the limitations placed upon Solomon when building his great temple was 'that no iron tool should be used' in its construction. A difficult task at this particular period of time. However, tradition comes to our aid by telling us that Solomon made use of a worm called *Shamir*, which had the ability to 'split any stone over which it crawled.'

The prophet Ezekiel described four 'living creatures' that 'had the likeness of a man, and each with, four faces and four wings.' Ezekiel tells us, 'As for the likeness of their faces, they four had the face of a man (= 'that of a human face symbolizing intelligence'), and the face of a lion (= 'indicating sovereignty'), on the right side: and they four had the face of an ox (= 'figuring strength') on the left side; they four also had the face of an eagle (= 'signifying immense vision and speed.') Thus were their faces: and their wings were stretched upwards; two wings of every one were joined to another, and two covered their bodies.' *Ezekiel* 1:11.

They are mentioned in **Revelation** 4:8 founded upon Ezekiel's prophecy as six–winged beasts as above. These are the four fixed Signs of the Zodiac, our old friends again. 'And the first was like a lion (= **Leo**), and the second beast was like a calf (= **Taurus**), and the third beast had the face of a man (=*Aquarius*), and the fourth beast was like a flying eagle (= **Scorpio**.) The Archangel Gabriel and Raphael are often connected with the order of the Cherubim, as have been Lucifer and Satan, not Lucifer/Satan.

It is thought in this adaptation, the prophet accommodated himself to the symbolism and art of the Assyro–Babylonians who decorated their palaces with composite figures of an animal and man. It was at the River Chebar (= 'great') in Babylon where the prophet lived among the exiles, ministering to them and it was here that he had his first visions.

If the Cherub's face corresponded to that of the ox, the other faces of the man, lion and eagle are given. This may account for the fact that the cherubim of Near East art are represented as four–footed creature. Besides their wings, Ezekiel also described their feet. 'And their feet were straight feet; and the sole of their feet was like the sole of a calf's foot: and they sparkled like the colour of burnished brass.' *Ezekiel* 1:7.

The four living creatures in **Revelation** are similar to the Cherubim and add very little to their initial description. The Cherubim are often identified with statues and art of other races in the near–East, which have various combinations of animal and human bodies with prominent wings, though none adequately represent the **Old Testament** Cherubim. The Church Fathers are generally agreed in regarding them as angels and most Fathers explain the word as meaning 'knowledge,' or 'the fullness of knowledge.'

In **Genesis**, they act as custodians and guardians. ' . . . And he placed at the East of the garden of Eden cherubims, and a flaming sword which turned every way, to keep the way of the tree of life.' 3: 24. Supernatural guardians were a common theme in near Eastern thought and in **Ezekiel**; the Cherubim were executors of divine judgement, spreading burning coals over a city. ' . . . Even under the cherub, and fill thine hand with coals of fire from between the cherubim's, and scatter them over the city.' 10:2–7. Again, as with the seraphim, we find burning coals and the Element of Fire prominent with cherubim.

Images of the Cherubim have been carried before the pope (as was the **Flabellum**) and among the Greeks, these were emblems of the spread of the gospel, as the evangelists are said to be prefigured by these symbols. The trisagion is sometimes called the Cherubic Hymn and sung in the Eastern Church at the entrance of the holy gifts, before the oblation. Let us pick up the word *flabellum*= 'a small fan' or 'fly trap.' **Flabellum Muscatorium**= a fan to keep flies away from the chalice, frequently made of peacock feathers. **Musca**= 'a fly,' **muscarium**= 'a fly flap, fly brush, more often than not made of peacock's tails, ostrich feathers and decorated with peacock's eyes to ornament them or hairy ox or horse tails.' In the Greek Church, the *flabellum* is sometimes made to represent a winged angel.

In ending, it is to be observed that in the many passages referring to the Cherubim in which God is said to dwell between the Cherubim, to ride among the Cherubim, to sit upon the Cherubim. Similarly, it has been suggested that 'they are poetical expressions alluding in figurative language to the fact that the Divine glory was specially manifested above the *Mercy Seat*, where Cherubim were placed.' Next in order of descent are the ...

## DOMINIONS

The Dominions are the 'dominions, lords or lordships.' This order is often given deference as being the oldest of the orders and by some, they are considered to be the 'original angels.' They do not seem to have attracted a great deal of attention to themselves despite this for little appears about them. According to the *Magus*, they are the *hashmallin*, probably because the chief of their order is Hashmal, though sometimes this is given as Zadkiel. Dionysius tells us 'they regulate the duties of the angels and are perpetually aspiring to true lordship; through them the majesty of God is manifested.' They are mentioned only once in the *Bible* in *Colossians* 1:6: ' ... For by him were all things created, that are in heaven, and that are in earth, visible and invisible, whether they be thrones, or dominions, or principalities, or powers.' The Dominions are said to receive their orders from the Cherubim or God, as they regulate the duties of the angels by making God's commands know to them. According to the *Zohar,* the term denotes 'an inner, supernal sphere, hidden and veiled, in which the celestial letters of the Holy name are suspended.' Again, according to the *Zohar* we read of the *hayah* (plural= *hayoth*) lit. 'Animal, living and one of the highest ranks of angels.' We next move on to the ...

## THRONES

Next, we have the second triple tier giving the fourth to the sixth levels starting with the Thrones who are the 'many–eyed ones.' Dionysius tells us it is through the Thrones that 'God brings his justice to bear upon us.' The Angel Iofiel — 'the beauty of God' — is one of the seven archangels and this angel is called the 'chief of the order of thrones.' In Agrippa, the Angel Iofiel is the ruler of the planet Saturn but Paracelsus says he is an intelligence of Jupiter. The Thrones are an enigmatic group of angels who are high in the hierarchy of angels as all are at the top of this three–tier level. The Thrones are also know as *ophanium* and *galballin* and these creatures are 'the chariots of God, which are driven by the Cherubs.' God is supported by them and they inhabit in the region of the Cosmos where material form begins to take shape

In early times, there was something special about sitting in a chair. Most of the people stood or reclined on couches even when they ate they sat on benches or on the ground. Only the king, ruler or absolute head of the household sat in a throne or chair. These angels are called Thrones because the authority of judgement is shown by a throne and Dionysius tells us 'they are bearers of God and wholly capable of undertaking all that is divine.'

A throne always belongs to someone and others did not sit in it, because it was not theirs and they did not possess the authority to use it. In a lesser degree, my father had 'his chair' in the house and others did not use it, at least not when he was there and you got out of it when or before he came in. All the other names in the hierarchies suggested a mobile power, not a stationary one as a 'throne' or seat usually does. Of course, there were portable thrones that were carried on certain occasions but these were a substitute throne and a representative of the true Throne of Power, which remained *in situ* and was rarely if ever moved. To take a realm, land or country at one time it was necessary to take the crown, throne and the person who sat in it preferably all.

King Henry is told 'God and his angels guard your sacred throne and make you long become it.' *King Henry V* Act.1: Sc.2. When his enemies start to gather against him King Richard asks 'Is the chair empty? Is the sword unsway'd? Is the King dead, the empire unpossess'ed?' *King*

*Richard the Third.* Act.4: Sc.4. In keeping with other commentators I cannot find it used as an explicit rank of anyone in the *Bible*, rather it seems to confer rank on those that owned it or sat in it.

In John's vision of heaven, we read that 'a throne was set in heaven' and next there was the 'one who sat on the throne.' *Revelation* 4:2. First, the throne is stressed then the one who sits in it, next we find the twenty–four thrones (today these thrones are usually reduced to 'seats') for the twenty–four elders, clothed in white with gold crowns on their heads and 'gold crowns' often go with thrones or important seats or once they did.

The ancient Syrians defined their world of Planetary Rulers in much the same way as the Chaldeans. The lowest world was under the Moon. Our earth was ruled by Angels, with Mercury ruling the Archangels. Venus was over the Principalities, with the Sun over the Powers with Mars ruling the Virtues. Jupiter ruled the Dominions and finally they set Saturn to rule the Thrones.

The angel of the church of the Laodiceans was told. ' . . .To him that overcometh will I grant to sit with me in my throne, even as I also overcame, and am set down with my Father in his throne.' *Revelations* 3:21. The line 'To sit with me' suggests a few interpretations. It appears to be a special privilege to be granted this. Did it bestow equal rank, a gesture of affection or a reward? It seems to be something that was granted, shared but not a right. These are only a few of the examples that can be found regarding the subject. We now move to the . . .

## PRINCIPALITIES

The seventh order of angels in the celestial hierarchy of the pseudo–Dionysius. This hierarchy is recognized in the *New Testament*: 'I am persuaded, that neither death, nor life, nor angels, nor principalities, nor powers, nor things present, . . . shall be able to separate us from the love of God' *Romans* 8:38-9. There was little found regarding the Principalities or Princedoms that have 'princely powers' and they are the protectors and defenders of religion and, according to the list, they 'watch over the leaders of people, the people' and help them to make the right decisions. Though it is regarded as doubtful by some Barret, in his work *The Magus*, says the 'principalities are the called by the Hebrews *elohim*.'

In part, Principality translates from the Latin *principalitas*= 'the first place, superiority, pre–eminence, excellence' and *principalis*= 'first, original, primitive' and 'first in rank, station or esteem, chief, principle' and 'of or belonging to a prince or ruler.' The are allusions in the recognized names of the Gnostic hierarchical systems of aeons or emanations. 'From Mind proceeded the word, **Logos**, then from this Virtue and Wisdom in Principalities, Power, Angels . . . so forth' from Basilidean philosophy.

The Principalities are often associated with 'countries or continents' St. Ignatius speaks of the 'hierarchy of principalities.' The Principalities is usually given over to the planet Venus and this agrees with the Angel Anael being given as the chief of the order of the Principalities. In a passage telling of the ancient Syrian scheme of hierarchies, the lowest world—Earth—is ruled by Angels; the sphere of Mercury by Archangels; that of Venus by Principalities; that of the Sun by solar gods termed Powers; that of Mars by Virtues; Jupiter, Dominions; Saturn, Thrones. Next, we come to the . . .

## POWERS OR POTENTATES

The Powers are the 'potentates, authorities or dynamis.' The *Septuagint* first applies the term powers to an angelic order *Dynamis*, 'a store, plenty' from Greek δυναμις, *dynamis*= 'power, might, strength, ability' to do a thing.). The principle job of the Powers is the see that order is maintained on the pathways to heaven and God's plans are protected from disruption because the demons try to bring chaos through people or individuals. According to the lists, the work of the Powers is to 'stop the efforts of the demons who would overthrow the world.' It was the opinion of Pope Gregory that the Powers regulate the demons. Next, we move on to the . . .

## VIRTUES

With the Virtues, we come to the third and last of the triple layered groups, taking in the seventh to the ninth tiers. The main duty of the Virtues appears to be 'to work miracles on earth' and they are 'the main bestowers of grace and valour.' An old tradition has two of the Virtues preparing Eve for the birth of Cain, escorted by twelve other angels. In Hebrew lore, the Virtues are equated with the *malakim* (= 'kings' commensurate with the virtues) or the *tarshishim* (= 'the brilliant ones') Michael, Raphael, Uriel and Satan are often found listed in this order. This term responds to the seventh kingdom of Cabbala. According to the hierarchical scheme of the Syrians, the Virtues correspond to the planet Mars. Next, the venture is moved a little closer home or nearer to our place in the scheme of things, which would be more accurate.

## ARCHANGELS

Archangel in the Latin is *archangelus*= an archangel and in the Greek it is *αρχαγγελος, archaggelos*= 'an archangel' from *αρχε, arche*= 'implying superiority' + *αγγελος, aggelos* = (1) 'a messenger' (2) 'an angel' making these angels a chief or higher angel in the original Order of Angels or Cosmic Powers. The Archangels are any of several chiefs, rulers or princes in the hierarchy of angels of the major Western religions, in particular Judaism, Christianity and Islam. In Christian legend, these angels number seven but in the Koran, they are four. In Catholic theology, they are the eighth of the nine divisions in the Divine Hierarchy. Jewish astrology associates the archangels with the planets.

Raphael with the Sun, Gabriel with the Moon, Michael with Mercury, Aniel (= Anael) with Venus, Samael with Mars, Zadkiel (= Sachiel) with Jupiter and Kafziel (= Cassiel) with Saturn. In medieval Europe, influenced by the Islamic system of *Averroes*, the planets of Michael and Raphael were reversed and this is the order found in Part 2 and as already said, the archangels parallel the Babylonian Planetary Spirits, the Zoroastrian *Ameshaspentas*.

I feel it would not be wrong to regard the archangels as the older brothers of the angels. They are probably the leaders of the group in which they are found and I do not think it would be unreasonable to assume that the archangels often guide the angels and give them advice because they have a greater perspective of evolution, especially ours, being the older and the senior ranking of the two.

This is not like family relationships where the younger and less experience seek out the older because they should have the greater experience and wiser in guidance? The archangels can remember a great deal more of the past than the angels can. Of course, all the angels know of a past when the world was being created and we had not made their appearance on the world's stage. Because of this I feel that we may hear perhaps without knowing it, the voice of the archangel speaking through the angel, just as I use phrases my grandmother used through hearing my grandmother and my mother's sayings and general views about life.

The simplest definition to give of the order of the archangels is the obvious one that they rank one division above the angels. The archangels are naturally incorporeal beings eighth in rank in the scheme of the pseudo–Dionysius, which we are using while the angels are the ninth. They are in the third circle, which puts them in the sphere of Mercury.

It is said the archangels guide the spiritual destiny of groups and nations, rather than individuals, which is the sphere of the angels. This may explain why the archangels are often found in art bearing formalised designs of cities in their arms.

The rank of archangel is given only twice in the **New Testament**. One of these is in 1 **Thessalonians** 4:16; 'For the Lord himself shall descend from heaven with a shout, with the voice of an archangel, and with the trump of God.' The other is in Jude 9, 'Yet Michael the archangel, when contending with the devil he disputed about the body of Moses.' This tradition was held to be familiar to the early writers, such as Clement of Alexander and Origen among others.

Only in the latter is Michael named as an archangel. In the **Old Testament**, Daniel tells us ' . . . but lo, Michael, one of the chief princes, came to help me.' **Daniel** 10:13. Although Daniel has not called Michael, an archangel, the words 'one of the chief princes' generally indicates this to be so and to confuse the issue for us just a little more. **Revelation** 8:2 John tells us of 'the seven angels which stood before God.' This is usually interpreted to mean the seven were archangels because they 'stood before God.' They are probably ' . . . his angels that excel in strength, that do his commandments, hearkening unto the voice of his word.' **Psalm** 103:20 and they may also be 'the chief princes' in terms of Daniel.

The **First Book of Enoch** (chapter 20), names seven angels and gives them as Uriel = 'Leader of the Heavenly Hosts and Guardian of Sheol, the Underworld.' Raphael= Guardian of Human Spirits. Raguel= 'Avenger of God against the World of Lights.' Michael= 'The Guardian of Israel.' Sariel= 'Avenger of the Spirits' — 'who sin in the spirit.' Gabriel= 'Ruler of Paradise, the Seraphim, and the Cherubim and Remiel (also called Jeremiel)= 'Guardian of the Souls in Sheol. Of these, two (the Archangels Michael and Gabriel) are mentioned in the **Old Testament** and two others (Archangels Raphael and Uriel) in the **Apocrypha**. Among the sectarians associated with the **Dead Sea Scrolls**, some of the Higher Angels embrace Angels of Light, Darkness, Destruction and Holiness.

This should warn the reader that other lists and spelling variations are extant and they are at variance with this one and the list we will be using later in Part 2. For example, later Jewish practice gives Phaneul as an alternative for Uriel. The list that we use for our work here I consider to be reliable and mature in use, long before my teacher, my School and me.

We find lists of twelve archangels and angels, one for each Sign of the Zodiac. The names of these angels and the Signs of the Zodiac they rule will be will dealt with, again in Part 2 with other matters only hinted in this part of the work. The pseudo–Dionysius tells us that 'the archangels are messengers who bear divine decrees.' We have come to the final rank in the Orders when we come to the . . .

## ANGELS

With the ninth rank in the third and last tier, we come to the angels from Greek *αγγελος, angelos*= 'messenger, envoy, announcer' and used in the **Old Testament** to translate the Hebrew word *mal'ach*= 'messenger.' In the Latin we have *angelus*= 'a messenger' or 'a messenger of God, and angel'and angelicus= 'suitable or pertaining to messengers' or 'belonging to angels or angelic.'

In Christian, Jewish, Islamic and other theologies, they are a messenger either of God, one of various hierarchies of celestial beings, a messenger of the king or ruler. The idea of a guardian angel or angels is also familiar as this work attests and it is the reason that it was written. However, the suggestion of hosts of formative powers, *rectores mundi* or other beings bridging the area between Divine beings, people and serving as intermediaries or a means of communication between people and the high spiritual entities has in the main vanished from popular Christianity though *Angels*, *Principalities* and *Powers* are recounted by Paul and the Archangel Michael is mentioned in *Jude*.

*Rector*= 'a guide, director, leader, ruler, master' + *Mundi*= 'the world, of the world.' *Angelus Rector.* Latin= 'Ruling Angel.' According to Kepler, the angel or divine being who caused a planet to pursue its course around the sun. The influence of the Gnostics, Neoplatonists and Jews on early Christianity gives and expands the importance of the word. Angels then are members of numerous hierarchies of celestial powers from the septenary formative host that emanates from the formative downwards, acting as intermediaries or envoys between the divine and the human or terrestrial.

We will deal with the angels who rule specific areas and conditions of human life on earth, not unlike overseers of departments and the workforce. We will discuss the planetary angels, the Four Archangels, the Auxiliary Angels, the Ben Ben Angel and finally probably the most important of the personal angels, your Holy Guardian Angels fully in Part 2. These angels have been with an individual from birth and are unique to them. This is why these particular angels will always be important to any human being.

The Seraphim and Cherubim may have contacted people and helped them, but you have to leave it to them to make the contact as I think you have little choice in the matter because they are usually performing duties of far greater import, which is why there are angels working under them and not the other way around. I think it would be rather presumptuous to think because we want it or command them that these higher angels or entities must put in an appearance. It would be another matter if they chose to do so and lucky the individual to whom this happens.

This does not mean higher angels take no interest in us. As said, regard the archangels as the older brothers of the angels. The memory of the angels is far beyond our comprehension and that of the archangels is even greater than this. The angels have a memory that takes them to a distant past when we did not exist and neither did the world as we know it. The angels were there in the early days of the creation of world. We do tend to forget that we are comparative newcomers in the universal scheme of things. We have been here a very short time indeed considering the time scale involved. Talent and hard work can attract the attention of those higher on Jacob's Ladder and with this vision Jacob saw the scale of the angelic hierarchy with God at its head.

Something like this can sometimes happen in large commercial organizations. From time to time, a high executive bypasses the hierarchical order because they have or something is justified. They may even send specific tasks down to see how they are dealt with or even if they are recognized and coped with at all.

I cannot believe this is unique or exclusive to this level alone so and if someone on a higher rung is satisfied with you — who knows what can come of their interest? If we are not aware of the existence of our personal Guardian Angels, this could be because it is inherent in their nature not to draw attention to themselves. They only appear when necessary or the need is great — not every five minutes and in response to every demand, whim or fancy and the somewhat perpetual —'I want' — no matter how much you want it.

It is the angels and archangels by far who have made the greater contact with our 'brave new world' and we 'the creatures in it.' The writer feels these two orders of angels are the more accessible and this is why we will be concentrating for the most on these two areas and levels. They are quite enough to satisfy anyone if contact can be made and this should be excitement enough for anybody. For someone to demand of the angels is patently foolish and I will keep on advising the reader to always remember who it is they are petitioning to help them — if they will

— this is an oft–repeated phrase throughout this work but it is worth the repetition if it gets the point home.

Glendower is reproached by Hotspur in **King Henry IV, Part 1** when he says 'I can call spirits from the vasty deep.' Hotspur retorts 'Why, so can I, or so can any man. But will they come when you do call for them?' Act.2: Sc.1 and as usual the Bard is as always straight to the point.

There is an old English proverb that speaks of 'angel visits' as an 'enchanting communication of short length and rare occasion.' 'How fading are the Joves (= 'joys') we dote upon . . . like Angels visits, short and bright.' (1687). Angels were used to practical and sarcastic account when speaking of your physician in the past. 'A physician is an angel when employed but a devil when one must pay him.'

Be sensible regarding your work and always request. Heed the Apostle Paul's advice in **Philippians** because it is good advice for any religion or any people. 'Let your good sense be obvious to everybody. The Lord is near. Never worry about anything; but tell God all your desires of every kind in prayer and petition shot through with gratitude, and the peace of God which is beyond our understanding will guard your hearts and thoughts in Christ Jesus.' 4:6–7. (**The New Jerusalem Bible. 1985.**)

The system of Angelic Magic being offered here is old and its growth and evolution has been slow and measured. It is based on old manuscripts and methods of working that have been in practise a very long time. There have been discreet and small changes in a few areas because the advice, relevant at the time when they were written, is not the same as the present time. I must stress that I have not, nor will I join the almost pathological haste abroad today to 'bring things into the twentieth–first century to make the work relevant for today' or 'brought up to date' because they have never, ever been 'out of date' and this has not always been shown to be an improvement. Remember, work of this nature has always been 'relevant.'

We will be using Kameas, seals, sigils, spirits, intelligence's, angelic signatures, some effective magical scripts, putting them all together and collating them from manuscripts, books, works, Schools and some measure of experience. There will be help to find the best days and hours for doing the work, with a Table of Planetary and Angelic Hours, incense, colours, perfumes, the Olympian Spirits and much more. Remember that all the, diagrams and lists, plans and tables mentioned throughout both parts are at the rear of the work in one place where they can be easily found.

Regard all this seemingly disconnected information as a large skein of wool in which the separate colours are tangled, just as they are scattered throughout the book in the various chapters of the work. The reader will find as they progress further that it is far from disconnected, as will be seen in Part 2. You seek the information required by sorting out from the skein the colour you want. For example, the Angel of Mars has red as his basic colour so pick out all the red strands to compose the material from which you will work, but more of this later.

Let me pass on a small trick I use in my Schoolwork in the past and still use because it is efficient. When I was in School learning, I marked any appropriate sections in their correct colour. I said above that red is one of the colours of Mars, light blue or green for Venus, purple or mauve for Jupiter and so forth. I bought a set of coloured pencils though now I use a cheap set of colour fibre pens or highlighting pens.

Using appropriate colours I would underline or highlight the references to connected subjects of a particular source, for example Saturn, the Archangel Michael and the rest. It should be unnecessary to say I never mark literary works in this way but textbooks are working books and manuals, they are used for a practical purpose, so they should be used in a practical way. Another way was to run these colours into the margins, opposite or in line the written material and taken the edge of the page so that it could easily be seen, even when the edge of the pages are flicked through.

This makes the information or the sections needed easily found when you want any relevant and connected information scattered throughout a School Course or the chapters of a working textbook such as this You simply flick through the edge of the pages and stop at the appropriately coloured sections. Having gathered the information on paper from the book or course, it was a simple task to chose the information I would use for the work in hand. Although the material is mainly connected to one source, as the colour example used, occasionally it belonged to more than one source.

If the main source was Mars, the first line was red, but if the material also had some association with Venus or Mercury, the second line was blue and the third bright yellow. This told me that this information belonged mainly to Mars (= red) but it had links with Venus (= blue) and Mercury (= bright yellow) and these colours are given in Part 2. On the edge of the page put a short red line across the page edge margin, next a blue and finally yellow. Remember, it is not always necessary to make use of all the material you find, an artist does not use every colour on his palette just because it is there — you are not obliged to do this — experience will give the best combination as this book cannot.

What can the reader expect from all this? A fair question but a difficult one to answer and I have had enough practise. In a world that seems at times to be having a nervous breakdown with probably more to come, perhaps the answer is that the angels offer a measure of peace, hope, stability and direction where there appears to be none or very little. The angels emerge as stability in a shifting world that seems to drift from one crisis to another, going with every new fad until a new one is found. Some I am sure (as I have) must have pondered the words of the Christ in *The Gospel According to Thomas*. 'If the flesh has come into existence because of the spirit, it is a marvel; but if the spirit has come into existence because of the body, it is a marvel of marvels. But I marvel how this great wealth has made its home in this poverty.' Log. 29

I have little doubt those undergoing the period that became know as the 'Black Death' here during through the 1300's thought their world would not get past that particular stumbling block of history but we are still here, though in saying this I do not hold the inhabitants of this planet to be indestructible or enduring for all time. There may well come a time when patience runs out somewhere and the cry heard is 'Enough'! 'No more!' I think we who populate the earth plane of this particular 'scheme of things' make one important error of judgement. We assume that the Creator's patience in acceptance of our shortcomings and lack of progress is limitless yet patience, whoever owns it is not an inexhaustible commodity. Further, I think that this is a mistake that could work against us and perhaps finally undo us but I hope of course, I am wrong.

Neither is it necessary for the world to end because we are no longer on it — another vanity — that we are necessary to the planet. When we find the sheet anchor of our life has been torn from its mooring, when we are adrift and seek stability, something or someone to hold on to that may answer our appeal to mediate on our behalf. It may possibly be then that the angels truly come into their own. Even the thought they are there is time and again comforting enough for many. From this kind of hope, very few are immune or self–sufficient, even though there are those who think they are. Yet, it is something that besets us all at sometime in our life, especially in the dark silent hours of the night just before the dawn, when everything seems twice as big and twice as ugly.

Faith is a term used to describe the attitude of the believer towards the object of their belief. This word has been beautifully defined by Saint Paul below. Although this definition is regarded as

Christian because of the book in which it appears — the **Bible** — nevertheless it would be a serious mistake to underestimate its wisdom because of this. Wisdom cuts across all barriers, it can apply to any faith and the mere covers of a book cannot imprison it or claim it as their own and if people think it can — this is poverty indeed. Wisdom or faith is not the exclusive property of any one group.

'Now faith is the substance of things hoped for,
The evidence of things not seen.
**Hebrews**. 11:1

Finally, going back to the beginning and what was said there. If after reading this closing paragraph of Part 1, the reader will take a look at the cover before moving on to Part 2 they will see that it was designed with a purpose and that purpose was given at the beginning on the opening pages. The work is called the **Summa Angelica** and that has already been explained. The words of the sub–title has been deliberately split up as the work has been and that was planned. The first part is 'The Angels . . . ' and this makes up Part 1 of the work, the section you are now finishing. The second part is ' . . . and their Magic' and this part makes up Part 2 of the work, which is the part we will be studying next. These two sections when together give us the purpose of the book and the book itself — **The Angels . . . and their magic**. Now let us move on to Part 2 where we will be found much to do and without doubt — it was not written for the idle.

# PART TWO:

# THE
# MAGIC

## PART TWO ... the Angels and their Magic.

'If there be for him an Angel to mediate,
One of a thousand,
To declare to man what is right for him,
Then He (= God) is gracious to him and says:
"Loose him for going down to the pit,
I have found a ransom." '
*Job* 33:23.

## THE PLANETS AND THEIR ANGELS

Now we must start to assemble our jigsaw and see how the pieces fit together into a workable whole to present an interconnected system. It is not as difficult as it appears and if this is new to the reader, there could considerable advantage in keeping the initial efforts of their work as simple as possible. You can add refinements and embellish later once the basics are firmly established. Always remember one thing, to break the rules you must first know them. What we are about to undertake is not unlike an attempt to ride your first bicycle. Easy for those who know how to do it, but a little daunting for those who may be taking their first steps in the matter?

When you started, in our example, you needed the confidence of knowing that someone was holding onto the saddle of your bicycle and keeping it stable, giving you their support, they would be there to catch you if you fell and this was so for most of us. One day your custodian decided you could go on your own and you were doing fine until you spoke to them and realized they were not there — then you lost your confidence — then you fell! What did they say to you next? 'Get up and get back on the bicycle straight away because that is the only way to learn' — it still is!

Throughout the work is given what the angels take care of in your life and in your world. Later will be found many of the things they rule such as trees, buildings, jobs, tools, people, professions, metals, perfumes, flowers, colours, gemstones, attitudes, feelings and so on because there is very little on earth that does not have a planetary rulership. Briefly, anger for Mars, love for Venus, eating well under Jupiter, eating little under Saturn, study, communication and reading under Mercury, enjoying yourself and socializing with others under Venus and so on. From the lists and suggestions given, it is relatively simple to select the angel whose help you are seeking for a particular matter or situation but sometimes you need something a little more personal in your life and your hopes and wishes.

Do you need help in writing in any form for example; the lists will show that the Archangel Raphael and the planet Mercury have such matters under their rule. Are you seeking help and guidance regarding writing, reading, education, facts, data, learning and the equipment associated with these matters again, seek the help of the Archangel Raphael (Gemini), especially if the information is regarding medical, dietary and health matters over which he also has rulership for this Archangel rules health matters in general and overall health (Virgo). If it is surgery, the Archangel Raphael cooperates with the Angel Samael, the Angel of Mars because this angel rules surgery, while the Angel Asariel of the planet Neptune rules anaesthetic and so on. You must be sensible in your appeals in these matters, for example, if you have lost a limb you cannot ask that a new limb grow in its place and expect it to be given just because you are petitioning an angel.

This is asking for something that will not happen and it is against Nature for human beings. You can ask for help for the best possible replacement to be found to enable you to get on with your life as efficiently as possible. The Angel Samael (= Mars, rules engineering, mechanics and strength) could be asked to assist with the finest construction and working. You can ask the Angel Anael (Venus= cosmetics and beauty) and the Angel Asariel (= Neptune, ruling illusion, who makes things appear what they are not) to find a replacement to will be as unobtrusive as possible. This example is given to illustrate that although the basic matter is a medical one that you can call upon other angels to add their portion to add to, assist and develop the fundamental requirement. However, in all matters do not make excessive demands even though they may be thought possible from the source petitioned, keep most of your invocations within the bounds set by the material plane you find yourself.

Are you seeking help or guidance from church, law, higher education, university, banking or insurance? Looking through the list will show that such matters come under the Angel Sachiel and the planet Jupiter.

Are you dealing with a death in the family or someone close, with all the duties, obligations and sadness that this entails? Such matters will be found under the Angel Cassiel and the planet Saturn, who rules death with all its associated matters, bereavement, cemeteries, the pine tree and the 'pine box,' old age, houses and estate.

Are you dealing with an affair of the heart in which you have lost your way or about which you are uncertain? This you will find is under the wings of the Angel Anael, who is the of the planet and Venus is the goddess of love and the affections. If it involves an older person than yourself, then ask the Angel Cassiel to add his wisdom to the love of the Angel Anael because the Angel Cassiel rules older and mature people. Always remember the possibility of love must either exist or be thought possible between both parties. Ask if any prospect of love that exists can be strengthened or if a bridge can be built between the two people involved.

Forget all these ridiculous and infantile spells, potions, herbs, lotions and incenses for 'commanding love.' One such incense claims 'sprinkle on the ground of a loved one and he will return to you' or it will 'compel the opposite sex to desire you.' Another tells you to 'sprinkle the incense on any person you wish to gain control over' and 'to place a spell upon someone you want to get even with.' This sort of thing sounds very grand and sell books, which it does because someone must be buying them or worse still — needing them! They are not found in any books that I write nor in the previously published book on *Ritual Incense*, which, at the time of writing is being revised as a new extended and edition.

Who in their right mind would want the kind of love that has to be commanded? If you have to command something to get it, you do not have it and never will because it was not freely given in the first place. If something is not freely given, you have taken it in some way and have something to which you have no right because it was and is under duress or subterfuge. Some things cannot be acquired in this way, especially regarding such matters as love, which has to be freely given or it is worthless, further you will lose it in the end and rightly so.

This is one of the ways that the lists should be used and you can extend them as your knowledge grows as many examples and hints follow. Do not be afraid to combine the angels because more than one angel may be involved as given in a short example above.

Love for the most part is ruled by the Angel Anael but if the affair involved someone younger than yourself, then add and invoke the Archangel Raphael of Mercury with the Angel Anael of Venus. If it involves someone who is older, this is under the Angel Cassiel of Saturn as given earlier.

Someone who is well established and mature in their middle age could involve Jupiter and his angel. If the person had an interest in occultism or astrology, then you could include the Archangel

Uriel of the planet Uranus because he is the angel who rules such matters and he always adds a touch of magic. If there is interest in Spiritualism, art, idealism then you should include the planets Moon or Neptune and their angels, who are the Archangel Gabriel of the Moon and the Angel Asariel of Neptune.

If the person involved is active, interested in sports, the martial arts, strenuous sport or in the Armed Forces, then add the Angel Samael of Mars, it is not as difficult as it looks, but do not strain the matter, use and experience will take over just as it did when learning to ride the bicycle in the opening example.

Now, even though I have given them above, you do not have to use combinations if you do not wish to do so. The purpose of the exercise above was to show that you can 'fine–tune' your efforts with the addition of other angels who rule elements that are involved in the matter. However, love is love no matter who is involved in the affair and love is primarily under the Angel Anael of Venus. Sometimes the Archangel Michael because this angel, his planet the Sun and his natural house in an astrological chart rules the 'physical heart and all the affairs of the heart. He also rules gambling and matters of chance including the gamble of love, which does not always pay off,' but when it does, the returns can be great.

Why give the all the above if it can be made as simple? To begin with to let the reader know these principles and alternatives can be applied to the matter in hand, the situation, its circumstance and that it is available for bringing into play should the reader wish to make use of them. Secondly, as said earlier, to show that your efforts can be given a form of 'fine–tuning' and we can give a better assessment of any situation when we have a greater command of what or who is involved — which is precisely what I am trying to do here. The greater the 'planetary or angelic vocabulary' the better you will be able to understand and say what is involved in the matter and make yourself understood and things you understand can be dealt with better.

In our everyday affairs, we unconsciously make use of astrological terms in our everyday speech. In the following, the reader will find lists of 'keywords' that are applicable to the planets rule, such as people, occupations and trades, colours, actions, perfumes and incense, gemstones, feelings and so on. You do not go to a food store to buy bricks; you go to a builders yard. Neither would you take your watch or clock to a plumber to have it repaired, nor should you expect to be able to do this. Normally you would go to a jeweller's where not only will you get what you want but you will be given advice regarding timepieces and service for your watch from their repair department because it is usually manned by people who know what they are doing regarding such matters.

It is much the same with matters related to human hopes and wishes when we need help and advice, we still have to know where to go to get or ask for that advice regarding these hopes and wishes. The principle involved is basically very simple in as much as you have to learn about who deals with what and not go to the wrong source. You will be surprised how quickly you begin to pick this up and it is important to know where to petition for what you seek and to whom. Let me suggest that you need not attempt to memorize these lists; use will familiarize you with them in the course of time.

Neither is there any need at this early stage, to read them all, though you can if you wish. Do not worry if you find some of the entries duplicated under different planets because quite often a matter is 'quite at home' with more than one planet and angel. This is not a mistake, marine matters are under the Moon and Neptune so use either, there is often a main source with support from elsewhere. You may decide as many do that the Moon is concerned more with seas and oceans, while Neptune is often given over to streams, rivers and lakes but the dividing line is not fixed and Neptune is a God of the Sea.

The pattern set is maintained for each planet and their planetary angels. These are short lists to help the reader begin their own. It was culled from the lists given in an earlier work *Talismans, Amulets and Charms* (*Regency Press* 1977) now much enlarged and being revised also for later printing I hope. These lists included occupations, objects, descriptions of things with people, situations, the actions they take and so on. Each of these categories is attributed to or is under the rule of a specific planet and its associated angel. This system seemed to be successful with readers of the other work, who found the method simple, so why complicate it with change for the sake of it?

The idea behind the original lists was to make the reader familiar with the diversity of matters the planet and angel rule. Showing some of the ways and areas that the planet operates and sometimes even what the planet can use in our lives. Incidentally, what is also being given are some of the 'signs' you may find after you have invoked or written your petition. It may be you are given or shown something that is in keeping with the planet and angels invoked. Unexpectedly or where you did not expect it — out of context — but coincidental with the petition or invocation, spoken about in greater detail later. You should add to the lists and personalize them. I repeat, do not, at this early stage if you are new to them, try to memorize them because drawing on them will make them familiar to you.


There are very few things in our lives that do not have a planetary rulership. So, let us start by giving some simple examples of how they were used in this work. This will help the reader understand the things the planet rules and to know the many signs that may be offered. In the examples that follow, we will show the principles involved and keep the examples straightforward. We will take one subject — buildings — and their planetary rulership.

The use of a building as well as its style often dictates the planet that rules both the building and its purpose. Abattoirs (slaughter, blood), barracks and military buildings or War Departments, areas used for manoeuvres are under the planet Mars including the military and what it uses, fighting, bloodshed and blood, guns, knives, protection, bullet–proof vests, protective armour and so on.

Pens, pencils, diaries, notebooks, envelopes, notepaper, books generally, textbooks for learning, and the places that sell them are under Mercury. The post, the people who deliver the post and post offices are also under Mercury. At one time, the winged figure of this deity Mercury in some form was prominent as some old post offices show — what we are using now in the British Isles I cannot imagine — perhaps the Pied Piper of Hamlin. I do not even know what it is and at the time of writing, the figure has neither rhyme or reason. Mercury is found on many of the uniforms of medical staff in the military or medical units of most countries.

Racing and breeding stables, gambling houses, churches, cathedrals, palaces, law courts, manors and grand houses are under Jupiter. Dairies, bakers and bakeries, breweries, shops and business that have to do with marine matters, boats, lines and sails, anchors and so forth are under the Moon and Neptune.

Occasionally in the descriptions, we have added words that are relevant to the planets and I have drawn attention to this and their use. When we remind someone of their duty, this is Saturn. When we speak of love and affection, this is Venus. When we suggest someone should use a more assertive approach in their life, this is ruled by a positive Mars. If we say they should control their temper a little more, the 'bad temper' is under a negative Mars and so forth. This is a fascinating subject and makes some conversations interesting beyond the surface meaning. Without deliberate eavesdropping in the usual sense, listening to the conversations of others and many you cannot avoid, say on train journeys, is an excellent and efficient exercise that passes both the time and increases learning.

All magnificent palaces, cathedrals, churches, ornate buildings, government buildings and buildings that are built on traditional or conservative lines. Prominent buildings built on high ground that dominates an area, sometimes at the end of a grand avenue, at other times protected and unapproachable by the public at large, places you 'go up to' as with the very rich are under the Sun and Jupiter (= often Government or Church).

Corner buildings are under Jupiter and these often deal in the things Jupiter rules like banks, public houses, wine–bars, insurance offices, off–licences, expensive or exclusive shops selling expensive lines, often one off creations and the like. These 'corner–site' buildings usually cost more to buy, insure, maintain and attract a higher business tax from the authority who administers the area — whatever they call it and these matters are generally associated with the planet. Jupiter usually means a lot of anything if he deals with it, whatever he gives — for good or ill — he is generous either way and either way there is usually a lot of it so take care what you ask for.

Many buildings when on a prominent corner location, especially in the older well–established areas were ornate, sometimes almost classical or baroque. They were well–built and substantial in their appearance to gives an air of stability and affluence, which is appropriate for banks and insurance offices. In new building developments, this design practise is ignored for the most and appropriate businesses seem to ignore this relevant position, which could assist them in their business. Even in small towns and villages, public houses, wine merchants and bars, banks and the like are often found on a corner site — 'the Jupiter site.' Obviously, as with all the things we will talk about throughout this work, there will always exceptions to the rule, which I accept and acceptance of the exceptions should be taken for granted in all the examples given throughout the work.

Under the rule of Venus are the shops and salons that deal with hair–dressing, clothes, jewellery, cosmetics and all things that benefit the overall appearance of people, their well–being, comfortable surroundings and their homes and area. There are premises that deal with the adornment of the home such as carpets, wall–coverings, furniture, lighting and so forth. Shops that supply the goods to make the home comfortable, relaxed and beautiful are also under the rule of Venus. In some areas, some of these shops can at times seem to be almost gaudy, 'over–dressed and over–painted,' which is a negative aspect of Venus, especially when she goes 'too far.' Alternatively, we often say of some places they need 'a face lift,' a 'lick of paint' or a 'cosmetic job' and again these are all terms of Venus.

Cramped premises and areas that are old, run–down with peeling paint, in need of repair or decoration and sometimes considered to be overcrowded and dingy are under the rule of Saturn. They are often found in the poorer parts of an area, perhaps down narrow, dark side streets, away from the bright lights, quiet, sometimes sombre. Undertakers funeral business's are under this planet because they deal with the end of someone's life (= Saturn) and the duty (= Saturn) of burial under earth (= Saturn). Cremation is a often a compound rulership with the death under Saturn while the fire of cremation is under Mars, leaving only the skeleton that brings us back to Saturn and the ashes are often scattered over the earth or buried under it somewhere (= Saturn).

If the 'fire' used for the cremation is gas then the means used are usually under Neptune who rules gas and oil while electricity is under Uranus and so forth and this primarily makes a crematorium under Saturn as a place dealing with the dead with Mars, Neptune or Uranus the means used, though it always ends with Saturn as ashes. The planet Saturn also rules the property, estate and land and the 'estate' to be dealt with after their owner is dead — all Saturn. Just as estates and estate agents, farms, agriculture, pits, caves and cavers all dealing with the earth. Learn to look for the 'components' that make things up, who rules them and then finding the 'rulers' will become so much easier and this can make a useful exercise while walking around — it was how I learnt.

As said, you can often find something under a dual–rulership, now and then there is a basic ruler and an secondary ruler and a good example of this is the ubiquitous quartz watch and clocks. Time and time–keeping are one of the things under Saturn's rule as is quartz that is the mineral used in these watches and both are under Saturn. The power to active and operate this accurate form of time keeping is stored electricity in the form of a battery that drives the exact electronics by the vibration of the quartz and the electricity and battery used and this is under Uranus, as is the admirable inventiveness of this form of time–keeping that is now produced so cheaply for all. This is an excellent example of dual–rulership of Saturn and Uranus, particularly as Uranus took over one of Saturn's Signs of the Zodiac — Aquarius. The reader can consult the lists for guidance on the particular matters and signs associated with a planet and their angels or archangels.

Now let us take some examples of how we can use this in our work. As said, we think the Internet is new and exciting and it is all this and more — but the Celestial Internet connecting everything was set in place a long time ago and it is even more exciting for that alone. In Anglo–Saxon times it was know as the **Web of Wyrrd**, but if you shake or disturb it in one place, you are not always sure where the reaction is felt, who feels it or what it may or may not bring, which could be in part, why we may not always get exactly what we are seeking, sometimes even after long experience, but we are getting better and what this work is attempting is to give you a few helpful 'addresses' to use.

Let us say you have petitioned the Angel of the Sun, the Archangel Michael and invoked for advancement in your career, you want to rise to a higher station. You check the lists to see the matters that are under the sway of this planet and its archangel. You do this to alert yourself to the mundane matters and objects that could be used as a 'sign' for you to become aware of the archangels possible interest in your petition. For example, it would not count, because the archangel rules 'royal' matters and items that fit in with royalty, if you deliberately strolled down the Mall to look at Buckingham Palace afterward undertaking your work. Likewise, it would not count if you deliberately petitioned the Archangel Michael just before you knew that you were going the Tower of London to see the crown jewels and the royal regalia, because you knew you were going there beforehand because this by my reckoning was manipulated.

**Prediction**, Latin **prædicere** precludes this by the meaning **præ**= 'before' **dicere**=' to say.' In other words — **prædicere** — 'saying before the event' or 'to tell beforehand' —to predict. The one thing I learned from Alistair Crowley was to use Skeat's **Etymological Dictionary of the English Language**; a work that was his regular companion for understanding words because it is important to have the correct meaning and understanding of them, which can usually be gleaned from how and why they are originally constructed because word meanings change over the years. I started early to do the same with words and I was most surprised the knowledge this added. Over the years, I have added other dictionaries and books of old words, some no longer used, from second–hand stores and given them a home to extend this practise.

There is now a well–know anecdote the when King George I first saw St. Paul's Cathedral in London for the first time he turned to Sir Christopher Wren and told him that his masterpiece was 'amusing, awful and artificial.' We may not regard this as not much of a compliment yet we are told that Sir Christopher was highly delighted with it. Perhaps this is because in Wren's time 'amusing' meant 'amazing'; 'awful' meant 'awe–inspiring or full of awe' and 'artificial' meant 'artistic' and this is why Wren was delighted.

Angels have responded in the past with the heavens parting and the radiance of the Glory flooding everything in sight with the heavenly luminous light of the **Shekinah** with heavenly choirs declaring its presence. Wonderful I agree but for the most, they will often use what is to hand — unless of course, you are the lucky one. Whatever is given or found has to be unexpected or fortuitous, a serendipity, but prominent, out–of–the–blue and persistent, more so than usual in your life. Something not expected, manipulated or planned because in such a case if you attempted such disreputable pettifoggery and trickery, I am sure that the angel or archangel would not respond at all and I would second such a resolve. To think in this manner is patently asinine as no such confirmation is being given because the 'signs given' are being stage–managed by you or others and anyone doing that and accepting this as proof of intent is fooling no one but themselves and in my opinion people and groups that do this patently deserve each other.

After writing your petition if you received a postcard from a friend that had pictures of royal palaces or royal regalia on the front, not necessarily even the British royal collection, this could be viewed in a different perspective and this is because the card and the subject were unexpected and you could regard it as possibly 'number one.' It was chosen by someone else, out of your hands and not planned. It was a coincidence, more of this word later because it is important.

If friends say, returning from holiday, brought you a vase, a brooch, a pendant, candlesticks or any present in the shape of a crown or with crowns on them, royal insignia or if they had images of the Sun or sun–disks on them. This could be regarded as a possible **connected–coincidence** regarding your invocation because they were chosen casually for you and not by any influence or stage–management by you. The present brought for you coincided with the circumstances and was not manipulated. The main criterion is that it should not be controlled by you in any way.

Of course, to attempt to organize the event by suggesting you would like such a present from them before they left for their holiday requires no comment from me that could be printed. I am sure such perfidy would be noted by the recipient of the invocation that is sent upwards and would be dealt with accordingly — downwards.

Common sense must prevail and a sharp eye kept for any deception, particularly for that constantly alert adversary called self–deception, which is ever present, widespread and extremely clever. Self–deception can bend and crop anything to make it fit and it can be hard to detect if you really do not want to do so or your desire blinds you, but at what cost?

Do the mighty angels and archangels use such simple devices as this? Is this really the way these mighty Angels and Archangels of God work? Is he telling me they cannot do better than this? Is the writer somewhat over–simplifying the matter and the method or is he simple–minded himself? Such questions would not surprise me because for some time I thought the same when it was first presented to me. Until experience taught me that for the most, the angels do not usually draw attention to themselves but quietly go about their business and I wisely learnt to do likewise. There are many ways in which the confirmation of a petition or invocation can be offered to you and it is reasonable to question if it is genuine or not, it is not only reasonable — it is the correct thing to do.

Things are not often given personally or with great splendour, but this does mean they could not be. More often, than not the angels will use what is to hand and they often use the 'library' they find within someone so, the bigger the 'library within,' the bigger the 'vocabulary' they have at their disposal to use. We use simple terms to children according to their understanding but persist with this into their teens and adult life and you will soon be told 'do not talk to me as if I am a child!' There are many reasons why 'signs' can often be overlooked, missed or dismissed altogether as being too trivial or trite, like something precious mixed in with the detritus or the proverbial needle in the haystack. You must not however, strain or force something to fit the mould of what you think is acceptable or what you would like it to be and sometimes this can be hard when times are desperate.

You have to be alert and prudent with what you are given or what you think you are being given —if you are given nothing —admit it and accept the fact by saying so. Further more, it has to be more than once, several times in fact and three is my minimum, persistent, out of the ordinary among the 'usual run of things.' Such things should alert you to the possibility that your awareness could be trying to be attracted. The *Moral Sayings* of Pubililius Syrus, a Syrian mimic poet and originally a slave, who flourished about 44 B.C. In what remains of his 'moral sentences' (some four hundred I believe) he counsels ' . . . it is well to moor your ship with two anchors' — I am suggesting that three 'anchors' would be better.

You could be looking for something that has the fundamental characteristics of a miracle on a smaller and not as grand but for many it is enough. This of course does not mean the angels could not use a miracle for their purpose, but what I am suggesting is that you are looking for something akin to the philosophy we apply to miracles, rather than a miracle itself. A miracle is frequently thought of as something that causes wonderment and given to an event that cannot be understood as being part of the natural order and sometimes this is precisely what the angels use.

In the beginning look for signs often use the natural order of things and what is to hand. Signs and symbols are necessary to comprehend the abstract and they are at times the only means of expressing abstract thoughts and incidents, something that can span the Middle Ground and be understood at both ends but more here at ours, after all they know what they are sending. Signs and symbols may testify to realities — but reality must be able to translate the signs and symbols because they mean nothing unless the reality behind them is understood. This is sometimes why they are not observed because they are taken as just 'another coincidence' and of little consequence. We will discuss the way the word 'coincidence' is commonly regarded later and the disparaging layer that now obscures it.

St Augustine believed miracles were expressions of the Will of God and a miracle was not contradictory to nature — it was due more to our imperfect knowledge of nature. Thomas Aquinas and 'the Schoolmen' continuing on similar lines thought there were two Orders in Nature. The order that was known to us and the order that was known to God. Those events properly called miracles seemed to contradict the lower order, because they were expressions of the higher order, known to God. Playing the heretic, we mention Spinoza, who followed the French philosopher Gersonides (Levi ben Gersonides) 1288–1344, the successor to Maimonides who, while defending miracles, limited their role. Spinoza argued that miracles could not happen since the Laws of Nature and the decrees of God are the same and any transgression of the Order of Nature would mean that God was contradicting himself.

Keep your 'Devil's Advocate' on permanent stand–by in case he is required in these matters, better to be thought a fool than be one. It is far better, in this particular area of endeavour to stand on the sometimes solid rock of disappointment, than sinking fast into the shifting sands of deception where all things die. Human hopes and aspirations can be wide open to manipulation and dishonesty because of the high expectations and hope it creates, which is understandable. It is something we want to happen and very few are immune from this no matter how hard and practical we want to appear to the world. Of course, this is why the manipulation of advertisements are so successful, even though some are akin to 'legalized mugging' but we hand them success on a plate by wanting it to be, so do not be too hard on yourself.

Again, do not try to force something to 'fit' because if you do the only one who is being fooled is you. Remember the crystal slipper in the fairy–tale *Cinderella*, those who tried to make the crystal slipper fit were trying to get something to which they were not entitled. They were found out, made to look foolish. They were termed 'ugly' in the tale, they became the object of ridicule and in the pantomime although we laughed at them, we forgive them in the end because there is a little of them in everyone.

Remember, 'one swallow does not a summer make.' I personally prefer to find a minimum of 'three swallows,' natural signs or *connected–coincidences* to be satisfied enough to start taking an interest in the matter. In time, experience will tell you what is working for you and what is not, if it is not right, it will not seem right. Books and teachers can give you the knowledge but they cannot give you the wisdom or their experience, not even this one. These things you have to hew out for yourself and learning what is wrong is the start of learning what is right. Sometimes the signs are quick in coming but if they take a long time appearing, so that you have to strain to find them and make them apply, then you should become guarded and feel this does not augur well for success in this particular venture. Not everything tried achieves success, even when it is sincere, well intended and well done so a time arrives when we have to let go.

## Coincidence

If you consider your invocation has been acknowledged or answered, there are some that will tell you that it was 'merely a coincidence.' Your answer to this is that this is precisely what it was — 'a coincidence' but not 'merely a coincidence' — at least not in the way your detractor means it. The word 'coincidence' has taken on a somewhat derogatory meaning today that assumes that 'it would have happened no matter what and only a fool would regard it as anything else, you are not only grasping at straws, you are deluding yourself.'

The word 'coincident' is from the Low Latin, *coincidens*= 'falling together' pr. par. of *coincido*= 'to fall together.' Coincidence is 'anything that coincides, corresponds or happens at the same time with another; a coinciding or corresponding combination of circumstances.' Figuratively: 'Happening at the same time, coinciding with, concurrent.' Coincidence is something that 'falls together' and I regard these matters as happening 'with the incident' and therefore 'as planned' and so 'not due to chance.' *Incident* from the Latin *incidens*, pr. par. of *incido*= 'to fall on, to happen' and *co*= 'with' and *incido*= 'to happen' or 'to happen with.'

As far as I am concerned if something happens frequently and is connected to what is being done and sought, it can be considered as being 'coincidental' without the disparaging overlay of 'merely.' To some coincidences are regarded as being simply chance acts that just happen. To those who know how to look deeper they can be evidence of possible contacts being made and listening to others over the years, I think 'significant' coincidences take place more than people are prepared to admit. In part, dismissal of them usually springs from the fear of ridicule or the charge that they are going soft in the head, simple minded, clutching at straws and being deluded so, do not tell them — I don't!

It is not 'a concurrence' in the sense of being 'purely casual.' An action usually causes a reaction somewhere and we are trying to see that our 'reaction somewhere' is as beneficial as we can make it and that the reaction is in keeping with the result(s) we seek in our actions by sending the matter to the right place, a 'controlled reaction.' Coincidences are events, little or large, that cannot always be explained or proven, but if enough of them occur in connection with something else, they alert the wise.

Carl Gustav Jung was enthusiastic about the concept of 'synchronicity' and so was the world including me, we have all used the word apace since then. He stressed the connection of apparently dissimilar or chance events with every other event they occurred with, he insisted that this simultaneous link was significant. It was not just a matter of coincidence. For the theory of synchronicity, there is no such thing as 'mere coincidence' in matters of import in your life.

 If the reader looks back over their life, I am sure they will recognize moments in time when this could be applied without any distortion or bending the facts to make them fit. The claim of synchronicity is that these 'coincidences' were not linked to the event merely because (afterwards) they 'happened at the same time' — but 'because they were influenced by and linked to the event.' The guaranteed way of missing such things is an insistence of not believing such things or a resolve to believe that such things do not exist.

We say again that for Jung, there was no such thing as a 'mere coincidence' in the important, uncanny and significant incidents or events in our lives. This is of course, why he placed so much faith in that wonderful work called — *I Ching* — translated as the *Book of Change*. This book has been my constant companion for many long years and long before it had its deserved popularity, starting with the James Legge, though it has been 'updated and made relevant for our times' it seems, though I have never considered there was ever a time when it was without relevance. I always felt that it was a wonderful and 'a most ingenious paradox' that the subject of this wonderful work is that change is one of the permanent and most dependable laws of my life.

The allegation that anything that has happened is 'merely a coincidence' may be resorted to once, perhaps even twice, but when the elements coincide repeatedly — coincidence may be considered more in line with conformity — rather than mere chance. Start taking notice of 'coincidences,' when, where, how they appear and work in your life. Do not take them for granted, many think coincidences are set in our lives to be helpful and point out things that could prove important. If 'coincidence' increases in your life while doing work of this nature or in prayer, it often suggests that you could be on the right path. This is why it is important to note them and not to dismiss them out of hand, never forget that when you are swimming against the current — you are usually going toward the source.


This line of thought brings us, as you would expect to premonitions or presentiments. These can take many forms and from time to time, they are a forewarning of an imminent event or to give warnings of danger or misfortune. Often they take on a prophetic feeling that some calamity is about to happen, which prevents or advises people from taking car journeys, using trains, ships or aircraft. Premonitions are not the same as pre–vision, presentiments are strong feelings rather than any visualization of the event and sight is not always concerned in the process.

Events on the physical plane may be heralded by causes that may not be perceptible to our physical senses, yet our more subtle, inner senses are conscious of them and it is trying to make us listen — a *Bat Qol* or the 'still small voice' if you will, as discussed in Part 1. Some people and a lot of animals have had premonitions of events long before it arrives, particularly earthquakes or tremors and in China, even today, certain animal behaviour is noted and considered reliable and relevant. On this and similar occasions the inner senses can recognize an event before it takes place on the physical plane and such cases are far too numerous and recorded for them to be lightly dismissed as being imaginary or 'mere coincidence.'

When the above becomes a mature, customary or a more reliable process it was usually considered to have developed into the Art of Prophecy. This is the power of predicting the future through mystic revelation or by possessing a knowledge of the cyclic laws often involved. Those versed in the latter can predict future cataclysms and events as positively as astronomers predict eclipses and predictive astrology (when it concerns future events) could be included in this heading. The word prophet originally meant one who speaks for another, this was usually a deity or Yahweh and this view is established throughout the *Old Testament* and other works

I have (often instinctively) held that **connected–coincidences** are more than just chance signs and regard them as a small part of the Cosmic Law and Web that all can be privy to at times and it is my terminology for them. They exist for a purpose but have no meaning for those who 'see but do not perceive.' If you try to instigate, alter, seek, wish or hope for certain circumstances in your life there is a good chance that coincidence will play its part in the affair. With this particular kind of work, you are attempting to change the matrix or the important relationships and matters of your life in some way. When you attempt to do this, you make 'waves or vibrations' because for something to happen something must move and change, it cannot remain static and change — that is a **non sequitur**. You make a vibration in one area and it is reflected elsewhere. The secret could be knowing how and where to make it, sent it and remove chance and the accidental as much as possible. Let us extend these thoughts about the 'vibrations' that are set up, the how and why.

Three giant maidens came from Giantland' in the Golden Age of German mythology and it is said they ended the Golden Age and this is because they brought with them — Time. They took time and divided it into three distinct elements. Urdr was the 'past' sometimes 'fate,' Verdandi was the 'present' sometimes 'necessity' and Skuld the 'future' sometimes 'being.' Together these three were known as the Norns or Nornir (**norn**= 'she who whispers) — the Nordic Fates — the spae–wives who determine a person's fate on earth from the moment they are born. Note the triad of the sisters, just as there are three groups of three in the angelic scheme of the pseudo–Dionysius. Spae/spay= 'to foretell, to foretell or divine to forebode.' A spae–man is a fortune–teller, a prophet, a soothsayer and the female the spae–woman. (Scottish).

Their home was the **Well of Urdr** that was found under the third root of Cosmic Word Tree — **Yggdrasil**. They are described in the **Prose Edda** as the daughters of Davalin, a dwarf who may have been one of the original guardians of the sacred tree. It does not seem unreasonable to suggest, as others have done, these sisters may have been a college of sibyls at Asgard whose students may have included the Valkyries.

The tradition of wandering wise women casting the fates of children and others may well have arisen from this, as well as godmothers or the spiteful hags in fairy tales. These weird sisters put in an appearance in Shakespeare's **Macbeth** when they forecast the future for Macbeth. The clarity of it all was not clear to the future Thane of Cawdor at the time because it had not arrived, which seems to be the way of most prediction, until it was shown how to how Birnham wood 'shall come against him' naturally he thought, how can a wood uproot itself and 'come against' me. Shakespeare gets it right (as usual) when Macbeth asks these ambassadors of Time and Fate. 'What is't you do? They reply as one voice 'A deed without a name.' Any deed without a name is something that is not manifest and if it is not manifest, it cannot be named until it is called forth from the future to be marked in the present or if it comes forth of its own volition.

Now, how does this assist us? The first clue is in calling them the 'weird sisters' as this brings the matter into the Anglo–Saxon because the Anglo–Saxons called Urdr by the name of Wyrd and this name is interpreted as 'fate' or 'destiny.' The power possessed by these three sisters or the **Wyrdes** or **Weirds** is immensely tenacious, as is the **Web of Wyrd** — as said, the 'internet' or 'web' is far from new, at least in principle.

The arrival of Christianity did little to weaken their power for a very long time and as you can see, it has not disappeared even in our day and it seems to be gathering strength. Today the expression is often put to use for witches and soothsayers or at least it was in Scotland as written above regarding the Spae–wives. The Anglo–Saxons would often see things as being connected by the *Web of Wyrd* and a 'vibration' in one place would be felt elsewhere by those who could feel it. The Creator of the Web, like the spider, always keeps in touch through one strand so that any 'vibrations' were felt when they were created no matter where from. I am sure that the *Web of Wyrd* spanned (or could be found) on the Middle Ground. Was it the Anglo–Saxon and northern tribe's method of negotiating this unknown territory to contact their Gods or the deities' messengers, which is a constant theme of this work?

In Nordic lore, the Nine Worlds form the Cosmos are all placed on the *Web of Wyrd* between roots and branches of the cosmic tree Yggdrasil.

1) *Asgard* is the land of the Gods.
2) *Ljossalfheim* is the world of the star elves, space.
3) *Muspellshheim* is the land of fire. It may refer to the Aurora Borealis or simply that the inhabitants had red hair.
4) *Vanaheim* is the land of fertility spirits;
5) *Svartalfheim (Svart-Hiem)* is the land of the elf smiths or black elves. These dwarfs play a very important role in Nordic myth because they are the artificers, craftsmen and inventors. They seem to have a similar relationship with the Celts and Slavs. These people had the skills and arts of working bronze and iron as well as precious metals.
6) There is *Midgard*, the middle ground or Earth that contained *Mannheim*—'the world of men' that was not inhabited by the dwarfs or giants. Midgard is set between *Svartheim* — the land of the dwarfs or elves and *Jotunnheim* the land of the giants—'between' these two lands, not above and below as written here. The *Midgard Serpent* spawned by Loki was known as Jormungard. Thor is often depicted fishing for this creature, which he finally kills.
7) *Jotunheimr* is the land of the giants. *Jötun* is the German appellation for gigantic demonic beings that possess enormous strength
8) *Niflheim* is a land of cold, mists, ice and fog. Some think this may have been based upon the description of hunters and raiding parties caught by the severe winter in the frozen wastes of the Arctic.
9) *Helhiom* is the Underworld where the spinning goddess Urd(r), the chief of the Nordic Fates though she may have been titular head of a college of sibyls at Asgard. She weaves the web and lives with her sisters at the foot of at the foot of the Tree Yggdrasil.

We have given the nine kingdoms above numbers to account for them but these numbers do not imply any approved or accepted order, nor must they be taken as such. Some of the order as given is implied within the descriptions, for example, *Asgard* is the 'land of the Gods' at the top, *Midgard* (= the 'middle ground or earth') is central while *Helhiom*, the 'underworld' has been set at the bottom. It should be pointed out that many world philosophies seem to have their 'serpent.' In Nordic mythology there was Nidhöggr (= the 'Dragon of Envy'), described as a 'corpse–eating demon' who is found in the underworld. He gnaws without rest the roots of *Yggdrasil* — the World Tree — threatening to bring it and all creation down, we still have a few of these people loose in the world today. As I have commented many times before, Chaos was here first and driven out by order and it wants its world back and returned to its original state, before Order was imposed on it from outside — ' . . . and the earth was without form and void; and darkness was upon the face of the deep. *Genesis*.

Many of the above 'kingdoms' contain nature spirits, the Elementals are said to exist within Nature and this is a common belief in most cultures throughout history. They are normally invisible to human beings unless they choose otherwise and are a part of the 'Life Force' so, 'may the Force be with you' was equally not new but very old. They are often found being ruled by the archangels and angels in Western Tradition and others for the most. They are by and large regarded as being benevolent but this does not mean that this convention cannot be totally reversed as the records show.

Nine is a magical number in the tradition and lore of so many of the nations of old because 'it is the number of fullness.' One example, taken from a future project on the magic and mythology of trees almost complete, tells us of a spring beneath the sea. This spring is fabled to be the origin of the river Shannon and under the spring, the magic lore of Segais could be discovered. Growing over the spring is found the 'poet's music–haunted hazels' and these were the nine hazels of Segais that bore the 'nine nuts of poetic art.' They grow in the 'land of promise,' in the red sunrise of the dawn on the edge of a well. The poet who eats these nuts learns a new style of poetic composition because they are 'the hazels of inspiration and wisdom.' Celtic paganism associates the hazel with fire, fertility, poets and poetry.

In astrological charts, the Eleventh House was called by old astrologers the 'House of Hopes and Wishes.' In early astrology, the Eleventh House was ruled by Saturn originally and you got your 'luck' only if you had earned it with a life of responsible and accountable living. Today the Eleventh House is given over to the planet Uranus who is a somewhat erratic planet to say the least. Uranus, discovered in 1781 by Herschel hence this name is found in some old ephemeredes is the complete opposite of Saturn because Uranus makes changes sometimes necessary and sometimes whimsical. You can rarely make changes without a break with the past (= Saturn) and even hazarding the future at times. Uranus moves swiftly when he acts and he is more arbitrary in giving his gifts and blessings, giving them or taking them away with equal fancy hence the greater stress on 'luck.' There seems to be a far greater element of chance in this particular area now when reading the expectations of very old books of astrology before Saturn was removed from this Sign of the Zodiac and Uranus took charge.

The Eleventh House of the astrological chart deals with the intangibles of life: your hopes, wishes, friendships, 'unbonded' relationships (= those who are not bound to us by the ties of family or marriage), which also makes it he 'House of Associations.' Most of the things found in the Eleventh House cannot be felt, weighed or measured, apart from the earnings you get from your career (Tenth House), but you know they are present in your life because of their results and influence. The cusps of any House are the lines drawn in the chart to show where a House begins and ends. This starting cusp is the threshold or the 'Gate of the House' because to enter that House a planet has to cross it. Planets found in the third house are often people and events that are 'in your neighbourhood' and when they approach or are close to the cusp of the fourth house, they may knock on your door — 'we were in the neighbourhood so we thought we would call in.'

Imagine this 'Eleventh Gate' as a good strong door, which it is and it is equally a door that cannot be stormed by force, so you can forget the example of the Walls of Jericho because it will not work here. Set in the middle of this door is a large combination lock and unless you have the 'combination' for your particular 'hope or wish,' the door will remain unassailably shut. However, you could ask for help through your Angelic Work and Invocations.

Let us assume in your life a sequence of 'connected meanings' began to line up (= *connected–coincidence'*) regarding the 'treasures' of the Eleventh House. This could be the sequence needed to open the combination lock or Kamea of the door. With a few gentle clicks, the combination lock operates and imperceptibly the door opens slightly. You may not even notice this because the gap is so small. You may even choose to ignore it but do not become upset if you miss it — after all it is just another of those meaningless coincidences that are of no consequence and can be ignored.

A degree of common sense must be used in interpreting the short lists that follow, the full lists are in *Talismans, Amulets and Charms*, which like earlier works I hope to reissue in the future. When you see that the Moon and the Archangel Gabriel have rulership over the 'willow tree,' it does not usually mean you will be given a fully–grown tree. The gift of a young willow sapling for your garden can be given by friends. You could be given some twigs with catkins that have been picked for you to display in a floral display. You could be given willow catkins represented as jewellery or a small representation of the willow tree. However, there would be little point in regarding the willow tree that you pass every day in your road for years as a sign because it has been there a long time. However, if I had written an invocation to the Archangel Gabriel I would give it a discreet but respectful nod as I passed by the tree in future. So, what could be regarded as a sign?

If, after you had written your invocation to the Archangel Gabriel, you were taken to a place on an overcast day where you had never been before and you came across a small group of willows around a small lake. If I saw these trees were suddenly bathed in the only strong shafts of sunlight to be seen, as if the sun was pointing them out, I would at least take notice. These particular occurrences are called the 'Fingers of God' because this name was given to such beams of sunlight that were often seen in Renaissance paintings, they often fall on an important building or place in the painting. I have always liked the effect in art very much but I was lucky enough several years ago to be arriving in Florence during the tail end of a storm.

We got there and were looking down upon the city when the rain storm suddenly stopped. Through the clouds edged with red and gold, the 'Fingers of God' broke through pointing to the dome of the cathedral only. I must admit, I have long loved the effect in paintings but it was the first time I had ever seen it in life. I felt I now knew the full meaning of the phrase and was sad to see it go as the clouds opened up to the blue sky. So, look for the 'Fingers of God' if you are attempting to deal with the Archangel Michael, whose planet is the Sun.

Is this light on the willows merely a coincidence? No, I would regard it as a connected–coincidence and 'sign number one perhaps?' Then I would be more alert for the possibility of finding signs two and three, which is my way of thinking and working because I like to find a minimum of 'three worthwhile coincidences' if possible and I now would be very careful in case I tried to make something fit.

Is this a fanciful scene stretching the point to make it fit the theory being expounded? Is not this one of the things against which I have been warning the reader? Am I ignoring it myself? If you think that, then you are just the one who may miss what is being given. If, having sent out your 'invitation' and you want the angels to come in, then try answering the door to see whose knocking, it could be them. Better still, leave it on the latch but as always, check the credentials of all callers. There are some that will try to gain entrance from other levels of existence in 'borrowed clothes.'

Let us define the words 'commit' and 'commitment.' Gurdjieff often did this in his works so there was no confusion in the meaning of the word he was using in his Work and how he meant it to be taken. If he used a word in his writing, it only had the meaning the Work said it had, there was no ambiguity and I have always liked his method because it often tells us much about the word being used. Therefore, 'commit' is from the Latin *commito= com*; *con*= 'with' and *mitto*= 'to send. 'To entrust, to give over in charge or in trust.' Commitment= 'The act of entrusting or delivering to one's charge or care' and this is precisely what I feel we are endeavouring to do in this work regarding some aspects of contact with the angels.

Let spend a few moments with the great German poet, playwright and novelist, Goethe (1749–1832.) Of interest to us are his comments on **Commitment** because they can also be tied in with 'coincidence' and I feel it has a bearing on the theme of this work.

He wrote ' . . . concerning all acts of initiative (and creation), there is one elementary truth the ignorance of which kills countless ideas and endless plans. The moment one definitely commits oneself, then Providence moves too. All things occur to help one that would never otherwise have occurred. A whole stream of events issues from the decision, raising in one's favour all manner of unforeseen incidents, meetings and material assistance, which no man could have dreamed would come his way . . . boldness has genius, power and magic in it . . . begin it now.'

If you find several *connected–episodes* (= *coincidences*) lining up in your affairs, there is a possibility that a 'connected–coincidence' has made an entry into your life, dealings and for a precise reason. You ignore certain forms of coincidence at your possible loss — but being able to recognize the right ones is an art gained by experience and only experience — what or who else can teach you?

I normally never give examples of a personal nature because, as with religious experiences and all events of such a personal nature I believe they are valid first and foremost only to the person to whom they happened. Further, at times they can be quite irrelevant to the reader because this sort of thing is what they want to experience for themselves. I do not believe they want to read pages upon pages about these matters regarding what has happened to someone else, including me, whose word they have to take on trust regarding the matter.

I think, no matter how well intended, many pages of experiences given to prove the point of a work or experiment can be at times discouraging, which is probably the opposite effect to what was intended. However, I will give just one very short example of what I mean only because it was pertinent and clearly and simply stated so it may have some value but more important, it was witnessed by my companion. I normally never write of episodes in my life where 'things happen.' In this rare instance, I will suspend my own convention because it has some bearing on the subject in hand.

While writing the manuscript that would become **Pan, Great God of Nature**, I hit a very fallow period for several very long days and things were not easy and the driving force present seemed to have departed before the first draft was done. Naturally, everyone has such periods and they think they will never write/paint/compose/sing again. Discussing the work and the problem over a meal with the dedicatee of the work and close confident over many years, though at the time she did not know she was the dedicatee, we left the restaurant. We were walking down a crowded Charing Cross Road in London. The street was very busy with people preparing for Christmas and only shop and street lighting as it was late mid December and very dark.

I said to my companion that I wish Pan would show me in some way that he was satisfied with the work done or at least that he found the direction being taken acceptable. If only he would show me this in some simple way that I could understand it would be so helpful and encouraging at this low period. After we had taken a some more steps in silence, my companion pulled me up suddenly and pointing down at my feet, she said 'Do you mean like that?' I could see something small on the pavement at my feet but whatever it was it was in the reading part of my bifocals and the street not well lit so I could not see what it was. She bent down, picked up whatever it was, told me to hold out my hand and stood a small plastic goat in centre of my palm. The goat was attractively formed, the sort usually found in a child's farmyard set.

We said very little walking back to the flat. The little goat stands on a table and I treasure it very much. The work progressed to the printing from that evening onwards and with little trouble I thought. Later, when the work was published, I received a very generous and complementary hand–written note regarding the Pan work from the American writer William S. Burroughs saying he was so pleased to read the book, he liked it and it was nice to know 'that Pan was not lost — only mislaid!' I sent him my sincere thanks for his kindness without delay, it was a delightful thing to do, the more so for being totally unexpected from a writer I did not know. Sadly he died later in the year but it was a very generous gesture on his behalf.

Was this a coincidence that started the above train of events? Yes, it was because it came in answer to a direct and sincere request and gave me more than I hoped for! It came or 'coincided' as a direct reply to a question or request formulated and spoken out loud to a close companion in a crowed street. This time there was an immediate answer to the request for confirmation. All the elements of question, time, place and an appropriate answer slotted into a textbook conclusion that could not have been manipulated so perfectly even with planning. Most important of all and this I cannot help you with, it felt right and when something 'feels right' for you — it is, but of course it was really just a mere coincidence. Now let us leave our little diversion and return back to the work in hand.

On the list of Mars and the Angel Samael, the reader will find he rules the panther, wolf and other hunting and guarding animals. There are many ways of representing this animal and I think you will be pleased to know the angels do not usually deliver the live animal into your lap to show you they have taken note. Powerful dreams frequently arrive at the appropriate time — just 'mere coincidence' of course. There can be day–dreaming with strong imagery or catching 'something' out of the corner of your eye. The ways that exist for the Powers to accomplish such things are limited only by you — most certainly not by them. For they are the ones who have to work with what is available on the physical lever.

No matter how wonderful we think it would be, to some the appearance of an angel in full splendour could scare some people half to death. This could have the same effect as the appearance of Zeus in full splendour to Semele, when she was tricked by the jealousy of Hera into demanding that her lover appear 'in his true shape.' Hera knew that Zeus had sworn this in the throes of ardent love and burning desire, to grant whatever Semele asked for. If it had the same result as the tale of Semele to us, it would somewhat defeat the purpose of coming. We have to accept that they will choose the method, the sign, the time, the place and that they know best.

It needs considerable caution, because it is very hard to lay down hard and fast rules regarding such matters and neither do I wish to disparage the claim of help given to other people. There are times when things were desperate in the extreme and it has been said 'I don't know how I got through it or managed?' Yet, you did because somehow help came in one form or another but was that because you did not give up at the first hurdle. You jumped them all, knocked a few of them down, but got through that particular obstacle course. All right, you may have come in last — but you stayed the course and more important — finished the race.

There are those situations that cause you to say 'my Guardian Angels must have been looking after me then!' An object found or given coincidental to your problems that helps you to go on in spite of appearances and obstacles or alternatively something warns you to withdraw or what to do. A book that appears when you need it most, which is the story of my life thank goodness and one gift horse I never look in the mouth.

Another thing many experience is money or help that appears as a gift or a 'windfall' when needed most. A windfall is a gift brought down 'by the wind' like 'fruit from a tree.' A windfall means 'an unexpected piece of good fortune, as an unexpected legacy.' The 'Walker on the Wind' is the Archangel Raphael, the Messenger of the Gods of the planet Mercury. Blessings from Hermes were called **ἑρμαιόν, hermaion**= 'a gift from Hermes, good luck, an unexpected find in the road, a windfall.' Is this a too simple an explanation and only fit for children? Well, it will be found that the Archangel Raphael and the planet Mercury also rules 'children.

As said earlier in the work some of the things mentioned in the lists may never be used, but they are given to paint as broad a picture of the source you are trying to contact as possible. Some of the things given are to help you to make further connections and one of the most important things you can do is connect This is done in the hope it will lead to a greater understanding of what is under the rulership of an angel and its planet. The original lists were of far greater length but what has been omitted was of greater import to talismans, amulets and charms, which was the subject of the earlier book.

I repeat, the ways are many so that the presentation of symbolism can be accomplished and you will have to keep alert to all the possibilities that can present themselves to you. Some you can accept almost without question others you hold in abeyance, while some can be dismissed. This said, always remain aware of whom you are trying to deal with because they are far more ingenious than we could ever be in such matters. We practise these arts within our anticipated three score years and ten, they have been doing so from the beginning of Creation itself.

## SUN:

The day of the Sun is Sunday and the Archangel Michael. The Sun's gemstone is the diamond, most yellow or golden varieties of any stones. The metal is gold and this is the setting for all solar jewels. The Sign of the Zodiac is Leo. The colours are gold, gilt, orange or dark yellow. His perfumes include; frankincense (= olibanum), heliotrope, laurel, acacia, ambergris, balsam, red sandalwood. Some of the things that he rules are:

Amber; Apollo (= the Greek Sun God); authority benign or otherwise; bay trees; royal circle at the theatre; brocades and rich materials, perhaps with gold thread; career and ambition; children; crowns and all objects made in this shape; a lover; diamonds; despots; desert plants and trees; fame and fortune; fine wines and rare liqueurs; fire and flames; frankincense; gambler; gambling and speculation, anything where the outcome is uncertain; brokers; executives; those in charge of things; genuine things, not copies or imitations; gilt and gilded objects; gold and objects of gold like rings, necklaces, bracelets or pendants; goldsmiths; gold–leaf; gold plate and plating; golden tinsel; government; the father or the head of large organizations; the heart and heart–shaped; the chest or torso of men; lion; the Law, of the land or tribe; lords; magistrates; mansions; marigold; monarchs; orange (the colour, fruit and tree); men in general; palm tree; parks; peacock and its feathers; pedigree (people and animals); privy council; places of entertainment and amusement; Ra (= Egyptian Sun God); rare (as with things of which there is only one or very few; rank and position; royal and royalty (coach, crown, sceptre and the like); the spine; the stage (= theatre);

entertainers; sun discs or shapes that represent the sun; sundials; theatre, the theatrical and theatrical performances; sunflower; throne; walnut tree and walnuts.

## MOON:

The day of the Moon is Monday and the Archangel Gabriel. The Moon's gemstones are the moonstone, pearls, the opal, milk–stone, white stones and in particular crystals. The metal is silver and this is the setting for lunar jewels. The Sign of the Zodiac is Cancer. The colours are silver, white, cream and the palest of greens. The perfumes include; white sandalwood, mandrake, frankincense (the same incense is often used for more than one planet so this is not a mistake), camphor, ginseng and jasmine. Some of the things the Moon rules are:

Babies and the very young; bakers and baking; boats, boating and boathouses; business's dealing with the public at large; grocers and groceries; housewife and housework; those who deal with dairy products; obstetrics; the stomach and breasts; sailors; canals; candles; china and chinaware; coronet or crown, especially when made of silver or a silver colour; crabs; crescent or crescent–shaped objects, especially when silver or white; Diana (= Italian Goddess identified with Artemis); fishermen; fish with scales; fishing; fountains; geese and goose; glass and glassware; harbours; homes and home–making, houses or anything that encloses or protects; Isis (= Egyptian Moon Goddess); lakes; lighthouse; maritime (= the sea and inland waterways); the mother and motherhood; family; feminine; night animals, night birds and flowers; owls; oysters; ponds and pools; public at large; rivers; sea, ships and mariners; silver and silver plating; silver tinsel; silversmiths; silver birch; streams and wells; tides, the Moon not only rules the physical tides but the 'tides' in many mundane and psychic matters; Clairvoyants; trees that have an association with water or rich in sap; sleep; turtles; women in general, conception, fertility; weeping willow; water lily; white; white–poppies.

## MERCURY:

The day of Mercury is Wednesday and the Archangel Raphael. The gemstones of Mercury are agate and yellow stones generally. Quicksilver is the metal of Mercury, but you cannot use this but you can use silver or silver plate or silver gilt. These can be used for setting his gemstones. The Signs of the Zodiac are Gemini and Virgo. His colours are bright yellows, silver (to represent quicksilver his metal). His perfumes include lime, lemon, clove, mace, tragacanth, dammar, camomile, mastic and storax. Some of the things he rules are:

Annoying and jumping insects; accountants; authors; autographs; acquisition of knowledge; books and book–shops; breath and breathing; brothers; Cain and Abel; carrier pigeons; caduceus; certificates; communications (= every form); correspondence; deeds and documents; diaries; disease or distress; dogs; distributors; education; errands; essays; foxes; greyhounds; hand–operated machinery; hares; herald or referee; Hermes (= winged God of the Greeks); information (= most kinds); jesters; juggler and juggling; journeys; kin (= your relatives); knaves; linguist; languages and their acquisition; letters, alphabets and what you write using them; mechanical toys and novelties; ambassadors; messages and messengers; mirrors; mischief; monkeys; neighbours and your neighbourhood; your nervous system and 'nerves'; news and newspapers; nut–bearing trees, not necessarily the edible kind; lecturers; orators; parrot; pencil and paper; power of reasoning; post and postal workers; post offices; reports and reporters, reporting and rumours;

schools; shorthand; sickness; sister; children; students; storekeepers; teachers; theft and thieves; travel and travellers; translators; typing and typists; twins; wit; words; writs; youth (yours), youth in general and the young; visitor and visiting; deliveries.

## VENUS:

The day of Venus is Friday and the Angel Anael. The gemstones are lapis lazuli, rose quartz, blue diamonds, jade and most light blue and green stones. The metal is copper but silver can be used. These metals can be used for setting Venusian gemstones. The Signs of the Zodiac are Taurus and Libra. The colours are blues and greens (the bright varieties), pink, turquoise and his perfumes include rose myrtle, red sandalwood, benzoin, damiana, musk and storax. Some of the things ruled are:

Almond tree; Aphrodite (= Greek goddess of Love and Beauty); apples and apple trees; architects; art, the artistic and artists; Astarte (= Semitic Goddess of Love and Fertility); beauty and beauty parlours; bed and the bedroom; brass (= the metal); brides, bridal dress; carpets (= especially Chinese, fine carpets and genuine ones not copies); cats; clubs (= especially social clubs); concerts; copper and copper coins; cosmetics; dancing; decorative objects that beautify; declared and known enemies in war or any dispute; dilettante; dressmakers; doves; elegance; emeralds; enamelled woods; entertainment and entertainers; figs and fig tree; florists, flowers and most things floral, especially bouquets; Freya (= Norse Goddess of Love and Fertility); friends and friendship; gardens (= floral, not vegetable); gloves; gowns; hairdressers; harmony and unity; Hesperus (= the 'Evening Star' and a name for Venus); jewellery; laces (= decorative); the kidneys and their disorders; light wines; love that results in marriage; lawyers; luxury furniture; marriage and matrimony; movable possessions, those you take with you when you move; music, musicians and musical events; opponents; orchestra; ornaments and the ornamental; partnerships of most kinds; parties; peach and pears and their trees; perfume, perfumer and the perfumed; pleasure in most of its forms; presents and gifts; poets; rabbits; ribbons; rose, rose petals, scents, soaps, incense; rosewood (= genuine first, the veneer second); sapphires; settlements; silks; social events of any kind; stringed instruments; tea (= especially light teas and Chinese); vases; Venetian; vines and light wines.

## MARS:

The day of Mars is Tuesday and the Angel Samael. The gemstones of Mars are rubies, garnets, fire opals and red stones generally. His metal is iron, steel and brass. These can be used for setting his gemstones, but so can gold and bronze. The Signs of the Zodiac are Aries and Scorpio (Scorpio is Pluto's in later astrology). The colours are strong, vibrant, bright reds sometimes mid reds, but no washed out or pale colours. The perfumes include opopanax, geranium, spicy substances that 'have bite,' tobacco, pepper, benzoin, sulphur, hellebore. Some of the things he rules are:

Adventure and misadventure; agriculture, especially in spring after winter when the earth is renewing itself; animals of prey; armour; anvils; arrows; army and armaments; artillery; guns and rifles; athletes; barbers; blacksmiths; blood and bloodshed; bow (= for arrows); boxers (= people, not dogs or shorts); builders; butchers; burns and scalds; cannon; cars and the internal combustion engine; carpenters; courage and recklessness; agitators; bailiffs; builders; butcher and butchery;

bullies; cutlass; carpenter; combat and combatants; critics, who cut with words; dentists; detectives; cuts and cutting; daggers; daring and defiance; darts; dogs (= particularly hunting and working dogs); drums and percussion instruments that are struck; eagle; engineers; falcon; fever and pain; fever and feverish; fire; gladiator and guard; gauntlet; guns; hawk; holly; javelin; knives; lance; locks, padlocks and locksmiths; machinery, especially engineering; metal workers; prize–fighter; missiles; motors; nettles; new ventures; panther; razor; redwoods; scarlet; sharp tools and cutting instruments; soldiers; spears; steam–engines; steel; swords and swordsmen; surgeons and surgery; swords; thistle; thorns, thorny plants and trees; tiger; vulture; soldiers; war and weapons of war; valiant and venturesome; wolf; woodpecker.

## JUPITER:

The day of Jupiter is Thursday and the Angel Sachiel. His metal is gold, silver and silver gilt. These metals can be used for setting his gemstones. The Signs of the Zodiac are Sagittarius and Pisces (Pisces is now ruled by Neptune in later astrology). It is possible that the reader will find the Angel of Jupiter given as Zadkiel (primarily), Tsadkiel or Tzadiqel, in particular accompanying *Cabbala* and Rabbinic writings, some believe Zadkiel is another form of Sachiel, which we use. This short explanation is to avoid confusion. The colours are all shades of purple, lilac, lavender and mauves. The perfumes include cedar, orris, galbanum, Balm of Gilead, oak, saffron, ambergris, storax, benjamin, olives. Some of the things ruled are:

Academics; advisors; adjudicators; aristocrats; ash trees; bank, bankers and banking; barristers; the Bible; legal books and Law books; bishops; cardinals; ceremonies; chancellors; charity; churches, their furnishings and dignitaries; colleges; councillors; court (legal and royal); courts of law; juries and juror; the crown and the crown jewels; all crown–shaped objects; Crucifix; diplomats; dreams; eagle; elephant; expansive and expensive; explorers who go to exotic places or places far removed from the place of birth; finance and financiers; gambling and gaming houses; holy objects and relics; hospitals; judges and the judiciary; insurance and the people connected with it; the mind, especially that part that deals with the intellect, academic and philosophical thought; kings, queens and their family; lavender (=plant and perfume); lawyers and the law; lime tree; the liver; 'luck' in general; magistrates; ministers; money; oak trees; officials; olives; pageants and parades; philanthropy and philosophy; prestige and social priests; profit and expansion; prominence; promoters; publishing and publishers; racehorses especially thoroughbred horses, racecourses and racing; religions; ritual; sports and the contestants; stocks, the Stock Exchange and shares; swans (= royal birds with royal protection in England) and swan–shaped objects; telegraph and telegrams; treasure and the Treasury; the 'turf'; touts; wealth and the wealthy; whales; wisdom; vines and wine.

## SATURN:

The day of Saturn is Saturday and the Angel Cassiel. His metal is lead or pewter. These metals can be used for setting his gemstones but pewter is preferable to lead if used next to the sking. Use a metal that has a 'leaden' colour or an 'antique' look, alternatively used gold or silver as a substitute. The Signs of the Zodiac are Capricorn and Aquarius. (Aquarius is ruled by Uranus in later astrology.) The colours are black, grey, dark browns and greens. The gemstones are jet, garnets, smoky quartz, corals and obsidian The perfumes include rue, myrrh, cypress, storax, yew, musk civet, asafoetida, mandrake, sulphur, black hellebore and aloes. Some of the things ruled are:

Age and aged, all things old; agriculture; animal husbandry; aspen tree; archaeologists and archaeology; bankrupts; bone and bones; calendar; chains (= not precious metals); coal; caves; cemeteries; Chronus (= the Greek name of Saturn or time, whose annual festivals were called **Chronia**); the career; chronometers; clocks, watches, clockmakers and their repair; clowns; death and Death as 'the reaper'; debts and what is owing in money, obligations or Karma; depression; desolation; duty; earth and the Earth; ebony; economy; elm trees; estate and estate agents; miners, especially coal especially coal mines and the metal lead; excavations, mines and pits, but not necessarily what comes out of them; excavators; farms, farmers and farming; fame and infamy; Fate; Father Time, as time itself; foundations (= of anything); gardens and gardeners, usually vegetable gardens and those that are utilitarian; graves, gravestones, gravediggers, sepulchres and vaults; grief and sadness; goats and Capricorn, the goat; the Government; houses and property; hour–glass; illnesses brought about by cold and damp; jailer, guard or warder; Karma; leather and goods made from it; masons and masonry; method and the methodical; mines; miser or skinflint; nails (= of the hands); night–watchmen; ordeals; old people, matters and things; 'the past'; patience, persistence and punctuality; pine trees and the 'pine box'; plumbers; poplar trees; recluse; responsibility and the reputation; rocks and stones; scapegoat; skeleton; stability; tanners and tanning; terminus (= the end); time, timekeepers and timekeeping; tombs; urns; vaults; wisdom, especially that connected with age being earned by experience; working clothes; worldly standing; yew trees; yokes.

This is the end of the seven planets of old astrology and these planets as given before consist of the Sun, Moon, Mars, Mercury, Venus, Jupiter and Saturn. This is not their astronomical order, but their order according to the days of the week that they rule and this order is used throughout the work. There are three more planets used that make up the ten planets of the astrology used today and they have rulership over many aspects of our lives and we do use them so we give them next. The missing planets from the lists are Uranus, Neptune and Pluto and these have been mentioned at various times.

The Archangel Uriel has sway over the planet Uranus. The planet Neptune has the Angel Asariel and the planet Pluto has the Angel Azrael. However, they do not have the usual signatures, Olympic spirits, kameas and this is why we remain with the older planets in some aspects of the work and this is because these three planets beyond the rings of Saturn go beyond these seven.

The Seven Planets of the Ancient World are the planets concerned mainly with you and your life here on this planet. They are often designated the 'personal planets.' The astrologers of the Chaldeans called the Sun, Moon and the five planets of old 'the Interpreters.' This is because they believed these seven planets made manifest 'the purpose of the Gods.' They called the twelve Signs of the Zodiac and its decans 'the Counsellor Gods' and the stars outside the Zodiac, beyond the range of Saturn were 'the Judges of the Living and the Dead.'

The Sun and Moon are the planets of Life, in your chart and they represent your parents. The Sun is your father and the Moon your mother. The Sun impregnates the Moon and she conceives, just as our parents do when they 'conjunct.' Every monthly New Moon is though of as a new beginning, a conjunction. The principle of life, according to the old astrologers, which breathed life into the human body that was of the same basic nature as the 'Fires of Heaven.' From these fires, the soul was said to get its condition and from the moment of birth, it received the qualities that determined its destiny here below.

The two planets of Sun and Moon lie next to each other in the Zodiac Belt as they do in physical life with the Sun in Leo and the Moon in Cancer. These two astrological houses, the fourth and the fifth are next to each other in the Zodiac, see the diagram below. The fourth house is the astrological house of the home, the mother and family in which the needs of the baby are tended, while the fifth house is the astrological house, among other things, of love and love affairs, mating and children.

The Moon represents the new–born babe who needs the nourishment of the mother. Nature equipped the Moon (= the female) for this and not the Sun (= the male), which is in part why we call Nature — 'Mother Nature' and of course, Nature has always had her male consort and partner if a correct balanced is to be maintained, as it must, when Nature goes into imbalance she is terrifying and destructive, not creative but destructive — *the principle of human birth*

Above the Sun and the Moon are the two signs of the planet Mercury, which are Gemini and Virgo. This planet represents the young child undertaking the Mercurial pursuits of schooling, learning, writing, reading, books (especially those that give information like schoolbooks), debate, conversation, lessons, communication and this is the Gemini House. The Virgo House gives matters of health, hygiene, dietary and health matters, lungs, the breath and bronchial matters, medicines, pills and tablets, remedies and cures — *the principle of the reasoning.*

Above Mercury are the two signs of Venus, which are the natural houses of Taurus and Libra. Venus represents the young person moving out into the world, going out and moving away from the enclosed protection of the family and the family home, learning the social arts of being involved with others and having to consider them through contact outside the family, this used to be called learning the 'social skills.' The emotions are being developed and the desire for harmony and unity with others not of the family is beginning to be developed. Eventually this leads to attraction to and of others for Venus seeks the complimentary balance (= Libra), which opens up the desire for social contacts whether they are for love or lust, for marriage or partnership — *the principle of love.*

Above Venus are the two signs of the planet Mars, which are Aries and Scorpio. Growing up requires we 'make our way in the world,' and this is under Mars who gives the young adults the need for a certain amount of positive assertion or aggression, to accomplish this. At this time, there is great passion and heat, enterprise and courage and to this added some risk and foolhardiness — taking your chance. This is a time of passionate causes, sport and outdoor pursuits, including the amorous. At one time, this would have involved the young males serving time in the military, a Martian occupation (= Aries). The second sign (Scorpio) gave passion and intensity, wilfulness, jealousy, violence and violence, smouldering and unseen passion that runs deep, revenge and paying back, hidden agitators, intense competition — *the principle of action.*

Above Mars are the two signs of the planet Jupiter, which are Sagittarius and Pisces. Jupiter rules the middle age of life when life should have stabilised and this should be a time of reaping the rewards of your labour, an easier and more comfortable life. Jupiter rules the spiritual and temporal conditions of the life. The rule of Law and a more settled conservative and philosophical approach to life. Often at this time, we notice the 'middle age spread' that the good living that the Sagittarian Jupiter can bring. The Piscean Jupiter is frequently a little more detached and less involved in life's mundane affairs, it gives the desire to be free, to roam and jump the fence, philosophy, religion, meditation and contemplation. Undertaking some form of gambling where the outcome is uncertain, a desire to be perverse and against the traditional and established because the principles of Saturn are being expressed through the Element of Air and not the Element of Earth but in some way — *the principle of expansion.*

Finally, above Jupiter comes the planet Saturn and he rules the last two signs of the Zodiac. Saturn rules the signs of Capricorn and Aquarius (old astrology). Saturn rules your old age. He can bring stability, wisdom, security and he is always seeking security and safety, even in love he is cautious, it may outlast all the other signs but it is wary and cautious. If you want no surprises and routine, where there is stability and a pension, then Saturn is your planet. Finally your physical death; possibly infirmity, stiff joints leading up to it and all that goes with it. For as Saturn is at the end of the planetary list, he is also the 'end of things.' His cold, sombre kingdom is placed as far as is possible from the warm life–giving planets of life within the 'circle of your life.' These circles is the chart of your birth and the 'circle' within which you live, breath and die and after the principle of expansion comes — *the principle of contraction.*

Early astrological charts were square. Like the *tertris* of Pythagoras, they were four–square because they had four sides. It represented the mundane earth on which we live. The square chart was later replaced by the now familiar circular chart, so perhaps the circle has already been squared.

The two Zodiac signs of Saturn and his Signs are in direct opposition to the two signs of Life, we climb from birth to death, see the diagram below. The Sun and Moon are planets that are warm and moist, masculine and feminine and they started your personal Cycle of Life. Saturn as physical death is cold and termed 'the Greater Malefic' and he will end your life, yet he is a better friend than many know. Saturn always wins though for he is the Lord of Time and another thing he rules is patience, all he has to do is wait, he has plenty of time for he is eternity.

These, simply put, are the basic facts in our journey from the two signs of life, the Sun and Moon and their pilgrimage to the opposite houses of Saturn, death and the end of the matter, including ours. Then the limitation and boundaries of Saturn are broken and we are set free from the circle in which our life was set, perhaps releasing us to the three non–physical planets beyond the limits of Saturn, who deal with the intangible things of life which Saturn cannot do.

The square chart had some merit and it was easier to read than people think. When we were low and appeared to be beaten, we were often told to come 'out of our corner fighting.' In a square chart you could, metaphorically do that and see what planets were in 'your corner' to help you do it.

If we take the planets of the list and set them out in the order I have given above you will see that they form the Belt of the Zodiac as we have it today. Even if we added the modification of what are termed the 'modern planets,' given later, its order remains the same. Let me put the list of the seven old planets into the order given in the text the better to show the reasoning behind it. I have added the astrological symbols for those who prefer them and those who want to learn them.

The columns in both lists show the natural progression of their construction building upwards from birth with the Sun and Moon, to physical death that ends with Saturn. If the reader will start with Aries near the middle of the left–hand column and follow the signs and planets anticlockwise, down the first column, up the other side, cross over at the top and end above where you started, with Pisces. You will notice the sequence follows the sign order of the natural Zodiac and the 'base' of the chart is supported by the mother and the father and it is the natural fourth house of Cancer (= the womb, the home and the tomb) with the father at the bottom of the right hand column with natural fifth house of Leo (= love, loving, creativity producing children and being parents) that gives a firm foundation to the life. The necessity of which is poignantly expressed in the following. 'The foxes have holes, and the birds of the air have nests; but the Son of Man hath not where to lay his head.' *Matthew*.8: 20.

| | |
|---|---|
| Saturn—Aquarius | Capricorn—Saturn |
| Jupiter—Pisces | Sagittarius—Jupiter |
| Mars—Aries | Scorpio—Mars |
| Venus—Taurus | Libra—Venus |

| | |
|---|---|
| Mercury—Gemini | Virgo—Mercury |
| Moon—Cancer | Leo—Sun. |

The reader will see these planets are all connected to the individual in some personal way and their progress through life. In many of the areas ruled by these seven planets but we can take control of our destiny and, with good judgement, change it. Saturn is the planet that sets the boundaries and limits, which is why the rings encircling him are the 'Rings of Pass Not' that encircle our life, just as the planets are set in the circle of the astrological chart, which is the circle of our life.

Let us reaffirm some facts regarding the 'seven rungs' of the **Ladder of Life** that uses the **Seven Planets of the Ancient World**, because this is why it is sometimes shown as being a 'ladder.' The Sun has only one rung or Sign of the Zodiac (= Leo) and he is completely male. The Moon has only one rung or Sign of the Zodiac and she is completely female, while the remaining five planets Mercury to Saturn have two rungs or Signs of the Zodiac each. One rung or Sign being male and the other female, positive and negative and so forth, as a result allowing its ruler two dissimilar paths of expression for whatever planet is found in the Sign.

Let us start from the bottom (of both columns) and climb. The bottom rungs rest firmly on the earth, our life starts with the mother (= the Moon, who represents all babes immaterial of gender) and the father (= Sun, creativity, children) or at least they did once. Though at sometime in the future I suppose astrologers, if things take the path they appear to be taking will soon have to start speculating whether their clients were born, donated, Internet purchased or cloned.

Moving up a rung to young children (= Mercury rules children) learning our 'three R's and our early schooling close to home, often with the help of our parents). Next rung, we spread our wings a little more outside the family, by learning the social graces of being with others and having to take others into account in our lives. There is usually a little more giving and not always so much getting (=Venus), manipulating parents is easier than manipulating others. Next rung, we have the young folk full of life and determined to make their way in world, everything is an adventure a spreading of wings and testing the water. Once this meant into the military for the young blades for a while at least, but open season for 'hunting' (= under Mars) partner(s) for whatever reason.

We move on to being established and comfortable in middle age, in our occupation, with a position in the world and the family is settled and making their mark (=Jupiter). Once, for those males who had not achieved any of this in the outside world and looked unlikely to do so, it was often in the Government or the Church (= Jupiter again). Last rung, retirement and starting to relax our grip on the world and its affairs or going into second childhood lost in the misty passages of the past, where all seemed better and more secure by being familiar (= under Saturn) and finally a 'new ladder?' This is your personal ladder, a ladder you were created to climb from birth to death and bear this similarity in mind when you read about the 'ladder' in the chapter **The Link** or **Jacob's Ladder** given later,

The three remaining planets of Neptune, Uranus and Pluto are outside this 'circle of our life' and because of this, they are also, for the most outside your control. These planets can lead you a merry dance, especially Uranus if he feels so inclined. They generally have powerful control over the areas they rule and they rarely relinquish it to the control of others. These planets require careful handling as much of the time their effects and power are not always of a tangible nature but they can become so when they filter down to the mundane level and operate here, because we have to deal with them and sometimes we do not know how, why, what it is or where its coming from.

This is why I have advised caution with these planets because they can sometimes leave you with residual problems with the cause out of reach or hidden. They often deal with such matters as occultism, magic, Spiritualism, astral travel, meditation, visualization and other associated activities, to name a few that are in keeping with this work.

These untold areas are regions where care is needed because the signposts and maps are fewer than the old seven on the physical level that we have been dealing with for some time from the beginning of our history. They are one of the few areas that remain unexplored to us and we are still mapping them. In some cases, they may prove the most dangerous regions left to explore. The counsel is simple and not at all restricting. Go forward in such matters of course, but with patience and vigilance — speak gently and few sudden moves.

Uranus takes the Sign of the Zodiac, Aquarius, from Saturn. Uranus has the Archangel Uriel as its angel. It uses the hours and the day of Saturn, which is Saturday.

Neptune takes the sign of the Zodiac, Pisces, from Jupiter. Neptune has the Angel Asariel as its angel. It uses the hours and day of Jupiter, which is Thursday.

Pluto takes the sign of the Zodiac, Scorpio, from Mars. Pluto has the Angel Azrael as its angel. It uses the hours and day of Mars, which is Tuesday.

So let us add these three angels to the lists already given above, which is not difficult. Following next, the reader will find a short list, modelled upon the lists already given above for the **Seven Planets of Old**, regarding the people, matters and objects under their rule. The type of information and order given for the seven planets above is used here.

## URANUS AND THE ARCHANGEL URIEL:

The day of Uranus is Saturday and his sign of the Zodiac is Aquarius. Uranus uses the same day as Saturn because he took over rulership of one of the signs Saturn originally ruled, Saturn's 'night house.' Saturn keeps Capricorn while Uranus takes his second sign, Aquarius. His colours are 'electric blue and green,' striped and banded colours or mixtures of many colours. Today he would rule colours that are termed 'psychedelic.' The gemstone of Uranus is chrysoberyl, cymophene, stones that are multicoloured, a mixture or flecked. His metal is platinum or chromium. Appropriate settings for Uranian gemstones are platinum, chromium and silver or blended and mixed metals. The perfumes can include Frankincense; myrrh; yew; musk; root of mandrake; black hellebore; alum; asafoetida.

I say 'can include' in the perfumes above, because the Archangel Uriel and his planet are not easy to give arbitration for, inasmuch as they can be very arbitrary. If any perfume or incense lifts you 'out of the ordinary' or has a touch of 'magic' about it, then that could be a perfume and incense of Uranus for you. It should be fast because Uranus does not do anything slowly and that is why he can upset Saturn and is the only planet that can. Some of the things that he rules are:

Magical forces; sudden change as with the 'Lightning Struck Tower' — the 'bolt from the blue' from a clear blue sky; an 'eleventh hour miracle' or 'in the nick of time when all feels lost'; new, modern and novel matters and inventions; inventor; liberal, liberty and licence; crises and chaos; divorce, separation and the 'divorced'; spasmodic; paradox and the paradoxical; occultists and the Occult; prophet and prophetic; pioneers and pioneering; original; magnetic; metaphysician; enlightenment, the sudden kind like a 'Road to Damascus'; fanatics and fanaticism; freethinker and freelance; genuine eccentrics; innovators; magic and magicians (= not the stage variety, which is illusion and trickery and under Neptune), but those who attempt to change or control their lives using natural or supernatural forces or otherwise subjected to training of will–power; fraternal clubs and societies; people outside the family circle, such as friendship; astrology and astrologers; antiquarians; anarchists; electricity and electricians; radio; the illegal, illicit and the illegitimate; radio–active; reformer; science and scientists; television; spectacular and spontaneous; strange; defiance; reformers; humanitarian; nomadic; non–conformist; hybrid plants and animals; utopian; unpredictable; unconventional; zeal, zealot and zealotry.

## NEPTUNE AND THE ANGEL ASARIEL:

The day of Neptune is Thursday (= the same day as Jupiter, but Neptune rules Pisces, Jupiter keeps Sagittarius) and the angel is the Angel Asariel. The colours are sea–green; pale violet; soft colours, pastel shades or vague or indistinct colours, those that imperceptibly blend. The gemstones of Neptune are green beryl and many light green or blue stones, especially jadeite and nephrite. Turquoise can be used. Those stones and gems that are artificial or those that look to be what they are not, especially the green, green/blue varieties. He has no real metal of his own so again, artificial metals or metals that are not what they seem, like metallic plastic. If you use something that is artificial, that may be what you get in return and it may be not what it seems, so you can use silver and silver–plate. These last two metals are appropriate setting for his gems and stones. His sign of the Zodiac is Pisces. His perfumes are: Storax; nutmeg; camphor; opoponax; ambergris; mastic; seeds of the Ash Tree; hyssop; Florentine Iris (= Orris root.) Some of the things that he rules are:

Clairvoyance (= passive); all people and matter connected with the sea; Poseidon; photographer and photography; mediums and mediumistic; receptive; prophecy and prophets; oracle; necromancer; parasites like the cuckoo and parasitic people, mistletoe that grows on its host giving nothing in return; the 'Astral'; crystal balls; spirit and Spiritualism; the mysterious, the unknown and the unexplained; psychic trance; catalepsy; vague, intangible, elusive and dream–like; inspiration and aspirations; idealism; enchanting and enchantment; imaginative; poetic; moral, immoral and amoral; hallucination and hallucinogenic; addicts and addiction; alcoholics and alcohol; anaesthetists and anaesthetics; distillers; bogus= (people, things, companies); opium and opiates; artificial, imitation and illusory; fakes and forgeries (= people and things); subterfuge; chaos; chemists; duplicity; ideals and idealists; illusion and illusionists (=stage magic); those who attack from ambush; 'self–undoing' through lack of judgement; all things clandestine; secrets; mountebanks; mystery, mysteries and mystics; recluses and hermits; sacrifice and the sacrificial; alms, charity and charities; idealist; tenderness; sublime; Utopia; sleep and slumber; exile, detention, hospitals, asylums and prisons; suicide; 'fog and night' — that which fogs and veils — disappearance.

## PLUTO AND THE ANGEL AZRAEL:

This is one of the comparatively new planets considering the age of the universe. The planet was discovered in 1930, though naturally, it has always been there and it is often thought that we are only just beginning to get the hang of him. What is given is well–established since his discovery and working with these facts over quite a long time has not yet proved it to be unacceptable or unworkable.

The day of Pluto is Tuesday (the same day as Mars, but Pluto rules Scorpio, while Mars keeps Aries) and the angel is the Angel Azrael. His colours are dark colours, perhaps a sulphurous yellow and the dark hues of red. The gemstones are black diamonds and pearls, possibly the tourmaline, especially the deep red variation and the fire opals, the darkest of red stones. Stones that have a reputation of being 'magical stones,' obsidian, especially the black, brown and red colours. Perhaps he may use the so–called magical stones of alexandrine and labradorite. The metal is radium with silver suggested for setting any of his gemstones. His perfumes include: Black peppercorns; absinthe; rue; geranium; lodestone; sulphur; hellebore root; pepper and tobacco; bdellium; dragon's blood.' Some of the things he rules are:

The underworld (=Hades) and 'the Underworld'— the worlds of the dead and the criminal; racketeer; rogue; the after–life; things that are hidden and out–of–sight; buried in the depths of your mind (= the sub–conscious) and the earth (= oils, gases, precious stones and minerals); secrets, secret and subversive ideas and people; a 'bringing–to–light' of people and matters; regeneration and recuperation; perpetrator; transmutation; the dead and death; enlightenment (= slowly, most things of Pluto are slow until the break the surface, then they erupt); the breaking up of the old to make way for the new (= again slowly, not like Uranus who is quick and sometimes violent.); the bringing of light to that which was hidden; fanatics and fanaticism; coroners and people engaged in tending the dead; baffling; germination; evolution and revolution; after–life research and interests; Mephisto or 'Mephisto natures'; metamorphosis; monsters; intense; relentless; temptation; virus; transformer and transformation; plutocrat= 'having great wealth'; psychoanalysis (= digging deep for what is hidden and known only by its results); abyss; enlightenment; fermenting; purification; treachery; intense; scavenger.

If the reader has read through the three lists above they will see there is a great deal there that can be considered intangible. There is little you can 'get hold of' as the saying goes, unlike the seven earlier lists where everything seem so solid and corporeal and most of it is set in our place in the scheme of things inside the 'rings of Saturn.' These last lists contain things you know about by their effect more than their cause. You cannot see a virus (= Pluto) but you know its results. Mediumship (Spiritualism= Neptune) can give uncertain results and it is often judged by the results or lack of them. Neptune often presents things and people, as you would like them to be — not as they are — Neptune may look at reality but if he does not like it, he does not always use it, only this planet could have invented 'rose–coloured' spectacles. Electricity (=Uranus), you know what electricity can do because you can measure it, but you cannot really see it only by the results. Readers will find some intangibles in the lists given for the Seven Planets of old astrology but certainly not as many as they will find in the lists of the last three planets. This makes these three 'outer' planets harder to 'pin down' or control. If you can use them do so, but use discrimination and caution or you could find that they may well use you.

It was not intended in the foregoing to give the reader astrology lessons, its purpose was only to make clearer the why and how of them and this is the reason why I have kept things as non–technical as possible. The response to this section in the original work in which they were first used was better than I thought from the readers and this is the reason why they have been used (in part) here. Now let us move on I am sure to an important part of the work for those who do not know the answer — who are my Guardian Angels?

259

# YOUR PERSONAL GUARDIAN ANGELS

Most philosophies and traditions say we have two Guardian Angels and all say at least one, so it seems reasonable to try and find out who they are because obviously they are very important to us. Tradition shows that other angels show a special interest in an individual and their life. This work proposes that there are five angels who have varying degrees of interest in a soul from their birth to their death and we will give the methods of finding this information and the reasoning behind the reasons for finding them.

These angels are taken from the personal details of an individual's birth, which makes them unique though even if someone were found to have the same angels, they still are not you and the odds of this are great.

When we have found these five angels, we use the information to form the basis of the **Angelic Pentagram,** which is unique to that person coupled with the **Personal Pyramid of Angelic Power**. The pentagram has a chapter devoted to it and will explain the method of the pentagrams creation and use. This chapter will also introduce you to your fifth and final angel in your personal angelic group — the **Benben Angel**.

Once we have found the Guardian Angels, we next seek the second pairing of angels called your Auxiliary Angels in this work to distinguish them from your Guardian Angels. We expressly use the word *auxiliary*= 'someone or something who gives help, rendering assistance, helping, aiding, subsidiary to.' We have chosen the term 'auxiliary' instead of 'lesser' because some may wrongly infer that the 'lesser angels' are inferior or lower angels. They are called 'lesser angels' only because their tasks for you are less than your Guardian Angels whom they assist and support when needed and never forget, your **Auxiliary Angels** are someone else's **Guardian Angels.**

So many words today have lost their original meaning, earlier the word naïve did not have any pejorative inference, it simply meant that something or someone was uncomplicated and natural, it was complimentary. Always remember that your **Auxiliary Angels**, although they play a 'lesser' role in your life they are nonetheless important.

The most important angels are your undoubtedly your **Guardian Angels** and many cultures say you are given these angels long before you make your appearance on the physical level, but more of this later. On the day of your birth, you gained a fifth and very important angel called the **Angel of the Ascendant** or **Benben Angel**. There will be more of this particular Angel in the appropriate place, just keep him in mind for now.

## Your Solar Guardian Angel

The first of your two **Guardian Angels** is the easiest angel to find because he is the Angel of the Sun in your birth chart. Most people who read their daily horoscopes in the newspapers know their 'Sun–Sign' from these readings, otherwise they would not know which forecast to read. Sun–sign predictions have a place in astrology as long as you remember it is only a brief and general guide to the possibilities of your Sign of the Zodiac for that day. The suggestions given represent a broad consensus of the daily possibilities regarding the planetary aspects to your birth Sun and its Sign of the Zodiac. The other nine planets do play their part and should be accounted for but this cannot be quite so accurately in this branch of astrology, though some do manage to do it very well.

The Sun Sign is with you throughout your life and it is taken from the sign of the Zodiac that the Sun was passing through on the day of your birth. Most know and accept from these lists that if someone is born between the dates of 24th of September and the 23rd of October they are born under the sign of Libra the Scales or the Balance. The sign of Libra is ruled by the planet Venus and this makes the Angel Anael their solar guardian Angel. I will not give a list for the Sun in the other eleven Sun Signs because these are given in most newspapers and magazines and are well known enough The reader will find variations for the changeover dates and this is why care must be taken regarding them. I have an old work that gives the above dates for Libra as September 20th to October 20th.

This system works fine for most people and the only people who need to take care and check the accuracy are those born on the day when the Sun is changing Signs in the Zodiac, leaving one sign to go into another. These dates are usually the first and last dates of the given period. In our example, this Sign of the Zodiac would be for those who were born on the 24th of September and the 23rd of October respectively. The Sun does not leave or enter a sign of the Zodiac at exactly the same time each year and there are sometimes slight variations in the timing. Let me give an example to show what is involved.

In most astrological columns, the dates for Sagittarius are usually given as November 23rd — December 21st and anyone using these dates would assume, if born on November 22nd, they would be a automatically be a Scorpio and use the Angel of Mars, they would read the forecast given for Scorpio and up to a point, this could be fine. Let us take November 22nd 1998 as an example because on this day the Sun did change signs going from Scorpio into Sagittarius.

Most people using these popular lists would assume a person born on November 22nd was a Scorpio and if they are in a habit of reading their daily stars, they would read those under Scorpio. Nevertheless, as our example for 1998 shows, they would only use Scorpio if they were born before 2.59 p.m GMT. Anyone born after this time on this day and this year would technically be a Sagittarian because the Sun will have moved into Sagittarius and this is why it is recommended and necessary to check these changeover dates.

The above only applies to people who were born on one of the twelve changeover dates given in the lists and not those born on the dates between these two dates. When people are born on any date of change of the Signs of the Zodiac, they seem to take a share a part in both signs, the one being left and the one being entered by the Sun. They are not a mixture of both signs, but more like someone living on the border of two countries and able to go into one or the other. Many ephemeredes have a table to show the times when the Sun enters a new Sign of the Zodiac in the back pages, they are easy enough to read and there are people who will do it for those who are not sure, especially in shops who deal with these matters.

## Your Lunar Guardian Angel

Your second *Guardian Angel* or your *Lunar Guardian Angel* is the Angel of the Moon. It is taken from the position of the Moon at birth and if you cannot read an Ephemeris or almanac (to give it its old name), it is perhaps a little harder to find because this planet moves faster than the Sun. The Moon stays in a Sign of the Zodiac approximately two and a half days. It is easy enough to read in the Ephemeris and it is the same, like the Sun above, when your birthday falls on a day when the Moon changes signs. The Sun changes Signs of the Zodiac twelve times in a year, while Moon changes Signs of the Zodiac twelve times in every month and one hundred and forty–four times in a year. The Moon usually gives a distinct emotional personality to each individual, for example the Moon in Sagittarius is totally unlike the Moon found in the next sign

261

of Capricorn and her position by the Sign of the Zodiac affects the personality presented to the world powerfully.

On your birthday, if the Moon falls on a change over date when she goes into another Sign of the Zodiac, you will have to find out if the time of your birth was before the changeover or after, exactly the same as above for the Sun. If this is a problem for you, then again someone who understands an Ephemeris will be able to help you — but even if you do not understand astrology, I would really recommend that you learn to read an Ephemeris.

It is not difficult to learn and the basics enable you to understand and add so much more to your work. Remember you do not have to learn astrology or be able to cast and predict birth charts and all the rest. All you will be doing is to know where the planets are at any given time of the day or night for any place on the planet Earth.

Remember you do something very similar to reading an Ephemeris when you read a bus or train table. These tables simply tell you where the train is going, what time it should reach its destination and whether a train is even going to the destination that you want. The timetable gives the times it reaches the intermediate stations between where it is and where it is going.

You only have ten 'trains' or planets to deal with in the Ephemeris and they are called the Sun, the Moon, Mercury, Venus, Mars, Jupiter, Saturn, Uranus, Neptune and Pluto and in this order they are dealt with and the Ephemeris will even give you where the planet Earth is at the time — it is in the opposite Sign of the Zodiac to where the Sun is and in the same degree.

These 'trains' or planets travel around twelve 'stations' or Signs of the Zodiac, which are all carefully marked in the Ephemeris and follow the Signs of the Zodiac as given in newspapers. It is only the unfamiliarity of the Ephemeris that makes it appear more complicated than it is, of course there are other considerations should you want to use them, but you learnt to read bus and train tables and found them simple enough and I am sure you will do the same with this 'planet table.' There are some specialist books that teach you only how to read an Ephemeris in easy stages. If you are interested in doing this and I think you should, a long standing primer (now updated with additional information) is *How to read Raphael's Ephemeris* by Jeff Mayo, published by *Foulsham's* that is easy enough to obtain — remember these books

However, back to our fictitious example and we will assume the Moon was found in Cancer so this would make the Lunar Guardian Angel the Archangel Gabriel. Now we have the Angel Anael as the Solar Guardian Angel and the Archangel Gabriel as the Lunar Guardian Angel. The Guardian Angels are the two main angels in this fictitious life and these angels are in yours, which is not fictitious and they are the Guardian Angels of your Life. These unique angels are said to be present before your birth, present at your birth, present with you throughout your life, present at your dying and present at your leaving it on your physical death — that should be enough for anyone!

**Your Auxiliary Angels**

Let us look next at to the two Auxiliary Angels. These angels watch over your life and its affairs with your Guardian Angels but they work with and under the guidance of your Guardian Angels. The second Auxiliary Angel requires more information to know which angel to use than the first. If you do not know or cannot find this information (and many cannot) there is a reliable substitute angel that can be deputize for the fourth angel and this follows later.

The first Auxiliary Angel is simply taken from the day of the week upon which you were born and this is easy enough to find. For our example let us assume you were born on Tuesday, this makes your first Auxiliary Angel the Angel Samael because Tuesday is ruled by the planet

Mars and the Angel Samael. If you were born on a Wednesday, your first Auxiliary Angel would be the Archangel Raphael because Wednesday is ruled by the planet Mercury and this Archangel.

The second Auxiliary Angel is taken from the hour of the day you were born. If you know this time, you consult the *Table of Planetary and Angelic Hours* to find out which planet and angel rules that particular hour on the day that you were born. If you were born on Monday at 9.00 a.m this angel would be the Angel Sachiel that rules the planet Jupiter. If it was 9.00 p.m in the evening on Monday this would be ruled by the Archangel Gabriel that rules the planet Moon. The way to use the *Table of Planetary and Angelic Hours* will be explained in more detail later

As said, the piece of the puzzle most frequently missing is usually the time someone was born. Normally, you can get this information from those old enough to be there at the time of the birth and obviously, the best person to ask is your mother if you are able to do so. Significant others are the older members of your family and this detail can be lost or become vague as memory fades or plays tricks. Taking to astrology early, I made sure to ask my mother and she said that the time was known without doubt because my first cry was augmented by the factory sirens with no mistaking the time — 'the 5 p.m shift was over.' A great many people do not know the hour of their birth with accuracy or at all. Often are there are phrases like 'it was early in the morning' and it is quite remarkable how many children were born on the hour, twenty past the hour or twenty to the hour. Some astrologers use rectification using major events later in the individual's life, but if this information is not known then you can safely use the 'delegated angel' or the 'Six o'clock Angel.

There are two reliable methods used to overcome this problem to fill all the angelic stations and we will deal with them both below and give the methods to use. Let us return the ways of calculating your Guardian and Auxiliary Angels when the details are known to strengthen the method and give a two examples to make the matter clear and to find these four angels that make you stand 'four–square' in life. This is an important subject and it rests firmly at the heart of the work being personal to the individual, so it must be understood and it is not difficult.

Let us deal with the two Guardian Angels and the two Auxiliary Angels for the moment. Let us take someone (fictitiously) born on the 3rd of March 1962 at 11.00 a.m, remember the person may be 'fictitious' but the method used is not. They would be born with the Sun in Pisces, which is ruled by Neptune whose Angel is Asariel. The Moon is in Virgo and this sign is ruled by Mercury, whose Angel is the Archangel Raphael. The 3rd of March 1962 was a Saturday and this day is ruled by Saturn, whose angel is the Angel Cassiel. The hour of 11.00 a.m on Saturday is ruled by the Sun, whose angel is the Archangel Michael. Daylight saving was not in operation at the time of birth (dealt with later in its place) so we use GMT throughout, which requires no adjustment to the *Table of Planetary and Angelic Hours* because it is calculated for Greenwich Mean Time.

The Angel Sachiel is their Solar Guardian Angel and the Archangel Raphael is their Lunar Guardian Angel. The Angel Cassiel is their first Auxiliary Angel and the Archangel Michael their second Auxiliary Angel, all the angels are derived from which Sign of the Zodiac their Sun and Moon were in and the day and time of the day on which they were born.

Let us take another date picked at random but one that involves Daylight Saving Time or British Summer Time (= BST) for the British Isles. If any form of Daylight Saving Time is in operation in the country or place where you are living that necessitates the alteration of the clocks for a period of time, you must take this into account or you will be wrong and one hour out.

Let us take someone born (fictitiously) on the 18th of July 1969 at 1.20 p.m. They were born when British Summer Time was in operation for the British Isles. During the period of BST in the British Isles, the clocks are advanced one hour during this time making them one hour ahead of Greenwich Mean Time. Being born when BST is in force means the true time of the birth was 12.20 p.m because one hour must be subtracted from clock time to take British Summer Time back to Greenwich Mean Time by removing the hour added.

Most astrological tables are written in Greenwich Mean Time and if you use British Summer Time or any form of Daylight Saving anywhere, you must revert back to Greenwich Mean Time to use the *Table of Planetary and Angelic Hours* or you will get the wrong information.

You could regard British Summer Time as being 'man–made' and Greenwich Mean Time as 'solar–made' and the correct time according to the Sun; British Summer Time is a 'convenience time' to give longer hours of daylight. More information about British Summer Time is found in the chapter *The Table of Angelic and Planetary Hours.*

In our example, this person would be born with the Sun in Cancer, which is ruled by the Moon and the Angel of the Moon is the Archangel Gabriel, therefore this angel is their Solar Guardian Angel. The Moon was in Virgo ruled by Mercury, whose angel is the Archangel Raphael and this angel is their Lunar Guardian Angel. The 18th of July 1969 was a Friday, which is ruled by Venus, whose Angel is the Angel Anael. The hour 12.20 p.m on Friday, the day of their birth is ruled by Mars whose angel is the Angel Samael. So this individual has the Archangel Gabriel as their Solar Guardian Angel and the Archangel Raphael as their Lunar Guardian Angel. The Angel Anael is their first Auxiliary Angel and the Angel Samael is their second Auxiliary Angel. These four important angels are based upon the day, month, year, day and time upon which they were born.

Your Auxiliary Angels can be invoked for the matters they rule as with any other angels. However, if you want to invoke an angel for a specific purpose and find the angel involved is one your 'personal angels,' then this could give them a greater interest in you and your affairs as a result of being in their charge. However, this does not mean you will automatically be given preferential treatment or *carte blanche* to get what you want. Did your parents or your family always give you everything you cried for? Sometimes they could not, sometimes they believed it would be unwise and said no, you did not like it but you got over it. If your family did this through their circumstances at the time or experience then so can the angels for the better reasons that they know even more than your parents did about you.

What would be the result of the Sun and Moon being in the same sign of the Zodiac? It would simply mean the Guardian Angel should be twice as strong, active or more prominent in your life and its affairs.

What would be the result if the day and the hour also gave you the same Auxiliary Angels? Again, this would make that angel stronger still because this would be like strengthening a pole by adding other poles to it and binding them together. I give the Auxiliary Angels (capriciously) three quarters to half strength of the Guardian Angels. This is an arbitrary figure only used to explain my methods regarding this particular aspect of the work. Could this happen and someone have all the angels in same sign as suggested? If all the angels were the same that would make this 'singleton' angel very strong and somewhat unique and to date I have not met it, however . . . I do not count that for aught.

Let us take another 'fictitious' person born on the 13th of February 1983 at 7.30 a.m. The Sun is in Aquarius, which is ruled by Uranus. The (New) Moon is in Aquarius ruled by Uranus, for this is the date of the New Moon. The puts the Moon in the same sign as the Sun, which is why this date was chosen. The 13th of February is a Saturday, ruled by Saturn whose day is also used by Uranus and the time of 7.30 a.m on Saturday is ruled by Uranus. This means that the Solar and Lunar Guardian Angels and both of the Auxiliary Angels are all ruled by the same angel. At least a person with this angel (four times over) should never be bored — I think they would like to be now and then — but they will not, as said in the previous chapter.

This particular individual would have a full complement of four angels. They would have the same angel for their Solar and Lunar Guardian Angels plus their two Auxiliary Angels and one angel will perform the duties of all these offices. To complete the picture we could have chosen a time that gave the Rising Sign (= or Ascendant) to the Sign of Aquarius and its angel for the fifth angel, the Benben Angel (discussed later) — guess who, yes — the Archangel Uriel and he would like that. This would have included the Angel of the Ascendant introduced in the chapter *The Angelic Pentagram* but only mentioned here and so all of the five angelic positions of this person is under one angel. Could this happen? As said, it is possible of course and very rare I agree and it could make that individual very unique if positive — but a pain in the nether regions if negative!

Now let us look at the methods of substituting the second Auxiliary Angel because we are without a birth time because it is not known and none know what it was, a frequent situation. We know where the Sun was, we can find out where the Moon is and it is relatively easy to find out the day when we were born but we do not always know the correct time, giving us the second Auxiliary Angel.

### The 'Herald' and the 'Six o'clock Angel'

There are two methods by which this problem can be 'got around' (according to some) or 'solved' (according to others including myself) and both are acceptable. Whatever of the two ways you chose, both methods are perfectly satisfactory.

The first way to set in place your second Auxiliary Angel because you do not know your time of birth is by far the simplest and it has been suggested throughout the work. You use the Archangel Raphael of the planet Mercury as a 'herald' for the fourth angel and you can do so with absolute confidence for the following reasons. The Archangel Raphael in some of his aspects and duties is very neutral, particularly when he is acting as the *Messenger of the Gods* or in the important post of herald, whether this is undertaken between antagonistic or friendly parties. I do not intend to go into this subject to deeply here, just enough.

In the Greek he is Hermes (Latin= Mercury) and he is the founder and head of the family of heralds (Latin= *heraldus*) and in the Greek κηρυξ, *kerux*; κηρυκες, *kerukes*= 'a herald, pursuivant, marshal, public messenger.' Ambassadors were authorized to give messages and they could negotiate matters— but not the heralds. The herald could circulate freely between warring factions, even during open war. They could open the way for negotiations and obtain the required permission and guarantees of safety to send ambassadors but first and foremost, their task was to deliver 'only what was said' — with 'no embellishment or additions whatsoever.'

The holder of the office of herald must show no favouritism or bias no matter what they may believe in the matter privately. They should deliver their messages and return the replies given without fear or favour, otherwise they would not be trusted by either parties, their own people who sent him as herald and those who received him. The king or sender expects and demands the person of his herald is held sacrosanct by the one who receives him because he is under the protection of the god Hermes/Mercury. The receiver of the herald honours him as the rule of civilized behaviour demands and naturally expects the same civilized practices for his own herald. To abuse or kill a herald while under the protection of his staff of office was beyond the pale and an act that was beneath contempt and retribution would sought. Witness the civilized treatment of the 'gentle herald' of the French, Mountjoy, in Shakespeare's **Henry V.**, which is an excellent example of the point in question. King Henry asks his name because ' . . . I know thy quality.' On being told his name, he tells the herald — 'Thou dost thy office fairly.'

When you invoke your personal angels, you can add to your invocation or letter the request or rider, that the Archangel Raphael as herald takes your wishes to your 'unknown angel.' There is a ten to one chance that the Archangel Raphael may even be the missing angel. You can rest easy, knowing your request and affairs have been given into completely safe hands especially if the Archangel Raphael is addressed as 'herald,' remember that heralds are his family. You must not forget the angels are a family and work together. The angels at times may appear to be at odds with each other because the duties of one may appear to conflict with those of another angel but only in the way they work and what they rule. This is only a surface appearance because fundamentally they all work together.

As always, let us squash any thoughts of laziness and do not think this suggestion is **carte blanche** not to bother learning anything or making the effort. Just invoke the Archangel Raphael, leave it all in his lap and sit back because he will do the job for you, after all 'that's what he does.' If it is not genuine, you may find something dumped in your lap for your impudence in thinking you can treat a mighty Archangel as a menial and I for one would have no sympathy. I have never attempted this and I would never be tempted. Your 'Green Bay tree' may appear to flourish for a time, but it will be cut down or uprooted in some way for your presumption. Perhaps you should remember what the 'wise American' Benjamin Franklin said — 'Despair ruins some, presumption many.'

Please forget the all too frequent picture of simpering angels who will overlook every transgression and carry on forgetting and forgiving regardless because 'it is their job,' that card has been played far too often in modern times to win any tricks. Do you have a limit beyond which you will not be pressed and how often have you warned someone not to push you too far? Do you have a certain standard and things you will not do?

Do not forget some have the Power to enforce their views and we can be extremely grateful it does not appear to be used very often. You rarely hear of a really genuine — 'road to Damascus' — a much–overused and theatrical phrase. Then there is that other over–worked and dramatic phrase — 'the Dark Night of the Soul.' Some people I have known seemed to have taken up permanent residence on the 'road to Damascus' or their souls are in perpetual darkness in the 'dark night of the soul' from which they seldom if ever appear to come forth and with some of them that could be a blessing in disguise.

Angels can be good or evil, according to what they had been sent to say or do, as we said in Part 1. The same angel or spirit could be sent to take away a million pounds or give it. Your opinion or description of the angel would match his deeds and you would report the contact accordingly. I think it would be reasonable to say we judge an angel as good or evil by their actions and what they do to us — of course, which does not necessarily make the angel so by nature. We sometimes have to do things demanded of us that go against our nature.

'It must be remembered in early thought, the spirits were considered vague with little or no moral character. They were considered neither angel nor demon, but it is thought they took their character from the duty they were given to perform and it is possible, therefore, that good and evil angels are often the same angel.'

The Archangel Raphael is a healing angel. This Archangel is invoked to bring the ease of healing but it must not be forgotten that he can also bring the *dis*–ease of affliction, plague and contagion if he was instructed to do so. 'Seven angels have the seven last plagues; for in them is the wrath of God.' *Revelation* 15:1 and ' . . . one of the seven, which had the seven vials full of the seven last plagues.' *Revelation* 21:9. Its been done before and could be so again. Therefore, it should not be taken for granted an angel cannot bring evil or be unpleasant if he is so instructed or if your actions or presumption invites it. If the angels can work positively, they can also work negatively.

Now let us consider the second method to use if you do not know the time of your birth. Your birthday is enough to give you three of your important angels, your Guardian Angels (the Sun and Moon) and the day upon which you were born will give you your first Auxiliary Angel, but the time of the day we were born is not always so secure but this does not mean that you cannot have your second Auxiliary Angel. Explained above is a satisfactory method of filling this position and next is another reliable method for the same problem.

We have taken an important time of the day in Hebrew astrology and tradition — 6.00 a.m, which has long been in use for astrological work of unknown times. This time is regarded as 'the first hour of the day' in both the *Talmud* and *Cabbala* and this hour and its angel can be accepted without hesitation. It is also mentioned in the chapter dealing with the *Angelic Pentagram*. This is recommended to you and is the method I would not hesitate in using if I did not know the time of my birth.

We have extracted for you from the *Table of Planetary and Angelic Hours*, the seven Angels that rule the hour of 6 a.m (= GMT) for each day of the week and there is no working out to be done though looking at the *Table of Planetary and Angelic Hours* for yourself would not hurt. All the reader has to do is to know the day upon which they were born. If someone does not know the hour when they were born, they can substitute the *Six o'clock Angel* from this table for their second Auxiliary Angel. The reader may ask if I prefer this method then why give the reader the first. The simple answer to this is because the alternative method exists and it also has equal merit. I try to give alternatives, even when my views differ regarding them, though not here. If I was somewhere where I did not have access to the table below or I could not remember it, I would use the Archangel Raphael without a second thought. The following list gives the angel ruling the hour of six o'clock in the morning for each day of the week

| | |
|---|---|
| For Sunday: | use the Angel Samael. * |
| For Monday: | use the Archangel Raphael. |
| For Tuesday: | use the Angel Sachiel. |
| For Wednesday: | use the Angel Anael. |
| For Thursday: | use the Angel Cassiel. |
| For Friday: | use the Archangel Michael |
| For Saturday: | use the Archangel Gabriel. |

*Remember not to confuse the Angel Samael
(= Mars) with the Angel Sammael (= often given
to the Devil or Satan.)

# DO YOU DEAL ONLY WITH YOUR GUARDIAN ANGELS?

No! You always take your problems or requests to the angel who rules whatever it is you are seeking help with. You do this irrespective of whether the angel is your Guardian Angel, Auxiliary Angel or not. The matter is not unlike going to ten shops to try and get the item you want (= attraction) or to try to get rid of things you do not want (= banishment) but you should keep one thing in mind. Even though your Guardian Angel does not rule the matter, you can still take the matter to him if you wish, especially if you do not know or are not sure who rules the matter. Sometimes we take problems to someone who, although they cannot always deal with the problem themselves, they have a wealth of experience and knowledge and they know where to go or who to see to have the matter settled or get good advice. Have we not at times told someone who has got us out of an awkward predicament 'they were a Guardian Angel.' Always go to the angel involved in the matter first, if they are a Guardian Angel or an Auxiliary Angel then so much the better.

The lists given for the angels are wide and they do not always rule material matters. Found within them are such things as authority, fertility, courage, social advancement, career, hopes and wishes, love, daring, intellect, philosophy, elegance, harmony and unity, pleasure, depression, patience and so on. Life does not consist only of those things comprehended by the five senses; if they were, if it was life would be much easier to deal with.

You know when you are happy and contented, but you cannot go out and buy a pound of it as you can biscuits. Depression cannot be thrown into a dustbin because you do not want it as you can a cracked cup. However, you have to be prepared to work with these things and resolve them because as most know, they are not like a coat that you can take off a peg when you feel like it or take off when you do not. There are a lot of people today suggesting that it is abnormal to be unhappy or to be despondent or depressed. Everyone feels these things now and then and if you do, you are not ill or odd because of it, 'black dog' and I are old friends. From this statement, I obviously exclude certain medical or psychological conditions.

There are many very talented people in the world but unless all the elements 'come together' in what we call 'luck' or being in the right place at the right time, then sadly talent is not always enough to guarantee success or reward. You only have to look at the entertainment industry and television in particular to see that success and talent does not necessarily go hand in hand.

It would not be wrong to regard your *Guardian Angels* as your intimate angels. If your *Guardian Angel* rules the problem for which you are seeking help, so much the better. In our affairs we have a select circle of people we often call our intimate circle. This is to differentiate them from casual people, friends and associates who we meet and get on with, as with work or our daily routine and of course, this does not prevent them from being helpful and nice people. The people we want to be with and close to are those in our intimate circle, which is why we put them in a circle or boundary and keep the outsiders — 'outside the circle.' Your intimate friends you bring inside and within the *Sacred Court* of your Temple, while the others stay in the *Outer Court* and you alone enter the *Temenos*. These principles are explained in the text and the diagrams.

'Experts' today are finding out something that astrology has known for years. They are suggesting that we should try and keep our intimate circle down to eleven people or less, twelve including yourself. A person can only handle eleven people or less in intimate relationships. Most winning teams in sport, commerce and so forth seem to be those that keep to or below this figure. Going beyond this number breaks the circle and causes its collapse and the reason for this is comparatively simple.

There are twelve houses in your birth chart. You are always represented by the 'first house' in the astrological chart, because your birth chart is your 'circle.' The other eleven houses or spaces can be filled with your intimates or 'the close friends of your circle.' It is like having eleven guesthouses around you where each friend has their room or liberty where they can come, stay and be with you. If you want to bring someone else into the circle when these eleven rooms are filled, a thirteenth person, there is no room or space for them, because all the places have been taken or filled because you have a 'full house.' Those brought in from 'outside the circle' will have to take or share someone else's place.

This is not always taken kindly because that person breaks the intimate circle and the circle or boundary now has to remain 'open' to admit them into this special circle that many hold sacrosanct and special. Then the words 'outsider, interloper, odd–man out, gate–crasher' and so forth can start to appear. When these words are bandied about, the circle really has been breached and wide open to the outside; it is unprotected and no longer intimate. It is no longer an closeed circle and in due course, it will eventually fail and fall. Christ had thirteen with his twelve disciples; one broke the circle and the enemies got in and betrayed him. However, he knew the 'betrayer' would fulfil the prophecy — 'as it was determined.' *Luke* 22:22.

Your Guardian Angels are the ones to whom you can turn in times of trouble, stress, depression and despair. We call them to witness our grief, loneliness, happiness and joy. We can trust them without question, they will listen and a very wise Turkish proverb tells us that — 'listening requires more intelligence than speaking.'

To add a few more categories to the lists that the angels deal with, the *Seven Angels of Old* in Medieval Occultism ruled 'seven magical works' and it is not difficult to place their angelic ruler. Magic was classified in seven groups. *Works of Light and Riches*; *Works of Divination and Mystery*; *Works of Punishment and Retribution*; *Works of Science and Skill*; *Works of Intrigue*; *Works of Love* and *Works of Malediction and Death*. Below is another early list, passed on without comment, which gives us:

Sun — Sunday: Gaining money or support; causing friendship
and harmony; finding buried treasure.
Moon — Monday: Operations of love; seeing visions;
necromancy; invisibility; operations connected with water;
travel.
Mars — Tuesday: Operations of death, destruction hatred and
discord; summoning spirits of the dead.
Mercury — Wednesday: Obtaining knowledge or discovering
the future; theft and deceit, commerce, merchandise.
Jupiter — Thursday: Gaining money, status or friendship;
becoming invisible; achieving good health.
Venus — Friday: Ceremonies of love; lust; pleasure and
friendship.
Saturn — Saturday: Ceremonies of death, destruction or
injury; summoning souls from hell; obtaining knowledge.

# THE AUXILIARY ANGELS:

Naturally, the Auxiliary Angels are useful in as much as they widen the range of angels who are considered to take a personal interest in your life, its affairs and if they rule your invocation, again this is though to be all to the good. The addition of the Auxiliary Angels give you four angels to stand 'four–square' for you. This model of the four angels standing four–square will be found again in the chapter on the *Pyramid of Power* where you will meet the important Angel of the Ascendant or Benben Angel. The day you were born is important because it marks us in the beginning for life and, like Cain; we always bear the mark of it. The Auxiliary Angels wait in attendance to see if they are needed to assist your Guardian Angels while they watch over us.

You can use your Auxiliary Angels if you require help quickly, especially if their days and hours are the first available to you, because they are linked to you and your Guardian Angels as helpers. However, if you find you have a genuine emergency on your hands, the simple act of lighting a candle of appropriate colour or using white is often ritual enough. If your problem is very urgent then invoke the angel of the hour and speak low. Use an appropriate incense if possible, if not then use frankincense as your 'emergency incense' because it is acceptable to all, rejected by none and it is the one incense you should always have in stock.

There is a list known as the 'Seven Planetary Ages of Man,' given by Shakespeare in his play *As You Like It.* Act.2: Sc.7. In the text Shakespeare only appears to give six planetary ages in the speech and not seven, but the Sun is there if you look for it or know what to look for it. The angels and their planets also rule certain ages in our lives. This is not essential information but any information that widens and extends the knowledge of the angels and our association with them is useful in my thinking and you can never know enough. From the lists, you can see that we are all living in a period of our life ruled overall by an Angel. This adds a background colour to that particular period that is sometimes recognizable.

We use a similar system in history to describe certain periods, saying one period was Elizabethan, Victorian, the Dark Ages and so forth. This often comes from the manner of dress, the language, the buildings and many other things and without their history; we have individuals like a leaf that does not know to which tree it belongs.

The age periods differ in some lists, but not a great deal. Hermes Tristmegistus and Ptolemy give the planetary periods as the listed below. We have added the appropriate Angels in parenthesis to the periods given.

The Moon governs the First Age, which is four years. (The Archangel Gabriel= the Moon.)

Mercury governs the Second Age of ten years, from five to fourteen. (The Archangel Raphael= Mercury.)

Venus governs the Third Age of eight years, from fifteen to twenty–two. (The Angel Anael= Venus.)

The Sun governs the Fourth Age of nineteen years, from twenty–three to forty–one. (The Archangel Michael= Sun.)

Mars governs the Fifth Age of fifteen years, from forty–two to fifty–six. (The Angel Samael= Mars.)

Jupiter governs the Sixth Age of twelve years, from fifty–seven to sixty–eight. (The Angel Sachiel= Jupiter.)

Saturn governs the Seventh Age form sixty–nine to thc end of life and the release of death. (The Angel Cassiel= Saturn.)

The modern planets Uranus, Neptune and Pluto were discovered long after this list was compiled by the ancients and some are mentioned indirectly in *Bible*. These three have been added to the above list by some writers to extend the old list for today's use and the reader will find them. I have always accepted the reasoning that these outer planets being beyond the limits of Saturn are concerned more with the part of the individual that does not undergo change, decay and death as the physical does. These planets do influence the physical just as our thoughts can indirectly influence our physical life and health. I agree with giving their rule over to the more intangible part of our nature and life generally, the spiritual, higher philosophy and the intangible matters of life. Uranus deals in part with Astrology, Occultism and Magic and the other matters in his list, Neptune with Spiritualism or the Spiritual including his list and Pluto with Regeneration on the deepest levels such as the true *Dark Night of the Soul*, not the one that some people seem to have every other week and his list.

Next, let us move on and discuss two important subjects that each can undertake for themselves, which should not prove difficult now that you have discovered the personal angels in your life. The *Pentagram of the Angels* and the *Personal Pentagram of Your Angels* — I have never been without either of these Pentagrams throughout my occult life.

## THE TWO ANGELIC PENTAGRAMS — ONE FOR ALL and A PERSONAL ONE

Magical diagrams are geometric designs representing the mysteries of the Deity and Creation. Some are reputed to have unique attributes in the Rites of Calling Forth in magic. The principal forms these designs take are the triangle, the double triangle, which forms the six-pointed star, the Seal or Sign of Solomon (= 'Signum Salomonius'). This hexagram is also called the Magen David or 'Shield of David' that is said to be the shape of King David's shield and now one of the most popular symbols of Jewish symbolism. If this symbol is taken from an historical point of view it is true to say that it has ancient origins but its origins are obscure because it has no reference either in the *Bible* or Rabbinical writings.

The device itself appears to be very old and can be found among other magical symbolism, as an amulet to attract good luck and avert evil it is found in use around the twelfth century. However, it did not gain any real significance as a Jewish symbol until the nineteen century when it started to appear on synagogues. The Star of David was adopted by the First Zionist Congress in 1897 and incorporated into the flag of Israel and as a result became a symbol of nationality, because of this adoption Jews were forced to wear the star as a badge to separate them from others faiths in World War II by the Nazis in Germany.

The most popular and practical philosophical interpretation of this 'interlocking star' is of the divine reaching down from its source (upper triangle, point upwards) and the response of humanity reaching upwards to embrace it (the lower triangle, point downwards.)

There was the tetragram or tetras (= 'the number four, a quaternion, tetrad'), a four–pointed star, sometimes formed of two crossed pillars and finally we come to probably the most used, pentagram. We are primarily concerned with the latter symbol and these signs were outlined on paper, parchment, engraved on glass, metals and consecrated to various and specific rites.

'The Holy Pentacles numbered forty–two, of which seven were consecrated to each of the planets Saturn, Jupiter, Mars and the Sun. Five each to Venus and Mercury and six to the Moon. The divers figures were enclosed in a double circle, containing the name of God in Hebrew and other mystical words.'

The pentagram is a five–pointed star sometimes called the pentalpha by the followers of Pythagoras because its angles are like five (= 'pente') alphas (= 'A's'). It is a blend of two and the three, the first even number and the first odd number after the number of unity. This according to some indicates on the universal plane, the union of cosmic material with cosmic intellect. As a union or unity of five elements, it stands 'for the heavenly man.'

Its five points correspond to the head and limbs of the human body and this same general idea lies behind the five wounds Christians ascribed to the crucified Christ. Sometimes, as discussed below, the five–pointed star is drawn with one point down and two upwards like horns, representative of the polar opposite of the above, an emblem of base and heavy matter and so black magic.

As with the symbols mentioned above, the pentagram is a very old symbol and traditionally it is a weapon of power in the arsenal of magic and occultism. The word is sometimes written pentacle, pantacle, pentalpha, pentangle or pentageron. In old works it is often referred to as a 'five–fingered figure.' It is explained that when the hand is opened it symbolized the Microcosm. The Four Elements are represented by the four fingers (= Hebrew – Yod, He, Vau, He) with the thumb indicating the Element of Spirit (= Hebrew – Shin). The hand when closed symbolized totality and the 'egg' from which all manifestation came forth.

The Seal of Solomon is held to have been 'a sapphire that contained within it a live hand that grasped a small serpent, which was also alive. Through the bright gem both were visible, the hand, and the 'worm' as they called it. When invoked by King Solomon ' . . . the fingers moved and the serpent writhed, and miracles were wrought by spirits who were vassals of the gem.' *Credulities Past and Present*: William Jones (1898).

The pentagram consists of three triangles intersected. Aubrey says the pentacle was 'heretofore used by the Greek Christians (as the sign of the cross is now) at the beginning of letters or books for good–lucks sake.' Jewish women were 'held to make this mark on their chrysome clothes.' 'Chrysome' is an old version of chrisom= 'A white dress, anointed with the chrism, which in the ancient Church was put upon children by the priest at the time of their baptism. It was afterwards carefully preserved as a memorial and emblem of innocence . . . the white dress put upon a child newly christened, with which it was also shrouded if it died within a month after its baptism, the child was then also called a chrisom–child.'

Rennet, Bishop of Peterborough (Lansdowne MS. 231) writes. 'The figure of three triangles intersected and made of five lines, is called the Pentangle of Solomon and when it is delineated on the body of a man, it is pretended to touch and point out the five places wherein the Saviour was wounded, and therefore the devils were afraid of it.'

The pentacle is the *druden fus* for writers of magic in Germany where it is regarded as a powerful talisman against the power of witches. They said it had 'its origins in the doctrines of Pythagoras, and thence transferred to Druidism.'

The pentacle from time to time is found described as 'a piece of linen folded with five corners according to the five senses, and suitably inscribed with characters.' This pentacle the magician extended towards the spirits when he called them forth, especially if they were stubborn, rebellious and refusing to acquiesce in the ceremonies and rites of magic. Some commentators say the pentagram was a headdress made of fine linen that was worn as a shield against demons in the act of conjuration.

When we draw the pentagram, (sometimes called 'the endless knot') with a single point up, it is a symbol of good, as we will be using it. It was believed to be a symbol of the dominance of the divine spirit (= the upward point) over earthly matter (= the four lower points) or the four elements. The number four was symbolic of the mundane world of the four elements and therefore, old books of magic said of the pentagram that 'it represented man' and the physical level of existence.

When the pentagram was reversed, with the single point down and two points upwards, it was regarded as a symbol of evil and attracted sinister forces. This is because when the pentagram is written upside down it overturns the natural order of things and demonstrates the triumph of matter (= the two points upwards) over spirit (= the single point downwards).

The reversed pentacle is sometimes found with the figure of a Goat contained within the outline. This arrangement is often called the Goat of Mendes. The horns are placed into the two upright triangles with the ears are placed in the lower two triangles. The beard of the goat was set into the single point, which was pointing downwards in this reversed form. The face of the goat was placed in the centre of the pentagram. This particular illustration is frequently found in horror films and books on Black Magic and this outline of the pentagram is always associated with the Devil, Satan, the Angel Sammael and the Black Magic Arts.

The pentagram is one of the symbols often found on the Ace of Pentacles in Tarot cards and this is usually given as the 'Root of the Power of Earth.' This can be found with two points upwards on talismans, especially when used for invoking for wealth, because wealth is an earthly Power, in all probability Mammon and not a heavenly power. Naturally, if anyone was found invoking for wealth using an inverted pentagram they would be said to be invoking Satan for wealth and bargaining for the expected reward of money with their soul, not strictly true of course.

'The pentagram, which in Gnostic schools is called the Blazing Star, is the sign of intellectual omnipotence and autocracy. It is the star of the magi; it is the sign of the Word made flesh.' *Transcendental Magic* – Eliphas Levi. This is because it adds the 'One' of the Godhead to the 'four' of material matter.

In European magical textbooks, a pentagram was recommended for keeping evil spirits at bay because the demons were frightened by any symbol with five points. Modern magicians make use of the pentagram for invoking good influences and banishing evil influences. The pentagram is considered a potent means of conjuring spirits. A banishing formula followed the same ritual model of the pentagram invoking ritual, but in the reverse order. The act of invoking the pentagram has often been used as a Morning Prayer with the banishing procedure as the Evening Prayer.

The banishing procedure was considered a very 'effective weapon against polluted magnetism' and 'for getting rid of beguiling or profane thoughts.' The Lesser Ritual of the Pentagram is found early in the Rituals of the Golden Dawn and the Banishing Pentagram used the same ritual in reverse direction of that used in the Invoking Ritual; see the works of Israel Regardie.

As said earlier, five is a significant number because it is considered to symbolize the natural, rhythm of life and order in the macrocosm. This is why so many amulets and talismans are constructed upon this figure because the pentagram is a sign of the microcosm. Five planets are important to the Chinese — Mercury, Venus, Mars, Jupiter and Saturn. The Chinese use five elementals not four as we in the West. These are metal, wood, water, fire and earth, also five colours, white, black, blue, red and yellow. This is a very practical arrangement and the element 'earth' is placed where it belongs — under your feet in the centre — where you are standing.

The number five is said to 'represent man after the fall,' but if it is applied skilfully to secular matters, it signifies health, advancement and love. The relevance of this number was expressed by Hildegard of Bingen who said 'man is inclined by the figure five.' Saying 'he had five equal parts in height and five in girth. He has five senses and five members that are echoed in his hand, which has five fingers.'

In the West, we work with the four elements that have been mentioned elsewhere. Honorius of Autun, an early twelfth century popular theologian, said the flesh and bones of a man are derived from earth, blood from water, breath from air and bodily heat from fire – *Elucidarium*.

These brief words of explanation have prefaced this chapter to add detail to what is to follow. I thought it better to explain, no matter how abridged, why the pentagram and the number five is important in most works of this nature.

The pentagram is a powerful symbol even before any additions have been added to mark them for a particular purpose. The writer has always regarded a blank pentagram similar to the 'key blanks' that locksmiths use. The blanks from which he cuts a key to the pattern that will open a specific lock or door.

We have mentioned the Roman god Janus elsewhere and keys are under the Janus, which name means 'a gate' or 'barbican' and Janus is usually mentioned in many of the things that I write To enter a city or a house you had to enter through the gate or a door. Janus became known as 'the god of beginnings,' thus he is found at the beginning of a list of the gods, in prayer, even before Jupiter.

When the god is not represented by a door, he is shown as having two faces, one face is looking to the East while the other looks to the West and his temple had two doors that faced in the same directions. Janus is held to rule the final twelve hours of the old year, when the New Year is initiated and we make our New Year resolutions, even today. One face looks back to the old year, when we review the past year, its losses, gains and the lessons to be learnt. The other face looks toward the future with our 'New Year resolutions' to make the New Year better than the old one that is passing see the earlier entry for more information, now let us end this short preamble and get to the practical part of the chapter.

Look at the 'Angelic Pentagram' diagram at the end of the book and put a bookmark so that you can refer back to it while reading the text. You can make your pentagram on a thin sheet of glass, though some protection may be needed for any sharp edges as well as some method of hanging if the glass has no frame. A plastic sheet or the thin acetate used for overhead projectors has served in the past. New materials are constantly being introduced that can be adapted for your use. You must always look at materials in a new way and do not see things for what they were originally intended, but how you can use it for your purpose.

I have found a photo frame with the back removed leaving only the glass in the frame is ideal and today these can be bought quite cheaply, especially in markets. You will have to put in a few small panel pins in the corners or some means of stopping the glass from falling out of the frame when it is complete, as the back has been removed. What you are aiming for is the pentagram is best set on a material that permits the light to shine through it, not put on a solid material that does not allow this.

Apart from the specialised artwork that you put on the glass, everything is there ready made and framed and there are so many sizes available. Some frames are in an attractive gilt, silver, coloured or patterned frames. You can paint your pentagram in watercolours or draw it in crayons on a piece of paper the size of the frame chosen and when you are sure your diagram is correct, stick it in the back of the frame and copy it on the front of the glass from your pattern. If you fix your pattern behind the glass, you can use a wax pencil to draw it on the front or paint it freehand and with your 'pattern' in place, this is not difficult. Alternatively, you can paint your pentagram on the back of the glass, which I prefer because this protects the design when cleaning the front of the glass.

Make and paint in full colours your design on a very thin white paper again using a size of pentagram that will fit the glass you have chosen. Fix the design to the front of the glass and shine a light through the paper. You can now paint the design, in reverse on the back of the glass. This prevents any mistakes being made when doing it this way. Of course, if you decide to paint the design on the back of the glass, you will have to reverse the order of laying on the paint.

When you paint the design on the front of the glass, you paint the background colours first and let them dry. Next, add the symbols on the backgrounds and finally the black outline to cover where the coloured sections meet and give a strong outline. The order of painting is background, symbols and outline.

If you decide to put your design on the back of the glass you will have to paint the black outline first and let it dry, then put in the signs of the planets in place and let them dry then finally paint in the background colours last keeping them within the outline. This is simply the reverse order of the above. This order of painting for putting the pentagram behind the glass is outline, symbols and background. Turn the frame around to look at it from the front and if all is well, you will have a blazing pentagram when it is held up to the light or the Sun, especially if you have used glass paint.

Glass paint is one of the best mediums to use because it is translucent and lets the light shine through to bring the colours and their form into the room functioning like a stained glass window, which it is. Make it to let the light of the sunshine come through the pentagram into your room. Remember you make this form of pentagram for the coloured light, the pattern the pentagram creates and the pentagram will have some light coming through it, even on the dullest of days.

On dark nights the light inside the house shines through the pentagram and out to the darkness outside. The pentagram will shine out, declaring that you and your home are for the angels and the house and its occupants are under their charge. Today's society is sometimes tolerant to a point of intolerance — tolerant when people and things agree with their tolerance. You will have to decide whether this open display is desirable or not because only you know your area and the people in it. If you are not sure or happy with displaying your pentagram, then I would not let it be seen to the outside.

From the Chinese practise of Feng Shui (pronounced fung shw'ay= meaning 'wind and water'), we borrow one of its principles. The Chinese have used this art for centuries to produce harmonious, living conditions for people, their homes and the land around them. Feng Shui was used to avert ill fortune and stress, bringing good fortune and contentment. You can hang round, faceted crystals in your window, as these seem to be the best design, though you can use other shapes. The crystal casts its refractive light into the room and that is their purpose. The round crystals cast the light over a much wider area and spread it into the darkest corners on a bright day.

There are many hanging crystals available now in art and gift shops and when these are hung where they can catch the sun, they are a source of energy and power. In sunlight these will project, the seven colours of refracted light, one colour for each the Seven Angels of Old that are reflected in your pentagram, throughout your room. The crystal will cast this light remarkably long distances. Your room is filled with refracted light depending on how many facets on the crystal. The more the merrier as far as I am concerned because they reflect the coloured light onto ceilings, walls and floor, but the choice must be yours.

If you can afford to buy only one crystal then hang it in a window that is facing West, if you have a Western window. It is through this window that the setting and dying sun, shines into the house. The crystal will energize and disperse this dying, weak light into the refracted light of the seven colours of the rainbow, which is vibrant and possessing energy. The Chinese people regard light from the West as harmful and threatening. My Chinese friends tell me that some Chinese people draw their curtains to prevent this light entering their homes with some not having a western window if it can be avoided, because in most religious traditions the Lands of the Dead lie in the West 'with the dying sun.' For this reason few Chinese will not (or are unhappy) living in a house numbered four because it has the same sound in Chinese as the word 'death' and a house numbered 444 is definitely out.

These faceted crystals supplement beautifully your hanging pentagram of the angels. Furthermore, any letter–invocation to the angels, left lying in the path of the refracted light of the crystal(s) or pentagram as the sun passes through the day is thought to be effectual and energizing for both the angelic letter and sender.

On your pentagram, you paint the sigils of the planets and the outline of the pentagram black. If you wish, you could paint the outline of the pentagram in gold if you are male and silver if you are female but do not paint the sigils in glass paint as they represent the traditional lead outlines. Glass paint is recommended for the background colours mainly because it lets the light shine through the colours and the solid colour used for the outline and sigils cast their shapes as shadow and this would be my choice. I used to get my glass paint from *Windsor and Newton Ltd, Artists Supplies* but there are other art suppliers now. This gives as said, your pentagram the appearance of a stained glass window, which is the effect you should be trying to create. Leonardo da Vinci, who knew something of colour, said the power of meditation was ten times greater under violet light falling through the stained glass windows of a quiet church than any other colour. This pentagram is made as a general Angelic Talisman of Protection, an Angelic Blessing and a permanent prayer to Providence working through the angels by inviting them into your home.

Always remember, you view the pentagram as if you were viewing someone from behind. Your right is the pentagrams 'right' and your left is its left. When you stand in front of someone, their right is on your left and vice versa and this is natural. It takes longer to explain then do.

Now let us consider the colours used for the Pentagram of the Angels. The single triangle at the top, represents the 'head' and this is coloured with a bright yellow background for Mercury because we usually regard thought, intellect and reasoning as being concentrated in the 'head' area.

The right 'arm' background is coloured red for Mars and his 'good right arm' of defence for it was the sword arm in the past. The right hand was offered in friendship and open to show it did not have a weapon in it.

The left 'arm' background is coloured light blue and given to Venus. It is gentler of these two planets and gave less offence for it was the 'glove hand,' decorative, friendly and sometimes regarded by some as the weaker of the two, which is reasonable if you are naturally right–handed.

The right 'leg' is under Jupiter with a purple, mauve or lilac background, it is this leg we use when we are told to 'put our best foot forward.'

The left 'leg' is under Saturn with a dark green background for it followed the right and is under the rule of Saturn. It is this leg we speak of when we say of someone is 'on their last legs' for as often said, the planet Saturn rules the end of most things, including life. When the Christ said 'it is finished' on the cross, he surrendered his physical life to Saturn as Lord of Death, because his physical life was finished.

The torso in the centre contains the Sun and it is the area of the Element of Fire so it has a background colour of orange and represents the chest and physical heart of the male, while the Moon represents the breasts and physical heart of the woman as the Sun rules the physical heart for both sexes. Love is under Venus but the 'seat of the affections' is the Sun and the heart, which the love of Venus frequently breaks or Mars overheats with the ardour of passion or lust.

Are you naturally left-handed in writing and most of the other things in your life? Is the left the stronger of the two sides for you? This causes no real problem! Reverse the left and right sides of the pentagram so that Mars, the planet that is everyone else's 'good right arm,' goes to the left and becomes your 'good left arm' putting Venus on the right. Reverse the order of the 'legs' and put Jupiter on the left so that your left 'leg' is your 'best leg to put forward,' which it is and Saturn goes to the right. If you are naturally left–handed then so should your Angelic Pentagram.

Remember to take the background colour over with the sigil of the planet and all will be well, otherwise you will have the right planet on the wrong background colour — messy! The other parts represented on the pentagram remain as they are because only the left and right sides change position. Your 'body' and 'head' remain constant no matter what hand is prominent and this does not seem to cause them any problems.

As said earlier, there may be circumstances when it may not be practical or desirable to hang your pentagram in your windows or put it out on open display. It would be foolish to think the 'breakers of bones on the rack' have left us and they have much more subtle ways now. This, however, need not be an obstacle to having the pentagram in your room. During the day, a pentagram is not noticed in a well-chosen window. At night, you can stand your pentagram with a candle or a night light behind it, which is excellent symbolism because, like the Sun, the candle is a living light.

You can paint extra pentagrams on paper, wood or any material suits your purpose. Use an appropriate paint for the medium used. Make up a suitable base and paint your pentagram on it in watercolours, poster paint, emulsion, gloss or enamel paints. If your pentagram is done on a wooden base then you can varnish the finished pentagram to keep it clean and for this, I personally prefer matt varnish because it reduces any shine. Hang or stand your pentagram wherever is convenient for you and remember just because it cannot be seen does not mean it is not there.

Placing your pentagram out of sight does not affect its efficacy or hinder its work. I made a small pentagram with a small wire hook on the back to hang on my headboard each night over my head, while I slept. The pentagram would be taken down in the morning and hidden away simply so because it did not require explanation. You can paint your pentagram on stout card. Cut a flap to fit on the back so that it stands up like a photograph frame by your bed. Hide a small copy of your personal pentagram behind a picture on your desk or hanging on a wall, if you want to take a pentagram to work. You can stick a pentagram behind a hanging picture in your room if you want to keep matters private, there are so many ways this problem can be resolved.

The foregoing section has dealt with a general Angelic Pentagram. This pentacle can be used by everyone because it is the same for everyone and it is like putting up a notice in your house or room that reads — 'All the Angels are welcome here.' The personalized pentagram is give next and is made personal for the one who makes it and is regarded as a powerful talisman to make up when it is charged and energized with power. It is not enough just to make your pentagram, without consecration, it would be like making a car and forgetting to put the engine under the bonnet. The simplest way to start charging your pentagram is from the very beginning through the concentration you put into the work while making it. Do not let people touch your pentagram while you are creating it, do not let them touch it after it has been made and the best way of doing this is not to let them know about it.

There many ways of performing consecration and dedication and if you already have established rituals for this in place, perhaps in the course of earlier work or previous study use them; particularly if you are satisfied with them. In matters such as these, the 'why' changes little but there are often numerous variations in the 'how' that can vary according to temperament, earlier teaching or past experience. It is not unlike ten people leaving their homes throughout the county to come to Trafalgar Square in London. Depending on where they are coming from, they can walk, cycle, drive cars, use planes, trains or buses and find almost limitless routes of getting to the agreed meeting place nevertheless, they will arrive at Trafalgar Square in London and if they were to loose their way, they will not.

For those who have no previous experience I give the following suggestions to help them and what follows has been used for a long time now with no reasons to change it. You can use either incense or light in the form of candles, both if you feel inclined. If your situation is say rooms within a house and you want to keep things private use the light, though incense is used more by people more that it was in the past, especially incense sticks. This was discussed in an earlier work on ritual incense, which is being revised and enlarged and from it I am going to take the 'Time Candle' used in magic because it that works well with many things were time can be used, whether for 'lights' or 'incense.'

## The Time Candle

I make up a Time Candle to use on an altar or for a ritual use where time is involved for it is simply a natural extension of the Clock Candle, which has a long history and this has been adapted and shortened from the original for use here. According to Hazlitt, 'There were no clocks in England in King Alfred's time. He is said by his biographer Asser, who is supposed to have died in A.D. 910, to have measured his time by wax candles, marked with circular lines to distinguish the hour.' *Faiths and Folklore*, 1905.

You make Time Candles up as required for anything that deals with periods of time. You can keep unmarked Time Candle in stock and in their box until required. Mark them in equal sections for the number of periods your ritual lasts, not necessarily in hours because it is not a candle to tell the time only to show and count the equal periods required for the work. Each marked section does not have to last an hour despite being called a 'Time Candle.'

You make a Time Candle by putting divisions on it according to your needs and I recommend it to you. This candle has only one purpose for being on your altar or being used, to give you equal time–periods for the work in hand. A ritual of seven days will have shorter periods than a four–day ritual because on the same size candle, the seven sections will be smaller than a four day. The size of this candle is up to you, as long as they are not taller than any Altar Candles being used but the bigger the Time Candle you chose, the longer the sections will last.

Always use a dark green candle for the Time Candle as it represents the planet Saturn who is the Lord of Time in all matters here on the material level. If you run out of dark green — use a white or yellow candle. Mark this candle with the requisite number of divisions for the length of the work you are doing. Remember its only function is to give equal set periods of time and its function in all rituals is the same, which is why it is set to one side.

When you mark your candles with these equal intervals, take the straight side of the candle. Of course, I have an opinion and a method that I use. I only use the straight side of the candle for the timing and start my equal intervals from there. Some candles do not have this and if this is so, take the timing from the wick to the base. I do not include the curved top if it is present and my reasoning for doing this is as follows.

The top of the candle is my 'Gratia Lux' and I made up this name to be the 'free light' for this part of the candle. When I burn this small section, it is given to the Unknown God(s) of whom I am mindful before anything else begins. My rituals start and the timing begins when the small top section has burned down to the straight side of the candle. This light is freely given on every occasion and for each candle used. The Gratia Lux is given to the *Αγνωτος Θεος, Agnostos Theos* or the Unknown God(s*)*. How the Time Candle is used will be more obvious in the examples that follow.

Now let us deal with some aspects of incense. You pass the pentagram through incense to dedicate it to the service of the angels. Ideally, you would need seven incenses, one correct incense for each angel and dedicate the pentagram to each angel in turn by asking their blessing on your work and its outcome. If you have the incenses of the seven planets and their angels. If you do not have these seven incenses, one for each angel, then use frankincense far all and all will be well.

To do this form of consecration, you start on Sunday and end on Saturday. This should be done on the day that the angel rules and in one of the hours the Angel of the day owns. You would start with the Archangel Michael on Sunday in one of his hours. You would use Monday for the Archangel Gabriel in one of his hours and so on, until you reach Saturday when you would end in one of the hours of Saturn and the Angel Cassiel and with this planet, the sequence would be complete.

You do the full sequence in the consecration despite the fact that some of the angels may not be represented on your Personal Angelic Pentagram. There are ten planets and angels from which you take the five angels according to the birth needed for making the Personal Angelic Pentagram. There are seven planets and angels in the Angelic Pentagram and these are all are represented. The maximum you use for Personal Angel Pentagram is five planets and angels. However, you ask the blessings of all the angels, whatever pentagram you are creating. Would you give a party and not invite all the angels to come and not uninvited. Let us take a run from Sunday to Saturday to show this and the ten planets and angels that can be used for this.

### The Angels and the Days of the Week they Rule:

| | |
|---|---|
| Sunday/Sun: | Archangel Michael. |
| Monday/Moon: | Archangel Gabriel. |
| Tuesday/Mars/Pluto: | Angel Samael and Angel Azrael |
| Wednesday/Mercury: | Archangel Raphael. |
| Thursday/Jupiter/Neptune: | Angel Sachiel and Angel Asariel. |
| Friday/Venus: | Angel Anael |
| Saturday/Saturn/Uranus: | Angel Cassiel and Archangel Uriel. |

Remember as explained many times throughout. In the beginning, there were only the Seven Planets of the Ancients, as used in the Pentagram of the Angels. In the astrology of today three further planets were added and these were Uranus (= Archangel Uriel), Neptune (= Angel Asariel) and last, in 1930 came Pluto (= Angel Azrael), as used in the Personal Pentagram of the Angels because this pentagram is constructed from your birth chart that uses the astrology of today — using ten planets — it is not difficult. To accommodate these three extra planets, they took over one Sign of the Zodiac from three of the old seven planets so this means they can also use the day and hours of these planets, which is why, in the above list you will find three days have two angels.

If you follow this scheme, you will devote a little time each day to consecrating your personal pentagram to the angel or angels of that day. I think this method is the best as it parallels the Seven Days of Creation mentioned elsewhere. You would mark your Time Candle into seven equal periods with seven horizontal marks. When the hour of the Archangel Michael starts by the clock do nothing, never start dead on the hour or time in any work of this nature, leave it a few minutes to let the new hour to establish itself. If you are using lights only light the candle and let the Gratia Lux burn down and this obviously only happens once for each candle. When the light reaches the straight side of the candle dedicate your personal pentagram to the Archangel Michael and when the candle reaches the first mark for Monday, cup your hand behind the candle and blow it out.

If you are using incense only, wait for the correct hour to establish itself and light the incense, pass your personal pentagram through the incense smoke and dedicate your it to the Archangel Michael.

If you decide to use light and incense, wait for the correct hour to establish itself, light the Time Candle and let the Gratia Lux burn down while you light the incense, pass the personal pentagram through the incense and dedicate it to the Archangel Michael. Let the incense burn itself out so do not use too much and when the candle reaches the first mark blow it out and repeat whichever combination you are using on Monday until you reach Saturday and the dedication and blessing is completed. On Tuesday, Thursday and Saturday you dedicate your pentagram to two angels so that in one hour on seven days, all ten planets and their angels have been acknowledged and your personal pentagram is fully consecrated. If you do not have a candle snuffer and they are easy to get now, blow out your candles by cupping your hand behind the light and gently blow, see the revised and enlarged ***Practical Book of Candle Magic***, out hopefully later.

As the reader can see, the consecration rite given here is simple, plain and would not tax anyone and that is the reason that it was chosen but this does not mean that it is ineffective or it should be done in a perfunctory manner for that. Much ritual work can be made elaborate or simple depending on the temperament of the user(s) and in cases the angel involved. The Sun and Jupiter love ritual, Mars wants you to get to the point, Saturn dislikes ostentatious show, Mercury (like the planet) is swift and to the point but leave out nothing due for that and so on.

In the matter of choice regarding this part of the work, I have always offered roughly the same advice. As a plant, tree or anything you want to grow in your life needs good roots, see that the roots or beginning of your efforts are sound and you will have growth. This is why at this point we are going to introduce another small but important ritual below that can be used when you feel the need.

The 'roots' of the above forms, although not written, are 'that Creation was started on the Sun's Day with the creation of Light and ended on the Sabbath, which should be for resting and that day is Saturday or Saturn's Day, when Creation was finished because as repeatedly said throughout, Saturn ends most things and if whatever what you are doing look as if it is lead naturally to this planet and angel, I feel it is probably closing along the right lines.

'God ended his work which he made; and he rested on the seventh day . . . And God blessed the seventh day, and sanctified it.' **Genesis** 2: 2. God started his work on the first day, the day of the Sun and the Archangel Michael. He finished his work and rested on the seventh day, which is Saturn's Day or Saturday, from sunset Friday to sunset Saturday, which is the Sabbath and he 'sanctified it.' He did not rest on the first day, Sunday, because that is not the Sabbath.

The Sun initiates things and Saturn finishes them. Sunday replaced the Jewish Sabbath primarily in remembrance of Christ's resurrection on this day and called the 'Lord's Day.' Observing this day as a day of rest began to be regulated by ecclesiastical legislation at the beginning of the 4th century, Constantine forbade townspeople to work on Sundays in A.D 321 though permitting farm labour because food was needed.

Start with the hour of the Sun for the Sun gives its life–giving rays to everything or they will die. Without light, all would be given over to darkness and back to Chaos.

To conclude, could the above Rite of Consecration be completed in seven hours instead of seven days? Yes, it could whether for this or anything else you are working with. I feel that this is best done again on Sunday, Day of the Sun. this time use the order of the planets as given in the Table of Planetary Hours and not the natural days of the week. This is the clockwise order of the planets taken from the Heptegon or Septangle of the Planets giving the sequence found in Table of the hours of the Angels and Planets. Whatever planet or angel you start with clockwise around the Heptagon, the order of the planets remains the same as it is given and is never broken.

We are starting with the Sun from the Table of Planetary and Angelic Hours and the Sun is followed by Venus, Mercury, Moon, Saturn*, Jupiter* and Mars* because this is their natural sequence and a future diagram will explain this order. Remember the planets, days and hours marked with the asterisk can have two angels on that day when you are using the ten planets of today instead of the Seven Ancient Planets, as explained earlier with the Table: *The Angels and the Days of the week they rule.*

Sometimes I use a small ritual devised a long time ago now, which has been in continual use and is adaptable for many circumstances where you want it initiate or create something. It is based upon and called the . . .

## The RITUAL of the FIAT LUX.

This small ritual I devised many years ago and it is small when it is stripped of the explanations and reasons for using it, often with these things, it takes longer to explain them than perform them. This has been in use by many others who, like myself, found it quite useful for the reasons given, sometimes with slight person variations but not in the main premise. I feel that it always helps and others do the same, to understand the words we use and to know why we use a word in a particular context. So let us take a look at the word 'fiat.' Under *facio* we find *fiat* listed and telling us it is 'an expression of assent, so be it, very good.' — *Lloyd's Encyclopaedic Dictionary*, 1895 — it gives me fiat, s. [Lat. 3rd pers. sing. pr. Subj. of *fio*= 'to be done.']

1. Ordinary language: An order or command for anything to be done.

2. Law: An order or warrant of a judge or the Attorney–General, authorising or allowing certain processes and signified by his subscribing the words *fiat ut petit*, that is 'let it be done as is asked.'

These lines give the key to the whole process that follows and a part of the above is incorporated into what follows. The word 'lux' has the meaning 'the light of the sun. The heavenly bodies or day, the sight of the eye.'

This ritual has been given in other works that I have written and to operate this ritual you will need a small table. Prepare it by setting out a clean cloth, a small tablecloth or use a large, good quality napkin would be ideal if you are limited for space. The purpose of the napkin is to define the area on which you are going to work. Defining an area brings us again to Saturn, who sets the limits, concentrates your work within a circumscribed area and focussed, so that it does not become scattered and therefore weak by dissipation by going outside the area.

Use a cloth that has not been used for anything before you use it and if it has been used then wash it. Soaking a used napkin for a while in a strong saline solution before washing it will sterilise it of its previous use. A new one bought and kept only for this kind of purpose is even better. The napkins other purpose is to give an area on your table that is clean and to isolate your work from the tables customary secular use.

Place your pentagram, talisman, charm, amulet and so forth in the centre and set out some incense in a suitable burner above the pentagram, opposite to you and you should be facing the East. Set a box of matches open with one match on the top of the box in front of your, under the pentagram

You need two candlesticks of glass or crystal. One candlestick should have an orange or gold candle (= the Sun–male), which is placed to the right of the pentagram. The other candlestick is placed to the left of the pentagram, with a white or silver candle (= the Moon–female). Set these items equally spaced at the sides of the pentagram so that it forms a balanced cross with the incense and the matches. The Christian Cross has one arm longer than the other arms because it was an unbalanced Cross of Sacrifice that was 'earthed' in the soil of Golgotha — 'the place of the skull,' a hill of death. Skulls, mountains, hills and death are all matters found under the rulership of the planet Saturn, you cannot avoid him. The reader will find, throughout the work, how so many things come back to this planet because if something has an end, as most things do, there you will find Saturn waiting as always.

Now why do we have two candlesticks with one candle dedicated to the Sun and the other to the Moon? We do it to accord with the words 'And God made two great lights.' *Genesis*.1: 6. We represent these 'two great lights' with the two candlesticks and their gold and silver candles, which naturally represent the Sun (= gold) and Moon (= silver).

We are further told 'And God made two great lights; the greater light to rule the day (= the Sun), and the lesser light (= the Moon) to rule the night: he made the stars also. And God set them in the firmament of the heaven to give light upon the earth, and to rule over the day and over the night, and to divide the light from the darkness: and god saw that it was good. And the evening and the morning were the fourth day.' *Genesis* 1:16-19.

The best day you for the FIAT LUX is again the Day of the Sun (= Sunday) starting on 'the evening and morning of the first day.' This simply means you regard Sunday as starting on sunset Saturday until sunset Sunday, when Monday starts and this is the way it was divided 'in the beginning.' Another day is 'the evening and the morning' of the fourth day when the 'lights' were created. Starting from Sunday this would be Wednesday, the day of Mercury and the Archangel Raphael and there is a cabalistic connection between the Sun and Mercury. Use the biblical and Celtic 'day' from sunset Tuesday until sunset Wednesday and not after that time, because after sunset on Wednesday would be the start of the evening and morning of Thursday.

Reckoning the days and nights using this order was acceptable for the style of life in those early times. Starting with sunset at the end of a day started the new day and it progressing from darkness into increasing light, this was a more optimistic and natural order with natural light. You slept in darkness at the beginning of the day and got up when the Sun came over the horizon, you then stopped working and the business of the day when the Sun set again. The progression from darkness to light and the new day starting again in darkness appeals to me, though I admit it would be quite impractical today. However, in occultism and magic you often have to live in two different times, the occult or ritual timing and the civic and everyday timing.

In the modern order, our day starts at midnight during darkness, goes into daylight and then goes back to darkness to start the new day at midnight again, which is clearly in the middle of the night. We still retain a remnant of this old order. Sometimes we say that we will meet someone in two weeks time or 'a fortnight.' This comes from the Middle English *fourt(en)*= 'fourteen,' and night. The old spelling was 'fort–nyte,' 'fourte–night,' 'four–ten–night' and 'fowrt–nyght'= 'a period of two weeks or fourteen days. It was the custom to reckon by night and winters (= Samhain), instead of days and years: thus we had *sennight*= 'seven nights, a week.'

282

As said, I admit the old order is no longer practical unless you are retired and financially secure, but I have always liked the principle behind it because it is a more natural order because it went with the Sun and Moon.

To fully discuss this old method of reckoning the days, the 'evening and morning' of the day, which would need a big deviation even for me. I am sometimes a little criticized for the 'detours' I take but it has done little to halt them. I love detours in writing, because they so often lead to such interesting places that may otherwise be missed. At times, I do agree that the criticism may be right and it possibly does take a little force from the writing, but I still do it, most readers never seem to worry about it and I am too old now the change horse mid–stream.

Now let us look at some further suggestions for the Fiat Lux. Do the ritual late at night and draw the curtains so that the room is as dark as you can make it, the darker the better. Do not do this ritual during the day for this is against all the principles of it being a ritual that 'calls up the Light.' Do the ritual in the old period at sunset on the previous day to sunset on the next day. If you find this method difficult then use the hours as used today for that is your time but you should try to enter the spirit of the old time. You will see that here and elsewhere, I suggest you never begin anything as the clock strikes the hour.

Always start after the hour or time you require has had time to established itself and does not have any mixed vibrations. If sunset was at 5.28 p.m you should leave things for a few minutes for the evening to become established and the time of the Moon to take over from the Sun and I wait until the sun properly below the horizon. When using a particular angelic hour of any set time, I have waited sometimes up to five minutes after the required time given.. Obviously, if the time you want is five thirty, half way through the hour, start when you wish because it is already within an established hour and it is not going to change and it is already well established. This was one of the first things I was taught and it has stood me in good stead, which is why it is here.

Never, unless it is unavoidable, use a lighter to light a natural light or candle. You should use a created flame from the Rite of Fire struck from flint and the closest to this is a match, because the fire is at least created by friction. I know many lighters use a flint to create the flame but they do not transfer the spark of living fire to the wood of the match, which was once a living entity.

Light your incense before you turn out the room lighting and when everything is in its appointed place, turn out the light. Stand for a time before your pentagram to allow your eyes to adjust to the darkness for a while. Try to imagine the whole planet in total darkness. You do not know what is out there in the darkness around your table. Imagine it is an unknown territory, not your familiar room. For your pentagram this is its personal 'in the beginning' of its Creation, with Chaos ruling around it without light or order.

When you feel ready raise your arms above your head and say out aloud (mentally if you prefer or circumstances require it), the opening words of **Genesis**. 'In the beginning God created the heaven and the earth.' This is the first physical manifested act of duality or division by Creation and Order. Next say 'And the earth was without form and void; and darkness was upon the face of the deep.' Pause a while and think upon those words, for there is much in them to ponder. Next say 'And the Spirit of God moved upon the waters.' Again, pause and feel or if you can visualize it better still, a light breath stirring around you and 'the waters' becoming a little agitated.

When you feel ready say 'Let there be Light' and strike the match left in readiness. The match flaring in the darkness may temporarily blind you, which is exactly the desired effect and it does not last long, the match represents the first created light — 'Let there be Light.'

Let your eyes grow accustomed to the light shining in the darkness, before going any further. You can now buy long matches that give more time for this than in the past. Again, try to visualize your small act as a 'beginning' with the darkness pierced by light and the darkness retreating from the light. Imagine the enormous authority of those Words of Power, their meaning and the awesome results when the original 'Light Bringer' brought Light down from on high to the planet below.

You must remember that in this small model of the opening of *Genesis*, you are acting as the 'creator' for this ritual. You are not God of course nor are you pretending to be for that would be a travesty. In this little model you will 'create the light' for it and then pass it on to the other 'two lights' you have put in place and named 'the Sun and the Moon.'

Next say 'And God made two great lights; the greater light to rule the day . . . ' At this point, you light the golden solar candle with the match. You can let the match go out when this candle is lit and burning well. Next, you take up the candlestick with the silver lunar candle in your left hand that represents the Moon. Light this from the candle of the Sun saying ' . . . and the lesser light to rule the night: he made the stars also. And God set them in the firmament of the heaven to give light upon the earth, and to rule over the day and over the night, and to divide the light from the darkness: and god saw that it was good. And the evening and the morning were the fourth day.'

The original 'Light' created with the words 'Let there be Light' is not the light, as we know it. When this command was given by God, he did not flick a switch as we do when we switch on a torch, an electric light. The Sun, Moon and stars did not appear until three days after this original Light 'to give light upon the earth.' The fourth day God created the things we associate with light. When we use our solitary match, it was the 'Light' of the first day (= singular and not the light of the Sun). The two candles are the 'lights' of the fourth day (= plural) because they represent the Sun and Moon. We cannot create light with our word as God created the Light with his Word, using the FIAT LUX — 'Let there be Light.' This is why I have suggested you ponder these words carefully and do not pass lightly over them

When your struck your single match that was the FIAT LUX — 'Let there be Light.' You then symbolically transferred the original Light to the candles, representing the lights of the Sun and Moon that came later in the scheme of things. We have condensed the first day of the original Light and the creation of the Sun and Moon of the fourth day into one ritual because our ritual is symbolic of the act of Creation. It is not intended to be an exact copy — but a symbolic representation.

When you lit the lunar candle from the solar candle this is, on a physical level, what the Moon does. She has no light of her own but carries the light of the Sun during the hours of night, for the benefit of her children on earth. She gives some light during the darkness to remind the Darkness that the Light exists and it will return. Naturally, most things need the respite that darkness brings. You next pass your pentagram through the smoke of the incense seven times, once for each Angel, using the old planets only (they only had seven planets in biblical times) going from the Sun and Moon through to Saturn.

Before passing your pentagram through your incense, I prefer to have a previously prepared and established form of speech applicable to all the Angels, so that you only need insert the name of the required Angel and this is hardly mass production. At this point in my ritual, I pick up a small sheet of best quality paper that I have prepared before the ritual on which has been written, in a flowing italic hand of old — *Fiat ut petit* –'let it be done as is asked' — this is my way. I hold the centre the edge of the paper in a pair of tweezers and light a corner at each end from the candles of the Sun and Moon and let it burn down before putting what remains of the still burning sheet in a suitable receptacle such as a saucer, in which to burn the sheet to ashes. I have transferred the 'light' from my representative Sun and Moon candle down to 'my world' and have respectfully asked *Fiat ut petit* — 'Let it be done, as is asked.'

Using the basic framework, you can make this ritual as simple or as elaborate as you wish. I have not put in full what I use because that is mine and not yours — it should be yours I feel. The same patterns are best for each of the seven Angels, but do not let familiarity make the execution of them mechanical and drift into a meaningless duplication and repetition. The FIAT LUX ritual is brief in actual use, in the *Bible* in fact it amounts to a few lines already given but it always takes much longer to explain on paper and read — most things of this nature do.

Having made the Angelic Pentagram for the house, you make a unique Personal Angelic Pentagram, which is activated in the same way as above. The gospel of perfection would be to make this pentagram active on your birthday, but this is a recommendation and not a fiat. Alternatively, you could always use the day of the week on which you were born perhaps using the time you were born on that day if you know it, always seek ways of making connections. This is because this pentagram is made up according to the personal details of your birth, which makes it distinctive and personal to you, using your date of birth, the day of your birth, the time you were born and your ascendant. Very few would have all the details exactly the same. This special pentagram is the subject of the next section and should cause little trouble with the making if you make the Pentagram of the Angels first. The only work additional to the first pentagram given earlier is the details that make it 'personal' to you the pentagram used what is personal to you and you will be using ten planets and the older seven planets because with this pentagram they are all available to you.

# YOUR PERSONAL PENTAGRAM OF THE ANGELS

This section deals with the Personal Angelic Pentagram that uses the full complement of your individual five angels of the ten available and here we are back to the important 'five' discussed at the beginning of the chapter and in part, this was why this number was discussed in detail. There it was said, 'five is a very significant number because it is considered to symbolize the natural rhythm of life and order in the macrocosm.' We are told 'if it is applied skilfully to secular matters it signifies health, advancement and love.' With the last three affairs, we are back to the basic 'three wishes' of most fairytales, legends and myths — health, wealth and love — because most wishes usually come back to these three.

The five important angels are your two guardian Angels, your two Ancillary Angels and a fifth additional angel – the Angel of the Ascendant or the Benben Angel. This last Angel is used in the chapter of your *Personal Pyramid of Angelic Power.* We have already given details of how to find your Guardian Angels and Ancillary Angels in the chapter of the Personal Guardian Angels. If you do not know your four personal Angels, we have explained elsewhere that there is a well–established method of completing them so that they can all be used. The Personal Pentagram is not a difficult diagram to make up and basically follows the principles given above.

As explained in the diagram of this pentagram, given at the end of the book, we have called the pentagram your Personal Angelic Pentagram to differentiate it from the general Angelic Pentagram. The latter pentagram is a powerful pentagram that is the same for all. This pentagram was the basis of an effective ritual drawn up some years ago, which is still in use.

It may be as well to take a look at the diagrams of this pentagram and put a bookmark in place while reading about it so you can refer back to it. As with the Angelic Pentagram, you fill in each part of the pentagram with the correct background colour according to the angel and the planet that will be placed there and you still write the sigil of the planet in black.

This diagram is naturally without any instructions regarding planets, angels or colours and it is, unlike the Angelic Pentagram, because it is waiting to be filled in and the text should make things clear. You will need to know the ascendant or rising sign of your birth chart, because the planet that rules the eastern horizon at your birth is placed in top triangle making it an important station to be filled.

For the Personal Angelic Pentagram you use the full ten planets of today's astrology from the Sun through to Pluto because these planets would be used if an astrologer were to set up an astrological chart for your birth chart today and all the other charts that come from it.

The ascendant is appropriate for top triangle in that it governs and 'colours' how we view people, circumstances, situations, how we deal with and react to them. It would not be wrong to say the ascendant colours our entire life because the ascendant is not unlike a magnifying lens through which the life is focused and therefore different for each person therefore it 'colours' a person's outlook greatly. The ascendant is the main factor making people different even those who have of the same birth sign so that those possessing the same birth sign are not all the same as the critics of astrology would have people believe. Within a Sign of the Zodiac, there are twelve further divisions that have to be taken into account by giving twelve perspectives of that one Sign of the Zodiac.

They show by such statements that they criticize a subject of which they know very little regarding it. Best given as the famous remark attributed to Newton who, speaking to Halley (of comet fame) who had expressed his doubts regarding astrology told him, 'Sir, I have studied it, you have not.' How can this be put better?

For those interested let us briefly explain the main point. Imagine a circular room where the wall is slowly revolving around a stationary chair, from left to right. In the wall are set twelve coloured windows, which represent the colours of the twelve Signs of the Zodiac. Let us sit a native of Libra, who is just about to be born in centre of the room, so that they look through each window in turn, as the windows pass before them. It will depend which window they were looking through at the time of their birth how they will see things throughout their lives. The particular window would be their ascendant Sign of the Zodiac and modify or 'colour' their outlook, how they view themselves, others and life in general according to its colour.

Let us say our native of Libra has Aries (= Mars), as their rising sign (= a bright red window) in their birth chart. They are under a cardinal Mars regarding their outlook of life, which would not give them for Libra, the usual 'peace-loving' or the 'peace-at-any-price label,' too often given as the main characteristic of all Libra's — not so! This combination will make them fight for what they want and take on anyone who tries to take it from them and Libra folk usually make the best generals in war or conquest.

Capricorn (= Saturn), as their rising sign (= a dark green window) would make our Libra very cold, calculating, cautious at times and a most sombre Venus because Saturn sits somewhat heavily on this light–hearted planet and Saturn is to cold and calculating for her. This Libra would have a Saturn outlook and 'the Scales or Balance' will not vary one iota from exactness, and even the addition of a grain of sand would be duly weighed for a full accounting. Not exactly the usual vacillating, indeterminate Libra, which Shakespeare's Hamlet may well have been. 'To be, or not to be, that is the question?' Libra with Saturn rising is more like the charming (when he wanted to be) ambitious and scheming Richard III — 'I can smile, and I can murder while I smile' and 'Can I do all this and not get the crown? Tut, were it farther off, I'll pluck it down.'

Libra does tend to vacillate in many things because they can see all sides of the problem not unlike Hamlet that ponders but does not always act (= Libra). Laertes acts but does not always think before he acts (= Aries, the sign that opposes Libra, so he opposes Hamlet and acts rashly, often without thought). Prince Fortinbras, son of the King of Norway calculates and waits until these two opposing signs destroy each other, he then steps in to pick up the pieces and does not even soil his hands (= Capricorn stands square between the other two Signs of the Zodiac where it can watch them both). As the reader can see, the Bard was no slouch in matters astrological or any other subject for that matter, which is why it is an unbalanced conclusion to the play when Fortinbras is sometimes omitted in the final scene.

What if our Libra had Aquarius (= Uranus) as their rising sign would they still be the quiet, peace–loving Libra, gentle, companionable and harmonious — yes, they could be when the mood takes them. However, with this combination of planets you will never know where the lightning will strike next or like Zeus, where they will throw the next thunderbolt. Independent, given to sudden change, self-willed, paradoxical, though because of Libra/Venus they can still be charming and loveable in their way, but a typical Libra? I think not! This pattern can be carried through for all the other signs of the Zodiac when combined with their appropriate ascendant combinations.

Libra rules the natural seventh house in the astrological chart. The House of Partnerships and the House of War and Open Enemies or those who have declared their enmity, which is bizarre for the house of partnerships and marriage. However, a Mexican proverb does say that 'marriage is the only war where you sleep with the enemy.' Do you want a 'typical Libra?' Probably the only combination in this particular discussion would be for our Libra to be born with Libra itself rising. If all the other parts are equal in the chart, they might just make the stereotyped typical Libra!

It may seem that the reader is being given astrology lessons but this diversion gives some of the reasons why the ascendant or rising sign is so important in these matters as is the angel that rules the ascendant. Few know of this angel, so they do not deal with him and yet he has such a marked and powerful effect on the life of the individual. His influence is felt every day in almost everything we do or say yet he appears to be more a 'hidden angel' for most, rather than the significant Angel of the Ascendant, who is born in the East where the Light is born.

This is the reason for spending some time with this matter and why the time of birth is essential because it gives not one angel, but two. The time of birth has an angel and the angel of the ascendant is taken from this time, as is the second Auxiliary Angel. We are discussing a key angel in our lives and it is to our advantage to get it right, if we can and to do that, we have to understand this almost 'hidden' angel and bring him into the Light. Now, let us return to the other parts of your Personal Pentagram. We will be closing this chapter dealing with help with the calculations to find the Angel of the Ascendant or Benben Angel.

You will be pleased to know there are a lot of similarities between the Pentagram of the Angels and the Personal Angelic Pentagram. First, you also regard this pentagram as if viewing from the back with its right and left sides agreeing with yours and if you are naturally left–handed you can reverse the instruction for the right–side and put them into the left side and vice verse, again remember when you transfer the signs, you must also reverse the background colours or they will be wrong.

If you have done the work in the earlier chapter of finding out your Guardian, Auxiliary and finally the Ascendant or Benben Angel than you will already have the personal information you need to fill the Personal Pentagram in. the outline of the pentagram and the signs are still painted in black and the background colours are in accordance with who your angels are. They are painted in exactly the same way as given for the first Angelic Pentagram and in use is much the same, but much more potent because they are so personal.

The main difference comes with the centre panel or the 'torso.' This is left clear of any background colour and you do not set the signs for the Sun and the Moon here as earlier. Where these would go is set the Kamea of the Sun and on this you place your personal Solar Kamea Signature as given in the section dealing with the Kameas, to make the pentagram 'vibrate' to you personally and no other. So now, let us start putting these symbols into the framework of the Personal Pentagram.

In the right 'arm' you put the Angel of the Day, the day you were born. In the left 'arm,' you put the Angel of the Hour you were born. These are you Auxiliary Angels, auxiliary (= of a person) 'who or what provides essential support' and this is the same for both pentagrams The right 'leg' takes your Solar Guardian Angel and the left 'leg' takes your Lunar Guardian Angel and again this is the same for both pentagrams. Your Guardian Angels are placed here because, like your physical legs they 'carry' and support you throughout your life and slow you down when they let you down. Now we come to the 'torso' of this particular pentagram, which had the Sun and Moon in it in the first arrangement. This section is left natural and uncoloured for the following reasons.

In the 'torso' or central section, you do not paint any background colour. You paint the grid of the Kamea of the Sun in gold or gilt paint and the numbers can be in gold or black if you wish. The Kamea of the Sun is a square six–by–six, filled with the numbers given, which go from one to thirty–six and this can be found in the chapter on the **Kameas in Angelic use**. The size of the Kamea will be ruled by the space you have and you do not have to slavishly copy the style of the diagram of the Kameas as given. Once you have written the squares of the kamea, you can fill the numbers in whatever style of figures you please. You put your name sigil on the kamea as given in the appropriate chapter on Kameas. Writing the sigil of your name on the solar pentagram aligns you with the considerable power of the Sun and other levels of existence. Everything that follows is simply variation that you can follow should you want to

You do not have to use black for the sigils on the pentagram. If your Solar Guardian Angel is the Angel of Mars then you could write his sigil in red. You would use the colours blue or pink for the sigil if it was the Angel of Venus and so forth taken from the planetary colours given in the work.

In the centre of your personal Angelic Pentagram, you have the magical form of your name and this can be black or written in the colour of your Solar Guardian Angel set on the Kamea of the Sun that owns this kamea, it already is his. When everything is in place, you have the Solar Kamea in the centre, on the Kamea is written the correctly coloured magic sigil of your name. This kamea sigil of your name is surrounded by the signs of your two Guardian Angels who are supporting you, your two Ancillary Angels who are aiding you, with the Angel of Ascendant, quite rightly at the top or 'in the ascendant,' lighting and guiding your way. This pentagram is not unlike five planets circling a central sun in your name and as they are your five personal planets, it should be regarded as your private microcosm — a personal map of your existence, the map of who you are.

This particular form of the pentagram is personal to you and to no other. It would be rare to find two pentagrams exactly the same but even if they were, they would still be different. Not unlike two excellent artists painting the same subject, the subject would be the same but not the method of creating the painting because each artist puts in something of themselves and their way of looking at things. There are some wonderful copies of the Old Masters that have fooled the experts, but there still are differences that are impossible to copy in the original. The pentagrams are not unlike an astral gate created for you and your home and it has to be carefully consecrated to the angels who have the right to use it and open it. The Personal Angelic Pentagram is created exclusively from the combination of your personal angels and this is why I do not display or show this pentagram to all but an 'inner circle' few, what you do in the matter is entirely your choice.

I said at the beginning an empty pentagram is not unlike a key–blank that a locksmith uses to cut the pattern of a key. A key blank is prepared to enter an appropriate brand of lock but it has to be cut to fit the internal pattern of the 'lock' or it will not turn and the door will remain closed. Whatever it would have opened onto will remain a mystery. It would not hurt to think upon Janus when you make and use the key, for such creations are under his jurisdiction. Making the Personal Pentagram is not unlike attempting to unlock the combination that is within from the time of your birth and personal to you.

The Angel of the Ascendant strongly influences your outlook and how you will tackle the concerns and affairs of your life. If you find the angel who rules this particular aspect of your life, you will have another piece of the jigsaw to understanding yourself better and your life. What makes you different from others born of your Sign of the Zodiac and you will have gained another useful ally on your journey through life — the powerful Angel of the Ascendant or the Benben Angel, which is why we have spent the time discussing this angel.

Make both pentagrams translucent, so if you wish they can hang them in a window or anywhere where the Sun or light can shine through them and carry the coloured light created into the house. Make this form your main pentagram and if only want to make one pentagram of the two, make it your Personal Angelic Pentagram. As before, you can place it in such a way that you can put a light behind it, which can be quite effective, an eastern window is preferred, though not essential, the more so if you do not have one.

This is another reason for creating the sigil of your name on the Kamea of the Sun. The sun gives your pentagram its 'light' and its 'life' as it does for all of us. You can make up other forms of the pentagram to put in the room, hide them somewhere or make them small enough to carry with you. These non-translucent forms I call 'solid pentagrams' to differentiate them from the semi–transparent variety. The 'solid pentagram' is the pentagram I have suggested that you lay on your invocation letter in the chapter *Your Letter or Invocation to the Angels*.

The Sun rules the 'heart' of our Universe as well as the physical heart of a human being. If your heart goes out, you 'go out' and go to the kingdom of Saturn where the Lord of Time and Karma waits. The Kingdom of the Sun on the Tree of Life (= the Kingdom of Tiphareth) is at the centre of the Tree and all the paths of the Kingdoms, apart from one, lead directly to it.

If the 'heart' of the universe goes out then all will 'go out,' our universe will die, as will everything that relies upon the sun for life. The Tree of Life would have no light at its heart to drive it and it too will die, because the Tree of Life is a Tree of Light — not Darkness.


If you know the hour of your birth, you can make the necessary calculations to find the ascendant by the simple method given next and as we have said earlier, it is a little like reading a bus or train timetable. If you become stuck trying to work out your ascendant, I am sure you can find someone who could do this for you. Someone studying astrology or a professional could give you the answer in less than a minute but it is not as difficult as it seems and you should make the attempt. The method used for an unknown birth time is given after this section.

Two things are necessary to undertake this part of the work. An Ephemeris and a Table of Astrological Houses both of which are readily available, you buy the Ephemeris each year for the information changes though it is not really expensive, especially when you consider at least in my case, the amount of work that it does. The Table of Astrological Houses you buy only once. Do not be overwhelmed by the information given because I have to assume that I am writing for someone who knows nothing of the method and someone who has never dealt with astrology, those who have will disregard these remarks.

Some Ephemeredes give a selection of House Tables somewhere with Raphael's at the end of the book and these cover quite a few of the major cities so you may not have to buy the House Tables at all, check first. Raphael's give three main latitudes and these are for London, Liverpool and New York for example those for London can be used for any places between 50° to 53° between which are found Antwerp, Berlin, Brussels, Leipzig, Rotterdam, Warsaw etc., so it is easy enough with an atlas to see what latitude you need. If a town is small find a city close to it, as there is some leeway, do the same for the other two latitudes given in Raphael's Ephemeris.

What does the Table of Houses tell you? These tables will give you the latitude of the place where you where born and the correct Sidereal Time for the place, which is why you need. Raphael's Tables of House for Northern Latitudes is very comprehensive and gives information at the back for using them for people born above the equator in the Northern Hemisphere and I cannot believe it is the only one that does so.

However, we are only concern is the Sign of the Zodiac rising at birth and the angel that rules that sign and its planet on the northern side of the equator. The degree of the sign is unnecessary for the work we are dealing with because we are not going to set up an astrological chart. We only need greater exactness if the Signs of the Zodiac are changing around the time we need, so we will know which the Sign of the Zodiac and Angel to use and has a change taken place.


I will give two examples of this method to help those who want to try it. An ephemeris is always given in GMT throughout but you will have to deal with Daylight Saving, if it was in operation at the time wherever you were born. Raphael's Ephemeris gives the information regarding BST (British Summer Time) on the title page. I am not familiar with the ephemeredes of other countries, but the people living there will know if any form or daylight saving is in operation during the year.

Sidereal Time, (pronounced= sigh-deer-ree-al) from the Latin sidereus, from sidus, genit. Sider = 'a star' and this is why Sidereal Time is sometimes called Star Time or ST= 'time reckoned by the stars.' Sidereal Time 'measured or determined by the apparent motions of the stars: as a sidereal day,' is only used by astrologers and astronomers.

For our examples, we will use the Table of Houses for London. You find the latitude for the place where you live from a map. Do not use longitude, which are the lines running from North and South. The lines of latitude are the lines running from East to West parallel to the equator. They are marked north and south to show on which side of the equator the distance is taken. If the place where you were born is small then follow the latitude along until you find a major city and use that city because it has the same latitude as your birthplace. When you find the correct latitude for your place of birth, make a note of it and keep it with your birth details as astrologers do.

Let us give examples of this. London is 51$^\circ$ 32' North of the equator. This latitude can be used for any place found between the latitudes of 50$^\circ$ and 53$^\circ$ North, which includes Antwerp, Berlin, Brussels, Rotterdam, Warsaw and the like. The latitude of New York in the United States is 40$^\circ$ North of the equator and can be used for places found near to this latitude. In the States, this will include Boston, Chicago, Denver, Omaha, Pittsburgh, Philadelphia, Salt Lake City and elsewhere, which can include Istanbul, Madrid, Naples, Peking, Rome and the rest. The degree of latitude does not have to be exact and two to three degrees either side of exact would not be too serious.

One thing you must always check is the hour of the day for which Sidereal Time is given. Many ephemeredes, perhaps most now, give the Sidereal Time for midnight, 00h 00m 00s a.m, which is the best system because it progresses from 00h 00m 00s a.m to 23h 59m 59s. If you want 6.00 a.m in the morning you add six hours to the Sidereal Time given to arrive at the right hour.

The British, Raphael's Ephemeris works differently because it gives Sidereal Time for noon. To get the Sidereal Time for 6 a.m in the morning you must subtract six hours from the given noon Sidereal Time because it is calculated for twelve hours later. If you use Raphael's Ephemeris you subtract the time if it is before noon, and add the time if it is after noon. This is why I prefer the time given for midnight, because it helps to lessen any chance of mistakes.

Let us take as our date the 1st of January 1994. Raphael's Ephemeris gives the Sidereal Time for noon from which you work out the hour you want. The Sidereal Time is given in hours, minutes and seconds. The time noon is 18h 43m 38s on this date at noon, you can omit the seconds because such accuracy is not needed for this work and only the hour and minutes will be used.

Let us assume our example was born at 9 a.m in the morning, which is three hours before noon. The noon Sidereal Time of 18h 43m and we subtract three hours to take us to the birth time of 9.00 a.m, which gives a Sidereal Time of 15h 43m. Turn to the Table of Houses for London and take the Sidereal Time nearest to this time is 15h 42m and this gives an ascendant or rising sign of 24 degrees of Capricorn.

You only need the Sign of the Zodiac rising and not the degree for this work because you are not going to make up an astrological chart. The only thing you have to watch is does the ascendant change signs at the time you are using and if it is, does it change before or after this time. Then you will have to use greater accuracy regarding the time. For the above date, place and a time of 9.00 a.m, the Sign of the Zodiac rising was Capricorn. The Angel is the Angel Cassiel for this example and this gives the Angel Cassiel as the Angel of the Ascendant or Benben Angel and the fifth Angel to complete the full complement of five angels.

Where does British Summer Time come into this when the clocks are one hour ahead of Greenwich Mean Time by altering the clocks by one hour for a set period during each year for the British Isles? The Ephemeris is written in Greenwich Mean Time throughout. The reader will have to check for any period when daylight saving is in operation and the dates for this are usually given in the front of the Ephemeris. I feel this deviation from GMT has been emphasized enough throughout the work. Obviously if the country where you are living operates any Daylight Saving time, this will have to be taken into account to convert to Daylight Saving Time into Greenwich Mean Time

Again, let us take someone who tells us they were born at 9 a.m in the morning of May 1st 1994, which is of course is still three hours before noon as above, apart from the different date selected, it looks the same — but it is not and that is why it was chosen.

We are told that this person was born at nine o'clock in the morning (according to the clock), but they were not because being born during British Summer Time all the clocks have had one hour artificially added to them to make full use of the daylight hours during the summer months. The real time of the birth in Greenwich Mean Time is eight o' clock in the morning, when we take off the hour that has been added to take the birth time to Greenwich Mean Time.

The Ephemeris deals with planetary time or Solar, while Daylight Saving Time is a man–made convenience time to make better use of the daylight hours as said; to astrologers it is an 'inconvenience' time, especially when you forget it or get it wrong. Now let us do the arithmetic for this time and date.

On May the 1st, 1994, the Sidereal Time at noon is 2h.36m in GMT. To arrive at 8.00 a.m we have to subtract four hours from the noon Sidereal Time given in the Ephemeris, because 12 hours minus 8 hours equals 4 hours. The Sidereal Time for noon on that day is less than the figure you will use for the subtraction of the hours. Therefore, you will have to do what you were told in school or I was, when taking a greater number from a lesser.

You 'borrowed' either ten or a hundred according to the amount involved. Here you will 'borrow' twenty–four because there are twenty–four hours to a day. You add twenty–four hours to the Sidereal Time to make it the greater so subtraction can take place. If twenty–four hours is added to the noon Sidereal Time of 2h.36m, you have 26h.36m. From this you subtract four hours because it is before noon to take the time to 8.00 a.m, which gives you a Sidereal Time of 22h.36m for 8.00 a.m on the date of our example.

In the Table of Houses for London, you find the closest Sidereal Time to 22h.36m, which is 22h.38m and this gives an ascendant of eleven degrees of Cancer, which makes the angel sought the Archangel Gabriel. Again the degree rising is not required for we only need the correct Sign of the Zodiac rising to know the Angel of the Ascendant or the Benben Angel.

Let me give a brief example of why care should be taken regarding this time from a true occurrence involving this subject. A friend asked me to do his chart as he had never had one and would like to have it. I did the chart but he said I had done the wrong day because it should be May 15th as given to me, not May 14th. We went to his mother, the best person to ask and she confirmed that without doubt he was born at 1.35 a.m on May 15th 1944 and she too was adamant that May 14th was wrong — after all she was there so she should know — true without question, but only up to a point. X was born in the last years of *World War II* and to aid production, certain years during the war were not only made British Summer Time adding one hour, but also Double British Summer Time adding two hours, which started on April 2nd in 1944. These two hours when subtracted from the given DBST time to give Greenwich Mean Time made his true birthday, 11.35

p.m on May the 14th. I have never asked him which day he uses for his birthday but if he has stuck with May the 15th — he is wrong.

N.B. In the past, some have made the error of taking the sign of the Zodiac given at the top of the column for the ascendant. Always go down the column to the Sidereal Time you want, to see if the Sign of the Zodiac has changed between the one given at the top of the column and the Sidereal Time you want. Otherwise, you will have the wrong Sign of the Zodiac for the ascendant.

We use the Seven Planets of the Ancients for the Angelic Pentagram, because this original pentagram is very old and only uses the seven planets and their Angels in its creation. The Personal Angelic Pentagram is later and so can use the ten planets found in today's astrology. Each angel and planet has their personal day, hours, perfumes, incenses, metals, precious stones and so on. The planet Uranus uses Saturn's days and hours with Saturn. The planet Neptune uses the days and hours with Jupiter, Pluto uses the days and hours with Mars and this is explained elsewhere.

## THE SIX O' CLOCK ANGEL

For those who do not have the time of their birth they use 6.00 a.m and we have given our reasons for doing this. I would be quite happy to use this angel if I did not know the time of my birth To get your second Ancillary Angel you substitute the 6.00 a.m angel on the day you were born or the Archangel Raphael, the Messenger and Herald of the Gods. We have given a table giving the angel for 6.00 a.m on each day of the week in the chapter *Your Guardian Angels* and explained the reasons for using it. If you use the 'six–o'clock Angel,' you use the same hour to calculate the rising sign or ascendant for the day and place you were born. Let us take one example that should suffice. Let us suppose someone knows their place and date of birth, but they do not know the hour of their birth. We will use the 7th of February 1962 in London, time unknown, using the ten Angels and planets for the Personal Angelic Pentagram.

On the above date the Sun was in Aquarius so that would make their Solar Guardian the Archangel Uriel (= Uranus ruler)

The Moon was in Pisces so that would make their Lunar Guardian Angel, the Angel Asariel (= Neptune ruler).

They were born on a Wednesday so that would make their first Ancillary Angel the Archangel Raphael.    (Mercury ruler.)

Because of the unknown time of birth we substitute the birth time of 6.00 a.m. on the day of birth, Wednesday,    which gives us the Angel Anael (Venus ruler.) This is their second Ancillary Angel.

Finally, we find the sign on the ascendant at the date of the birth. Raphael's Ephemeris is used, giving the Sidereal Time as 21h.08m for noon. For our example, we need six hours earlier. This gives us a Sidereal Time of 15h.08m because we have to subtract six hours to arrive at 6.00 a.m. In the Table of Houses for London, a Sidereal Time of 15h.08m gives us Capricorn as the rising sign of the ascendant. This makes the Six o' Clock Angel of the Ascendant the Angel Cassiel. (= Saturn ruler), with this final piece of the puzzle, we have the compliment of five angels for this imaginary person. The two Guardian Angels, the two Ancillary Angels and the Angel of the Ascendant or Benben Angel.

The above method shows that even without a known time of birth, it is possible to fill all the angelic stations of the Personal Angelic Pentagram and perform the Angelic Ritual of the Pyramid of Power. This is a reliable method of working, it goes a long way back into the past and I recommend its use to the reader.

N.B. Remember the difference between the two forms of pentagram. The Angelic Pentagram applies to everyone, it only uses the seven planets and the seven angels of old astrology and this is because it was created when only the seven planets were used in astrology.

The Personal Angel Pentagram uses the ten planets used in modern astrology today, because we are creating this pentagram with a system in place today because these ten planets apply to the important time, day, month and year of the birth of the individual for whom the Personal Angel Pentagram is made.

I hope those readers who know their time of birth will work out their ascendant and its angel for themselves because it is not as difficult as it appears, it only appears so because there is so much to explain for those who have never done it before. A good method of practise is to work out the ascendant of known charts so that you know the answer before you work it out and you can check that your answer is correct, this will give you more confidence. If your answer is wrong, you have the right answer because that was how you knew it was wrong, to check where you have gone wrong. Many astrological magazines give examples of this and all you need is the date, time and place of birth. Most things appear more difficult than they are on paper but once you have done a few times you may well wonder what all the fuss was about.

Practise and making mistakes will give you the necessary experience in the matter — mistakes and correcting them if they happen is the only thing that will. Practise and perseverance will lead to experience and with experience, we are back to Saturn again. Remember that I have repeatedly said most things in the physical end with the planet Saturn and the Angel Cassiel. You can rarely escape the attentions of this planet while you live. You definitely cannot do so when you die for he is one of the Angel's of Death and the Lord of Karma. This is why I recommend repeatedly throughout whatever works I write and because Saturn is involved, never invoke for justice — you just may get it. Always ask for justice tempered with mercy that involves Jupiter — you may need it!

# YOUR LETTER OR INVOCATION TO THE ANGELS.

Many people regard prayers and invocations as the same thing with a fine line dividing the two, nevertheless this line is not fixed and where it is set depends upon the circumstances or teaching, not unlike the tuning cursor on a radio that tells you what station you are listening to. *Invocation*= 'to call upon, to address in prayer.' To direct your prayer to a specific source, though sometimes with invocation this includes trying to call up the source as well as 'calling upon' the source. *Prayer*= 'to ask, supplicate or implore something be granted' hence someone or something is being implored or supplicated through prayer. Obviously, prayers are directed to a specific source in accordance with the religious customs of the petitioner and in the done in the way of the religion they espouse.

Sometimes, invocations and prayers are spoken though silent invocation and prayer has long been used. However, whether it is a 'silent prayer or invocation' words are still being used. Words are the servants of the mind and the mind would be mute and somewhat incoherent without them because signs and gestures can only go so far.

Prayer is usually perceived from a purely religious point of view. In the West, occultists and pagans are said to 'invoke' their Gods, while Christians and those of other established religions 'pray' to theirs, yet I sometimes wonder what the difference is supposed to be apart from the position from which it is viewed. Prayer has long proven itself to be a substantial and beneficial aid and it has over and over again been shown to have positive results regarding the well–being of those who use it for a fitting purpose and wisely — so none have need to justify its use to another. What is the more important is what is being done and why, coupled with the faith and hope that it bestows.

Prayer can be used at any time and for many reasons. Some people prefer morning and evening prayers and those done at sunrise and sunset are considered to be the most powerful. Ritual invocation usually has a definite aim because most invocation is directed to a particular source and for a particular purpose, typically after the matter has been given a great deal of thought, clearly defined and considered to be necessary to the situation or circumstances. It is frequently planned and sometimes it has additional customs to support it, such as incense, colours, a certain day, time and the direction faced — often the East to attract matters and the West to banish them and quite often it is the 'how' that causes dissent, not the 'why.'

Perhaps in the above the important words are that 'it is frequently planned.' this shows that the centre of attention is fine–tuned and the ritual has been developing for some time. The old injunction was to 'inflame thyself with prayer' and this is still a powerful recommendation. Among the ancients, repetition of certain formulae in some rituals was considered effective in proportion to the number of repetitions and this is common in many religious philosophies even today. We read that in India, 'if an ascetic speaks in one month the name Radha Krishna or Ram one hundred thousand times, he cannot fail to obtain what he wants.' The prophets of Baal called out 'Baal, hear us' to their god from morning until night in the same manner. 'Pray without ceasing' is found being advised in 1 *Thessalonians* 12:16.

However, in the *Sermon on the Mount*, Christ warns his listeners against thinking that the effectiveness of a prayer depends on the number of times it is repeated saying, 'But when ye pray, use not vain repetitions, as the heathen do: for they think that they shall be heard for their much speaking.' *Matthew* 6:7. However, any new dispensation habitually reverses previous practises and if the earlier method of prayer — *βαττο–λογεω, Batto–logeo* — had not been a well–established practise, this admonition would not have be needed. Christ did not actually write anything down as mentioned earlier. This makes me suspicious of just one short line, which I think may have been put in by the reporter of Christ's words — 'as the heathen do' — making me think this was not in the original but put in to make a point that Christians were not heathens or pagans, now unacceptable to the new dispensation.

*Βαττος, Battos* was a king of Cyrene and according to some, the name *Βαττος, Battos*= 'stammerer.' A name given from his stammering' is considered to have been derived from *βατταριξω, battarizo*= 'to stutter.' King Battos had an impediment in his speech and according to *Herodotus* and his name is thought to have been formed from the sound. Therefore, *βαττο–λογεω, batto–logeo*= 'to speak stammering, to say the same thing over and over again (*New Testament*) or excessive talking' hence *batto–logeo* as given above.

Angels, especially the personal angels have unique and overall knowledge of that person's life, their circumstances, the world in which they live, why they are set in an appointed place and what is happening to them. Although it may appear unfair and unjustifiable to us, we have to accept that the angels do not automatically grant every request just because we ask them and at times, they even seem to ignore both the request and us and now and then, they even seem to go against the invocation completely. Not knowing why or understanding why this is done is often the hardest part to bear. To make matters worse, they rarely give reasons for what they do or what they do not do and I agree, this can be very frustrating. When people explain why the answer is no, we may not like it but at least we know why and can even at times accept it.

Now and again, there is a common belief abroad that angels must do what we ask of them because this is 'what angels do' and we are the 'reason for their existence' — looking after the planet and us, but this is not so, even though we are certainly included in the equation. We are not the sole duty of the angels, even those appointed to us because the angels existed long before we arrived on the scene and we are 'in addition to.' As pointed out earlier, originally some of the angels were not particularly pleased that we were here at all with their dislike starting with Adam; some even thought we were a mistake.

However, even we decline to help others, to answer their questions, choose not to answer a letter sent to us and refuse to comply with the wishes of the writer. Sometimes we do not have the means or the ability to do so even if we wanted to. Sometimes we think it would not be in their best interests or ours and we do not give the reasons for our actions or decisions because our reasons would not be too well received and equally, not understood. Therefore, I believe that others, no matter who they are can do the same whether I like it or not.

The angels have a lot more answers than we do and many more to questions we know nothing about. Further, they are not limited as we are and see more than we do. Will what we ask for be wise, remember the previously mentioned 'gift of Midas.' He was given exactly what he asked for and he was delighted with it — until he started to use it seriously, after he had finished turning plates, goblets, statues, furnishing and the like into the gold he loved so much, he touched his beloved daughter. Despite being given exactly what he asked for, the king implored that the 'blessing' be removed, quickly and at any cost.

Remember your fairy tales and how in many of these stories, three wishes are granted for some help or a kindness unselfishly given. In many of them, the three wishes that would have 'solved everything in their lives at a stroke' but they were either lost or wasted by the people involved. They spend the rest of the tale and their lives mourning the chances so foolishly let slip but then — yet we are adults not children and we finished with fairy tales long ago — or did we!

It has been held for a long time that there are basically two kinds of prayer — the 'spoken prayer' and 'the prayer of silence.' It is thought that King David speaks of them in the *Psalms*. 'Let the words of my mouth (= 'spoken prayer'), and the meditation of my heart (= 'silent prayer'), be acceptable in thy sight, O Lord, my strength, and my redeemer,' (19:14) and perhaps we should heed the advice given in the *Zohar* that tells us that silent prayer is the deeper and more powerful of the two forms.

In many Schools to present your invocation or plea, you wrote a 'letter' or 'petition' just as you would in your everyday affairs, because there is little difference in principle, but a great deal in the method used, not unlike presenting your case for consideration. Sometimes people write down their spoken invocations before they use them in speech. This is done to make sure that it is correct and proper in content. I often do this to get my thoughts in order and to make sure I am saying exactly what I intend and it cannot be misconstrued in any way — people who do this are sometimes termed 'Occult Lawyers' —I call it prudence and common sense.

I have always thought this was reasonable learning of Apollo and some of the ways he worked, it was a caution that had to be taken with the cryptic predictions of Apollo, which is why he was sometimes called *Απολλω Λοξιας, Apollo Loxias,* 'the oblique or ambiguous one,' a surname derived from his convoluted and ambiguous oracles at times.

Time and again his most cleverly constructed 'contact' or answers were like a box within a box, within a box and if you did not act with great care with his responses, you could quickly lose any advantage given and end up with nothing that you wanted or found yourself where you did not want to be. *Απολλω Λοξιας, Apollo Loxias* that is either from *λοξος, loxos* or from *λεγω= lego, λογος= logos* = 'the Speaker, a prophet or Speaker of Zeus.' *Λοξος, Loxos*= 'slanting, crosswise, aslant.' Latin, *obliquus*, *λοξα βατης, loxa bates*= 'going sideways' as a crab that walks obliquely or sideways. Of language 'indirect' and of oracles 'ambiguous.' Lucien.'

In your personal affairs, you write letters asking for information, request a good turn or advice, to express sympathy or affection, happiness or to thank someone for a kindness. Then you put your letter into a post–box with a stamp on it and send it, you wait for a reply if it needs one. Your angelic letter is not 'posted' in the same way as a letter by using the postal services, but it is still carefully prepared and 'posted' nevertheless. You still have to wait for a 'reply' up to a point and hope that it will come. To save space the term 'letter–invocation' will be replaced with 'letter.' Just remember that what you are writing is 'a letter of invocation' to an angel or angels, if more than one angel involved.

The first thing to discuss is what to use and the method of writing your letter. The basic methods given here are well–established and they are not difficult once they are understood but here they are broken down into their component parts to explain them and this usually makes something simple appear complicated but it is not.

A letter is a letter no matter what and apart from personal touches and it has a fundamental form. The angelic formula is much the same as conventional letters and consists first and foremost of three basic parts. (1) The one to whom the letter or invocation is being sent. (2) What the writer has to say and why it is being written and (3) the salutation and signature identifying the writer of the letter showing who sent it. There are various ways you can 'post' an angelic letter and we will deal with some of them later in the chapter, you will have plenty of opportunity to exercise your inventiveness. Next, let us deal with some of . . .

## THE MATERIALS

Paper is the material that we use and there are many excellent papers available today. Some are made to look like parchment, while others have deckle edges in gold or silver. Some papers have a smooth, rough or matt surface and finished in many colours, some are made to have the appearance of stone, cloth, marble, silk and so on. An enquiry to a paper supplier can bring a very useful product catalogue and frequently some excellent samples. Some works of this nature make great store that 'virgin parchment' must be used and in my opinion, far too much fuss is made of this.

Anything is 'virgin' as long as it remains unused, intact, unmarked, unsullied and in its original state because this is all the word 'virgin' means and it applies to many other things as well as paper. Paper remains virgin if you do not use it and this principle applied when the material used was parchment. It is understandable why this was recommended because if a parchment had been used previously then it was in danger of contamination from the previous writing (see below). I have seen large amounts of money being asked for virgin parchment in the past as now, but I have rarely felt the price is justified now as it may have been in the past.

When skin was the material used for writing, it was very expensive so people would often use a parchment more than once by erasing the first writing. The second use made of a skin was called in the Greek a *παλιμψηστον, palimpseston* or 'palimpsest,' *παλιμψεστος, palimpsestos*= 'scraped again' or a parchment from which the writing has been erased by being scraped it off to make room for new writing. Pref. *παλιν, palin*= 'taken back, restored' and the Greek *ψηστος, psestos*= 'rubbed, scraped;' *ψαω, psao*= 'to rub or scrape.'

It is a term applied to parchment from which the writing has been removed and something else written in its place. Obviously, the previous writing on a skin could be erased or scraped off more than once or until a skin became too thin to be used any more. In the same way previous thoughts or alterations have been found under an oil painting by x–ray testing but these were simply painted over rather than removed.

We use paper because paper is the material of our time and it is satisfactory for our use because there are now many fine papers. Good paper is still not cheap so these exacting circumstances are still with us because if you want the best you have to pay for it. Parchment is rarely used now, apart from purists, official or special celebratory occasions where the cost and use is justified.

Just remember, all new paper is virgin, unused, untouched, unsullied or we would not buy it 'as new paper.' Recycled paper today is so clean it could almost merit being called a palimpsest because the paper has had 'the previous writing and material removed' so that it can be used again and the technique of recycling is sometimes so well done I feel is better than 'scraped' and perhaps the word 'reconstructed' would be more appropriate. If you think the latter argument does not satisfy you then do not use recycled paper for your work but always use new paper in a sealed box, which would be without doubt be 'virgin paper.'

## INKS AND COLOURS

You can use white paper and black ink though letters can be made personal by using white paper and a coloured ink appropriate to the angel you are trying to contact. Use the colours given in the lists supplied and the selection of coloured inks available now includes gold, silver and even 'psychedelic' inks, which should more than cover all your needs. When you have established who your Guardian Angels are later, you can buy their inks and a black ink and keep these in stock as a minimum requirement for you.

Use a gold, dark yellow or orange ink for the Sun and the Archangel Michael. If you cannot get an orange ink, then add a little red ink to a yellow ink using an eye–dropper until you get the colour that you like, add it drop by drop and test by writing until you get the colour you want. This is like adding 'fire' (= red) to the 'gold' (= yellow) of the Sun, but today I am sure this will be unnecessary, remember to wash clean your dropper.

For the Moon and the Archangel Gabriel, use silver, a light or pale green or mauve ink, no dark inks, if you are using white paper you cannot use white ink for obvious reasons despite being a correct colour that you could use, you could use a white ink on suitably coloured paper.

For Mars and the Angel Samael use a bright, lively red ink, do not use a dark red unless it is for Mars in Scorpio is needed or you need a negative red ink for Mars.

For Mercury and the Archangel Raphael a bright yellow ink, again no dark inks use the brightest you can find.

Use a rich purple, mauve or lavender inks for Jupiter and the Angel Sachiel but because he is another of the 'royal' planets and like the Sun, you can use gold.

Use a light or medium green, a royal vivid blue, pink or royal blue for Venus and the Angel Anael; once again avoid dark green inks as these are best kept for the next planet.

Use a dark green, dark grey or black ink for the planet Saturn and the Angel Cassiel, but no light inks. If you do not have a dark ink then simply then add a small drop of black ink to bright inks as shown above. Again, add the dark colour in one drop amounts and test until the required shade is achieved, remember it is easier to add the darker colour than remove it once its mixed, too dark an ink then throw it away.

Any inks for the planets beyond the orbit of Saturn are easier said than done but not impossible. For Uranus use any ink that is unusual such as 'day–glow,' psychedelic or a metallic inks, any ink that is bright, out of the ordinary and what could be termed 'eye–catching.'

Neptune is easier to deal with because this planet is similar to the Moon because both are water planets and the inks of Neptune can be just a little darker than the Moon but not too much, enough to distinguish the two. Neptune is often regarded as a higher octave of the Moon.

Pluto can use a jet–black ink, a metallic black looking like pewter if you can or a very deep red, never bright red, again no light colours. Alternatively, use invisible ink. No! This is not a mistake — you have found a legitimate use for invisible ink at last.

*Pluto, Hades, Αιδης, Aides* poetic of *Αιδνος, Aidnos*= 'the invisible, the unseen' or 'the god who makes invisible,' in Greek mythology is the Prince of the Underworld= *Hades* and the god of the lower world, sometimes confused with Plutus. Another name for Pluto is Orcus who was a deity of the Underworld who punished perjurers. Because Orcus had a distinct personality and duties, it is thought that originally he may have been a chthonic Roman god of the Underworld that became identified with the Greek god Hades just as Pluto may have been.

Orcus carried men off to the lower world and kept the dead imprisoned there and he was not unlike a form of 'an Angel of Death who slew the dying' and remember there are quite a few angels doing this particular duty. Dead gladiators were sometimes carried from the gladiatorial arena by a man dressed to represent Orcus.

Pluto loved and lost a nymph called Minthe, the daughter of Cocytus. When his wife Persephone discovered Pluto's infidelity and she transformed the nymph into the plant that we call mint, which is why this plant and odour can be used for him. Having mint growing in the garden, I often rub a mint leaf on any letter to the Angel Azrael, Angel of Pluto. If I use the Folding Letter, I sometimes put a small mint leaf inside the letter before folding and sealing the letter.

You can use this practise for the other angels and planets, get the herbs that are ruled by the planets. A short list would include. Acacia, bay, birch, oak, laurel, heliotrope or vine for the Sun. Lily petals, willow, snowdrop, moon–wort, white flowers for the Moon. Thistle or thorns, tiger–lily, geranium, cactus spines for Mars. Vervain, herb Mercury, nut–bearing trees (= not necessarily edible) for Mercury. Olive, shamrock, oak, vine leaves, laurel for Jupiter. Ivy, fern, fir, pine or cedar for Saturn.

Let us take as an example from the above lists birch used for the Sun for the Archangel Michael. The bark of the birch is resinous and it is this resin that makes the tree smell wonderful after a shower of rain. Take a small amount of birch bark and burn it in a suitable container its blue flame will scent the air and you can pass your letter to the Archangel Michael through the smoke.

This is like the romantic letters of old being given a dash of perfume so that the sender would be known to the recipient before the letter was even opened. Your angelic letter is given the perfume so they will know it is for them as with the above examples.

It must be remembered long before the expensive resins and perfumes were imported and used, wood, resins, leaves, petals and so forth were used, because that is all that there was. The distillation of perfumes and the harvesting of fine resins and so on came later so do not be afraid to go back to the root of things as they have stood the test of time by still being there and they are still very much used in incenses.

Rose petals are for Venus, better to use red or pink. You could use white roses for the Moon. Orange and yellow roses are for the Sun and Mercury, follow this idea through. Roses are always under the overall rulership of Venus but the colour of the rose makes them acceptable for use by other the other planets and their angels. For example, a yellow rose for the Archangel Raphael of the planet Mercury is given to show love for the Archangel and acknowledge his presence.

This is given to show how extended connections can be made by expanding what is given. Yew, cypress, aloe, hellebore, pine or nightshade can be used for Saturn. Myth, legend and folklore often give excellent pointers regarding what to do or use for what or who. Traditions are more important than people given them credit today and they are being dismissed a little too glibly as time and the future will eventually prove. They are not outdated rituals, they tell you who you are, where you have come from and quite often how to act in a given set of circumstances or situations — as D.H Lawrence said in *Women in Love*, ' . . . even when you're wrong, you can still be decent.'

The present rests on the past and the future is constructed from them both. An opinion I frequently express now as this is why history is so important to us or should be. It stops us from being narrow in our views, doing things the way we say they have always been done and it prevents us from thinking that our way is the only way. History often shows that matters have (on occasion) been done quite differently in the past, it can tell us that what we are doing or believe is not as original as we think it is — sometimes it is the exact opposite. History does not restrict us — it sets us free.

Those who live low on the *Tree of Life*, below the Sun (= 'Tiphereth') and do not extend themselves that much or raise their eyes upwards usually find there is very 'little new under the Sun' in their lives and there never will be.

White is a most useful colour in that it contains the other all the colours of the spectrum. White is a neutral colour and is usually safe for use with all so use a white candle if you are uncertain what colour to use, alternatively use a yellow candle of Mercury because (as discussed earlier) he is the Messenger or Herald of the Gods who has access to all but he is not the only one. There are other messengers, especially Mercury's 'traditional' son, the God of Nature, Pan.

The origins of Pan are claimed by many and he is found with a diversity of parents but the pair that seems to have prevailed over the time is Mercury and Penelope. When Pan was born, his father wrapped him 'in the Skin of a Goat' and carried him up to heaven. The gods were enchanted with Pan who delighted them all with his musical skills and always remember that 'Pan' means 'all.' What is sometimes forgotten is the that 'the gods made Pan their messenger like his father' Hermes/Mercury, who is mentioned frequently and in detail elsewhere.

Frankincense is a splendid and safe incense for you to use for everyone, so use this incense if you have run out of a particular incense or if you are in doubt about which one to use. Frankincense is acceptable to all and offends no one, you can regard it as an emergency incense and keep it by you because it is possibly the greatest single ingredient you can have in you store cupboard. This has already been said and it will be until the final full stop that heralds the end of this work, all the other works written — or me!

Your work written inside the temenos is set within a secure four–square base, probably the most secure base available to you on any level because (like the threefold base) it has great stability with its centre of gravity set within the dead centre of the pyramid base. A wide base makes the structure sound and stable. This, as with most other things often suggests that it is the best course of action to take regarding the work found in this book and many other matters, circumstances and situations in your life. If something is attempted without a stable base or support, it does not usually stand long, because it was born defective to begin with and can be easily be unbalanced and toppled. Without this base, so many things cannot get off the ground , which is why they are invariably found scattered (in pieces) all over it.

All your work should contain a minimum of three props to support it and give it stability, nothing less will do, though four props is even better. Always remember, 'three props' are the minimum to support your work — 1: DECLARE, 2: FINISH and 3: EARTH and if you succeed in these three you could get the fourth prop — 4: SUCCESS!

The first number you can use to make something stand by itself is three and four gives added strength. Something with only one support can stand if it is secured or held, but it requires help and support to prevent it from falling in any direction if it is to be left unattended

Something with two supports has more stability than one, but if unsupported it too will fall to one side or the other. It still requires help if you want to leave it unattended as above, but its getting better.

Something with three supports can stand on its own without any assistance as can four, which has even greater stability. Remember in the opening remarks of this chapter we wrote 'the letter consists of three basic parts and never less' because if your letter/invocation has less than the three basic parts, it will surely fall.

Three or four can be left unattended, witness the pyramid form given here and the material pyramids themselves, which if left alone would stand without any support till the Crack of Doom. The pyramid contains these three important numbers — four, three and one. The pyramid has a four–square base. Three is contained in the sides of the pyramid because they are made up of four, three–sided triangles, which rises upwards ever decreasing in material content to the Ben–Ben or Sacred Capstone at the top — where they unite to make the One and pointing up into the air in the direction of the celestial. The formula is a wonderfully simply sum. From four at the material base or level built on the earth moves to the three and the ubiquitous Holy Trinity of the four sides and finally resolves itself in One — the culmination and path to the Supreme Deity or 'the One.'

The writer has always advocated the use of three simple 'props' based affectionately upon the principle of the tripod of Delphi calling the sequence of three — 'Declare, Close and Earth.'

DECLARE THE WORK: Declare your intentions when you begin your work by announcing who you are, what you are attempting to do and respectfully, who you would like to deal with. This is not unlike presenting your credentials to someone from whom you hope to solicit help. Do not demand, because more often than not in this category of Work you are not able to do so. 'Invocation proceedeth of the good will of man and of the heat and fervency of the spirit: And therefore is prayer of such effect with God.' You will pick up this statement near the end of this chapter. Remember its you who are doing the asking and they who are doing the giving — if they will. These words have written many times before and they will many times again — are you bored with them? Get used to them because they will be back!

CLOSE THE WORK: When you have finished your work. Thank them for their attendance and interest, which you hope will be beneficial and offer them the peace of (their) Creator in the hope this will be sustained between them and you. Ask who ever you are dealing with or any entity or entities who may be in attendance, whether you know of them or not, to depart to whence they came from in peace and stillness. This part is often omitted, yet is the part that should be done without fail. The wise races of the ancient world raised an altar to the Unknown God(s) in case they may have been left out and be offended by the omission. The ancients were excellent 'legal draughtsmen' on all levels — including religion. We will address the matter of the 'Unknown Gods' in greater detail after this section and the 'Unknown God' was spoken of in Part 1.

EARTH THE WORK: Finally, 'earth' your work in a manner that is both simple and effective. Electricity is grounded to make it safe and it should be able to find a prepared path whereby it can run harmlessly to the earth should something go wrong and not harm the user. Therefore, you should ground matters upon ending your Work in case something should 'leak,' remain as 'static power' or go awry. There is little difference in the principle involved. When you are finished your work, one simple way for you to 'earth or ground' it by stamping your feet hard upon the ground several times.

If this is inconvenient, say you live in a flat where stamping on the floor would probably not be welcome, clap your hands hard and feel them physically sting as this makes you aware of your body and its place on the earth. Devise a method on similar principles depending on your circumstances, but feel the stability of the Earth under your feet, supporting your body and you. The object of 'earthing' however it is done, is to bring you firmly back to earth, the physical and the place from where you started. You must always 'buy a return ticket' when undertaking this sort of venture because you live 'here' and not 'there.' Attempting to outstay your visit 'there' will bring you untold troubles — you are *terrae filius* — here is where you belong and trying to run away does not solve anything, it only usually creates more problems.

You could use a number for stamping or clapping in 'earthing' that is appropriate to the angel invoked and some relevant numbers associated with the planets that can be used for this and there are suggestions at the end of this chapter. By earthing your work, you show that you are (colloquially) back on *terra firma* and as said, standing on your two feet again in the place where you started from and therefore, where you belong. If the work done was lengthy then have some form of hot drink (a flask is ideal) and a few sweet biscuits because actions such as eating and drinking set you firmly back in the material level and 'back home.' It also replaces any energy that may have been spent doing the working, some use more than others. These are some suggestions for 'closing' your work.

There are two forms of letter/invocation and they are similar up to a point. They are called the Folded Letter and the Pyramid Letter and although the Pyramid Letter is the more elaborate of the two, this does not in any way invalidate or take away any value from the Folded Letter and both letters have their use. The Pyramid Letter requires greater preparation and concentration but sometimes you are not able to give the time to the Pyramid Letter depending on circumstances. Urgency and experience will eventually dictate which of two letters is best suited for your needs, situation or circumstances. I must point out that I believe the Pyramid Letter to be the more powerful of the two forms given, but only because of the extra time and effort invested in it and how it is used.

# THE FOLDED LETTER

The first of the two forms of angelic letters used in this work is called the Folded Letter — for reasons that will soon be evident. The reader will probably be glad to know that both letters have a great deal in common regarding fundamental layout and principles. The chief difference being the important addition in the Pyramid Letter and the way that it is used.

The Folding Letter can be carried with you if you wish because of the way it is made up, the Pyramid Letter cannot, it has to be set up and left in a secure place until the matter is resolved one way or another, however long this takes. The Folding Letter does not have to do this, so obviously the Folding Letter could be much more convenient in some circumstances. You may live somewhere where privacy is not all that you wish, perhaps you share accommodation, you do not want to show your private studies or feel the need to explain them and the best way of doing this is to keep them out of sight and private. Critics of the this kind of study always demand that you justify yourself to them and seek their approval, while you want nothing from them but to be left alone and this tells the wise something.

The Folding Letter is quicker to create and if you are writing a letter in an emergency this would be the quicker of the two forms. The Folding Letter can be put in an envelope, sealed and put away until the matter is concluded. Sometimes people have posted the Folding Letter to themselves and leave it unopened when they receive it.

For a better understanding of our subject, we must give our attention to the three squares in both letters because they are the same in both letters and have the same reason for being there. The first square is the one in the centre drawn in a thin line of appropriate colour. The second square surrounds this central square and is always drawn in a thick black line at all times and the third and final square is not drawn because it is the edge of the paper and defines the limit of the area within which you work — three concentric squares.

The first square is in the centre of the letter and this area is extremely important because it is where you set down your invocation or the 'place of meeting.' This enclosed area is the focal point of all your work and this square is called the temenos, which is taken from the Greek. Let us stay with this word to make sure we understand it and the way it is used and quite often understanding the word used is the way to ensure this.

Greek, τεμενος, temenos= 'a piece of land dedicated to a god, the sacred precincts (within it stood in the temple).' Τεμενιξω, temenizo= 'to make or consecrate a sacred grove.' Originally, a temenos was a piece of land taken out of public use and appropriated to support a king in the Heroic Age. It could also be 'a piece of land taken out of public use and dedicated to a god.' The temenos in later years became regarded exclusively as the god's sphere of influence. The word sometimes includes within its meaning 'the temple buildings.' In a narrow sense, it is the sanctuary, a holy place or περιβολος, peribolos= 'going round, compassing, encircling, a precinct.' It was the enclosed, consecrated quadrant surrounding 'the god's altar and the centre of worship' and this is exactly how it is regarded here. This area was the place where rites of passage, the rituals of transformation and invocations forms of invocations were performed. Naturally, there were a variety of holy places built because sometimes they were created for an explicit purpose or dedication.

Some were erected for healing illness and an important temenos was the one for the rites of incubation. Some were specially built for the conscious initiation of dreams and psychic contact with the gods. When the *Temenos of Dreams* became 'unscientific' and sacrificed on the altar of Science, it was a great loss, more so than people think. In my opinion dreams, dreaming and practical dream work are important. At least they are to me and were while writing most of my 'paper staining' and particularly this one. It is something I have attempted for a great deal of my life and this enterprise will only stop when I do. Now let us start constructing our letter and deal more fully with the temenos and its place in the scheme of things but before we do.

There is another excellent Greek word that could have replaced *temenos* with little difficulty and I am sure that many readers may have already met with it — adytum. The word *adytum* in the Latin form gives us 'the innermost secret part of a temple, the sanctuary, which none but the priests could enter and from which oracles were delivered.' I believe the Latin came from the Greek word *αδυτον, aduton*= 'the innermost sanctuary' from the adj. *αδυτος, adutos*= 'not to be entered' so naturally they all mean the same thing. The meanings are given as 'not to be entered, the innermost secret part of a Temple, the sanctuary, which none but priests could enter and from which oracles were delivered.' It was sometimes also used for 'a grave or tomb' or 'the innermost recesses.' If this word appeals to you more than temenos, there is no reason why you should not use it.

As always I advocate that you are consistent in use, once you have established this word in your work, simply so that you and everyone else knows what you are talking about and doing, I do not mean that you must never change it, only not every five minutes. In Occultism, the word is used for much the same meaning — 'the holiest area, the temple or the place of initiation where you make your sacred vows.' Now let us make a start on the first of our letters and as always, we will find that it takes longer to explain than actually do and as always, it is the explanation that takes the time and not the doing.

Use a good quality white A4 paper to make your letter. Mark the oblong paper into a square by measuring 8·5" or 21cm down the length of both sides of the sheet and draw a line across the paper. The line drawn across the bottom shows where the excess paper will be removed to make the oblong sheet into a square sheet. The paper itself does not have to be an exact square but the squares you will draw on it must be. The reader may ask why not use a square sheet of paper to start with? Making the oblong sheet into a square one is a symbolic act that is connected to a past practice, which is explained in the Pyramid Letter dealt with later, where it has greater import. Just remember it and accept this statement for now.

Start by drawing an 7" or 18cm square on the paper with a thick pen using black ink, which is a colour of Saturn and the Angel Cassiel and this is done for both letters. You naturally set this square equidistant from the edges of the paper to make it central and balanced on the square part of the paper, the square that you made when you drew your line across the bottom of the paper.

The only thing to remember about this square is that the line must have no breaks in it. If you put up a fence or boundary, you would not leave gaps in it, because this would let what is inside free to go outside, because the fence would not contain it. Any breaks would also enable what is outside to come in and this would defeat the purpose of putting up a fence or boundary in the first place because what came in would pollute the inner areas and contaminate them and make them worthless, wasting everyone's time.

The square can be bigger if you wish to do so, these measurements are the size I use and but the measurements are not written in stone. The main thing is that they must not go right to the edge of the paper as will remove the space that indicates the Outer Court or the Court of the Gentiles. There must be three distinct areas shown on the both letters that are clearly defined in both diagrams and your letter is not valid without them. 1: The Outer Court 2: The Sacred Court and 3: The Temenos or Adytum

You place a second square measuring 5·5" or 14cm inside the larger thick square. The line of the second square is drawn in the colour of the angel you are invoking with your letter (the diagrams are in black and white so this is not shown) and the area inside the second square is called the temenos or adytum, these two words were discussed earlier and again this square must be centred with regard to the other square.

So, what you now have is an A4 sheet of paper with a line drawn across the bottom to square the paper off, equidistant within this area you put a square drawn thickly in black without any breaks and within this black square, you place another square drawn in the colour of the angel that you are invoking. This gives the paper with two concentric squares making three squares in all because you include the edge of the paper. These three equal areas give you the Court of the Gentiles, the Inner and Sacred Court and the centre square is the temenos or adytum called the Holy of Holies or Inner Sanctum

## WHY THE SQUARE MARKED IN THICK BLACK?

Why is the first square black? The Angel Cassiel is the Lord of Saturn and he rules, among other matters, limitation, form and the enclosing of things. Saturn rules the skeleton that supports the body and gives it its shape. He rules your skin, which is the limit of your body and your shape by which you can be recognized. Any break in your skin allows what is contained inside to come outside where it does not belong, likewise bacteria can enter the body through the breach made unless it is protected or closed because if it gets inside it can cause disorder, which is against all the principles of order and containment for which Saturn stands.

It therefore follows that the Angel Cassiel rules fences, walls, boundaries, frontiers and the limits set to anything that says 'this far and no further.' In addition, this angel rules 'the final act of anything' such as the final full–stop I will place at the end of this manuscript to show 'it is finished.' The full stops preceding the final one are simply 'breathing spaces' and these are under the Archangel Raphael who rules the lungs, breath and writing, but the Angel Cassiel rules the end of the matter and the end of our matter.

Every character in writing including full–stops are under the rule of the *Angel of Scripts and Writing* that is the Archangel Raphael of the planet Mercury — but he does not own the very last full–stop because it is this full–stop that says ' no further, it is finished.' The words 'it is finished' are found in *John* and with those words 'he gave up the ghost.' *St. John* 19:30. Even here, we are still with the Angel Cassiel, who is the Lord of Death and the end of things. For the 'ghost' (= 'the spirit') had left the body, which remained behind as it must staying in the physical kingdom where it was created — where else should it go but by burial or cremation, back to the earth from which it came or as ashes?

It should be obvious by now the Angel Cassiel rules the outside square as this square is the 'fence or boundary' that contains the people connected with the work done in the centre quadrangle of the letter, which is the temenos or adytum. Outside this line is the Outer Court where the multitude gathers. It is this court where Christ overturned the tables of the moneychangers and those who sold doves and he told them, 'my house shall be called a house of prayer; but ye have made it a den of thieves.' Nothing connected with the letter must go over, be done or go outside or beyond this boundary line and it must never be broken or breached. If it is, you may as well save your time by doing something useful elsewhere.

The second of the two squares, the centre square is drawn using a thinner line of the colour of the angel being invoked to differentiate it if you wish. The space between the two frames can be varied depending on how much work you are going to put in the central square. It should be obvious the more room you leave yourself to work with the better, however, if you are going to put any angelic symbolism between these two lines or the areas down the sides of the square, then sufficient space must be left for this. For this you must exercise judgement and gain your experience.

This is why it is always better to work out what you want to say on separate paper to get it right and this will also help to dispense with any superfluous detail, repetition or words. Making sure that the meaning is not ambiguous and on a practical level, to see how much you are going to write on the page and the space needed for it. The size of any symbol drawn between these two lines is adjusted to fit the available space because they or anything else does not necessarily have to be 'writ large.' After a while, these trial runs can be dispensed with because you will not need them because fluency with the work will take over. The minimum requirements for the symbolism of an angelic Folding Letter or any angelic letter are fundamentally three.

1: Set the Angelic signature at the top of the letter, both letters, nothing goes above it and it has to be the highest thing written on the letter.

2: Set at least one symbol on either side to keep the letter balanced and using the Intelligence or Spirit of the Planet is fine as is any other suitable symbol connected with the angel and planet being invoked and what is being invoked. These symbols or signs are set between the limiting square of Saturn and the angel's line of the temenos, but they are never put inside the temenos or outside the outside the thick black line of the boundary see diagram.

3: Set the Kamea of the Angel at the bottom of the letter on which you finally place the sigil of your name (this is explained later). This action seals the letter and nothing must be done to the letter after this is done because — 'it is finished.'

The Angelic signatures are given in the diagrams at the back of the work with the others supplied. Doing this on the top, sides and finally the bottom is like placing symbols in the first in the East (the top of the letter) then the North and South (the sides of the letter) and finally in the West (the bottom of the letter). You are marking and clearly defining the sacred space of the letter, which surrounds the temenos where you will work, inside the boundary line just as you would under the physical conditions of a Temple. You can add to the minimum requirements above as you wish but never give less, you can make your letter as simple or elaborate as you wish, as long as these simple rules are observed as a minimum. Everything you use must be connected — all the sigils, signs, line–drawings, the symbols or colours must belong to the angel you are attempting to invoke and no other — you cannot ask for chalk if you want cheese.

For those readers interested in the physical orientation of their 'letter' it is as follows and this applies to both versions of it. When it is placed in front of you, the Angel's Signature is the East (= the top of your letter, the direction of the Archangel Raphael, planet Mercury). The North is on your left (= the direction of the Archangel Uriel, planet Uranus) and the South is on your right (= the direction of the Archangel Michael, planet Sun). The kamea of the Angel is set in the West (= the bottom of your letter, the direction of the Archangel Gabriel, the Moon). This is also the reason why you should place at least one symbol on either side of the your letter so that the cardinal directions compass (North and South) do not remain empty.

If you can and you should always try to sit facing the East when writing your angelic letters because this is the direction from where the Light is born each day at dawn and a (cheap) compass will give you this. The name for the celestial entities that were thought to bring the light of the dawn to the earth daily by the ancient Egyptian's was the Uben. The baboon in mythology was fêted in mythological tradition because the Uben welcomed the Light of the Dawn each day.

When you start writing your invocation at the top of the letter, this is in the East of your letter where the sun rises at dawn because you are facing the East. You write down the page towards the West from left to right, where the sun during its daily journey 'dies' each evening at dusk and it ends in the West, where your task of writing your letter will eventually come to an end.

When you have completed your letter, which is your invocation or the part that tells the angel what you want to say, you fill in the kamea of the angel underneath it all with its numbers. You should have prepared your letter by placing the 'grid' of the kamea there before you started writing your letter. You put the 'grid' of the kamea in place first because you write around it, never across it or touching it — you never disfigure a kamea.

Your signature as a sigil does not disfigure the kamea because it was 'born and taken' from the kamea being used. Your signature makes the kamea personal to you and the method of setting a signature on the kamea is a long accepted practise. Placing you name on the kamea is taken up in the appropriate place and fully explained in due course, so just accept this for now until you have all the pieces.

Finally, as said above, you activate the kamea by putting the number code in place when your letter is complete by using the code of the sigil of your name. You place upon the kamea the sigil of your name as a 'magical signature' and this is absolutely the last thing you do.

You write no *post–scribo* under your signature because this would have to be written after signing and closing the letter. This practise is all right for normal letters as afterthoughts, but never here because you must completed the letter you leave it. If it is wrong or at fault in any respect, you destroy it (preferably by fire) and start anew at another time.

If you had a precious liquid, you would carefully place it in a container that did not leak or was in such a bad shape that it might. You would risk losing it all and this is why the repeated stress is made that there must be no breaks in the thick black line that keeps the Sacred Court distant from the Outer Court of the Gentiles. You are placing your alchemical formula — your invocation or the 'seed' you want to flourish — within the boundaries set on your letter to contain the mixture. Regard the sigil of your signature on the kamea as a 'cork' that will seal your 'alchemical flask' and you leave your 'mixture' to brew for the appointed period.

When you write your sigil on the Kamea of a planet or angel this should be the last act done to complete the work. Do this only when all the work is finished because as said nothing should be done after it — I say, 'it is finished!' Now you will see the importance in the early stages at least, of writing a draft to check that nothing has been omitted. Once you have gained experience, this will probably not be needed.

You can, if you have genuine difficulty with your personal kamea signature sigil but do not regard this as an 'escape clause' for idleness, use your usual signature. Your personal signature is individual to you on the physical or material level where it has its unique vibration — but it has far less power at higher levels. You can write your signature across the kamea preferably from bottom corner left to upper corner right across the kamea or underneath, just as you would a personal letter, but remember this has less power than the kamea sigil of your name written properly on the kamea, which has been taken it to other levels above this one. Your ordinary signature stays on this level because the mundane and physical is where it was created at birth and where it has authority — but not elsewhere.

The sigil of your name written properly on the kamea is more powerful because your name on it in sigil form is linked with the source of the kamea and where the kamea was created. Remember, even on its own, the kamea is 'a prayer or a talisman.'

However, if you have genuine difficulty with this, again a genuine difficulty, not 'I can't be bothered' difficulty or it is an emergency letter where speed is essential, then your signature could be used. As said, your signature is personal to you and it 'marks' you and who you are because it is 'your mark.' Even someone with the same name would not write it the way you do. It would be very rare to find such exactitude, unless it is intentional, which could mean a forgery and a 'negative' signature.

As far as writing the invocation is concerned, this is really all there is to it. Make your Folding Letter as simple or as elaborate as you wish once the basic requirements are in place. However, never place anything higher than the angelic signature at the top, which is in the East the place of the rising Sun, where Light is born and the angelic signature must be the highest thing on the letter always.

You are attempting to invoke an angel and anything placed above the angelic signature is placing whatever it represents, above the angel and reducing the angel in importance.

The information given here applies to both forms of letter. The supplementary instructions for the Pyramid Letter given later are additional to what is given here. If you get the Folding Letter right and understand it, the Pyramid Letter is already ninety per cent understood.

## Making letter templates

If you have a computer, you could make up two templates, one set for the Folding Letter and another set for the Pyramid Letter because the Pyramid Letter has a variation in its assembly. I would not worry too much about making up some paper templates in readiness for your letters in this age of computers but if you have an aversion to this then make up the letters as and when you require them. As long as you do not use the prepared letter templates in a perfunctory way, all should be well.

Regard your templates as personal notepaper printed, created and part prepared for your private letters for special occasions and used for one purpose only. People still have personal notepaper and matching envelopes printed for their private correspondence. Store these templates in a large envelope or box of appropriate size so that they can lie flat, kept clean and not creased or folded. You should store your paper carefully out of sight and preferably somewhere high in your room. Obviously, others should not handle this paper and this is simply accomplished by not letting them know that it exists.

It is not exactly mass–production to prepare one pre–drawn square in thick black and the other square in the colour of one of the seven angels of old, with the outline of a kamea grid without the numbers set in place or any written details on a sheet of paper. You still have a great deal of personal work to do before it is presentable and acceptable for the purpose for which it will be used.

Your prepared letters should only be a 'skeleton outline' of the letter, leaving the personal details to be written in by hand and a minimum printing on them that would not tell anyone what they were being used for if they did see them, as there should be no words or numbers printed on them because this should be done by hand.

Forms dominate our life today that are sent out from a multitude of people who have nothing else to do but ask about us for one thing or another and it seems they can never have enough information. However, to the point being made. Even though printed to receive the relevant information asked for, until these forms have been filled in they are useless pieces of paper that look like all the forms without information because they say nothing until the personal part has be done, without the personal information on them, they belong to nobody and of themselves they are nothing

Further, even when you have filled in the information asked for or demanded the forms are still not acceptable or official until you sign them and they have been sent back and received. Only when you sign papers, sometimes in the presence of others as witnesses if they are really important, is it acknowledged that what is contained on them is acceptable, legal and official. I repeat, if this small amount of preparation beforehand bothers you, then use blank paper and do everything at the time of writing your letter but you will need more time to complete them and this should be allowed for, I do not feel that either way is wrong but your feeling happy about the issue is more important.

## THE KAMEA

Let us now get the use of the Kamea into perspective for both letters. Some of the Kamea must extend across the inner line of the temenos and go into the temenos, but it must never cross over the outside, thick black line, everything must remain within this border. As the kameas get larger, more of the kamea goes over the line into the temenos unless you make your kameas very small. The Kamea of the Moon is made up of eighty–one squares in all and on one illustration the kamea has only has nine squares, which of course is why I chose it.

The reader will find it easy as the diagram shows to incorporate the line of the temenos into one of the lines of the kamea being used, but this does not have to done. How much of the kamea you put over the line into the temenos is up to you and the size of the kamea used, but obviously, the minimum amount of the kamea put inside the temenos must be one line.

Just remember, the kamea must never cross over, touch or break through the outer thick line (nothing must) and with the Kameas must be kept inside the Sacred Court and that is the deciding factor on how many lines of the kamea goes over into the temenos of Holy of Holies.

Everything that is sacred must remain inside this thick black line and nothing must go over it or touch it, as it would be in contact with the Outer Court and back in the secular world of the Outer Court of the Gentiles. Putting the kamea over the inner line is like making a bridge from the Sacred Court into the temenos.

Using the magical scripts given later, you write your invocation within the square of the temenos and write the numbers in the squares of the kamea next. You place the sigil of your name on the kamea to 'close' the letter and ***this is the last thing you do***; this is constantly stressed because it is important. The signed kamea is thought of as setting a cartouche in place and closing the letter. This action corresponds to the 'closing' of a physical pyramid and sealing it when the work within is finished and when all that was intended to be within the pyramid is set in place. This is the reasoning here and this rule will be taken up in more detail when the Pyramid Letter is discussed in due course, though the principle is the same and important to both forms of letter.

## CARTOUCHE OR 'CLOSING THE LETTER'

The cartouche is an interesting word and an interesting article; let us see how it concerns us in the present work. French *cartouche*. Italian *cartoccia*= 'an angular roll of paper, a cartridge, from the Latin *carta*= 'paper,' *charta*= 'chart'; Greek, χαρτης, *chartes*= 'a leaf of paper.' 'In Egyptian Antiquity a cartouche is an oval seal found on ancient monuments and in papyri containing hieroglyphics expressing royal names and titles and occasionally those of the deities.' The original Egyptian symbol I understand is designated by the word *shenu*= 'that which encircles' or 'an oval frame encircling the royal names of the king/pharaoh and representing the eternal powers of the god Ra.' It is the endless circle of Ra and is 'without end or eternity' having no beginning or end and represents the eternal powers of the highest god, Ra.

It is interesting to read that the cartouche encircled precise royal names of the Egyptian kings, contained five distinct essentials illustrating the kings association with the gods and incorporated the following parts. It began with the ***Horus name*** touching upon the king's right to being the true agent of Horus on earth; the second was the ***Nebti name***, demonstrating the right of the king to rule over the Kingdoms of Upper and Lower Egypt. The third name is given as the *Golden Horus name* maintaining the king to be the representative of the gods on earth and the fourth *Nisut name* declaring the king as the Lord of the South and the North. Finally, the fifth name was the *Son of Ra name* or the king's name that was given to him at birth, which shows his right of succession and his right to be included in the annals of the royal lineage of Egypt.

It is interesting to find that in our personal angelic line there are also found 'five elements or names' belonging to the five individual or personal angels relevant to us and our lives. These are made up of the two Guardian Angels, the two Ancillary Angels and the important Angel of the Ascendant or the Benben Angel, all discussed in their appropriate place. These angels were taken from the map of the heavens, set up for the time and place of your birth and placed in your 'cartouche' (the circle of your birth chart) and a pentagram, which encompasses and contains the five angels and their symbols (= hieroglyphics?) for your personal use and descent, just as the true cartouche 'contained five elements' that left the royal lineage in no doubt.

Having been given the template to use, how do you start to set down on paper what you want? First, I must clear up something because it has bothered a few people in the past. You are not expected to reproduce the things found exactly as they are in this book or any other book you use. You make a fair representation of what is here to the best of your ability, it does not have to be a photographic copy, though you can trace things if you wish.

Your signs and symbols only have to be understood for what they, what they are meant to be, say and able to be recognized. You use whatever artistic skills you have and do the best that you can as we all do because we cannot do more. What you are doing is not going to be marked, accepted or rejected on its artistic merit because honesty of intent will stand you in far better stead.

Look at a child's drawing of a house. Often this is basically a square with a triangle on the top for the roof. The windows are squares with crosses in the them with an oblong placed between them for the front door. Sometimes there is a path with a chimney that has curly lines for smoke. The drawing is regularly out of proportion but it is simple, effective and most important of all, no one is in any doubt what it is — its a house!

There is no need to finish your letter all in one go as long as it was started at the right time, because a good start gives a good finish. If you are slow worker or you want to take your time, start your work in the day of the angel and in their hour. Pick up the work again in the hour the angel rules in the same day or continue in the hour that the angel rules in the day of another angel. Just use the angel's hour on the following days until the job is done and a Table of Planetary and Angelic Hours is given at the back of the book with directions how to use it.

If you want to finish your work in one session, you can. As long as you start your task on the right day and hour, you can continue until the work is done, even if this means working through the hours that follow because although the following hours do not belong to the angel. If you start your work on the right day and time, then the correct angel has 'marked the work' and it will bear his 'mark' always.

Most letters should be completed within an hour without any problems, even a very full letter once you have gained experience. If you do not finish, running into the hour of the next angel will not be a disaster and you are not being timed and neither is it a test. Do not worry about it and remember the angels are all one family and work together for the most. Just start in the right hour on the right day, which is more important, and carry on until the letter is finished. As you see, you have several alternatives that you can chose to finish the work. These matters are all explained in their due place, treat them all as pieces of a jigsaw puzzle which, although they appear to be scattered in the various chapters will fit into a whole when the parts are assembled later.

The symbols you set down the side's of your letter are like 'columns' that support the 'angelic lintel' across the top, not unlike a door that you are trying to open with the 'lintel' with the angel's name above it showing which 'angel's door' it is.

These side drawings can be the Sign or Signs of the Zodiac of the angel, the sigil of the planet the angel rules, a line drawing of something the angel rules, the spirit of the planet and so forth. For example, the Egyptian gods have equivalents that can be used, Ra for the Sun, Isis for the Moon with Thoth for Mercury, Horus for Mars, Hathor for Venus and Anubis — the 'Lord of the Mummy Wrappings' — for Saturn.

Do not underestimate the value of using simple line drawings created for things that the planet rules, a crown, a sun, a heart, the Eye of Ra, a drawing of a throne representing power and majesty for the Archangel Michael, Angel of the Sun. In the past, when they started in the School, some students (including myself at times in the beginning) thought this particular style of drawing was to certain extent unsophisticated, rather fanciful and not unlike a child's drawings.

Now I know to bear in mind not everything you do has to be high ceremonial magic filled with pomp and circumstance, robes, wands and chalices, using only Latin, Greek, ancient symbols and signs and 'the barbarous names of evocation.' I think this has more to do with pre–conceived notions of what people think 'magic' should be rather than any practical issues. The simpler forms of sign and symbol puts the work within the reach of all, remember the parable of the Widow's Mite.

## REASON FOR USING SQUARE PAPER FOR YOUR LETTERS, NOT OBLONG

Why not leave the oblong paper as it is or use square paper to begin with? A fair question, so let us try to give a fair answer.

Using the square form for your angelic letter and the particular method of folding it to keep the square shape as given here is symbolic. The square is used to represent the material world and when something or someone is stable in the world even we say that they stand 'four–square.' The square represents the square area occupied by the base of the pyramid on which the pyramid was built and that is what it is. Even with the Folding Letter, you are symbolically closing your pyramid over your letter and you do this when you close over your letter the four triangular flaps. Strangely enough, a rather flat pyramid I admit, but symbolically all the elements of the Pyramid and the Pyramid Letter are there and I did say it was a symbolic form with this letter. This method enables the letter to be carried or put away out of sight, something you cannot do with the second form of the letter. Just accept this for the moment, when we get there it will all be explained and it is not complicated as it appears on first reading as you have made a good start with the Folding Letter.

Barrett tells us 'The Pythagoreans call the number four *Tectractis*, and prefer it before all the virtues of numbers, because it is the foundation and root of all other numbers; when, also, all foundations, as well in artificial things, as natural and divine, are four square . . . it signifies solidity.' *The Magus*. This does not exhaust all the reasons behind the choice, but it gives some of the most important ones.

Until modern times, the Chinese conceived the earth as square as did many of the older races. They knew that a straight line of the same length if bent to the right, then again and yet again would come back to its starting point and close the figure it started. Therefore, a square was an assembling of identical straight lines on the same plane. This thought is expressed in the very old Chinese proverb — 'Heaven Round, Earth Square.' This may be why the old circular Chinese coins had squares cut in their centre but this is pure speculation.

We represent the heavens with the Signs of the Zodiac as a circular chart around which we set the twelve signs, a very daring diagram indeed which brings the vast space of the universe down to a diagram the human mind can manage. Originally, astrological charts in the past were square in shape and they were not difficult to read being logically laid out. The Fixed Signs of the Zodiac as said were often called the 'pillars of the Earth' or the 'cornerstones.' If we drew straight lines between these four signs naturally, this would make a square within the circle or 'squaring the circle?' the Egyptian's were well aware of this concept because they recognized the Four Corners of the Earth and we have mentioned from *Job* in the *Bible*, the Four Corners of the Earth and their foundations. The Egyptian's built this into the construction of so many of their building and monuments, especially the pyramids. They had their gods of the cardinal points as we have our angels and archangels and these are Sopedu (Sopdu), Horus, Seth and Thoth, briefly . . .

Sopedu is a guardian deity and a god that protects the eastern borders and the eastern desert. He is linked the Pyramid Texts with the hawk god Horus and frequently shown as falcon. He was associated with the star that was identified by the Greeks as Sirius, whose appearance heralded the inundation of the Nile.

Horus is one of most universally important gods in the Egyptian pantheon that was born at Khemmis in the region of the Nile delta. Through her magic, Horus was born of Isis from his dead father Osiris. His symbol is a falcon or a hawk, a form of Sun–god, found called 'Horus of the Horizon' and an implacable enemy of Seth, his rival. The Eye of Horus is regarded as one of the most powerful symbols in all Egypt.

Seth, in the Greek Typhon, the Egyptian god of Adversity and Chaos is the son of Geb and Nut. He lusted after the women of the gods of light causing havoc. He killed his twin brother Osiris and fought a protracted battle with his brother's son, Horus and his mother Isis that ended with his humiliation before the Celestial Court and he ceased troubling them to trouble us instead.

Thoth is the ancient Egyptian god of writing, learning and wisdom, the patron of scribes and usually associated with the Moon. Among the many titles he owns are found 'the Lord of the Heavens.' He is said to have invented every intellectual skill, which required organization, astronomy, astrology, music, law, magic, medicine and especially writing. Having no body or shape of his own he entered the body of the baboon or a man with the head of the ibis that are the main forms usually shown.

## SEALING YOUR LETTERS

To seal your Folding Letter you fold the corners of your letter in towards the centre and this is how this particular letter got its name. You can seal the other corners to the first fold with a small touch of gum. If you use this method, you take the first fold a little over the centre of the letter so the three other folds can be stuck to it. You obviously do not stick down the first fold as this would stick the corner to the letter itself. Putting a touch of gum on the second, third and fourth folds so that they stick to the back of the first. Alternatively, you can use the seals as explained next, which is my chief method.

Sometimes a letter is a request to attract or to banish something and attraction and banishment are discussed in greater detail in the chapter on the *Pentagram*, though they are not used only for these two matters.

When I want to repel or banish something from my life, I start folding my letters from the bottom left–hand corner, next bottom right, top right and finally top left, sealing the folds in an anticlockwise order, which is widdershins or 'against the sun.'

If the letter is to draw or to attract something to me, the first fold starts with bottom left–hand corner of the letter to top left, to top right and finally bottom right, This makes the folds in a clockwise or deosil order, 'with the sun.'

The anticlockwise action repels (= widdershins), the clockwise action attracts (= deosil) and these are well–established movements in most types of Work of this nature and have been so for a very long time.

The number four represents the material place where we live and breath because it is a number significant of system and order. Within a square, we can find the four cardinal points of the compass, the four elements, the four seasons, the four Archangels or Throne Angels and so many other significant groupings of four.

Some examples taken from Part 1 of the work are of angels that are often found as groups of four or seven, 'And after these things I saw four Angels standing on the four corners of the earth, holding the four winds of the earth.' *Revelation* 7:1. The 'four corners of the earth' are usually taken to mean the Four Great Fixed Signs of the Zodiac giving Taurus, Leo, Scorpio and Aquarius, taking in the four elements, in the same order. The Element of Earth, the Element of Fire, the Element of Water and the Element of Air.

When we say of someone they are 'four–square' we mean they are solid and reliable like the earth itself. It takes a lot to move those born under the Earth Signs, especially Taurus because being a 'fixed earth sign' it takes a lot more to move them into raw anger. When it does happen the folk of Taurus become the proverbial 'bull in a china shop' when roused. If they are moved then stand well clear, because they erupt like an earthquake without thought for the consequences, just as the earth does and like the earth and they bear the scars of the eruption for a long time to come.

## USING LETTER SEALS (OPTIONAL PRACTISE)

I often seal my letters with self–adhesive artistic 'seals,' which can be bought in stationers, gift or art shops in the appropriate colour for the angel being invoked. Some of these seals copy the style of the seals on old documents, which used sealing wax over ribbon but there are other shapes now.

The word seal is from the Latin. *Sigilum*= a seal, a mark; prop. Dimin, from *signum*= 'a sign, a mark'. Anglo–Saxon *sigle*= 'an ornament.' Using seals on your angelic letters are not obligatory but it puts a subtle finishing touch to the letter; it is an optional act and I do not always do it. I started fixing 'seals' on my angelic letters from my habit of saying of a completed letter that it was 'signed and sealed.' Therefore, I decided I would do just that.

You can use a ribbon of the same colour as the seal or a different colour. If you want to use only one ribbon for your seal, you could use either white or yellow. Again, as said before white contains the other seven colours and yellow is a good colour because it is the colour the colour of Mercury, the Messenger of the Gods, but I like using red ribbon to imitation the sealing wax of old. Cut a length of ribbon. Trim the ends of the ribbon and fold the ribbon as if a 'V' and the ends of the ribbon need not be even. When you seal the letter you can set the ribbon in place, hanging downwards I feel looks best and stick the self–sealing 'seal' over the ribbon to hold it as in the diagram, it is not difficult to do. This is shown in the diagram *'Making Letter — Invocation Seals'* found in the diagrams and tables grouped at the end of the work.

Occasionally the reader will find the words 'if you wish' attached to some of the statements I make. You do not have to use everything that is given here and some things are only given as suggestions. If something is important, it is stressed so and there is little doubt about it. Please use your judgement and work within reasonable perimeters and make you letters personal to you. If you do not want to use an optional self– adhesive seal then do not do it.

All your work should be guided by one word — *CONNECT* — the word 'connect' for this writer is absolutely paramount. The word is repeated and repeated regularly for which I make not apologies if it gets the message home for that is what is intended to do. What has gone before and what is to come should be connected to what you are doing now and your intent because we rarely do things in isolation in work of this nature.

If you have some fine beads, you can arrange them in order but they cannot be picked up, handled or worn until they are strung on a cord or connected. The cord holds them, their pattern and their form together. So should everything you do in this kind of work. Always look for the 'connecting cord' running through things because it holds everything together and without it, things would simply fall apart and scatter, as the beads would if the cord was broken.

You can make your letter as simple or elaborate as you wish but connect everything used to the angel being invoked, the aims, objectives and what is being invoked. You should be able to say to anyone who asks why something is there or being done. I admit some things are done at times because it has always been so and the reason is sometimes lost in time, but if it has lasted that long and had continual use, criticism of it and changing it for the sake of it sometimes sounds a little like nit–picking.

## SYMBOLS AND LINE DRAWINGS

Let us now discuss the line drawings that you can use on your letters to establish which angel the letter or invocation is being addressed. These symbols are usually put down either side of the letter and if you look at a 'letter' to an angel there should be little doubt where it should be sent by what is found written on it. On a mundane level, you can hardly mistake a bedroom for the kitchen because they are furnished for the purpose for which they are intended and your letter of invocation should show much the same broad principles.

Cursing tablets have been found on a reasonably regular basis and these were simple both in construction and purpose. Usually they were small 'plates of lead,' roughly about the size of a modern playing card and thin. There was often a hole in them where they had been nailed somewhere, in rooms, on posts, barns and buried in fields. Because of the association of the metal lead with the planet Saturn, they were not always meant to wish someone or something the best of luck. Lead is a malleable metal and curses or ill–wishes could be scratched on it with reasonable ease and they often contained simple diagrams of their intent. Such 'simple pictures' have been used long before books existed to carry the information far and wide to those who sought such knowledge and could read it.

Naturally, words have been found written on them with other symbols and (in early times) this may have shown the help of a professional consulted in the matter. For example, if a farmer had a cow with one horn and the cursing tablet showed such a cow lying feet up at the bottom of a steep ravine, it was not meant to wish the cow or its owner the best of luck.

Outlines were simple and they were understood, if early people were invoking for a cow — they drew a cow, a horse, a cart or a barn. This cannot always be certain with some of the old medieval works translated from Latin or other languages with symbols of angels or demons they did not understand. Of course, if you have made study of such things to this level that is a different matter, but you started your studies with your 'ABC.'

In the Courses in the School in which I was involved and worked in for so many years, there was a Course dealing with Angelic Letters and associated subjects and this course included a very basic *Invocation Tablet* and a *Banishment Square* for the use of the students and these made use of simple line drawings in their creation. Of course, the illustrations used in the School are not given here, but line–drawings are a far older practise than many of the Schools that teach them or use them even now, which is why they are being discussed here

Many Chinese characters were of this 'pictorial' type as were Egyptian hieroglyphics. We use something similar today with signs of warning to point out danger, fire hazard, electricity, hazardous chemicals and other things. A skull and crossbones does not need words because the picture gives its meaning to all people. There are times when situations must be understood quickly by someone who may not understand the language of the country they are in. Other universal and agreed signs shows disabled facilities, hospitals, picnic areas, parking spaces, a car crossed out with a red line shows no cars allowed and so on.

They are simple but effective signs that say what they mean without words and for the most, they are intuitively recognized without the need of language and proof of this is their use today. There is little confusion what is intended when someone twice your size and looking twice as ugly, comes at you from afar waving clenched fists, pointing at you, certainly ranting something about your immediate future even though this is in a language unknown to you. Such 'signs' mean the same whatever the language —get a good head start and run like hell!

A warrior or great fighter was represented by the weapons they used, a spear, a bow, arrows, a shield, a dagger or sword and so on. The Sun was shown by a round disc and the Moon by a crescent, a black disc starting to go over a white disc was an eclipse. A king was shown by a crown or the distinctive headdress worn and further examples are obvious.

For the planet Sun, you could draw a crown, a palm tree, a lion, a heart, a disk representing the Sun (with wings sometimes), a sceptre, a sunflower. The sign of Leo the Lion, a peacock, a swan and these symbols are taken from the lists given for the planets. If your symbols were drawn in the colours of the Sun, orange, there would be little doubt what was intended.

Draw a crescent moon, a lighthouse, a boat, an owl, a willow tree, a turtle, a water lily or white lilies. Geese, hens or night birds, a pumpkin or melon for the Moon because these fruits contain a lot of water.

For Mars you can draw a gauntlet, the one you throw down to challenge and wear for protection. A spear, a lance, a shield, armour, fire, a dagger, sword or knife. A ram, a falcon, a woodpecker because this bird is the sacred and prophetic bird of Mars, a thorny plant such as a cactus or holly because these plants 'defend' themselves, a drawing of Horus the falcon–headed Egyptian deity, remember you can use symbolism from any period, the only requirement is that it is the right symbolism.

For Mercury you could use a fox, a parrot (= a 'talking' bird), a monkey or a hare. The caduceus or wings. If, for example, you need a book draw the book and put the title on it and wings to show it 'winging its way to you.' A herald, a jester or juggler who can keep several things in the air at the same time and to do this they need a quick mind and nimble fingers.

For Jupiter you can draw a mitre, a crown, the orb or sceptre and if this was done in purple, the planet would be known. An archer, an eagle, a whale, a horse or a swan. The crucifix, the *Bible* or any holy book, any holy object, a church or ceremonial building, an oak tree or an acorn, a mace or anything that represents the rule of Law.

For Venus you could draw apples, roses, a dove, a heart for love, a pear, peach even a rabbit all of which are under Venus. However, drawing a sword through a heart was more likely to be a quarrelsome love or kill it than conquer it, though once popular I always thought this was a somewhat dubious tattoo, think carefully before you use things, especially in combination.

For Saturn you could draw a goat, a clock, an hourglass, a yew or pine tree or a gravestone. For example, if you are invoking Saturn for something you to want get rid of, then write on your 'gravestone' what you want 'dead and buried' — no, not a rich relative or someone you do not like — be nice to former and avoid the latter. A knot to represent a problem or blockage that you appear not to be able to undo unless you become an Alexander, an urn, some bones, a skeleton or a house you want to buy or somewhere to live.

315

Uranus, the lightning flash, a ceremonial magician (not stage); Neptune, a trident or any mythical creature of the sea and Pluto, an active volcano and the like.

The study of the angels and the angelic is extensive, wide–ranging and all–embracing but it is a generous philosophy and the means can be found no matter how small to suit the abilities and temperament of most people. Somewhere can usually be found where they can belong and work 'in the vineyard' as best they can and add their portion and that is all anyone can do so. If all could paint like Michelangelo, every city, town and village would have a Sistine Chapel and what was brilliantly unique would become commonplace.

The point being made is if a planet's rulership is taken down to its fundamental and material level, the angels will be found to have rulership over some extremely basic, everyday things and concerns by default. This is because these are some of the concerns of our daily lives like it or not that we have to deal with them. We cannot spend all our days walking and floating around in Elysium Fields high above these dreary and routine affairs no matter how desirable, especially when there is an unblocked drain that needs our attention or bills to be paid.

You use a symbol that vibrates to the angel and the planet with anything that will reinforce the identity of the angel and planet. This coupled with the colour of the paper, the colour of the ink and if you wish, the incense you are using will do this — leave no doubt and connect everything you do to one source. Some of the system is very simple while other parts are not, but this does not mean that the simple is the less effective for that.

You write your request, plea, prayer and even your thanks in one of the magical scripts. There are more magical scripts than I have supplied but the ones given are reliable and quite sufficient for what is being attempted here. Suggestions have been made regarding which script to use for the various angels and this discussed in the appropriate place.

You should not be writing to the angels for help for every little thing only for the important things, stressed many times. Those matters in your life that are in crisis and you are appealing for help because you have done all you can to resolve it for yourself, your back is to the wall and you cannot see any way out. The angels were not created to solve every trivial problem in our lives, solving our problems is what we are supposed to do and one of the reasons for our being here.

Writing to the angels for help should be a 'last resort' as (for example) when consulting the *I Ching* or any other recognized form of help, advice or counsellor, certainly not used for every little problem that appears in our lives. The reader should remember the interpretation attached to *Hexagram* 4 in the *I Ching* — 'Youthful Folly.'

The oracle cautions that at the first time of asking guidance will be given and the seeker will be told, but if they ask repeatedly, then the oracle regards the seeker as abusing the privilege. They have become irreverent, annoying, will not be helped and any further seeking will be ignored. The

*I Ching* does not seek them out, they seek out the Oracle nevertheless, if genuineness is shown, the oracle will reply but not to repetitious or trivial demands.

I have written before that you do not always have to ask. Say thank you when things are going well and you are pleased with yourself and your life. I am sure you have blossomed when you received a pleasant letter, pleasing comments or a small gift that said thank you for something done or given and sometimes a good listening ear is enough — there are not many of these around today. Good advice in a difficult period, help when it was sorely needed or just for being there when you were needed or who you are. You felt that you were not being taken for granted and you were appreciated, so why keep this feeling to yourself. Show that you too can be a generous 'giver' and not always a 'taker.'

If you find a particular magical script does not give you the letters for some of the words in your request then use another word, series of words or even another script. Most languages are rich in alternatives, but there is a tendency today to be somewhat lazy despite this remarkably flexible choice. You hear the same tired old words today such as 'hassle' for 'trouble,' 'on–going' for 'continuing', 'up–coming' and 'guys' for everyone as if men and women do not exist any more, everything is 'up for grabs' and the rest, all of which to my tired old eyes and ears shows an inordinate laziness regarding a beautiful and expressive language.

For the most seek out simple words because they are usually the best for this and most other work. For instance you could write 'Scintillate, scintillate, infinitesimal celestial globule' but 'Twinkle, twinkle, little star' is better by far. Now let us move on from the Folding Letter to the second form of letter with you will find that it has much in common with the Folding Letter and the reader will see why it is called . . .

## THE PYRAMID LETTER

The instructions 'given' regarding this form of letter were 'to place a pyramid over the temenos to enclose its contents from 'the sight of men as it was with the original Holy of Holies' and this is the reason for using this title as you will see later. As with the Folding Letter, the Pyramid Letter starts being made up on good quality A4 paper. Some of the instructions have already been given but will be repeated with additional information to make the section self–contained.

Measure the paper as before, outside this square is the Outer Court or Court of the Gentiles and no work is ever done in this area because it is outside the temple and the sacred area and it can be used by anyone who happens to be there, including storing their animals for sale or sacrifice in the original construction, including money–changing and the rest, which is why Christ overturned their tables and beat them saying ' . . . my house shall be called the house of prayer; but ye have made it a den of thieves.' it must be represented and be present or the three becomes two. There are three distinct areas and none should be omitted, remember, three elements are the least you can work with.

As before, inside the first square you place your second square using a thinner line this time, again this line is drawn in the colour of the angel you are invoking. The space within this area is called the temenos, which is 'the place where rites of passage and rituals of transformation were conducted.' The area around these squares should be equidistant from the outside edge of the paper. This central area (the temenos or adytum) will be covered by the pyramid — not the outer square. You will be making a pyramid to cover this central area so it would be best that it remains uniform in size. The other small difference between the two letter forms is shown in the Pyramid Letter diagram and it will be explained later. Again, let me assure the reader that this letter of invocation is not difficult.

Solomon's temple was thought to be a duplicate of an Egyptian temple, having the Holy of

317

Holies set within the central, third compartment and the pylon in the front supported by the two pillars of Boaz and Jakin. The Temple of Dendra is described as having three parts and again, the central, inner and third compartment was the most holy containing the statue of Hathor — the 'Lady of the Sycamore' — or Neith — the 'Opener of the Ways, the Mother or Nurse.' Only the chosen or initiated could behold the statue, the ordinary people could not even enter the gate or be inside the temple and could only look in from the outside.

You make your pyramid to cover the temenos of an appropriate colour especially if you are going to make a pyramid for each planet and angel, making ten pyramids in all. More of this later, including some practical shortcuts to make the task easier. Choose a card of suitable thickness so it will stand firm when assembled. The base of the pyramid measurements given here will obviously have to be 14cm along each side so that the base will cover the square of the temenos, for the measurements given here. The height of the pyramid should be such to maintain 'the Egyptian pyramid shape,' try 7cm to start with. If you make the shape of your pyramid too high or squat, it looks ridiculous, a pyramid so short it looks as if it is collapsing or too high, it seems unable to make up its mind if its a pyramid or the beginning of an obelisk, which does not come to a point but has a pyramid on the top.

However, as long as you maintain the inner square measurements for the base, you can increase the height to an obelisk if you wish, better though to make a short obelisk because if it is made too tall it will be liable to fall over. An obelisk is perfectly acceptable but two rules are 'written in stone' for both obelisk and pyramid — the base must cover the temenos square and the Benben stone (the small pyramid that tops it) must always be gold whatever form is chosen.

A simple way to make the pyramid is to get some card and cut a 14cm, square and draw a line from corner to corner and cut out the four triangles that will measure 14cm along the base and 7cm high, which usually does the job, the for triangular shape is joined together, I put strong tape inside the pyramid and join them together when flat. I then put the tape on half of the last join so when the final sides are married together then you only have one side to join. Having said this in the hope of being helpful naturally, the reader is free to construct their pyramid in any way that suits them, as the results will be the same. Whatever height of pyramid you decide, the base must cover the square of the temenos completely, so that what is inside, cannot be seen — apart from the Gate of the East at the top and the part of the Kamea at the bottom, half under the pyramid and half outside — all explained later.

This fundamental order shown must never be changed and the pattern must remain, the edge of the paper plus two squares making three distinct areas with each square concentric within the others as the diagram shows. If you change the size of the squares then you will have to change the size of the pyramid used to cover the square of the temenos with the Pyramid Letter so it would be better to standardize your template and keep to that size. Otherwise, if you do keep varying the size of the areas, you will have to keep altering the size of the covering pyramid so that it will cover the new measurements. The Pyramid Letter, which is the more powerful of the two forms.

## THE BENBEN STONE

Let us take a brief look at the Benben stone. You must make one small Benben stone, approximately three or four centimetres across the base and this small pyramid must be made from a gilt or gold-faced card or covered with gold leaf that can be bought in art shops and this I recommend because the Benben stone is important and very special. This was made up to fit and crown the pyramid to represent the original gold capstone, the pyramidion or Benben stone of the original pyramid. The capstone is made removable because it is used for all your 'pyramids' for the

Pyramid Letters no matter who or what you are using it for. The capstone or Benben represents the important Angel of the Ascendant and it must always be gold and no other colour. This is why we sometimes call the Angel of the Ascendant — the 'Benben Angel' — when used in this work because of this angel's unique position on the pyramid. The Angel of the Ascendant takes the station of the highest in the pantheon — any pantheon!

The Benben will be explained in greater detail later for any reader not familiar with the term so that we understand how and why we use it. There will some more information about making your pyramids to set upon your letter and this will also be found later with instructions for making them in an alternative way. Be patient and all the scattered pieces will be drawn together but first they have to be gathered, set out and arranged, just as you lay out a jigsaw puzzle. I agree that it does look rather a lot but it is less than you think and I do admit this takes time, especially to explain it all. Once you have all the pieces laid out, they should fit together with a little patience and in time, you will use them with ease because they are not as difficult as they at first appear and use means that you will not have to keep referring back.

At the time of writing the instructions given were. 'The kamea must not touch or cross the boundary line' (= the thick outside square) and 'one (= minimum) or more rows of the kamea must cross the inner line, which will take the kamea into the temenos and under the pyramid' (= the thin coloured central square). The above is shown in the all diagrams referring to the Pyramid Letter.

The other difference between the Pyramid letter and the Folding Letter is at the top of the Pyramid Letter in the East, there is a distinct break in the temenos wall allowing clear entry to the temenos from the Sacred Court on the Eastern side (the Eastern Gate) and this 'entrance' is seen going under the pyramid even when it is covered by the pyramid you place over the temenos and it emerges on the opposite side through the kamea in the West (the Western Gate).

When the Pyramid Letter is complete, your last act is to place the pyramid over the temenos to hide its contents which only you have seen; you leave it safe and you leave it alone. This does not mean that cannot go to your pyramid or the place where it is and by ritual, invocation or prayer reinforce your work when you want to do so, but you do not move the pyramid. This limitation will govern where you place this particular form of letter for it must stay there for the allotted time (suggestions given later), until the invocation has been answered in full, in part or you feel that the project is 'cold' and/or 'finished.' This is in keeping the original pyramids once they were constructed and sealed because they were not intended to be opened again but left in peace, neither were they moved because this would have been impossible to do so you do likewise.

**For the Folding Letter, the minimum requirements for the symbolism to be used are three:**

Set the Angelic signature at the top of the letter
Put at a minimum of one symbol belonging the angel on either side of the letter
Set the kamea of the angel at the bottom of the letter. Part of the kamea should be inside the square of the temenos. On the kamea, you place the sigil of your name.
The kamea must not cross the outer square. Signing the kamea is the last act you       perform after everything else is written on the letter just before you fold it, seal it and close it. Once it is sealed you add nothing else to it. If you open it or attempt to add something to it then it has been defiled, like a sealed tomb that has been broken into by robbers so throw the letter away and a new start made. This is why  before writing your letter you were advised to make a draft of the work.

**For the Pyramid Letter, the minimum requirement for the symbolism used is three plus one.**

If you are using the Pyramid Letter method of writing your letter, you add to the above three instructions one further requirement, putting in the position the Eastern Gate, which gives admission to the pyramid in the East and this is placed second in the order.

Set the Angelic signature at the top of the letter

Under the angelic signature at the top you add in the centre of the inner line, two parallel vertical lines (the 'Eastern Gate') that break through the temenos line as shown in the diagram, giving access between the Sacred Court and the Temenos.

Set them wide enough apart to take the Seal of the Planet of the angel being used.

The line of the temenos is not drawn through these lines, because it is a passage so it must be left open and unobstructed or it cannot be used. It is a passage not a cul de sac having an entrance and exit. Put at least on symbol of the angel on either side of the letter. Set the kamea of the angel at the bottom of the letter. Part of the kamea should be inside the square of the temenos and hidden under the pyramid. On the kamea, you place the sigil of your name (the 'Western Gate).

The kamea must not cross the outer square. Signing the kamea is the last act you perform after everything else is done. Finally, set out the paper flat somewhere private and safe, then you cover the temenos with your pyramid. It is left in place until the matter has been resolved, the time limit has be passed or you feel it is a 'dead letter.'

Between the vertical lines put the Seal of the Planet, half outside and half inside the Sacred Court and the temenos, because this is a gate giving admission the closed pyramid but not for us. It is 'the Angel's Gate' for the Angels of Light. As said, do not put the line of the temenos through this 'gate' because it 'must be left open and not blocked' and this the only time this inner line is ever broken or left open. In the Pyramid Letter model, make a break in the inner square to let the vertical lines pass through from the Sacred Court into the temenos, see the diagram. This additional instruction inserted in the second instructions for the Pyramid Letter is one of the requirements different from the Folding Letter, the 'plus one' of the subtitle. The second variation is covering the temenos with the pyramid from which this letter takes its name and the last is placing the Benben stone on the apex of the pyramid. However, having made your covering pyramid, you will use your Benben stone for all the Pyramid Letters in accordance with the angel being invoked no a matter what their personal colour is.

## TEMPLATES

If you prepare templates for your letters — I do — then you will have to make up two sets, one for the Folding Letters, there are seven versions of the Folding Letter, one for each of the seven Kameas used according to the angel, the framework of the kamea is set in place but the numbers are not. The other templates are for the Pyramid Letter, which also has seven versions, one for each of the seven kameas as above — if you decide to use both forms of letter. This would mean fourteen part–prepared letters with their outlines only showing. All other work done to them would be done by hand.

As written earlier and I repeat, prepared templates should not cause you any disquiet because prepared templates are to some extent like forms with which we are all familiar from birth to death living in a modern society and the governments we give ourselves. They are simply pieces of paper prepared in readiness and until the relevant information is put on them, they have no validity or identity whatsoever, they are 'dead things' and they have to be signed after they are filled in to make them personal, valid and possessing authority.

It is best to regard these templates as personal notepaper for the angels only and no other source. Keep them in an A4 box or envelope, flat, clean and they are only handled by you. As said earlier, you keep fourteen in stock (seven of each letter with nothing written on them part from outlines in the appropriate colours) and replace the one that you use.

## THE BENBEN STONE

We are told by those of authority that the root of the word 'ben' or 'Benben' can mean 'human sperm, ejaculation' or 'placing the seed in the womb.' Long before Herodotus visited Egypt, the original Benben stone had disappeared from history and departed for realms of legend. The Benben stone appears to have given its name to the apex stones, capstones or pyramidions, which were placed on the top of pyramids and obelisks. An obelisk ends with a small pyramid at its tip because they did not simply come to a point. It had a small pyramid at the top to finish it off and it held this Benben stone high above the ground or above the mundane.

The original Benben Stone is chiefly associated with Heliopolis and this name means 'the City of the Sun.' This connection has led some Egyptologists to conclude that the pyramid shape is essentially male and a solar symbol and that it portrays the rays of the sun coming down to earth through a break in the clouds, spreading out from a central point to wide base — a triangle.

As said, the pyramid form is regarded as a male symbol. This symbolism is stressed further in the pyramid and obelisk form with its Benben stone or 'seed or sperm' at the tip and pointing erect to the sky, which hardly requires any interpretation, see below. Let us look at another connection and some thoughts regarding this.

The Egyptians did not use the generally accepted Creation order of today that the Earth is created from a female deity or source. The deity Geb is one Egypt's most ancient gods and was known as the 'Great Cackler.' This is because he was often shown as a man with a goose on his head to show that it was he that had laid the first Cosmic Egg of Creation, the male not the female in this instance but not the only one found.

In mythology Geb was sometimes regarded 'as being unwise because he was a little too curious.' He opened the box containing the Uraeus of Ra and he was badly burned by the power of the Serpent Cobra, which destroyed his companions. This is reminiscent of the 'burning and destructive power' of the Ark of the Covenant of the Hebrews that stuck down even those who where trying to protect it from falling when touched or when opened by the unauthorized.

Geb is honoured as the father of Osiris, Isis, Seth and Nephthys, with the help of Nut of course. Geb is the brother–husband of the goddess of the sky, Nut. They were inseparable in the fullest sense of the word, far too much so for Ra who sent Shu, the ancient god of air to separate them, because nothing was getting done at least not with Ra's Creation. Therefore, Shu — 'Air' — placed himself between Geb (= earth) and Nut (= sky) to separate the earth and the sky, which is the arrangement we find today.

Geb was inconsolable because of this and because of his loss, he wept so much that his tears formed the seas, oceans and rivers of the world. The body of the god Geb is represented lying on his back and weeping for Nut represents the mountains and valleys of the earth. Many standing stones, maypoles, obelisks and so forth are firmly planted erect and supported in the earth (= Geb/male) and pointing to the sky (= Nut/female), just as Geb is still shown doing in art.

A similar example to Geb, from the Chinese this time, is the god Pan Gu, the creator of the universe and the earth. He is said to have 'chiselled the universe for 18,000 years' increasing each day until his body became the universe. His eyes became the sun and moon and his head became the mountains. His limbs are the four quarters of the world, his flesh became the soil, his blood became the rivers of the world and (not very complementary for us) 'mankind was created from his body lice.'

The pyramid represented the idea of resurrection and some writers think the symbol of the Benben influenced the builders of the pyramids of the Old Kingdom. The Egyptians called their phoenix — the bennu. The root word ben is sometimes used by the ancient Egyptians to denote sexual procreation, 'to copulate, to fertilize' or the 'seeding of ideas.' Many races possess the legend of the phoenix and the symbolism of this fabulous bird in most of them remains reasonably constant. The phoenix is often portrayed as a symbol of divine procreation, rebirth and resurrection. There can be little doubt that the Egyptian Phoenix is Osiris. In the ***Book of the Dead*** we are told by Osiris — 'I am the great phoenix that is in Heliopolis.'

The meaning of 'bennu' is sometimes often given as 'self–creation' and it is found in the accounts of the Egyptian creation myths, the bird that flew from the light into the darkness. The use of the term 'self–creation' appears to come from the ashes of its death at the city of Heliopolis, as a facet of the Egyptian Sun God Ra. This was strengthened by the information given to the Greek Herodotus by the Egyptians making him associate the bird with the phoenix who, flying out of the light of the primeval fire at the destruction of the universe, the only thing that did survive and settling on an 'earth mound' to resurrect creation. Many creation myths have life being brought into the darkness from the light for rebirth or resurrection, see the opening lines of ***Genesis***.

The phoenix is credited in legend with being the first creature to exist, its flight into the darkness brought with it both warmth and creative energy — its cry is said to have been the first sound that was ever heard. In the art of Egypt, the bird is often represented as a yellow wagtail or the Nile heron, with feathers rising from its head like two spears. The bennu is often found engraved on gemstones and interred with bodies, to help them the deceased to attain a subsequent existence.

Herodotus (***Histories*** II, 73) said that the phoenix came from Arabia carrying the parent bird 'encased in myrrh' and this ball was 'as big as the bird could carry.' It hollowed out the ball to take the body of the dead parent and it takes the myrrh 'sarcophagus' to the Temple of the Sun where it buried the body and the bennu shelters in the sacred Persea tree at Heliopolis, a tree that is associated with the cat that slew the legendary serpent Apophis.

It should hardly be necessary to point out that the Egyptians used myrrh resin in mummification and that this ingredient is under the rulership of the planet Saturn and the Angel Cassiel. This angel is an Angel of Death (there are many such angels) and is the angel that rules decay, death, the duties of burial, burial grounds, the end of things and the like, being ever–present he is a hard angel to avoid — especially by the living for he is their end.


The reader by now may be wondering if they have bought book on Egyptology instead of Angelology. So, let us explain why we have spent some time with the Benben stone and introducing the Angel of the Ascendant or the Benben Angel. What follows applies only the Pyramid Letter; the reader will have already seen that both letter forms are immersed in many parts of Egyptian culture, but the Pyramid Letter is the only letter that uses the pyramid and the Benben stone and this is given in the hope it will clarify some of its more important principles. It will also give a better understanding of the methods used in the angelic letters as given in the work and why we do things the way we do.

As said, the pyramid and the obelisk are regarded as solar and therefore male with the Benben stone, the 'seed' or 'the power of generation' at its tip because the Benben is placed at the tip of both pyramid and obelisk. The 'seed' you want to germinate is your invocation, which you have set inside the darkness or 'womb' of the pyramid, the female part inside the pyramid. This is sent out and upwards through the Benben Angel who is an 'Angel of Pure Light' and therefore he represents Ra (or Re nowadays but I am used to the former), the Sun–god and the solar gods generally who are usually found heading the pantheon.

If the fertilization being sought is successful, the 'fertilized seed' will be return to the dark womb of the pyramid and prepare for gestation and birth into the physical world (= attraction). Alternatively, the 'fertilized seed' can be prepared for being sent out of the physical world (= banishment), if this was the request made. Just remember, when the Angel of the Ascendant occupies the Benben station he uses the colour and the metal gold, which to the Egyptians represented sunlight, the rays of the Sun and the golden disc among other things.

In all other usage, other than the unique Benben station on the Pyramid Letter, the Angel of the Ascendant uses his own colours given throughout for the Angel of the Ascendant for all other work.

This has been to show some of the importance of the Benben stone of the original pyramid, your pyramid and to explain that what can happen on one level of existence can often be found mirrored on another. If something is present or has been created on the higher level, the main task is to try to bring it down intact to the physical and sometimes this is quite an undertaking.

The four sides of the pyramid contain the four Elements of Earth, Air, Fire, Water and these four Elements give the pyramid and our lives, a firm wide base upon which to stand. A pyramid is one of the most sound and stable constructions with its centre of gravity firmly placed at its centre to make it secure. This does not make a pyramid indestructible, but we should take note of how long they have lasted on the physical level. The damage being inflicted on them now comes more from our presence on earth than the natural elements set here before us. It would also take a lot to bring us down if we could manage to set our centre of gravity in the midpoint or the King's Chamber of such an ample and stable base.

The four Elements are 'four–square' as they must be if they are to support us in the physical where we live and work. The Benben stone represents Spirit hovering over the four elements just as it was in *Genesis*. The elements can be made to rise positively, drawn together and focused at this focal point—the Benben — the pyramid shows the culmination where the combined elements can rise to work in harmony towards their highest principles. If the Four Elements can be made to ascend above the physical, then they could take us, our hopes and wishes up with them, because they are within us and we are in them. The Element closest to the Spiritual is the Element of Fire, especially the Spiritual Fire hence the old injunction, one of many, to 'inflame yourself with prayer.'

An very old arrangement takes the human body and divides it roughly into four equal sections. The feet and the legs are of the Element of Earth because they have most contact with the earth and support the structure — us and we often say of people who fail use that they 'have feet of clay.'

The next division, roughly from the legs to midriff are under the Element of Water as a great deal of the emotional life takes place here for one reason or another, emotion and panic can often upset the stomach area one way or another.

The next section containing the heart was the seat of the Element of Fire with its all–consuming fires of love, a burning infatuation, with heaving of chests or bosoms among other things or the entry of Spirituality into our lives that burns the dross.

The final division is just below the neck up to the head and takes the Element of Air, the location and focus of voice and speech, thinking and where the activity of the mind is concentrated. This is brief I admit but it is only intended to show the point.

Most seem to agree that life on our level (the physical) probably began in the sea and water is an element that is strong in us as it is the largest element. We are born in Water and the Element of Water is often given as the symbol of Truth and the medium in which creativeness takes place.

We are born of earth and to the earth we return. A reconstructed papyrus in Berlin tells us of a sacrament of Amen–Ra at Karnak, the modern name for Nesut–Towi —'The Throne of the Two Lands'. When the celebrant 'goes into the sanctuary and kindles a light in his censer they were in the presence of the Earth God Geb' mentioned earlier ' . . . Given to thee is thy head, given to thee are thy bones, established for thee is thy head upon thy bones in the presence of Geb.' We are born in Water, in bodies of Earth. We think and communicate through Air and raise ourselves in Fire above the earthbound — upwards to Spirit — these ideas are not new.

We cannot divorce ourselves from these Elements and there are two strong Angels of Fire and Water who attend us from before our birth and after our death. Our two Guardian Angels are a Solar Angel (Sun–Fire) and a Lunar Angel (Moon–Water) and these two angels are so important to us because we are frequently told that the Angels themselves are 'born' of fire and water.

### THE PYRAMID COVER — IT IS NOT ALL HARD WORK.

We said earlier that we would discuss some suggestions for simplifying the pyramid used for the Pyramid Letter. You have ten planetary angels today so technically you should have ten pyramids in ten colours should want to include all the angels given in this work, one for each angel and archangel as given and you can do this if you wish. If you think this would cause difficulties for you then remain with the original seven planets of old. The choice is entirely yours.

It is mentioned elsewhere that the three later planets of Uranus, Neptune and Pluto took over one Sign of the Zodiac from the seven old planets, see the bottom line of *The Table of the Planetary for the Planets and Angels*.

Uranus took Aquarius from Saturn who retains Capricorn; Neptune took Pisces from Jupiter who retains Sagittarius and Pluto took Scorpio from Mars who retains Aries and this information is given when you arrive at this chapter. If you decide to use these three planets, they are treat in the same way as the old seven planet scheme. The way I have found to overcome the fact that these three planets do not have a kamea to call their own is to use the kamea of the three planets they already share their days and hours. It seems to work all right and does not seem to have created any problems that I know of to date.

Whatever system you choose, there is a more practical way to deal with this if you wish and one that I used a good few years now to save have many pyramids by having only one basic pyramid with seven (or ten) covers to put over them.

Make up one strong pyramid in a thick *white cardboard* — it must be white because if it is not white it will add whatever colour it is to colour scheme of each angel and white contains some proportion of the other colours. If you make you single pyramid black, you are adding Saturn to the scheme, if red Mars, if bright yellow, Mercury and so on so it must be white which is neutral.

After making one such sturdy pyramid to cover the temenos, I then made seven or ten covers in good quality cartridge paper to neatly cover the white pyramid base according to the colour required for the angel used. Naturally, only one golden Benben capstone is made up for use with the pyramid, which is correct whatever you do. You can make the Benben of gold card or white card upon which you lay gold leaf. This gold leaf is genuine gold not a likeness and it can be bought in small amounts in art shops of bookbinding stores and it is used for gold lettering on books and bookbinding — remember the Benben represents the highest and the supreme deity. It is not cheap I admit but whatever the philosophy be generous with this single important object and this is why I recommend that you use this gold leaf if you possibly can and do not worry to much if you cannot.

So we have one basic white card pyramid plus ten covers in good quality coloured paper, one for each of the ten angels and archangels to cover the white pyramid, one golden Benben capstone in gold leaf if possible, otherwise use gold or gilt card. These items can be used to make up seven or ten pyramids of the required colours and stored until they are needed.

Many excellent patterns are printed on good quality paper today and inventiveness can make up extra pyramid covers for special occasions or invocations for example if it was printed with holly, it could be used for Mars and so on. I love taking something and using it for something else for which it was never intended. Remember, small variations to the original scheme are not a 'stoning' matter as long as it is reasonable and builds on the original scheme. You do not have to change the system at all if you do not want to because everything you need is there in the ten angels and archangels as given. I believe it is inventive to take something for a new use and if it is done properly, I think the angels and archangels like inventiveness on there behalf — especially the Archangel Uriel and Raphael.

The possibilities are infinite and quite a few materials can be adapted if the symbolism is right with the correct connection of colour and design. This is why the lists given are fairly wide to stimulate your imagination. Now I want to broaden the philosophy and information regarding the Eastern Gate that leads from the Sacred Court under the pyramid and into the temenos and strengthen the reasons for using it.

## JANUS — THE TWO–FACED GOD.

No, the above title actually means what it says and it is not given as a derogatory view of the god Janus; we have already spoken earlier of this interesting, important and a somewhat neglected deity. The two vertical lines through into the temenos — the Eastern Gate — between which you place the Seal of the Planet and angel you are invoking, symbolically represents a passage that is open, like Janus at both ends and looking in both directions. This is why this particular path is under the aegis of the Roman god Janus (=Mars and the Angel Samael.) Janus 'the one by whom all things were introduced into life' was figured as dual–faced or 'time past,' 'time now' and 'time to come. Janus is the 'I was,' the 'I am' and the 'I shall be.'

Mentioned elsewhere, Janus is the god of doors, gateways, thresholds, alleyways and passages that are open at both ends. *Janua*= 'door, door–jam, entrance' and he was 'Heaven's Doorkeeper.' Janus was often found as a statue on the doors of Roman houses and often carved directly from the door–jam itself. The festival of *Janarius* (= 'belonging to Janus') was the first day of the New Year and was the festival on which the Romans presented their good wishes to each other. It was also customary to begin any undertaking on this day. It was a time when we look backwards in reflection regarding the old year passing that is passing. We make our New Year resolutions at this time of the year to make changes in the future and to correct the mistakes of the past. Janus and Mars are deities of initiatory endeavour and new beginnings for the future. Janus protected the beginning of all operations and actions as well as the beginning of human life for at that time he is called *Consivius*= 'the propagator.'

On New Year's Day, the principle festival of Janus people took great care to see that all they thought, said and did was beyond reproach and favourable since everything was portentous for the occurrences of the whole year. People wore festive garments, abstained from cursing and avoided quarrels. They greeted everyone they met with favourable words, gave presents to one another and performed some part of what they intended to try to do during the New Year that was fast approaching.

Their presents consisted of sweetmeats, such as gilt dates, figs, honey cakes and copper coins and the coins had on one side the double–head of Janus and on the other, a ship. This is the ship recalled in the old blessing given at this time of the year — 'may your ship come in.'

*Janua*(ry) was the first month of the year or the 'door or entrance of the year.' A threshold is the symbol of transition between one state and another, even on the physical levels the transition from the outside of a building that leads to the inside of the building. In the case of a temple or any place of worship it was symbolic of leaving the physical and mundane and entering a place that has been spiritually dedicated to the deity. This is symbolically shown by the Eastern Gate on your letter.

The importance of this principle is often stressed in architecture with the portal, porch or entrance of a building, which is very often grand and ornate, as if to prepare you for the grandeur that will be found within the building. The door in front of a temple usually reached from floor to ceiling to allowed the worshipers to view (from without) the entire statue of the divinity and watch the rites that were performed before it without their view being impeded in any way, nothing came between them and the representation of the deity. Further, the whole light of the building was commonly let in through the same door or a hole left open in the roof and this was not inappropriate for a god of the Sun, while the temple of the god Terminus had no roof at all and this left the god open to the elements, which he normally was when he was outside, as he quite often was.

This is all in keeping with the dualism of the god Janus represented by his two opposing faces, which look in opposite directions at the same time, representing inside and outside, peace and war, east and west, past and future so the two–headed eagle is often associated with Janus.

He is the god of good beginnings, which the Romans believed ensured a good ending, a term often found throughout this work. As the 'God of Beginnings,' it would not be unreasonable to connect Janus with the word '*genesis*' and all these attributes are in keeping with the planet Mars and the Angel Samael. The **Morning Prayer** was addressed to him in all domestic enterprises and his help was sought in every home. *Genesis*, Latin *genesis*= 'the name of the first book of the *Bible* in the *Vulgate* version and Greek, γενεσις, *genesis*= 'origin or source, beginning, race, descent, creation, created things.' from γενναω, *gennao*= 'to begat to engender,' γιγομαι, *gigeomai*= 'to come into being, to be born, to be produced.'

Never make the mistake of regarding the god and planet of Mars only as a God of War, Strife and Bloodshed as some astrological books give sometimes and they do this god a great disservice for this is the Greek, Ares (= 'thong of war') overlay. This is a very unbalanced view of this planet and god and it is time it was challenged. Originally, Mars was a chthonic god connected with the fertility of the Earth and he was called upon to protect the fields and those who worked in them. He is foremost a great God of Nature and at the Spring Equinox, Nature calls upon him to assist her to renew the Earth.

Every bud, flower, fruit and leaf that burgeons into new life is evidence of a battle for life and survival successfully won with the help of Mars, sometimes under very difficult conditions in which they may not survive, but they do. Nature could not do her work her miracles without him and many enterprises, including yours and mine, can fall by the wayside without calling on him at the beginning for aid, which is why we do this — or should!

As written, because the deity Janus is represented as having two faces that are looking in opposite directions, he rules alleys, streets and the like, which usually have two entrances or exits depending on the one you used to enter. The main temple of Janus was found in the Forum and it had two sets of doors, one set facing east and west, standing for the beginning and ending of the day.

Like the temple of Janus, your Pyramid Letter has 'two doors.' One door is in the East — 'for the beginning of the day' where things begin and the other in the west — 'for the end of the day,' where things end. His statue stood between these two doors that were set so that his two faces gazed through them, one facing east and the other west. He was invoked at the beginning of wars, because he can be the benign intercessor and defender in times of war and not necessarily the aggressor. During war, the doors of his temple in the Forum always stood open and the cry for war was heard 'Open Janus.' When Rome was at peace or a war was not sanctioned to be undertaken, the doors were closed and the cry was 'Close Janus.'

Janus holds a key in his right hand and a staff in his left and he is invoked as the 'guardian of the gate or the road.' Because Janus was the 'god of beginnings,' his name is at the beginning of the list of gods in prayer, he was even above and named before the name of Jupiter. He is associated with the rising and setting of the sun, each new season, with the dawn of each day sacred to him.

He presided over the start of a New Year where he held the number 300 in one hand and the number 65 in the other. As the god of beginnings, he was publicly invoked on the first day of January and the first month was named after him because it began the New Year and significantly Janus rules the last twelve hours of the old year, the hours that are a 'bridge between the old and new year and a time of reflection.' This brief twelve hours of time could be called the 'middle ground' between the years where the old and new mix and the old year is weakening to relinquish its hold and giving way to the New Year being born.

Like Janus, this is a time when we look back to the old year and review what has come to pass while we look forward to the New Year and make our New Year resolutions in the light of what experience has taught us. We resolve to do better and initiate the resolutions we feel are required for the future to be better and to 'initiate' anything we usually need from Janus, Mars and his Angel.

All these matters are under Mars because Janus is a Martian god and keys are under his care, it is from the god Janus we get the 'keeper of the keys' in the American States as the 'janitor' and the gods made him the 'janitor of the seasons.' Zeus gave him a peculiar form of immortality — circular — but he did not really enjoy it. As soon as the old year died, the New Year was born and this was endlessly repeated by going around in circles. Janus rules keys and those who make them; there will be little surprise that two crossed keys are one of his symbols.

Long ago, when men went off on long pilgrimages or wars, they would foolishly attempt to lock up their 'love' by various means for safe keeping until they returned and one method was the chastity belt. This did not always seem to work as expected, perhaps because the locksmith often made more than one key that he sold to the highest bidder. I am sure this practise gave birth to the saying that 'love laughs at locksmiths' to which should be added chastity belts. When the ardent Mars sought the chaste Venus, a little thing like a key was not going to stand in his way — then or now.

The Quadrifon Temple of Janus was said to be a perfect square with a door in each side representing the four seasons. Each side had three windows making up the twelve months of the year or the twelve Signs of the Zodiac in their four quarters, spring, summer, autumn and winter. Quadrifron is also an epithet of Janus and an image of him has been found with four heads, to represent the fact he is the divinity of the four seasons of the year.

Legend gives Janus as a son of Apollo and his birthplace is given as Thessaly. Janus is said to have founded the city of Janiculum, which is a prominent ridge on the West Bank of the Tiber. I hope this brief résumé has show you that Janus is a god well worth keeping in mind when you begin a new venture or initiating something new — especially as is associated strongly with the Angel Samael, the Angel of Mars. Keep him in mind or invoke him when you draw and use the entrance under the pyramid into the temenos from the Sacred Court in the Pyramid Letter from the East. Janus has no counterpart in Greek mythology. If you only write one letter a year do it at this powerful, time of change in the year for the reasons presented above, you have twelve hours on December the 31st, to try to make a good, fresh start, which is why this has been given the time it has here and in all came from one word, the name of the god Janus.

## SOME FURTHER OBSERVATIONS THAT MAY HELP

The paradigm of the temenos bears a strong resemblance to many ancient tabernacles and temples. The central square, the 'cube' is the 'Holy Place'. The Holy Place was 'oblong' in the Hebrew model, but the 'cube' was created by positioning a veil across the centre of the Holy Place. This cube had the cherubim (do not confuse these with cherubs) as the symbolic guardians of the sanctuary.

'And he made a vail of blue, and purple, and scarlet, and fine twined linen: with cherubim's made he it of cunning work. And he made thereunto four pillars of shittim wood, and overlaid them with gold: their hooks were of gold; and he cast for them four sockets of silver. *Exodus*. 36:35.

The veil was set across the Holy Place making the Holy of Holies a perfect cube of (approximately) fifteen feet by enclosing half of the area the Holy Place. The Holy Place occupied an area of thirty feet by fifteen feet,' precisely double the area of the Holy of Holies, a magical double cube or double ashlar, just as many magical altars are a double cube. The most important undertaking was to create the 'cube' or square within this oblong structure. This is why I said earlier that it was a symbolic act to cut the oblong paper of the angelic letter, even though it is not to the exact scale of the Holy of Holies, down to its square form —a symbolic act, more than an exact one. Your square represents the Holy of Holies, which is the 'heart' and focal point of your efforts. It should be regarded in this way even though it is symbolic as a highly sacred site and given the respect it merits and guarded accordingly.

It is said that great observance was taken in the Hebrew model with the overlapping joints and the layers of material of the Holy of Holies. It would appear that darkness and privacy was especially important within the innermost shrine. God was surrounded in darkness and carefully isolated from unauthorized sight. 'Clouds and darkness are round about him.' *Psalm* 97:2. This was done either for Creator or the Ark of the Covenant, which is the same to many commentators. Once a pyramid has been sealed there are few things on earth possessing greater darkness, silence and isolation than a sealed pyramid and these principles should be regarded as operating in spirit for our smaller model, if not in reality, the symbolism and principles are there.

Most ideas germinate in the dark just as seeds do that are buried in the earth. Seeds develop hidden and protected until they are strong enough to come into the light to stand or fall on their merit to become productive through growth and evolution. Books, music, art among other things are formed unseen from 'seeds' planted in the darkness and isolation of the mind of their creator, which is the 'womb' that succours them and only when they are brought out into the light are they 'born.' These are the 'children of the mind,' not unlike the children of the body, though you often have greater control over the way they will turn out and develop for good or ill. If you want to secure the future — put it in the past and it will be.

As said, many temples consist of three parts. The first is the porch, then the temple proper and lastly, hidden from the sight of all, the holy of holies or inner sanctum (= the temenos or adytum). The temple often had 'three courts,' the central temenos or Holy of Holies, next the court of the priests or Sacred Court and finally the Outer Court of the people and 'the court of the foreigners.' Sometimes described in magical literature as 'the court of the hewers of wood and the drawers of water.' All these 'courts' revolved around the ever–present, Holy of Holies.

The largest part of King Herod's temple was the Court of the Gentiles, though unlike the measurements given throughout this work that are all ideal, equal and balanced, Herod's was of irregular shape. The court was given as being wider at the northern end than it was in the south. This part of the temple was open to Gentiles as well as Jews though a notice was posted on the partition wall instructing the Gentiles not to stray into the inner courts of the temple and it was usually guarded to prevent this. Perhaps the Court of the Gentiles was a juncture in the scheme where critical measurement was neither necessary or needed, see *Revelations* below.

In this part of the temple, the Court of the Gentiles, the animals for sacrifice and other purposes were sold and the money changers plied their trade and as said earlier, it was more than likely it was here where the 'cleansing of the temple' by Jesus took place in *Matthew* 21:12; *Mark* 11:15 and *John* 3:14.

The Gentiles were the *goy* or *goyim* (= plural) people, a nation or nations sometimes euphemistically given as 'cattle.' The Israelites were regarded as 'the chosen' nation and considered other nations to be on a lower level and less privileged than themselves. The terms uncircumcised, uncircumcision were sometimes used here but with a deeper meaning to designate those who had no share or lot with Israel in her special privileges but in fairness, the prophets frequently predicted of their future participation in its blessing. Because they were mainly heathens and because of other matters, the Gentiles were looked upon as unclean so unnecessary contact with them was frowned on, intermarriage was not acceptable and it was unlawful to eat with them.

*Revelation* tells us 'And there was given me a reed like unto a rod: and the angel stood, saying, Rise, and measure the temple of God, and the altar, and them that worship within. But the court which is without the temple leave out, and measure it not; for it is given unto the Gentiles: and the holy city shall they tread under foot forty and two months.' 11:1–3.

Even in the *Bible,* Solomon's temple had three rows in the inner court, 'and he built the inner courts with three rows of hewed stone and a row of cedar beams.' 1 *Kings* 6: 36. Further 'And there were windows in three rows, and light was against light in three ranks. (7:4.) 'And all the doors and posts were square, with the windows: and light was against light in three ranks.' (7:5.)

The temenos of the Holy of Holies is within the lines of the inner square and these lines are coloured according to the angel being invoked. Only the High Priest entered the Holy of Holies, which in the Jewish form contained the Holy Ark of the Covenant. The High Priest in the Jewish model is you for you are the High Priest and entry is your right of office. One student in the School asked for advice about how to approach any work done inside this particular area and my instinctive suggestion was 'move very slowly and do not make any sudden moves!'

I want to return briefly to a section of John Dee's work and take an extract from his diaries. It is taken (in part) from Dee's recorded conversation with the Angel Mapsama regarding the above advice, giving due respect at all times, how can any advice I give ever gainsay that of an angel? When I read it, coming to this conclusion beforehand, I felt I may have stumbled on the correct course to use and it was confirmed:

'You called for wisdom, God hath opened unto you, his Judgement: He hath delivered unto you the keyes, that you may enter; But be humble. Enter not of presumption, but of permission. Go not in rashly; But be brought in willingly: For, many have ascended, but few have entered.'

The Holy of Holies was at the West End of the Temple. In the Temple of Solomon, it enshrined the Ark of the Covenant, which was the most holy symbol embodying God's special relationship with Israel and at the entrance to the Holy of Holies stood a small cedar altar that was overlaid with gold.

The Holy of Holies in Hebrew is **Qodesh Ha–Qadashim** and it is also called **Devir**. As said, it is the innermost and sacred region of the ancient Temple of Jerusalem and was accessible to the High Priest only. On one day of the year, the Day of Atonement (= **Yom Kippur**), the High Priest was allowed to enter the square enclosure that was without light from any source, to burn incense and sprinkle the blood of a sacrificial animal. At this time, he wore only white linen garments, abandoning the ornate vestments used during the year whenever he officiated at services. With this, perhaps the most solemn act of the religious year, the high priest atoned for his sins and those of the priesthood. As I have said before many times, an idea can often be quite simple but explaining it and translating it into practise on paper is not and it is done and understood only with patience, application and now once again, we must come back to our angelic letter dealing with the completed letter and the final act of the ritual.

You can place Pyramid Letter on a small table in a private place or anywhere convenient for this where it will not be disturbed. I personally think it is better if you align your pyramid with the cardinal points of the compass as given on the diagram. For those letters for the Archangel Raphael, I set a statue of Hermes given by a friend and brought back from Greece on my table and, as with many of the things I do, Pan is never neglected. The combinations for which the Pyramid Letter can be used appear to be most fruitful.

You could make and experiment with a configuration that makes up an Elemental Pyramid of the Four Elements by making up a pyramid cover with the four elements on the four sides in their correct order. The Element of Air on the East, the Element of Water in the West, the Element of Earth in the North and the Element of Fire in the South. This kind of information is liberally scattered throughout the work and now you know why. Another suggestion is a Pyramid of the Four Seasons, setting signs on the four sides to show the natural progression of the year and your aspirations for those particular times. This you do by facing the side of the pyramid with the symbolism of the time of season we are in.

You could use a pyramid of the Tarot Suits, using the four aces of initiation and beginnings or any four appropriate cards in sequence expressing a course of action or wish, perhaps the past, the present, the future and the outcome hoped for. You can set out a sequence of four Tarot cards as a wish for the New Year on December 31st, using the last twelve hours of the year under Janus. Using deosil for attraction — this sequence is clockwise; widdershins for banishment — this sequence is anticlockwise. The diagrams show the progression of this form of movement. Perhaps, you could decorate the pyramid using appropriate Rune symbolism and these are only a few of the more obvious suggestions. The Hebrew Script has meanings attached to each letter and I am sure that these could be used by the inventive.

As I have suggested (repeatedly) in the chapter on **Magical Scripts**, a true account should be kept of all your experiments, with all the relevant details good, bad and indifferent. These details should be kept in a diary used only for this purpose, no other — keeping a 'magical diary' is a very old practise, it is regularly mentioned in most of the things that I write. If Dr. John Dee had not kept a meticulous diary and records, I could not have put his dictionary in print. Record in your magical diary, which angels were involved, the days used, the hours, invocations, incense, phases of the moon, the results, success or failure and so forth. Remember, also as repeatedly said, write only what is — not what you would have liked it to be — as this fools none but you and this diary is personal only to you.

## INCENSE, CHARMS, SYMBOLS, ETC.

Can you burn incense? Certainly, it is an excellent practise to pass your letter through an appropriate incense smoke when it is finished and you can burn it while doing your work. Try to get an incense appropriate to the source you are trying to contact otherwise use frankincense. A list is given of appropriate perfumes.

Wash your hands before attempting any serious work of this nature; it has a parallel with a surgeon operating with unclean hands and contaminating what they are doing and weakening it. Never work with dirty hands, a good quality soap is sufficient but some can be bought with appropriate perfumes, for example, rose, musk, lavender, pine and the like. You could put a small amount of an appropriate perfume or oil on your hands to make them smell sweet and clean.

I have sometimes used a good coal tar soap for work that is for cleansing and clearing out anything that is unwanted. I was brought up with this soap when young and it does not matter if this attitude is the result of the advertising of my day. The smell and using this particular soap is associated in my mind and childhood with being 'clean, fresh and germ free' so it always feels right to me.

You can rinse your hands in water to which a small amount of salt has been added, this will clean them of most mundane and unacceptable vibrations. Use a stronger saline solution to wash a talismans, charms or any other object from which you want to remove the vibrations and use of a previous owner and this is especially useful if you are not sure what it may have been used for previously or who owned it. If the item has materials that you cannot immerse in salt water, check the material and if it is safe, wipe it with the saline solution. Obviously, if there was a paper, parchment or vellum on which ink had been used then this would not be practical.

This practice should be done if your talisman or charm has come from an uncertain or unknown source. Shop bought charms, charm bracelets, crucifixes and the like, should always be washed this way before wearing them. This has the effect of 'cleaning' the vibrations of those who have handled them purely for commercial gain but if you are using bought charms purely for decoration then this does not matter, I know there is some repetition here but it cannot always be avoided and if it works and reminds people, it has served its purpose and is a lesson well learned.

## SENDING ANGELIC LETTERS . . .

How do you 'send' your angelic letter because there are no 'post boxes' to the angels into which you can conveniently drop them into for collection in the normal way of posting things? There are no agencies to guarantee that they are delivered for you. There are ways of attempting this and we give a few examples, but you are limited in this only by your imagination. We must divorce ourselves from the postal services and our way of doing things, as we know them. It is hard at times to accept that your letter has been 'posted' when your eyes clearly tell you it is still there but this is a nettle that has to be grasped and understood, it is not easy at times I agree.

On the other hand, you do not post prayers, it would be nice to know how many oral and silent prayers are 'sent up' in only five minutes, yet, nothing is really seen to be collected, go or be accepted but this does not invalidate them for those who pray. A prayer can be given as: ' . . . to make or address petitions to the Divine Being; to offer prayers or supplications to God; to address the Supreme Being with reverential adoration, confession of sins, supplication of mercy and thanksgiving for mercies received.' Another view given is 'if I should never pray to him or worship him at all, such a total omission would be equivalent to this assertion — there is no God, who governs the world, to be adored.' Woolaston – ***Religion of Nature.***

Praying machines, mills or wheels are not a new invention but interesting. They are an

331

apparatus used mainly in Tibet and other parts of the East as a mechanical aid to prayer. The are of various forms, the commonest being a cylinder or barrel of pasteboard fixed on an axle and inscribed by prayers. The devout give the barrel a turn and each revolution counts as an utterance of the prayer or prayers transcribed.

'It is common enough to see them fixed in the bed of a running streams, as they are then set in motion by the water and go on praying night and day, to the special benefit of the person who has placed them there. The Tartars also suspend them over their domestic hearths, that they may be set in motion by the current of cool air from the opening in the tent and so twirl for the peace and prosperity of the family.' *Travels in Tibet*. (1844) again nothing is physically taken.

Every time someone expresses a wish in any way, they are hoping that someone or something will listen and grant what they seek. A lucky horseshoe, a rabbits foot or charm will grant that undefined key called 'good luck' that opens the appropriate door will be heard and open a channel to us for luck to make use of. The 'how' used is different in each case but the 'why' remains' reasonably constant and the method rarely questioned — 'it worked before!'

I accept that it would be very satisfying and comforting to actually see that the 'letter' has gone as when we post it and it is collected to be delivered. However, we are not only dealing with the familiar on our level, its laws and our way of doing things but other levels that are not always familiar and do not operate the way we do. I would be among the first to admit this can be extremely difficult at times, especially when faith is more than a little threadbare and doubts decide to call for a visit, create a rumpus and upset things.

In the philosophy and teaching of past Schools developed over the years, the letter that remained was simply considered to be a 'shell' from which the 'essence' had been taken. If you leave a letter on a table for a lengthy time, you may suspect that it has been read by someone, it has obviously been moved and a letter does not have to be taken away to be read, only the information it contains.

This is much the same with a letter of invocation, the information is taken and the medium is left, it is the information we need to send and for this in the past we have used smoke signals or a flashing mirror (a heliograph), the information got there.

Let us look at some suggestions for this particular facet of the work and while it is true, some of the ideas are in keeping with the work *Practical Candle Magic*. There is some overlapping of application, system and knowledge that can be combined or utilised for more than one aspect of the work; this overlapping will be found and they are not errors.

In part, associate your letter with appropriate items. A letter for money can be placed under a candlestick burning a purple candle. This candle should be lit during the appropriate hours of Jupiter and the Angel Sachiel, with your prayers/invocations and concentration focused upon the contents of the letter and to whom it is addressed. A personal use is to place a pound coin, which I polished brightly to represent gold or representing a guinea coin, under the candle to represent a 'golden' guinea. This coin was once a highly valued gold coin and the gold standard of the British Isles, when our money had some value. The coin should be washed in strong salt water before being used to remove the mundane vibrations of everyday barter.

Place the coin on a flat base appropriate and practical for burning a candle safely, perhaps a decorative or purple saucer, oddment bins in stores are very useful at sale times. Light your candle and drip the purple wax over the coin until it is covered with it. Let the wax cool a little and then set the candle on top of the warm wax covering the coin. You can drop the coin into the sconce of the candlestick if the sconce is big enough to hold it and you are using a candlestick. As the candle burns down it brings the release of the coin (= the money being sought) in fullness of time, which is symbolically what the petitioner is seeking. If your Folding Letter concerns money and because the Folding Letter is flat, you can put the letter under your candle; these are simple little rituals but they are none the less effective for that.

Examples of a faulty petition for money are too obvious to give and are as variable as the people asking. 'Enough money' or 'sufficient money' is a reasonable request. Experience has shown this is often better than stressing a specific sum though this does not mean you cannot do so if a specific sum is what you need — but with a specific amount, remember the word 'need' — not 'want.'

When the invocation is complete and the coin released you should not spend it. Clean the wax from it and, when you go out next put the coin in the first charity box you see. If you do not find one then throw it into water, preferably running water, but do not bring the coin back home with you. Someone will find it and use it, considering the find a windfall or good fortune. Windfalls come from Mercury (Latin) or Hermes (Greek) *'Ερμης, 'Ermes*, as gifts, like fruit or wind–falls blown down from a tree.

*'Ερμαιον, 'Ermaion*= 'god–sent, wind–fall, reputed to be a gift of the god Hermes.' Hermes, hence the proverb *'Κοινος, 'Ερμης, Koinos 'Ermes* shares your luck!' (In common, Hermes shares your luck!') Theophrastus. *'Ερμης, 'Ermes= Messenger of the Gods= διακτορος, diaktoros=* 'an epithet of Hermes or Minister of Zeus.' Homer. He was *εριουνιος, erioynios=* 'guiltless, gracious' and *ακακητα, akaketa=* 'the ready helper, luck–bring,' which are both epithets of Hermes as the 'giver of good luck.' *Λολιος,* dolios= 'crafty, deceitful, treacherous' hence the use of the epithet for Hermes as the *Λολιος, dolios=* 'the god of all secret dealings, cunning and stratagem.' Hermes is the tutelary god of all arts, of traffic, markets, roads and of heralds. Hermes bust, mounted on a four–cornered pillar was used to mark boundaries. His office of *Psychopomp* has already been discussed regarding the section the Angels of Death, more could be written but I feel that this is enough to put him into perspective for our purpose here.

Wise teachers of astrology tell their students that although Mercury (Hermes) is a smallest planet in both size and mass and great linear speed, they would be very foolish indeed to underestimate the planet and his power. Regarding this God and planet I heed *Cicero — 'Cujusvis hominis est errare; nullius, nisi isipientis, in errore perseverare.'* ('Any man may make a mistake; none but a fool would persist in it.') *Philippicae.*

The reader they must not limit their imagination and extend their work so that the base of their knowledge grows. You must always be adding to the information in the library of the mind, the bigger the library you have inside you the better you can handle things but the options must not be of capricious nature. They should not be done just to show how clever or inventive you are or for the sake of doing them. They must be shown to be standing on the bedrock of sound reasoning in relation to the matter you are dealing with and that they can stand examination of why they are there and be supported by a sound explanation if one is required or requested — 'whatever' is not an answer it is an evasion. There may be some disagreement about the 'how' of a thing — but there should be none regarding the 'why' of it?'

I would not want to live in a world where we all used the same official words, read the same books all written in the same way and thinking the same thoughts. Perform only sanctioned acts or speak only in a sanctioned way — I would die of boredom in less than a week. We got rid of our Puritans some time back in our history in England, but it seems the New Puritans are back with us with a vengeance in our lives — everywhere like fleas on a feral dog or cat. The American journalist, literary critic and essayist, H. L. Mencken (1880–1956) knew them well when he said, 'Puritanism is the haunting fear that someone, somewhere, may be happy.' He also said, 'The objection to puritans is not they try to make us think as they do, but that they try to make us do as they think.' I have long liked this man. Now let us return again to our letters and some more suggestions . . .

A letter to the Moon and the Archangel Gabriel can be left where the rays of the Moon can fall upon it. Use the New Moon to full for those things that you wish to grow and want to attract to you. For those things you wish to contract and dispel from you should use after the Full Moon to last quarter. Do not use the day of the Full Moon for lunar work as the tides of the Moon are neither one thing nor the other and your affairs will be likewise — confused and erratic. Do not use the three days before the New Moon as these are known as the Dark of the Moon. These hours are said to be 'given over to those powers that are not friendly or agreeable to the hopes and wishes of mankind.'

Any letter to the Archangel Raphael has many paths to use. You can post the letter to yourself, inside a normal envelope, on the day and hour of the Archangel Raphael. You have written a letter that asks for a 'reply' and have shown a way by which a 'reply' could come back through the post in some way. As said above, Mercury rules 'the post, letters and those who process, collect and deliver them.' You can light a yellow candle with appropriate incense, in the hours of the angel, in an act of expectancy, while waiting for the letter to 'come home.' Your letter has symbolically been sent and received and I put it away sealed until one way or another it is resolved.

In the summer months on dry days, I have put the letter to the Archangel Raphael on a nut–bearing tree, particularly a hazel, though any other nut–bearing tree can be used, not necessarily edible. Sometimes the letter will have a small bell attached to it, which would ring in the breeze, as the Archangel Raphael rules the wind and breath. One of the old titles of the Archangel Raphael mentioned throughout is 'the Walker of Wind' where he 'leaves no footprints.' It is better if he comes from the East, not the West. When he comes from the East this is his natural station. When he comes from the West, he comes as the psycopomp from the dying Sun and the Land of the Dead, which is not a good direction, particularly for hopes and wishes or things you want to evolve.

This is generally done in the privacy of my garden or a secluded and wild place where few people go look especially for single trees that have grown apart or are singled out by appearance. It does not matter too much what happens to the letter if someone finds it because it will mean nothing to them. Mercury 'likes tintinnabulation' as do many of the angels and this is why I use a set of small Tibetan bells at home, chosen by testing for their wonderful sound. They are in two halves like small heavy cymbals, which are joined by a leather thong as said, this set of original Tibetan bells was chosen for their particularly beautiful sound from the selection offered. Always try out things like this before buying them and you will know the ones you want, they will 'speak' to you. If the sound is discordant, you are inviting the goddess Eris (= 'discord') to the feast and you do not want her there.

Strike the bells gently whenever it seems appropriate, sometimes loud and if when they are vibrating you place one bell over, under or near the other, you can vary its vibrations get some quite wonderful variations in the timbre. The number of times you strike your bell is a matter of choice, do whatever feels right to you, it need not be the same every time. Again, each planet has a number given to it and these numbers would be a good guide for the number of 'strikes' according to angel and planet involved. I have repeated the planetary numbers from the chapter **Kameas** at the end to save you going back to that chapter.

Mentioned earlier, Aleister Crowley in his **Book 4** mentions these Tibetan bells and recommends them for use. He calls such bells 'Astral Bells' and he tells us ' . . . during certain mediation–practises the Student hears a bell resound in the depth of his being. It is not subjective, for it is sometimes heard by other people. Some Magicians are able to call the attention of those with whom they wish to communicate at a distance by its means or, so it is said.'

Any letter to the Angel Cassiel of the planet Saturn can be placed under something made of lead, pewter, a piece of coal, rock, slate or granite. You can place it under a clock because the Angel Cassiel rules Time. An hourglass would serve equally well as would a dish of earth from the garden or wild place. You can find suitable symbols from the lists given.

Do you visit the grave of someone you love? Take a small amount of earth from the grave and put it in a suitable container to stand on the letter. Is this being morbid, not in the least, the Angel Cassiel rules graves, graveyards, the dead, remembrance of the dead and death, this is simply being practical, which is another thing he rules. If the wish was granted you can scatter the earth taken on your garden, in a window box or a house plant to make a connection with the earth taken and your home. The Angel Cassiel does not rule over–sentimentality for he is an austere and practical angel. He does not like waffle or flattery, so they will get you nowhere with him. I am sure it was this angel who must have said — 'flattery you taste — but you do not swallow.'

Eloquent language is for Jupiter who loves ceremony and display but this will get you nowhere with Mars who likes things short and forceful, he hates frills and verbiage and will cut through them. He simply wishes you to cut out the waffle and come to the point. The position of Mars in your birth chart will sometimes show what is 'cut out to be cut out' in your in you life and its affairs. Cosy, gentle, affectionate and warm is for Venus with a touch of eloquence and civilized manners. Every day, homely, protective, nurturing and comforting is for the Moon, while grand, generous, vital and majestic is for the Sun. The tale is best given plain with the facts for Mercury as he rules news, gossip, details and facts, leave out nothing because he does not like to miss anything, to Mercury nothing is trivial and all news is grist for his mill.

If your problem concerns love and its many aspects, then you can leave your letter under a vase holding a single rose or several roses preferably pink for Venus, but love is a red rose, Venus and Mars combined in harmony and beauty. A pink or blue vase is best for Venus though not essential and if the vase is the right colour, you could omit the flowers and put the letter inside if it is rolled up to size. Jade, lapis–lazuli, rose–quartz or anything made of copper or something heart–shaped. These are some of the things under the domain of Venus and Angel Anael.

Roses are predominantly under the rule of the planet Venus and the Angel Anael, but you can use roses of appropriate colour for the other angels. Love can be expressed through the medium of the other angels. Simply pick a colour close to the angel, such as a purple rose for Jupiter and the Angel Sachiel, an orange rose for the Sun and the Archangel Michael, using white for the Moon and the Archangel Gabriel. Yellow for Mercury and the Archangel Raphael, a light or vibrant red for Mars and the Angel Samael and a colour as dark and as close to black as you can or a dark, dark green for the planet Saturn and the Angel Cassiel.

The planets rule various woods so you could buy a suitable wooden box that will be kept for putting in your letters Folding Letters and used for no other purpose. The gospel of perfection would be to have seven of these boxes, not unlike seven 'post boxes,' one for each of the planets of old and their angels. To guide those who may want to gather such boxes, here are the main woods to use.

As a guide for the Sun, you can use oak, bay or birch. For the Moon, you can use willow, ash or any trees with an affinity with water. For Mars you can use hawthorn, any redwoods or trees bearing thorns. Use hazel, mulberry or myrtle for Mercury. Use oak, birch or vine wood for Jupiter.

For Venus use rosewood (genuine if possible otherwise a veneer), myrtle, apple, fig or wood of fruit trees. For Saturn use yew, elm, beech or cypress.

If you can only afford to buy one box or only wish to use one then choose the wood of the planet Mercury and the Archangel Raphael. Mercury has the ear of all the angels as Herald or Messenger of the Gods as we have often said. Again, if you are uncertain the angel that rules the subject of the letter you have composed put it in the box for Mercury and then you ask that it be taken by this angel to the relevant source. The Archangel Raphael and his planet Mercury, who delights in ingenuity and inventiveness, because this is something that this planet not only rules it, but actively encourages it.

To repeat previous warnings, this Archangel knows if he is being used to save you from learning what or who rules what or what goes where without making the effort. He also rules rogues, thieves and tricksters and he can dissemble better than all of these types put together because he invented the practise so, he will trick you if it suits him or if you try to do this to him. Please believe me when I tell you there is nothing you can teach this Archangel and very foolish you would be to even think of trying — he rules thinking and thought and if you find a way of hiding that from him it would be interesting.

The possibilities for this part of the work are almost endless and nothing would be better to find that each book owned had personal variations attached to them. If you devise a successful system for yourself this is all to the good. It will be personal to you, your efforts and will form a strong connecting link with you and the work you do, so stay with it and build upon any gains you make that prove successful and if any deadwood is found do not hesitate to cut it out.

If this principle of working is not legitimate then millions of people perhaps for an similar amount of years have wasting their time, profit and labour, foolishly leaving food for the dead, burying horses and chariots, goods and furniture supplied for use in another world. A sun barge as with one for Cheops (Khufu) and if you think our pre–packed objects that are assemble later are new then go and see the Cheops Sun–barge at Ghiza, study the photographs of how it was 'flat–packed — then look at what was 'unpacked' and assembled — and marvel!

Leaving a pebble or small stone on the memorial stone to 'show' that you have been to visit, tying prayers to the branches of sacred trees, the crutches and artificial limbs left to give thanks for help given. Examples are as varied and as never–ending there are people on the earth.

We try to construct our letters from the knowledge and experience gleaned by those who have gone before and we must try to add to that knowledge. We must try to comply with the fundamental laws that pervade all levels from the highest to the lowest and to the best of our ability understand and cooperate with them.

A fundamental note contains all the harmonics or overtones within itself, which extends upwards to levels we know nothing of yet, probably passing through signs and symbols, colours, minerals, flowers, perfumes, incense, time, a particular day all going up to the planet, the angel and beyond. It is possible these Laws vibrate far beyond our level, past the Music of the Spheres where one wrong note or chord makes harmony into discord, out of key and the chain weak. If there is a false rung in the 'ladder' or the harmony distorted then the power is short–circuited and earthed from where it came.

The unbroken progression from above comes down and was set in place 'in the beginning.' We have to try to build a new 'Jacob's Ladder' by which to ascend. As said, one false rung, a rung out of place, one that does not have the strength to bear your weight or which does not belong in the scheme or order and the striving is blocked and probably thwarted. What we are attempting to do is something that goes far beyond the confines of the physical level upon which we live and breathe.

Sometimes, when you start this kind of work you begin to realize just how limited and limiting this level can be, beautiful though it can be.

Regarding the way you set out your letters, I again refer you to the entry taken from the **Angelic Dairies** of Dr. John Dee and Edward Kelly. This is the record of their conversation with the Angel Ave. The Greek symbol 'Δ' (**Delta**= 'D') in the following obviously stands for Dee. With John Dee his notes and annotations in the margins are often as illumination as the book itself, he is a margin writer and in text books so am I, he is a good teacher by example and despite the time scale between us I am learning from him. The entry is for '**Julii** 2. After Noon, **Hora** 1 ¼.' (1584) or July 2nd 1584 in the afternoon at 1.15pm.

| | |
|---|---|
| Δ | As for the form of our Petition or Invocation of the good angels, what sort should it be of? |
| Ave - | A short and brief speech. |
| Δ | We beseech you to give us an example: we would have a confidence; it should be of more effect. |
| Ave - | *I may not do so.* |
| E. K. - | **And why?** |
| Ave - | Invocation proceedeth of the good will of man, *and of the heat and fervency of the spirit: And therefore is prayer of such effect with God.* |
| Δ | We beseech you, shall we use one form to all? |
| Ave - | *Every one, after a divers form.* |
| Δ - | If the minde do dictate or prompt a divers form, you mean. |
| Ave - | *I know not: for I dwell not in the soul of man.* |

I have always felt the above is good advice and I have always kept it in mind when preparing all my work and I have passed it on to others who have asked for advice. The key words here being 'a short and brief speech' which 'proceedeth of the good will of man' and done in 'the heat and fervency of the spirit.' If we accept the authenticity of the source from where this advice came, it surely has to be excellent advice. *Ecclesiates* gives the same excellent advice. 'Be not rash with thy mouth, and let not thine heart be hasty to utter anything before God: for God is in heaven, and thou upon earth: therefore let thy words be few. For a dream cometh through the multitude of business, and a fool's voice is known by multitude of words.' 5: 2–3. Always bear in mind that brevity does not necessarily prevent eloquence from the right person.

Some students thought it better to leave their letters always in the same place, especially if it had a connection with a particular angel, saying it was like having 'letter boxes' all around their house and garden. Remember you should do all within your power to reinforce anything that could prove a successful link and strengthen it. Whatever system you are working remember — connect! Everything should be connected, unless it is the last or closing part of the ritual, which belongs to Saturn that says — 'it is finished.' What you are doing should always be connected with what has gone before and it should lead on to what comes next. I think it will serve you and your efforts well if you only remember this dictum.

## DISPOSAL OF YOUR LETTERS

How do you dispose of your letters when you feel that the matter is finally closed one way or another? Some people felt they should not just be thrown away and I wholly agree with this, which is why I have used the word 'disposal' above. When my letters have run their course and by this, I mean they have been answered, answered in part or not answered at all. I file them away, write my comments on the back and keep them for my records and this system has much to recommend it.

There are several ways of disposing of a letter. I own up that my main method is a simple one. I burn them and scatter the ashes to the wind over a flowing stream or river. Not a stagnant pond, it must have movement. I do this because the angels are so often described as 'creatures of fire and water,' first the fire and then the water. Before someone puts pen to paper, I do not think a extremely small amount of ash crushed to a fine powder and sprinkled in a flowing river can be construed as a major ecological disaster. The letter's remains are natural ash and not a non-degradable material, but I feel someone will have to have their say to let me know they are watching what I write. As the angels are of the Elements of Air, Earth, Fire and Water, these four elements alone should suggest ways of dealing with your written invocations.

## HOW LONG DO YOU KEEP THE ANGELIC LETTERS...

Now let us come to the vexed question of the timing, which is a notoriously difficult thing to judge. I have often thought this is because the angels have been there since the beginning of Time itself and they will be there at the end of it. I sometimes think the angels forget we can only rely on our biblical 'three score years and ten.' We, therefore have a greater sense of urgency than they have regarding our life and its affairs. The Angel Cassiel of the planet Saturn can be notorious with time because he *is* Time and Eternity, I sometimes think the periods days, months or years are not even in his vocabulary, though they feature prominently in ours. It is hard for us to accept or realise that our lives, important as they undoubtedly are to us, are but a blink in the eye of eternity and sometimes I have thought that the angels may forget how short our time appears to us compared to theirs.

Let us consider some reasonable guidelines and suggestions regarding how long to keep your letters or before we feel we are unlikely to get an answer and the matter is closed. What follows is based upon advice given in earlier works written.

The advice has been shortened, but the reasoning and the results are the much the same. Some people like to keep a permanent letter to their Guardian Angels and there is no reason why you cannot do this. Your permanently written letter would be acting more as a talisman, amulet or charm. One copy could be large and ever present within the home, perhaps the other small enough to be carried about with you or one small enough to serve both purposes.

Using a letter as a talisman is also discussed in the chapter on the pentagram and to a large extent what is said there holds good for here. A good place to hide such letters perhaps made larger and artistic for this reason is behind a picture or a mirror; the fact that they are 'hidden' does not make them less effective. Symbolically a mirror is a good choice as Mercury rules mirrors or more accurately, the quicksilver once used for 'silvering' them. In using a mirror for magical work, it was the quicksilver and the Spirit of Mercury who pervaded the other planes that made the mirror under the right circumstances capable of reflecting these planes within it. You can still buy these old mirrors with a quicksilver backing to be used for this purpose only; it does not have to be new because it is being used for your Work, not your vanity.

You can put your letter inside or behind a wardrobe in the bedroom where you sleep because this is good protection while you sleep, because in sleep you are 'loose in the body.' You can put your letter behind the headboard on the bed, assuming it is a solid headboard, which is and excellent place. I have seen an angelic letter–invocation pasted on a wall of the room before the wallpaper was pasted over it. Others have been put on the wall near a window in such a way that the curtains hide them when they are open or drawn, under drawers. It is a letter for the well–being for all within the house and those who come there, offering service to the angels and your God(s).

I find it ironic that if later tenants decorate that room and find the angelic letter pasted behind the paper and hidden from sight, they will brand the previous occupants as practitioners of the Black Arts and they obviously had dealings with the Devil and Satan, even though nothing could be further from the truth. Now to the question of time and most of what follows is common sense really and is based upon astrology, but it has proven a good foundation in the past with which to work

## THE SUN AND THE ARCHANGEL MICHAEL

The Sun takes one year to move through the Zodiac therefore, one year is his natural time. The Sun starts growing in strength at the Winter Solstice around December 21st and when he moves on to around March 21st, he enters the Spring Equinox. The Sun mounts to its greatest strength at the Summer Solstice after which time his power starts to wane. The Sun moves to the Autumn Equinox before finally arriving back to the Winter Solstice once more. When the Sun comes back to the Winter Solstice, he is weak in the Northern Hemisphere and is preparing to start the whole cycle again. The Sun does in effect 'wax and wane' just like the Moon but the difference between the two planets is that the Moon does the same cycle each month and at greater speed, so it is more obvious, while the Sun takes a year to do the same thing.

From the Winter Solstice through spring to summer is a period of heat, light and maximum growth. The strength to grow is strongest during the first quarter from winter to spring, which time is used for the beginning of germination and waking from the winter sleep, though mostly unseen under the earth, it is there. When spring arrives, this hidden activity burgeons forth above the earth to be ready for the height of summer, with maximum light and the creation of new growth or it did once when the seasons seemed to be more settled — this six months is the 'Bright Fortnight.'

From summer through autumn to the Winter Solstice the light and growth slowly withdraw from the earth, in readiness for the seasons of rest and cold, when life is suspended and hibernation begins for many things. At the Autumn Equinox, the seasons are balanced. After autumn, the darkness strengthens its hold on the earth and the withdrawal becomes faster — this six months is the 'Dark Fortnight.'

Do not regard the apparent period of decline as negative. It is true little grows during this period but you can use the time preparing for when the cycle of growth returns. The earth needs is rest and you should take your rest during this period and do so at least during the last quarter of winter. The brief suggestions given here of the type of solar power operating during the annual solar cycle give some indication of the use that can be made of the four quarters of the year and the type of 'power' available. Tie the above in with the remarks given to the Moon's periods that follow, because they reinforce each other while one is slower than the other.

The main difference between the two planets, as said, is that the Sun's cycle is yearly while the Moon's is monthly. These are some of the arguments, now for the results. Keep any letters to the Sun and the Archangel Michael for a maximum of a year and a day, no longer. The minimum acceptable period is usually regarded as being three months for this planet and its archangel.

## THE MOON AND THE ARCHANGEL GABRIEL

The Moon is the fastest moving body in the heavens used in this work or astrology. We regard and call the Moon a planet, even though technically we know it is a satellite of the earth. This does not matter and knowing this does not diminish the importance of the Moon in our lives of this work, astrology or magic. For the force of magic is governed by the lunar tides so it as well to know them. As said, the Sun takes a solar year to go through the twelve Signs of the Zodiac while the Moon does the same thing in one lunar month or twelve times a year.

The Moon stays in each sign of the Zodiac for approximately two and a half days. She moves through twelve signs of the Zodiac to the Sun's one sign. The Moon is not unlike the 'minute hand' of a clock, which moves through twelve divisions or 'hours' on the clock face (= the twelve signs of the Zodiac in a month). During the same period, the 'hour hand' (= the Sun) moves one division for the hour (= one sign of the Zodiac in a month). It is therefore, not surprising that these two planets are known as the 'Clock of the Heavens.'

Many folk know the Moon has two all–important phases. The first is from the New Moon to the Full and the second is just after the Full Moon to the end of the Last Quarter after which we are with the Dark of the Moon, three days before the New Moon again. At the time of the New Moon people noticed that crops, seeds and many circumstances in our life appeared to wax and prosper just as the Moon did. Therefore, people aligned themselves with this period for the same reasons. For the Moon, like the Sun, the period, from the New Moon to the first quarter is the strongest. With the second phase from first quarter to the Full Moon though the Moon is still growing it has less strength for the phase is beginning draw to an end and a change is starting to set in. For growth in any lunar work it is thought that the nearer you work to the New Moon the better, so the first quarter is usually given as the best time.

After the Full Moon, the Moon begins to wane and die and it was thought that many undesirable things could be invoked to do likewise. Ending a relationship or asking for some unfinished business that is holding on or obstructing new growth, to wane and pass. As the Moon 'passed on and diminished,' she would take these things with her and their influence would go or wane from your life. Pliny the Elder held to the almost general belief that growth was improved during a waxing Moon, while cutting, harvesting and getting rid of things, were enhanced during a waning Moon.

As you can see, the have noticed, when speaking of the Full Moon I always used the phrase 'after the Full Moon.' I never advocate using the night of the Full Moon for important matters. Most people will recall the saying that lunatics are affected by the Full Moon. The term 'lunatic' or those affected by the Moon, comes from the Latin word *Luna*= 'the Moon.' This is because at the night of Full Moon the power of the Moon is neither one thing nor the other. The Moon and its tides are neither waxing or waning — it is Chaos.

Just as the tides of the seas falter and stop, before reversing their direction, this is analogous to the influences prevailing at the time of the Full Moon because they are neither one thing or the other and running in all directions. Because of the prevailing trends at this time, you just do not know whether people, circumstances or situations are coming or going because they lack direction and so will you. Of course, if you deliberately wanted to cause confusion and the like, this would be the time to attempt it. People tend to get more emotional around this period, some a lot more than others. It is a time when bad decisions are made because they are based upon emotion not logic. The heart and not head and in many cases, things are not thought through well enough. Leave any work for this one day, especially so if it is important work. In all matters given throughout the work where time is concerned never start anything you attempt exactly at the time the clock strikes the hour, always leave matters a few minutes to give the new hour a little time to establish itself before using the new hour.

Now let us take note of the important three day period before the New Moon when the Moon does not 'show her face in the heavens.' It has long been advised that you do nothing during this period because this time is called the 'Dark of the Moon.' In the past this was thought to be a period when evil things were done because the 'eye of the Moon was closed.' The Moon was not in the heavens to see what went on in the hours of darkness. Magical work could be reversed by Forces that were unfriendly and spiteful to you. An old manuscript tells us this was because the Forces of this time are 'antagonistic to Mankind and their hopes and wishes.'

Again, these are some of the arguments regarding the Moon and time, now for the results of them. At the most, the period of the Moon is three months and a day or one–quarter. Generally, a period of one lunar month is reasonable and note if the Moon changes Signs of the Zodiac during the period and leaves the Sign of the Zodiac she was in when you started as this could shorten the time period.

## THE PLANET MERCURY AND THE ARCHANGEL RAPHAEL

The planet Mercury has a natural period to circle the twelve Signs of the Zodiac of about a year. If you need information, data, contracts, books, papers all things connected with writing then the Archangel Raphael is your angel in his Gemini aspect. Here he is the 'Newsvendor of the Zodiac,' no issue is too insignificant for his attention and as oft repeated throughout, he likes to be the first to know and the first to tell. His is the ability to communicate on all levels, the nervous reactions of the body, the mental reaction to people, life and its circumstances; he gives the desire and urge to communicate. He is the Messenger of the Gods — wings on his of feet and the Caduceus in his hand, it should come as no surprise that his metal is quicksilver that takes the shape of the vessel into which it is poured and bearing the 'shape' of the last strong mind that he was with for a time. He is the head of the family of heralds and their strict rules of conduct, impartiality and honour, which are good advice to use and how to act in some situations especially in those places where we are the guests. If it is for matters of hygiene, diet, illness and medical matters these are his Virgo aspect.

If Mercury is retrograde (marked RX) at the time you are performing your work, expect delays — you will get them whatever it is, whether you like it or not and if something is given during this period (for any planet) something will be held back, only given in part or not given at all. I personally take a maximum of one, two or three months for him and even this at times has proven too long. If you work when he is retrograde (when Mercury appears to be going backward because of the swifter movement of the earth), you can frequently double these times because of it. Sometimes he appears to do things twice or repeatedly when retrograde. He acts quickly, fleeting and shifting like his metal and he is the Walker on the Wind and a Shape–Changer. Watch for him because he can be so quick and for those who can, watch the direction he comes from, if it is the East more often than not this is the best direction — if he is coming from the West, he can be doubtful in some matters, this has been mentioned earlier.

## THE PLANET VENUS AND THE ANGEL ANAEL.

Venus and the Angel Anael is the chief planet of love, a subject that seems to defy explanation and thank goodness for that. It is a glorious madness available to all for the asking and sometimes even without the asking. Those who keep calling for an explanation about it or demanding constant reassuring about it by the minute will soon destroy it because they did not have any grasp on it in the first place.

Venus as most know is the Goddess of beauty and love. During our years of adolescence, the time in our lives that Venus rules, she gives us the desire to be attractive to others and to attract others to us. This is a time when we start to make friends of your choosing outside the intimate circle of the family and the home, it a time of 'us' meaning you with 'someone else' that is not family. Someone of 'our choosing' for good or ill and it hurts when it all goes wrong because we are playing with one of the most powerful emotions ever created and one, as legends sometimes show has even been able to conquer death itself and their are few that can melt the heart of that particular angel. Sometimes with Venus, it is a partnership of business and enterprise, which, if successful could bring in enough money for a comfortable or luxurious life style and all that goes with it — though each thing can bring its own set of problems.

We want to have our possessions that we have bought with our money because the things are of our choosing and if we leave home to be with another, it is these we take with us. As you can see this involves being with someone else and not being alone. Venus rules beauty, art and the collecting of such possessions, social affairs, relationships, partnerships and being social, the good and pleasant people and things in life, all forms of affection. She is adaptable, tactful, gentle, graceful and peace–loving but not always pleasant when she is upset whether male or female. She also shows a persons ability to attract affection, love and partners, including harmony. Venus in astrology is called 'the Lesser Fortune.' She has a time scale of roughly a year at the most and there are subdivisions within this period — a month, three, six or nine months for the most, but not beyond a year and a day.

## THE PLANET MARS AND THE ANGEL SAMAEL

The planet Mars takes about two years to pass through the twelve signs of the Zodiac, so he remains in a Sign of the Zodiac roughly about two months. Mars being a fire planet his actions are usually quick, not unlike an inflammable liquid thrown on a fire or a fire made of straw, a bright display but quickly over unless their is something to sustain it. With Mars, things become heated in some way and take on energy, activity, fervent, zealous, over–enthusiastic, feverish with a temperature and the like. His efforts are not sustained unless he is supported elsewhere as said and this is why Mars rules feverish complaints in people and those quick outbursts of temper, he has very little patience. To read the mythology of Mars and any of the other planets is usually very helpful with sections like this. If you intend to initiate or take some action that is courageous and pioneering then you need the help of this planet. Forget the usual that you have read about Mars and never regard the god, the angel or the planet of Mars only as a God of War, Strife and Bloodshed as some astrologers and writers often present him, that is an overlay of *Ares* and this too has been mentioned earlier. There is a very unbalanced view of this god and it is time it was challenged. Originally, Mars was a chthonic and agricultural god connected with the fertility and growth found in the battle of life and survival. These things are successfully won with the help of Mars and Nature could not do her work without him. Many enterprises, including yours, would fail without calling on him for aid, which is why we do this or we should because he gives initiative, enterprise and drive.

I would place a time limit of about two months on Mars. Alternatively, you can take the length of time he is in the Sign of the Zodiac in which you wrote your letter. If there are no results during this time then I would burn the letter because fire is his Element and try again another time, it may not have been the right time.

342

## THE PLANET JUPITER AND THE ANGEL SACHIEL

Jupiter is regarded as a good planet from our point of view because of his overall *noblesse oblige* and if your wish is granted, there will be little doubt that he has heard you. Jupiter is called 'the Greater Fortune' in astrology, mythology, legend and the rest but the one thing about this planet that many tend to forget is that Jupiter is 'expansion' — no matter what it is, he expands it — no matter if it is good or bad, wanted or not, like it or not you will get a lot of it. This planet does not discriminate about the results or what it is because he just expands it because its one of the things he does. So, get it wrong and you will have an awful lot of it to deal with whether you want it or not, his gifts are mostly for good. He rules opportunity, cheerfulness, joviality, well–being, optimism and prosperity.

Strange though it may seem, as he is such a beneficial planet, you should think carefully about your hopes and wishes before you write to this angel. Make sure your letters are written very clearly and not liable to any misinterpretation or ambiguity like the Sun — remember *Apollo Loxios* and the moral tale of King Midas mentioned elsewhere.

Midas got what exactly what he wanted to overflowing but at a cost that he found hard to bear because he did not think it through. It was only afterwards that he found out it was not such a good idea after all. Today the golden sand of Pactolus, a celebrated river in Lydia that rose in Mount Tmolus is said to bear witness to Midas willingly washing away his gift, to be free of his 'blessing' at any cost. (Ovid *Met*. II, 90ff).

Remember, we may not have a Dionysus appear to give us the necessary advice of what to do about it if we got into so much trouble and grant our release from it. The planet Jupiter takes twelve years to traverse the Zodiac, so a year is usually considered his time but a month or while in a Sign of the Zodiac could be used as a more practical time.

## THE PLANET SATURN AND THE ANGEL CASSIEL

This is the final of the seven old planets and their angels in the old planetary scheme of the ancient world upon which so much of this work was built. When we come to Saturn, we meet the slowest moving of the original seven planets. Saturn, as in the case of Mars, often has an ill–deserved reputation, justified if you chose to live up to the negative side of his nature. Never forget all the planets have a negative side, everything that has been written about them can become negative and often he seems not to give us what we want

Saturn teaches us experience and he rules Time itself. He usually gives us the time to be taught, though our time on earth is nothing compared to Saturn's concept of time. He is often found called the 'Celestial Schoolmaster' and although his lessons can be hard, they are enduring and without him, our education would be sadly lacking, though we are not so philosophical while he is teaching us these lessons — for our own good naturally —because he can weigh very heavy at times. He is your ability to bear hardship and difficulties with patience and fortitude, even though you may feel they seem to go on for ever at times. He gives responsibility and expects you see it through to that end if you accept them, the responsibility of partnership, the duty of contracts, work accepted, home, family, your children, promises given and your word.

He can cool things and limit them like health into illness and will try to keep you within these limits but not if you can pass his set restrictions. He draws the boundaries of your life in and narrows them so that you get less for longer but the wise can surmount this. He is the 'Wise One' and wisdom is one of his gifts to the wise that learn to work with him so that the lesson is learnt. Often if we knew why, it could be easier, but he is a hard planet to work out although he and his actions are well listed and he is fair and bills must be paid to the last farthing. His 'mills grind slow' and the grind 'exceedingly small.'

Saturn stays about two and a half years in a Sign of the Zodiac on average, but his time can be between two and a half to four years if retrograde motion occurs and it usually does. He takes about 30 years to circle the zodiac. This may appear a long time but he can take as long as this to operate and it is no good being impatient, for one of the lessons he teaches is patience. He rules patience because it is one of his 'gifts,' and he can 'wait it out' longer than we can. Take four years as the maximum as that is as long as it can take, if Saturn chooses. Two years and a half is often the average or moving out of the Sign of the Zodiac that he was in when you started, whatever is the shorter.

## THE THREE PLANETS OUTSIDE THE RANGE OF SATURN

In astrology these planets, unless prominent and intensely focused in the birth chart, which they can be, are thought to influence a group or generation more than individuals because of the time they stay in a Sign of the Zodiac. The house position is thought to show where they will affect the individual or group most, also when these planets are in aspect from other planets, especially the heavy planets, if it is the swift moving planets as a rule only produce annoyances that swiftly pass, which to some are not even noticed.

The planet Uranus, Neptune and Pluto take a long time to traverse the twelve Signs of the Zodiac or even passing through one sign. As written, they are outside the confines of Saturn and outside the circle of our physical lives and so it is they are often call the non–personal planets for this reason. Because these three planets are outside the boundary of Saturn, the planet of Time, they are also outside any idea of time, as we know it by being a law unto themselves. We must remember where these planets are concerned to forget time as we regard it. Time is our problem and not theirs.

Uranus is approximately seven years in a sign. Like all the planets, he can take much longer if he goes retrograde many times in his journey. Neptune takes around fourteen years and Pluto some twenty–eight years to go through a single sign, minimum. A suggested time for them is almost impossible, but I will try to give you some suggestions and guidelines about their effects on the material level, which may help and experience is your only teacher.

## URANUS AND THE ARCHANGEL URIEL

Uranus is the planet of magic (not the stage variety) but the 'magic' attempted by those who work through the Will to try to change the circumstances in their life and enable them to control their own soul for good or evil. Magic has the power the make the seeker 'God–centred' and a influence for good. However, it can also make some a influence that is self–centred and channel for human malevolence. Uranus rules revolution, change and sudden upheaval so he can work his ways like 'magic' through unusual and unexpected methods, twists and turns.

He is a very erratic planet who considers that rules are there to be broken or short–circuited by far quicker methods. All the planets rotate in the same direction toward the east but Uranus does not rotate like the other planets with its axial rotation retrograde. There are no 'seasons' on Uranus as he presents his poles to the Sun alternately and this gives each pole a 'summer' of forty–two years and the opposite pole a 'winter' of forty–two years — one or the other with very little in between.

Uranus can act very quickly and be perverse, being a non–conformist conforming to very little, original, unpredictable, inventive and spontaneous especially with those things or people he thinks have outlived their usefulness because he has little time for them, their activities or the people that used such methods.

This of course immediately put him at odds with Saturn, who is 'the immovable object.' Saturn is conservative, traditional and dislikes change, if the established order is working well then why do it. Only one planet can shift the planet Saturn and that is 'the irresistible force' — Uranus and the Archangel Uriel. Once Saturn digs his heels in, Uranus is the only planet that can make him let go, which is something the other planets may try but some would not even attempt it.

Handle Uranus and the Archangel Uriel with the proverbial 'kid gloves' and remember he is the 'Lightning Struck Tower.' If you can, take a look at a traditional Tarot Card 16 in the major arcana on which there a tower being stuck by lightning from of a blue and cloudless sky. This is the familiar 'bolt from the blue' that can reduce you, your carefully laid plans and the patiently built 'tower' to rubble in seconds. He sends the sort of event that makes people say 'I just didn't see it coming!' why should you, if Uranus sees you looking in one direction, he will come in from the other.

In the Tarot card mentioned, notice how the people are being 'brought down' from their strong fortified tower, immaterial of their apparent station in life. One of the figures is wearing a crown in some designs of this card. This makes little difference to the Archangel Uriel. He probably invented the phrase — 'O how the Mighty are fallen' —none are immune from the actions of Uranus or his Archangel Uriel. He will never bore you even though you wish he would at times.

Saul of Tarsus, later Paul the Apostle, was immovable in his mission and would not yield or deviate from his zealous path of persecution. The Archangel Uriel is the 'irresistible force' and he particularly loves those 'immovable objects' called zealots. He delights in bringing them to their knees because it is something they do not think can happen to them — to others but not to them — because they are always right and on a permanent 'holy crusade.'

Guess which archangel was waiting for Saul 'on the road to Damascus' and at the time of the Archangels most active period — 'And was come to Damascus about noon.' *Acts* 22:6. In passing, Pan is not at his best about noon either, when to sun is high because at this time he is best left alone with no sudden noises. Not even the shepherds (whose protector he is) played their pipes at this time — in issues such as these — discretion *is* the better part of valour.

Uranus is for completely doing away with the old and on with the new, so he will rearrange things and reform them, leaving no stone standing upon another if he thinks it is necessary. His problem is that he loses interest once the novelty has worn off and he goes off to find other things to do. When he has levelled things to the ground for a 'clean start' there is nothing left for him to do so he just moves on to pastures new there he starts all over again.

It is then that Saturn moves in and builds it all up again. Saturn has what Uranus lacks — patience and staying power beyond the call of duty! Uranus is the 'eleventh hour' miracle — the kind that arrives just in the nick of time and saves you. To be fair to him, some things do need his management because long after they have outlived their usefulness, they will not let go — another trait of Saturn — and that is the polarity of these two forces but Uranus could use a little more discrimination and finesse at times. As a rule with the Archangel Uriel, it is usually the case of no sooner the word than the blow!

As said, this angel requires great care in use and cooperation so it may be just as well, in many matters and in peoples lives that he often 'does not bother.' If he does decide to take an interest in you and your affairs, you will be in no doubt that he has and matters may never be the same again. One thing is certain, as said earlier, if he does take an interest in you and your affairs, you will not be bored rigid and sometimes his gift is the 'stroke of genius.' It is not a cliché to say that you can expect the unexpected with Uranus. If he is your ruler, he will lead you a merry old dance and down some interesting paths.

Negatively he tends to eccentricity, determined to be different at any cost, rebellious, perverse and veering from the accepted norm in some respects just to upset it and perhaps with a nervous breakdown thrown in for good measure. Positively, he is a touch of magic, he will transform the mundane into something you could never have conceived and your world will never be the same again and neither will you. His response is usually quick and to the point! He is, on average in a Sign of the Zodiac seven years or stay with it until he leaves the Sign of the Zodiac he was in when you wrote your invocation — if it helps.

## NEPTUNE AND THE ANGEL ASARIEL

Neptune is an idealistic planet and is often is somewhat impractical because he usually sees things and people as he would like them to be, rather than how they actually are, even if it cannot be and what is more, he often persuade you to do likewise.

Do you want to see it white when it is black? This is no problem for this planet and angel because he is a visionary, intuitive, artistic, imaginative, acting more on feelings than logic. If the fiction is better than the facts then the fiction is what he will use because he does not a like 'two and two makes four' existence and he personally invented 'rose–coloured spectacles.'

He can give and encourage artistic ability, imagination and beauty, which will enhance everything he touches and it can be better, if it is not allowed to get out of hand — remember the important 'return ticket' to get back from where you started because he rules the *Lotophagi* of Homeric legend — the 'Lotus Eaters' — and you will forget family, home, country and dream only beautiful things. Artistic people of all kinds and those who appreciate their skills have much to thank this planet for. He can be your dreams or your worst nightmare — prepare for either.

He can make your world a positively magical and beautiful place in which to live if he finds the right material with which to work especially if you are in the arts and are artistic. More to the point, he can give to an individual under his sway sensitivity to the arts, literature and music in all its aspects, theatre, dance, painting, design and all things associated with this. Quite often, the problem is not the gift itself but the need to learn to control what he gives and not be controlled by them. Used properly what comes from all this can border on true genius, because you would be responding to one.

Neptune works slowly and sometimes it is so subtle you will hardly know what he is doing. Like the sea and marine matters, which Neptune is his kingdom and he shares it with the Moon, he will slowly wear away the land and the strongest rock. He rules anaesthetics and drugs that change your perception depending how you use them and why, legal or otherwise. He will come in fog and mist, dreams, imagination and intuition.

Negatively Neptune can be deceitful, forgetful, indiscreet, diffuse, self–deceiving, drugs, impracticality and unworldliness. The planet Uranus and the Archangel Uriel above rules occultism, magic under Will and Magicians of stature. The stage variety belongs to Neptune and the Angel Asariel who rule stage magicians, the masters of illusion and sleight of hand, where things are not as they seem and you are left wondering how was it done; an acceptable form of deception and he has plenty of other forms and tricks like this if needed.

Contact with the dead and is under his guidance and Spiritualism is usually under guidance and not Will if Neptune is aiding your efforts and you may have to look for the 'strings' that are attached sometimes. If matters take on a somewhat ethereal glow and you have a feeling of gentle

346

drifting then this angel could be taking a hand. Often it is a kind and tender hand when positive that gently guides you into the harbour you seek and he has so many ways of getting you there but he does tend to creep up on you.

Neptune doubles the times Uranus is in a Sign of the Zodiac — fourteen years so its getting harder to suggest. Try not to rely on a time scale too much and more on observable circumstances in the matter with which he could be involved.

## PLUTO AND THE ANGEL AZRAEL

Pluto and the Angel Azrael can confuse the issue, whether it is a single issue or all of them at once if he feels like it. He can cause you to take wrong turns or inappropriate actions so that you waste time, money, effort and end up miles from where you want to go, sometimes you will even find you are facing in the opposite direction or back where you started and wondering how you got there. He can compound trouble and complicate matters of the past, present and the future. He frequently complicates your present affairs through the past, which he is not averse to dragging up if it suits him.

This planet and angel can drag up things, issues and people you thought were long buried and forgotten, but never believe that because if they exist, he will find them no matter how deeply they have been buried. Just when you think you are safe, you could face them again and they are back to stare you in the face once more. I am sure this planet was in at the birth of the Gypsy proverb regarding the past fashioning the present. 'You have to dig deep to bury your father.' He has his particular touch of magic, which can regenerate, rejuvenate and make something new from old. Pluto can transform your life out of all recognition and beyond your wildest dreams — for good or ill — if he chooses.

He works like yeast in bread, hidden under the surface but working unseen. His working is at times known only by its results. He exerts a pull on things and suddenly they erupt into sight from the depths when he takes the ground from under your feet. He did this, as the Greek Hades and Prince of the Underworld, when he took Persephone. She was fascinated by a very unusual flower, which he had planted there for just that purpose to attract her curiosity. You can at times deal with the results with varying degrees of success but you could deal with them a lot better if you could find what caused and there's the rub.

Like Uranus, Pluto is the planet that makes you say 'Where did that come from — I didn't see it coming?' Pluto usually works slowly and protracted in your affairs with a degree of dexterity. Uranus is swift, Pluto is not and this is how the planet was originally discovered — indirectly!

Pluto's mass was such that it produced erratic effects on the orbits of Uranus and Neptune and because of their orbital deviation a reason was sought. It was then that Pluto was discovered to be the cause, lurking in the darkness of the outer limits, unseen but exerting its power by deviating things. When he is active in your life he can, not always, echo this process and turn you from your orbit so that you arrive where you did not intend to be as said. Finding yourself with something or someone that you did not really want or for which you did not ask in your affairs, though not always. Pluto is in a Sign of the Zodiac about twenty years and takes two–hundred and forty eight years to pass through all twelve Signs of the Zodiac, which is why I said, when dealing with these three planets, they are hard to give periods for and to expect or hope for speedy results (though they can give it) seems a little optimistic to say the least. Like the two above watch for matters in your life in which they may have a hand or are exerting their sway.

347

The three planets above like all the other planets can work negative or positive from our point of view and the comments given above will show some of the ways that they could operate. If you think any of these planets are making an appearance or an interest in your life and its affairs, fortunate you, especially if it is positive. Watch carefully to see if they persist or present themselves more than once as suggested at least three promising examples perhaps, this could suggest that they may be taking an interest in your affairs if they are involved in your invocation. Keep your diary, it could help you in the future and guide you how these three high planets beyond the range of Saturn will demonstrate how they are showing up later for you, possibly they may even use the same methods each time to establish a rapport with you as this has not been unknown. In this intuition and instinct are you best allies in the matter. If, regarding these three planets you start saying 'I feel,' you could be on the right track.

Let me repeat, the planets beyond Saturn are difficult to give suggestions for how long should you keep their 'letters' before they are 'dead mail or when they may act?' In truth, they are a law unto themselves, I depend entire upon my instinct regarding them and I feel that you will have to do the same. Experience is something this work cannot give you as this precious asset cannot be given, though we have tried to as much as we can. Be prepared to modify things as you gain experience and when we come to experience, we are back again with Saturn yet again. It is rare not to end with this planet or angel for when you finish or end most things in life and your affairs, Saturn is always there waiting to close the matter.

## TABLE OF PLANETARY NUMBERS

Each planet is considered as having a particular vibration, which gave it a characteristic and distinct personality, which evolved from it and revolved around its centre. A very old table from earlier manuscripts, often found in old works of Numerology gives the numbers as follows: Sun= 1; Moon= 2; Jupiter= 3; Uranus= 4; Mercury= 5; Venus= 6; Neptune= 7; Saturn= 8 and Mars= 9. Naturally, the reader will find opinions and other tables that can differ from the above, but the table here has long use and it is deemed reliable. This table has already been given in another chapter and they are repeated here to make the table easy to find for the work found in this chapter.

# YOUR PERSONAL PYRAMID OF ANGELIC POWER.

This section of the work extends the knowledge the reader has gathered concerning their five angels. You now know that these five Angels are your two *Guardian Angels*, your two *Auxiliary Angels* and the *Angel of the Ascendant* or *Benben Angel*. This is why you have again found the word 'personal' included in the title. These five Angels are very powerful in the life of the individual, from the time of their birth and the Guardian Angels before their birth. They watch over their charge through the journey of their life, interfering as little as possible, only when they must and even appealing for their help does not always guarantee immediate response, it could do so but even they must consider when help becomes interference.

In the end, they gather at the death of their charge just as they gathered for the birth of the life that started their guardianship. They discharge their final duties and obligations to the life that was given to their safekeeping with the nativity. The last angel to arrive is the Angel of Death who, at this point in the proceedings, has unconditional authority over all because he will close the account in the *Book of Life* that was opened for the individual.

Most of the things we meet on the material level of existence are usually subjected to two fundamental and on the face of it opposing forces — action and reaction, attraction and rejection and all the polarities we have to deal with during our lives. You have to decide which of the two forces offered you will use at a particular period and situation because you have Free Will.

These two forces of themselves are neutral and it is often your circumstances and your hopes and wishes that makes them be regarded as good or bad. The Element of Fire is neutral but circumstances make it good or bad. On a cold winters evening a big roaring fire in the grate or cooking food is wonderful but if the fire is in the middle of the carpet it is a different matter and similar examples are easy enough to find for most things.

In 'attraction,' you try to get it and keep it. Naturally, there are things in life we have to accept and get on with it. We would like to be rid of it but neither wishing, tears, tantrums, pleading, praying or ritual will make it any different. They seem to have been set for us and sent by a 'court' that has no system of appeal or one to which we have no access to plead our case, it seems we cannot make a case against the sentence other than accepting it and making the best of it, other examples are obvious.

These two principles are the *raison d'etre* for the kind of rituals that are called the Rituals of Attraction and Banishment, their principles are old and they may prove to be one of the oldest forms of ritual or magic. They are listed among those basic rituals that gave a simple 'yes' or 'no' answer such as sortilege. We still use a form of this ritual today when we 'toss a coin' or leave the matter 'in the lap of the Gods.' I doubt if anyone can say when they made an appearance in human affairs. It is only the method that changes because the basic principles behind this form of ritual change little and both forms basically consist 'of asking.'

It is not the ritual but the results that are beyond our control. We have some control over a ritual, what it is for, when to do it, what to use and so forth. Rituals of this nature are being attempted because we have exhausted all the courses open to us and we need help from outside. We use ritual and all that attends it to try to influence the outcome in our favour, supplicating something or someone that we think can influence the result in our favour and give us what we want. There is little to choose between ritual, invocation, prayer, service, entreaty, supplication, solicitation, flattering and the rest of the tricks in the pack. Usually we find only the 'how' changes — but not the 'why.'

I have seen and read of new rituals for 'new magic' that are naturally advocated by the people who have devised them or used them. Sometimes, they seem to have simply reversed the order or made matters opposite to the earlier ritual — frequently I feel they have elaborated something basically simple into something more complicated for the sake of it with the tenet that the more complicated the better because the more impressive it will be.

Let us take an example of the point I am making by having a look at the following words. 'Desire; wish or wish for; long for; desiderate; yearn for, hope for, pine for, sigh for; hanker after, have a yen for, covet, fancy, have a fancy for; have an eye to. To be attracted to, have a mind to, have at heart, be bent upon, set one's heart on, ask for the moon; crave, hunger for, thirst for, lust after, burn for. *Informally*: be wild or mad about.' The foregoing is roughly half of the alternatives given in a ***Thesaurus*** for one small word — ***want!***

The rituals in this work are not the form of rituals used by my old School, though parts are parallel. The rituals here are firmly based upon basic principles established by work completed within the School on an almost daily basis for many long years but even these rituals were not invented by the School because they have been in use long before today's Schools existed.

I have always worked with these basic principles introduced many years ago. I accepted them then and I do now because they have stood the test of time for me and most who have gone before. Of course, I have slightly modified them in places or come to them from a different direction over the years to suit my particular way of working, my viewpoint, my experience and temperament but I arrive roughly at the same place. The basic principles remain the same but this does not make them a straight–jacket to the wise. It makes them a firm foundation upon which to build, to expand and to build on rock — not sand.

A wise teacher will come and look at the foundations and footings of a students work but if they are sound then what they build on them will stand. You may not like the 'building' but if it does the job and the principles are sound, it is enough. Naturally, you make proposals, give hints, suggest alterations, give reasons why but all such matters must be able to stand the test of scrutiny.

It is said that 'the basis of all good magic is simplicity and perseverance, like water dripping on stone which, in the end will make its mark or break the stone.' These are the two powerful forces that combine to bring about the desired result.' People often say these expressions are trite or blasé but that does not make them any the less true, they appear to have become pedestrian because they have lasted and made commonplace by frequent use, but when you look at the new sometimes it is the same with a new coat of paint. Often though, it shows how grand some people have become by being unable to accept the simple forms they now feel are beneath them. Simplicity of expression is a direct force as is its continual application and perseverance. Occult students are probably following one of the most ancient faiths among the faiths, preferring to use the ancient rituals — because they have stood the test and lasted.

It would to advantage if the two diagrams ***Personal Pyramid of Banishment/Attraction*** were examined while reading what follows and all diagrams are at the rear of the work and in one place. You do not write in the compass points given on your work, you line them up. These are there to show you the alignment of the diagram to the East and the other important cardinal points.

The diagrams are identical, apart from the direction of your work shown by the numbered arrows. The direction of the arrows changes according to the intent of the user. One movement and direction is clockwise, which is ***deosil,*** while the other movement and direction is anticlockwise or ***widdershins.***

Deosil or clockwise goes with the Sun while widdershins or anticlockwise goes with the Moon. In many instances, deosil is sometimes found the slower in response of the two, this is not guaranteed but it can be found and should be taken into account in timing of things. The reason for this is easy enough to explain, the Sun moves slower than the Moon and therefore his responses are likewise slower but unlike the Moon they are less liable to change. Using astrology, the Moon passes through the twelve Signs of the Zodiac in a month and in that time, the Sun moves through only one Sign of the Zodiac. This explains the point — the Moon moves faster than the Sun and this is sometimes why lunar rituals work faster than solar rituals.

Once you have established which angels occupy the five stations of the pyramid, they are personal to you and no other, the station of the angels remains constant in both rituals.

1) In the *Pyramid of Banishment*, the movement is anticlockwise, widdershins or 'against the Sun' and the movement is called widdershins because it was considered to be 'against the natural order of things or the natural course of the Sun' in earlier times

2) In the *Pyramid of Attraction*, the movement is clockwise, deosil or 'with the Sun' considered to be the natural progression of going towards the Light.

3) In the *Ritual of Banishment*, the power is widdershins. It goes from our world, up the pyramid to the Angel of the Ascendant to be sent out through the capstone of the pyramid. As the power ascends, the material of the pyramid diminishes until it comes to the single capstone or golden *Benben Stone* high above your material world and from there away. The unwanted is sent up from you and hopefully — out of the material or your world.

4) In the *Ritual of Attraction*, the power is drawn down through the *Benben Stone* of the pyramid; the power descends through the increasing material of the pyramid into the 'material world' to the foundation upon which the pyramid firmly rests, the earth. The capstone, pyramidion or *Benben Stone* is the station of the *Angel of the Ascendant*. The path is down from the single capstone to the strong wide material base upon which the pyramid stands and rests, through the four angels at each corner then optimistically —it materializes into our world.

5) Remember the two basic principles given above. The power when drawn down from the *Benben Stone* to the pyramid base — *Attraction* (4) — increases materially with the increased material construction of the pyramid, in preparation for its appearance in the material world and into your life.

6) The power, when sent upwards from the pyramid base to the *Benben Stone* — *Banishment* (3) —as it rises through the decreasing material construction of the pyramid and getting lighter in preparation for its

351

disappearance from the material world and out of your life. If this part of the ritual was successful in the School, we would say that it had *'Gone With The Wind.'*

## Important — to me!

There is one thing I must make crystal clear to the reader. The above observations are not meant to suggest in any way that what is given here is the purpose of the pyramids or why they were built. The pyramid allies itself with the expression of certain philosophical principles I use and I am not inferring in any way that I have found the purpose for which the Great Pyramid of Khufu was built, which naturally everyone else has missed.

The above philosophy simply associates itself with some of the principles inherent in my work, which fits in with the pyramid construction and not the other way around.

The pyramid construction materially decreases as it rises from its base to the Ben–Ben Stone. It increases in its material form from the Benben Stone as it descends to the base depending on the direction that you take and work. I have always seen the pyramids as being set on a strong four–square base that is resting firmly in the material world upon the 'four–square earth.'

The figure four has long been given to represent 'the material, the ***Four Pillars or Corners of the Earth*** even in Egypt giving in a word — stability. The four sides of the pyramid are four triangles, as each has three sides. The equilateral triangle was the symbol of perfection among the Egyptians and represented the ubiquitous and important Trinity in the many religious philosophies of so many races. The pyramid diminishes in size as it rises and eventually merges from the base and 'the many' to focus at the apex and 'the One' — the Supreme Deity, the Sun God Ra — who was originally represented by the golden ***Benben Stone***. This is my view and philosophy of what I see and use and (as a construction), it has long been important to me. It beautifully, efficiently and symbolically expresses in one perfect symbol many of the viewpoints I hold and use in much of my life and the Work I follow. Further and this is important to me, I also feel that these views have respect for the original creation and it does not abuse the edifice or those to whom it belongs. It has with generosity only been 'borrowed' because it expresses what I want better than I can convey it and because I just love the pyramids — especially the Step Pyramid at Saqqara and its remarkable and respected builder — Imhotep.

There are many things that create an atmosphere of peace, deep thought and contemplation. They are personal and not the same for all people. Churches are quiet as are libraries to encourage meditation and study, concert halls and rock concerts have their own ambience and please those who are there or they would not go there. There are intimate places, small restaurants and opulent premises each offering what there clients require and seek and those that do not succeed do not last long. I think the reader can see were this line of thought is leading.

There are several suggestions to help to promote or bolster the ambience to help your personal work. There are many pieces of music giving individual qualities according to needs that I use and one unique of its kind piece that has been with from the day of its first hearing and is still is almost instantaneous in its results, with the right recording. It gives me sixteen minutes thirty–three seconds of elation with my recording and the repeat button gives me all the time I may need. People can have a love of certain powerful symbols, paintings, sculptures, candles, incenses or the spoken word; I use a lot of music while writing but 'the task of filling up the blanks, I'd rather leave to you.'

The ultimate objective is to have your five personal Angels present at the ritual in 'the god form' assisting you with your hopes and wishes. Petitioning their help and advice and do not forget to ask them what if anything you can do to assist them in the matter, but offer. Small aids can be used to create the appropriate atmosphere and state of mind to help these forms.

Let me enlarge a small exercise you could try, which is not elaborate unless you make it so. You could make a square of white or yellow linen or cotton, better still you could use a square tablecloth of appropriate size to cover the floor area of the room where you are working. I bought a good quality damask tablecloth at my local market that was not expensive. Wash the material before you do any work with it by soaking it in water first in which a generous amount of salt has be dissolved and then wash it in the usual way. You use this cloth to 'insulate' you and your work from the floor where you and other people may have been walking with shoes that are not 'clean' having been outside and who knows where. It goes without saying that you will take off any footwear when you step on the cloth and put them back on when you leave to keep your feet clean. I bought a light pair of slippers and they are used only on the white cloth in this exercise and kept with the cloth.

Little oil lamps have a magical charm all of their own, those with the wick and chimney are ideal and their light is sufficient. Keep these clean, wipe up oil immediately so it will not smell and keep the wicks trimmed and short. You can write on them in paint or marker pen, the names of your personal Angels or their signs on the base of the lamp because this will show you where they are to be set and you can regard these as your personal Angel Lamps. The white or yellow cloth representing the 'base of your pyramid' will naturally be governed by the space available to you.

An alternative is to place four nightlights (in saucers) or candles (in candlesticks) at the corners where the angels are in the diagram to represent the four corners of the pyramid and this will naturally be your personal angels. I will use the term 'lights' from now on, because the choice of the 'sacred fire' is yours as long as it is a 'living flame.' Please avoid electricity if you can, only use electricity as an absolutely last resort. Electricity for this sort of work is very artificial and 'soulless.' Electricity is useful and I value it in my life and would not like live without it now as our lives are aligned to it so much, but it has very little if any soul, yet it 'fires up' my computer with which I have a real love/hate relationship at times.

You can, if you wish, hang the fifth light above your head over where you will sit, kneel or stand, which by proxy represents 'the Kings Chamber.' The smallest of hooks in the ceiling is hardly noticeable and if it is noticed, say it was left over from the Christmas decorations. This is mentioned to show how you can personalize the ritual with your own touches. However, if necessary put the fifth light/lamp on the floor in front of you inside 'your Pyramid' square and because you should be facing the East as shown in the diagram, a light in this position will be set in an Eastern direction from where comes the source of all Light.

White candleholders with appropriately coloured lights or white lights in appropriately coloured holders. Even though these lights are set in a holder, you could still place them in a saucer filled with some water for safety or put a small amount of water in the holder before putting in the light. Whatever safety measures you feel necessary are in your hands.

N.B. Because of the obviously danger of fire, you should always be in attendance and do not leave unattended any naked flames unless they are secure. Use common sense precautions with fire always. It should not be necessary to have to write this sort of thing and it was not found in the books that I read as certain self–evident responsibilities would be taken for granted by the reader — today however is a different time.

You could put the signs of the angels in the four corners with the symbolism of the *Ascendant Angel* in front of where you sit, towards the East. You can sit, kneel or stand just behind it facing the East. Spread this cloth out as shown in the diagram and use the cloth for nothing else because you want to build up the power in the things that you use. Use your imagination and be comfortable with what you do.

If you wish you can buy some attractive place setting cards, put the names of your Angels on them and use a magical script (given later) if you wish. Not unlike setting an appointed place for your invited guests, you would put these at the place (= station) where you would like your guests to be. Set the place setting card for the *Angel of the Ascendant* before you on the floor so that the card is set facing the East, because this is the mundane and astrological position of this Angel.

There are five angelic stations in the *Personal Pyramid of Angelic Power* and there is an addition preparation you can practice and whether you decide to use this is entirely up to you. Make up on good quality paper the necessary Seals of the Planets, found with the Kameas, one Planetary Seal for each Angel and planet at the stations of the Pyramid. These need not be big, about the size of a visiting card would be fine, for this is how you should regard them. The pentagram is like a passport to request admission, while the 'planetary seals' are the addresses or 'letters of introduction' if you are admitted. You may not have to use the 'planetary seals' or 'letters of introduction' but you have them with you should they be required and could this be because they were carried? In any journey, it is well to be as prepared as possible.

What if two of the stations of the power pyramid is occupied by the same angel? Should those 'planetary seals' be duplicated, one for each station? No, this is not necessary. Just make sure you have one seal for each of the angel's and planet involved in your personal circumstances. In the chapter on finding your *Guardian Angels* we gave, as an example, an imaginary person having all the stations occupied by one angel and planet. This I feel would be rare, but it could happen and that person, imaginary or otherwise, would only need to have one 'planetary seal,' because there is only one planet and one angel involved for all five stations of the pyramid.

However, one light would still be placed at each station and because one planet occupies all the stations, they would all be the colour of the angel but you should 'light up' your pyramid. If you found the five stations of the pyramid occupied by three angels and their planets then you would only require three 'seals' for those three angels and their planets, this would mean that two of the stations are occupied by one angel and a light of that angel would be set in both places — no matter what the circumstances you must always have five lights. How would you use the seals, no matter what number they are, I personally set the seals around the Ascendant light that is in front of you.

This is given to show how the principles could be extended in form as long as the principles are correct and linked with what you are doing, the form can be varied to suit the practitioner making the matter personal. The skeleton of a human being is basically the same but the variation Nature adds to it is beyond credence as the 'variations' with the human races show.

There is another purpose for which the pyramid can be used, especially when you feel things are getting on top of you. It can be used to give you some rest and respite symbolically from your world, by sitting in a small part of their world, which is another reason for keeping the area used as untainted as possible of mundane vibrations of this level. After all, you want to leave your troubles outside the pyramid, not take them in there with you; otherwise, you may as well stay where you are and not bother. Try to make the only thing from the mundane world in your pyramid — you! Make a pact with your mind by asking that its fretting and troubles should stay outside the pyramid for a while, you need a rest and you will pick them up again when you come out. I have been making such bargains for years. Remember, I use the word 'pyramid' for the square cloth set in place for the base and facing the East, do everything within the base and assume or visualize 'a pyramid' of appropriate height above and around you.

When your are finished roll or fold the cloth up and put it in something to keep it clean. A silk or cotton bag with draw strings would be ideal or just fold it and wrap it in a piece of the same cloth, prepared the same way and used only for this purpose.

You can wash this if it becomes grubby with use because ordinary washing does not remove the power, but salt water does and you would only use salt water again if you felt the cloth had become contaminated in any way to remove this contamination. This method has the advantage of being able to be put away from prying eyes and once things are out of sight, you would never know they were there but sometimes, even to the most mundane, there is a residue that they pick up. Once more, you are limited only by your imagination in this part of the work. Within the general design and relatively few rules, there is considerable scope for making the ritual personal, simple, complicated, practical and a thing of beauty, especially if it uplifts you for a while from your routine life.

Now let us turn our attention to the diagrams of this chapter and to the arrows placed around the pyramid in the diagram and explain the order and reasoning behind them. As discussed before, there are two forms of movement in the **Pyramid Ritual** and this movement is not unique to it because it is found everywhere.

The movement in the top diagram is the movement associated with banishment, anticlockwise or widdershins. In this, what you do not want is gathered up around the base outside the pyramid to be sent away through the capstone and from you, your affairs and your world.

In the lower diagram, the movement is associated with attraction. In this, what you want is drawn down to you and your pyramid, through the capstone and sent around the pyramid base and out into your world, where you want it to go like water at the inundation of the Nile to nourish your land and make things grow. In truth, it is as simple as that but do not let the simplicity fool you.

I have sometimes seen a simple ritual made more elaborate than it need be in the initial stages of teaching, otherwise some of the members of the Junior School would not be interested in the work. We often had a hard time convincing them with some of the rituals — 'that's all there was to it.' Remember this is why I have given the excellent example of the centurion and the Christ from **Luke** from the **Bible**, later in the chapter.

Too many horror movies and lurid books were part of our theory for this. When the juniors 'graduated' into the senior School it would be explained the reasons for doing so because, by then, they understood better. Gurdjieff was sometimes asked why he charged so much for his teaching and he said (more or less) that 'people did not appreciate or value what was given to them cheaply or for nothing.'

Rituals have the powerful effect of lifting people and carrying them along with the occasion, because that is what a ritual is in part. An 'occasion' and something out of the ordinary, after all we have lived with the commonplace most of our life. After a splendid uplifting ritual, life can seem a little dull for a few days afterwards.

I did not feel impressed by some of the 'simple' tasks I was given when I started as a foundation member in the Junior School, until I learned the value of simple rituals and how they usually gave the more complicated rituals a firm base upon which to build much later in the work. Learn your alphabet, study your primer until you can write joined up letters and read and spell well, cultivate good habits in your craft that will never leave you all your life and it will move under its own power and all you will have to do is use the reins gently to take it where you want to go.

I think simple rituals and prayers often work better because at times, it is an act of simple faith that is needed and sometimes it is all you have. I write so glibly the words 'simple faith' as if it is that easy. 'Simple faith' is one of the hardest things to understand, get hold of, maintain and it is one of the first things you lose. It is so often discarded with ease and indifference, far too easily and far too often. I have had to go back, pick it up where I dropped it and eat humble pie when younger, I am a little more careful now. Many people find it hard to accept that a simple act can cause, at times, some remarkable results.

You often feel that you have not done anything or enough and I could not understand it in the beginning so that I could explain it later on — when I was supposed to know better. If I falter in my resolve, which I still can sometimes, I am not completely upset because it shows I have not finished learning and my mind has doubts and is not closed. I always call to mind the principles expressed in the example of the centurion's servant who was ill and dying in *Luke* 7:1–10, mentioned earlier.

He had heard of Jesus and sent the elders to plead with Jesus to save his dying servant. The elders told Jesus although he was a Roman he had built a synagogue and 'loved our nation.' Jesus went with them but when he was close to the house, the centurion had already sent friends to meet Jesus to tell him:

'Lord, trouble not thyself: for I am not worthy that thou shouldest enter under my roof: wherefore neither thought I myself worthy to come unto thee: but say the word, and my servant shall be healed. For I also am a man set under authority, having under me soldiers, and I say unto one, Go, and he goeth; and to another, Come, and he cometh; and to my servant Do this, and he doeth it. When Jesus heard these things, he marvelled at him, and turned him about, and said unto the people that followed him, I say unto you, I have not found so great faith, no, not in Israel. And they that were sent, returning to the house, found the servant whole that had been sick.' There is little if anything you can add to the principles involved in this no matter in what religion it was found, which is why it is here.

1) In banishment, you ask your *Solar Guardian Angel*, to draw the undesirable matter to him and he sends it around the base of the pyramid anti-clockwise creating a vortex at the base of this structure representing the world we are in. After a complete revolution, when it returns to your *Solar Guardian Angel*, he sends it up, through diminishing material and obstruction to the apex and capstone of your pyramid. From here, it is hoped your *Benben Angel* will dispel the matter away from you, your life and its affairs and out of your world.

2) In attraction, the procedure is the reverse of the above. This time you are attempting to draw down what you desire from above and outside your sphere — down to you. This is drawn down by the *Angel of the Ascendant* or *Benben Angel*, one of the directors of your life, who passes it down through the pyramid making it more material to enter your world through your *Solar Guardian Angel* who sends it around the base of the pyramid, as before, but

clockwise this time. When it has completed a circuit around the base of the pyramid and comes back to your solar Guardian Angel, it is hoped it will slowly spread outwards from the pyramid base into your life, into your world and its affairs. As said, this is like the life–giving Nile inundation that brought growth and fertility to our world

The circuit of power of banishment is completed when the revolution around the base of the pyramid returns to your **Solar Guardian Angel** that makes a vortex and he sends the force upwards to the **Benben Angel** with the request to banish it. This anticlockwise circuit marks and powers the action as lunar, widdershins and banishing from you. What we have is the creation of the circuit of power and then the desired action.

The circuit made in attraction starts only if the invocation is granted and if the force is sent down to your **Angel of your Ascendant** occupies the station at the apex of the pyramid, at the all important and powerful, golden **Benben stone** and then down to your **Solar Guardian Angel** and at first this appears to be different, but it is not so. What we have first is the desired action and then the circuit of power to bring it down to the pyramid base. It is natural that the two actions of attraction and banishment should mirror each other in reverse, because attraction and banishment are opposed to each other although they are the same force but different use —two sides of the same coin. Here we have the desired action and the circuit of power for the act requested.

When the **Angel of the Ascendant** takes the Benben station, it is the only time he does not use his own personal colours. The **Ben–Ben Angel** always uses the colours of the Egyptian Sun God Ra, which is gold and this why we always use a golden **Benben** or capstone whoever the angel. The colour gold is used for this station because it is the station of the Sun–God who cannot be usurped or tarnished, just as his metal is incorruptible. This is the principle behind these rituals.

It does not matter really how they materialize to the individual as the appearance and details of it will vary according to your lights, your heritage, traditions and the internal material with which the angels have to work. There are no restrictions or rules how the 'skeleton' of the ritual will be 'clothed.' They will 'clothe' it with what they find within to work with and the richer the 'library and vocabulary of myth, legend, literature, signs and symbols' found within, the richer will be what they use to help you to understand. We should strive to give them the largest and finest 'vocabulary' we can assemble — each according to their lights!

If these rituals are given sufficient power, they either draw together the negative influences, which is preventing things from growing or prospering and disperse them up and away through banishment. Alternatively, the ritual can 'water' the barren areas of your 'land' and life with the positive influences brought down, which can make things flourish and blossom, as with attraction. This is their purposes and the reason they are invoked. One thing does not change regarding what is given here because it is too obvious and basic to change, we are back to the beginning of the chapter — attraction is done to bring to you and banishment is done to send away from you.

What gives the pyramid its power? The link with the pyramid is your personal pentagram because it is from this figure that we took the five angels who make up the five angelic stations of the pyramid. They are the personal angels 'locked' within you from your birth until your death. You are after all a living pentagram and the personal combination of your special key was created at your birth. I believe the 'lock' of the pyramid can be turned by taking this special key, your personal pentagram, into the pyramid. You have the unique combination that only fits the lock of your pyramid, your *adytum* or *temenos*, because it was created from this combination.

This is why it has been stressed how to make that personal key or the 'skeleton key,' made by using the Six o'clock Angel if the time is not known that will open the lock. The pyramid as a structure and a concept is so perfect — it is also so generous in accommodating those who come to it with respect and an open heart.

You were shown how to make this particular pentagram in the chapter — *The Angelic Pentagrams*. This is the 'solid pentagram' form that you carry with you into the pyramid not the alternative translucent pentagram that is made for hanging where the light will catch it. The solid pentagram is painted on card, wood or any suitable material, large or small enough so that it can be put around your neck or carried with you into your pyramid. Make the cord long enough so that the pentagram lies over the heart area for both sexes, which is ruled by the Sun. Alternatively, you can paint your pentagram on good quality paper and carry it with you. It is this form of pentagram you can place on your letters and invocations to act as a 'personal key' in the chapter *Your Letter or Invocation to the Angels*, where I asked you to keep this in mind.

The personal pentagram is the connecting link between you, your personal pyramid and the Angelic Kingdom. The pyramid should be regarded as a structure to be found on the 'middle ground' where you are attempting to make contact. To do this you must first find the 'middle ground' and the pyramid in your meditation or its physical form or attempt to create such a place. Some people find this easier than others and if it does not come immediately, patience and persistence are the dual keys to use. Please do not try to 'force the lock' because this will get you nowhere, always remember — what you take you have not been given and it will never be yours paradoxically, even though you have it.

There are three centres, hearts or Suns involved in this ritual, and these are the 'three hearts, suns or centres' of the three worlds you are trying to bring into alignment, remember that important word — alignment. First, there is *your* heart, representing you physically as a human being, over which you have placed the pentagram with its unique symbolism.

Your physical heart is the centre of your being and you are operating from the 'heart' of your pyramid. The heart or centre of the pentagram represented by the Kamea of the Sun on which you have written your solar signature. The heart or 'King's Chamber' of the pyramid is where you are standing, sitting or kneeling. It is the *Astral Gate with Five Locks*, which you will attempt to open with the 'combination lock' you have been carrying with you from birth, which has been made corporeal in your created *Personal Pentagram*. It is the combination that you had to find and if the combination is right and you are right, you may be given sight of or contact with the Angelic World.

Let me give you an allegory. Imagine you are sitting in a circular room that has a small window in it. Outside that room, there is another circular wall with a small window in it, with other concentric walls beyond that — in fact seven concentric walls and windows in all. Imagine the six outer walls are slowly rotating at different speeds, you can naturally see the second wall through the small window of the first wall and think this is all there is.

Sometimes two or three of the windows line up and you can see further than before but still, always another wall to block your sight though it has (or should) have whet your appetite for more. However, if all the seven windows lined up you can see through the limitations, that surround you and no matter how fleeting the alignment, to scenes and worlds you never knew existed. Your vision is extended to a point you would never have thought possible and taken beyond the seventh concentric wall of Saturn and his **Rings–of–Pass–Not** that limit your physical world in the first place and made it more restricted than it need be. You would not have believed anyone who told that this could be done, just as others will probably not believe you if you say you have accomplish it.

When this happens you may have some wonderful insights into life, your life and its purpose. You get some idea of what can lie outside the relatively narrow confines of your life (= your small window in the first wall of your chamber) with your limited physical sight and the understanding it gives. With all seven windows aligned, you are as one inspired at times and the answers seem to come easier for you, for this is one of the rare times when 'you know.'

You hardly put a foot wrong at times like these, but try to be even more sure footed at these times, for they often do not last and if you fall it could be from a quite a height if you are not prepared. You will have seen where you want to be—not 'here' any more.

This can often be a blessing and a curse at times because you will know there is more than you have. The variable movement makes the windows slip out of alignment and the view is blocked once more. Like the salmon, you are filled with a 'divine homesickness' for the place of your birth and you would swim upstream, with all its possible dangers and death of spawning to try to go home to die but you know it exists and you can rely on one thing in this. You know that you do not belong here, you want to know where you came from and you want to get back. When you swim against the current, at least there is a good chance you are swimming towards the source of the river.

You must still use discrimination in this and remember the Magic Theatre in Hesse's **Steppinwolf** where 'the price of a ticket is your mind,' that could be a big price to pay if its the 'wrong' or 'a bad play.'

Your pentagram acts as the key that can connect or align you and the Angels of the Pyramid. Your pyramid can be opened with the unique combination of angels, colours, day, month, year, hours that are individual to you and other people may carry part of the same key, but it would be exceptional to find someone who has exactly the same combination lock as you.

The pentagram acts as a bridge or gate connecting the Mundane, Astral and the Angelic to use general terms, so it may prove that the 'middle ground' is in the area of the Astral and Astral Gate. The Astral can be a very deceptive place if it wishes to be so and it often does wish to be. The material of its making is very malleable so great care must be taken to find what is and not what is hoped for by the traveller, enjoy but as already said do not become a Lotus–eater, forgetting loved ones, friends and country of birth.

It is obvious that the stronger this bridge is the better, so we must do all we can to build it strong and true. This is another reason why we have spent so much time with this aspect of the work, whether you have used your known hour of birth= the 'original key' or the perfectly valid **'Six-o'clock Angel'** or the 'skeleton key.' Your key is valid, personal and unique to you and you can use it or not.

I have not given any prayers, pronouncements or invocations to use because those that I use are personal to my circumstances, philosophy, experience and to me. They are important in my life, my circumstances, the people in my life and to me. I know to those starting out this may be thought unhelpful, but words from the heart can frequently outweigh someone else's words in this respect. Sometimes giving prayers and invocations frequently gives the beginner the impression that this is the way it must be done, word for word with terrible penalties for any mistakes and I find this a little constricting. If you are in a Group this is a different matter for it is necessary for all in the Group to know what they are doing otherwise things could become chaotic, time wasting and 'free–for–all.'

There are some individuals and Groups today think that this is fine but it is not for me, I have never found order restricting and it is sometimes it is most surprising how much leeway within order and agreement there is with imagination and invention. Order does not prohibit development and those who do not see this are the more restrictive, order in so many cases in point is simply agreement and agreements can be changed. There is to me, little point in putting out your hand for something required in a ritual and you hear the person say 'what do you want!' People are not in their appointed places, stations are not filled and I am sure I will come back to this 'thorn in my side' later.

Try this excellent little guide, used successfully by so many in the past, for any work of this nature for the tongue–tied. Write out in the form an intimate letter to a trusted friend to whom you can pour out your innermost thoughts, hopes and wishes. When it is written, extract the heart of the 'letter' and discard the address and the ending (head and tail it) and you more often than not have an excellent basis for any prayer or invocation and as you grow in experience, so will your confidence.

The reader must have some close, intimate friends that they trust, well how do you speak to them when you are in trouble, when you relax your guard, forget your ego and open your heart. How much more so can you be honest when you pray or invoke the angels because you cannot hide or dissemble from those you are attempting to contact because to try to do so would be both pointless, foolish and they will not betray you. If you cannot trust the angels above all other things then this work and the writing of it was a pointless exercise.

If you cannot be completely honest in what you attempting with the angels —with whom can you ever be? Now and then, I vary the basic word pattern. Otherwise, through repetition, your invocations can become mechanical and lose some of the power that first created them. If you are not very careful your invocations can with the best will and intention in the world, become mechanical.

Spontaneity within the pattern is not to be completely frowned upon, especially when rituals are private dealings, but it is less desirable, some would say taboo within group rituals and with good cause. The agreed and established pattern lets everyone know where they are, where they should be and what they should be doing; I said I would probably return to this point.

Further, I see no reason why the reader should not make their own invocations and many works give good models to work from and there are suggestions throughout. Your words will have the advantage of coming from you to your angels. You know your circumstances and situation better than I do. You know why you are attempting to make the contact and what you are striving to achieve. I offer one criterion when dealing with such matters — always give respect! Even Mephistopheles stood on the hem of his cloak as a mark of respect to God while he was in heaven.

I stress that that you should never forget that you start from the disadvantage of being the one who is asking and hoping the angels may give. Would you give to people who called you and demanded from you that you give them what they want, saying it is their right to receive and yours to give? You would quickly send them off with a flea in their ear for their impertinence and presumption and (like the pharaoh of Moses) will 'harden your heart.'

Many people have a pass with honours regarding their Rights and Free Will with an abysmal failure regarding their Responsibilities and Obligations. If you chose to erect an *Altar to your Rights and Freedoms* as is your right, then another *Altar of Responsibility and Obligation* should immediately be erected opposite the other altar with duty given to them both, as is their right. You cannot erect an altar to one without the altar to the other. Many people do not do this and wonder why they fail. By the end of this work or any other work that I write, readers may get sick of the repetition of this but it is important as far as I am concerned and this is why I stress it so much or I would not do it. In my early days, my 'fuse' tended to be shorter than many — but I promise I am much better than I was.

# THE LINK OR 'JACOB'S LADDER'

What follows is quite straightforward but as usual, it takes longer to explain than make use of, most matters of this nature do although it is agreed that a great deal of associated information is drawn into the matter for discussion and explanation. This section deals with possibly one of the interesting sections of the *Bible* that has some of the most powerful imagery in the work. This part includes the story of Jacob wrestling with the angel and although incidental, this part is not used here. We can make a start by quoting the appropriate chapter and verse from the *Bible:*

> 'And Jacob went from Beer–sheba, and went toward Haren. And he lighted upon a certain place and tarried there all night, because the sun was set; and he took of the stones of that place and put them for his pillows, and lay down in that place to sleep. And he dreamed, and behold a ladder set up on the earth, and the top of it reached to heaven: and behold the angels of God ascending and descending on it. And, behold, the Lord stood above it, and said, I am the Lord God of Abraham thy father, and God of Isaac: and the land whereon thou liest, to thee will I give it, and to thy seed; and thy seed shall be as the dust of the earth, and thou shalt spread abroad to the west, and to the east, and to the north and to the south: and in thee and in thy seed shall all the families of the earth be blessed. And, behold, I am with thee, will keep thee in all the places whither thou goest, and will bring thee again into this land; for I will not leave thee, until I have done that which I have spoken to thee of. And Jacob awaked out of his sleep, and he said, Surely the LORD is in this place; and I knew it not. And he was afraid, and said How dreadful is this place! This is none other but the house of God, and this is the gate of heaven.
>
> And Jacob rose up early in the morning, and took the stone that he put for his pillows, and set it up for a pillar, and poured oil upon the top of it. And he called the name of that place Beth–el: but the name of that city was called Luz at the first.' The only words of interest in what follows this are '. . . then shall the LORD be my God: and this stone, which I have set for a pillar, shall be God's house.' *Genesis* 28: 10–22.

In all probability, what is in this chapter can be found in one form or another in other religious philosophies and some examples and symbolism will be dealt with at the end of this short chapter. Many spiritual philosophies are about climbing and raising yourself above your present state to a higher and more refined state of consciousness. As I said in the opening chapter, a great deal of the information regarding the angels uses biblical terminology because the *Bible* is the prominent religious philosophy and the *Holy Book* of my culture, it is a work I love and it is second nature to me for which I make no apologies. All that is given here is easily adapted to other religious philosophies with little trouble really for those who wish to do because the principles are universal. Now let us take the important points from the biblical verses to see how they apply to our present quest and while creating a link or Ladder may be optional to some extent, it is strongly recommended.

First, we reiterate some things already discussed. When you send a letter through the post, you know how it gets where it is going and once your letter is posted, the delivery is taken out of your hands. Considering the volume of mail handled every day by the postal services, it is really successful but it would be foolish to say that nothing ever goes wrong or gets lost. To guarantee really important letters getting where we want them to go, we sometimes use a special guaranteed delivery service, deliver them ourselves or have a special messenger deliver them for us.

Once you have done your Work on your angelic letters using either the *Pyramid* or *Folded Letter* form, the Work also moves to a level that is outside our control. It moves from the physical level on which we are living, where we can touch and feel the physical letter to levels where we cannot or the levels where the 'essence' of the letter is placed. These other levels are not under our control nor are they even using our laws therefore, we appeal for help from those who can use them because the Laws sought are theirs and not ours.

We have already discussed these matters yet one thing that often perplexes the tyro is that their letter remains after it has been 'posted.' It is not taken away for delivery as it is with the post we use but, of course, it is obvious we are not using the 'post we use.'

We, however, can only deal with an angelic letter up to the point of preparing it to be sent and offering or 'posting' it in ways suggested elsewhere. If the Power or angel you want to contact lived in a house as we do and we knew where it was, then we could use the obvious methods available to us to see that it reached them — but they do not, so we cannot.

Many people have the belief that if you want something hard enough it could come to us, the wishing creates a vacuum (which Nature abhors) so she fills it. There is the other side of the coin, there always is because a coin has two sides and to pick up the coin, you have to accept both. If you have fears and apprehensions about unpleasant things, they also seem to attract that which you fear and it too can be drawn to you. If such things are in the form of a mental image, powerfully visualized or strongly controlling the mind, you quite often attract that which you fear. Strong visualization sometimes brings what you seek closer than you think by putting it on the Astral Plane.

Things have appeared and disappeared from places such as the séance room but great care must be taken to see that such *apports* are not fraudulent and are being used by the unscrupulous for their ends. These people are always with us, so there must be work for them and profit in it.

Despite the above this does not mean that the letter is not read or the contents noted because, considering to whom they are being sent it is not necessary for the receiver to take it as we take delivery of letters to know what they say. Taking in the contents of the letter is not hard for angels or us really. We read public notices on notice boards where information is put up on a regular basis and we go to these places because of this, we know information will be there. Placards, posters, advertisements, signs and information are set up to tell us what, where and when, free or by ticket something is going to happen. We are told what we can or cannot do, where to go and the point this is leading to is that we take away the information without taking away the medium on which it is written.

Very few people have any trouble with the principles of prayer, a form of ritual that is regularly used whether in private or communal prayers at a place of worship. We have sent our prayers and assume that they are heard by God or the angels and we hope they will be acted upon. The words used in prayer are spoken and presumed heard even when silent prayer is used. In an angelic letter, we use words but the principle is one and the same.

In prayer, the first thing we usually do is to address the Source to whom we wish to speak or we call upon them to attend us if they will. Often we ask for this through the goodwill of other agencies such as the Christ, the angels, the saints and so forth asking them to intercede on our behalf. We do this to help our cause because these agencies are usually thought to be nearer to the Source than we are. They act as a 'bridge' or the Middle Ground.

We give their name, title, rank and a form of address. We ask for help, guidance, granting a wish, to express our devotion, to confess our faults and sins, to beg forgiveness or to offer service. There is often an established mode of speech and a prescribed posture, such as lying face down, kneeling, clasping the hands together, bowing the head, facing in a certain direction, sometimes this has to be performed in a certain place at assigned times and so forth.

The books of the religious philosophies of the world are filled to overflowing with the forms of address used and by many this is done with honour and respect. With some, it is done in fear, flattery or the hope of gain. The form of address is different according to the status or rank of the one we are addressing. In other words, we use protocol according to the rank and importance of the one being spoken to. The formula of prayers is thought to be magically effective because ritual and ceremony are the 'symbols of the soul.'

I could remove the word 'prayer' from the foregoing and substitute 'invocation.' I could have taken it further and suggested its use as an invocation to a god, to the deities, to the gods of Nature under Pan. Your personal *daemon* (used in the classical sense as spoken of elsewhere and not *demon*, see Part 1) and so on but doing this, we would make the foregoing blasphemous to many eyes, pagan, heathen and the 'work of the Devil.' It may be worth repeating a few lines from Part 1 here:

*'Qui croit à la Providence et à l'efficacité de la prière doit se rappeler qu'il accepte tous les principes sur lesquels repose la divination antique.' Historie de la Divination dans L'antiquite. (4 vols.) 1879–82.* Auguste Bouché–Leclerq.

(*'He who believes in Providence and in the efficaciousness of prayer ought to remember that he is accepting all those principles upon which stands archaic divination.'*)

Making a link or Ladder does not guarantee success but it makes a good start and in the opinion of the writer, anything that improves the chance of success should be undertaken, especially in Work of this nature. So it would serve us well to understand what is involved in making our link or Ladder and why — magical or religious. At the end of this section, the main points of this chapter will be listed in an abridged form — giving the 'essence' of it for the reader, extracted and collated for you.

The reason for Jacob being at the place where he had his remarkable vision was that he was fleeing for his life. He was at the end of his tether because of the animosity of his twin brother Esau, who was the firstborn and older. Esau was planning to kill Jacob on the death of their father because of Jacob's treachery and deception in taking what was not his to take by right. Rebekah (Jacob's mother) learning of Easu's intent advised her son to flee to her brother Laban. So, what was it that Jacob had wrongly taken?

Jacob had robbed Easu of his birthright through his mother's scheming. Jacob had wrongly taken the blessing intended for Esau from their father Isaac 'whose eyes were dim, so that he could not see.' The name Jacob is sometimes explained as 'a supplanter.' An oral blessing had legal validity regarding inheritance and once it was given, it could not be revoked — right or wrong. The blessing should have been given to Esau as the eldest son who tells us it was the blessing from his 'father's soul.'

Jacob and his story has been regard as a symbol of the soul's path (= represented by the ladder by which we are attempting to climb). This path goes from the lower nature (= represented by earth on which it was resting) to the highest nature (= represented by heaven where it was touching, with the angels active between these two points.)

At the beginning of the tale, we find Jacob leaving Beer–Sheba and on his way to Haran because he is at the end of his tether and he is trying to flee from the unbearable circumstances that he has helped to create. This is how it should be when we are trying to contact the angels. We (like Jacob) should be 'at the end of our tether' and feel we cannot face up to the difficulties we are contending with that threaten to overwhelm us, even when they are of our making, though not always.

We have tried everything but cannot see a way out of our dilemma and now we are trying to seek contact with the a higher authority for help and this is not the first thing we should try in our difficulties — *but the last.* We should not attempt to make a link or Ladder for every trivial matter in our lives especially when we should be trying to solve these problems for ourselves and this may be the reason they were given to us. This has been fully discussed and stressed elsewhere. As far as this writer is concerned, the angels are not our servants but our helpers — *if they will* — it is not a right that we can demand!

In the next part of the tale, we are told Jacob 'lighted upon a certain place.' What can we infer from this sentence? We know that darkness had descended upon him 'because the sun was set.' If you do not know the land then it is advisable to wait until you have some light so that you can at least see where you are going and what is under your feet. We often say when we are in difficulty that we are 'in the dark' and do not know what to do but often the thing to do is to stay put until there is 'some light in the matter.' However, 'a certain place' gives the impression that it was something special from the other places on his journey so far. Jacob names the place Beth–el after his vision, almost as an afterthought or in honour of what happened, ' . . . the name of that city was called Luz at the first' so he was renaming the place.

Perhaps this 'certain place' was a barren place or a shrine (some think it may have been) outside the walls and to the East of Luz. It is thought the name Bethel — 'House of God' —was passed on to the city and to the surrounding area later. Luz is the ancient name for Bethel, 'Luz' has the meaning of 'almond or almond tree' and this tree has enough symbolism of its own. In the *Bible* the almond is referred to as *shaked*= 'to watch or to be alert.'

The tree is possibly so named because of its early blossoming as if it is watching for the approach of Spring. It is the first tree in Palestine to flower in January with the flowers appearing before the leaves and this is similar to the use of 'May' for the hawthorn, which usually flowers in that month in Britain. The word 'Luz' which occurs in *Genesis* 30: 37, which has been translated as hazel but is thought to be another name for the almond.

Light was the first created gift after the creation of the world—the *Fiat Lux*—because the almond is 'the tree of watchfulness and of light.' The budding and blossoming almond was an apt model to be selected and imitated in some kinds of ornamental carved work used for making and decorating the golden candlestick for use in the tabernacle. Each of the bowls (= sconces) was shaped like the calyx of the almond *Exodus* 25:33–34 and 37:19-20. This is because it is through light alone that religion can fulfil the duties of life 'for the light shineth in the darkness and the darkness comprehendeth it not.'

This information is given in *Genesis* 28:19. 'And he called the name of that place Beth–el: but the name of the city was called Luz at first' There are quite a few important allusions to the almond tree and its fruit scattered throughout Scripture.

To the above, let us add a further suggestion that is relevant to what we are trying to accomplish. The 'certain place' on any such a journey can be anywhere or at any time. If this is so, how do we know that we have arrived at such a place? Perhaps it comes when our strength has gone and we have reached the day of reckoning. We can go no further and 'here is as good a place to die as anywhere else.' Exhaustion had brought us to our knees, sometimes a good place to start from with all the levels of our life are hovering just above zero. Again better expressed by Prospero in the lines, 'Now my charms are all o'erthrown, and what strength I have's mine own, which is most faint.' Epilogue from Shakespeare's *The Tempest*.

Now we could be at our most receptive to what is offered because Ego has long fled the scene because how can it take the centre of the stage when there is neither stage or audience. At this time, we could be listening instead of talking, fretting, cursing, blaming and demanding. Speaking for myself, I do not live in an Ivory Tower that was demolished many years ago when young and so few assaults on it. Quite candidly, I did not feel it was worth rebuilding because it was a fragile thing at best and the maintenance of it was far too expensive.

When Jacob sent his sons for the second time to Egypt for corn, he gave them presents for Joseph, which included almonds. Elsewhere, each tribe was commanded to 'take of every one of them a rod according to the house of their fathers . . . and write thou every man's name upon his rod,' which made twelve rods in all, one for each of the twelve tribes. Moses commanded ' . . . and thou shalt write Aaron's name upon the rod of Levi.' These twelve rods were placed 'in the tabernacle of the congregation before the testimony.' The man chosen will be the one who owns the rod that had blossomed. In the morning, the Rod of Aaron of the Tribe of Levi had budded, blossomed and brought forth almonds confirming him and his tribe to their sacred calling within the twelve tribes. *Numbers* 17:1–9.

Was this Jacob's 'certain place' because of the almond trees? Though he does say of the place later in the story, 'I knew it not' perhaps he instinctively felt it. The words in *Ecclesiastes* 12:5, ' . . . and the almond tree shall flourish' are thought, overall, the correct rendering. The white (pink–white) blossoms are used as a symbol of the white hair of the aged man who had arrived at wisdom. The almond was well known in Palestine and was a delicacy esteemed in other countries, especially Egypt who imported the fruit.

When you have finished creating your letter to the angels you are advised to be 'watchful' and 'vigilant' — *shaked* — like the almond, for any valid signs or *connected–coincidences* that could suggest your letter has been 'taken up' or 'interest shown.' Jacob returns to Bethel later, the place where God and the angelic ladder first appeared to him. God said he would 'bring him again to this land.' Jacob builds another altar to God and calls the place *El–beth–el*= 'the God of Bethel.' In doing this, he not only renews the name he gave it first, but strengthens it with even greater power. Each night you renew your 'Bethel' and strengthen your link or Ladder during the period your *Personal Pyramid* stands or while your letter is written and the planetary period for invocation is valid.

When Rebekah's nurse Deborah dies, she is buried under an oak below Bethel, which is called afterwards *Al'lon–ba'cuth*= 'the oak of weeping,' from the deep and sincere grief of those for the one who was buried there. *Al'lon* is a word that properly signifies the oak tree and the idea conveyed by the word is of strength and durability. Some commentators explain the word *al'lon* as 'terebinth' the — pistacia terebinthus. The terebinth is a deciduous tree with straggling branches much like the oak tree, especially when leafless. The terebinth was venerated with the oak tree in ancient times because of its considerable size and great longevity. Many commentators firmly believe terebinth (= *elah*) is meant for oak (= also *elah*) in the *Bible*.

Why have we written above 'his remarkable vision or dream?' We did this because of the importance of it. Jacob of course was not the first to have a dream or vision and nor would he be the last in the *Bible* and dreams are mentioned a little later. 'And Joseph dreamed a dream, and he told it his brethren: and they hated him yet the more.' *Genesis* 37: 5. Those who are the 'dreamer of dreams' are nearly always set apart as 'not being of this world' and this is said kindly or otherwise depending on the speaker. They are thought to live in a world of their own that is somewhere in the Middle Ground, an important term in this work and mentioned many times.

Let us listen again to England's 'gift of the gods' — William Shakespeare — and stay with *The Tempest.* Shakespeare has Prospero tell us ' . . . we are such stuff as dreams are made on, and our little life is rounded with a sleep.' In the Homeric poems Sleep, in the Greek *Ύπνος, Hypnos* is fatherless though the twin–brother of Death and sleep is often called 'a little death.' According the Homer, he lives in the underworld and never sees the sun 'but in contrast to his brother he comes softly and is sweet for men.' He is human at first before changing into a bird of the night, even making the mighty Zeus sleep. There is a representation of Night (= *Nyx*) holding a sleeping boy in each arm. Sometimes they are shown holding two inverted torches in their hands. The boy on the right hand is white and symbolizes Sleep, while the other boy on the left is black and symbolizes Death, who in the Greek is *θανατος, Thanatos.*

*Έρμης, Hermes* is the name given by the Greeks to the Latin god Mercury who is among other things, a god of sleep and he has authority over the dream gods. Dreams are the children of Nyx= *Night* and the brothers and sisters of Death and Sleep. Hermes (= Mercury) whose planet and angel (= the Archangel Raphael) 'collects spiritual sustenance from above and the experiences from below.' The Archangel Raphael is the Archangel who gathers intelligence or news. If there is one source that can tell us what is happening or what we want to know, then it is to the Archangel Raphael that we must turn because he usually hears about such things first.

Before Jacob's dream the passage of the Spiritual and Holy was for the most, a rather one–sided affair in as much as it usually came from above to below with very little interchange (if any) in the opposite direction. With Jacob's dream there appears to be a change because the movement on the ladder shows commerce between the earth and heaven and in both ways, which was something of a rarity before this time. This suggests the 'created' is being shown a path to the 'Creator.'

In Jacob's dream, the angels are descending and ascending the ladder that was between heaven and earth, up one side and down the other and it is this twofold path of which we take special account. There seems to be an element of partnership between the two levels, because God tells Jacob. ' . . . I am with thee and will keep thee . . . for I will not leave thee, until I have done that which I have spoken to thee of.' It is easy to see this is a contract and God intends to keep his part of it. The undertaking is no longer one way but in both directions.

Dreaming has a positive function in our lives, especially in the Spiritual and is an important technique of finding and bridging the Middle Ground. If you dream true and find the 'certain place' you may find Jacob's 'gate of heaven' and it is one thing to find a 'gate' and another to open it and pass through. To arrive at this point is a positive gain without doubt, which should not be lightly dismissed. Most things, before Jacob's Ladder appeared not knowing where the lightning would strike next.

We had the *Garden of Eden* early in Scripture where no appeal, repentance, mitigation or regret was accepted or countenanced and there was an angel wielding a flaming sword to bar the way back if this was attempted. Whatever happened before Jacob's vision, even when it was a timely warning to people about future events or people's safety, the people had very little say in the matter. God appeared to brook no discussion, only obedience to the commands of his angelic messengers or suffer the consequences. Witness the destruction of Sodom and the death of Lot's wife for her disobedience and just because she looked back.

Now we come to an important question, who sets the link or Ladder in place? The ladder came from heaven to the earth and it was 'set upon the earth, and the top of it reached to heaven.' How do we create the required link or Ladder? It is created as it was in the tale of Jacob in your dreams while you are symbolically lying on your 'pillar of stone' taken from the 'stones' at 'Bethel.' Do this each night just before you sleep so you can try to take your 'Bethel' into your dreams with you. This point is midway and bridges the physical and the dream–world, just when you are midway between sleep and waking. This is why holding it in your mind as your last thought just before you slip into sleep is thought to be best.

The Hebrew system of *Gematria* is mention in the chapter on the ***Kameas in Angelic Use***. The system of *Gematria* is a technique by which a word is associated or compared with a different word for the reason that the two words have the same numerical value. The possibilities of *Gematria* are endless it has to be admitted. It is a form of 'religious mathematics' to some seekers and a serious study for others. Some commentators have said that *gematria* is derived from the Greek and its similarity with geometry has often been remarked upon, but many scholars today are indecisive regarding this etymology.

'The Hebrew word for ladder, *sulam* is made up of the letters S–*samekh* (60) + L–*lammed* (30) + Moon–*mem* (40)= 130, the same numerical value as (Mount) Sinai= S–*samekh* (60) + I–*yod* (10) + N–*nun* (50) + I–*yod* (10)= 130 that was on 'the ladder' of Mount Sinai that Moses climbed to met his when God who and Moses listened. This gives one interpretation of Jacob's Ladder and it is said it represents the giving of the Torah on Mount Sinai and the angels who 'ascend and descend.' Moses could go to the highest point with Aaron going about halfway up the mountain (=ladder).' How far up you can climb is dependant upon the individuals highest personal 'rung' or how far you have extended your ladder' and more often than not the stage of progress may be found represented in symbolism by that rung of the ladder reached at a certain period or the figuratiave emblems displayed on a road or bridge, etc.

Many philosophies express similar teachings, heaven is intuition so linking with heaven elevates and exalts us, then we come back to earth to find a safe place perhaps our Bethel or personal House of God. These two poles are heaven and earth and where they are fixed there is a path between them. Remember the Archangel Raphael 'collects spiritual sustenance from above and the experiences from below.'

The Greeks and many of the ancient races had ***Temples of Incubation*** and the purpose of a number of these was principally for healing. A temple where people came to undertake a ritual sleep and were assisted by priests. They tried to make contact with the healing god of the sanctuary so that a diagnosis or cure would be suggested or achieved. A god of dreams was subsequently worshipped and represented in works of art, sometimes with Sleep and was honoured, especially at the seats of the dream oracles at the health resorts of Asclepius.

Jacob 'called the name of the place Beth–el' and 'he was afraid.' He said it was a 'dreadful' place because it filled him 'full of dread,' apprehension, awe or great fear, not because it did not please him aesthetically. He said it was 'the house of God' and 'the gate of heaven.' ***Beth*** is the second letter of the Hebrew alphabet and is a contraction of the Hebrew word signifying 'tent' or 'house,' the outline of which is preserved in the Phoenician, see the diagram of the Hebrew Alphabet. The suffix 'el,' which has been added, signifies 'belonging to God' and this is why as said many times is why so many names of angels end with the suffix 'el'= 'belonging to' or 'of

God.' Therefore, in Beth–el we have a 'House belonging to God' or 'God's House.' Some small churches can still be found retaining this attractive and powerful name and its a pity it is not used more often. Now let us list the main points, in abridged form, as promised earlier . . .

**CHAPTER SUMMARY**

1) We should try to create a link or Ladder only when we are at the 'end of our tether' and not for every trivial affair we cannot be bothered to deal with thinking the angels should do it for us. I am sure this attitude will not get us very far in the present, any more than it did in the past. All the information we need for this part is given in the story of Jacob and his dream of a ladder set on the earth and going up to heaven.

2) Jacob's Ladder is a passage open in both directions (remember Janus) as shown by the angels ascending and descending or it would not serve our purpose or Heavens and this is why we use Jacob's Ladder for this Work. Remember that 'certain place,' which was possibly an altar to the East of Luz.

3) We should take heed of the Hebrew word *shaked, shaqedh* or *shaqad* (= 'the almond or almond tree,') that was applied to city of Luz. Traditionally the symbolic interpretation of the almond meant to be 'vigilant' and 'watchful,' and for our purpose, this was to be vigilant for any signs or *connected– coincidences* appearing as suggested in the chapter *The Angels and their Planets*.

4) The link or Ladder as a two–way path appears to be confirmed by God's promise to Jacob that he will keep his part of the bargain and give Jacob what had been promised and to keep watch over him. God will not leave him until he has done what he has said he would do.

5) We 'watch' for the link or Ladder and the Ladder was 'set up on the earth, and the top of it reached to heaven.'

6) Why is the use of the link or Ladder suggested? It is suggested because it helps to focus the Work being done in your *Personal Pyramid*. You should try to make a link or Ladder between your Work (= Earth) and the Source (= Heaven) that you are trying to contact and try to achieve a connection by spanning the Middle Ground between Heaven and Earth. Anything that helps this should be tried and not be dismissed too quickly or out of hand.

7) How do you make a new link or Ladder or strengthen an existing link or Ladder already being used? How long do you create or sustain the link or Ladder? You make your link or Ladder as in the original, at night and during sleep. You create your link or Ladder each night before you go to

sleep. You continue each night to try to sustain a link or Ladder for the period you are working with your Pyramid and/or Angelic Letter according to the angel and planet with which you are working. The times of the angels and planets have been given in the appropriate chapter.

If circumstances beyond your control prevent you from doing your work what would happen if you miss a night. Nothing really — but the secret of the Work will probably prove to be a sustained pressure, which should be maintained to aid success. If you miss too many nights, particularly if they are in succession, then the pressure becomes weaker and this makes it harder to sustain the power. Further, any gains from previous nights will also be weakened, becoming less effective and perhaps lost overall in the long run. This is why it is stressed that you should not undertake this kind of Work unless you are prepared to devote the necessary time to it — sustained pressure is one of the important secrets of this kind of work.

Students in old Occult Schools were taught and reminded, particularly in the beginning of study, to understand how much they must be prepared to sacrifice to realize their purpose and not flit like moths back and forth between the brightest candles — that is how you get your wings burnt and that's the least of it.

You try to find Jacob's 'certain place' that could bring you to the 'the gate of heaven' and link you with the Source you seek. Deceptive dreams come forth from the *Gate of Ivory*, while true dreams come through the *Gate of Horn*. As said, the gods and especially Hermes have authority over the dream–gods and sometimes they send dreams though one gate and sometimes through the other.

The Greek *ελεφας, elephas* = 'ivory or of ivory ' with *ελεφαιρομαι, elephairomai*= 'to cheat with empty hopes' said of the false dreams that come through the *ελεφας, elephas, ivory gate* (Od.), generally, *to cheat, overreach* — hence the *Gate of Ivory*, for deceptive or false dreams. The Greek for 'horn' is *κερας, keras*= 'the horn of an animal, as of oxen or as a materia, *κεραεσσι τετευχαται, keraessi teteichatai*= 'of the horn doors through which the true dreams came.' Remember always try to find the *Gate of Horn* because through this gate comes forth true dreams, while deceptive dreams come through the *Gate of Ivory* and if this is what you find, do not enter or pay heed. Now let us deal with some . . .

## Further Examples and Symbols.

The conception of a ladder or staircase reaching from the earth to heaven is not only found in the *Bible* and the biblical Jacob's Ladder can be found in other forms and in various places. We could have chosen an example from our very rich northern mythology using *Yggdrasil*, a giant Ash Tree or World Tree, which connects the heavens, the earth and the underworld and we are back to the word 'connect', you cannot really go far from it.

The tree holds the various worlds below the realms of the gods with its roots in the underworld, the birds, animals and people scurrying between heaven and Hel (= 'hell?') There was a rainbow bridge joining the people below to the gods above because a bridge is some form is a constant element in the world scheme and like a bridge, a ladder connects you from 'below' to 'above.'

As said we have said, a ladder set up from earth to heaven has always been regarded as symbolic of the path of the soul. I have sometimes thought (earlier in my studies) that the children's game of *Snakes and Ladders* may have been based upon the biblical story of Eden. You 'fell' by the snakes (= expelled from the 'Garden of Eden') and climbed by the ladders (= the 'Ladder of Jacob at Bethel,' which took you past areas of danger and 'raised' you.) We use a ladder to climb and try to reach something we want that is out of reach, so we need help to reach it.

Attempting this often requires a measure of courage and taking chances, which makes the timid falter because we are trying, like a Prometheus, to gain what we want from heaven and bring it back to earth. According to legend, Prometheus took a chance and if he had lacked courage and faltered in the attempt the gift of fire would have been longer in coming because it was most jealously guarded. Although he won the Sacred Element for us, he paid a heavy price for his impudence to the gods

It is said similar advice was given to Sir Walter Raleigh concerning climbing high and being afraid of falling by Queen Elizabeth I. Raleigh wrote the line on a window pane. 'Fain I would climb, yet fear I to fall.' A very earthy, practical and unsentimental Queen Elizabeth, born under the Sign of the Virgin with Capricorn rising saw it and wrote under his line — 'If thy heart fails thee, climb not at all.' Fuller – *Worthies* (1840), which would be a characteristic reply for her.

Angels ascending a ladder are often thought of as our aspirations, prayers, invocations — this includes our 'letters to the angels.' The angels descending the ladders were regarded as the Divine responses to those prayers or invocations of the soul. The ladder is a very old symbol and is found in the *Book of the Dead* – Wallis Budge. 'Homage to thee O ladder of the God, homage to thee O ladder of Set. Set thyself up O ladder of Horus, whereby Osiris appeared in heaven, when he wrought the protection of Ra.' (*Papyrus*), Set is sometimes given as Seth both are understood.

Some think we should avoid setting up a 'ladder to Set' because this god stands for all–powerful desires and the principle of evil, whose Egyptian name is translated as 'the instigator of confusion.' In the conflict of Set and Horus, when it came to the division of the stars, Set took all the circumpolar stars (= those that never set, just as evil and confusion never sleep and are ever alert for conquest). While Horus took those stars that rise and set (= like the sun, activity and light alternating with rest and darkness, lucky and unlucky, in other words, the duality we so often find here on the material, I feel.)

Perhaps this is why we are always advised to take great care regarding our reasons and our intentions. We are always advised to try only to mount the *Scalae Perfectus* — *Scalae* (= 'a flight of steps or stairs, a ladder') *Perfectus* (= 'a finishing or perfecting, perfection') or the *Ladder of Perfection*. Because of some recurring dreams, my teacher advised me to 'always remain alert and use caution regarding any ladder, stairs, trellis and the like found on other levels.' She said, 'If you can climb up something, then something can come down — but what?'

In the Egyptian example, we meet an earlier symbolism of a 'ladder hanging between this word and the next.' There exists a belief that Osiris encountered some difficulty in getting up to the 'iron plate' because of his feebleness. It was only by means of the ladder that his father Osiris, if he had to strength to climb it could finally ascend to heaven. On one side of the ladder stood Ra and on the other Horus, the son of Osiris and Isis, and all helped Osiris to climb the ladder. According the Budge the original guardians of the ladder were Horus the Elder and Set.

The sign called the '*Two Fingers of Horus*' was used by the Egyptians as a blessing, granting peace and the blessing of good faith and it is interesting to find this sign is still with us. The same two fingers are used in the ecclesiastical benediction or blessing of Christianity. Raise the index and middle fingers of the right hand and keep them close together. Draw the third and fourth fingers into the palm of the hand and put the thumb on top of them. Now the hand is formed into the symbol of assistance, benediction and help. Then as now Horus used these two fingers to assist Osiris to mount the Ladder of Heaven, he assisted and lifted his father into heaven — or to the 'higher world.'

Wallis Budge tells us, 'This amulet is intended to represent the two fingers, index and medius, which the god Horus employed in helping his father Osiris up the ladder up to heaven.' From

371

*Egyptian Magic* and this amulet was made to represent the *'Two Fingers of Horus'* is often found interred with mummies and are sometimes tucked in the wrappings. Stairs and the staircases obviously have much the same meaning as the ladder. I sometimes use a staircase in my Work because Osiris was called 'the god at the top of the staircase' in the *Book of the Dead* – Wallis Budge.

There are various manifestations of Horus (some six or seven principal forms) that can overlap from time to time, so the problem of disentangling them is not always easy. Basically, there are two gods of importance who take the name of Horus. The first is the Solar God and brother of Set, while the second is Horus the child of Osiris and Isis and these are the most important two for the reader to keep in mind. *Horus* is a Latin form of the Greek *Hores* and taken from the Egyptian *Hor*. Horus is a portrayed either as a falcon or a man with the head of a falcon and he is a very powerful god and he is not a deity that you deal with without due consideration or lightly do so and you could well get a 'short sharp shock,' which is why I brought my excellent copy back from Egypt. The 'iron plate' mentioned in the above represents 'the firmament' or the 'floor of heaven.' In the *Bible*, it is called a 'molton mirror.' *Job* 37:18. St Bernard tells us 'Whosoever therefore thirsteth to see his God, let him cleanse from every stain his mirror, let him purify his heart by faith!'

In many religions there is found the symbolism of mounting a cosmic tower as a ritual. High towers are often found in the centre of most Babylonian cities. The primary blueprint for such towers was that 'it's pinnacle shall reach to the heaven.' This tower was a model of the heavenly sanctuary of the religion. Its levels were sometimes the 'the three regions of the Universe, or the seven spheres of the planets, rising to the highest heaven, which guided the seeker to the seat of the *Summus Deus*.'

In the mysteries of Osiris and Mithra, the tower is replaced by the ladder and in the Mithras cult. The 'ladder of seven metals' corresponded to the seven ancient planets and the seven grades of Mithra. The ceremony of the *Bema*, ascended by the devotees is a similar mystery. There were five steps, corresponding with the number of the ancient planets 'less the unpropitious two.' βημα, *Bema* = 'a step, pace or stride' and it is thought the climbing of these was an act for which the gods apportion a reward.

There is a story of the Buddha's descent from heaven with the help of golden steps and he is sometimes shown at the top of a ladder as if seated in heaven. Strengthening previous observations given throughout the work that the Physical or Material plane is represented numerically by the figure four and is 'four–square' are strengthened. The lower planes are represented by 'square platforms' with 'four temples at the corners or quarters.' The Egyptian concept is given as a 'square iron plate' supported by four columns fixed at the four cardinal points and (later) these were thought to be under the direction of four gods. The *Pyramid Texts* presumed there was a flat slab of iron forming the sky, which was the 'floor' of the home of the gods. Jung believed the quaternary — rather than the Trinity — was the symbol of wholeness and this I have long believed, thinking of the Trinity as the symbol of perfection and balance.

Another well–known example we could have used is the *Tree of Life* of the Hebraic philosophy of *Cabbala*, with its four levels of world with each world having ten kingdoms and many important angels. The Tree of the lowest level of four has a bridge of Kingdoms between the Kingdom of Heaven (= *Kether*) and the Kingdom of the Four Elements (= *Malkuth*), which is mentioned in the main text. In this Hebrew philosophy and tradition, there is a tree by which people climb to reach paradise on the eve of the Sabbath. Christ is often spoken of symbolically as a 'ladder' as in

'Hereafter ye shall see the heaven open, and the Angels of God ascending and descending upon the Son of Man.' *John* 1:51.

The Ancients envisaged a ladder between heaven and earth; its major rungs were the seven planetary spheres. The basic and traditional view of the universe was of earth encircled by the seven planets with the fixed stars and zodiac above these.

Astrology was not originally taught primarily as a means of fortune–telling as many think it is today and this lessening of the skills came later. I find that when people take up the Teachings and start to use astrology properly as an guide to the **Occult Sciences**, symbolic language and so forth that can be used to unlock the mysteries of the soul does astrological prediction take its rightful place, as a useful and helpful force when used properly, but a little lower down the list and at the top.

The Hermetic Law with slight variations is 'as it is below, so it is above' or 'as on earth so it is in the sky' or 'as above, so below.' It was thought that what happened in the heavens was reflected here on earth and what you know, you can handle better or accept it.

These seven steps, grades, initiations are found in many forms and in many philosophies. These are quite clear and mentioned earlier in the cult of Mithras the 'mediator' as a ladder with seven steps and seven gates with an eighth gate at the top of the ladder. The first rung and gate was of the metal lead, the second of tin, the third of bronze, the fourth of iron, the fifth of an alloy, the sixth of silver and the seventh of gold.

These metals of ascent are not too difficult to work out being already set in order. The metal lead is for Saturn, the tin is for Jupiter, the bronze is for Venus, the iron for Mars. The alloy was used to represent Mercury because how can you make a 'rung or step' of the quicksilver or mercury of the planet Mercury finally silver for the Moon and gold for the Sun. This ladder order may well take us in reverse this time, from physical death as the first rung is under the rule of Saturn to the Sun, Moon and the stars in cosmic rebirth and freedom and not to physical rebirth and death again.

For a long time, magicians and alchemists have used these metals, their planets and a similar order for a great deal of this Work including those of talismans, amulets and charms and so many other philosophies, paths and Work. It is for this reason that I always suggest that people take up astrology, but for the old teaching reasons, primarily because it is a tried and tested ladder that has been honed and strengthened by centuries or work by some very remarkable people though some astrological work of the past is possibly still being neglected. The mysteries of Mithra and his Temple was only open to men and the grades started from *Corax* (= 'Raven'), *Nymphus* (= 'Bridegroom'), *Miles* (= 'Soldier'), *Leo* (= 'Lion'), *Perses* (= 'Persian'), *Heliodromus* (= 'Courier to the Sun') to *Pater* (= 'Father'). The Raven wore a raven's mask, as did the Lion, while the Persian wore a Persian cap and so on to show the stage that was being worked and those grades if any that had already passed. At the end of each successful initiation, the candidate was offered a wreath, which he would reject by saying that 'Mithras was his wreath.' This is only a small part of one of the many examples that could have been chosen.

Now let us look at the important symbolism of 'the pillar of stone' upon which Jacob laid his head to sleep and dream. Stone is a symbol of faith in the underlying spirit for which stone and rock are often used to represent the spiritual nature that depends upon Divine support. Some may wonder why something so heavy and inert as stone is used for such matters; it seems an unlikely candidate for use in representing the ethereal Spirit or the unearthly Spiritual.

Stone or rock was frequently taken as a symbol of the Spiritual because the material is not impressionable but firm, resolute, resisting the fickle winds of change and if change is made it is a slow process by the measured wearing away of what was, into what will be. This is the opposite of matter, which is very receptive to the acceptance of impressions, imprints and it is undecided or unstable.

Jacob was symbolically being supported by an underlying Spirituality by resting his head on a 'pillar of stone.' Matter is unstable compared to the Spiritual, stone or rock is the sustaining of eternal life that knows neither the limitation of time or decay. Like the Spiritual, the material stone changes slowly, if considered necessary and sanctioned from above and not from our end of the ladder, as vanity often assumes. The symbolism of a 'rock' is not wasted in the **Bible** and there are many concepts that could be chosen but one will do — 'for they drank of the same spiritual Rock that followed them: and that Rock was Christ.'

If the Source or Contact of a School (= on a small scale) or a Religion (= on a large scale), decides to withdraw its authority then you are left with an empty shell with equally empty words that lack Power and the all–important Authority that gave it its life and reason for existence. It can easily become a shell occupied by unbalanced forces and used as seen fit by those that use and guide it because there is nothing in attendance to keep them in check or stop them. These lifeless shells sink to the realm of the **Qliphoth**, which become the 'evil and averse Sephiroth' of the **Tree of Life** — 'these are awful forms, dangerous even to think upon.'

Neither must it be thought that the religions of today are automatically excluded from the possibility of such a drastic action from a Higher Authority, the Source of the religion and the Path once adhered to. The past has shown that these 'shells' are dangerous because they have no guiding hand or overseer to check how it is used or in what cause.

As said, such organizations can be put to any use by those who wish to manipulate them for any purpose that suits them, best expressed by Lady Macbeth. 'What need we fear who knows it, when none can call our pow'r to account.' Act 5:Sc. 1 — often the way of governments. As always in such circumstances it is the 'believers and seekers' that suffer and I have always regarded such zealots or mountebanks as Banquo did the witches, staying with **Macbeth** 'What, can the devil speak true?' . . . 'And oftentimes, to win us to our harm, the instruments of darkness tell us truths, win us with honest trifles, to betray us in deepest consequence.' Act.1: Sc. 3. Heed this well.

In the past, strong and powerful religious forces wielded great power in the land and over millions people of their time. They left their mark and their monument, but where are they now? We read of them in books and I am sure many think this could not happen now or to us but just as they did in the past, they too thought they were secure and safe, take nothing for granted. Spirit, Nature and Life in my opinion, operates a **Law of Degeneration and Atrophy** on those things that are not productive or which appear to serve no apparent purpose. In my view, the human race must continue to develop or perish. 'Be not troubled with the time . . . But let determin'd things to destiny hold unbewail'd their way.' **Antony and Cleopatra**. Act.3: Sc.6. I know I love Shakespeare but it is simply because he has usually said it first and so much better — why apologize?

'Tertullian tells us in his time there were several temples that had no statues. Shapeless stones were worshiped, to pillars of stone and other things of that nature' and this we learn from several authors. The Phoenician historian Sanchoniathon tells us that the most ancient statues 'were nothing but unhew'd stones' that he calls 'bætilia.' This word may have come from Bethel the name that Jacob gave to the stone he set up for an altar after his wrestling with the angel. 'Baetyli' were stones believed to be animated and were consulted by some fanatics as oracles, a form of teraphim . . . thought by some to be fictitious. Pausanias speaks of the statues of Hercules and Cupid that were nothing but masses of stone.'

'The same author adds that there were seen in one place thirty square stones, which had the names of so many divinities. Some believe the stone swallowed by Saturn was the god Terminus and that this stone was vomited up by him. It was preserved near the temple at Delphi, where care was taken to anoint it every day with oil, and to cover it with wool that had grown on the days of his Festival.' The sections given above are taken from *Mythology and Fables*, Abbé Antoine Banier (London, 1739.)

Stones were thrown as an expression of hatred and punishment for crimes, including 'death by stoning' that was a punishment among other things, for idolatry, possessing familiar spirits, cursing and certain forms 'of a lack of chastity.' Gemstones were often described in the *Bible* as 'pleasant stones,' 'stones to be set,' 'glistening stones' or 'stones for inlaid work.' This was a practical and non–technical description rather than one of a precise or accurate sense and the Hebrew itself is not always clear.

Precious stones were largely used in the Temple and were often a 'seat of revelation.' In the *Old Testament*, some of the first altars were made of unhewn stone and rock. The mysterious *Urim* or *Thummim* was 'four–square' and made of precious stones, it was enclosed within the folds of the High Priest's breastplate, which 'none but the High Priest ever beheld.' These gems or precious stones were symbolic of the higher qualities of mind and emotions however, a precise identification of the stones on the high priest's breastplate or any of the other stones mentioned are not easy to define with any confidence. Some of the ancient names for example give a general description of appearance and colour, but a red stone could be one gem among four or five. Take the following examples, (3) *bareqeth*= 'the flashing stone.' (5) *Sappir*= sapphire (?) but modern sapphire was unknown in ancient times, so lapis lazuli is suggested and (6) *Yaholom*= 'the hard stone' and so forth.

The *Ten Commandments* or '*The Ten Words*' (Δεκαλογος, *Dekalogos* already explained) were written on stone (twice) and the Black Stone of the Kaaba is a extremely holy artefact to a large section of earth's people is of unknown origin other than legend. In the *Bible*, we find 'Thou are my father, my God, and the rock of my salvation.' *Psalm* 89:26. Moses produced an abundance of life–giving water for the people and the animals by striking a rock twice with his rod in the desert. *Numbers* 20:11. This rock as given earlier is called a 'spiritual Rock' in 1 *Corinthians* 10:1–4. 'For who is God, save the Lord? And who is a rock, save our God.' 2 *Samuel* 22:2. Caves are sometimes given as a symbol of the lower nature of the soul in which the Self is born. Caves are usually dark because they are held not to contain the Light of Truth to lift and lighten the Darkness of Ignorance. A rock cave used as a sepulchre is devoid of life, holds the lifeless and so it too is thought to be lifeless.

We have only scratched the surface of the symbolism that comes with the words 'stones, rocks and ladder.' There are two reasons for these suggestions being here and the first reason is the lesser of the two. We have given enough information to aid the understanding of those readers who do not want to go into the matter further than what is given here, while the second is the greater. I hope the reader, seeing what this simple taken–for–granted word 'ladder' has hidden within it and the symbolism that it contains will dig deeper not only this word but so many others — if words do not speak to you then so that we understand them — what is their point?

Perhaps readers will never again look at a sad, old ladder leaning against a wall for support, without looking at it in a new light, even the humble ass had its day with palm fronds under its hooves. It will 'speak' to them and no longer remain insignificant and ignored, these readers will find the world is full of such sights waiting to be discovered — if their 'inner eyes' are open to what is there for the finding but remember — having found the 'ladders' to look out for the 'snakes.'

# THE KAMEAS IN ANGELIC USE,
## (WITH THEIR SEALS, SPIRITS AND THE INTELLIGENCES,
## WITH THE ADDITION OF THE OLYMPIC SPIRITS AND THEIR SIGILS)

I have written in the above title that the kameas are being applied here 'in angelic use' and this has been put in the title to draw attention to the fact that what is given in this chapter is not the only way that the kameas can be used by any means. We are attempting to ally ourselves with the angel of the planetary power that we are trying to contact and each of the Seven Planets of Old has its own personal kamea, which is a very powerful symbol.

The kameas are the magic tables of numbers of the Seven Planets of the Ancients; the later planets of Uranus, Neptune or Pluto do not have kameas. We have pointed out many times during this work and others published that originally only these Seven Spirits before the Throne would have been used in any work of this nature in the past so it is not surprising they are called the Sacred Tables of the Planets. We use a range of ten planets today as often said and while we can use, include and incorporate these additional three planets (outside the orbit of Saturn) in our work, they do not have any *traditional* kameas.

I have often thought because these three outer planets use three Signs of the Zodiac originally used by other planets, as well as their days and hours, it may be acceptable for them to temporarily use their kameas, not to own them but not unlike leasing or renting a property for a while to someone you know when you are not using them. I feel there is a possibility that in the end there may well be an attempt to have twelve planets in use, one for each Sign of the Zodiac, especially with astrologers now beginning to include Chiron the Centaur, the Dark Moon Lilith and the asteroids in charts, it is easy to put the planet Earth in a chart as it takes the opposite Sign of the Zodiac and the same degree as the Sun. whether this option would improve things or complicate at this time, I am not sure.

We are instructed in early volumes that if these sacred tables are correctly constructed, they will be invested with the many remarkable virtues of the heavens. They represent the divine order of the celestial numbers and have been impressed by the 'ideas of the Divine Mind, by means of the Soul of the World and the sweet harmony on those celestial rays.' *The Magus*: Barratt. These are some of the considerations that govern the reasons for using and including them here as the kameas are said to be very powerful talismans and the word kamea is often found translated as 'a talisman, a charm or a prayer.'

This linked line is known as a *sigil*, which contains 'the essence of the name of either a spirit or a person.' Sigil is from the Latin *sigillum*= 'a sign, a mark.' Once the sigil has been created, it can be used on the kamea or by itself and disconnected from the kamea from which it is created for other magical purposes, just as a charged battery contains a reserve of power when disconnected from its charger. When the sigil has been created, its use is not limited to being written on kameas only. Many of the sigils of the spirits were revealed through their sacred numbers from these magical squares, proving the enormous application and use numbers they have in Cabbalistic work, this will be taken up later in the chapter.

Other fine examples of such work undertaken were the Angelic Tablets that originated from the magical work of Dr. John Dee and Sir Edward Kelly. These are the magical squares or quadrangles and they are part of a very extensive system of Enochian Magic. The system of using the Enochian

Tablets is far beyond the scope of this work and their study is greater than is required here, though it is touched upon where it was felt to be necessary. We have given a small part of the Enochian system but compared to the magnitude of the subject, not much really, apart from the Enochian Alphabet.

Kameas are used in talismanic work, which is why I advised the reader at the beginning that their use for angelic work is not the only way kameas can be used. Let us give an example of their talismanic use and for this we will use the Kamea of Saturn. 'If it was a fortunate table of Saturn it would be engraved on lead, which is the metal of Saturn and it was reputed to be helpful with child-birth, for making any man secure or supreme, to give success with petitions with princes and powers. If it was unfortunate table, it would hinder buildings, planting and the like. Cast a man from dignities and honours, cause antagonism, quarrelling and scatter an army.'

This basic pattern could be given for the other six tablets and they would be used when the specific celestial power was at its most influential to effect what was being sought. Timing is significant to so many things, easy to say but often hard to judge and the cause of much failure, which is why Shakespeare gives to Brutus better advice than I can give.

'There is a tide in the affairs of men,
Which, taken at the flood, leads on to fortune:
Omitted, all the voyage of their life
Is bound in shallows and miseries.
On such a full sea are we now afloat;
And we must take the current when it serves,
Or lose our ventures.'
*Julius Caesar*. Act.4: Sc.3.

Too many people consider that a higher or more powerful source is limitless in an endless largesse it can shower upon those below that ask for it. The higher sources and powers do appear limitless from the point of view of someone who has less. Of course, the Angels and Archangels are limitless considering what is the source of their creation and power and let us take a simple example to illustrate this.

Electricity is not taken into our home directly from the power station that creates it. This is because our home and we with it could be a burnt to a cinder if we attempted it. Electricity at source is too powerful to be taken direct without adjustment and the power is gradually stepped down to various strengths according to the needs of the user. At the end of the chain, where the power has least strength and (if handled carefully) is easiest to handle, because it is down to what is called 'domestic voltage.' It can still be dangerous at this level and must be treat with respect, which is a good suggestion to keep permanently in mind throughout this work or any other work of this nature.

It is ill–advised to try to plug into the supply higher up the system than the domestic level unless you know what you are doing and this is why in life we find order, responsibility, the required knowledge and experience. Premises such as factories have powerful equipment to drive and they need to take greater power. They must take greater precautions and know what they are doing when connecting the equipment that can receive the higher power or they could in trouble and take the consequences — as always.

If there was suddenly a strong power surge sent down the line from the main generator, usually one or more of the safety cut–outs wisely set in place to safeguard those lower down in the scheme of things would trip and protect the transformers beneath them and the domestic user at the end of the line. The transformers lower down the chain would receive nothing from the source and cause least harm. This is what teachers try to do for their students in Schools and elsewhere when operating the schemes and order set in place. In the electrical systems and experience over the years, we have learnt how to deal with many of the foreseeable conditions because we made the system but this of itself is still no guarantee that nothing will or can go wrong.

With regard the level we want to align ourselves and deal with, we are in a system we did not make. It was in place long before our 'seven handfuls of earth where gathered.' Although we have studied the system, we do not always know how to run it properly or get it right.

You may ask 'what can I possibly give when you think about the level I am trying to contact?' We all have something we can give and even the offer of sincere service, honest work, love, respect and the offer of help in whatever capacity we can is a form of giving — the Widow's Mite — giving whatever you can. From a true source service and not servitude is often all that is asked. The offer of help pleases everyone from the highest to the lowest and what a pleasant change it must be for them — someone asking them 'what can I do?'

Some may charge me of being pedantic regarding this particular theme. If this is what I have to be to get across the principles I believe in, which are basically good manners, civil behavious and the respect I feel is due to the subjects of this work, then so be it, I can live with it!

We have already given lists of people, situations, circumstances and matters under the rulership of the Seven Planets of Old and their Planetary Angels. Let us extend them a little more and take a look at some classical models from the **Greater Key of King Solomon**, given first, followed by the equivalent sections from **The Magus** of Francis Barrett:

The Days and Hours of the Sun are very good for perfecting experiments regarding temporal wealth; hope; gain; fortune; divination; the favours of princes; to dissolve hostile feeling; and make friends.
Barrett: To be graven on a plate of pure gold, being fortunate, renders him that wears it renowned, amiable, acceptable, potent in all his works, and equals him to a king, elevating his fortunes, and enabling him to do whatever he will. But with an unfortunate Sun, it makes one a tyrant, proud, ambitious, insatiable, and finally to come to an ill ending

The Days and Hours of the Moon are good for embassies; voyages; envoys; messages; navigation; reconciliation; love and the acquisition of merchandise by water.
Barrett: This, the Moon being fortunate, engraven on silver, makes the bearer amiable, pleasant, cheerful and honoured, removing all malice and ill-will; it causes security in a journey, increase of riches, and health of body; drives away enemies and other evil things from what place soever thou shalt wish them to be expelled. But if the Moon be unfortunate, and it be engraved on a plate of lead, wherever it shall be buried it makes that place unfortunate, and the inhabitants thereabouts, as also ships, rivers, fountains, and mills; and it makes every man unfortunate against whom it shall be directly done, making him fly his place of abode (and even his country) where it shall be buried; and it hinders physicians and orators, and all men whatsoever in their office, against whom it shall be made.

The Days and the Hours of Mercury are good to operate for eloquence and intelligence; promptitude in business; science and divination; wonders; apparitions; and answers regarding the future. Thou canst also operate under this Planet for thefts; writings; deceit; and merchandise.
Barrett: If, with Mercury being fortunate, you engrave it upon silver, tin, or yellow brass, or write it

upon virgin parchment, it renders the bearer there grateful, acceptable, and fortunate to do what he pleases: it brings gain, and prevents poverty; helps the memory, understanding, and divination, and the understanding of occult things by dreams; but with an unfortunate Mercury does everything contrary to this.

Barrett: With Mars being fortunate, being graven on an iron plate, or sword, makes a man potent in war and judgement, and petitions, and terrible to his enemies, and victorious over them; and if he engraves upon the stone correola, it stops blood and the menstures; but if it be engraven, with Mars being unfortunate, on a plate of red brass, it prevents and hinders buildings, it casts down the powerful from dignities, honours, and riches; causes discord and hatred amongst men and beasts; drives away bees, pigeons, and fish; and hinders mills from working i.e. binds them; it likewise renders hunters and fighters unfortunate; causes barrenness in men and women; and strikes terror into our enemies and compels them to submit.

The Days and Hours of Venus are good for forming friends; for kindness and love; for joyous and pleasant undertakings; and for travelling.

Barrett: This being engraven on a plate of silver, Venus being fortunate, promotes concord, ends strife, procures the love of women, helps conception, is good against barrenness, gives ability for generation, dissolves enchantments; causes peace between man and woman, and makes all kinds of animals fruitful, and likewise cattle; and being put into a dove or pigeon house, causes increase; it likewise drives away melancholy, distempers, and causes joyfulness; and this being carried about travellers, makes them fortunate. But if it be formed upon brass, Venus being unfortunate, it acts contrary to all that has been said.

The Days and Hours of Jupiter are proper for obtaining honours, acquiring riches; contracting friendships, preserving health; and arriving at all that thou canst desire.

Barrett: If this is engraven on a plate of silver, with Jupiter being powerful and ruling in the heavens, it conduces to gain, riches, and favour, love, peace, and concord, and to appease enemies, and to confirm honours, dignities, and counsels; and dissolves enchantments if engraven on coral.

In the Days and Hours of Saturn thou canst perform experiments to cause good or ill success to business; possessions; goods; seeds; fruits; and similar things, in order to acquire learning; to bring destruction and give death, and sow hatred and discord.

Barrett: This table being with a fortunate Saturn, engraven on a plate of lead, helps child-birth; and to make any man safe or powerful; and to cause success of petitions with princes and powers; but if it be done, Saturn being unfortunate, it hinders buildings, planting, and the like, and casts a man from honours and dignities, causes discord, quarrelling, and disperses and army.

The Tables of the Days and Hours of the Angels and Planets will be found at the end of the book, but before leaving *The Greater Key of King Solomon*, perhaps it may be meet to repeat the following injunction, so read, mark learn and inwardly digest:

'I command thee, my Son, to carefully engrave in thy memory all that I say unto thee, in order that it may never leave thee. If thou dost not intend to use for good purpose the secrets which I here teach thee, I command thee rather to cast this Testament into the Fire, than to abuse the power thou will have constraining the Spirits, for I warn thee that the beneficent angels, wearied and fatigued by thine illicit demands, would to thy sorrow execute the commands of God, as well as to that of all such who, with evil intent, would abuse those secrets which He hath given and revealed unto me . . . and so forth.'

The kameas are seven squares consisting of numbers or in some cases Hebrew letters. Each square is given over to one of the seven planets –– the Sun, Moon, Mercury, Mars, Venus, Jupiter and Saturn.

'There are certain magic tables of numbers distributed to the seven planets, which they call the sacred tables of the planets; because, being rightly formed, they are endued with many great virtues of the heavens, insomuch that they represent the divine order of the celestial numbers, impressed upon them by the ideas of the divine mind by means of the soul of the world, and the sweet harmony of those celestial rays; signifying, according to proportion, super–celestial intelligence's, which can no other way be expressed than by the marks of numbers, letters, and characters; for material numbers and figures can do nothing in the mysteries of hidden things, but representatively by formal numbers and figures, as they are governed and informed by intelligence's and divine enumeration's, which unite the extremes of the matter and spirit to the will of the elevated soul, receiving (through great affection, by the celestial power of the operator) a virtue and power from God, applied the soul of the universe; and the observation of celestial constellations to a matter fit for a form, the mediums being disposed by the skill and industry of the magician.' *The Magus:* Barrett.

## THE NUMERICAL RANGE OF THE KAMEAS

Use the following tables to check the range of numbers that are available on each of the kameas will save you having to look for them. They will tell you if any of the names you wish to use, represented by their numerical value or power, will fit the particular kamea you want to use. This is explained later so just accept the statement for now. They will also tell you if the numbers will require 'reducing' by an old method of using them on kameas given later.

The Kamea of the Sun is a square 6 x 6 making 36 squares that use the numbers 1 to 36. Each line adds up to 111 horizontally, vertically and diagonally from corner to corner.

The Kamea of the Moon is a square 9 x 9 making 81 squares that use the numbers 1 to 81. Each line adds up to 369 horizontally, vertically and diagonally from corner to corner.

The Kamea of Mercury is a square 8 x 8 making 64 squares that use the numbers 1 to 64. Each line adds up to 260 horizontally, vertically and diagonally from corner to corner.

The Kamea of Mars is a square 5 x 5 making 25 squares that use the numbers 1 to 25. Each line adds up to 64 horizontally, vertically and diagonally from corner to corner.

The Kamea of Venus is a square 7 x 7 making 49 squares that use the numbers 1 to 49. Each line adds up to 175 horizontally, vertically and diagonally from corner to corner.

The Kamea of Jupiter is a square of 4 x 4 making 16 squares that use the numbers 1 to 16. Each line adds up to 34 horizontally, vertically and diagonally from corner to corner.

The Kamea of Saturn is a square of 3 x 3 making 9 squares that use the numbers 1 to 9. Each line adds up to 15 horizontally, vertically and diagonally from corner to corner.

If the reader wants to make sure a kamea has been written correctly, they will simply have to make the additions given above and check the totals. The kameas have other important numerical values and each kamea has four numbers connected with it and to illustrate this principle let us take as an example the Kamea of the Sun. The pattern given is the same for all the remaining kameas.

The four numbers associated with the Kamea of the Sun are 6, 36, 111 and 666. The first number is from the number of squares that make up the four sides of the kamea. In this example, the first number is six because each side of the kamea consists of six squares.

The second number is 36 because this is the total number of squares that makes up the kamea, 6 x 6 is 36.

The third number is 111 and this number is obtained by adding the figures found in the squares of the kamea, six lines horizontally, six lines vertically and two lines diagonally by adding the numbers in the squares from corner to corner only.

The last number in the group is 666 for the Kamea of the Sun. First, you add together the numbers in the six squares that make up a sides of the Kamea of the Sun, this is 111 (the third number). You multiply this number by the number of squares that make up the side of the kamea, which are six squares in our example (the first number). If you multiply 6 x 111, you get 666, which gives us the final figure in the set of four.

This pattern is followed in the same manner for the remaining kameas. The Kamea of Venus has four numbers 7, 49, 175 and 1225; the Kamea of Mercury has 8, 64, 260 and 2080; the Kamea of the Moon has the numbers 9, 81, 369 and 3321 and so forth. Simply follow the method explained above and the four numbers of the seven kameas can be worked out with little trouble.

Each kamea has a Seal, a Spirit and Intelligence of the Planet. These sigils are given at the end of the book with their associated kamea. The sigils of Seal, Spirit and Intelligence can be placed on your Letter of Invocation to the angels in similar manner to the kamea though they are not as significant or as prominent as the kamea, this is how I use them, this has already been explained in the chapter *Your Letters of Invocation*. As it has happened in the past, what do you do if you decide to use only one symbol of these three, say the Seal? To maintain balance put the Seal on both sides (left and right) of the letter of invocation and this is fine. Do the same with any single symbol you like to use of a planet or angel for your letters, just balance them off.

The Seals, Spirits and Intelligence are additional to the kamea and they must be kept with their kamea and obviously not mixed with other kameas to which they do not belong. They give additional strength to your essay if space permits and if it is felt right to do so. My treatment regarding their strength is in the following order of using the Seal of the Planet first, followed by the Sigil of the Spirit and finally the sigil of the Intelligence. You could start with this arrangement, alter the method as experience and use dictates.

A little later, we will be using the method of converting letters and names into the value and power of numbers. We do this to make seven planetary sigils of your name, one name sigil from each of the seven kameas and their planetary angels. These will give you seven powerful signatures or sigils, one each for each of the Kameas, Planets and their Angels of the Ancient World through which you can attempt to connect yourself to that power.

You can use the sigil of your name away from the kamea once you know it, because it was originally created on the kamea and it will still carry the Power of the Kamea within it, even when it is not written on the kamea that created it.

The power of numbers, letters and words has greater depth for study than is presented here. There is the Hebraic Gematria, Notaricon, Temurah and other forms, enlarged upon a little more later. Books are available giving details for this specialized subject if you desire to increase your knowledge. The works of d'Abano, Agrippa, Barrett (*The Magus — Talismanic* chapter), A. Crowley, Dion Fortune writing on Cabbala. *The Hermetic Order of the Golden Dawn* (Vol.4: Bk.7) uses much from the earlier writers, so its writings make an excellent starting point for study. These and other works would give the reader a greater understanding of the principles involved should they wish to enlarge upon what is given here. For those who want to go deeper into Cabbala the works of the following writers and teachers works will not disappoint. Z'ev ben Shimon Halevi (Warren Kenton) provides an excellent groundwork in the subject, as will the works of Gareth Knight (including other subjects), Gershom G. Scholem (Professor of Jewish Mysticism) and Dion Fortune. Omission from this short list does not imply criticism, today the lists of such works are now great and I have not read them all.

## THE HEBREW ALPHABET

'The Hebrew characters have marks of numbers attributed to them far more excellent than any other language, since the greatest mysteries lie in the Hebrew letters, as is handled concerning these in that part of Cabbala which we call Notaricon.

Now the principle Hebrew letters are in number twenty–two, whereof five have various other certain figures in the end of a word, which, therefore, they call the five ending letters, which, being added to them aforesaid, make twenty-seven; which being then divided into three degrees, signify units, which are the first degree; tens which are the second; and hundreds, which are in the third degree.'

'The divine order of the celestial numbers, impressed upon them by the ideas of the divine mind by means of the soul of the world, and the sweet harmony of those celestial rays; signifying, according to proportion, super–celestial intelligence's, which can no other way be expressed than by the marks of numbers, letters, and characters; for material numbers and figures can do nothing in the mysteries of hidden things, but representatively by formal numbers and figures, as they are governed and informed by intelligence's and divine enumeration's, which unite the extremes of the matter and spirit to the will of the elevated soul, receiving (through great affection, by the celestial power of the operator) a virtue and power from God, applied through soul of the universe; and the observation of celestial constellations to a matter fit for a form, the mediums being disposed by the skill and industry of the magician.' These two sections are quoted from *The Magus*: Barrett.

It is now time to look at the Hebrew alphabet with its equivalent and more familiar Latin, along with the numerical value, power and the descriptive meaning of the letters. Sometimes these diagrams are altered to fit the personal philosophy of a writer or teacher. For example, one writer gives the letter 'E' the same numerical value as 'A' or Aleph, which is '1' and places the letters together. 'O' can be found as can 'I' and this choice must always be the readers. A good teacher would explain their views and reasons for these changes. The diagram given here does not have the letter 'E' listed, it is simply an earlier listing and the one that I am used to.

My teacher was an associate and friend of Aleister Crowley. Although she was never a member of the **Golden Dawn**, much of her early teaching was influenced by this particular School, many teachers and pupils of her period were. It is natural that students after a time 'find their own voice,' which will have some variations from their teacher but if the teaching was sound there will still be a stable thread running through it. This 'thread' is not broken often and if it is, it is more like found running parallel with the subject than running away from it or breaking with it completely. Sometimes there is a feeling that to prove a separate individualityidentity people have to change things to show this, even when it is unnecessary — if you have been given a good ship why sink it? This does not mean your 'ship' cannot evolve into something bearing your own individual stamp this is natural and a tribute to those who teach or guide you.

Pupils more often than not start their initial studies by taking what they are given and trusting the teacher in what they say. If the teacher is good, this will serve them well and what they learn can be used as a foundation on which to build their future efforts. The Hebrew diagram used in the School is the one found in the papers of the Golden Dawn and in many other Schools. It has served me well for a long time now even before I joined the School or knew of the Schools existence after all, this diagram was not exactly a close kept secret.

Let us discuss briefly the systems used by the Hebrews to interpret the hidden meaning believed to be encoded within the Divine Words of Scripture and such books have now enjoyed quite a flowering and here is not the place to discuss them. It was long assumed that the letters and words of Scripture had an vital Spirit and essence at their concealed heart, which had to be discovered and decoded. Cabbalists briefly used three main methods (there are others) to discover this concealed or secret meaning. Gematria, Notaricon and Temurah and we do not use the last two coded scripts because they use intricate procedures of abbreviation, substitution and transposition, not used in this work.

In Cabbala, Notaricon uses the abbreviation of words by using the initials and the finals of another word or the initial letters of a sentence are combined to form a word. These methods appear to have as their chief aim abbreviation, brevity and hidden elements.

Word exchange based upon numerical values is the basis of the Temurah system. Some regard the cryptograms of Temurah the most complicated and this can involve, according to strict rules, an interchange of up to twenty-five letters. These systems can be quite mind bending and are mentioned to show the reader there is a vast field of learning, study and material regarding scripts and alphabets well outside the range of this work for their investigation if they wish to investigate them. The study is there should they wish to go further than they find here.

We will be making part–use of the fact that every Hebrew letter has a number assigned to it by which the letters of a word can be converted into their numerical power and the word into its numerical power by adding these together. Here it has only been modified on three minor points where an alternative letter was numerically represented twice and apart from this, it is identical with the original.

Gematria (as said) is a Caballistic system of interpreting the **Bible** that consists of in finding the numerical value of a word or words — the twenty–two letters of the Hebrew alphabet each has a numerical value — and substituting another word whose numerical value is the same to the one to be replaced, an example was given in **The Link or Jacob's Ladder**, we repeat it here:

'The Hebrew word for ladder, **sulam** is made up of the letters S–**samekh** (60) + L–**lammed** (30) + M–**mem** (40)= 130, the same numerical value as (Mount) Sinai= S–**samekh** (60) + I–**yod** (10) + N–**nun** (50) + I–**yod** (10)= 130 that was on 'the ladder' of Mount Sinai that Moses climbed to met his when God who and Moses listened. This gives one interpretation of Jacob's Ladder and it is said it represents the giving of the Torah on Mount Sinai and the angels who 'ascend and descend.' Moses could go to the highest point with Aaron going about halfway up the mountain (=ladder).' How far up you can climb is dependant upon the individuals highest personal 'rung' or how far you have extended your ladder' and more often than not the stage of progress may be found represented in symbolism by that rung of the ladder reached at a certain period or the figuratiave emblems displayed on a road or bridge, etc.

We will be finding the numerical value of words but we will not substituting another word, so it may be more accurate to say we follow Gematria in part. To use the table for the original Hebrew would require a knowledge of writing and reading Hebrew and to know which of the correct letters to employ and which of the alternatives to use, when and where. Most of the time for our work, we use a transliteration of the Hebrew to give numerical values into English.

As discussed in the chapter *Jacob's Ladder* from the Hebrew letter Beth (= house) we get the name Bethel (Beth= 'house' + el= 'God' or 'of God') meaning 'The House of God.' I have already mentioned 'el' is often found as a suffix of the angelic names as with the Archangels Michael, Raphael, Uriel and Gabriel, because they are 'of God.'

In the table, there are one or two unfamiliar variations that are not difficult to use. First, there are the combinations 'Aa' or 'Ngh' (16) or 'Tz' (18). It is true that today we will find little use for such combinations in languages, we must leave them in their position because some of the older words, invocations, angels, spirits or demons among other things sometimes use them, as with the example 'Tz,' shown later.

In most of today's Christian or given names, Surnames or family names there may be little use for the combination Aa–Ngh –70 in English, but the original language was not English but Hebrew. There could occasions however when it may be needed for some of the ancient names, especially some that are found in Cabbalistic literature or other esoteric systems. We do not by and large change things for the sake of it because there is quite enough of that going on today without me adding to the chaos. We only want to clarify small points to make the table easier to use and understand, other than this, the changes are very small and hardly noticable.

Five letters and their finals have two positions in a word and this is why they are called 'double letters,' because they can be found in two places. Depending on where they found in the word their numerical value is different and this is not only simple, it is logical. For example the Greek character *sigma*: σ= 's' is used when the this letter is within a word, but if it is found at the end of the word then the final form is used ς= 's' (= final 's') and I am sure there are other examples that can be found in other languages.

### The Five Final Letters . . .

In the Hebrew, there are five extra letters in the diagram under the column headed 'final.' These five are K–final K; M–final M; N–final N; P–final Ph and Tz–final Tz. You will also notice they have different numerical values and two distinct outlines. Put simply 'final' means exactly what it says. The second outline given for these five pairs of letters are called 'finals' because they are placed last in a word or in the 'final' for these five letters. They are additionally marked with a star to draw attention to them but the 'star' is not used in any way. Barrett calls them 'the five ending letters'

If the first of these five characters is anywhere within the word, the single form is used with its numerical value. If the letter is found at the end the end of the word, the 'final' form of the letter is used with its numerical value and that is all there is to it.

An exception to the rule is the 'ph' combination. If you find the combination 'ph' at the beginning of a word (as in phantom) or within a word (as in typhoon), the letters are used separately. If the word actually ends in 'ph' (see example below), because the Final Ph combines these two letters with a different form and a higher numerical value of 800, you use it. Let us list these five final letters and give examples of their use, it is not difficult:

K (or C) and Final K — Kaph has the value 20 when used at the beginning or within a word, but the final K placed at the end of the word has a different form and a value of 500. For our example, we will use the word 'comic.' The initial 'c' has a value of 20, as would any 'c' found within the word. The final Kaph takes a different written form and a value of 500 only when it is found at the end of the word.

M and Final M — M has the value 40 when used at the beginning or within a word, but the Final M placed at the end of the word has a different form and a value of 600. For our example, we will use the word 'madam.' The initial 'm' has a value of 40, as would any 'm' found within the word. The final M takes a different written form and a value of 600 only when it is found at the end of the word.

N and Final N — N has the value 50 when used at the beginning or within a word, but the Final N placed at the end of the word has a differen written form and a value of 700. For our example, we will use the name Norman. The initial 'n' has a value of 50, as would any other 'n' found within the word. The final N takes a different written form and a value of 700 only at the end of the word.

P and Final Ph — P has the value 80 when used at the beginning or within a word, but the Final Ph placed at the end of a word has a different written form and a value of 800. For our example, let us take the Angel Pharzuph. You use P–80 + H–5+A–1+R–200 + final Ph with a value of 800 at the end of the name. This is because 'ph' is a final only so it can only be used as a final. The combination 'Ph' is not available for use at the beginning of a word or anywhere within a word because 'ph' is only used at the end. If you do not do this, then the name would have both the wrong numerical value and vibration. However, I cannot think for one moment why you would be transcribing the name of the Angel Pharzuph — seeing he is an Angel of Lust and a Genius of Fornication.

The last combination and double letter is Tz and Final Tz. Tz has a value of 90 when used at the beginning or within a word, but the Final Tz is only placed at the end of the word when it has a value of 900. This was a difficult word to find an example of but the modern word 'hertz' is a good example of using the 'Tz' final, which gives it a different written form and avalue of 900. This particular combination probably arises more frequently within ancient words like 'the barbarous names of evocation,' which are sometimes used in works of this nature. The name of the Intelligence of the Kamea of Mars, Bartzabel (= B–a–r–tz–a–b–(e)–l), is another example of using this obscure combination but this time the 'tz' is within the word. When the 'tz' combination occurs within the word, it takes the first value of 90 and as it does in Bartzabel. if 'tz' is was found at the end of a word it is the final Tz and takes a different written form and the second value 900. These are shown in the column headed 'Finals.' Remember the word 'final' and its meaning, and that is all there is to it —because final simply means what it says — last! The uses of the finals can only occur in five instances and we hope we have covered it all

I can almost hear you say this is all very well and I can see the important vowel 'a' but where are the other four vowels and in particular the valuable vowel 'e' as is a very useful one? The vowels are not there because the early Hebrew alphabet does not give them. In the original Hebrew, the vowels were not clearly shown and this is why Hebrew appears to miss out some of the vowels at times. The reader's attention is drawn to this discussion in Part 1 regarding the name Jehovah (a made up word) and Yahwah (the right word) and the chapter *Tetragrammaton*.

For example, take the name John. In Hebrew the name John was rendered as Yochanon (= spoken Yo–*car*–non) so we have Y(o)chan(o)n — Yod, Cheth, Aleph, Nun and Nun (final). As you can see in the early Hebrew, the name Yochanon (= John) does not have 'o'though it is sometimes found included in some Tables at Vau–6, which is the spelling of the name. Today we would use the spelling according to some later westernised tables, which does supply the missing 'O' and add the value O–Vau–6, but this is a later practise and something the reader will have to decide according to their lights and experience — no, this not evasion.

The differences were thought by some commentators to have occurred because of the different Hebrew dialects that have, as they do in most countries, very distinct tones. Israel Regardie, writing in the *Golden Dawn Papers*, considered that the dialect of the Ashkenazy of Germany and Russia gave the best transliteration into English. In Spain and the Mediterranean areas, Sephardic was the prominent dialect. Cabbala was prominent in Spain and a vast amount of the system was recorded in this area. The Golden Dawn used the Sephardic pronunciation but the pronunciation of Hebrew is academic to the present work because we do not use any Hebrew pronunciation in it so as you can see, this problem for us is academic but it shows that the problems of transliteration has been with us for some time and I feel still is.

Information is frequently given because the reader may come across the problem or ponder it and this at least attempts to make them aware that it exists but in doing so I hope I have not added still more confusion to the subject matter. This can be resolved easily by beginning with what is given here and researching the differences and alternatives if you want to go further in your studies.

This preamble will point you in the direction and that is what was intended. As always, study and experience will be the final arbiter in deciding any matter for you and taking this point we will be using the letters as given in the Table at the back of the work. All Hebrew letters have a numerical value or power and these have many uses but we are interested in one practical use. How to place a name, which has been converted into its numerical values, on a specific kamea.

Let us illustrate some names like Andy (this is used more than Andrew) rendered A–1 + N–50 + D–4 + (Y)= 55; Alan rendered A–1 + L–30 + A–1 + final N–700= 732 and Martin rendered M–40 + A–1 + R–200 + T–9 + I–10 + final N–700= 960.

Next, the addition of two female friends Pat as P–8 + A–1 + T–9= 18. We use 'Pat' even though her name is really Patricia though I can never remember anyone calling her by that name so we use the name by which she is usually known, which is a part of the full name as given at baptism for the Christian faith or 'given names' can be used.

Finally, we take the name of a friend of many long pleasant years — Mrs Mona Vincent. Mona is another founder member of the School, which of course was where I first met her. Mona is rendered M–40 + (O) + N–50 + A–1= 91 and naturally the principle is the same whatever the gender.

Certain letters, mainly vowels are not catered for in the Hebrew alphabet (some lists today include extra letters and are given values, if this is the list you use — you use them) and they are omitted but this does not mean that you cannot include the missing letters in brackets and write the name in full as shown in the relevant examples above, but they do not have a numerical value therefore, they are not included in the sigil created. We have added the numbers of the letters together in the examples to show the words numerical value, although we do not use it but remembering the example of 'ladder' and 'Sinai' given earlier.

We discussed the construction of the kameas earlier and gave the reader the numerical range of each kamea or the numbers available for use. Let us make a short list repeating the numerical range of the kameas, to save referring to the earlier list. For now, we must start dealing with the subject in greater detail. Do not let this worry you because eventually you will use it automatically and without thinking for it is not difficult. Especially the method of reducing any large number so it can be accommodated on all the kameas, even though a kamea may not have the number within its numerical range. It is a very simple method and I am sure that it will cause the reader little difficulty. As with most things it takes longer to explain than accomplish

The Kamea of the Saturn has a numerical range of 1 to 9.
The Kamea of Jupiter has a numerical range of 1 to 16.
The Kamea of Mars has a numerical range of I to 25.
The Kamea of the Sun has a numerical range of 1 to 36.
The Kamea of Venus has a numerical range of 1 to 49.
The Kamea of Mercury has a numerical range of 1 to 64.
The Kamea of the Moon has a numerical range of 1 to 81.

The above tables show the highest number available on any kamea is 81 but the *Table of the Hebrew Alphabet* shows the highest letter value in the alphabet is Tz–900 and no kamea has the number 900 within its range. What do you do if you find that you needed this letter and number? This has all been taken care of by the system a long, long time ago before anyone living now came onto the scene and we will discuss this next. If you remember the Tz–900 combination was mentioned earlier in the name Bartzabel, the Intelligence of the Kamea of Mars. What square would we use for the Tz–900 combination as this numerical value is not included in the numerical range of any of the Seven Kameas? It can be included on all the kameas using a system that is undemanding in its simplicity

This is where the 'System of Reduction' comes into operation. You reduce the figure by simply striking off the end zero until it will fit the kamea that you want to work with. If you strike off the last zero, you now have a figure of 90, but even this figure will not fit any kamea. Therefore, you strike off the second zero, which gives us the fundamental figure of 9, which fits all seven kameas.
The figures 90 and 900 are simply multiplications (shown by the number of noughts added to the fundamental root figure of 9), which is the root from it sprang and from which it still draws its power. As said, a single nought shows the root has been multiplied by ten (x10) while two noughts would show a multiplication of one hundred (x100) and so forth.
As it is with all growing things, it is the root that is important because the roots give life to what springs from it. You can trim plants, trees or hedges but carelessly cut the root and its lost for ever and this is why I have constantly stressed the need for the basics to be learnt thoroughly because they are the 'roots' of your endevours. Ignore this and for a while, you may well flourish

like the proverbial 'green bay tree' but in the end, it will all wither and give up the ghost. I have seen it happen so often and some very promising good stock was lost in the bargain — end of lecture!

Let us return to the name Alan to further illustrate this principle. It is a short name but it contains a high final number. Numerically the name Alan is A–1 + L–30 + A–1 + Final N–700= 732. The above tables tell us that none of the seven kameas go as high as 700 or have a square of that numerical value to take the the Final letter of this particular name. Therefore, we reduce 700 by the removal of the last zero, which takes it down to 70. Only one kamea has the square 70 available for use and that is the Kamea of the Moon because its range is from 1 to 81. If you wanted to put the name Alan on the Kamea of the Moon, square number 70 is available and therefore it can be used. The number 70 is not available on the remaining six kameas but the number seven is and to use this 'final letter' and the name Alan on these tables so you reduce the 70 further by the removal of the last zero to make it 7. This number is available on the remaining six kameas.

On the Kamea of the Moon the final N–700 is used by reducing 700 to 70 because this kamea has this number. On the remaining six kameas 70 does not exist so the 70 is reduced further by removing the second '0' — reducing 700 to 70 then to 7 — which will fit all the remaining six kameas and this is why it is called the — 'System of Reduction.'

So placing the name Alan on the Kamea of the Moon would start the sigil on square 1 then go to square 30, then back to square 1 and end on square 70. On the Kamea of Venus the name Alan would go from square 1, to 30, back to 1 but this time it would finish on square 7. However, we do have one more problem with this name, if Alan was to be placed on the Kamea of Saturn the value for the letter L–30 is not available but 3 is, so you 'reduce' the 30 down by removing the zero to take it down to 3. The Kamea of Saturn has a range of 1 to 9, which includes the figure 3 and that is the square you use for the Final N. The sigil for the name Alan would start on square 1, go to square 3, back again to 1 and finish on square 7.

The same reduction would apply to the Kameas of Jupiter and Mars because neither of these kameas have the numerical values 30 and 70 in their range, so they are not available. The numbers 30 and 70 would have to be reduced by removing the zero to get the numbers 3 and 7. Now they can be used on these last two kameas. For the moment, do not worry about how you mark the kamea to make your personal sigil. We will give the method and some suggestions for dealing with this later.

Let us take the letter R–200 because no kamea has a figure to the power of 200. For those kameas that have 20 on them you strike off the last zero to reduce the 200 to 20 and use the 20 square. The Kameas of Jupiter and Saturn do not have the reduced 20 because it is not included in their range. You strike off the second zero to reduce the 20 down to 2 and use that square. If the kamea will accept 20, you do not reduce it because that would be using the wrong square. If the kamea you want to use does not have 20 in its range, you reduce the 20 to 2 and you will have the right square.

If a kamea will not accept a large number, reduce the until it can be used. As said, no kamea can use 200 so it is reduced down to 20 and if the kamea can accept 20 then no further reduction is necessary. However, if it only has 2 and does not have 20, then reduce the 20 to 2 so that it can be used and really that is all there is to it.

I believe these examples are enough to demonstrate the method involved in placing names on a kamea, the System of Reduction and how to make a specific name into the sigil of a selected kamea. If it does not fall into place at once, do not worry about it, every time you use the system it will become more familiar, easier and clearer. How many times have you failed while learning something new? One day something took over and it became almost automatic and you wondered what all the fuss was about. We all had the same problem when we started but as time passes experience takes over, you stop looking at books to check the way it is done and simply do it — I do and so will you.

## NICKNAMES

Now we must take up the question of 'nick-names' because people have always been given them, I was and use them for others, most people do. The question we pose here is can they be used on your kameas. There is nothing wrong with using a diminutive of your name, providing it is a diminutive of the name you were given at birth in some way. Leo is short for Leonardo or Leonard, Pat for Patricia, Ray for Raymond, Ros for Rosalind and so forth as these I feel have a legitimate use particularly if they have frequency of use. If this applies in your case, decide if you wish to use a diminutive or your given name, I believe a diminutive of your name to be acceptable, but no nicknames please that have no connection with your name and more with your character, no matter how much it is used.

I would not use nicknames such as Crusher, Tinkerbell, Spud or any other unprintable epithets despite their frequent or affectionate use and your acceptance of them because you answer to them. Nevertheless, I recommend that they are avoided. Do not think by this I am against nicknames and remember to some these were thought to be 'Old Nick Names' or Devil names in the past.

I have had enough of these names in my lifetime, but I would not think of using one of my early names at school, even though it was complimentary and the affection of its use. It is not really my name, my sigil or signature and it is not legal really because I cannot sign anything with them. Therefore, I do not think they should be used for this particular type of work. I would not, for example, even think of addressing the Archangel Michael as 'Mike,' the Archangel Gabriel as 'Gabe' and I hope you would not think this way or contemplate its use — don't even think about it! Now let us move on to the methods of making you sigil from the kamea you will be using for your Work.

## THE CONSTRUCTION OF YOUR NAME SIGIL

When marking your sigil, which must be written as a continuous line, it is best to mark the beginning in some way to show which end is the start of the sigil. You put another mark at the end to show it is the end just as your name begins its initial letter and a final letter, doing this will show the number where the name begins and the number on which it ends. Knowing the beginning would also show the order of the numbers within the name, as your signature shows the order of the letters.

The method I use is to put a circle at the beginning of the line and a short line at right angles across the end of the line, to show where it stops. This short line across the end is not unlike a *cul-de-sac* on a map, the line across the end shows where the road ends and goes no further because it has an entrance but does not have an exit at the other end (therefore not under Janus —no through road, a deadend). The circle at the beginning shows on what square and number the line began and you follow the line to show the squares and numbers to which the sigil has moved and the line at right angles on the end shows on which square and number the sigil has ended.

Do you want to begin the sigil with a triangle or diamond and end with a small square or circle or the other way around? Fine but be consistent, so you and others in your group (if you are in one) agree and know what you are doing and your work has uniformity, choose whatever you wish that has artistic appeal. Just do not keep swapping and changing about as the mood takes you, if people can get fed up with then so can others. For obvious reasons you cannot use the same mark for both ends. I am not saying that you cannot change your symbols later to new symbols as experience, just do not keep on doing so, especially during work being done at the time.

You mark out your sigil in the unbroken order of the numbers and if this means a line has to cross over itself to get to the next number you want, then that is what it has to do. What do you do if the three numbers were in a straight line? How would you show that the line has passed over the second number? One way is that you start on the first number go to the second, make a loop in the line, a zigzag or something, which shows that this letter is included then move straight on to the third number and mark the end. The loop or mark in the line shows another number is between where the line starts and where it ends.

What do you do if you have the same letter twice in a word, which follow each other? Let us say your name was Bennet. To show the 'n' has been used twice in the middle of the word you can mark the square with two arches and the double loops will show that the letter has been used twice and consecutively, you can make an arch on one side of the line and the second on the other side. Alternatively, you could put a double circle in the square by drawing a circle and putting a smaller circle inside the larger. Devise a sign that you will repeat to show there are two consecutive letters in the square, a circle on one side of the line and another on the other like a figure of eight, equally you could drop the line at right angles before going on to show a double, consecutive letter. The main thing to remember no matter what pattern you use is this and this rule is never broken. The line has to be continuous with no breaks. Whatever you decide to use it must be guided by this strict criterion — the line must never be broken.

This does not mean you cannot lift your pen and hand from the paper to move it around. As long as the final result is an unbroken line. You can put dots on the squares you are going to use to the side of the numbers to make the sigil clear before you join your lines in sections as long as there are no breaks. If you keep in mind the idea of a railway track, it will help. If the word has five letters, it has five 'stations' and as said, you can mark their position on the map (= the numbered squares). Then connect the stations with the track (= line) using a rule, which must be continuous when it is finished, even if it was built in sections as many railways were and still are, otherwise, the train could not complete its journey from the first station to the last because the 'train' or Power cannot reach its destination and neither will you, it is these small things that are important.

Because we are dealing with the planetary angels, their planets and their numbers I repeat a small a list from *Numerology* given elsewhere before leaving this section. We will not use this information in the present work, for this is not a book of Numerology. This list is put here for reference purposes only and it may prove useful. Each of the planets in Numerology is given a number:

1= Sun; 2= Moon; 3= Jupiter; 4= Uranus; 5= Mercury;
6= Venus; 7= Neptune; 8= Saturn; 9= Mars.

One example of using the above table could be as a guide to some practitioners, that strike a small bell in their rituals as I sometimes do — a *tocsin* — to draw attention to the ceremony, in particular it can be used to attract the planet or angel who is involved by using their number, I use these from the above table. The above table may prove of use as to the number of strikes according to the planet invoked, which I use. The bell finds its place in religious ceremonies also, such at the Elevation of the Host; see also *Book 4* – Aleister Crowley. A tocsin is an 'alarm bell, Old French *toquesing*= 'an alarm bell, from *toquer*= 'to clap, to knock, to hit' — 'a sign, a mark, a bell rung as a signal.'

The last of these additional notes are to give further information that some may find value with some readers and covers the negative and positive numbers and the numbers of the four Elements: Fire, Earth, Air and Water. The positive numbers are given as one, two, five, six and nine. The negative numbers are three, four, seven and eight and we are told, 'in any matter of conflict, contest or a question as to who is master out of two people it will be found that the negative overcomes the positive.'

The numbers of the Element of Fire are one, five and nine. The numbers of the Element of Air are two and six. The numbers of the Element of Water are three and seven and finally, the numbers of the Element of Earth are four and eight and this ends the numerical notes given to add extra information to the subject matter in hand.

This ends the chapter of placing names on the kameas or making a magical symbol of names called 'a sigil,' which can be used with or, without the kamea if you choose. You must remember that a sigil of a name still carries the power of the kamea on which it was created, even though the kamea is not present. This is because the sigil is personal to the kamea and you, just as you are your parent's child. From this you will see that you can have seven planetary signatures taken from the kameas and when you are dealing with the planetary angels, you should use the correct planetary version of your name taken from the kamea of the angel. You do not have to stop at your name created on a kamea. Let us suppose that you would like a positive attribute from an angel or planet.

Find out which angel and planet has rule over the attribute you would like to draw upon. Would you like the stability, firmness or methodical ways of Saturn or the expansion, religious or philosophical ways of Jupiter? Take a suitable keyword for the angel and planet, something that you are seeking. Reduce the letters to numerical values and write them in the same way as your name on their kamea.

You could make a talisman to wear or carry with you with the keyword written on the kamea of that you are seeking. It would consist of the appropriate kamea with its 'keyword' sigil written on it. Remember at the beginning of this chapter, I told you that the kamea is 'a talisman, prayer or charm.' You can write this 'short note' as a letter-invocation in the suggested manner. Set your name as a sigil of the kamea underneath the kamea of the angel, write on the kamea what it is you seek, seal your letter and follow the recommendations already given. You are limited by your imagination, not by what is available or given here.

As I have said elsewhere, the whole process of building the system is not unlike gathering similar strands from a tangled mass of coloured wool. Every piece you find gives you more wool to work with and the more you collect, the more you can do with the material that you have gathered.

In any form of written angelic communication it is continually stressed that one of the most important items to use for those who elect to follow the system given in this work are the kameas. The kameas are not the only symbols you can use for your invocation or letter to the archangels and angels. It is, however, one of the principal symbols used and as far as this writer is concerned, the kamea should *never* be omitted because it acts like an address with the sigils, signs, symbols as additions.

The reader will find when the kameas are given in books they often have underneath them three or more symbols representing the Seal of the Planet, the Spirit of the Planet and the Intelligence of the Planet and these are useful adjuncts to use with the kamea. You do not have to use these three sigils or all of them and their omission will not invalidate any work done.

Barratt in his *Magus*, using the Kamea of Saturn for this example, tells us ' . . . are set such divine names as fill up the numbers with an intelligence, to what is good, and a spirit to bad; and out of the same numbers are drawn the seal and characters of Saturn, and of the spirits thereof, such as is beneath ascribed to the table.' Chapter 28. The pattern is the same for the remaining planets. The 'spirits thereof . . . ascribed to the table' mentioned in the above example are their names, which are given in the appropriate place.

The Intelligence's are usually regarded as equivalent to the Angels of the Sephirah, which are the Kingdoms of the Cabbalistic Tree of Life. The reader will find the intelligence's frequently referred to as 'the planetary intelligence's,' as they are here. Spirits, on the other hand, can be good or bad, but in either instance, they are always regarded as pure spirit. Whether a spirit is good or bad depends for what purpose the practitioner is using them or being used by them. 'And the spirit of jealousy came upon him . . .' *Numbers*. 5:14 as given before. A spirit is a disembodied or conscious being who is operating in people's affairs for good or ill. This is why I have always regarded the spirits with a little prudence.

The illustrations of the Seals, Intelligences and Spirits of the kamea are sometimes placed under the kamea in illustrations. However, it was thought it would make things easier by putting them on a separate page, because the choice of whether the reader uses them is a matter of personal taste. I usually add them to my work.

Some people write expansive and familiar letters. Others prefer to keep their letters precise and short, giving only essential information (= Saturn). Others are direct and get straight to the point (= Mars), one reading is enough, not unlike business or impersonal letters. Some are imaginative in form, pleasant to read (= Venus) while others are Authorative (= Sun), how they are written can be associated with the working of the planets. How you write your letters will depend upon you and in this I interfere as little as possible.

The kameas are the one thing you must put in your invocation and in this, I am inflexible because as far as I am concerned, which is why it is repeated — often. When I was younger in magic than now I regarded my kamea not unlike a manual telephone exchange where the operator plugged in the connections as it was once, even now with all our wonderful technology we can still misdial, get a wrong number or be cut off in full flow. The kamea was not unlike the angel's 'switchboard and number.'

My name sigil was regarded as the 'connection lead' between the angel and myself because it was written on their kamea and written in an order unique to them and myself on valid squares that represents my name (= sigil) and connected to those squares on their personal switchboard (= kamea). You will find your signature does not have the same form for every kamea but a different form for each kamea and angel. As already pointed out, your sigil for the Kamea of Saturn will not fit the Kamea of Mercury because the sigil would fall on squares and letters that do not belong to you or your name and so on.

I imagined the sigil of my signature as being 'plugged' into the kamea to 'make the connection' on the numbers from which it was produced and in that order and these numbers was different for each kamea. The kamea is the common meeting place where the angel and the sender of the letter–invocation could 'connect.' This is why you must be accurate and not 'dial the wrong number' and what is being attempted is precarious enough without adding to the difficulties. Now let us look at the second part of the title of this chapter, namely . . .

## THE OLYMPIAN SPIRITS AND THEIR SIGILS

The Olympian Spirits and their sigils are often used like the kameas in talismans, amulets and charms but their use is not restricted to this work any more than the kameas are. The Olympian spirits, sometimes called the 'Stewards of Heaven' were presented in a magical ritual in Latin published in Basle in the year 1575 called the *Arbatel* or the *Arbatel of Magic*. Although the writer of the work is unknown, it is thought that he may have been Italian in origin, some commentators thinking the work was influenced by Paracelsus and it is Christian in context, not Hebrew.

The size of the original work is given as nine volumes of which only one volume — the *Isagoge* — has come down to us. The title *Isagoge* is usually rendered as being 'essential instruction' by older writers. The work gives instructions for the rituals of the Olympian Spirits who dwell among the stars in the Element of Air and these Olympian spirits are said to 'govern the world.'

According to the *Arbatel of Magic,* the universe is divided into one hundred and ninety–six Olympic Provinces and ruling over these provinces are the seven Olympian Spirits. Each Olympian Spirit rules in a sequential order, a period of four hundred and ninety years.

These spirits are sometimes called the 'supreme archangels' and have natural authority over detailed regions of the material world, but when outside these spheres of duty, they perform identical work through the power of their magical expertise. For example, Och is the Olympian spirit that governs all affairs that are of a solar in nature. Materially, Och rules not only the natural formation of gold in the earth but magically and alchemically also so he has authority over the preparation of gold especially by alchemical procedures in the magic laboratory.

The Olympian spirits are thought to be privy to many of the hidden and potent procedures of magic. Many commentators regard the powers possessed by these spirits as infinite and some say they have access to all matters. The Olympic Spirits work in seven layers in multiples of seven as will be seen in the list below, which is said to show their office and powers.

Aratron, governing Saturn, rules over forty–nine provinces.
Bethor, governing Jupiter, rules over forty–two provinces.
Phaleg, governing Mars, rules over thirty–five provinces.
Och, governing the Sun, rules over twenty–eight provinces.
Hagith, governing Venus, rules over twenty–one provinces.
Ophiel, governing Mercury, rules over fourteen provinces
Phul, governing the Moon, rules over seven provinces.

We will not be going too deeply into the aspects of or become too involved into the magical aspects of the Olympian Spirits or their rituals because these are not required in the present work. We will use, optionally, the Seals of the Olympian Spirits in our invocation to the angels. How can the reader consider the Olympian Spirits the better to understand them? I have always thought of them as governors of the planet more than 'governing' the planet as is usually written.

I would express the matter this way using our level. Rome was the seat of government and the power of the Italian State (= the Angel and Ruling Planet). Herod (= the Olympian spirit) was the governor of the province of Judea acting, on behalf of the power of Rome, over this parched land of

Messiah's, Hebrew prophets, rocks and scorpions. It is obvious they are connected with the angels and planets and so can be used in conjunction with them, their hours and so on, which is how I use them.

The Seals of the Olympian Spirits are given at the end of the work and their use is optional, but I think their use strengthens the angel and planet involved with the invocation and anything that does this should be considered and studied. We have mentioned some of the matters Och has under his rule. Now let us expand the concerns of the seven Olympian Spirits. Each Olympic Spirit rules over an established number of Olympic provinces, the following is taken from old works

**ARATRON** rules those things that are ascribed astrologically to Saturn. He can petrify any living organism, animal or plant in a moment of time. He can in an instant turn coal into treasure and the reverse. He reconciles the subterranean spirits to men and gives familiars to them. He can teach alchemy, magic, medicine and can impart the secret of invisibility. He makes the barren fruitful and confirms (or can give) a long life. He is invoked in the first hour of the day on Saturday, using his symbol.

**BETHOR** governs and administers all things that are the affairs of Jupiter who is said to respond soon when he his called. In keeping with expansive Jupiter, he has at his command, 29,000 legions of spirits. In keeping with Jupiter, Bethor has command over kings, princes, dukes and the like. He can exalt the character to positions of great eminence and can provide great treasure. He can exalt to illustrious positions and he reconciles the spirits of Air to man so that they will give true answers. He can transport precious stones and compose medicines having marvellous effects. He is invoked in the first hour on Thursday, using his symbol.

**PHALEG** governs those things that are under the rule of the planet Mars. This is why Agrippa refers to him often as 'a war lord.' The persons who possess his character and blessing are raised by him to great honour in military affairs and any concerns of business. In positive magic Phaleg is one of the 'Stewards of Heaven.' He is invoked in the first hour of the day on Tuesday, using his symbol.

**OCH** oversees the affairs of the Sun who, like the other six spirits can prolong and give a healthy life. Six hundred years to be exact we are told, if a person could live that long. He can grant wisdom and good familiars. He creates perfect medicines and transforms any substance into pure metals and precious stones, which special interest and talent have earned him the name 'the prince of alchemy.' He can impart great wisdom, gives gold and 'purse gold,' he is described as 'springing with gold.' He can cause those whom he blesses 'to be worshipped as a god by the kings of the world.' He is invoked in the first hour on Sunday, using his symbol.

**HAGITH** rules the concerns of Venus and has rule over 4,000 legions of spirits. Any person blessed with his character is 'adorned with all beauty.' Hagith can transmute metals, changing copper into gold in an instant and he will give you faithful serving spirits. He is invoked in the first hour of his day, which is Friday, using his symbol.

**ORPHIEL** rules all those things that are attributed to Mercury. Orphiel gives familiar spirits, teaches all the arts and empowers those blessed by his spirit to change quicksilver into the Philosopher's Stone. He is invoked in the first hour of the day on Wednesday, using his symbol.

**PHUL** has command over all lunar interests and transmutes all metals to silver. He is called 'the lord of the powers of the moon and supreme lord of the waters' and provides you with 'spirits of water who will serve men in tangible and visible form.' He cures illness that has an excess of fluid. He is invoked in the first hour of the day on Monday, using his symbol.

There are legions of spirits (considered inferior) under the command of each of these governors who also have kings, princes, dukes, presidents and ministers under them. I have given the day of the Olympian Spirits and the magic of the Olympian Spirits is performed in the hour and day of the planet that is in correspondence with the Olympic Intelligence in keeping with usual use. I think there is enough for the reader to start their studies regarding the Olympic Spirits.

The invocation of the Governors is relatively simple and it is done in the day and hour of the planet, which has correspondence with the Olympic Intelligence as it is for the angels. There are extant prayers to use for Olympic Spirits and they are given in several works, upon which you make your judgement as I have mine, so repetition here would serve no purpose.

The diagram, showing the ***Characters of the Olympian Spirits*** is at the end of the book. As always, do not attempt to be photographic in your rendering of the sigils of the Olympian Spirits or any other sigils and symbols found do the best to can to make them close to the originals but the main thing to remember is that they are able to be recognized. They have many variations in printed works as the reader will find, just do the best that you can.

The perfumes of the Olympian Spirits have been modified and the animal parts of the original have been omitted. I have written earlier in the first publication of the book concerning incense (1980) now being prepared for future publication. If animal parts are given in any incense recipes, replace them with the albumen of an egg. This is representative of life and it has the added benefit of binding the materials together much better, which is much more acceptable all around.

Barratt, in his ***Magus***, using the Kamea of Saturn as the example tells us ' . . . are set such divine names as fill up the numbers with an intelligence, to what is good, and a spirit to bad; and out of the same numbers are drawn the seal and characters of Saturn, and of the spirits thereof, such as is beneath ascribed to the table.' Chapter.28. The pattern is the same for the remaining planets. The 'spirits thereof . . . ascribed to the table' mentioned in the above example, are their names, which are given in the appropriate place.

The Intelligence's are usually regarded as equivalent to the Angels of the Sephiroth, which are the Kingdoms of the Cabbalistic Tree of Life. The reader will find the Intelligence's frequently referred to as 'the planetary intelligence's,' as they are here. Spirits, on the other hand, can be good or bad, but in either instance, they are always regarded as pure spirit. Whether a spirit is good or bad depends for what purpose the practitioner is using them. 'And the spirit of jealousy came upon him . . .' ***Numbers*** 5:14 is but one example of those found throughout. A spirit is a disembodied or conscious being that is operating in people's affairs for good or ill.

# THE MAGIC SCRIPTS

It now seems rather absurd to call some of the magical alphabets 'secret' any more and I have given here a small selection of these scripts, though enough for what it needed of the best known and authentic of them. My studies of these scripts show there may well be some three hundred or more on record and there are enough books to serve the curious should they want them.

The fact that there are a large number of scripts could suggest that many of them may possibly be spurious. Several of them do seem to be based upon others in the group, enough so to be regarded as almost copies because the variations found are so small. Some scripts are obviously the invention of a particular School wishing to keep its secrets, which may make them 'secret' rather than 'magical.' Some do not seem to have been derived from a sacred source or contact and some of them are definitely the creation of an over–inflamed medieval mind.

Some of the scripts have stood the test of time with their authenticity recognized and regarded as proven. They are accepted by many including myself, which naturally is the reason for their being here and other works of this nature. It is the job of the writer to filter out to the best according to their competence and experience, things thought to be of dubious origin, without bias and if a bias is shown, it should be declared I feel. One of the main alphabets used is the Hebrew and the Runes are particularly suited for those of Northern European descent who by their birth have an affinity with these particular Gods and their traditions. Therefore, they naturally and instinctively feel comfortable with them.

Quite a few scripts in early works are found with the overall name 'Chaldean' but many of these appear to have little in common with the Chaldeans of history or their cuneiform script. It often had more to do with medieval terminology because the term 'Chaldean' was often found synonymous with the word 'astrologer and astrology,' which may account for its frequent use. The reader should remember that when modifications are acknowledged to exist in some of the scripts then only one from the group is selected for use and that choice naturally will be the one that I use myself — bias declared.

Many magical scripts are obviously derivative of the Hebrew, while others are connected with Greek and Roman models, apart from the runes. Several scripts used in this chapter are found in the works of Henry Cornelius Agrippa in his *Three Books of Occult Philosophy*. I have an original copy of the English translation published in London in 1651. This source book is frequently met with today, as in a facsimile copy of *The Magus or Celestial Intelligencer* of Francis Barratt, originally of 1801, however, these works are now available in paperback.

One of the questions frequently asked is 'Can I write my letter to the Angels in English?' The simple answer to this is yes you can if you wish. You can use whatever language is your mother tongue and the one that are most familiar with and understand best. Nevertheless, you should always try to use the correct magical scripts, signs, symbols and sigils as others have done in the past and there are several answers to this question but I feel the most important one is continuity.

Each of the seven planets of antiquity has their own personal sigil and charms of the planet were customarily made by engraving the seal or sigil of the planet on a disc of metal that was appropriate to the planet. This work was usually done at a time when the power of that planet was exercising its greatest influence for good and not when it was being adversely aspected by other planets that would lessen the good effects. The charm was worn to acquire the help or influence of the genius of the planet and to give the wearer protection and assistance against evil influences.

One of the main reasons for using magical scripts is the source and origin of the scripts, where the scripts are said to have come from and by whom they were given. For example, if you made contact with a spiritual entity, you were happy with and trusted the contact and the spiritual entity gave you a set of signs, sigils and some scripts through which they said you could make future contact and communicate with them, would you use them or reject them? The form of the letters has a special vibration, which is stronger in combination. Some commentators regard each letter as a sigil in the meaning of a small picture or image and these sigils were thought to carry a philosophical and inner meaning that goes beyond the boundaries of the given image.

The word sigil has been used throughout this work, particularly so in the chapter *Your Letter or Invocation to the Angels* where the word is further explained. In the chapter on *The Kameas in Angelic Use,* you are shown how to convert your name into a sigil, which is a single design containing the letters of your name and often constructed by using a kamea or other designs. This sigil is, therefore, personal to you or those with the same name.

The word *sigil* has a special meaning in works of this character and astrology that rarely seems to appear in other forms of writing and has already been discussed. If you regarded the characters of the scripts as sigils more than letters of an alphabet, this may perhaps be better to aid understanding. They are already charged with power that has to be released by correct use, which means precisely for the purpose for which they were created.

For example, there is little point of trying to open the door of the planet Jupiter using the 'key' of the planet Saturn. First, it would not fit so you would be wasting your time, but even if it did fit, what Jupiter gives, Saturn invariably takes. Jupiter and Saturn bring the opposing principles of limitation and expansion and it is not that they are enemies and cannot work together; they just work in different way and use different methods. However, if the influence of each planet is balanced then the common sense they bring is of great help. Little point in having an exhilarating high–speed car without having a brake to bring it safely to a halt. A balanced approach often produces results — I do not think this is the first time that this has been mentioned.

Certain numbers and their combination were held to possess magical power because they represented divine and creative mysteries. The same principles hold true for magical scripts and their correct use, which is why they should not be taken lightly or used indiscriminately. The blending of letters is important in all languages. Words vibrate to patterns, if they did not we would not be able to recognize them. The name Len has three letters as has Leo, both are male names and the first two letters are the same, but Len lacks the final 'o' of Leo so I would not answer to it because the sound tells me this name does not belong to me.

I have long felt that this is one of the prime difficulties and at times a real and present danger, inherent in dealing with the gods, the magical names and invocations, particularly of another culture. Every nation has its Group Soul and Mind and the Group Mind is the gateway leading to the Group Soul.

It is not that a person comes from this place or that place because this has absolutely nothing to do with the matter. It is a traditional and natural way of thinking that places someone. Not because they are regarded as 'outsiders' or 'them and us' and this applies to us all. None of the above precludes contact, cooperation, co–existence or amity in any way.

Names and vibrations in another tongues can be confused by the user, unless they are highly skilled in that particular language. Therefore, who are they summoning, what are they invoking? Often there is something missing even in the fundamental tone in the original and a native speaker would know the words were being pronounced wrong.

When I visited Madeline at Torrington Place, she told me that early in her studies, being very hungry and having very little money when she and her partner started the School invoked for 'some fish'. An hour later, she said a neighbout arrived with a present of two fish — two goldfish — and they had to spend their last coins to feed them, but they did see the funny side of it.

In this flat in London, there was clause in the lease that said nothing had to be changed or altered in any way. Yet, when you called and looked up from below in the street, theirs was the only flat in the block that had beautiful stained glass windows when the lights were on, which were more often than not they were. It was great fun when the landlord called because he nearly took the bell off the wall. Madeline would open the windows and sweetly say she would be down.

The landlord would rush up the stairs while lecturing them on the unauthorised changes they had made and Madeline would still be sweet, agreeable and charming but when he walked through the open front door — nothing! While she was slowly going down, the 'stained glass' from the windows was removed, beautifully painted on acetate sheets that hung on the curtain rail, weighted at the bottom to keep them straight. They had already been rolled up and hid behind the big cushions on the sofa and there was nothing there, no holes had been drilled or marks made.the landlord never worked it out though we used to see him outside checking at times.

This does have something to do with the angels because they were of the four Archangels Michael, Gabriel, Raphael and Uriel and painted in glass paints as given in the pentagram chapter. This is here to let the reader know that our magical studies were not all straight-laced and deadly serious and neither were the angels, sometimes when I look in the mirror I think — 'God, they must have a sense of humour.' Let us remind the reader of an example already given regarding the correct use of the voice and the pronunciation we were discussing above concerning the legend of the Patriarch Moses, mentioned elsewhere.

The way we used the magical scripts in this work gives everyone who uses them equal advantage because the script is not required to be spoken. Written words have no possible mispronunciation unless spoken—misspelling is possible but that can be corrected by writing the script in draft form to get it right, which is why this is recommended. The spoken word is like an arrow, once fired (or said) it is not capable of being withdrawn or called back. This means everyone can use the written magical scripts because it is only required that we write them accurately — we do not having to pronounce them accurately.

In the past, learned people used Latin for their books, writing and the exchange of ideas because other educated people and scholars could read and understand what was written no matter what their native language. This of course is the main principle behind *Esperanto*. We are told today by some 'that Latin is a dead language' and if this is so then so is a great deal of the English and other languages because it seems impossible to avoid this 'dead' language, which is still having so much to say for itself.

The magical scripts can be thought of as a method of communication between two distinct spheres of operation and evolution, to be used on the 'middle ground' mentioned in Part 1, where the two kingdoms meet and merge and magical scripts are like a 'middle ground language.' They can be regarded as 'diplomatic scripts.' I have long thought there could well be seven true scripts one script for each of the Seven Angels and Planets of the Ancient Knowledge I have included four of them in the list. The Theban, Passing of the Rivers, Malachim and the Celestial as these would without doubt be included for consideration in such a scheme.

The magical scripts require concentration to use them because of their unfamiliarity, which is another practical reason for using them. These are special scripts with a special 'vibration' and should be only used for this purpose or a similar exercises.

Let us list the scripts we will use. There are nine scripts in all given in the chapter *The Kameas in Angelic Use*. The scripts listed below will be found the end of this chapter:

THE THEBAN SCRIPT (1531).
THE 'PASSING OF RIVERS' OR THE TRANSITUS FLUVII (1531)
THE MALACHIM SCRIPT (1531).
THE CELESTIAL SCRIPT (1531).
THE CABBALA OF THE NINE CHAMBERS OR 'AIQ BEQER.'
THE ROYAL CYPHER SCRIPT (1877?)
ENOCHIA — THE ENOCHIAN SCRIPT (1583)
THE HEBREW ALPHABET. (AGELESS)

These scripts are more than adequate for the work in hand. We have not exhausted all the scripts available, but as said at the beginning of the chapter there are well over three hundred scripts and to discuss them all would need another book.

The *Enochian Alphabet* recorded and presented by Dr. John Dee and Edward Kelley and it is mentioned in Part 1. I would consider this a script of all the Angels, which can be used right to left. This is why it is often called the 'Angelic Script' and the language of Enochia is very powerful. The alphabet and language has been discussed in greater detail in *Gmicalzoma — An Enochian Dictionary* (1972 – first edition; 1992 enlarged and new edition further enlarged, 2002 *Authors OnLine*). I think this script should be used with great respect, much as you using a very sharp knife that seems at times to have a mind of its own. I feel it is definitely not a script for trivial things, careless use or on impulse, but neither are all the other things that can be dangerous, if made use of without caution — electricity, cars, fire, petrol, knives, pointed sticks, gas and so forth, they all require careful use.

Look at the diagram that gives you the first four scripts at the rear of the book. These four scripts are the Theban Script, the Celestial Writing, the Writing called Malachim and the Writing called the the Passing of the Rivers. The first of these reads from left to right and has already been transliterated into the Latin alphabet in the Agrippa work. The remaining three scripts are written from right to left and given the names of the Hebrew alphaet and you can take these names from and translate them from the Hebrew alphabet already supplied in the same section.

The Hebrew forms are written from right to left, but I have seen them written (by those not of the Hebrew faith) from left to right. Try to master the correct way (right to left) but if you choose one or the other, perhaps it would be best to remain with it. Remember that the Hebrew, in common with other early alphabets, had no vowels and this may account why (commented on by other writers) that alphabets were sometimes found combined, even the Greek alphabet has numerals connected with its letters. The following four scripts are among the most famous and reliable as far as the writer is concerned. They appeared in the *Three Books of Occult Philosophy of Agrippa* of 1531. These were reproduced in Barret's The Magus in 1851 and this put them before a wider public. Now let us look at these four scripts.

One of the most popular scripts used for letter–invocations is the Theban Script and I was taught to use this script especially for the Archangel Gabriel and all types of lunar work. I find no fault with this and do, but you do not use it only for this archangel and planet. Teachers have their reasons for doing things but they do not always pass their reasoning on to those they teach. I would suggest in the initial stages you use it for all matters under this particular archangel and planet and see how matter's progress for you. The Theban Script is to magical scripts what frankincense is the incense — it is a good script to use if you have any doubts about which script to use, because it can be used with confidence or offence for all sources.

We have already touched upon the Theban Script, which is perhaps one of the most celebrated of all the Magical Scripts and it appears in Agrippa. We have said above the Theban script is one of the safe scripts because it offends none and if you are at loss which of the scripts to use for a particular Angel, use the Theban Script. It only needs me to repeat that even if a Script is suggested for a particular Angel, the other Angels can use it. I am not suggesting exclusivity to one source by giving an example of use. A magical script may be found under more than one Element and this is not a mistake. For example, the Malachim Script will be found under the Elements of Earth and Fire, because it is happy with both.

The Malachim Script and the Runes work well with the Archangel Uriel and the Angel Cassiel because they both hold sway over the northern quarter of the planet. The Archangel Uriel has this quarter and Aquarius, while the Angel Cassiel has the Sign of the Goat, which is also the Sign of the Zodiac for the God of Nature Pan. This script is good for the Fire and Earth Angels and the Northern quarter is Earth. The Element of Earth is used for the Angel Anael the Angel of the Sign of Zodiac, Taurus. The Archangel Raphael is Angel for the Sign of Zodiac, Virgo and the Angel Cassiel is the Angel for the Sign of the Zodiac, Capricorn.

The Passing the Rivers is a good script for signs that are ruled by the Element is Water. This script, like the Theban Script, is another of the famous alphabets, obviously related to the Hebrew Script. It has various names in Occult works including *Transitus Fluvii* or Crossing the River Script and our title. As with the Malachim Script, this script has small variations, but we have used the Agrippa of 1531 also given by Barratt, not the later versions with their minor additions. Usually given over the Element of Water so this can be used for the Archangel Gabriel is the angel for the Sign of the Zodiac, Cancer. The Angel Samael is the angel for Sign of the Zodiac, Scorpio the second Water sign and the Angel Sachiel is the angel for the Sign of the Zodiac, Pisces

The Malachim Script is one of the scripts that seem to have been obtained from a Cabbalistic tradition. The reader will notice two symbols for the letter 's' in this script and this is not an error. The first symbol is given by Agrippa in 1531, while the second was recorded by Bartolozzi in 1675 — *Biblioteca Magna Rabbinica*. There is nothing to show that the token is wrong, I use the Agrippa but this is personal. The Malachim Script appears to work well with the Element of Fire. The Element of Fire has three Angels and all the Elements have three Angels. The Angel Samael is the Angel for the Sign of the Zodiac, Aries. The Archangel Michael is the Angel for the Sign of the Zodiac, Leo and the Angel Sachiel is the Angel for the Sign of the Zodiac, Sagittarius.

The Celestial Script, again scripts in this class have a strong resemblance to the Hebraic writing. A number of these scripts are called 'angelic, celestial, even super celestial' and they can be found in some texts. Some versions follow the Roman alphabet but the script given here follows Agrippa, which is the best known and used of the group. It was used in many Schools. It is suggested for the Element of Air so this can be used for the Archangel Raphael the Angel for the Sign of the Zodiac Gemini. The Angel Anael is the Angel for the Sign of the Zodiac, Libra and the Archangel Uriel is the Angel of the Sign of the Zodiac, Aquarius.

The Cabbala of the Nine Chambers can be used with all the Angels as can the Royal Arch Cypher and no particular Angel's or elements are suggested for their use. In operation, these two scripts work much the same, so the instructions for using one can be used for the other. The Nine Chambers uses the Hebrew alphabet and has the five final letters. This can be used as a magical script because it is firmly based in Hebrew and is used in the same way as the Hebrew alphabet an alphabet that deserves our respect. The Aiq Beker can be regarded as a coded method of using the Hebrew alphabet.

The Royal Arch Cypher differs from the Cabbala of the Nine Chambers because it uses the Roman alphabet instead of the Hebrew as its foundation. It is similar in use to the Aiq Beker because a symbol represents the required letter, within a representation of the chamber in which the letter is found. This has led some (not unreasonably to think this script may be used for privacy but its use for this work does not seem to have been proven wrong though I feel it is not a powerful script — personal bias.

The Enochian Script is a special alphabet that can be used for all the Angels. However, I like to use it particularly for the Archangel's Michael and Uriel as they appeared frequently to Dr. John Dee and Edward Kelly, though so did the Archangel Gabriel. These two Archangels are powerful angels and the Enochia language is a powerful script and I consider it should be used only for very important things in your life because it is not a language that should misused and ignorance is not a defence. This opinion is not meant to restrict the reader but it is meant to apply the brakes to any fanciful use of it. This script, like the Hebrew, can be written from right to left. The above two Angels are recorded quite often in the *De Heptarchia Mystica* of 1582, while other entries in their records, mention the Angel Anael. Dee and Kelly have been given an accounting in the chapters *First Things First* in Part 1 and *Your Letter or Invocations to the Angels* in this section, Part 2.

I feel I should mention the runes, which are fascinating symbols as the amount of books written about them show. I do not intend to add much to them because this is not the subject of this work. One general statement regarding them seems to be agreed by all — 'their origins are obscure' but in the mythology of the northern races they were given to Odin (or Wodin) because of his voluntary sacrifice on Yggdrasil, the World Tree. They are one of the earliest alphabets used among the Gothic tribes and were often used in divination.

It is thought the word may have been derived from the Gothic *runa*= 'secret' or the High German *raunen, runa*= 'to whisper, a secret council.' The Anglo–Saxon gives *rún*= 'a rune, a mystery' and this is in keeping with the Icelandic *rún*= 'rune, a secret.' Middle English *roun, round*= 'to whisper.' The rune symbols are easy to find if you want to use them.

There is little doubt that the runes and rune–magic were used by the Scandanavians as rune wands show. These wands were made of willow with runic characters inscribed upon them in magical rites. The use and transliteration of the runes is no longer a mystery and if the reader wishes to know or use them, there will be little difficulty in this. The alphabet is easy to find tranlated into the Latin alphabet.

The Hebrew alphabet has already been given in the chapter regarding the **Kameas in Angelic Use** so it is not repeated here. Again, I stress that Hebrew is a sacred alphabet and should always be treat with the respect it merits. It is an all–embracing script as some scripts are and can be used for all the angels, immaterial of rank or station, as it has in the past. As already said, the Hebrew alphabet is definitely an alphabet that should be used with care and treat with respect, especially when it is being used for sacred matters because it is a holy script. I cannot stress this enough because it has a long history and the ways of using it in the past more or less demand this. The reader may ask am I suggesting there could be consequences from misuse of this script for Work of this nature. I would not know because I have never misused any scripts other than with respect. I recommend that the reader does the same and I can only offer the advice to the reader but I cannot make the reader take it.

The **Sepher Yetsirah** — the **Book of Creation** — sometimes obscure but it is held to 'describe anything' such as how God created the world. It was created by numbers and letters from one to ten combined with the twenty–two letters of Hebrew, these are 'the foundation of all things. God created and 'revealed the letters'and he 'hewed them, combined them, weighed them, interchanged them and through them fashioned the sum total of creation, all were created from them as everything that was yet to be created.

The characteristic method of writing the Hebrew alphabet should be noted and this method of writing should be used if possible. Hebrew it is written and read from the right to left. Apart from the method of managing the Hebrew alphabet 'finals,' using the scripts requires little if any explanation. The English words are transcribed into the script you wish to use. Some have missing letters according to our alphabet, particularly those that appear based upon the Hebrew. This aspect of the Hebrew has alrcady been discussed in the chapter dealing with the **Kameas in Angelic Use**, to which the reader is referred. Often you can substitute another word that may not require the letter and here your ingenuity is required to overcome the difficulty. This is something that will not be difficult for crossword puzzle fans but it is not a major obstacle to working with the scripts.

The first script that may require some clarification is the code called the Cabbala of the Nine Chambers or the Aiq Bekir. This latter name is taken from the order of the three Hebrew letters in the top line, in the first and second chambers (from the right). Remember we are reading as the Hebrew is written from right to left and not left to right as is usual for us. In the first chamber there is Aleph (= A), Yod (= I) and Qoph (= Q), then Beth (= B), Kaph (= K) and Resh (= R), you have (without the some vowels) the name Aiq B(e)k(e)r.

This order was regarded as significant in the pattern of the sigils and symbols from the names of the planetary Spirits. If you look at each chamber, you will see it contains three numbers that consist of units, tens and hundreds. In the first chamber, this starts with one, ten and one hundred, in the second chamber two, twenty and two hundred and so on to the ninth chamber. We use this script to add power to what we write and achieve a certain amount of privacy to something that is personal and confidential. Your work regarding the angels is not a three–ring circus where all are invited to buy tickets, witness the performance and applaud. As secret codes go, the 'code' is not difficult and it would probably take an experience code breaker all of five minutes to unravel.

We use a mark for the letter and the shape of the chamber in which it is found, to write our angelic letter, look at the diagram at the rear of the work while you read this section so you can understand it better. The first diagram gives the original scheme that uses the Hebrew letters. The second diagram gives the Hebrew letters replaced by the English equivalent. All you do is to replace the letters with a dot or some other consistent mark to show which of the letters in the chamber you mean. A maximum of three letters per chamber, one mark per letter to show which letter it is being used in a chosen square.

If you want the first letter in the chamber, you have to show which chamber you want by writing its shape. You then indicate the first letter by making one mark. For the second letter from the right to the left, you would put two marks and if it is the third letter from the right, you would put three marks. Remember to read from the right in the Hebrew manner, not from the left as we do in the West or you will show the wrong letter.

Only one chamber has four sides and that is in the centre chamber. The four corner chambers have only two sides that are like the letter 'L.' The four middle chambers on the outside have three sides, like the letter 'U.' The top chamber points upwards, one to the left and one the right, while the last of the chambers point downwards, like a 'U' upside down.

The distinctive form of each chamber is because the diagram does not have an outer border. If a border was put around the diagram, all the chambers would have four sides and look the same and if all the chambers were square, we would not know which chamber was being used or what letter was meant. The lines or 'chambers' of the diagram looks like our game of 'noughts and crosses,' and that is how it must be kept. The diagram shows this better than describing it because this is always lengthy, most descriptions are — while pictures and illustrations are not.

Let us use some examples. If you want the letter 'n' then you would draw the centre chamber, which is a square with four sides. In this you put two marks, dashes, dots, circles or what you have chosen for your marker, just be consistent with your symbol, which would show you want the second letter from the right hand side of the middle chamber.

If you want the letter 'a,' this would be the top right hand chamber, written like a conventional 'L' with one mark in it. If you wanted 'P' this would be in the centre chamber of the bottom rank, which has three sides and is written like an upside down 'U.' In this chamber you would place two marks to show it was the second letter from the right that was wanted and so forth. You can see it is not difficult.

In this script, you still use the five finals if they appear at the end of a name or any other word, with the Hebrew alphabet. So if the name ended with an 'm' that would be the 'final m,' this letter is in the last chamber to the left of centre on the second line. The required square would be written like the letter 'u' on its side with the opening to the left and in this you would place three marks to show the 'final m' position. One mark in this chamber would indicate the letter 'o/u/v,' while two marks would denote the letter 's.' Apart from using the Hebrew alphabet or transposing these symbols to the Roman alphabet, you write the words as usual. If you want to keep to the spirit of the system you would write your words and sentences from right to left but some use left to right if you wish. Now let us take a look at the Royal Arch Cypher.

The Royal Arch Cypher Script has a similar arrangement as the Nine Chambers Script and almost mirrors it in shape and use. It is used in much the same way but it is easier because it is based upon the Roman alphabet and so naturally reads from right to left. This script contains most of the letters I am using here and it does not use any final letters. Use 'c' for 'k' and 'j' for 'i' 'u' and 'v' could be used for either because the context will tell you what the writer intended, as it often is in shorthand and these letters are often found close in alphabets.

The Royal Arch Cypher has the 'noughts and crosses' frame but withonly two letters per chamber not three and there are four extra chambers in the Royal Arch Script because the Roman alphabet normally has more letters (26) than the Hebrew (22) though a few letters are missing. The extra letters are placed within a large cross that has only one letter per chamber. In the Royal Arch Cypher, if you want the first letter in the chamber you only draw the chamber with nothing inside. If you want the second letter, you draw the chamber and add one symbol. For example, if you want 'e' you would draw an 'L' shape only, but if you wanted 'f' then you would draw the 'L' shape with a single symbol in place. Often a heavy dot or short down stroke is used with this alphabet as the reader may find in some works, but this does not limit you to the same. Alternatively, you can draw the required chamber and put one mark in for the first letter with two marks to show the second letter is being used and as long as it is clear and you are consistent, you can use either method.

The letters in the large X are dealt with in several ways and the method suggested for this work is given in diagram of the script. As said, one of the main uses of this code appears to be privacy, this is why this script is sometimes found grouped in the 'secret scripts 'rather than the' magical and this is where I feel it should in fact be. There are many of these scripts used for this purpose and I thought that at least one reliable example should be included from this particular group.

The Cabbala of the Nine Chambers and the Magical Scripts can all be used to code your name or anything else in the language of the Powers, having the added advantages of keeping your affairs and study private. The best way of keeping such matters private has always been not to put them on public display, which regularly invites discussion and sometimes argument. Some people flaunt their studies and appear to invite discussion and/or argument. This shows they do not seek any privacy and in truth wish to draw attention to themselves. I have some friends of many long years who still do not know of these studies to which some appear to have varying degrees of antagonism or indifference or that I have written a few books. I feel it is totally unnecessary to say anything.

It makes me wonder what is the true purpose of the contemplation of the former. Is it the genuine study of the Arcane Teachings or the self–aggrandisement they think such studies confers on them. The word 'Arcane' and 'Arcanum' means 'secret, a mystery' and this should surely preclude overt show and public statements. This unashamed soliciting is often done to secure the awe afforded them by the ill–informed and gullible regarding such matters — I think both are easily pleased and quite candidly — they deserve each other.

# THE TABLES OF ANGELIC AND PLANETARY HOURS

'To everything there is a season, and a time to every purpose under the heaven.
A time to be born, and a time to die.
A time to plant, and a time to pluck up that which is planted.
A time to kill, and a time to heal.
A time to break down, and a time to build up.
A time to weep, and a time to laugh;
A time to mourn, and a time to dance;
A time to cast away stones, and a time to gather stones together;
A time to embrace, and a time to refrain from embracing;
A time to keep and a time to cast away;
A time to rend, and a time to sew;
A time to keep silence, and a time to speak;
A time to love, and a time to hate;
A time of war, and a time of peace . . . and so on.'
*Ecclesiates* 3:1-9.

There is a correct time for all things and when things go wrong in our lives, it is quite often the result of bad timing. This is why we frequently hear it said that the secret of success is 'he was in the right place at the right time.' Many people are often in the 'right place' but at the wrong time — they know 'where' to be but not 'when' to be. We know the 'timing' of our close friends, relatives and family. When they are at work, home for lunch and the time that they usually go to bed and we adjust our contacts with them accordingly. We work with their time and not against them, unless something unusual crops up. Our dealings with them are successful for the most with them.

Knowing these facts does not always assure success because they may not be available due to unforeseen circumstances. They may have gone out for the evening or decided not to answer the telephone to be undisturbed. There are many elements of the puzzle to fit together to try to make everything successful. You can hardly give the angels a ring to see if they are at home, as you can family and friends, nor can you speak to them or call around to see them to discuss your affairs.

Shops are open at certain hours and days. These times are displayed and if you want to do business with them, it must be done when the premises are open at their times for business. If we try outside these hours, we will not succeed. We have to try to get the timing right, particularly so if it is something important. A similar principle applies equally to any attempt at angelic communication — the timing is all. Shakespeare as usual is succinct regarding such matters. In the much quoted lines from *Julius Caesar*, he gives Brutus to say to Cassius:

'There is a tide in the affairs of men,
Which, taken at the flood, leads on to fortune;
Omitted, all the voyage of their life,
Is bound in shallows and miseries.
On such a full sea are we now afloat;
And we must take the current when it serves,
Or lose our ventures.' Act.4: Sc.3.

405

The ancient writers stressed the importance of getting the timing precise in many of their writings and emphasized the need for using the correct time for actions and this is why they spent so much time with the subject. There is a whole system of astrology devoted purely to this art called Horary Astrology. *Horary*, Latin *horarius*= 'pertaining or relating to the hour.' *Horalis*= 'of or belonging to an hour.' In the definition of the word *horalis* lies most of the secret. You have to make sure that what you are doing belongs to the hour or you will obviously be wasting your time at the most or not helping or losing your cause in the least.

This particular problem occupied a great deal of their time and labour as said and it is why it is still be stressed here. Traditionally it was necessary to perform all rituals, invocations, making incense, talismans and so on at certain times, using certain hours and days or at least to start at times held appropriate for your purpose.

It was thought 'a good beginning brought a good end' and this carries within it a great deal of common sense. Not to try and use the correct time or trusting to luck could make your efforts fall somewhere between ineffective and invalid. Many teachers, including mine and me thought it pointless to attempt this work if the timing is wrong. I add my voice to this sentiment in the belief we should use everything available to us to further our cause and increase our chances of success even though it may not give success, it will not be for the want of trying.

The method of working with these tables is to select the day ruled by the Angel whose co-operation is being sought. His power and influence are strongest when he is 'Lord of the Day.' This day 'vibrates' to the Angel, it is 'marked' by him and to do this he always rules the first hour of it. The angel's power and influence are strongest when you use the hours over which he has personal charge on his day.

If you are unable to use the personal day then you can use the hours the angel rules in the days of the other angels. Some think an angel is less effective when he is away from 'home,' but on this, I reserve judgement. You use the hours of an angel within a day that is not his when the matter is urgent, which is like leaving a message at a 'branch office' when it is open and somewhere you can do your business. When the day and hours come around that they do rule, you can reinforce your message, which is like leaving a message of confirmation at the 'head office.'

Let us assume it is the Archangel Michael you wish to petition. This archangel's day is Sunday and as well as ruling the day, he rules four hours on that day. If you wanted to petition the Archangel Michael on Thursday, you can use his hours within that day and that will give you another four hours to use, just as the other angels have their hours in his day, Sunday. You would work in this way for any angel you want to connect with. There are two ways of using the Table to find the hours of the angels as the end columns show — 'after sunrise' and 'clock time' — and these will be dealt with soon.

The counsel of perfection would be to work only on the day the angel rules and in the hours ruled by the angel. Usually this is easier said than done, unless it is something that has been planned well ahead of time and there can be many reasons why this cannot be done. If it is a Monday and you want to invoke the Archangel Michael perhaps you cannot wait until the following Sunday, it would be perfectly valid for you to use the hours ruled by this angel on the Monday or any day following. This is why they are there and have been given.

The one thing that must always be remembered is that the angels are a family. They may operate and use methods at times in ways that seem opposed to other members of the family, but if this is looked at carefully this is not so, they are complimentary and not unlike a human family in many ways.

An angel has greatest authority in the property he owns in the day he owns, just as we all do because we have the greatest authority in our home. In the house of a friend, we do not act as we would in our home because we are in someone else's house and we should always respect this. Our behaviour is often governed by where we are—or it should—in some houses we can 'treat the place as if it were our own' but even then there is still a line over which we should not go by turning liberty into license or friendship into enmity.

You can start the work in the hour of the angel and keep working with breaks for refreshments if you wish, until the work is done even if this means you are working into the hours of the following angels. This is perfectly acceptable as long as the work was **started in the right day and hour**. Simply regard the overlapping as 'overtime' to get the work done. The angel of the day and hour has 'marked' the work as his because whatever is born in a time bears its mark and vibration. Jung wrote, 'Whatever is born, or done, in this moment of time, has the qualities of this moment of time.' **The Secret of the Golden Flower**. Now let us take a look at the first of the ways of using the Table.

The first method of timing uses the column on the far right of the chart headed 'Clock Time'and this is the most popular system because it is the easiest to use. This column represents the hourly divisions consecutively, as shown on the face of a clock. This column gives the hours of the day from midnight (the first hour) to noon (the twelfth hour) then back to midnight (the twenty–fourth hour) when a new day begins one second after 23 hours: 59 minutes and 59 seconds.

This lets me mention an important point already given, which briefly is this. Never start anything as the clock strikes the hour. Always give the new hour time to settle for a while and take on its own character— wait two or three minutes — then start. Let the new hour have time to take its coat off and put its slippers on — how do you feel when someone starts on you the moment you come through the door without as much as a by your leave.

There is no need for any working out with the Clock time system apart from when daylight saving is in operation or when we put the clocks forward one hour (British Summer Time) during the spring and summer months, then put them back (Greenwich Mean Time) for the autumn and winter. The first hour is from midnight to 1.00 am, the second hour from 1.00 a.m to 2.00 a.m and the third hour is from 2.00 a.m to 3.00 a.m and so forth.

For each hour, in the centre seven columns under the seven days of the week, you will find the planet and the angel. If you want to work with the planet Mars and the Angel Sammael on Thursday and want to know what hours are available to you. Go down the column for Thursday and when you find Mars/Samael go across to the Clocktime column and it will give you the hour. There are four times available on Thursday: 1a.m–2 a.m; 8 a.m–9 a.m; 3 p.m–4 p.m and 10 p.m–11 p.m.

Not unlike the mileage charts often found in a road atlas where you find where you are, then where you want to go and where these two lines intersect you will find the approximate mileage between the two. For those readers unfamiliar with astrological symbols a key has been placed at the end of the book in one of the diagrams and scattered in the text, as it would be useful to the reader to be familiar with astrological symbols if they are not because I feel it would be helpful.

To find an angel that rules the hour on the day in which you are interested is not complicated. If you were working with the Angel Anael of the planet Venus the table shows this Angel has rule over Friday. Always remember the angel and its planet rules the first hour of their day whether you are using clock-time in the right column or the first hour after sunrise in the second system in the left column and this is why the Ruling Planet and Angel marks their day.

To find the hours on the day ruled by this angel you move down the Friday column until you find entries for Venus: Anael. Having found the planet and angel, you go along the line to the right hand column (or the left if you were using the second system) to find the hour of the day the panet and the angel rules and that is all there is to it. It is simple so one example of this should suffice and take a another example.

Let us assume you want to work with the Archangel Gabriel and the Moon on a Wednesday. Use the column headed 'Wednesday' and find the entries for the Archangel Gabriel and the Moon. When you have found the entry, you move along the line to the column on the right hand side where you will find the first hour is 1- 2 a.m. The second is 8–9 a.m; the third hour is 3–4 p.m and the last hour is 10–11 p.m.

We again remind the reader they must take British Summer Time (= BST) into account during the period it is in force. During this period all the clocks have been artificially put forward one hour for daylight saving. All astrological tables including this one are given in Greenwich Mean Time (= GMT) and British Summer Time, when the clock is put forward by one hour must to be taken into account or your calculations will be wrong.

The reader may have noticed in the **Table of Planetary Hours for the Planets and Angels** seems to have an odd or broken planetary sequence. The table uses a sequence of Sun; Venus; Mercury; Moon; Saturn; Jupiter and Mars and this sequence, wherever you start is not broken. This order always sets the correct planet in the first hour of the day that the planet rules and gives the correct sequence of the days, Sunday/Sun; Monday/Moon; Tuesday/Mars/; Wednesday/Mercury; Thursday/Jupiter; Friday/Venus and Saturday/Saturn according to the first hour of the day. This is not difficult to explain because it was originally taken from a scheme called the **Heptagon of the Planetary Days and Hours**, which is not difficult to understand. This diagram is given at the rear of the work and is really self–explanetary.

Now let us consider the second method available. This part of the Table at first glance, appears to be the more difficult, but it is not. It only needs one piece of information to use it and its use is not complicated. When this table was originally created life moved at a slower, less complicated pace than today and time measurement was in its infancy. The measurement of life was the natural cycles of the seasons and primarily the Sun and Moon. The Sun ruled the day hours and the Moon the night hours.

Then, as now, we had long days in the summer and short days in the winter. People, generally working in agriculture worked hard from sunrise to sunset during the spring and summer sowing, gathering in the harvest and preserving meat from hunting. Making wine in readiness for the autumn and winter months when food would be scarce. This store of food would have to serve the people when everything was reversed. The days were short and the nights long and cold because this was a time of the year when the grain did not grow and you lived on what you had grown, gathered, stored, or preserved. Fuel was stored for light and heat during the long winter nights when the animals were hibernating making game and fresh food scarce.

The 'After Sunrise' Table is the older of the two systems. Some people like to use it to try to attune themselves with the old methods of working, which is why it is given. Today, electricity and modern lighting systems make the night as bright as day and we no longer need be ruled by the Sun and Moon as in the past. The seasonal growth and supply of so many foods do not effect us any longer in our brightly lit supermarket's, unless something goes wrong, then there is panic and people do not know what to do.

The new day in the modern world begins at midnight but this was not so with the earlier system. The day had not begun while the 'Lord of the Day,' the Sun, was below the horizon and could not be seen in the sky. The day only began when the Sun was above the horizon and shedding his light at sunrise and the night hours only began when the Sun had gone below the horizon once more. It could not be accepted, as now, that the first hour of the new day was midnight, because your eyes clearly told you it was the middle of the night and you should be asleep.

To operate the older system all you need each day is the hour of sunrise for the locality where you are living or doing your work. Once you have found the time of sunrise in your locality, it must follow that one hour after this time is the first hour of the day after sunrise. One hour after that is the second hour of the day after sunrise and so forth. When the twenty-third hour was complete, then the whole process begins again with another new day.

This is how the column to the extreme left is used, which is headed 'after sunrise.' The time of sunrise would change slightly each day getting earlier each day from the Winter Solstice to the Summer Solstice. Then from the Summer Solstice back to the Winter Solstice the time of sunrise would get later. This gave lengthening days during spring and summer, with shorter days during the autumn and winter. Local sunrise is often given in diaries, calendars and some newspaper and this information is always given in an astrological ephemeris with Raphael's having its Sunrise and Sunset Tables with examples of their use.

Let us give an example of this system in use. On the 1st of January 1995 in London, sunrise was timed at 8.06 a.m. The first hour after sunrise therefore is from 8.06 a.m to 9.06 a.m; the second hour after sunrise is 9.06 a.m to 10.06 a.m. and you carry on this pattern, which will start again at the time of sunrise on the next day, with minor adjustments because sunrise is not constant. You must check the time of sunrise for each day used for the Table to be accurately used.

On the 25th of June 1995 in London, sunrise was timed at 3.43 a.m. This is because in the summer the sun rises early, making long days and short nights. The first hour after sunrise therefore is 3.43 a.m to 4.43 a.m and the second hour after sunrise is 4.43 a.m to 5.43 a.m. As above, the day continues until sunrise on the next day when you check the sunrise time for that day. The caution that applies here is regarding British Summer Time because the above date, June 25th 1995 falls in the period when British Summer Time is operation in the British Isles, which is why it was chosen. All clocks during this period have been advanced one hour ahead of GMT. Therefore, for 3.43 a.m in Greenwich Mean Time the clock shows 4.43 a.m because clock time is one hour ahead of Greenwich Mean Time. Use clock time without removing the hour means that you will have to wait until the sun rises at 4.43 a.m.

In the British Isles, the changeover from GMT to BST takes place around the end of March. The change back to GMT from BST takes place at the end of October. The clocks are changed at 2 a.m on the morning on the date given, a Sunday morning, these periods are recorded and the times to change are announced throughout the media of all kinds.

| BRITISH SUMMER TIME At the end of March, at 2 a.m in the morning, the clocks are advanced one hour. | GREENWICH MEAN TIME At the end of October, at 2 a.m in the morning, the clocks are put back one hour. |
| --- | --- |

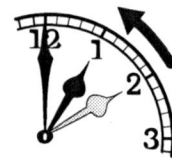

Which of the two methods offered you decide to use is something you will have to resolve for yourself according to your circumstances and temperament. A period of experimentation will determine the matter for you and show which method you feel comfortable with or prefer. It will not be resolved in five minutes. You should run both systems for a set period for a while and see which of the two 'feels right' for you.

The one thing I do suggest (as always is) having decided which of the two systems you prefer to use — stick to it. Do not swap and change around with every whim and fancy for it will only cause confusion to all concerned. Obviously regarding this, I do not mean your decision is irreversible and can never be changed. If you want to change later, considering experience or personal preference, you can. Do not swap and change every other day or just as the fancy takes you. You should, if asked by someone, be able to give sound reasons for your decision and your reasons should be able to stand up to scrutiny and debate.

# SOME THOUGHTS WHEN CLOSING THE WORK...

Naturally, though some will disagree, I think most experiences of a personal nature in works of this kind are relevant only to the individual who experienced them as I have said elsewhere. This is why I have always felt that these experiences are of limited value to others and in this, I include my private experiences. They are valid to me but I cannot assume they will be of equal value or of interest to others and of course, in many cases they have to be taken on trust. Many such examples could have been included but they have been omitted for the above reasons or kept to an absolute minimum. I believe throughout, only two incidents have been given.

Perhaps the most important myth to dispel is that all you have to do is to sit down and write a letter to an angel, sit back and then wait for the answer that will solve all your problems without any effort on your part. The desired answer will come post haste and will fill your life with the wealth of Croesus and you will never have to work or want for anything again. I am sure this kind of result has been given to some.

I can read a book on surgery or veterinary practise but I do not think that would make me a surgeon or a vet. Books can supply theory, advocate practices, give what is required to the best of the writer's experience, suggest methods to assist and try to help their readers all they can. However, it is the reader who has to supply the work and gain the experience the hard way because books cannot do this for them. I would like to be able to say books can do this but they cannot — not even this one.

This work contains a method of working that has been used for a long time in various guises but the basic form is much the same despite this. The important rudiments of the scheme were not invented by the writer. They were here long before he appeared on the scene and I believe they will be here and going strong long after he has gone across the sands of time leaving his footprints for the wind to obliterate. At times, the system has been revised, honed and constructed along the personal thoughts of a writer or teacher, for what they consider the needs of people and the period in which they live. I do not put blood or the liver of birds in incense; however, I have definitely not 'brought them up-to-date.'

There is a contagious fever abroad at the time of writing, as far as this writer's thinking is concerned, which shows little sign of abating as yet. It is an urge to 'bring things into the twenty–first century and up–to–date.' This is why we have so many tarot packs at the time of writing with probably many more to come and I hesitate to make some sarcastic suggestion for a new pack — just in case. I am sure the themes thought worthy of development are far from exhausted. I have tried to keep the presentation and development of the material as much as I can, close to the original thought. The system is one path and bridge to a particular destination and there are others.

Sometimes a system is modified to follow the philosophy of a School and its teacher or the writer who is presenting it. One thing is certain, it will please some and displease others, but this has always been so and it probably always will be. However, as I have already said elsewhere, I have now reached an age where I can face the twin onslaughts of abuse or flattery with surprising composure, given the planetary positions that rule my temperament fortunately short lived — *Sine Ira Et Studio*.

You cannot use the angel's to demand a house then sit back and wait for it to be delivered on a silver salver without any effort on your behalf. I was taught from the beginning that the angels may serve and help if certain criteria are filled, but they are not my personal servants to satisfy my whims, fancies, demands, neither were the angels put in place to replace or bypass my personal efforts.

411

Further, I was not to confuse service with servility. In similar fashion if a Power asks you for a service, this can be a reasonable request 'for a gift demands a gift' and 'nothing for nothing is an Occult Law' or in our School it was. If a Power, however, demands servility in return for what they offer, I was told that this should make me cautious, if not a little suspicious of the intentions of the Source, perhaps even to start questioning the Source itself. In the intervening years nothing has caused me to change my mind regarding this advice and I still consider it is excellent advice as it was when it was first given.

If you need a house, there are estate agents, housing agencies, newspapers, deposits to be gathered, regular employment is needed and budgets to pay for it, the acceptance of the responsibility undertaken and all the rest. These avenues and the services of the various agencies must be fully exhausted of what is being undertaken before you take to writing your letter 'to those on high.' When you have genuinely exhausted all the channels open to you, then you can attempt to play what you hope will prove to be your 'trump card.'

Take particular note of the word 'genuinely' in the above, a frequent admonition throughout my work and others written. You can fool people if you choose and in many examples, you may even succeed. However, to attempt to pollute an angelic channel to the Creator with duplicity should not even be contemplated and it would be a foolish thing to try. Only the Holy Ancient One the All–hidden One can 'make the dew to descend into the Holy Apple Trees' though some still try and get Dead Sea Apples for their troubles. To even think it could be done and got away with does not bear thinking about — at least to the wise.

You must use a high degree of common sense so as to keep your feet firmly on the ground. This is another regular phrase throughout the work. Keeping your feet upon the ground means that you must always come back to where you started by having a return ticket. I am not unsympathetic that 'other worlds' can often be preferable to what you or we have here. Some of them are more acceptable and exciting, but it is here where we were born, live, work and will die and this type of work no matter how desirable is not a way to escape from it — but to help you make a better job of it.

We all need help from time to time, sometimes the circumstances are so great that they threaten to overwhelm us and sometimes we do not know how to solve the problems set through lack of experience, ability or sheer fatigue and exhaustion. You must however show that you have exhausted your ingenuity and strength regarding the matter before you admit defeat in the matter. Then you have a clear conscience when asking for help, that you have done your best and no one can do more, it is enough.

When others work things out for you, it is they who gain experience from the situation and not you. It is true you can often gain valuable experience from observing how others handle difficult situations, because it is a valid method of learning through good examples and wiser people. Example is an excellent teacher, if we have the wit to be taught by it but it can be a hard taskmaster. Illogically, good experience is usually taught by bad experience.

We often spend much time looking for the place where our small piece of the 'jigsaw' fits and we tend to forget that the angels see the whole picture and there have been times in my life when I have even wondered if I am in the right puzzle.

We do not always understand how altering a small part of the picture may have such a serious effect elsewhere of which we are completely unaware. When we throw a very small stone into a pond and to us, it makes very small ripples on the surface that are not unattractive. However, to the unseen dwellers around the edge of the pond these ripples could be tidal waves of biblical proportions, making the Red Sea look like a puddle. It is a matter of degree.

Those who are spiritually inclined should remember that Karma is not there to be accepted without question as a burden to break people, as too many seem to think. Karma is to be taken up and actively worked upon if any benefit is to be gained by the exercise because Karma is usually defined as 'action.' Too many people use this word or any difficult action of the planet Saturn, as an excuse to do nothing. Many people slip into an almost permanent catatonic inertia saying 'This is karmic, there is nothing I can do about it, nothing will change it no matter what I do, I must bear it.' Why do you think you were given it in the first place, if was not for you to do something about it?

Karma is Sanskrit from the verbal root *kri*= 'to do, make, denoting action. Action, the causes and consequences of action; that which produces change' but to a lot of people karma is total 'inaction' because they think it is a burden from which they can never be free. Karma, if it is included in your system of belief is frequently thought of only as a burden that must be stoically borne. I believe, you have to work to resolve karma and more important to get rid of it and not take it up again or what would be the point of the exercise. It must not be forgotten there is 'good Karma,' which is the rewards for good actions. Karma in a number of minds is always thought of as nasty and heavy — it can be at times — but is it always.

Saturn and the Angel Cassiel is why we pay in full until the debts are cleared to the last farthing piece in our scheme of things. I am sure it is the Angel Cassiel who is spoken of when it is said 'the mills of God grind slowly, yet they grind exceedingly small.' It has to be dealt with, otherwise you will be given the task repeatedly until you do deal with it and solve it. I do not know what the possibility of those words do to the reader — but it scares the hell out of me to the point where I think I suppose I should try to do something about it.

Naturally if you do not subscribe to the principle of Karma given in *Galations* 6:7. 'Be not deceived; God is not mocked: for whatsoever a man soweth, that shall he also reap' or the introspection written here. You can put such thoughts out with the rubbish in the morning and get on with your life in the way you think you should be dealt with.

We have now reached that point in time where our journey together like the book is finished. This is a complex subject with an enormous amount of related facts, it has been quite a long journey and if you are reading this, splendid!'

Now both must go their separate ways, both will I hope, seek out and invite other journeys or adventures to begin elsewhere. I give my closing words to Prospero as I have done to other writings in the past, because they always seemed so appropriate at this point in the proceedings, because it is the Bard, I cannot do any better, which is why he speaks for me so often:

' . . . Now I want
Spirits to enforce, art to enchant:
And my ending is despair
Unless I be relieved by prayer,
Which pierces so that it assaults
Mercy itself, and frees from faults.
As you from your crimes would pardon'd be,
Let your indulgence set me free.'
*The Tempest*: Epilogue.

# DIAGRAMS:

CONTAINS THE DIAGRAMS AND  TABLES
ASSOCIATED WITH THE CHAPTERS.

# THE CABBALISTIC LORD'S PRAYER

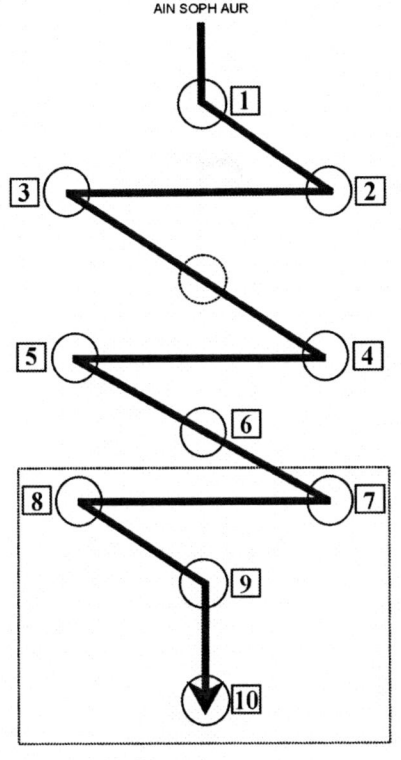

THE DESCENT OF POWER THROUGH THE KINGDOMS (THE PATHS HAVE BEEN REMOVED FOR CLARITY) IS SOMETIMES CALLED THE FLAMING SWORD OR LIGHTNING FLASH.
THE 'FALL' CAN BE VERY RAPID BECAUSE THE LIGHTNING STRIKE GOES THROUGH THE KINGDOMS ONLY AND DOWN TO EARTH. THE ASCENT, THROUGH THE SERPENT WISDOM CAN BE PAINFULLY SLOW BECAUSE THE SERPENT CLIMBS THE TREE OF LIFE CROSSING THE 32 PATHS AND THE KINGDOMS UNTIL THEY ARE ALL CONNECTED ONCE AGAIN.

WE ARE INTERESTED IN THE FOUR KINGDOMS OF THE TREE WITHIN THE MARKED AREA.

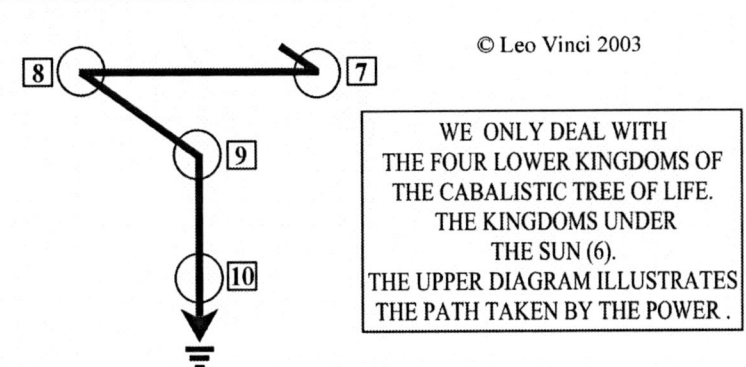

© Leo Vinci 2003

WE ONLY DEAL WITH
THE FOUR LOWER KINGDOMS OF
THE CABALISTIC TREE OF LIFE.
THE KINGDOMS UNDER
THE SUN (6).
THE UPPER DIAGRAM ILLUSTRATES
THE PATH TAKEN BY THE POWER .

## THE TRINITY OF CHRIST - THE CHRISTIAN.

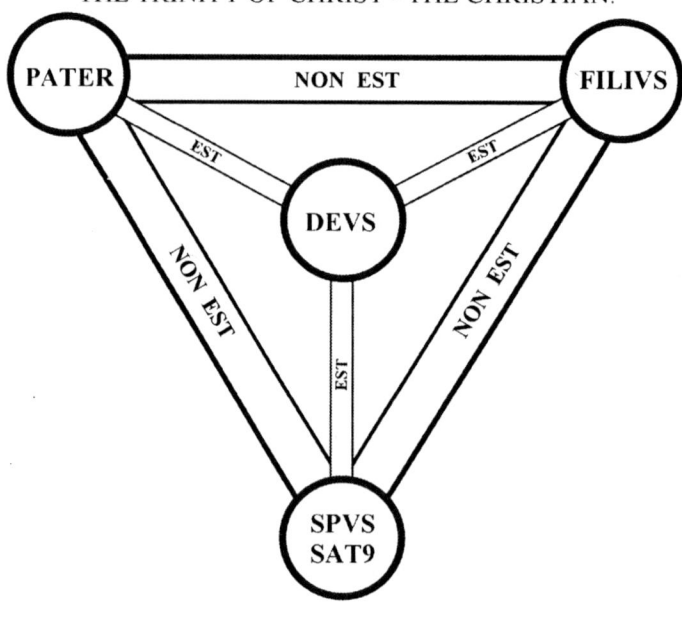

## THE TRINITY OF CHRIST - THE CABBALIST.

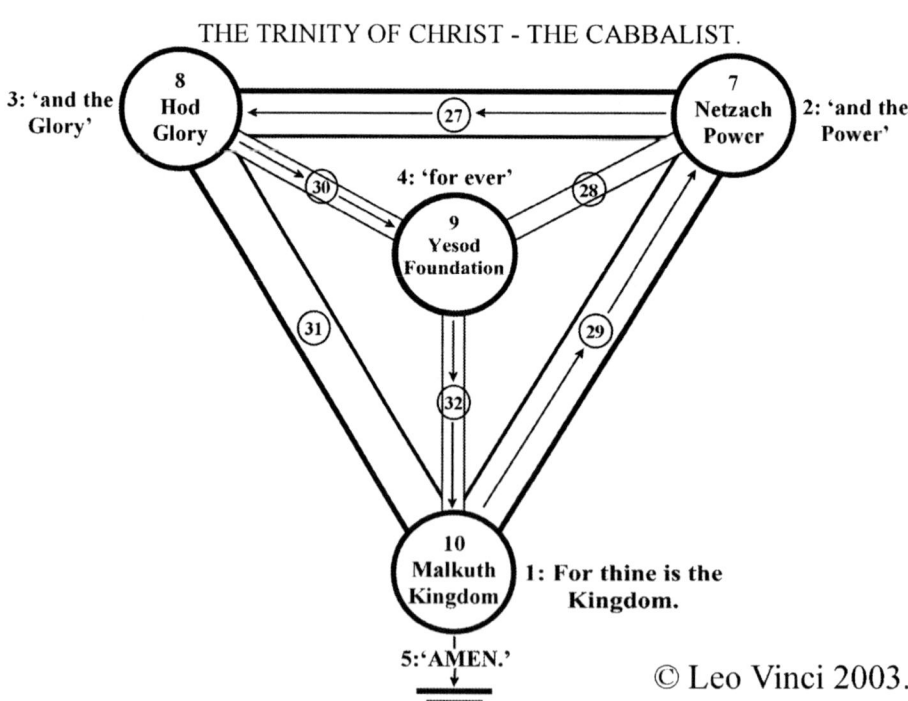

© Leo Vinci 2003.

# Angelic Pentagram

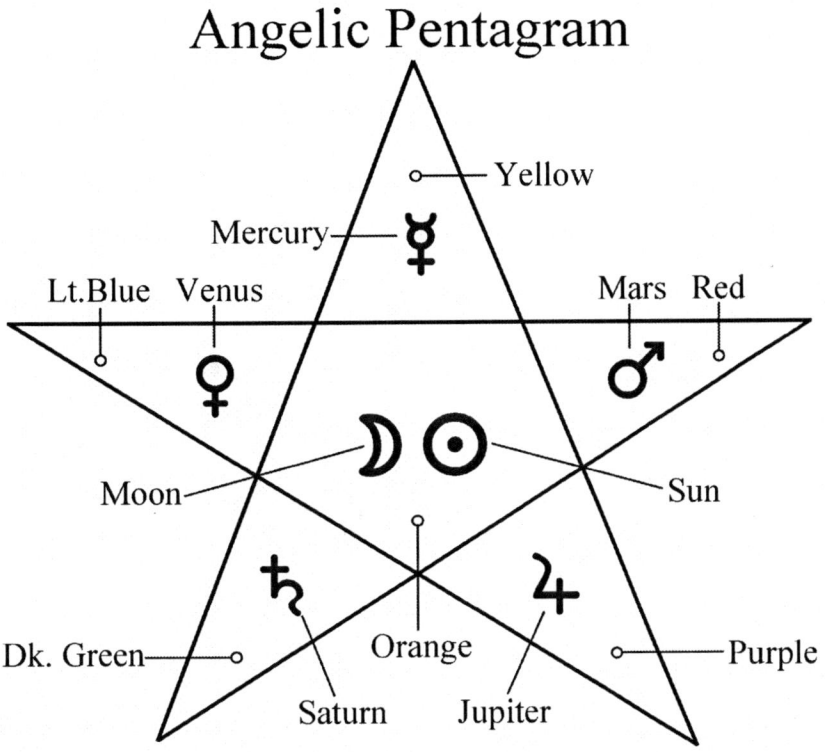

This diagram frequently represents the human body in Occult and Magical Tradition and used as a powerful talisman against evil. The pentacle is the human body with the head, torso two arms and legs. The pentacle is viewed as if looking at the back of someone. This makes the diagram's 'right arm,' your right arm and so on. The sigils of the planets with the background colour fare given. The pentagram and planetary sigils are painted in black. It is ideally painted on thin glass or acetate with glass-paints, framed and hung in the window, as recommended in the text, so that it will catch the light of the Sun. This gives the pentagram the appearance of a small 'stained glass window,' which is ideal. If it is made large enough (the size is your choice), it will throw a pattern of light into your room and this you should be striving for. The best position for the pentagram is an Eastern window so it catches the first light of the Sun in the morning, acting as a permanent invocation for the new day. The second choice is a Western window to catch the rays of a the dying Sun as it sinks into the Land of the Dead in the West, a protection during the hours of darkness. If neither of these are convenient then you can place it wherever it is best for you because, we cannot always achieve the ideal. This talisman has other uses and tthis must not be taken as its only use. The pentagram is used as a sign of the Microcosm and is considered a most powerful means of conjuration in any rite and it can equally represent evil. With one point at the top, it is the sign of good and the Christ. With two points at the top it is the sign of Satan or the Devil. By using the pentacle in one of these positions either the Powers of Light or Darkness are invoked. With one point high it is judged the highest to which the physical can aspire, God, the undivided source and from this point the pentacle issues and comes down to us. Two points upwards gives choice, duality, left or right and hence uncertainty because, from which of the two points does the pentagram originate and with whom are we dealing. 'Can two walk together except they be agreed' — 'No man can serve two masters: for either he will hate the one, and love the other; or else he will hold to the one and despise the other.' This does not exhaust the symbol on this page but what is here serves its intended purpose.     © Leo Vinci 2003

417

# Personal Angelic Pentagram

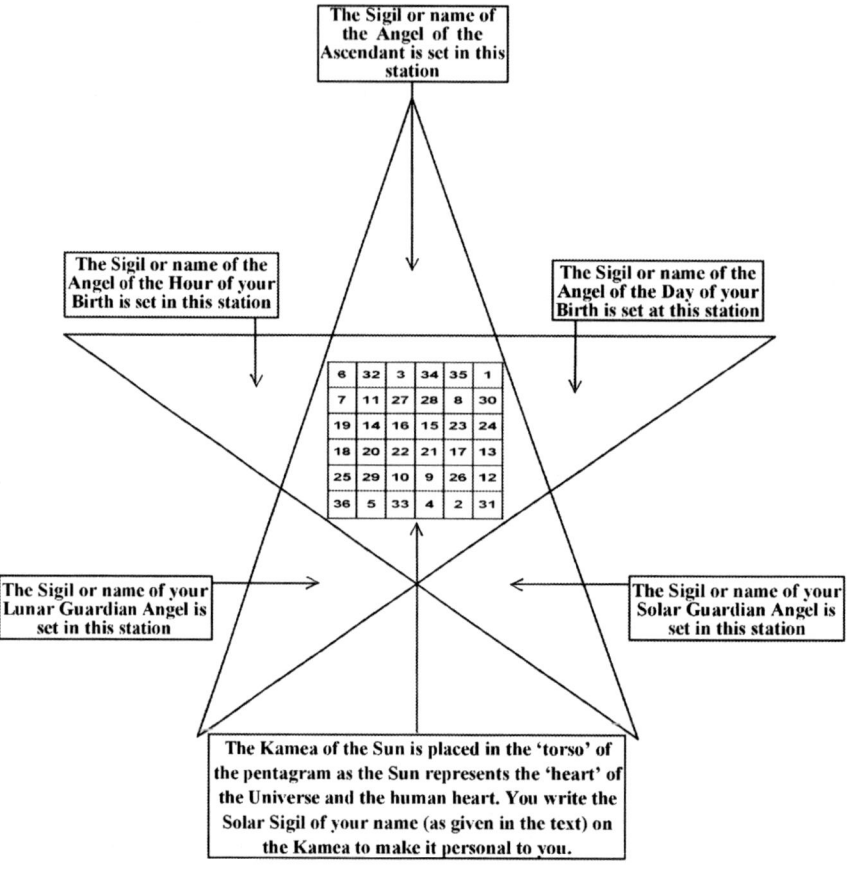

The Sigil or name of the Angel of the Ascendant is set in this station

The Sigil or name of the Angel of the Hour of your Birth is set in this station

The Sigil or name of the Angel of the Day of your Birth is set at this station

The Sigil or name of your Lunar Guardian Angel is set in this station

The Sigil or name of your Solar Guardian Angel is set in this station

The Kamea of the Sun is placed in the 'torso' of the pentagram as the Sun represents the 'heart' of the Universe and the human heart. You write the Solar Sigil of your name (as given in the text) on the Kamea to make it personal to you.

There are two methods of writing your information into this Pentagram. You can place the appropriate planetary symbol in the station given and this would be the symbol of the planet over which the Angel has rule. Alternatively, you can set the Angel's name in the required station of the Pentagram. If you chose the latter method then you convert the name into the Enochian Script, which is a very powerful Angelic Script, perhaps the most powerful. In some sections, such as the top station, you could write the characters under each other to read downwards and give yourself more room. In the two top stations they can be written straight across in the normal manner. With the two lowest stations, they can again be written downwards with the characters placed under each other. Another method would be to write the characters in the usual manner, sloping upwards in the left section and sloping downwards in the right section. The baseline of the characters would be facing inwards. Do whatever you feel is best regarding this and what you feel suits your artistic or intuitive feelings. Setting the Angelic Sigils or names in the correct station is far more important than any artistic discussion or merit and this is discussed further at the appropriate place in this chapter. Note well: if you are going to write the names of the Angels in Enochian, it is not, on this Pentagram to put their titles and sigils, only the Angelic name. © Leo Vinci 2003

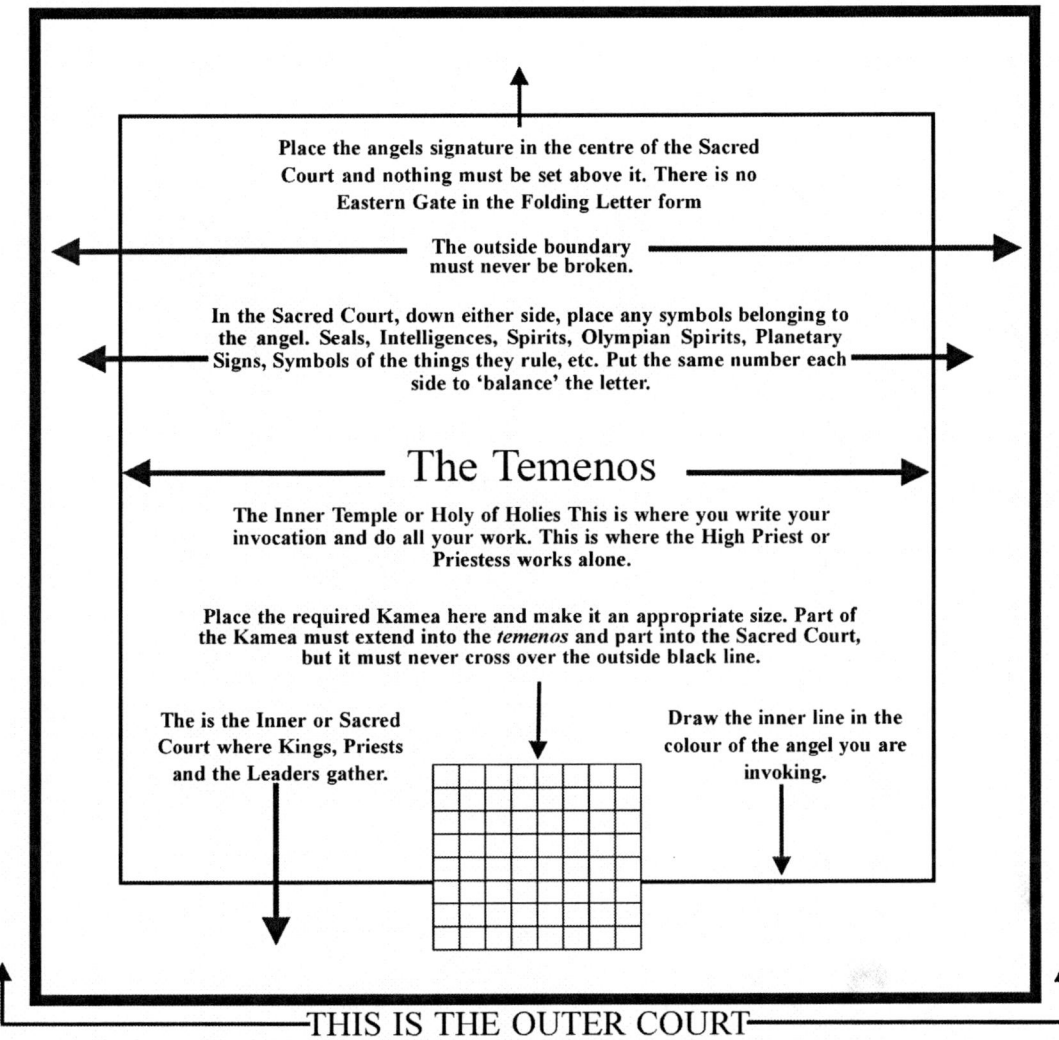

Place the angels signature in the centre of the Sacred Court and nothing must be set above it. There is no Eastern Gate in the Folding Letter form

The outside boundary must never be broken.

In the Sacred Court, down either side, place any symbols belonging to the angel. Seals, Intelligences, Spirits, Olympian Spirits, Planetary Signs, Symbols of the things they rule, etc. Put the same number each side to 'balance' the letter.

## The Temenos

The Inner Temple or Holy of Holies This is where you write your invocation and do all your work. This is where the High Priest or Priestess works alone.

Place the required Kamea here and make it an appropriate size. Part of the Kamea must extend into the *temenos* and part into the Sacred Court, but it must never cross over the outside black line.

The is the Inner or Sacred Court where Kings, Priests and the Leaders gather.

Draw the inner line in the colour of the angel you are invoking.

## THIS IS THE OUTER COURT

This is where the people and multitude gather. The number of people decreases as you move towards the *Temenos* and the Holy of Holies, until there is only one at the centre under the capstone.

CUT OFF ACROSS THE DOTTED LINE.

# THE FOLDING LETTER

This is the template for the Folding Letter on the A4 format given in the text. It is shown with the grid of the Kamea of Mercury set in place the place of the Western Gate, without its numbers, to show how the Kamea is set within the *Temenos* from the Sacred Court. The main difference between this letter and the Pyramid Letter is that this letter does not have the Eastern Gate set in place as shown in the Pyramid Letter, which gives access from the Sacred Court to the Temenos, see the main text.

419

# MAKING LETTER SEALS (OPTIONAL.)

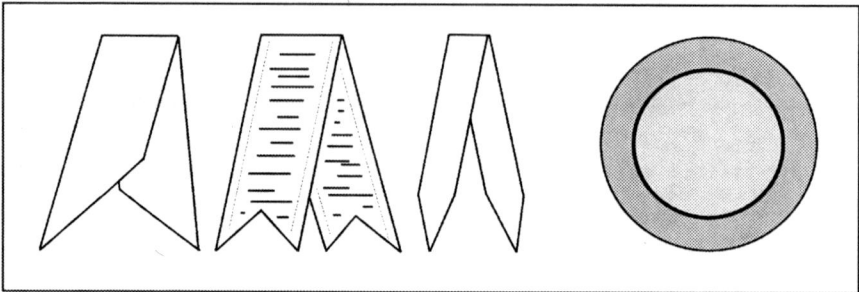

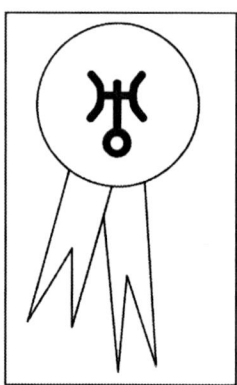

Making and using these 'seals' is optional. They are something that I like to do and are mentioned in the text. I believe that the more time and concentration you spend on your letters the better your chances of success. You feel appreciation when you see that someone has spent time and effort to do something special for you. These seals put the finishing touch to the letter. Resorting to this form of letter is special because it should only be written for insoluble problems for which you feel the need to ask special help because all else has failed. You are at your wits end and like Jacob, fleeing from the problem. You are attempting to build a bridge and the stronger it is the better because the more it can carry. You are trying to act as Pontiflex. You would not build a bridge of matchsticks to carry an elephant for obvious reasons, a fly yes, an elephant no !

Your ribbon should be of appropriate colour for your intent and can be of any width, thickness or texture that you find pleasing. The self-adhesive seals can also be of a material that you like, paper, foil and so forth. I like foil because, with a fine ball point pen and a light touch, you can inscribe it with any suitable, sigil, sign, signature or line drawing suitable for the letter you have written and the Source that you are trying to contact and influence. However, if the letter and circumstances are special, I often place the ribbons in place and seal them with a coloured sealing wax, which is easily obtained in many colours now, including gold and silver. The seal should be of an appropriate colour to the Angel to whom the letter is addressed. Alternatively, you could use the colours of your Guardian angels, the solar colour for the seal and the lunar colour for the ribbon. If you want to use only one Guardian Angel only, then use your Lunar Angel who rules the 'tides of magic.' The ribbons can point in any direction you please, not only as shown.

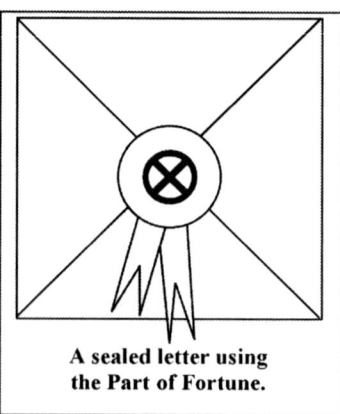

**A sealed letter using
the Part of Fortune.**

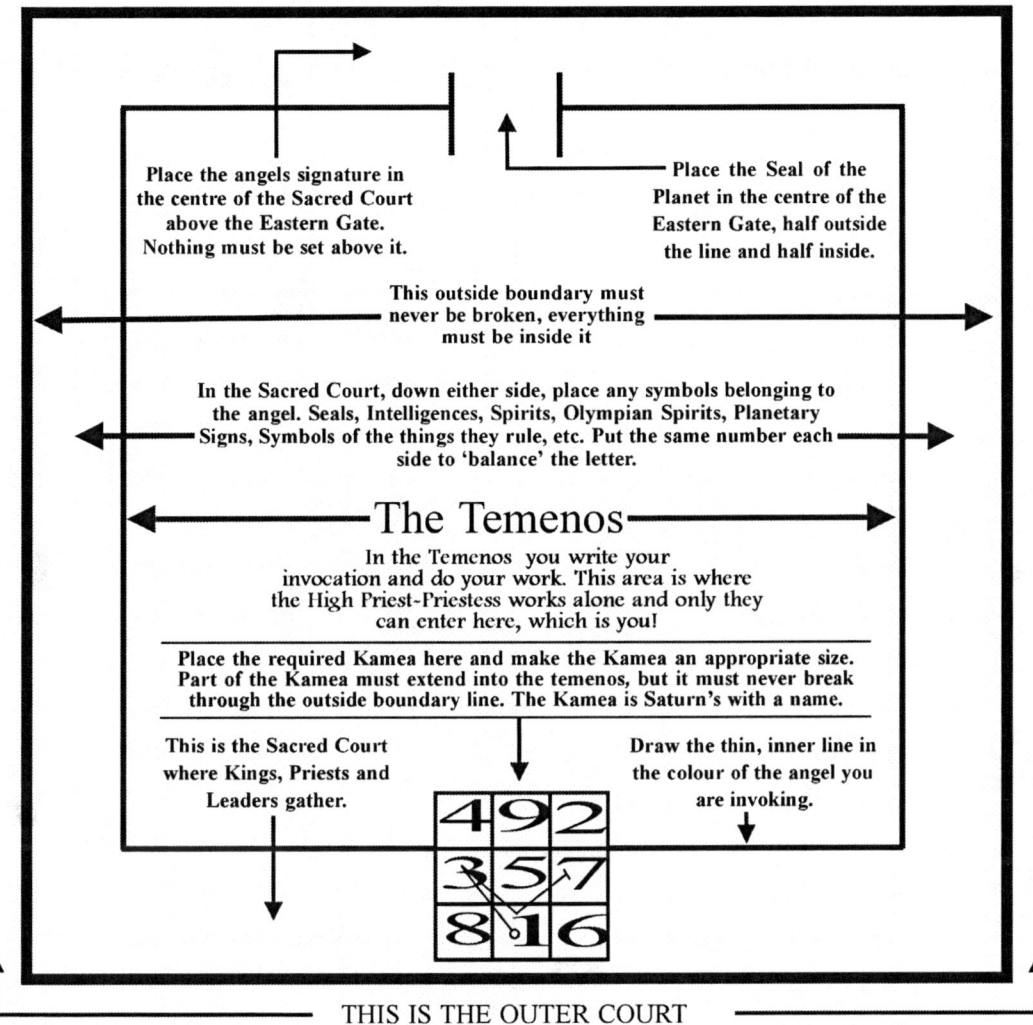

Place the angels signature in the centre of the Sacred Court above the Eastern Gate. Nothing must be set above it.

Place the Seal of the Planet in the centre of the Eastern Gate, half outside the line and half inside.

This outside boundary must never be broken, everything must be inside it

In the Sacred Court, down either side, place any symbols belonging to the angel. Seals, Intelligences, Spirits, Olympian Spirits, Planetary Signs, Symbols of the things they rule, etc. Put the same number each side to 'balance' the letter.

## The Temenos

In the Temenos you write your invocation and do your work. This area is where the High Priest-Priestess works alone and only they can enter here, which is you!

Place the required Kamea here and make the Kamea an appropriate size. Part of the Kamea must extend into the temenos, but it must never break through the outside boundary line. The Kamea is Saturn's with a name.

This is the Sacred Court where Kings, Priests and Leaders gather.

Draw the thin, inner line in the colour of the angel you are invoking.

THIS IS THE OUTER COURT

Outside the people and the multitude gather. The people decrease as you move inwards to the Temenos and the Holy of Holies, until there is only one at the centre under the capstone.

CUT ACROSS THE DOTTED LINE.

# PYRAMID LETTER

This is the template for the Pyramid Letter on the A4 format suggested in the text. It is shown with the grid of a Kamea set in the place of the Western Gate, which is opposite the Eastern Gate, to show how the Kamea is set within the Temenos. The Eastern Gate is not set in place in the Folding Letter. These two Gates go under the Pyramid, when it is set in place, giving an entrance and exit to the Temenos from the Sacred Court. The Pyramid should be set in line with the East so that the Sun (symbolically) 'enters' the Eastern Gate and 'leaves' the Pyramid by the Western Gate.

© Leo Vinci 2003

# TEMPLATE FOLDING LETTER FOR JUPITER (EXAMPLE)

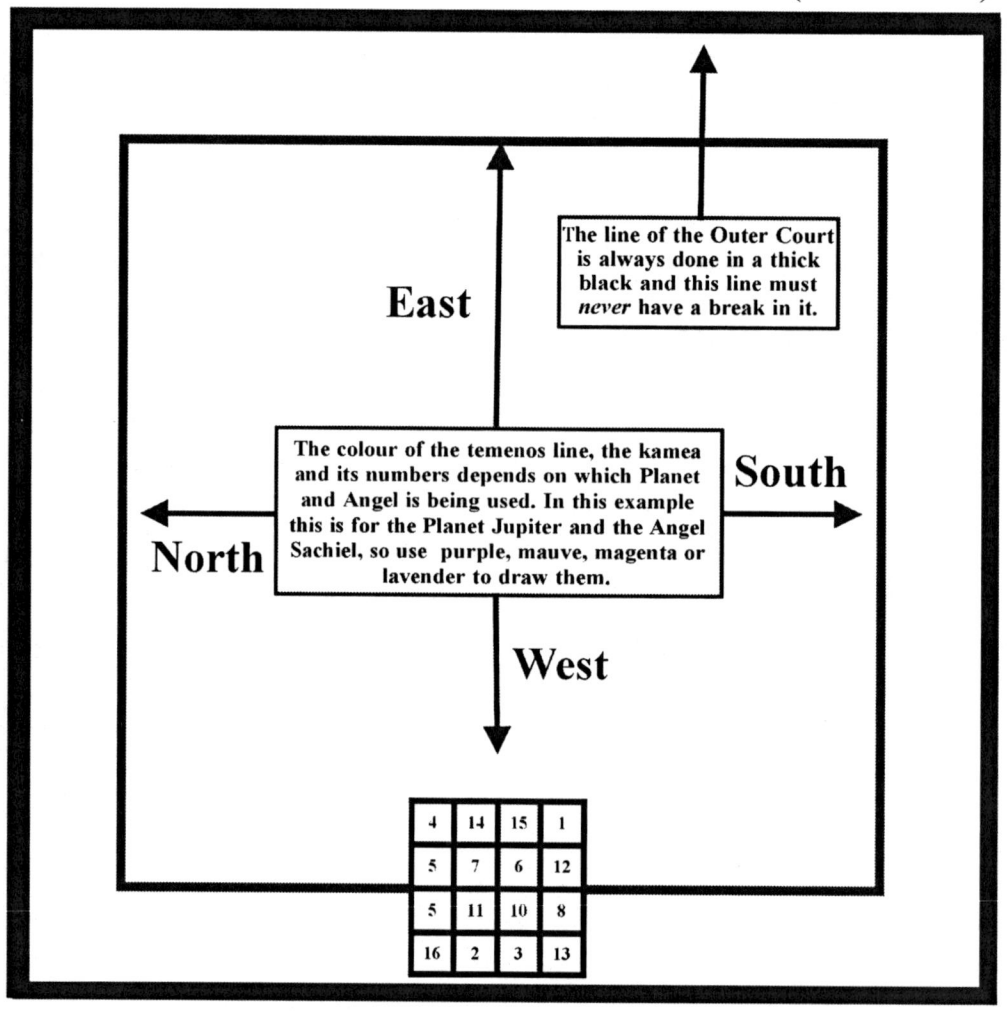

East

South

North

West

The line of the Outer Court is always done in a thick black and this line must *never* have a break in it.

The colour of the temenos line, the kamea and its numbers depends on which Planet and Angel is being used. In this example this is for the Planet Jupiter and the Angel Sachiel, so use purple, mauve, magenta or lavender to draw them.

| 4 | 14 | 15 | 1 |
| 5 | 7 | 6 | 12 |
| 5 | 11 | 10 | 8 |
| 16 | 2 | 3 | 13 |

- - - - - - - - - - - - - - - - - - - - - - - - - - - - - - - - - - - - - - - - - -
**CUT OFF**

## PRE-PREPARED FOLDING LETTER TEMPLATE (OPTIONAL)
Folding Letter template for the Planet Jupiter, the Angel Sachiel with the Kamea of Jupiter set in place. The directions and arrows are not written in. Only the two squares and the Kamea for Jupiter. The black square is constant to all letters, the inner square of the Temnos and the Kamea changes colour according to the Angel being invoked, as given in the text. Everything else you need to finish the letter has to be put in by hand.

# ANGELIC SIGNATURES

| DAY OF THE WEEK: | PLANET: | ANGEL/ARCHANGEL: | ANGELIC SIGNATURE: |
|---|---|---|---|
| SUNDAY | SUN | ARCHANGEL MICHAEL | |
| MONDAY | MOON | ARCHANGEL GABRIEL | |
| TUESDAY | MARS | ANGEL SAMAEL | |
| WEDNESDAY | MERCURY | ARCHANGEL RAPHAEL | |
| THURSDAY | JUPITER | ANGEL SACHIEL | |
| FRIDAY | VENUS | ANGEL ANAEL | |
| SATURDAY | SATURN | ANGEL CASSIEL | |

423

# Ground plan of the PERSONAL PYRAMID of BANISHMENT

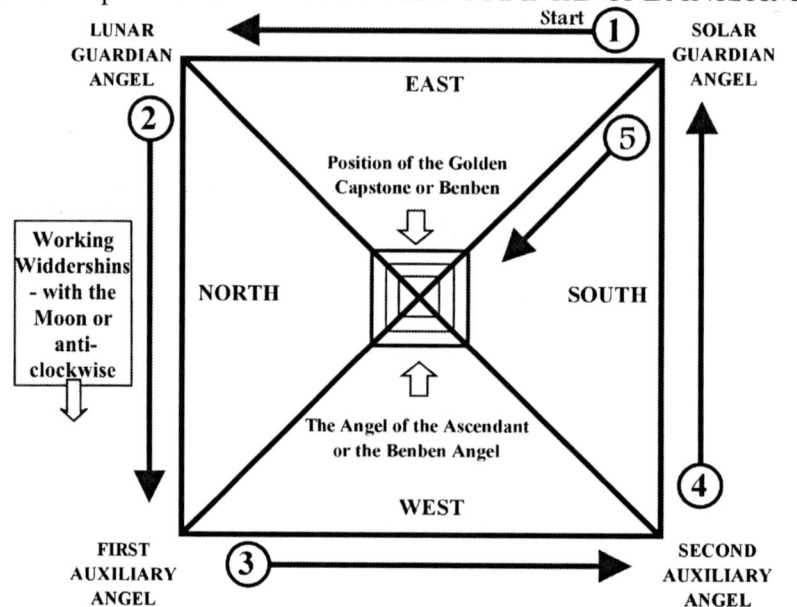

# Ground plan of the PERSONAL PYRAMID of ATTRACTION

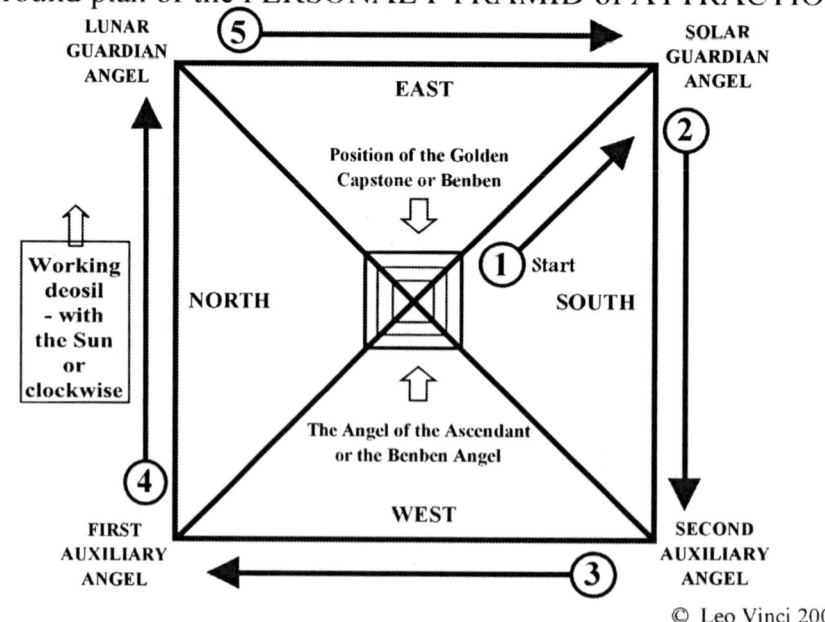

# HEBREW ALPHABET AND ITS CORRESPONDENCES

| No: | Latin: | Hebrew: | Name of Letters: | Numerical Value: | Significance: |
|---|---|---|---|---|---|
| 1 | A | א | Aleph | 1 | Ox |
| 2 | B | ב | Beth | 2 | House |
| 3 | G | ג | Gimel | 3 | Camel |
| 4 | D | ד | Daleth | 4 | Door |
| 5 | H | ה | He | 5 | Window |
| 6 | V | ו | Vau | 6 | Nail or Hook |
| 7 | Z | ז | Zayin | 7 | Sword or Armour |
| 8 | Ch | ח | Cheth | 8 | Fence, enclosure |
| 9 | T | ט | Teth | 9 | Serpent |
| 10 | I | י | Yod | 10 | Hand |
| 11 | K | כ | Kaph | 20 | Fist |
| ☆ | Final K | ך | Kaph Final | 500 | Fist |
| 12 | L | ל | Lamed | 30 | Ox-goad |
| 13 | M | מ | Mem | 40 | Water |
| ☆ | Final M | ם | Mem Final | 600 | Water |
| 14 | N | נ | Nun | 50 | Fish |
| ☆ | Final N | ן | Nun Final | 700 | Fish |
| 15 | S | ס | Samekh | 60 | Prop |
| 16 | Aa,Ngh | ע | Ayin | 70 | Eye |
| 17 | P | פ | Pe | 80 | Mouth |
| ☆ | Final Ph | ף | Pe Final | 800 | Mouth |
| 18 | Tz | צ | Tzaddi | 90 | Fish hook |
| ☆ | Final Tz | ץ | Tzaddi Final | 900 | Fish hook |
| 19 | Q | ק | Qoph | 100 | Ear or Back of head |
| 20 | R | ר | Resh | 200 | Head |
| 21 | Sh | ש | Shin | 300 | Tooth |
| 22 | Th | ת | Tau | 400 | Cross |

☆ = Five Final Letters

# The SEVEN KAMEAS of the ANGELS and their PLANETS.

ħ

| 4 | 9 | 2 |
|---|---|---|
| 3 | 5 | 7 |
| 8 | 1 | 6 |

SATURN

♃

| 4 | 14 | 15 | 1 |
|---|----|----|---|
| 9 | 7 | 6 | 12 |
| 5 | 11 | 10 | 8 |
| 16 | 2 | 3 | 13 |

JUPITER

♂

| 11 | 24 | 7 | 20 | 3 |
|----|----|---|----|---|
| 4 | 12 | 25 | 8 | 16 |
| 17 | 5 | 13 | 21 | 9 |
| 10 | 18 | 1 | 14 | 22 |
| 23 | 6 | 19 | 2 | 15 |

MARS

### KEY TO PLANETS AND ANGELS

⊙ = Sun/Archangel Michael.
☽ = Moon/Archangel Gabriel.
♂ = Mars/Angel Samael.
☿ = Mercury/Archangel Raphael.
♃ = Jupiter/Angel Sachiel.
♀ = Venus/Angel Anael.
ħ = Saturn/Angel Cassiel.

426

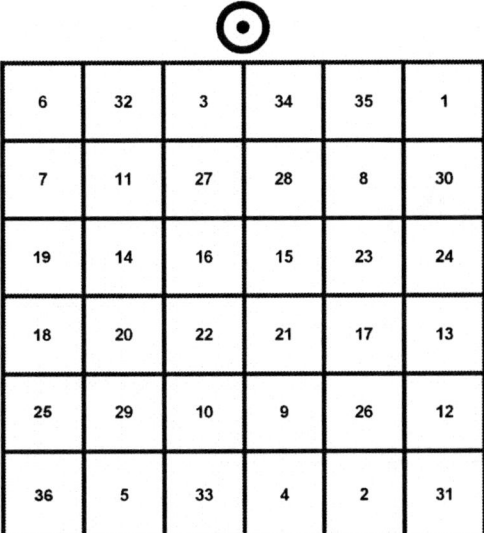

| 6 | 32 | 3 | 34 | 35 | 1 |
|---|----|---|----|----|---|
| 7 | 11 | 27 | 28 | 8 | 30 |
| 19 | 14 | 16 | 15 | 23 | 24 |
| 18 | 20 | 22 | 21 | 17 | 13 |
| 25 | 29 | 10 | 9 | 26 | 12 |
| 36 | 5 | 33 | 4 | 2 | 31 |

SUN

| 37 | 78 | 29 | 70 | 21 | 62 | 13 | 54 | 5 |
|----|----|----|----|----|----|----|----|---|
| 6 | 38 | 79 | 30 | 71 | 22 | 63 | 14 | 46 |
| 47 | 7 | 39 | 80 | 31 | 72 | 23 | 55 | 15 |
| 16 | 48 | 8 | 40 | 81 | 32 | 64 | 24 | 56 |
| 57 | 17 | 49 | 9 | 41 | 73 | 33 | 65 | 25 |
| 26 | 58 | 18 | 50 | 1 | 42 | 74 | 34 | 66 |
| 67 | 27 | 59 | 10 | 51 | 2 | 43 | 75 | 35 |
| 36 | 68 | 19 | 60 | 11 | 52 | 3 | 44 | 76 |
| 77 | 28 | 69 | 20 | 61 | 12 | 53 | 4 | 45 |

MOON

427

♀

| | | | | | | |
|---|---|---|---|---|---|---|
| 22 | 47 | 16 | 41 | 10 | 35 | 4 |
| 5 | 23 | 48 | 17 | 42 | 11 | 29 |
| 30 | 6 | 24 | 49 | 18 | 36 | 12 |
| 13 | 31 | 7 | 25 | 43 | 19 | 37 |
| 38 | 14 | 32 | 1 | 26 | 44 | 20 |
| 21 | 39 | 8 | 33 | 2 | 27 | 45 |
| 46 | 15 | 40 | 9 | 34 | 3 | 28 |

VENUS

☿

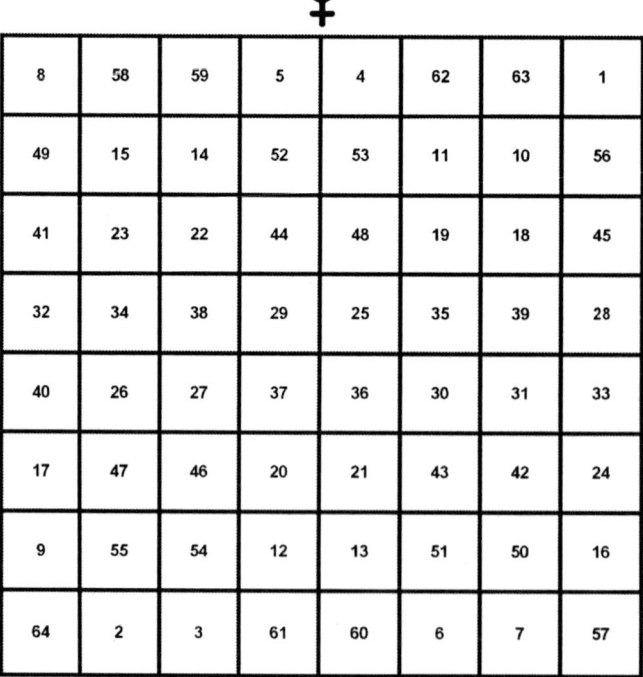

| | | | | | | | |
|---|---|---|---|---|---|---|---|
| 8 | 58 | 59 | 5 | 4 | 62 | 63 | 1 |
| 49 | 15 | 14 | 52 | 53 | 11 | 10 | 56 |
| 41 | 23 | 22 | 44 | 48 | 19 | 18 | 45 |
| 32 | 34 | 38 | 29 | 25 | 35 | 39 | 28 |
| 40 | 26 | 27 | 37 | 36 | 30 | 31 | 33 |
| 17 | 47 | 46 | 20 | 21 | 43 | 42 | 24 |
| 9 | 55 | 54 | 12 | 13 | 51 | 50 | 16 |
| 64 | 2 | 3 | 61 | 60 | 6 | 7 | 57 |

MERCURY

428

The Magical Seals and Characters of the Planets and their Intelligence and Spirits.

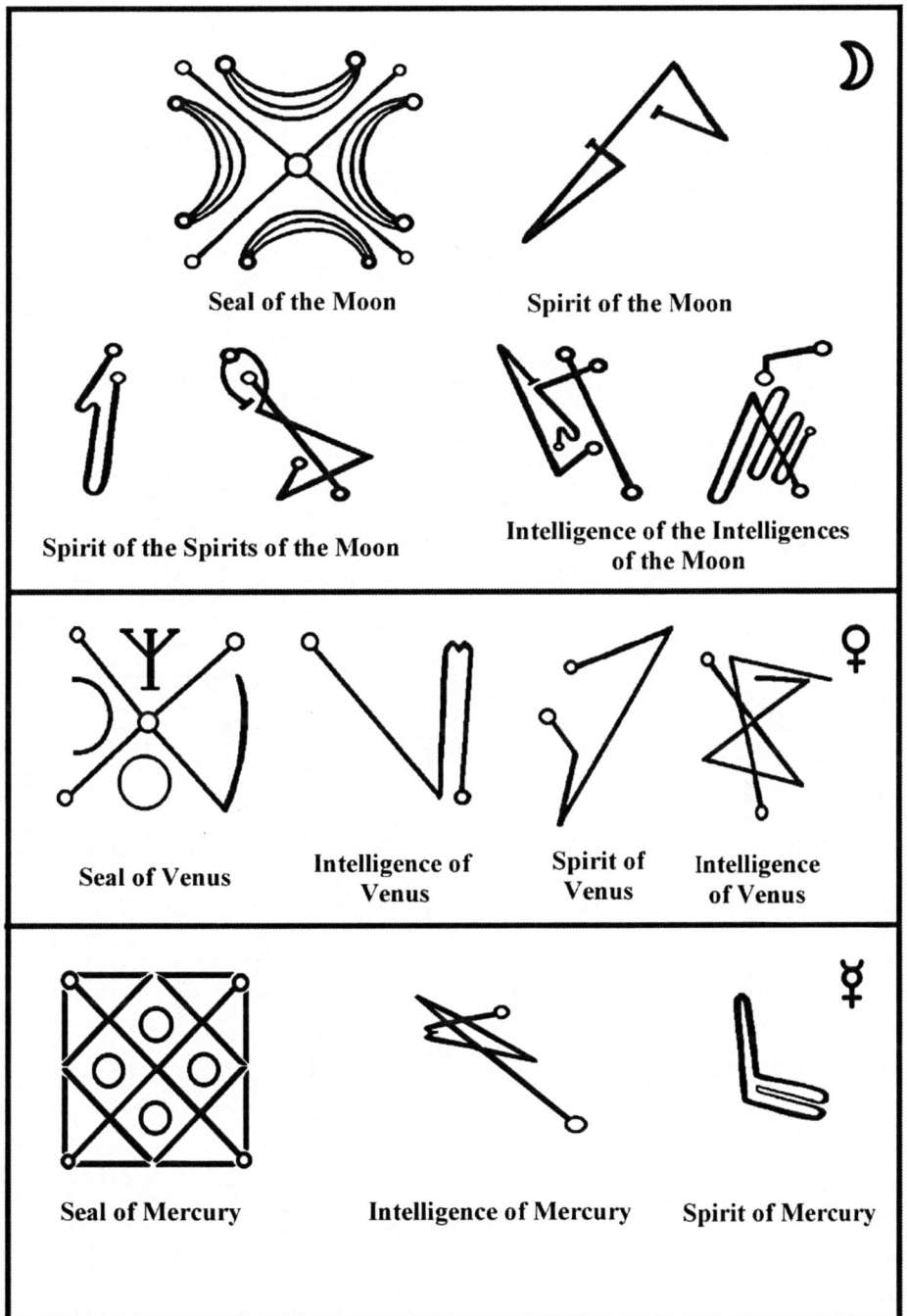

Seal of the Moon

Spirit of the Moon

Spirit of the Spirits of the Moon

Intelligence of the Intelligences of the Moon

Seal of Venus

Intelligence of Venus

Spirit of Venus

Intelligence of Venus

Seal of Mercury

Intelligence of Mercury

Spirit of Mercury

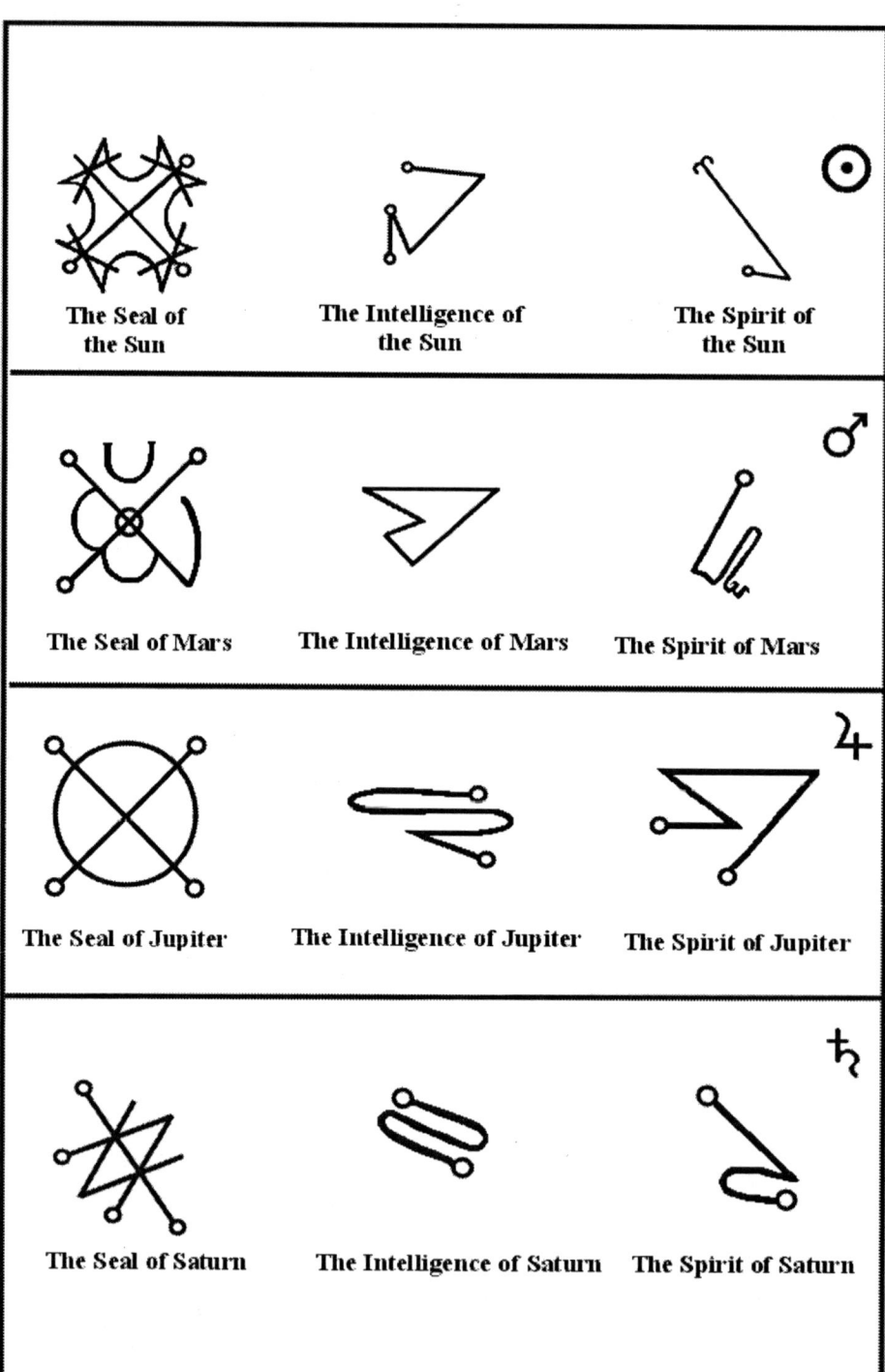

The Seal of
the Sun

The Intelligence of
the Sun

The Spirit of
the Sun

The Seal of Mars

The Intelligence of Mars

The Spirit of Mars

The Seal of Jupiter

The Intelligence of Jupiter

The Spirit of Jupiter

The Seal of Saturn

The Intelligence of Saturn

The Spirit of Saturn

# THE SYMBOLS OF THE OLYMPIAN SPIRITS

**CHARACTER OF ARATON**

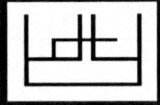

**LORD OF SATURN:** Perfume: Saffron; Aloes Wood; Elder or Pine seeds/leaves; Civet; Myrrh; Assafetida; Sulphur.

**CHARACTER OF BETHOR**

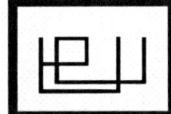

**LORD OF JUPITER:** Perfume: Sandalwood; Onycha; Saffron; Agrimony leaves; Cloves; Nutmeg and Henbane; Orange and Citron dried and powdered

**CHARACTER OF PHALEG**

**LORD OF MARS:** Perfume: White Poppy; Camphor; Calomile flowers; Pepper; Sandal red, white and black; Balsam; Tobacco.

**CHARACTER OF OCH**

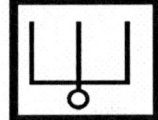

**LORD OF SUN:** Perfume: Black Pepper; Sulphur; Frankincense; Mastick; Musk; Benjamin; Amber; Storax.

**CHARACTER OF HAGITH**

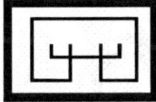

**LORD OF VENUS:** Perfume: Juniper berries; Red Sandal; Cinnamon; Benzion; Aloe Wood; Musk; Elder leaves; Rose; Violet; Crocus and sweet flower essences.

**CHARACTER OF OPHIEL**

**LORD OF MERCURY:** Perfume: Ash Tree seeds; Aloe Wood; Mandrake root; Scullcap herb; Cinnamon; Cassia; Storax; Cloves; Laurel bark; Mace and sweet seeds.

**CHARACTER OF PHUL**

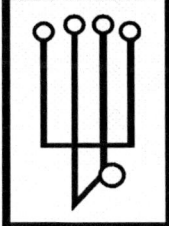

**LORD OF MOON:** Perfume: Myrtle; Jasmine; Camphor; Lignum Aloes; Laurel; Mandrake; Valerian herbs; Essences of sweet flowers.

## The Script delivered by Honorius called the Theban Alphabet

A  B  C  D  E  F  G  H  I  K  L  M

N  O  P  Q  R  S  T  V  X  Y  Z

## The Script called Celestial Writing

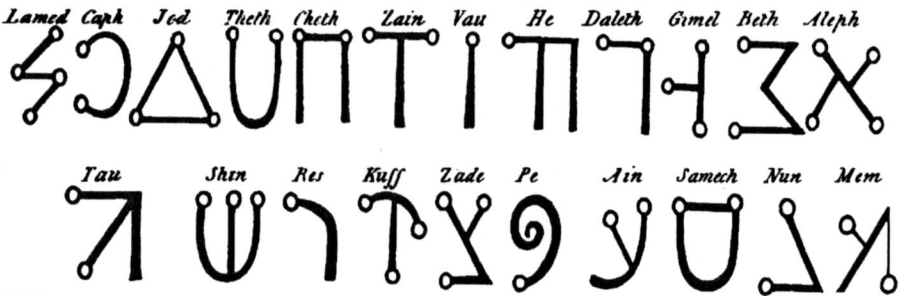

Lamed  Caph  Jod  Theth  Cheth  Zain  Vau  He  Daleth  Gimel  Beth  Aleph

Tau  Shin  Res  Kuff  Zade  Pe  Ain  Samech  Nun  Mem

## The Script called Malachim

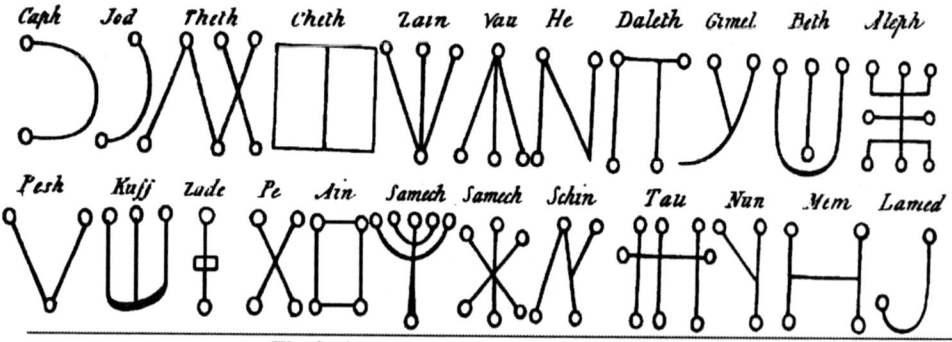

Caph  Jod  Theth  Cheth  Zain  Vau  He  Daleth  Gimel  Beth  Aleph

Pesh  Kuff  Zade  Pe  Ain  Samech  Samech  Schin  Tau  Nun  Mem  Lamed

## The Script called the Passing of the Rivers

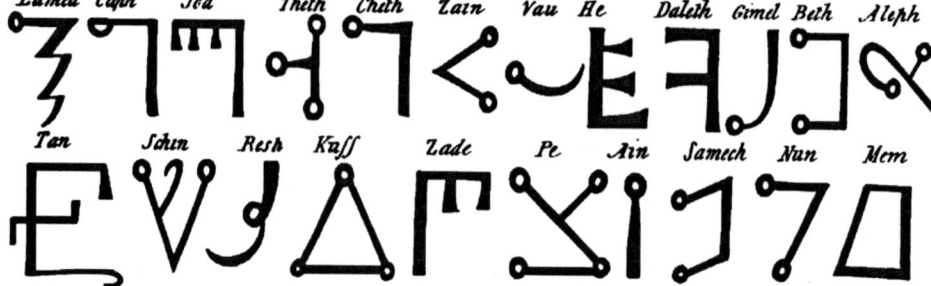

Lamed  Caph  Jod  Theth  Cheth  Zain  Vau  He  Daleth  Gimel  Beth  Aleph

Tau  Schin  Resh  Kuff  Zade  Pe  Ain  Samech  Nun  Mem

# The Aiq B(e)k(e)r or
# Cabbala of the Nine Chambers

|  |  |  |
|---|---|---|
| ש ל ג | ר כ ב | ק י א |
| ם ס ו | ך נ ה | ת מ ד |
| ץ צ ט | ף פ ח | ן ע ז |

| | | |
|---|---|---|
| Sh L G<br>300 30 3 | R K B<br>200 20 2 | Q I A<br>100 10 1 |
| ★<br>M S V<br>600 60 6 | ★<br>K N H<br>500 50 5 | Th M D<br>400 40 4 |
| ★<br>Tz Tz T<br>900 90 9 | ★<br>P P Ch<br>800 80 8 | ★<br>N O Z<br>700 70 7 |

★ = the 5 Finals

The lower diagram is an interpretation of the top diagram, the *Aiq Bkr*, and gives the numerical values and the equivalent Latin letters for the Hebrew.           © Leo Vinci 2003

# THE ROYAL ARCH CYPHER

## The Royal Arch Cypher

The *Royal Arch Cypher* has a similar pattern of use to the *Cabala of the Nine Chambers'* and works in much the same way. The main difference being that the Royal Arch Cypher uses Roman letters instead of the Hebrew, which is used in the *Aiq Beker*. The model given here is not the only version extant, but it is an often used scheme and used in past work. Like the Hebrew version, you draw the outline of the chamber containing the letter that you want to use but this time, if you want the first letter you draw the 'chamber' and leave it empty and this indicates the first letter. If it is the second letter you want you put one mark in the chamber and this indicates the second letter. There is no 'k' so you would use 'c' which has the same sound. 'I' and 'j' have long been interchangeable. Finally the letter 'u.' this letter can also be substituted for 'v' and 'w.' For 'u' leave the chamber empty, because it is the original letter. For 'v' you place one mark in it and 'w' you place two marks in the chamber to show there is a double letter - or 'double u' - the English name for the letter 'w.'

You could, as others have obviously done, make minor alterations as long as they are consistent in use and you do not keep swapping and changing, a frequent admonition of the writer. One of the main uses of this script is to make private what has been written and to keep your work confidential from the profane. Not all scripts used are 'magical' and seem to have this purpose, though they are put in with them, but use has made them valid. This code was not overtax a code breaker of today but it still serves its purpose for the most and basically this is why it is here - privacy.

© Leo Vinci 2003

# ENOCHIA
## ALPHABET OF THE ANGELIC LANGUAGE

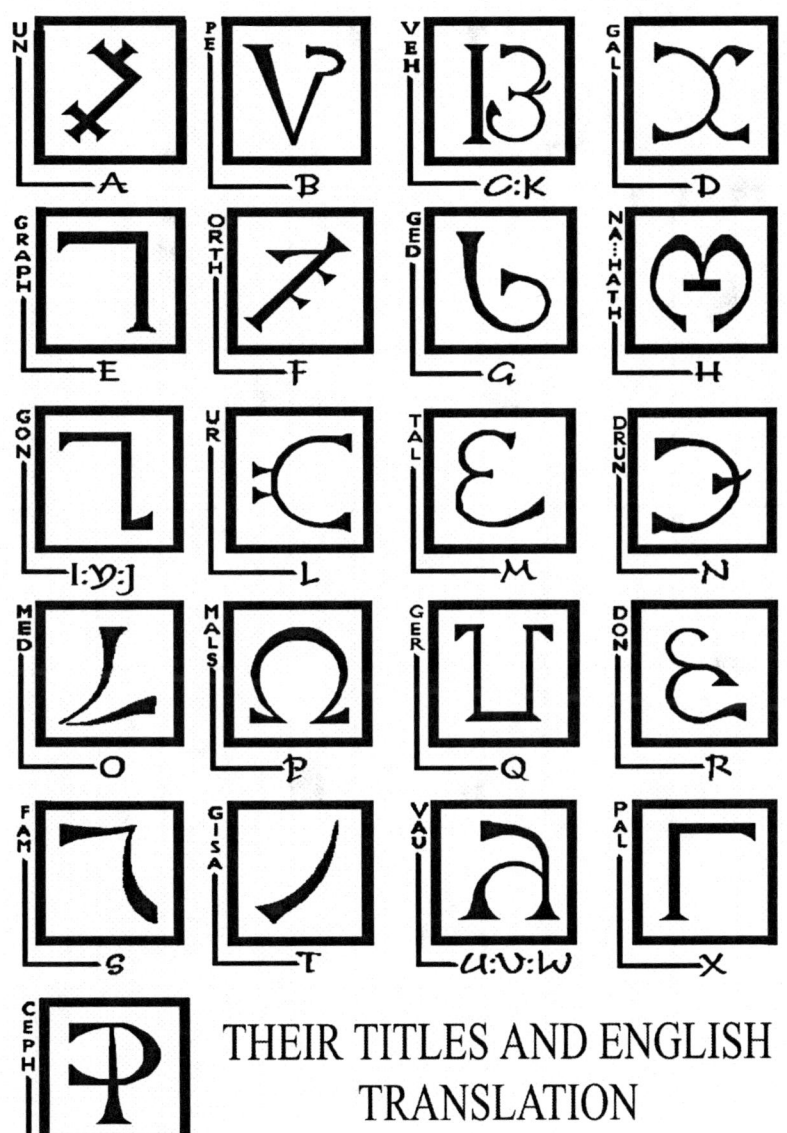

THEIR TITLES AND ENGLISH
TRANSLATION

## The Table of Planetary Hours for the Planets and Angels - Midnight to Midday

| AFTER SUNRISE | SUNDAY | MONDAY | TUESDAY | WEDNESDAY | THURSDAY | FRIDAY | SATURDAY | CLOCK TIME |
|---|---|---|---|---|---|---|---|---|
| 1ST HOUR | SUN: MICHAEL | MOON: GABRIEL | MARS: SAMAEL | MERCURY:RAPHAEL | JUPITER: SACHIEL | VENUS: ANAEL | SATURN: CASSIEL | 12AM to 1AM |
| 2ND HOUR | VENUS: ANAEL | SATURN: CASSIEL | SUN: MICHAEL | MOON: GABRIEL | MARS: SAMAEL | MERCURY:RAPHAEL | JUPITER: SACHIEL | 1AM to 2AM |
| 3RD HOUR | MERCURY:RAPHAEL | JUPITER: SACHIEL | VENUS: ANAEL | SATURN: CASSIEL | SUN: MICHAEL | MOON: GABRIEL | MARS: SAMAEL | 2AM to 3 AM |
| 4TH HOUR | MOON: GABRIEL | MARS: SAMAEL | MERCURY:RAPHAEL | JUPITER: SACHIEL | VENUS: ANAEL | SATURN: CASSIEL | SUN: MICHAEL | 3AM to 4AM |
| 5TH HOUR | SATURN: CASSIEL | SUN: MICHAEL | MOON: GABRIEL | MARS: SAMAEL | MERCURY:RAPHAEL | JUPITER: SACHIEL | VENUS: ANAEL | 4AM to 5AM |
| 6TH HOUR | JUPITER: SACHIEL | VENUS: ANAEL | SATURN: CASSIEL | SUN: MICHAEL | MOON: GABRIEL | MARS: SAMAEL | MERCURY:RAPHAEL | 5AM to 6AM |
| 7TH HOUR | MARS: SAMAEL | MERCURY:RAPHAEL | JUPITER: SACHIEL | VENUS: ANAEL | SATURN: CASSIEL | SUN: MICHAEL | MOON: GABRIEL | 6AM to 7AM |
| 8TH HOUR | SUN: MICHAEL | MOON: GABRIEL | MARS: SAMAEL | MERCURY:RAPHAEL | JUPITER: SACHIEL | VENUS: ANAEL | SATURN: CASSIEL | 7AM to 8AM |
| 9TH HOUR | VENUS: ANAEL | SATURN: CASSIEL | SUN: MICHAEL | MOON: GABRIEL | MARS: SAMAEL | MERCURY:RAPHAEL | JUPITER: SACHIEL | 8AM to 9AM |
| 10TH HOUR | MERCURY:RAPHAEL | JUPITER: SACHIEL | VENUS: ANAEL | SATURN: CASSIEL | SUN: MICHAEL | MOON: GABRIEL | MARS: SAMAEL | 9AM to 10AM |
| 11TH HOUR | MOON: GABRIEL | MARS: SAMAEL | MERURY: RAPHAEL | JUPITER: SACHIEL | VENUS: ANAEL | SATURN: CASSIEL | SUN: MICHAEL | 10AM to 11AM |
| 12TH HOUR | SATURN: CASSIEL | SUN: MICHAEL | MOON: GABRIEL | MARS: SAMAEL | MERCURY:RAPHAEL | JUPITER: SACHIEL | VENUS: ANAEL | 11AM to 12PM |

FOR NEPTUNE/ASARIEL, USE JUPITER/SACHIEL • • FOR URANUS/URIEL, USE SATURN/CASSIEL • • FOR PLUTO/AZRAEL, USE MARS/

## The Table of Planetary Hours for the Planets and Angels - Midday to Midnight

| AFTER SUNRISE | SUNDAY | MONDAY | TUESDAY | WEDNESDAY | THURSDAY | FRIDAY | SATURDAY | CLOCK TIME |
|---|---|---|---|---|---|---|---|---|
| 13TH HOUR | JUPITER: SACHIEL | VENUS: ANAEL | SATURN: CASSIEL | SUN: MICHAEL | MOON: GABRIEL | MARS: SAMAEL | MERCURY: RAPHAEL | 12PM to 1PM |
| 14TH HOUR | MARS: SAMAEL | MERCURY: RAPHAEL | JUPITER: SACHIEL | VENUS: ANAEL | SATURN: CASSIEL | SUN: MICHAEL | MOON: GABRIEL | 1PM to 2PM |
| 15TH HOUR | SUN: MICHAEL | MOON: GABRIEL | MARS: SAMAEL | MERCURY: RAPHAEL | JUPITER: SACHIEL | VENUS: ANAEL | SATURN: CASSIEL | 2PM to 3PM |
| 16TH HOUR | VENUS: ANAEL | SATURN: CASSIEL | SUN: MICHAEL | MOON: GABRIEL | MARS: SAMAEL | MERCURY: RAPHAEL | JUPITER: SACHIEL | 3PM to 4PM |
| 17TH HOUR | MERCURY: RAPHAEL | JUPITER: SACHIEL | VENUS: ANAEL | SATURN: CASSIEL | SUN: MICHAEL | MOON: GABRIEL | MARS: SAMAEL | 4PM to 5PM |
| 18TH HOUR | MOON: GABRIEL | MARS: SAMAEL | MERCURY: RAPHAEL | JUPITER: SACHIEL | VENUS: ANAEL | SATURN: CASSIEL | SUN: MICHAEL | 5PM to 6PM |
| 19TH HOUR | SATURN: CASSIEL | SUN: MICHAEL | MOON: GABRIEL | MARS: SAMAEL | MERCURY: RAPHAEL | JUPITER: SACHIEL | VENUS: ANAEL | 6PM to 7PM |
| 20TH HOUR | JUPITER: SACHIEL | VENUS: ANAEL | SATURN: CASSIEL | SUN: MICHAEL | MOON: GABRIEL | MARS: SAMAEL | MERCURY: RAPHAEL | 7PM to 8PM |
| 21ST HOUR | MARS: SAMAEL | MERCURY: RAPHAEL | JUPITER: SACHIEL | VENUS: ANAEL | SATURN: CASSIEL | SUN: MICHAEL | MOON: GABRIEL | 8PM to 9PM |
| 22ND HOUR | SUN: MICHAEL | MOON: GABRIEL | MARS: SAMAEL | MERCURY: RAPHAEL | JUPITER: SACHIEL | VENUS: ANAEL | SATURN: CASSIEL | 9PM to 10PM |
| 23RD HOUR | VENUS: ANAEL | SATURN: CASSIEL | SUN: MICHAEL | MOON: GABRIEL | MARS: SAMAEL | MERCURY: RAPHAEL | JUPITER: SACHIEL | 10PM to 11PM |
| 24TH HOUR | MERCURY: RAPHAEL | JUPITER: SACHIEL | VENUS: ANAEL | SATURN: CASSIEL | SUN: MICHAEL | MOON: GABRIEL | MARS: SAMAEL | 11PM to 12AM |

FOR NEPTUNE/ASARIEL USE JUPITER/SACHIEL • • FOR URANUS/URIEL USE SATURN/CASSIEL • • FOR PLUTO/AZRAEL USE MARS/

# THE HEPTAGON OF THE PLANETARY DAYS AND HOURS

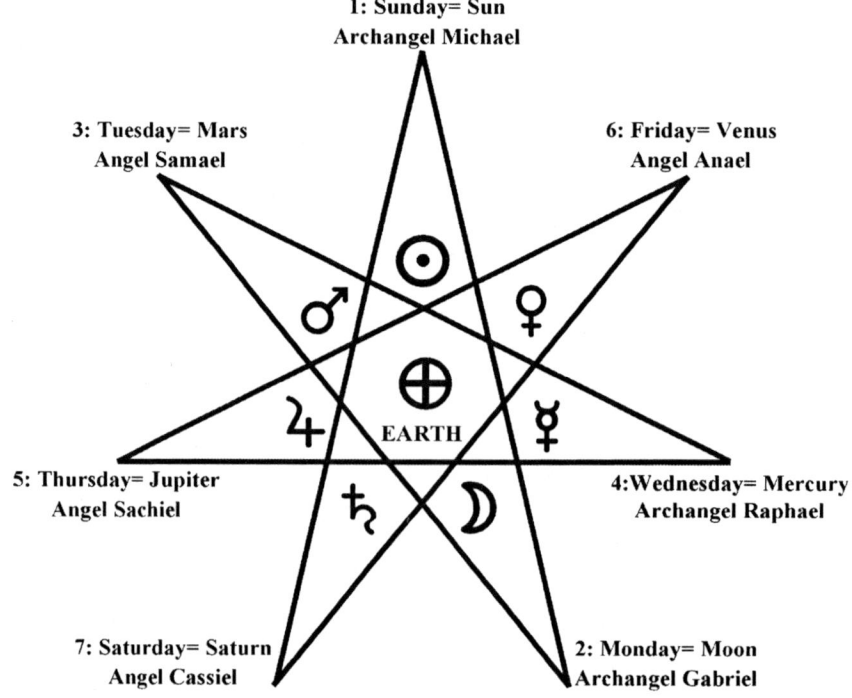

**1: Sunday= Sun**
**Archangel Michael**

**3: Tuesday= Mars**
**Angel Samael**

**6: Friday= Venus**
**Angel Anael**

**5: Thursday= Jupiter**
**Angel Sachiel**

**4:Wednesday= Mercury**
**Archangel Raphael**

**7: Saturday= Saturn**
**Angel Cassiel**

**2: Monday= Moon**
**Archangel Gabriel**

EARTH

This diagram helps to explain why the planets do not appear in their weekday order in the Tables. Some readers may question why the planets appear in the odd order they do in the *Planetary Hours Table*. The order of the days of the week (numbered) on the Heptagram goes from Sunday, down the right side to Monday, back over to Tuesday, across to Wednesday then back over to Thursday, up to Friday, down to Saturday and back up the left side to Sunday once more to start the sequence all over again. This arrangement gives the seven planets in their seven days of the week sequence, the succession of the planets is clockwise or deosil (= 'with the sun') as shown in the list below. We naturally start the *Table of Planetary Hours* and the week with Sunday and the first hour of the day is always ruled by the planet that rules that rules the day. In this way, the Angel and the Planet 'marks their day.' The first hour of Sunday of the twenty-four is ruled by the Sun and the Archangel Michael. The first hour of Monday is ruled by the Moon and the Archangel Gabriel. Following this order, the last hour of Saturday in the Table of Hours, is ruled by Mars and the Angel Samael, which brings us back to the first hour of Sunday once more to start the sequence of the week again. The cycle of the days starts with Sunday/Sun/Archangel Michael. Monday/Moon/Archangel Gabriel. TuesdayMars/Angel Samael. Wednesday Mercury/Archangel Raphael. Thursday Jupiter/Angel Sachiel. Friday/Venus/Angel Anael and Saturday/Saturn/Angel Cassiel, as they do if you take the sequence of planets in the numbered clockwise direction ar*ound the symbol for the Earth above.* Using the points of the heptagram from the Sun gives the order of the planets used in the *Table of Planetary Hours* that are Sun, Venus, Mercury, Moon, Saturn, Jupiter and Mars and *this order of hours is never broken when used, wherever you start* . This diagram explains the two sequences, the planetary hours and the days of the week.

© Leo Vinci 2003

438